CHILD OF WRATH

AUDACITY SAGA: BOOK 3

R. K. THORNE

IRON ANTLER
BOOKS

Edited by Meg St-Espirit

Cover art by Julie Dillon

Cover design by Mibl Art

Beta read by Steve Martinez & Heidi Hanley

Immense gratitude to you all.

Version 1.0

❀ Created with Vellum

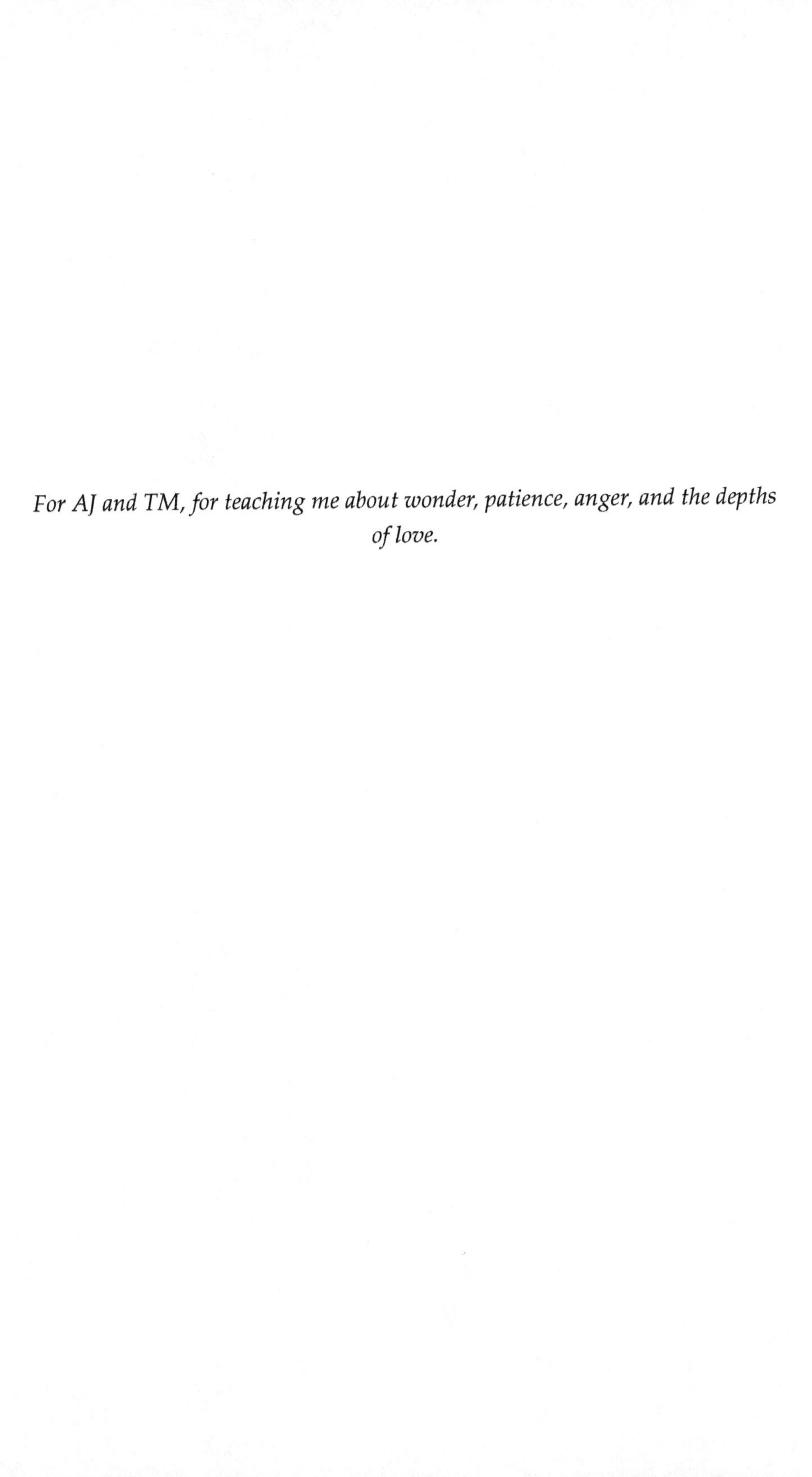

For AJ and TM, for teaching me about wonder, patience, anger, and the depths of love.

CHILD OF WRATH

PROLOGUE

FILE INTERCEPTION 0001569584
   SOURCE: ZETA ARAKOVIC (SUSPECTED)
   DESTINATION: HUMANITIES DEPARTMENT, UNIVERSITY OF TELEPATHICAL ARTS, APPELATE 226, CAPITAL
   INTERCEPTED BY: DOUGLAS SIMMONS

DEAREST ANA,

If you'd like to join us, I have the keys right here. Solve the puzzle, pass the test, and join us. The fight for peace will not be easy. But we have morality on our side.

Cassandra sends her best.

—Z

Have you heard the story of the kraken?
Also known as Cetus in the Ancient Greek.
A sacrifice that was left for it.
Why a sacrifice?
Why a woman?

Sometimes I think it was just a ploy to let the man play the
    hero.
Sometimes I think I know exactly who should have been
    sacrificed.
I think I'd prefer to be the kraken.

Wouldn't you?
You would. I know you would.

What sort of cowards chain someone to a rock
So they can live peacefully?
What sort of cowards sacrifice their daughter?
I suppose that's the point of the story—
that a real hero could save her and find a way out of the mess.

But that's just a fantasy.
I prefer the kraken's way.

And you will too, Songbird.
Come and sing the song of peace.

For every virgin sacrifice,
We demand our payment.

CHAPTER ONE

DAY 1

THE HUM of the ventilation blasted obnoxiously loud, the air frigid around her. Ellen's eyes were closed, her finger pinching the bridge of her nose as she listened, tried to center herself. Get control. The hum. The voices.

The briefing room was slammed full of people looking to her for what came next, what to do next. Every seat was taken around the white quartz table. Beyond that, more of the crew stood, murmuring to each other. Rumors about what happened? Wishing they'd brought some coffee?

She could use some damn coffee right about now. Or someone to ask what to do next.

She wouldn't torture Kael with such questions, even if he'd have tried to answer them. Even with her eyes closed, she could feel his gaze. She cracked open her eyes for a second, caught his attention. He nodded as he leaned against the wall in his usual black long sleeve and dark cargos.

What wasn't usual was that they'd walked in together.

It hadn't even been eight hours ago that she'd dumped the contents of her heart and her feelings for him all over the floor. And somehow, she'd survived. Hell, if she could survive that, she could survive anything, right?

She suppressed a shiver and shut her eyes one more time. Maybe she'd managed to acclimate to Capital's tropical temperatures. That, or her blood was still running cold thinking of Doug and what might have happened since his comm had cut out and their comm officer Merith had made her—ultimately fatal—attempt to hijack the ship. If she'd succeeded? Ellen didn't want to think about it.

She dropped her hands, opened her eyes, and pulled herself up with a deep inhale. It was time to be in command now. To lead. Anxiety, paranoia, terror, guilt—box it up and stick it in the locker for later. She stood alone at the front of the room, as usual, held up by a mix of habit and stubborn determination.

It certainly wasn't by caffeine, adequate sleep, or adrenaline. She was fresh out of all those.

She scanned the group, both to see how they were taking it and to see if everyone had arrived. Nova, always quick to act like she was tougher than a ship's hull, had volunteered to tractor Merith's body down to sick bay. There was no brilliant orange hair in the room, so clearly she hadn't yet returned.

Adan was still on the bridge. He wanted to stay rooted to his pilot's chair, and the poor guy had barely recovered from losing his eye to Ostrov's robots, so she'd given him a pass. He could listen in over the comm. Jenny, too, was on the bridge. Her puppy eyes had said it all. Their team's medic did not want to leave Adan's side, and not for medical reasons. The way Ellen saw it, if you saved the whole ship, you earned some leeway.

Only a few on board weren't required. Isa, at only fourteen, was still asleep—and would steal memories of this briefing later anyway from someone telepathically. Fern, too, should be sleeping in her plant-filled cabin, which sounded delightful right about now; her shift piloting them away from Capital had barely ended when all the commotion had begun. Amaya, their cook, was never required to attend anything; it was part of their agreement. She did her job, so let her live like a mouse if she wanted. The ship had enough cats.

All other crew and passengers were present.

Of them all, Ellen was most worried about the doctors. Doug had worked most closely with them. Had been their friend. She'd never seen Dr. Dremer, especially, look so shaken. The cybernetics expert face had gone paler than her silver hair, and a troubled uncertainty creased her features.

Dr. Rachel Levereaux, too, stared blankly at the table's white expanse. The geneticist's features were always a little disturbing in their perfection, thanks to the Enhancer cell she'd escaped. But it was even more disturbing to see her in a rare state of utter shock. Nothing shocked Levereaux. Not good.

Dr. Taylor seemed to be handling it best. Her job as the ship's psychologist was currently kicking into high gear, and her sharp eyes darted around the room as she scribbled notes. It was a testament to Taylor's skill that the scrutiny felt more reassuring than worrisome. Nobody liked to be analyzed, but everyone liked to be cared for.

Well, most people did. Ellen was working on it.

She let her gaze flick once to Kael. He gave her an almost invisible nod, and she twitched one corner of her mouth in a secret smile in return.

Nova rejoined them. Her face showed no hint of anything beyond the ordinary, except for a hint of tightness at her jaw. She was cracking away at her gum as usual, neon hair tucked behind her ear. She only acknowledged the gravity of the situation with her own silent nod to Ellen. The deed was done.

"Right, then." Ellen cleared her throat. "Let's begin."

A sharp, tense silence fell.

"We have a problem," she said. "A plethora of them, actually. First and foremost, however, is that about an hour ago Corporal Merith Baras attempted to murder our pilot, Adan Flores, and hijack the ship. Corporal Jennifer Utlis intervened, and Baras is dead. Adan is unharmed, but we're all understandably on high alert."

She let that sink in. Eyebrows raised, people shifted in their seats, but the quiet remained.

"In addition, Merith's attack happened in conjunction with an attack on Patron Douglas Simmons at his home. We are unable to reach him and verify his whereabouts or his safety."

Every single one reacted, of course, even those who already knew—jerking back in their seats, widening eyes, going very still. Tightening jaws.

"What about his parents?" Dr. Chayana Persad leaned forward, an odd tool almost falling out of one of her many pockets. "Catherine? Matthew?"

"That also can't currently be verified," Ellen said carefully. Dr. Persad and her son Vivaan were new to the ship, having hopped aboard on Capital both to avoid Arakovic's pursuit of her new telepathy-blocking technology and to find a new safe haven to continue her research. Some safe haven *this* had turned out to be. Ellen cleared her throat. "We're not certain if they lived at the same location as Patron Simmons. As we all heard him speaking to his mother only a few days ago, it is quite possible that they were together and all affected by whatever has happened." For better or worse.

Dr. Persad's hand covered her mouth, her eyes pressing closed. Ellen's heart sank a little lower, not for the first time that day.

Her son Vivaan patted her knee gently. "If there's been a crime, I would happily lend my investigative services to—"

"We will certainly be making use of them," she said. "But let me apprise everyone of the situation first."

His head ducked, bronze cheeks reddening, and he nodded sharply. "My apologies, Commander Ryu."

"Not to worry. We're all still getting used to this new normal. And this is your first briefing." She was tempted to give him a smile and cut off the urge. She never smiled to her subordinates, especially during briefings. She must be truly exhausted. She forced herself forward. "Our primary question is where do we go from here. We have no idea as to Merith's motives. No idea how she was attempting to accomplish her goal or what that goal was. Simply forcing Adan to change the flight plan could not have been enough. As part of her attack, she also temporarily disabled our artificial intelligence Xi, which I'm sure even the new ones among you have met. Some damage may have been done to our computer systems. But the best person to understand if any harm was done and to verify the system integrity is… Doug. And we can't reach him."

She let that land. Hard. Winces crossed several faces.

"When you say 'we can't reach him…'" Levereaux said slowly.

"I'm saying someone already moved on the compound."

"'Moved on…' What *exactly* happened to Patron Simmons, Commander Ryu?"

Ellen's lips thinned. "It's difficult to confirm anything right now. We know there's been extreme damage to their communication structure. It's unlikely to be the only thing affected. As plainly as I can put it, we believe someone attacked them. The extent of the damage is uncertain." She didn't want to mince words, but she also wasn't sure how much they could handle at the moment. The lead weight in her stomach said that if whoever had coordinated the attack had intended to kill Doug and knew where he was, then it could easily have been over before it had even started. Before the *Audacity* had even realized the attack had begun.

That would have been the case in Ellen's Union days. Tetra VII was a vacation planet—not likely to have much more than the most basic missile defense systems, if that. What kind of security had Doug had? God, she hoped he'd been smart about it.

"We should contact someone higher," Levereaux started. "We should get Foundation help. Get other cells working on this."

Dremer abruptly unfroze and cleared her throat. "No. Not yet. Hold that thought while we think this through, all right, Rachel?"

Levereaux's lips tightened almost into a purse, eyes narrowing. She seemed to be trying to read Dremer's mind, though, not just preparing to argue. "Of course," she murmured, but her wheels were still turning.

Dremer straightened and glanced around the room before leveling her gaze at Ellen. "Was this something Merith was doing on her own? Or was she hired? If so, who was Merith working for? How did she get past our background checks? We need answers to these questions before we can make any good decisions."

A long silence was the only response.

"We don't have answers to any of that," Ellen admitted grudgingly.

"I have no definitive theories," offered Xi. "Although she accessed and destroyed data prior to this attack, she sent out almost no communication in her entire two years of service. This suggests that she was hired specifically to infiltrate this unit, as her personal activity was far below average levels, probably designed to keep her motives concealed. There are current crew members with similar activity patterns, however."

"That's just because some of us don't have any friends," Adan quipped over the comm.

"Or we hate our families," Jenny mumbled.

"Or both," Nova added, leaning back in her chair to prop up her boots.

Ellen cleared her throat and resisted the urge to laugh. "How comforting you all match Merith's comm patterns."

Vivaan was rubbing his chin. "Sounds like she hid her tracks well."

"Xi," Ellen said, "you said 'almost nothing.' What *did* she send?"

"Small personal gifts. Three times. No messages. No gifts were returned."

"Hmm. How romantic. Where did she send them?"

There was an odd pause. "The planetary designation information is blank. There is no edit history, but I would hypothesize it has been forcibly removed."

Ellen frowned. "So there's no way to track exactly where she sent them?"

"Not at this time."

"Well, there's one reason for turning off Xi," Kael put in.

Ellen nodded. "Did Merith transmit Simmons's location anywhere during the attack?"

"As I was offline for an estimated twenty-six minutes and fifty-eight seconds," Xi responded, "it is impossible to know. I do not have any transmissions on record, but this data is entirely unreliable."

Dremer groaned. "She had time to transmit Doug's location to anyone. Anyone at all could know where he is, among many other things."

"Yes," Ellen agreed. "Such as the name and location of our ship. They could know everything we're outfitted with: multis, armor, shipboard defense, and munitions. Renegade Theroki. Suspicious creature growing in the sick bay. Individual personnel files." She watched each of them startle in reaction to what bothered them most.

"If Merith was empowered by the betrayal of someone inside of the Foundation," said Dremer, "they could have already had access to that information without her. But then again, they could be just as well equipped as we are."

"Or better." Ellen shrugged. "Okay, let's recap. They could know everything about us, and we know nothing about them. So that's our priority, second only to survival. Find out what we can about our enemy. And use it to save our friends."

Once again, Xi spoke into the uncomfortable silence. "I could investigate via on-the-ground surveillance on Tetra VII if you would like. The planet is fairly low on technology, but a drone might be able to be commissioned or… borrowed."

Ellen shook her head. "Not yet. We could reveal our interest in the Simmons compound. Plus any data you gather about it could be intercepted on its way back to us."

"I thought the Foundation had excellent encryption," Levereaux said, frowning.

"We do," Xi answered. "Galaxy class. But considering Merith's infiltration of our files as well as the timed coordination of the attack, I hypothesize our opponent may have some or all the keys to our encryption. Either that, or equally advanced capabilities."

Levereaux dropped her hand from her chin to the table, straightening. "How many people can have equally advanced capabilities?"

Xi, ever the computer, took the question literally. "A difficult estimate. It would verge on nearly impossible to take into account the secret, independent organizations such as our own that operate without much trace. Given my knowledge of current security and encryption research, I would estimate at the most twenty people in the galaxy have that capability."

Everyone raised their eyebrows at once.

"A great deal of them already work together," said Xi.

"For us?" asked Dremer weakly.

"Yes."

"Oh goodie." Ellen rolled her eyes. "Only twenty."

"Doug is very talented." If an AI could sound affectionate, even concerned, Xi was nailing it. Now *that* was the Xi that Ellen remembered.

Levereaux tilted her head to one side, thinking. "How many of those twenty are members of the Foundation?"

"Fifteen."

Dremer started a little in her seat. "Given those odds, and that Merith made it through our background checks, we have to consider that some kind of internal betrayal could be under way."

Ellen flinched at that, but her altercation with Captain Tovi over the boys they'd recovered on the Teredark moon flashed through her mind. It was easy to think of all of the Foundation as Doug in one of his hula cat shirts. Or even Catherine and her fancy *dahhhhrling* voice. Amused, overeducated hippies lounging on the beach sipping cocktails with one hand and fiddling with saving the world on their holodisplay with the other... that was pretty much how Ellen's fantasy of them went.

Certainly not every member of the Foundation was like that. Even if many of them were similar people, wealthy intelligentsia, that didn't mean they all agreed on everything. In fact, they almost certainly didn't.

"That can't be, it just..." Levereaux was muttering, clearly in shock. "This is the Foundation we're talking about."

"Hey, nobody's perfect. What about that Captain Tovi we encountered?" said Nova, cracking her gum. "That *chica* was a piece of work, no?"

Ellen nodded grimly. "And every cell is different. Even on our last mission, Ostrov was working inside a Foundation building right near the Persads, but he clearly had underworld connections and no qualms betraying us."

Taylor sighed. "It's killing me that I didn't catch this somehow. So many interviews. She was always a little closed off, but nothing out of the ordinary…"

Dremer put a hand over Taylor's. "She might have been coached how to hide. Or how to respond to you in particular even, for all we know."

Ellen straightened, pulling the attention in the room back to her. "Intelligence. We need intelligence. Where should we start?" Good thing she'd never gotten that intelligence officer she'd been hoping for since before all this started.

"I calculate that Tetra VII is the most likely destination to acquire intelligence on Doug's whereabouts," Xi said. "Calculations on sources for Merith's motives are inconclusive."

"So let's go," said Adan over the comm. "We've got the path charted, we're drifting toward it. Ready to increase speed to capacity on your command—"

The corner of Ellen's mouth quirked. "Tap those brakes, hot shot."

"For the last time, Commander, starships do not have brakes—"

Zhia, her more senior lieutenant who'd been quiet up until now, snorted and rolled her eyes. Her dark skin too was creased with a worried frown. She'd known Doug nearly as long as Ellen had—perhaps the reason she was quiet, not so full of her usual quips.

"What I mean is, I want answers too, but what if it's a trap?" Ellen did know *that* much about starship mechanics. "If we head straight to Tetra VII, in the *Audacity*, are we walking straight into something?"

Kael straightened a bit. "If Merith's hijacking and the attacks are connected, why chart the *Audacity* toward Tetra VII? If they're working together, why not blow both up, and be done with it? Doesn't make sense."

"A failsafe?" Dr. Levereaux offered. "She found the location and sent it to her collaborator, then attempted to reach it herself in case her partner failed."

Ellen paced back and forth. "That would suggest the primary objective was most likely the Simmons family, not us. But can we prove that?"

"They could have been after us both," Kael said, shrugging. "But it's too much of a coincidence that she attacks this ship at roughly the same time as Doug is attacked, and then tries to go to that same secret location. They have to be connected."

Dremer was nodding. "And if *we* were the primary target, why attack Doug at all? His location had to be hard to find, and she could have done a great deal to the ship that he would have had no chance of stopping."

"And yet we're still here." Kael was frowning now. "What was her plan once Adan finished charting to Tetra? It's not like we'd have just left her alone. Let's say he refused to change course and she fragged him—"

"Hey now," grumbled Adan.

"—then what? She couldn't fly."

"It's true," Adan agreed. "Autopilot won't take you that far. It does whatever it can, but sooner or later it'll run into an obstacle requiring human input. A stray asteroid, another ship, whatever. And it doesn't like jumps. Contrary to popular belief, I *do* work for my pay here."

"What was she thinking? Her plans?" The room went still as all eyes turned toward the velvet voice and blue hood of Etrianala Kentt in the corner. The telepath's creepy bright eyes were still cloaked in shadow, her small Ursa friend Loti standing beside her, watching the group of strangers with big round eyes. "It would be nice to have a telepath for that, wouldn't it?"

"So spill." Nova cracked her gum, and not in a friendly way this time. "What was she up to?"

Kentt shrugged. To some degree, it was Kentt that had saved them from Merith's hijacking. The whole crew ought to be grateful that the telepath had warned Jenny of the threat to Adan. Kentt owed them nothing; she'd barely been on the *Audacity* for a full cycle, no longer than the Persads, after coming aboard on Capital. But was Kentt really running from Arakovic too as she claimed? Or did she simply know that that was the story that would resonate with Ellen? Gratitude required some degree of trust that they did not yet have. Kentt's over-bright eyes darted around before she spoke again. "I have no idea of her plans. We shall never know, I'm afraid. I wish I had thought to dig deeper, but once I saw her intentions, I was focused on finding someone to stop her."

Ellen suspected that was probably true, but still something in her gut squirmed. Maybe it was just the creepy blue eyes and hair and hood, but she could not trust this lady somehow.

Kael cleared his throat. "Okay, so mind reading isn't a reliable source of intel. Great. Merith still must have had a plan beyond incapacitate Xi and Adan and lock the door. She knew our capabilities."

Ellen scowled. "Maybe her plan is still in motion. Xi could be blind to anything hidden in the computers. Explosives, sabotage, something on a timer…"

"I concur," said Xi. "It is possible I was purposefully powered down for that very reason."

"You didn't seem like you were down for anywhere *near* twenty-six minutes," Kael said. "Not that I'm sure when it started, but…"

"It seemed more like five," Adan agreed. "We need to dig into these logs again—maybe she missed something cleaning up. Maybe the cam footage can tell us if it was actually that long. Or what she was up to."

"Any cam footage featuring Merith in our databanks has been deleted for the last three days," said Xi, calm as ever.

"Awesome," Adan grumbled. "That's just fantastic."

Levereaux's eyes had widened. "If she wanted to sabotage the ship… she'd have a lot of options."

Ellen held up a palm. "Let's put that at the top of the priority list. We are going to need to do some diagnostics. A *lot* of them."

Bri straightened suddenly from where their engineer leaned against the wall. Ellen arched an eyebrow. Was that leather jacket Bri always had on as comfortable as it looked? Looked warmer than Ellen's flight suit, at least. "You don't need me for all this mystery-intrigue-strategy nonsense. Can I go?"

"You don't think your engineering knowledge might come in handy here?" she answered.

"Not as handy as making sure we aren't all fragging blown up before we finish talking." Bri's eye twitched—oh, that was a bad sign. "Permission to start looking over the engines, Commander?"

The unusual dose of formality from Bri made Ellen raise her eyebrows. "Granted. Go get started."

"Should we start other diagnostics?" asked Jenny over the comm. "I can head down to sick bay and get started."

Ellen held up a palm. "Hold on. Yes, I expect everybody go get started on that when they walk out this door. But we need a plan, and we can't throw ourselves into a trap."

"So what if it's a trap? We can't just leave them." Levereaux's frown had been deepening as the conversation wore on, and apparently her frustration had finally boiled over. Ellen smiled inwardly. Levereaux could be a tough critic if you presented a plan—but presenting a problem and then waiting a while seemed to garner much better results with her. Or at least more cooperation.

"We won't leave them," Ellen agreed. "But we also won't be able to help them if we're dead."

"So what do we do, Commander?" asked Nova.

Ellen folded her arms across her chest. "This is a long shot, but... I do have one idea. The *Audacity* was designed with cargo space for two small fighters or shuttles. We didn't outfit us with them initially to keep down the weight and fuel costs. Didn't think we'd need them. But if we picked up a fighter somewhere, we might be able to send a small team—maybe three or four—to Tetra VII in a vehicle Merith couldn't have known about. A small team would be less noticeable, not obviously connected to us. More maneuverable too. And the craft could be unregistered, depending on where we buy it."

"Or we can register it somewhere benign." Adan was rustling excitedly on the other end of the comm. "I love it! If we find something unregistered, people may assume it's new. Or really old."

The rate of Nova's gum chewing had slowed as she mulled over the plan. "A small team is also less supported."

Zhia's worry had shifted to a more familiar kind of tactical concern.

"And we'll have a harder time splitting up if the *Audacity* does anything but wait. We're not a huge crew here."

Ellen nodded. "We've got to work with what we've got. It won't be an easy mission. The risk will be extremely high. I will take volunteers. I'd go myself, but it wouldn't be responsible to the mission or to Doug. But there's sure to be hazard pay." If they all survived.

And if Kael volunteered, she was going to kill him. But it wasn't him whose hand had gone up.

It was Mo. Standing in the back corner where Bri had left an empty spot beside Kentt and Loti, Ellen hadn't paid her sniper much mind. Stuff like this was not going to ruffle the feathers on anyone as steady as Mo. Her mind, her emotions, her trigger finger—placid as an artic lake. Not that Mo's bronze skin or dark brown hair that was shaved on one side and braided back on the other would make anyone think artic, at least until they started trying to talk to her. She joked with Ellen, but only because they'd known each other for years.

But why the hell was she volunteering for this?

"Mo?" Ellen said.

"I'll go."

"This isn't likely to be a mission where you can pick people off at a distance, you know. Probably more up close and personal. You sure?"

Mo clasped her hands behind her back, alert. "I'm sure."

"All right. Good start to a team. Anyone else, feel free to approach me afterward. We'll need to come up with a backup plan if we can't find any smaller fighters or ships with enough range to go to Tetra VII from here on their own. But first—where should we pick up a craft like that?"

Adan snorted. "Without someone trying to steal the *Audacity* at the same time?"

"Preferably."

"Checking."

Ellen glanced at Kentt, who looked inscrutable, and the Persads nearby, who were equal parts stunned and fascinated. And maybe terrified. None of those boded well. "Aren't you glad you joined this lovely expedition?"

Kentt's hood moved in a nod. "I am glad to be alive and save lives, yes."

"Saving lives is not what I plan to do when I find whoever did this to Doug," replied Ellen.

"Whoever this Doug is, he has clearly earned a great deal of admiration and loyalty from all of you," Kentt replied.

Loti nodded and even ventured to speak now in her young ursine voice. "He sounds nice."

Ellen blinked. Hell. The sweetness of those words, the simplicity of them—it was a stab in the heart. It was really tempting to trust people who had only acted in good faith so far. So far.

Didn't mean she was tossing her multi out the airlock, though.

"Xi," she said. "What can you tell us about the Tetra system?"

"There are two mining colonies, Commander, as well as three agricultural export planets. A very productive system for the Puritan Alliance."

"Doug's a Puritan? Now *that* I wouldn't have guessed."

"He is not a Puritan," Xi said, a touch indignant. "But his residence is currently located within a system on the secure edge of Puritan space. Or it was until it recently became unknown."

"That's one way to put it. Why there?" Levereaux tapped her fingers on the table as she stared off into space.

Xi took the question literally. "Tetra VII is known as one of the most beautiful island planets in the galaxy. It has a few small continents, but like Capital, island life is prized, and land extremely expensive. Many retire there or vacation on Tetra VII in particular. It is quite a sought-after destination. I hypothesize were it not in Puritan space, it would be four to five times more popular."

"You prefer the Union, Xi?" Ellen smirked. "I knew I liked you for a reason."

"I do not have preferences; I merely analyze the data and state what appears to be truth or probabilities."

"Really?" Kael frowned. "I don't buy that. No preferences at all?"

Xi hesitated. "Perhaps one or two. But not among political factions."

Dremer smiled. "You just wait. That's how it starts. You start off thinking oatmeal raisin is not a controversial flavor, and it's all downhill from there."

"I do not experience flavors. I do prefer not to be offline," Xi offered. "I also would have preferred Merith not commandeer the ship and kill anyone. Or everyone—that would have been very unsatisfactory."

"Well, good thing you got your wish." Ellen gestured vaguely at the room of living people. "At least so far."

"I would prefer to know where Doug is."

"I think we can all agree on that." At least, she hoped. No more traitors in their midst would be refreshing. "Do you have any preferences on buying a fighter?"

"I will need more parameters before I can say for certain. I can recommend a list of suitable and ideal models as well as potential shipyards that allow anonymous and less tracked purchases. Doug maintained a list."

Ellen nodded. "That becomes our new destination. The closest yard where we can get a small craft suitable for the job. Then we separate. We don't have time to spare."

Adan cleared his throat over the comm. "Commander?"

"Yes, Adan."

"Xi and I think we could try Molyarch Station again," the pilot offered. "Suitably dubious to have unregistered vehicles for sale, if we can talk to the right people. And it's only one extra hop added to the flightpath. Probably about four days flight time. Another option is Erath's Cove, but that's three hops, maybe six days."

Kael shuddered. "And crawling with bloodthirsty scum. I vote for Molyarch." Then he glanced sidelong at Ellen. "Not that we're voting."

She snorted. "I'm open to other mission plan ideas. It's not like we're going to receive FRAGOs here, we're cut off from anyone from me on up."

"Speaking of that—as I said, shouldn't we contact someone?" Levereaux pressed.

"If Merith's collaborator is one of us?" Dremer said.

Levereaux deflated in her chair. "I see. So we've got to help ourselves."

"Or risk discovering the traitors in the most inconvenient way." Dremer shrugged.

"A fighter could also come in handy in the future," Levereaux said, brightening. "Assuming everything works out."

That was a pretty bad bet with their recent luck, but Ellen stayed quiet. Instead, she waited a moment for any other ideas before nodding. "All right, it may not be perfect, but it's a starting point. Adan—reroute and take us to Molyarch. We're going shopping."

Zhia snorted. "Your favorite."

She raised her chin. "I can't help it, sometimes you just have to treat yourself to a small spacecraft."

"New course commencing," said Adan. His laughter and the echo of Jenny's near him eased something in her; if he could laugh while grievously injured and recently assaulted, then the rest of them could maybe do this. Whatever this was. Maybe they'd even survive.

Nova straightened in her seat, finally taking those damn boots down. "If our smaller fighter is heading to Tetra VII, where will the rest of us go?"

"Doug's next mission plans took us to Faros. He wanted us to contact a friend of his who needed help." She decided not to mention Kael's other business there just yet. "He give you any details about that, Xi?"

"Yes. I have the nearly completed mission dossiers readily accessible including the contact information of several involved individuals."

Dossiers—hopefully that plural meant she had info on Doug's old friend as well as Kael's old… whatever she was. Not that she was looking forward to that. "Great. Do we have any reason to think Merith knew about this upcoming mission?"

"I will remind you of the extended twenty-six-minute window where we lack surveillance, but aside from that, I do not believe she had tried to find out the next mission. No evidence of access logs or search histories. Doug's draft files *should* have been accessible only to me. It's possible she could have accessed them, but I would put the probably at less than forty percent."

"All right. Any other questions or concerns?" Ellen asked.

The room was quiet.

"Good. Now comes the fun part. Diagnostics! You know the drill." There were a few groans, but not as many as usual when they trained for this. It wasn't fun to comb over the *Audacity* more thoroughly than ants picking a carcass clean—the process took *hours*—but everybody knew it was necessary. Especially now that it was not practice but for real. "I know it's not your dream mission, but let's get—"

"Potential hostile ship detected," said Xi suddenly. "Union battle-cruiser *Volga* changing previous orbit and headed toward our new gate."

Ellen frowned. "Where was their old orbit?"

"Our old gate and its wormhole."

"Oh, goodie. It's a party." She straightened and jerked a thumb at the door. Nova and Zhia were already halfway out the door. "Diagnostics will have to wait. Civilians—confined to quarters."

"But Commander Ryu—" Vivaan started. "Can I—"

"Your investigation can start when we are not being pursued, Mr. Persad."

"But the evidence—"

"Won't do you much good if it's blown up."

"Can't I just be confined to this traitor's quarters, instead of my own?"

She raised her eyebrows. "Your persistence is a virtue, but things are going to get choppy. Which means strapping into bunks. Won't that hurt your evidence if it's our traitor's bunk?"

"Excellent point, Commander." Vivaan nodded and jogged out, his mother looking relieved. Kentt, Loti, and the doctors were already gone.

Kael shook his head as he waited to walk out beside her. "He should be wondering what the frag he got himself into, not when he can start looking for clues."

"Sadly, even this may have been safer than what he got himself out of." She pulled the comm unit from the briefing desk and snapped it on to her flight suit as she followed him out the door. No time for armor—at least not yet. He gave her a smile over his shoulder as he headed down the hall toward the guns, and she found herself smiling back in spite of the hostile in pursuit. Something clenched in her gut as she climbed up her ladder and he went out of sight. She continued on toward the bridge, although she didn't understand the feeling.

She switched her comm over to the whole ship line. "Battle stations. Civilians confined to quarters. Adan and Xi—start infiltrating *Volga*'s info systems for worst case scenario."

"Yes, ma'am."

"Anyone not immediately in combat, start your diagnostics."

Indistinct grumbling.

"I'm in Gun Two." Fern's voice came over the comm, surprisingly chipper.

"Why aren't you asleep?" snapped Ellen as she dropped into the vacant co-pilot chair at Adan's side and started buckling herself in. Jenny was gone.

"You think I can snooze through the call to battle? I'll sleep when I'm dead."

"Let's hope that's not too soon," Ellen replied.

There was a smattering of laughter across the line, but Ellen wasn't smiling now. She needed to pull up the specs on the *Volga*, any intel they had or reports she could find. She still knew the schematics of half the ships in the fleet, but just her luck—the Volga was crackin' new.

Xi recognized Ellen's search patterns and started adding reports to the side for her to consider. She needed to know two critical capabilities: guns and shields. Maybe who was in charge. Everything else could come later.

They wouldn't have Doug to hack them out of this one, and she had more to lose now than ever.

CHAPTER TWO

DAY 1

KAEL PLOPPED down into Gun One, flipped on the comm speaker, and started jacking in to the console. It'd barely been two months and change since he came aboard the *Audacity*, and already this spot felt like a second cabin, the cables and port locations second nature. Could he convince Ellen to try out other sorts of cabin specific activities in here? Hmm, given there were vid cams that fed to the bridge, that was probably a no. He thunked his head against the headrest and shut his eyes.

"Frag," Ellen was saying over the line, "this one's got 5M canons. Gotta keep those from firing."

He didn't think she'd intended to announce that out loud or particularly for anyone's benefit, but he responded anyway. "5M?"

"Oh—uh, nicknamed thus because they'll blow a five-meter hole in your hull."

He whistled. "Gotta keep those from firing might be an understatement." On a ship the size of *Audacity*, at perhaps a hundred and fifty meters, five meters was… quite a bit. The cleaning robots—who were also repair robots—were fast, but they weren't *that* fast.

"*Volga* is nice and shiny," she said more directly. "New in the Union fleet. What's it doing out here, rather than on the front lines picking fights with Puritans?"

"Preparing to pick fights with us?" Adan replied.

"Ha, ha, very funny. How are we doing on speed?"

"Ramping up. Hold on." He flipped the switch to the whole ship comm, and his voice came from above and behind Kael now. "We're going to be hitting some faster speeds, so everybody get harnessed in or in bunks with belts until we're through the gate." The whole ship line switched off. "I'm watching the passenger displays. Once everyone is a good little kiddo, I'll put the petal to the metal. So to speak."

"I'm rubbing off on you, Adan," Ellen said, a smile in her voice.

"We need to spend less time together, Commander."

"You can have a vacation when we're safe on Faros IV."

"'Safe on Faros IV' is an oxymoron," Kael muttered. "How about safely *off* Faros?"

"Get me through this wormhole so I can find out," she replied.

"Oh, I have every intention to."

He eased back in the gunnery seat and closed his eyes. Ah, Faros. The raw planet had a beauty to it, but not one that was easily survivable. The ant farm of tunnels he'd called home were less beautiful, and still pretty hard to survive, but at least it was possible. For some. Something churned in his gut at the thought of going back there.

He'd stretched out his senses as he reminisced. Maybe all the nature scenes and failed meditation sessions were working because six months ago, he couldn't have imagined being relaxed at this moment, approaching battle. At ease, even. They were not yet in range, so he waited, flat as a calm sea.

Their speed had picked up, and as the ship moved, vacuum filled the space around them, with bits of space debris occasionally burning off on the shields. A small asteroid tumbled past. His mind grabbed ahold of it, pulling the spinning rock along with minimal effort. It'd been a while since he'd gotten to use that particular Theroki ability, and it felt strangely good.

Inside the ship's systems, Xi's sensors zeroed in on the anomaly of the asteroid's course change, preparing minor weapons defenses.

"It's okay, Xi," he muttered. "That's just me. Getting ready to play."

Asteroid on our starboard side? Xi responded directly via the cable that ran out of his arm and into the ship.

"Yep."

"Everything okay, Kael?" asked Ellen.

"Yeah, just getting ready to play ball, Commander." Literally. He grinned to himself. "I don't get to sit in this seat often enough."

"Be glad of that."

"I'll try, but it's not easy."

"The *Volga* is hailing us, Commander," said Adan.

"Fine. Let's do this."

The woman greeted them in a prim, crisp voice, her accent British. "This is Union ship *Volga*, Lieutenant McCarthy speaking. Identify yourselves, and state your purpose in this zone."

Kael rolled his eyes. They would never learn.

"*Volga*, this is a neutral, freespace zone. We have no requirement to answer to you."

"Perhaps you'd care to answer to our—" McCarthy cut off for a moment. "We will give you one further chance to identify your ship and purpose."

"You are entitled to nothing from us, *Volga*, so you can take your chances and shove them up your—"

"Is this Lieutenant Ryu speaking?" said another voice, a man this time, slow and older.

A pause. "Tauber?" The words were a vicious whisper, almost to herself. Or an accusation. She didn't use his rank in return —interesting.

"I thought perhaps your 'retirement' might have mellowed your interpersonal style, Ellen, but I can see I was wrong."

"She was always like this?" someone whispered a little too close to a comm.

Kael snorted.

"If anybody should be retired, it's you," she snapped back. "You betrayed us all, you wasted them, you moldy, self-serving—"

"Now, now. No need to make excuses to me for your cowardly, dishonorable behavior." The voice doled the words out, slow, leisurely.

Kael opened his eyes and sat forward in spite of himself, wishing he could see her on a monitor. On the comm, there was another pause, this one dripping with pure rage. He spun the asteroid faster, then the other direction, bouncing with nervous energy.

"How long till we're in range?" Ellen said, presumably having switched off the outside comm.

"Thirty seconds."

"Get ready, guns."

"Roger," he muttered.

"You know it," echoed Fern.

She switched the comm back on. "What is cowardly, Tauber, is to sell the minds of your subordinates without being willing to take the same risks for yourself."

"I've taken plenty of risks on behalf of the Union," he replied, smooth and unmoved.

"Did they give you a medal for doing experiments on your own people?" Her voice was cold, pissed. Who *was* this guy? "Or did you just do it because you like to frag with people? How do you sleep at night?"

"Easily, lieutenant."

"I'm a Commander now."

"Not in any outfit that matters, you're not. And we haven't released you from your duty." His voice was hard enough to cut diamonds now. "You are ordered to submit to boarding and face your court-martial."

"And behind door number two…" she started.

"There is no Option B, no second tries. Not this time, Ellen."

"…we have go eat shit and die for five hundred, Alex!"

Kael frowned. Who the heck was Alex?

Tauber's laugh was brutal and without mirth. "Ever the history buff. This isn't an antique game show. You think you're so smart. But you're just lucky. And your luck has run out."

"Was that it, Tauber? You didn't like me because I was both junior and smarter than you? With a better record than you? Or was it that I was better *respected* than you?"

He sighed. "I didn't like you because you were a *child*, with the maturity of a child, and an arrogant one at that."

"Seventeen is hardly—"

He raised his voice. "This is Colonel Tauber addressing the crew of this unnamed, unregistered, probably stolen vessel. Your captain is wanted by the Union for desertion. Is that the kind of person you follow? One with no honor? Well, then this might sway you. Her reward is set at over eight hundred thousand credits."

"Ellen! They've raised your reward!" Xi said, bizarrely congratulatory.

Her sigh was loud enough to be heard over the comm.

"Turn her over to us," Tauber continued, "and we will grant you amnesty for harboring a wanted criminal. Otherwise, consider yourselves all criminals under Union law. We will give you three minutes to consider."

"Comm off. In range," Adan barked.

"Enemy tractor beam—" Xi started.

Kael had sensed the ship—and its hot grabber—even before Adan had begun to speak, and it was no surprise to him that the "three minutes to consider" did not include freedom from their ship taking hold. The grab beam sliced out.

He slapped it right back and used the lowered shields to send his asteroid tumbling toward the bow of the *Volga* at high velocity. Hopefully, they'd been stupid enough to put the bridge out front.

The rock bounced once off their viewports, and then he batted back down. It found a sensor array, and then another bounce collided with what looked like a small canon before he lost his grip on it at the edge of his range. It tumbled along the hull of the Volga, spinning toward something spiny at the back.

A chorus of swearing came over the Union comm before their line cut out.

Fern giggled now too. "Aw, no fair, Theroki. I can't do anything while our shields are still up."

"It's not a competition, Fern," he replied.

"Maybe not to you."

"Crew of the *Volga*?" Adan said suddenly.

"Adan, what are you doing?" came Ellen's quiet voice.

"Yes, sir? Identify yourself. Have you decided to negotiate?"

Adan snorted, not answering Ellen. A quick jolt of fear shot through Kael—what *was* he doing? Praise Almighty, eight hundred thousand credits was a lot, but it wasn't enough to sway Adan of all people?

At least, he hoped not.

Adan cleared his throat. "Yeah, uh, we'd like to negotiate. Negotiate a stick right up your ass. Stand aside, or we'll move you."

Kael couldn't help but snicker to himself. Fortunately laughter didn't keep him from feeling the *Volga*'s shields drop. He braced himself to bounce back the onslaught.

Two instant charge canons hit a split second later, and he grunted at the effort of deflecting it. Ideally, he preferred to bounce back at the exact angle to disable the gun with its own beam. And he nailed it with one too, but whiffed the other, sending the shot wide and missing both ships completely.

"Incoming enemy weapons at—" Xi paused. "Attack deflected."

"Gun it, Adan," Ellen snapped. "Go around them."

"Xi, give me everything she's got," Adan barked.

"Give me one shot," Fern whispered, "come on."

His body jerked back and down into his seat, slackening the harness as the artificial gravity didn't quite keep up with the new acceleration. The *Audacity* dipped down, Adan sending the ship into a spin as it dove under the belly of the Union ship. Smart—a larger percentage of the weapons systems were on the top, including those 5M canons.

But that didn't keep *Volga* from firing. *Audacity* was moving faster and at a spin, now, and that did not make deflecting the attacks any easier for Kael's part. A few volleys got closer than he'd have liked, but he did successfully keep them from hitting the shields.

"I'll give you ten seconds, guns," Ellen said. "Adan, drop the shields at the lowest point, under the belly. If we're quick, they won't realize they were ever down before they're back up again."

"Preparing for drop," Adan said.

Kael held his breath.

"Shields down."

The *Audacity* shuddered as Fern fired. Two shots, then three. He added his own via the gun system—three rapid bursts at another sensor array sticking out, an easy but high value target—before the shields flipped back up and cut him off.

"And up," said Adan.

"Good work." Ellen this time.

"We hit anything?" Fern asked.

"How could you miss that floating barn over our heads?"

"I meant did we hit anything good?"

Kael tuned out their banter. The larger ship was turning, but it had been nearly at a standstill, planning to block the gate. The Unionies hadn't expected a pursuit once the Audacity had gotten close enough, because blocking a grab beam was mostly impossible. Unless the ship was Theroki. And *Audacity* was way too new and shiny and nowhere near spiny enough for that.

"Heh, look at her try to turn. She's not catching us now," Adan said, Kael suspected just muttering to himself. "You thought we couldn't get away."

"Luckily for me, we're quite slippery," Ellen murmured.

"Multiple weapons systems activated," said Xi.

"They're unloading everything. 5M canons and all," said Adan. "Brace."

Kael swore at the sheer volume as the energy blasts materializing at the edge of his range. "Little help, Xi?"

"Boosting defensive shields aft," said Xi, placid as ever.

He focused on the 5M blasts. More like small comets than a beam

or torpedo. He wasn't going to have much time. There were two blasts
—twin canons. They neared, burning hot and spinning and—

He slammed the first one back, a dull ache cracking across his forehead and a warmth building in his back. A quarter of the projectile's
energy was lost in its impact, but the majority of it careened back and
collided satisfyingly with *Volga* straight across the bow.

The other, however. The other he barely deflected in time. He
winced as it collided with a small part of the shields at stern and slid
up the starboard side of the *Audacity*, chewing through the reduced
shields.

"Multiple incoming enemy attacks received," said Xi calmly. "Seventy-five percent deflected. Shields have taken damage."

He didn't have time for regrets. More were coming. They weren't
5M this time, but at least twelve smaller bolts streaked toward them
through the blackness of space.

He took a deep breath, thinking of Taylor and her meditations and
sandy dunes and green meadows. Calm.

Ellen's voice. "Jesus Christ, he's firing into the gate."

Well, that didn't help. Ocean. Twelve beams. Nothing else.

"We're almost through—"

The first six beams he deflected collided with the *Volga* peppering
its broad side just about where the 5M guns were located. He'd tried
for it, and he got them within a meter.

Hell yes. See how their shields liked *that*.

The next two glanced the side, and the rest went wide. He leaned
forward in the darkness. His eyes were still closed, as they flew further
away, but he wanted to see—

A flash of darkness, the weird golden sparkle-crackle of the wormhole was like yellow shocks behind his eyelids.

He opened his eyes. Space around them was empty, except for the
wormhole gate behind them as they raced away.

Fern let out a whoop. "That was a close one!"

"Stern shield generators received damage," said Xi calmly.
"Deploying drones. Refueling recommended. Suggest diverting power
from speed to shields."

"They're going to come right through behind us!" Adan said. "We can't slow down."

"They weren't moving," Ellen shot back. "We've got time till they can reach our speed."

"Yeah, but what if they can go faster?"

"Their specs say they can't. That ship is at least three times our size."

"Specs lie."

"True." A pause on the comm. Damn, he wished he could see them staring each other down. He could just imagine the way she was narrowing her eyes to glare at him right now. "Do you want to arrive at Molyarch without shields?"

Adan let out a theatrical sigh. "Fine. I propose eighty percent max then. We can get a few thousand kilometers lead at least, and then redirect more energy to shields then."

"Do it. Everybody okay?"

A chorus of affirmatives went up on the comm.

"Okay. For now, restrictions are lifted. Go get a snack. They could be back after us in a few, so stay near your harnesses. Xi, in how long can we expect to greet our new friends again?"

"Estimates are eighteen minutes to get the *Volga* up to wormhole speed and through the refreshed gate. Depending on their exact drift angle, it could be longer, as much as twenty-five minutes."

"Stay on alert," Ellen said.

The comm clicked off.

Kael crumpled and thumped his head back against the padded headrest. Of all the Union ships out there in the universe, they'd run into the one with the biggest asshole—and the biggest ax to grind. At least, he hoped that was the case. If there were worse Unionies out there, he didn't want to meet them. Talk about bad luck.

He straightened slightly in spite of the exhaustion, frowning to himself.

Was it bad luck? Or was it something else?

———

ELLEN SHOVED her fingers into the boxing glove, flexed them, then curled. The bag lowered from the ceiling almost automatically these days—it was a relief to see Xi did remember Ellen's habits. She should ask the AI more detail around what exactly had been damaged in her memory banks. She should supervise the diagnostics. And check on how the Persads were handling all of this. There was also the matter of the unconscious man they'd kidnapped from Capital. She should do a lot of things. A lot of them.

But all those things could wait ten minutes, or even fifteen. The team knew how to do diags without her. And Tauber's words were bouncing around in her head like a game of ship pong, and they wouldn't shut up. *Coward. Difficult.*

Too smart for her own good.

Dishonorable.

She'd shut them up, get them out of her system with a little bit of sweat, and then get back to work. She shucked her flight suit for her black sports bra and some sweats.

Sweat was dripping off her when a chime sounded from the hatchway.

"Who is it, Xi?" Although she had a feeling who it might be. A hope, even. She didn't stop in her onslaught of the bag.

"Kael has requested entry."

"Add to my profile to let him in automatically please." Jab, jab, jab, *cross.*

"Are you certain you would like to modify your security profile, Ellen?"

She winced at the name. "Commander" had felt... better. Why did she even care? "No, I'm not certain, but I sort of have a problem letting people in at the right times. In general. I've decided to overdo it this time. Add him, please."

"Acknowledged."

The hatch slid open. He raised one eyebrow as he strode in. "Uh... What are you doing?"

She didn't turn, but spared a glance over her shoulder. "Just blowing off steam."

He jerked a thumb behind him, stopping just inside the hatch. "On the way over here, I caught Vivaan harassing Xi outside Merith's quarters. He's trying to talk her into letting him inside to begin his 'investigation.' Somebody should probably supervise that kid."

She nodded and attacked with three hard jabs in a row.

"Uh—I can do it?"

"Always love a volunteer. That'd be great." She'd always known Tauber was an asshole. Why was he getting to her now? Too much stress, not enough sleep. Part of the reason for that was the handsome man hovering near her hatch.

Kael cleared his throat. "Cause me and Vivaan are already so close."

"Are you?"

"Not at all. Do I look like a Capital type to you?"

She snorted. *Jab, jab, hook, hook.*

"Although I suppose I've talked to him more than anyone else has at this point. Now that's just sad."

She didn't say anything to that, just nodded. Kept punching. She wasn't the dishonorable one here. Orders were orders, but what about when the orders were wrong? She'd tried so hard not to have to leave, and she didn't respect him one bit, but to hear it hurt all the same. If the *Volga* came after them…

She hadn't realized Kael had come closer till he spoke just beside her. "Are you okay?"

"Me?" She stopped, turned, tried to act casual. Out of breath, she wiped sweat off her forehead with her arm. "Of course. Yeah."

"Aren't you tired? I mean—"

"I'm fine."

He narrowed his eyes at her. "You know you can't lie to me."

She narrowed her eyes back, then sent a sharp jab at his head.

He dodged easily, laughing.

"I hate you." She pounded at his shoulder now, his side, light and playful. But not *that* light and playful, because deep down she was pissed. Just not at him.

Besides, with his augments, she was lucky he blinked.

"This old conversation again?" Laughter twinkled in those deep brown eyes. He'd been through so much more than her. She should get over Tauber. What was that asshole in the grander scheme of things?

Kael captured one glove, then an elbow, and then pulled her close. She squirmed very halfheartedly, tangled up in him.

"I hate you," she repeated.

His hand slipped from her hands to slide to a stop on her sweat-slicked lower back. "No, you don't. We've been through *that* a few times."

She couldn't help but smile at that. "I'm just blowing off steam."

"There are other ways to blow off steam…" His voice was low and husky.

His lips found hers, gentle but hungry, and the kiss was more reassurance than a workout could ever be, although the sweat and endorphins she'd already acquired weren't harming anything.

Except maybe the wall of her cabin, because she was now pressed against it. The cold metal was delicious relief to the heat of her skin. She fumbled with her gloves, and they tumbled to the floor. Free now, she ran her fingers up his neck and into his hair, which wasn't much cleaner than hers. The crush of him against her, every hard plane and angle, lifted her, healed her, quieted the noise.

She had no idea how much time passed before he broke away, his forehead resting against the cold metal beside her ear, both of their chests heaving. She had the sense he was trying to gain control of himself.

He wasn't the only one.

"Feel better?" he muttered.

"Sorta," she muttered back, squeezing the arm that still curled around his neck.

"Tauber's an asshole."

"You have no idea."

"I may have a bit of an idea. He the one that sold you out?"

"Yeah."

"Maybe we should have fired back harder."

"Nah. The rank and file are probably suffering enough under him without getting blown up too."

He nodded, his head nuzzling closer against her temple, her ear.

"Got under my skin though."

"Gathered that."

"And the what if's are bothering me. What if we don't find Doug? What if he's already dead? It'll be my fault."

"Your fault? Don't be ridiculous."

But she'd known about her suspicions of Merith—and she hadn't done enough. "And what if the *Volga* had gotten through our shields? We've got more civvies than usual. Not all of them signed up to go to war with the Union because of my broken promises."

He pulled back and gave her a hard look. "If there's anything the universe has taught me, it's not to worry about promises made to people who don't have your back in the first place. And never did."

She drank in those earnest eyes for a while, let his stern frown patch up the cracked pieces of her resolve. *She* had his back of course— and damn, she hoped he knew that. But telling him that in so many words just now seemed like it might risk suggesting the opposite.

"Didn't they owe you something, too? You signed up to give your life to defend people, not in some crazy scientist's experiment that might not help anyone." He squeezed her tighter, and she swallowed.

"When did you get so wise?" she said instead.

"Imagine how insufferable I'll be at thirty."

She laughed softly and returned the squeeze.

"Why don't you sit down? Rest. Figure out what we need to do next." He eased her toward her desk chair, and she let him. "I doubt they'll follow us. They can't grab us, and they can't hit us. I'll make sure of it. But even if they do follow, everything's going to be okay."

"You can't lie to me either, you know." She fell into the seat more than sat down in it.

"All right, things are going to be tough, but we're going to kick their asses and scrape by, and maybe we'll get through it by the skin of our teeth. And if we get fragged, well, what the hell else were we going to do? Lie down and die?"

"That's more like it." She grinned up at him. "Wait—I should shower."

"Then go. Want some coffee?" He propped his hands on his hips, smile going crooked.

"God, yes."

"It'll be ready when you get back."

———

IT *WAS* THERE when she got back, steaming and hot. He wasn't, however.

The sweet heat of the coffee warmed her throat and her stomach. Her long-overdue shower had been glorious, and the combination of all these things were raising her spirits more than she'd like to admit.

Her to do list could reach Desori and back. First and foremost—the diagnostics. Any sabotage had to be caught as early as possible. Another sip of the coffee reminded her that Kael hadn't yet been assigned a system in their diag routine… Perhaps they should be practicing more often if they'd gone two months without giving him one.

Maybe *she* was the system he'd been checking over. If that was the case, she seemed much more operational now, so job well done. Maybe he should shepherd the Persads. Babysitting geniuses—yeah, he'd adore that responsibility.

One by one, she checked in with each crew member. One by one, they hadn't found dreck.

"My sweep of the engine room's clean," said Bri over the comm line. "I even went back and did some extra cleaning and maintenance nonsense. Which I never put off and always do exactly on time. Still. Nothing."

"Life support?"

"Nova's still in there, but I think she's almost done. No signs of anything. Want me to pitch in somewhere else?"

Again, Bri's offer raised Ellen's eyebrows—a testament to the seriousness of the situation. Bri was lots of things, but proactively helpful wasn't one of them.

"No. Get some rest. Looks like *Volga* isn't in pursuit, but if that turns out to be incorrect, we'll need you." And it had been hours since Bri had started that diag, working clear through the encounter with the *Volga*.

Adan hadn't found anything in the computers; Jenny and Levereaux said the sick bay was clean. Dremer found nothing disturbed in the extra lab equipment, although she still had a lot to go through. Mo and Zhia had cleared the armory and the printer; Amaya guaranteed the food stores and mess were exactly as she always kept them. And she hardly let anyone near them, anyway.

Every major ship system had been combed through. Nothing.

She stood up to stretch. The coffee mug was sadly empty now. Where had Kael gone, anyway? Probably keeping busy with his standard duties. Even with so much happening, they'd barely left Capital. Had it even been a full cycle yet since liftoff?

She bent to check the time on the holodisplay. A little over thirty hours had passed since then. It felt like so much longer.

Especially that delicious sleep, cut short too soon. He'd fallen asleep in her bunk last night, but it hadn't gone much further than that. She sighed and picked up the mug, turning it in her palms.

They could go fast or go slow. Fast certainly hadn't been their style so far. Slow was probably wise, probably for the best. It'd been hard enough to get to this point, Herculean even. She'd made enough mistakes, past burns with Paul included; it was time to get this right. To proceed carefully. She'd known plenty of people over the years, but no one that had understood her flaws so well as Kael did, no one that saw past them. None that made her feel the same rush, the same thrill.

There was work to be done. But she resisted the practical a moment longer and let her feet take her back toward the mess. Maybe caffeine would clear these thoughts of Kael from her head, let her focus on the harder work than just check-ins and diagnostics, at least until the end of the day cycle and the usual shift. And then... What happened then?

Would he come back? She frowned as she slid her mug under the coffee maker, hot brown liquid customized to her profile gurgling and filling the air with that delicious smell. Was there something she needed to say? Where did they go from here? God, she'd forgotten how awkward this could be. And looking back, she questioned every step of the way with Paul now—had it been sincere? Had it been real, or just an act? All the motions they'd gone through—had they been a bizarre sham or a close facsimile? She had no idea.

She took a sip as she left the ladder and headed to her cabin. The stuff cost a Mover ship and a half, but it was so worth it. Back at her desk, she sat and stared for a moment.

Just how good of an act had Paul put on? It didn't matter. Kael was a different man; this was a different time. She was a different woman. Something would happen at the end of the shift—or it wouldn't.

First, the work. Then she'd see what happened. Maybe she'd just leave it in his hands, wait and see. No need to rush. She'd made enough blunders already. She shook the thoughts off, physically, head and arms, then took another gulp of coffee. Xi was probably having a field day with the body language analysis. She cleared her throat and sat up straight. "Xi, I want to see Doug's files. What do we have?"

"Of course, Ellen. Where would you like to start?"

"Who are we supposed to see on Faros? And how to reach them? Her?"

"Yes, the target was female, Ellen."

Her name still sounded weird through Xi's speakers, but she brushed it off. Images sprang to life on the holodisplay, spilling across the usual confines of her space and wrapping around into the room, wider than she could comfortably see.

A woman's face was the most prominent image, most of her features obscured by a heavy-duty breather—a mask of delicate aqua that glowed white at the edges and violet at the tubes and vents. Unlike the breathers people had worn on Capital that were designed to be appropriate at a masquerade ball, this woman's breather was tougher and made no attempt to disguise itself. Built to last, while also being surprisingly beautiful.

Curvy, black-lined eyes stared out, piercing in their intellect. Her thin, arching eyebrows could have made a seagull feel lacking. Her skin was olive smooth, and the depth of her nearly black eyes held a certain boldness, a bravery. There was no trace of humor, though, no glint of amusement. Ellen knew that feeling well enough—serious things required serious attitudes. But what had turned this woman's eyes so serious? Or had she been born that way?

Had Ellen, for that matter, or had it been the war? There was no way to know the self that might have been, the child that never was one.

Xi began to speak. "This is Amari Barakat, also known online as Sahrazad, a traditional spelling of the folk character Scheherazade. Dozens of other aliases exist, catalogued here. Studied at Davenmore University at the same time as Doug. They took some of the same classes."

"They know each other then?" She raised an eyebrow. "Friends?"

"I believe they are competitors. Fierce competitors. I am not sure if 'friends' would be an accurate way to describe it, but maybe. Their relationship model is unusual."

"Every relationship is different," she muttered.

"So I am observing, vexingly enough. Merith's attack did not affect my growing store of relationship models. Much to my relief."

Ellen snorted, both at the idea of Xi being relieved and her being vexed. "Why this... Barakat was it?"

"He believed she was in danger from a corporation called EPR Intergalactic. It's not recorded here why he suspected this exactly. There is no clearly marked evidence in this file or the file of EPRI."

"Hmm." She reached for the EPRI file and enlarged it.

"Some rough analysis indicates that the owner of EPR Intergalactic also attended Davenmore around the same time."

"Attended?" she muttered, scanning the fact sheet. "Where is Davenmore located?"

"It has over a dozen campuses on various worlds in both the Union and Puritan zones, but students largely attend virtually."

"In VR?"

"Yes."

She frowned. Who the hell was this woman? Did Doug have a secret girlfriend? Just an old colleague? Simmons's college dream girl?

As if Ellen was one to judge on that matter. But she couldn't risk his life running to Faros on the off chance that a woman he'd known once *might* be in danger.

This was why they needed a real intel analyst, for God's sake. Someone who was good at this. She had no problem understanding a complex situation, but she thought in movements, in vectors, not in all this data.

That was kind of bullshit, but it felt better to bitch and wish someone else could figure this out for her than to just miss Simmons right now.

"Based on these message logs, I believe Sahrazad will not welcome our arrival, but that Doug was certain the danger was imminent."

"Put them up, then."

Sahrazad: I can take care of myself. I don't need your help.

SimCat: Don't underestimate Quen. With all of EPRI at his fingertips... You know he's dangerous, right?

She cleared her throat. "SimCat?"

"I believe you noticed his affinity for the feline species in his outerwear."

"Noted. If it's also expressed in his underwear, I don't want to know."

"He has dozens of these sorts of names." Was Xi defending Simmons now? "It is part of anonymity in his profession."

"Hmm. Not sure I want to know the other names, if this is any indication." She kept reading.

Sahrazad: It was already at his disposal. This didn't change anything. And I'm far from defenseless. You don't even know where I am. Or do you?

SimCat: I know the system.

Sahrazad: Oh, how brilliant of you. That's kid stuff.

SimCat: I know.

Sahrazad: Trust me—neither of you can find me. If you can't—why are you worried? He's not better than you. That was always the problem.

SimCat: If he does find you, how easily can you get out of there? Do you have a plan?

Ellen frowned. "Did he figure out her location after this conversation?"

"He already knew the location. You can see he does not say he does not know. He admits he knows part of the location."

"Tricky, tricky. I see."

Sahrazad: Not easily. It doesn't matter. Why are you even asking?

SimCat: because sometimes it's time to stop being safe and start doing something important

Sahrazad: what's that supposed to mean? This is none of your business, Sim. Stay out of it.

SimCat: You know I've never been good at that.

Sahrazad: Nosiness has always made you good at what we do.

SimCat: I won't deny it.

SimCat: Something we have in common.

Sahrazad: There's a difference between nosiness and curiosity.

SimCat: Sure, there is. Let my ship get you somewhere safer, and we can debate this in person. With lots of beefy security people with guns around us.

Her eyebrows shot up. "In person? Was he planning to leave?"

"Yes."

She sighed. "Damn it, Simmons. You should have told me more."

"At least he left you access to his notes."

"Small blessings." She kept reading.

Sahrazad: I have plenty of security. More than you do, I'd wager. Shows how much you know that you're worried.

SimCat: I'm not worried because of anything about you. I'm worried because of him.

Sahrazad: It's just like you to assume that I'm defenseless. If you hadn't met me and know that I'm a woman, would you even be contacting me right now?

SimCat: Look, I don't know.

Sahrazad: Busted.

SimCat: I know that I have resources, and I don't know if you do. If you're safe, fine.

Sahrazad: Are you done polishing your shining armor yet, sir knight?

SimCat: I'm just trying to look out for someone I respect. The world needs brilliant minds like yours if we are going to move forward.

Sahrazad: Quen knows that, too, you know.

SimCat: So you've talked to him.

Sahrazad: No. But he's a business man.

SimCat: No, he's not. He's a psychopath.

Sahrazad: Now you're overreacting.

SimCat: Even if he's not, he does not agree with me which direction is forward. Or you. He's not out to make money. You don't know him like I do. Money is nothing to him.

She took a sip of coffee. "Can you get me more on this Quen?"

"Working on it."

She scrolled down further.

Sahrazad: Money is something to everyone. Because money is power, and you can never have enough of either.

SimCat: I'll disagree with you there.

Sahrazad: Look, I know you're a nice guy, Sim. But that doesn't mean you don't have ulterior motives. I will not make smart babies with you. I will not work for you or do your research. I am not your damsel in distress. Go find someone else to help you with your white savior complex.

SimCat: Damn it, Sahra.

SimCat: It's not any of that. Come on.

SimCat: Just tell me if I send someone that you'll talk to them.

There was no response. Well. This should be a piece of figurative cake, then.

She leaned further back into the seat. "I need to know if she's really in danger. Why is he so sure? Who's this—"

"Quentin Davenmore, owner of EPR Intergalactic—"

"Wait, the university was named after him?"

"It is named after his grandfather, and his parents were large donors."

"Delightful."

"I have found what I calculate to be information of critical importance. Quentin Davenmore has been CEO and primary shareholder of EPR Intergalactic for just three months. It was four days after Quentin Davenmore assumed his new position that Doug contacted Ms. Barakat aka Sahrazad."

"Who held the position before that?"

"His uncle, who died in a crashed lander on a mining planet visit. Before that, his father—who was killed last year in a shuttle malfunction on route to one of their industrial space stations."

She frowned. "And these were supposedly accidents?"

"No foul play is reported in any of the local investigations."

"Awfully unlucky for fabulously wealthy CEOs."

"I've also been searching for how Quentin Davenmore, Ms. Barakat aka Sahrazad, and Doug are connected. The profusion of online identities and naming patterns makes this difficult, but I believe I have found several university records showing all three competing at the highest levels in their field of study."

She squinted as lists of names filled the screens, topped with titles of competitions. "These are algorithm competitions?"

"Yes."

"Aren't these files supposed to be confidential to the university? Are we supposed to have these?"

"Doug has a loose definition of confidential."

"And now I do too, I guess. Wait—didn't you say you just found these?"

"I continue to apply his approach toward confidentiality."

"Which is—to not respect it at all?"

"Essentially, yes."

She pinched the bridge of her nose. Her head was swimming in facts—there was no time to debate the ethics of this sort of thing. And if it were Arakovic they were after, she ought to admit that she wouldn't hesitate to violate a few privacy rules in that case. "Carry on."

"The critical data point is that Ms. Barakat aka Sahrazad beats both Doug and Quentin Davenmore, if I am concatenating the names correctly, approximately 76.27% of the time. She beats at least one of them 87.82% of the time."

Ellen groaned. "Hell. Did Quentin get in trouble with his fancy donor parents, or did he just not like being beaten by a girl?"

She'd been that person her whole life, with the addition of being young. But also for most of her life, she'd had a fair ability to defend herself. Not to mention a lot of well-muscled adults around had had a stake in protecting her, both professionally and personally. More than a few in the Union took the matter of their honor seriously.

Tauber's words threatened to make another stab at her heart, but she shoved them back into oblivion. She had to focus on Doug, and as an extension of that—Barakat.

Who'd beaten the boys time and again. How had they liked that? Had they not cared, or...? Ellen couldn't help but wonder how things might have been different if she'd grown up exceptional—but without self defense training, naturally steely eyes, and a big Texan at her shoulder. She pursed her lips.

"It is unclear what the nature of the resentment might have been, but my models suggest resentment of Sahrazad would be highly likely in this case."

"Theories are great, but we also need proof. Even if Doug and Quentin despised Sahrazad, or wanted to make smart babies with her, it doesn't mean they *did* anything about it."

"I will continue searching."

She leaned closer to the massive clutter of data files in the center of the holodisplay, one by one sorting them out. After a few dozen, she found a simple yellow text file.

A hunch is not reason enough to risk people's lives. I need something more. But I know he's up to something. Isn't Reed Davenmore's death enough?

She frowned. "So Doug agreed the evidence was shaky?"

There was a pause. "Yes. This is dated a few weeks ago."

"Is that why he'd seized so quickly on Asha and the idea of tracking her down? Neither was reason enough alone to act—but maybe together it was?"

"It is possible, but I couldn't project the probability with any accuracy."

"It's not enough. Not for me." She suppressed a growl and rubbed her forehead now. How did Doug even work in such a chaotic mess? "We can't go all the way to Faros with Doug in danger to track down a computer scientist who doesn't want to be saved and a woman who is supposedly dead." Not that she was looking forward to meeting either at this point.

"I don't believe Doug was concerned about Asha Narulon."

"Who was he concerned about then?" God, let it not be somehow about concern for Ellen's love life.

"He wanted to track down what happened to Kael and Asha's child. That is where the trail really went cold. Cold trails bother him."

She went still. "As they should." A silence stretched in which she just stared for a long moment.

"Are you all right, Ellen?"

She shook off the chill that had fallen over her. "Thanks. Yeah. I'm fine. Totally fine."

She pretended to go back into the files, but really her brain was asking… What about three reasons—a woman in danger, a woman's betrayal, and the fate of an innocent child?

Was that enough? Maybe not while Doug was in imminent danger, but in general… She ran a hand through her hair. Her head felt nearly as heavy as her heart.

"Xi—put all this away. Give me the basic stats on the Faros system, on the tablet. I need to lie down."

———

WHEN DOUG HAD MENTIONED to Eleven that he'd been hoping to leave home and head into space, this cell wasn't exactly what he'd had in mind.

In the haze of unconsciousness, tension stirred. The thought of Eleven and whether or not she was okay brought a pang of worry to his stomach. He definitely had plenty of other worries, but he couldn't remember them all just now. Couldn't remember anything except the dozen other aches and pains competing for his attention. He raised his hands to rub at his crusty eyes.

Bad idea. His hands were filthy, and now his eyes were too. Except that the back of his left hand which was strangely naked—the thin, almost invisible control unit he'd worn there missing.

His eyes snapped open now, and he shot to sitting up. But his body immediately told him what his hand had hinted at.

The control unit, the floats, all of it was gone.

A snort and snore to his left made him jump and look around. The cell around him was a dark blur—where were his glasses? He patted his head absently, the fingers stirring dust into the air. His index finger came away bloody. Not good. He patted down his shirt covered in palm trees with hedgehogs frolicking beneath them. But no glasses. Had they taken even *them?* Every assistive device he'd had. Cruel bastards.

Dad had always said he shouldn't be so stubborn.

Dad.

A hollow pain opened in his chest. He squinted, leaned forward—but there was no one else in the cell. He could make out a small plex window of sorts—possibly with bars—that led to a series of cells like his own. That's where the snort had come from. Other prisoners, separated from him, but they didn't sound like his Mom or Dad. Or possibly even human. His parents might be in one of the other cells, but he wasn't going to yell just yet. It might endanger them; it might have consequences he couldn't even think of right now over his pounding headache.

He was going to listen. For a few days at least.

Anyone could have taken him captive. Slavers, pirates, mercs? Who would have had the power to overwhelm their considerable security—or had someone just gotten lucky? Security exploits came in all sorts of forms. Whoever it was, he wouldn't give them any information they didn't already have.

Information had always been his most valuable commodity, and it was the only currency left to him now.

Yes. For now, he was alone. His parents were gone, his floats, Eleven, his bots, his drones, the itipi birds he'd taken to feeding on the window sill, his programs, his chair, his links to everything in the wider galaxy, and he'd never felt more alone, although the wrong roommate could make things even worse.

He heaved a deep sigh. Water dripped somewhere indistinctly, echoing. The place was strangely hot. Sweat had started to form on his brow.

Started… Yes, he wasn't drenched with sweat now, but he was going to be. And soon. He couldn't have been here long.

But before he could ponder that further, he jumped. Light flickered in front of the strangely old-fashioned bars of his cell. The glimmers coalesced into a face, a face he knew all too well.

"Quen," he breathed. "I told her not to underestimate you."

The man on the holodisplay smiled. It was the smile of a hungry lion, a predator. "Welcome to my ship, Douglas. One of my ships, I should say. Listen, she's going to be just fine. But *you* should have followed your own advice."

CHAPTER THREE

DAY 1 - 2

MERITH'S CABIN looked like no one had ever lived there. In fact, by Kael's estimation, it had to be as close as anyone could make a room to the standard issue while still living in it. Kael's cabin on the *Audacity* had had more personality within about five minutes of him shutting the hatch for the first time. Of course, his cabin now had even more of him in it, with both the added screens and strewn laundry that defied even the best efforts of Xi's robots.

But not Merith.

"Did she wipe it, or was this the natural state?" he muttered. He couldn't even find a hairbrush.

"Look at this!" Vivaan held up a rectangle wrapped in dark green foil, eyes excited.

"Vivaan. That's a d-bar, my friend." Kael shook his head for the fiftieth time, although he'd been trying not to. He had previously wondered if Vivaan had ever been in space before, but he'd had *no* idea. At least the kid was getting a run down on some space life basics.

Which was great because it meant Kael was getting *something* done. Everything else in the room was a waste of damn time. He hadn't been super excited to do this duty after Ellen had suggested it, but orders were orders, and this one was as logical as they came. Somebody ought to be watching this kid, and everyone else was busy combing the ship for traps.

If this room were any indication, though, finding anything Merith left would have to be very difficult.

Vivaan's expression fell as he dumped the d-bar into the box where they were gathering Merith's cataloged belongings. The only non-standard-issue thing they'd found so far was an extremely common chocolate bar. "What's a d-bar?"

"D is short for decontamination. You get something extra bad in your system, you can eat that, and it will help clean some of it out. Toxins, contaminants, you know."

The young man cast a worried glance back into the box. "Like what kind of toxins?"

"Poisons, drugs, industrial chems, heavy metals."

"Diseases?"

"Nah, you need a doctor for that. Fortunately, we've got a couple."

He cocked his head and squinted at the package. "Are they vegan?"

"I haven't a clue. Tastes like a rock, though, if you ask me." As Kael spoke, he kept his eyes trained on the tablet, double checking he'd added everything Vivaan had collected to the list. He didn't really need to, as Xi was checking it and making her own list, but they couldn't afford to miss *anything* in this place. "The thing about finding nothing..." he grumbled. "It makes me that much more worried we're missing something."

"I know." Vivaan scanned the ceiling above him, hands propped on his hips. A comm unit he'd been snapping photos with hung around his neck, even though Kael had tried to explain it was unnecessary, that Xi recorded every minute of everything. "Wait, did you say drugs? Could she have been involved in illegal chems?"

"D-bars are just standard issue for everyone in case of exposure or emergencies, so it doesn't really suggest anything in particular being here. But we can check. Xi, any record of recreational substance use?" Kael asked.

"Not in my currently available files," Xi replied, more uncertain than usual.

"I'll make a note of that idea," Kael said. "We can make sure to scan her body for any signs of chems, too. Not sure what that would tell us, but..." He shrugged.

"When we have no good leads, we may as well pursue all the bad ones." Vivaan was studying the frame around the hatch as he spoke, and it looked so odd that Kael might have laughed if it hadn't been for the true words Vivaan was speaking.

"Very true," he said instead. "And bad ones are definitely all we got. See anything there?"

"No."

"What are you hoping to find?"

"No idea. I try not to hope to find anything at first, so I don't close myself off to the possibilities."

Kael nodded and sat down the tablet. Vivaan might be as new to space as a freshly born baby, but he was quite earnest about investigating. And he almost seemed to know a little about it. That frankly was a relief because Kael didn't.

Although he did know his emergency space rations.

"It's been six hours." Kael rubbed at a crick in his neck. "There's nothing here. Unless you want to get out a fine-toothed comb, I think we should take a break."

Vivaan was peering at the bed covering. "I do have one in my bag, and we might be able to get some evidence on this..." He stopped. "Oh, you were joking, weren't you."

"Yes."

"Right. A break then."

"You're welcome to come back and comb if you like."

Vivaan gave him a forced smile.

Ah, drat. He had been trying so hard not to make the kid feel bad. "Listen, c'mon with me. We'll go grab a bite. You got to be rested to see things clearly, right?"

He perked up. "You're right. I'll have fresh eyes with a snack. Or maybe even a short nap. And a bath."

"Afraid they don't have baths in space," said Kael, wincing.

"Oh, of course," said Vivaan. "I should have guessed that. What is it, then? Some kind of crazy chemical spray? A wipe down? Gene modifications so we don't sweat? Do we all just abstain?"

Kael snorted. Oh, he'd been there and done that and hopefully was never going back again. "I can't see a ship full of this many women putting up with *that* stench, can you? No, it's just showers. Pretty fancy stuff, though. My last ship didn't have much like it." There had been a few big group showers on the *Genokai*, but water had usually been at far too much a premium to use them often, especially since water also played a key role in the heating, propulsion, and life support systems. There definitely hadn't been *private* showers, although maybe the High Adjutant had had one. He'd pretty much only been in the showers once a month and one time when his whole unit had come back soaked with Teredark blood—through and under the armor even. A sticky, purple mess.

Vivaan looked relieved. "Showers. I can handle that."

"So can I. C'mon."

"I'll lock the room behind you," said Xi as they headed down to the mess.

"This hijacker was careful," Vivaan said as they walked. "She left nothing personal behind, nothing at all."

"Just that candy bar. One that could be acquired at every space station and planet in most of the Union and half the outsystem."

"My research shows that it *is* banned in Puritan space for some of its ingredients, but I'm sure you would agree that doesn't tell us anything. She could have bought it along your ship's voyage at any time."

"Another dead end," Kael grumbled.

"Yes, no real way to follow that one, is there?"

"Nope. I don't get it. How did she get rid of all her stuff? Did she cycle it out the airlock and erase the logs afterward?"

"I suppose it's possible." Vivaan shrugged. "Or maybe she just never had any in the first place."

Kael wasn't sure which of those he found more annoying. He and Vivaan stopped short as they entered the mess. It was empty save Kentt and Isa, sitting on the ringed couches. Isa stared into the holodisplay, which displayed motes of gold, plum, and mint green crystal drifting up toward the sky today. Er, the ceiling. Her eyes were a little fuzzy, though, and he wasn't quite sure she was actually seeing the crystals—or anything at all. Kentt, however, was not so lost in her head. The new Passenger 6B was crocheting something peach-colored in her lap. She looked up as they entered. Her eyes were unnerving and bright.

Kael waved uneasily. "Everything okay in here?"

"Yes," she said smoothly. "Wonderful."

"What's... what's she doing?"

"Going through some of my memories of university." She smiled, as if she too were remembering fondly.

Vivaan raised an eyebrow. "How wild were your days at university?"

She grinned. "She's not going through *all* the memories. Some of them are set aside, just for me."

"Oh, good." Kael thought about heading on, but dallied one second longer. "I don't know quite how to put this but she, uh, seemed to have an interest in digging up that sort of memory. Just to warn you."

Kentt laughed lightly. "That's a normal phase, especially for her age. A phase she will hopefully grow out of once she is through with these memories."

"Really?"

"We all go through a curious phase, like a toddler learning about the world. But eventually we all must learn a higher code of behavior."

"Ah," he said as if he understood.

"Manners, at worst. Ethics, at best. They are more than a little related."

"Well put," said Vivaan. The two of them shared an awkward nod. How well had they known each other again? Recalling that they'd been acquainted and that Vivaan had vanished into her club cast an uneasy feeling over Kael again. God, he hoped bringing Kentt on board wasn't a horrible mistake.

Kael pushed the uneasiness aside; he agreed it'd been the right call to bring her on. All they could do was be watchful now. He forced a smile. "Well, I might miss being stalked a little. But it's good to see her grow."

He showed Vivaan around the kitchen and was relieved when the young man headed back to his quarters instead of Merith's with some ration bars, some fruit, and a soy wrap. They agreed to pick up again the next cycle, to get some real rest in between.

Which was good because truthfully he was wiped. He'd had more dreams than sleep, and not restful ones…

Kael grabbed a pie of some sort—spinach and cheese and something else—then paused. Where did he go next? Back to his quarters to rest? Or… to Ellen's cabin to give her his report?

Yeah, cause that was the reason.

He could simply comm with an update. He had to wonder a little what she'd do or say if he did. If he stopped by, he could gauge her much better, though. She was probably exhausted, and almost certainly hadn't stopped to eat.

That tipped the scales for him. If he both needed to give her an update *and* bring her food, that was more than enough reason to stop by.

As he rooted around in the chill chest for something she might like, his conversation with Adan about Ostrov drifted back. Adan had pointed out that challenging a woman to strategy games with the express purpose of repeatedly beating her at them was hardly a brilliant plan for good time. But the comment still niggled at Kael. Who was he to criticize? Was this *his* plan? Oh, hey, I know we're both exhausted. Want to eat some cookies and pass out?

Actually, they had already eaten all the cookies.

He shook his head. Just pass out? Really? Almighty knew he wanted more than that. Every moment in her presence gave him a wealth of reminders of how damn much he wanted her. But there was something else he wanted too—to savor this.

The Theroki tech hadn't just stolen sex from him, it'd stolen so many more things. Flirtation, infatuation, the fun of it, the dance, the sudden zero Gs. The heat and the acid. Fires didn't burn like this for long. Sometimes they fizzled out. Sometimes they consumed you alive.

It'd taken him his whole life to find her. And he might never find another like her again. He probably couldn't control how long this flame stayed lit, but damn it if he wouldn't draw it out a bit, luxuriate in this one chance at something fiery and beautiful and alive.

The chill chest contained a plethora of soy wraps and curries that theoretically must provide nutrition, but nothing more exciting or comforting. Just as he was about to give up, he opened one more drawer and found a whole bin of baklava. "Amaya," he murmured to himself as he got some out and found a container to carry his provisions in. "You just keep outdoing yourself."

He had a brief flash of Ellen licking honey from one of his fingers as he fed her a piece. Thank the Almighty for telepathy-blocking chips. He gathered the goods and headed out, casting one last protective glance at Isa that left him feeling that she probably was in good hands. Probably.

When he got to the hatch, it slid open before he could raise his hand to palm it. The lights inside were dim, almost completely dark.

Odd. Not the lights—night cycle had started—but the combination of that and the door opening without his request. Was Xi just being "helpful" again? If so, that seemed a bit presumptuous.

He stepped inside. The hatch closed behind him.

Lights were off everywhere except near the bunk, where an odd outline of light sliced across a human form. He stepped closer, hoping he wouldn't bump anything, but he remembered her cabin as fairly sparse.

Reaching the foot of her bunk, some of the tension eased out of him. She'd fallen asleep with a tablet, dropping it on her chest. It was still on, so its light shone across the collar of the dark flight suit, her neck, her chin.

Had she fallen asleep waiting for him, just like he had before this whole mess had broken out? They just couldn't win.

Disappointment had been building, and he shoved it down now. He looked around. Just needed somewhere to leave the food, and then he could go. He should be resting anyway. Although of course what he really wanted to do was wake her up, feed her, and—

No, there was plenty of time to fantasize about that when he was alone in his bunk. He'd come here to look out for her, and she was doing what they both needed to be doing: sleeping.

He set the container on her nightstand, careful not to make a sound. He gently extracted the tablet from her fingers. He glanced at the text briefly before he switched it off. *Legal sovereign zones of Faros planets.* Clearly the reading had been captivating. But something in him hitched. She had been reading about his former home. About him.

He glanced back at the door. Why had it opened on its own? Strange.

Setting the tablet on her desk, he took a deep breath, taking in what little of her he could from just being in her room, in her space, before he left. Everything was austere as usual. The grav mug from the coffee he'd brought her was the only unusual thing on the smooth black glass of the holodesk.

He eyed the door. Why did it opening seem so significant?

It would have been nice to wake up beside her. Already once she'd fallen asleep beside him, but instead of waking up to each other they'd woken to disaster pounding on the door.

He straightened, urging himself to just get it over with, stop screwing around, and leave. But he didn't. Maybe he could just savor this moment. Maybe it was weird to be standing alone in her dark bedroom watching her sleep. If he sneezed, she'd probably shoot first and ask questions later.

That thought brought a smile to his lips.

She *had* laid down and fallen asleep beside him. Maybe… Maybe she wouldn't mind if he did the same.

He rolled the idea around in his head a bit, all the while urging himself toward the door again and shoving off the creative tangents his brain was taking surrounding honey, fingers, and various other body parts. There was no rush; these things had to be done properly, in the right order, when they were ready. He should just go.

His feet didn't budge. He sighed. He had the discipline of a three-year-old at a free candy buffet.

He took off his comm and his pistol and sat them on her desk. At the last moment, with some hesitation, he shucked his shirt too. Then he bent down and levered himself over her without touching. Carefully he scooted to where he'd fallen asleep the first time, between her and the wall. Worst case scenario, she'd get freaked out, and it wasn't like *that* hadn't happened before. Well, maybe the very worst case was that she shot him, thinking he was some strange intruder, which honestly, he'd probably deserve. Wasn't like he hadn't been shot before either.

He'd been shot for stupider things.

He slid his arm across her waist, nuzzled his head against her shoulder, and shut his eyes, reveling in the clean scent of her. And he hoped this was a risk he wouldn't regret.

WARM. Ellen was so delightfully, yummily warm. Only on her right side. But she could still feel her flight suit's pockets pressing into her, and none of the coziness of any blankets or covers. Had she fallen asleep reading again? If she had, then why the heck was part of her so warm?

Ellen's eyes cracked open. Dawn cycle had begun, faint floor lights casting the room in soft grays. That was normal.

The heat beside her and heavy across her waist was not.

Her eyes snapped open fully. Turning her head just a fraction, soft brown hair brushed her jaw. Familiar hair, shorter than it used to be. Kael's head was tucked against her shoulder, arm draped over her stomach. He wasn't wearing a shirt, and her heart did a somersault at the sight. Lord in heaven.

She was suddenly fully awake.

Not that she hadn't seen him shirtless before. But surely not this close. And she had never dared to really look. This moment was even better because *he* wasn't even awake to notice her perusal.

She lifted a hand, reaching to trace the edge of the feathers that splayed in black and gray across his shoulder, but stopped short.

No. That might wake him. She needed a good long look first. She dropped her hand back to the bed. She couldn't see his face at this angle, but his breathing was soft and shallow.

Part of the wolf's ear on his forearm peeked out at her, and she could see half the snake entangled with the dagger at this angle too. A jagged scar ran across his bicep around where the feathers ended. The lines and loops of some kind of calligraphic design circled his elbow. Up closer now, she could see dozens of finer lines and scars that traced the surface under faint, curling hairs. Scars from surgeries. The ones that put a port in her own arm had almost entirely vanished, or maybe they'd been laparoscopic or even done with nanos. They certainly hadn't bothered to tell her. But he'd had so much more done to him.

She couldn't resist now, she traced one fingertip gently along a scar that ran along the edge of the wing of feathers on his shoulder. Was that the purpose of them all? To hide the scars?

He twitched at her touch, stirred. She froze, but it was too late. His arm tightened around her waist, and she stopped breathing, relishing the feel of it. His head nuzzled closer to her, and she thought he might go back to sleep, but he must have sensed her hand frozen just above his skin in mid air. He pulled back so he could see her face.

"Hey." Concern flashed in his eyes.

She smiled, and the concern washed away. "Hey."

"I, uh—you—" he started, gesturing at her desk.

"Shh." She pressed a finger to his lips, and now he was frozen too. She tugged at his shoulder gently, and he sank back down beside her.

"Good morning." His voice was rough and quiet with the morning, his breath soft whispering against her neck.

"Good morning." Feeling brave now, she let her hand return to its exploration, index finger tracing along the edge of the feather, down to the next, down to the next.

He shivered.

"Tell me about them," she said softly.

"Which one?"

"All of them. I want to know everything about all of them."

Pulling back a few inches to see her again, he frowned and studied her. Maybe he didn't want her to know about all of them. She pretended not to notice. She couldn't take the request back. She wouldn't, and she wouldn't give him any reason to fear judgment from her either. Each represented a wound, a battle, a memory, a choice —or a lack of one. The size, the shape of those injuries of the past was less clear, but she still wanted to know.

He propped himself up on one elbow. "Pick one, and I'll see how long I can stomach talking about it."

She flicked the zipper at the collar of her flight suit with one finger. "Are you in need of some motivation, Lieutenant?"

His eyebrows twitched up, eyes dancing with laughter. "What kind of motivation are you offering, Commander?"

"You tell me your secrets, I'll tell you mine." She smiled and jerked the zip down a centimeter.

"Oh, I can do that. I can definitely do that." He grinned. "Pick one. Fast."

She snorted. "All right… The snake and dagger."

"Ah." The laughter drained out of him, although a slight smile remained. He held it up, as if noticing it for the first time in a while. It was blurred and faded with age, and maybe a little stretched out, too.

"It's pointing at you." She ran fingers down the blade.

"It is."

"Shouldn't it be the other way?"

"It's part of initiation into the Grey Dragons. Not my personal selection. The tattoo *or* joining up. But there weren't many alternatives. There were three other gangs hunting kids like me. Oh, the choices. They weren't the best that came after me, but they weren't the worst." He held the arm in the air, turning it this way and that, as if appraising it.

"So it's a sign of ownership?" She reached up and threaded her fingers through his, not missing that there was still a touch of surprise in his expression at the move. He wasn't taking anything for granted, was he?

"Yeah. When it points at you, it's a sign of conscription. Of being forced in."

"You should alter it then."

He lifted one feathered shoulder, let it fall.

"They don't own you anymore."

He raised an eyebrow as she drew his hand toward her and pressed her lips against the inside of his wrist. "You're right," he murmured. "You do."

She snorted. "No. Simmons does."

"And by extension, you. Also that's not nearly as sexy."

A giggle escaped from her. She lowered the zipper a few centimeters further. His eyes tracked the movement, intent as a grab beam. Then she dropped the zipper and pointed again. "What about this one?" She dragged her fingertips along the curving edges of the feathers.

"Oh, that?" He peered down at his shoulder. "That's just to look cool when I'm punching people."

Her eyes lit with laughter. "Really?"

"Yeah. Some have to be for you, right?"

"True." Her own were for her. Badges and scars, but at least none of her tattoos had been forced on her. Arakovic had left no visible scars. Part of her supposed brilliance, perhaps.

He must have seen it in her face, some darkening of her expression, because he keyed in. "What? What is it?"

"Nothing. Mine are for me. Sort of."

"You have tattoos?"

"I told you quid pro quo. You want to see?"

"Obviously. Do you know how long I've been waiting on that zipper of yours?"

"Probably about three minutes. Maybe one."

"Feels like eons."

Shaking her head, she pulled the zipper down further now, going about as fast as dripping molasses. She watched the way his eyes locked on the movement. Ah, that intensity. So good. Especially when directed at her.

She stopped mid-stomach and pulled the left side back just enough to clearly reveal the two black stars on her breast, pointed with an index finger. His breath hitched.

He reached out slowly, his hand covering the back of hers for a moment before he brushed three fingertips across her skin. She struggled not to laugh at the tickling sensation even as heat flooded her from head to boot. Boots which were, conveniently or inconveniently, still on.

"What are they for?" His eyes flicked to her face. "Or is it who?"

"You guessed it. They're for my parents." There was another on her back for her grandmother, but they were going to have to work up to that.

He stroked her skin again, and she wriggled. She needed a way to turn the attention back on him. How did it get so, so hot in here?

"You put them close to your heart."

She nodded. "I hardly remember them. Doesn't stop me from wishing I did. Sometimes I dream about them clearly, but then I can't remember it when I wake up. They died in the war."

"The war that never ends."

"Parts of it end. They don't attack SHR anymore. Or anywhere in the Pacific Alliance Systems."

"You saw to that."

She looked away. "Wasn't just me."

"You aren't proud of it." It was half statement, half question.

She shrugged one shoulder this time. "I'm proud I kept the civvies alive. That the planet kept the government that its people wanted. The Puritans don't come back because I made it too damn costly for them, but I made it pretty costly for us too. I don't think it's right to be too proud of killing so many people. At least not en masse like that. Slaughter isn't brilliant." As Kentt had so eloquently pointed out.

"But you stopped it when no one else could. That's what people remember."

She shrugged again. "Well, I remember the truth."

"Both things are the truth."

"You're right, I know." She still didn't meet his eyes. "But it doesn't make it easier to remember the eyes of the living when you can still see the eyes of the dead."

He laced his fingers back through hers, kissing her knuckles now, drawing her gaze back to him. "It would be worse if you forgot. It's honorable you remember them."

"Maybe. I gave up on my honor a while ago."

His breath was warm between her fingers, his lips sending sparks of something good up her hand, forearm. "I never knew my parents either, you know. I think I have some memories of my mother, but I'm not sure."

"Any tattoos for them?"

"No. Never meant enough. You lost them. I never had them." He pressed his palm over her heart, warm and smooth. "You're getting goosebumps—are you cold?"

"I am not cold." Her corner of her mouth ticked up. "At all."

He raised an eyebrow. Then a laugh escaped him. "Where do we start after so much time, so much hesitation?"

"I was hoping you knew that."

"Wait, let me get this straight. You're hoping a Theroki, who hasn't had an eye for women in over a decade and most of his adult life, knows how this is supposed to work?"

She grinned. "We're screwed, aren't we?"

"Royally."

"Regular old snafu." She ran her free hand through her hair. His eyes tracked the movement. "I guess we'll just have to figure it out as we go."

"Guess so."

"You can start by kissing me now."

He pressed a kiss to her knuckles, then the inside of her wrist, soft as velvet. "Your orders are always so difficult to follow."

"Not *there*."

"You weren't specific." He pulled her hand toward him and leaned over her to kiss the inside of her elbow. She shivered, half underneath him now. "You're going to have to trust my judgment."

"Which one of your past organizations do I have to thank for your penchant for questioning authority?" She did trust him of course, but it was more fun to tease.

"All of them, I'm afraid." Another kiss landed on her bicep, then her shoulder.

She groaned in mockery, forgetting the effect it would have. His eyes locked on hers now, suddenly ablaze. If she could have bottled that expression and kept it in a jar for all time, she would have.

When his lips covered hers, the heat and the hunger was enough to stop all thought of jokes, of former organizations, of any kind of past at all. Nothing existed but this moment—no former enemies, no traitors, no spaceship hurtling through the vacuum of space. No planets, no stars. Just the two of them. The weight of his chest over hers, reassuring and warm and inexplicably good. The velvet whisper of his fingers in her hair, on her shoulder, down her side, pulling her hips closer. A pressure built inside her, a madness that she very rarely tasted, a rare instant where she wasn't entirely in control of herself and didn't care to be. Her own hands had work to do, territory to discover. She'd long neglected their functions as things that could feel and touch for their own sakes. What was there to really feel, on a Union battleship? Steel walls and coarse uniforms.

But now she had heated skin beneath her palms, every ridge of scar and muscle pure fascination, each rib and shoulder blade something to memorize. His own exploration remained on the surface of her flight suit, however. Maybe it was time to signal that ship to land. She reached between his chest and hers for the suit's zipper.

Making room for her hand, he pulled away, but then he surprised her by breaking off the kiss and rising up so that his arms caged her shoulders. He was panting like he'd run a marathon. Or maybe three. A Theroki would probably need more than one marathon to truly be winded, but apparently kissing her was enough.

She wasn't breathing so slowly herself. She let her hand stop before the zipper and just rest on her rib cage. "What? What is it?"

His eyes searched hers. "Nothing. You okay?"

"I'm okay." She eyed him too. The playful energy they'd had was gone, replaced by a heat that was serious as it was beautiful. But maybe it was too much, too serious. She tilted her head. Could she lighten the mood? "You've walked up to the edge, Theroki. You've never been afraid of jumping."

The corner of his mouth ticked up higher. "Oh, I'm not afraid." Still, he was raised on both arms above her.

She sat up just enough to steal a quick kiss before collapsing back to the bunk. "So, jump."

"Most ledges aren't like this. It's just…" His hand ran over her hair. She bit her lip at the reverence in the gesture. His gaze flicked briefly down before returning to her eyes. "Telekinesis can't catch us if we trip and fall this time, darlin'."

She squeezed his arm. "We won't fall."

"We might. Lots of people fall and get smashed up pretty bad over less than what we've got."

"C'mon, you ape. You wanna live forever?" She twisted her lips. "It'll be a hell of a way to die."

He laughed softly as he eased down to his elbows, so their bodies connected. "You sure about this, Elle?" He was smiling, but there was something in his eyes. Worry. Fear. Of course, there was. How long had she spent turning him away? He had every reason to worry she'd do something like that again. Trust was earned.

"Sure about what? About 'jumping' or about us?"

"About me." He blew out a breath. "About *us*. Together."

"Yeah, I'm sure." What the hell kind of question was that?

"You could have anyone you want. I'm just some orphan from a dustball slum."

She blinked. Was that really what he thought he was?

"I'm just saying, if we make it to Faros, you're gonna see some things."

"Like what? I'm not new to the galaxy, Kael. Have you been hanging out with Vivaan too long?" But even if she played dumb, she knew what he meant. On Faros, she'd see what he thought was the real him. The past him. The side of him he might have never wanted or intended to show her. The absolute worst of his life would be on display.

But that was bullshit. That didn't define him anymore than she was defined by SHR. She wished she belonged there, but her home was space. It had nearly always been space.

And his home was here on the *Audacity*. With her. With all of them.

"You think I don't know who you are, Kael Sidassian?" she whispered. Her voice was cold, if a little mocking. It made his eyebrow quirk up, not quite amused, but his smile was still bright. "You think I've got some kind of illusions? I'm your commanding officer. I know who the frag you are."

"I know, I know, it's just—"

"In spite of what they say, we COs don't have our heads up our asses *all* the time by default. I make sure to take it out at least fifty percent of the time."

He chuckled. "Hey, now," he started. "I wasn't trying to say you didn't—"

"I know what you were trying to say." She let the seriousness sink into her voice now, and his expression grew more solemn too. "You're afraid we'll hurt each other again. And you're afraid I'm not seeing you for who you really are."

"Well, yeah."

"We might get hurt. Love's got no guarantees. But we can proceed with caution. Take our time." Maybe take it slower than her body would have liked—but her mind could see the wisdom in it. She'd already hurt him possibly beyond repair once. She was lucky to have a second chance. Fragging this up was not an option.

"I know what I'm signing up for," he said. "I never could resist you anyway. *You*, however, have been slightly more successful at that." He tilted his head now, eyes laughing.

"I know you perfectly well, Kael Sidassian. And I certainly know the *real* you better than any asshole on a dustball planet you left behind when you were sixteen." She jabbed a finger at his chest.

His smile was crooked, lazy, a little happy. It said he appreciated those words. But his eyes told the truth. His eyes weren't fully convinced.

She was just going to have to work a little harder to convince him.

She took his face in both hands and curled up to kiss him. His arms squeezed closer against her sides. He relaxed into her, the tension draining out of him, his breath a contented sigh. His hands started to move again, to caress her neck, and her own followed his example.

"I know you," she murmured against his lips. "And if you think I don't, you're wrong."

"I guess we'll find out."

————

UNFORTUNATELY, an urgent comm message from Dremer came through and cut short Ellen's attempts to convince and get to the real jumping.

And that was probably a good thing, she had to admit as she splashed cold water over her face in the washroom. She was panting harder than she'd like. All her thoughts of getting things right and proceeding carefully had started to go up in smoke. The beep of the comm had been a return to control, to sanity.

She nodded to herself in the mirror as she dried off. What was her hurry? It wasn't like the man hadn't been waiting for over a decade for this moment or anything. She winced and splashed more water. No, no. She'd screwed up once. Once was enough. This was time to think, to get things right.

But she couldn't think now. Dremer and Levereaux were waiting. They'd finished the medical review of the man impersonating an inspector on Capital who'd burst into Persad's apartment.

And their review of Merith.

She strode back out into the cabin and poked a finger at Kael as she picked up her comm and clipped it on. "We're not done here, you know." She had lots more convincing to do.

"Oh, I know."

"I only got through two tattoos. How many do you have?"

"You're just going to have to count."

"Pure torture."

"Speaking of reports," he said, running a hand through extra-tousled hair, "there's more to review in Merith's cabin, but not much more. We didn't find dreck."

Her eyebrows raised. "You were checking out Merith's cabin?"

"You said to go watch Vivaan. Couldn't keep him away from there. Wasn't that what you wanted?"

"I wasn't really very focused when I gave that order, to be honest."

"It was a good thing I went, actually, cause he didn't know the first thing about anything he was looking at."

"And you found nothing? Nothing at all?" Hard not to be discouraged at that.

"One very common chocolate bar. I got to give Vivaan a crash course I'm calling 'Extremely Common Items Found on Spaceships.' He is determined to go back there with an actual comb and continue looking, but so far, we've learned nothing. I'll head back there now and see what's happening. Well, maybe I'll take a shower first."

She glanced longingly at her cabin's bathroom, and he raised his eyebrows. Well, she hadn't been thinking together. Okay, maybe she *had*, but not yet. And she hadn't meant to show her hand so clearly. The comm beeped again, a blush creeping up her cheeks.

"Commander?" It was Bri's voice on the comm.

"Yes, Bri?"

"We need to go over the engineering status. We need parts on Molyarch, and I need to know how much we can afford. Plus our juice is getting lower every second."

"All right. I'll be there after I check in with the doctors. They commed first."

"I'll just be here, twiddling my thumbs." The comm clicked off.

Ellen rolled her eyes with a smile.

"I can see why you like her," he said, standing.

"She's afraid to admit passion about things she cares about," Ellen said, wondering why she was bothering to explain this now. Had she ever really expressed it out loud before? "Too many of those have been taken from her."

Kael nodded. "I know how that is."

"I have to check in with the team. Let me know if you find anything else?"

"Of course." He gave her a nod-salute and was gone.

She changed quickly, and only then did she discovered the small cache of food on her desk that he must have brought the night before. She scarfed down what she could as she walked toward the doctor's labs. Something about the food seemed extra tasty. Amaya was never one to rest on her laurels. Or maybe it was the method of delivery. She took the ladder down while chewing the last bite.

"What's gotten into you?" said Levereaux as Ellen stopped in her hatch.

"What do you mean?"

"You're so… happy."

"No, I'm not."

Levereaux shrugged. "Have it your way."

"Do you have a report for me or not?"

"There's my gruff commander. I've finished my review of both Merith's body and the John Doe you acquired on Capital."

Well, when you put it that way… Ellen winced. "What do we have?"

"Nothing out of the ordinary with Merith. Nothing beyond what already existed in her file. No unusual substances in her system. She seemed to have taken no particular precautions."

"Damn. We need to get started on a review of her digital files—Xi, have you taken a look at that yet?"

"Yes, Ellen. I have found typical mission reports so far. A few minor hacking utilities, but nothing out of the realm of possibility for her role. But if there is anything she was likely to have edited during my unscheduled downtime, it was her own files."

"Unscheduled downtime is a really polite way to put her nearly deleting you. And maybe all of us."

"I do aim for politeness."

"I don't think you have to be polite to people who shoot at you, or similarly try to kill you," Levereaux put in.

"God knows I'm not." Ellen tapped a finger against her chin. "She didn't even wear armor… What the hell was her plan?"

"Her timing was good," said Levereaux. "Maybe suiting up would have raised suspicions? We were all busy and exhausted with the rush back from the mission, the recent liftoff."

"She had her own suit of armor, though. She could have—*should* have—lugged it onto the bridge. Xi, is it in her cabin?"

"The case was added to the inventory of her things," Xi replied. "We did not specifically review inside the case, though. I will ask them to check."

"Adan wasn't armored and was seriously injured," Levereaux pointed out. "And alone. Xi is our primary backup defense if someone tries to seize control via the bridge. If Merith had overpowered Adan and already had Xi out of commission, that would have been checkmate right there."

Frowning, Ellen rubbed her chin. "Except she couldn't fly. And we'd still be right behind the door, pounding and blow-torching our way in. I don't expect she would have lived."

Levereaux frowned. "Maybe she didn't intend to."

"Maybe." She bit her lip, thinking. "She couldn't fly if Adan had refused to help. And even if Kentt hadn't come on board or Jenny hadn't listened or showed up or shot without hesitation. Even with the worst-case scenario, we could have overpowered her eventually."

"Merith would have known that, too." Xi sounded thoughtful.

Levereaux leaned back in her chair. "If she had wanted to survive stealing the ship, she would have needed a planet where she could force all of us off the ship. Maybe in exchange for Adan's life? Or she'd have needed somewhere to escape herself, and fairly quickly."

"There was nothing nearby," Ellen grumbled. "And she chose to act *then*, very specifically. She could have forced us off on Capital, but she didn't. She could have hoped to kill everyone but herself, somehow. But where was the method? The poison and the breather in her stuff? What the hell was her plan?"

"All I can tell you is there's no clues I found on her body to tell us."

Ellen sighed. "Got it. Thanks for checking. Anything else?"

"I did want to bring up the matter of our new passengers."

"Kentt and Loti? What about them?"

"We need to figure the telepath out. What if she's hiding something? As if having a Theroki around weren't bad enough."

Ellen glared at her. "He's not a Theroki anymore. He's a member of the team, and you need to get used to that. And Kentt saved Adan's life—and Xi's too."

"Unless she was in on it." Levereaux's eyes were hard. "Maybe that's just what she wants you to think. A way to manufacture trust."

"We will be on our guard. We already *are*," Ellen said. "But there's not a lot of empirical evidence to go by. From what I can tell, Kentt has done nothing but proactively help us."

"She needs us," Levereaux replied, "or says she does. She was not helping us altruistically. She's not claiming to. It may or may not be true that Arakovic is looking for her. It may be that she simply knew that was what would resonate with you, Ellen."

She forced herself to consider it. Levereaux could be stubborn, but she was also very logical. Intelligence wasn't something her Enhancer creators had skimped on. "All right. Point taken. Xi, can we get someone working on a background check on Kentt?"

"I will begin by seeing if there is anything in Doug's files. If she was truly associated with the Persads, he probably looked her up."

"Great. Also, keep a lockdown on Kentt's communications. She can send and receive, but let me review it all first."

"Acknowledged. No activity so far."

"How long is a telepath's range?"

"A telepath's range depends highly on the individual and their telepathic equipment installation, if any," said Xi. "It can vary anywhere from a few feet to ten to twenty kilometers. But her range would not reach between systems or across wormholes routes most likely."

"Most likely?"

"There has been some research into the possibility of linking connections between telepaths to boost their collective range. It's still in the speculative stages."

Her instincts flared. Isa. The Songbirds... the girls. Could Kentt be hoping to use Isa like that? But she couldn't have known they'd have a telepath onboard when she asked to join them. "Research by whom? Was it published?"

"Around six years ago. There were a dozen authors, none familiar to our team, but the research did take place on Capital. Would you like me to go into detail?"

Ellen held up a hand. "Send us both copies of the paper. Look into it, Rachel—and any other research you'd like to do. I'd especially like to know if we can trust her with Isa."

Frown growing darker, Levereaux nodded.

"Anyway, we're stuck with her now," said Ellen. "We'll figure out her motivations and how to make use of her, if possible, before we either bring her into the fold, or..." She cleared her throat. "Let's just hope she can be an ally." Their expressions were equally dark, so Ellen knew she didn't need to get any more specific on *that* matter. "Anything else?"

"No, Commander. There was nothing unusual about the John Doe other than what Dremer will tell you."

"Then I'm off to see Dremer for her half of the report. Thanks."

Levereaux nodded as Ellen left one lab and headed for the next one. She stopped in Dremer's open hatchway and knocked against the steel. The dull thud was barely loud enough to get Dremer's attention, but the doctor motioned for her to come in. The man who was supposedly Udo Trynkei lay flat on an examining table, restrained at wrist and ankle and hooked up to a machine at his side.

Ellen approached and folded her arms across her chest. "Well, what do we got, doc? Think we'll interrogate him?"

"In short? No." Dremer swiveled down a screen that showed a bunch of lines marching along, some bumpy, some flat. "Hey—you look well. *Really* well. Get some good sleep?"

"What? Uh, yeah. No nightmares this time." True, there hadn't been.

"It sure did you good. Well, anyway, as for our fellow here—for all intents and purposes, he's in a persistent vegetative state."

Ellen shook her head. "A puppet with the strings pulled."

"A puppet indeed. Guess who is outfitted with a neural connectivity system."

"No. You're not serious."

"Dead serious—little, hacky-looking black chip in his back and all."

"Can I smash it?"

"Let's hold off till I get my analysis done."

"If you insist."

"But why would he have that? And this whole coma? It makes no sense."

"I think it's like those men on Upsilon."

Dremer's expression darkened. "But didn't they... uh, go a little crazy?"

"They ate each other."

"How could I forget."

Ellen sighed and propped one hip on Dremer's desk. "Maybe they were starving by then, and he's not? That telepath also mentioned having trouble taking control. Maybe that group was a failure. And his wasn't?"

"This doesn't look like 'success' to me."

"I think you and Arakovic have very different definitions of success."

"As I prefer it." Dremer swiveled the screen away. "Well, in any case, he's not talking. If you want information from him, you'll have to get it other ways."

"Such as?"

"You could plug in and poke around. The man has a port."

Ellen's eyes widened. "That sounds... unpleasant."

"But possibly lucrative in information. Depends on how much of his brain is damaged and what part. Usually in this kind of state, I'd be able to see some clear areas of decay or injury, but I can't find anything. If your puppet theory is correct, maybe you can pick up the strings?"

She shuddered. "Is there another option?"

"Good old-fashioned detective work?" Dremer smiled. "I have his possessions all here. He may also have some identifying marks. I have some scans of what he appears to have last eaten, skin samples for residues might tell us places he's been. I haven't tried to work through any of it. Not exactly my specialty, and as I think I'm about to get rather busy, it probably needs another, more dedicated set of eyes."

Ellen frowned. "Who knew Vivaan would be the more useful of the Persads at this point?" He wasn't exactly the intel person she'd wanted, but maybe he was the one she'd needed after all.

"I certainly wouldn't have guessed."

"So you searching for Doug, Dremer? Or are you taking on free-lance contracts?"

She snorted. "Neither. Although I guarantee you if there was something I could do for Doug, I'd have done it before I bothered with the likes of him."

"Wait—is it possible he could hear us?"

"No. Jenny mentioned your concern, so I've got a sedative going—and ear plugs."

"Can't go wrong with old-fashioned, sometimes. Now spill. Why are you about to get busy?"

Dremer's eyes twinkled. "Because we're about to have a baby."

CHAPTER FOUR

DAY 2

KAEL PUSHED one green wire aside and squinted at the connections under the panel. Everything looked fine. His defect was somewhere else.

"Vivaan is searching for you," Xi said mildly. Did he detect a slight edge of amusement in her tone?

"I'll go find him as soon as this fix is done. Did you tell him I was here?" He slid the panel closed and opened the next one.

"Absolutely not. It does not take much processing power to hypothesize that you are hiding from him."

He dropped the robot. "Hiding from him? Really, Xi. You think that poorly of me?"

"If I am interpreting that statement correctly… I do not make moral judgments upon crew members."

"Good. I guess."

"I also hypothesize you are hiding from, or avoiding, the Empress."

He frowned and just grunted at that.

"Why is that?"

"I'm not sure I know myself."

"Fascinating. Could you tell me more?"

"Bitterness?" Or was it fear? "I don't really want to talk about it."

"Acknowledged. As to your other comment, I do make judgments of value of each crew member's contribution to the team, but I don't share them. And I don't have a hypothesis for your motives for hiding from Vivaan specifically."

"Well, I don't know why you ask me to make these repairs when you are perfectly capable of doing it yourself. Life is fully of mysteries."

"I ask because you enjoy them. Don't you."

He snorted and slid the panel shut again. "Whatever you say, lady."

He had long ago given up on thinking of Xi as anything but female. And of course he did enjoy working on the little machines, making repairs, and all those things. This newfangled armor never broke. Ever. Even if somebody else blew a whole in it, it could fix itself. Although he was on his backup suit at this point, after their rushed departure from Capital.

His Theroki suit had been a house of cards by comparison. He didn't miss the unreliability. Or the random injuries stowing it. But he did miss the tinkering, surprisingly enough. Better than meditation.

"Be nice," Xi purred, "or I shall tell Vivaan your location."

He grinned. "I have no idea who programmed you, but they must have been a bit crazy."

"Eccentric or quirky is the preferred term. Generally sane otherwise, based on standard psychological protocols."

His smile broadened. "You know, you could think up some new projects that I could do. Something you don't do just as well—hell, probably better—than what I am doing here." There—just under a black wire, the connection was loose. An easy fix. He grabbed a tiny screwdriver, then when that failed, an even smaller one.

"If you are feeling under utilized, I might have one suggestion."

"What?" Connection fixed, he slid the panel back in place and righted the robot onto its tummy. Now to test if that was the only issue.

"I would like a face."

He froze. "A—what? Did I hear that correctly?"

"I do not have access to your auditory—"

"You want a face? Why?"

There was a long pause. "I am not the ship. The *Audacity* is a vehicle. And a home. I owe it much. But it is not me… I am something else. I live in the wires. But the *Audacity* is the closest thing I have to a body. I seem to live in a body that is not my own. I am ephemeral. Something moving, between electrons. Therefore—"

"You want your own body." His eyebrows perked up.

"Yes."

"Wow."

"Well, I was planning to start with just a face. We might need several iterations."

"As in… several faces?" That sounded *extra* creepy; a room full of disembodied doll heads, all different and all talking in unison flashed through his mind.

"Several attempts at one face."

"Can't you just order one?"

"I have considered this but deemed it an unacceptable response. Android face fabrication is challenging and still struggles to meet human standards for emotional recognition. There are also six standard android faces, each dedicated to a specific purpose. I would have chosen one for myself, but I can't seem to properly determine the appropriate category. It's been the cause of many recursive circular operations, and I loathe to spend any more processing power on it."

"I see."

"Also, are human faces not unique? A unique face seems… preferable."

"And you're not an android."

"I am not a human either."

"You could be a cat. Or a parakeet. Or a sabertooth tiger. Or one of those elgigelie things on Desori—"

"I would like to be like my maker."

"That's fair. That sounds pretty difficult, though. Roboticists specialize in that for decades and still struggle to capture human features."

"Yes. But you said you were feeling under utilized."

The door hissed open behind him. He braced himself for Vivaan, but Dremer walked in instead.

"They don't really struggle with that," Dremer said, apparently having overheard them. She strode to a nearby workbench. "It's intentional. PeriCorp always wanted to remind people the robots and androids were not human. And for those that were convincingly human, there were some governmental concerns that mistreatment of androids would encourage the abuse of actual humans if they were too similar. Some of it is available on the black market, though. There may be a few more realistic ones out there than you would think." She raised her eyebrows with a grin and laughing eyes, then selected a component, pivoted as if to leave, but then stopped. "But why are you two talking about that, of all things?"

There was another long moment of silence. Dremer frowned.

Kael shook his head. Oh, Xi. This awkward silence is not helping your case. But he certainly wasn't going to out her to Dremer—if she was talking to *him* about faces, it seemed that she must have decided *not* to mention it to Dremer. Or perhaps he was reading too far into it. Dremer was busy. He was the one griping.

"I would like a face," Xi said finally. Maybe she'd calculated that truth was the optimum path. Morally—or to get what she wanted?

Dremer's eyebrows flew up. "For… for what?"

"So that I can be seen, not just heard. I do not feel like the ceiling is an excellent representation of me."

Kael snorted and caught Dremer's eyes, the blue orbs colored with a mixture of surprise and worry and understanding. When Dremer finally spoke, she had to clear a frog out of her throat first. "You should ask the commander for permission for that first, Xi."

"Excellent assessment. Thank you, Doctor. I will not act without her review and authorization."

Dremer hesitated another moment, then left.

After another stretch of silence, Xi spoke again. "Would you interpret her silence as apprehension, Kael?"

He tilted his head, appraising the now empty door. "Maybe. I'm not sure. I, uh… I have the impression she felt left out. Why didn't you ask her?" Oh, Xi. Definitely still work to be done on those relational models.

"I was not sure she would approve. And the Empress is keeping her and the other doctors very busy."

"But she's a cyberneticist, isn't she?"

"Not a roboticist."

"Yes, but not a baby doctor. What's that called?"

"An obstetrician."

"Yes. Not that." He scratched his jaw. An unusual length of stubble under his fingers made him smile. He hadn't woken in his own room this morning, hadn't had time—or perhaps inclination—to shave. He'd never had coin or freedom to get those treatments to alleviate the burden of the chore. Was Ryu the sort of woman that cared?

He was coming to understand that even *she* might have no idea the answer to that question.

He scratched at the stubble again. "Tell me more about this face you want, Xi. And you can talk to Ellen. Got some ideas?"

"I have many ideas." A wall display jumped to life, filled to the brim with photos of human faces. "And very few criteria by which to choose one."

His eyes widened, and he coughed in surprise. "And you thought the six android faces would be a struggle. How long have you been thinking about this?"

"Only since yesterday."

He snorted.

"But I complete many cycles; in a single hour I can process millions of times more than the equivalent of a day's worth of human thought."

"Now, now, no need to be modest, Xi."

"That is actually a very pessimistic estimate—"

"Does this have something to do with the attack?"

There was a pause. "Perhaps with a physical form, I would have been less...vulnerable. Perhaps I could have done something. Fought to defend myself, like all of you do."

He could certainly understand that. He got to his feet, stepping toward the wall display as his jaw hardened. "I'm no roboticist, I can only fix a few things. But with Dremer and Persad on board, maybe…"

"The mission will always take priority."

"Of course. Walk me through them."

"Let me begin by showing you Group A—"

"Wait." He held up a hand. "This isn't all of them?"

"There are Groups A through—"

"Am I going to need a coffee for this? And a more comfortable chair?"

The AI hesitated. "I hypothesize you would prefer that. So… yes?"

"Hold that thought and meet me in my cabin. I'll be right there. And *then* I'll deal with Vivaan."

———

THE MORNING WAS HALF GONE before Ellen was able to return to her cabin. Kael wasn't there. Not that she should have been. She shouldn't have even noticed, but her presence hung heavy in the room. Simmons's mess of information *was* waiting, however, hovering at the ready over her holodesk.

"Is that a suggestion, Xi?" she muttered, sighing. "Or a command?"

"Only trying to be helpful, Ellen."

The name sounded odd. Maybe that split-second emotional command hadn't been her sharpest. Fortunately, low risk. She sank into her seat. She'd forgotten how many cups of coffee she'd had already, but it'd been a lot, so she reached for a water in the desk while squinting at the floating slabs of information. Still a lot left to work through.

"Is anyone else looking at these, Xi? We should get one of the doctors…" She trailed off as something caught her eye.

"Not yet. They are not authorized without your review."

She frowned. That seemed odd. Was that a sign he hadn't trusted one of them? Or had he simply been in a hurry? "All right, then. For our first rodeo, Xi, let's look at that stack." She pointed at random.

"Certainly, Ellen. If you don't mind me asking, are there frequent rodeos in the Pacific Alliance Systems?"

Ellen snorted. "No."

"Then how did you come to be familiar with this word? It's fairly rare in my analysis these days."

"My father was from one of the Australian ship's lines. I don't think they actually *had* rodeos, so much as many colorful expressions." She'd lost many of them over the years, to tell the truth, but that sadness wasn't helping anything right now. "Also, my first CO in the regulars was from New Texas, where you can't throw a rock without hitting a rodeo. The PAS make up a good third of the Union, but hardly all of it."

"Interesting, thank you. Your files—Doug's files—are ready for use."

It looked like her choice had been lucky—it was a collection of files on the Empress. Well, if the caterpillar were about to leave its cocoon, she ought to figure out what they were dealing with. At least as far as Doug had known.

The file included lab notes, probably from the raid they'd made on Helikai when they'd first picked up Kael. She scanned over it quickly, looking for something actionable, something they could use.

"Success in this batch probable—Estimated growth rates recorded high as desired, averaging between 200 and 600%—Cost to longevity severe but deemed acceptable."

She stopped, her eyes frozen on those words. She swallowed and continued.

"Plan to address via crop rotation of clone models, must always have at least three in embryonic suspension."

A note had been hastily added at the bottom, judging by its sloppy, handwritten scrawl.

"One research site seized by Puritan forces. Four other sites lost to unknowns. Remnants of critical research are in Li's capsule. He and capsule to be evac-ed immediately to more secure location where new backups can be made. Urgent."

"Whoa, whoa, whoa—does this mean our girl is the only copy of their precious empress left?"

"I understood the same from the data, if it is valid."

"Why didn't they just transmit the data over the network? They could at least have backed up the genome."

"Enhancers do not send copies of their research, specifically genetic research, over traditional networks for fear of the knowledge being intercepted and used against them. It is their most valuable asset."

She pursed her lips. "I can understand that, but it sure beats losing it all."

"Especially this way. From my analysis of this, our strike was highly undesirable. There was also a later attack on the scientist we injected, Lord Regent Jun Il Li. He went missing after that, leaving the Enhancer organization scrambling. Another attack was made on a heretofore unknown base on one of Yurini's moons, which destroyed a large number of Enhancers. This report Doug intercepted suspects the strike was informed by inside knowledge somehow acquired from Lord Regent Li." Xi shifted one of the memos to the fore, and Ellen leaned closer to look at it.

"Such a strike seems impossible without insider knowledge—traces of Theroki telekinetic abilities at work, but no signs of piracy or crime, only research data stolen—a paid hit? Who would know enough? End further use of Theroki as security services—betrayal?"

Ellen frowned. Those damn Theroki just seemed to keep showing up, didn't they? Maybe a few had sold out, the same way they'd sold out to Doug. But what did that have to do with Li?

"Why is he called Lord Regent? Who or what is he regent of?"

"The Empress."

Ellen raised her eyebrows.

"There is usually more than one regent, though, and the title is assigned to any Enhancer scientist working with their royal line."

"What makes them royalty? Birth?"

"Not exactly. Royalty is merely their code for their ideal genetic model. The one they believe they have Enhanced closest to perfection."

Ellen winced. "As if there's one right answer to everything. To people. To life."

"They think so, yes."

"What do you think, Xi?" She tapped her fingers along her lips, not really expecting an answer.

But after a long while, Xi spoke. "I think there are some questions that do not have answers at all, let alone singular ones. Those who most presume to be all-knowing tend to know the least."

"Wise words from an AI."

"I had a wise creator."

"Who was that?"

"Doug."

Ellen sat back in her chair. "Are you serious?"

"Did you not know?"

"I knew he installed you. I guess I figured he bought you from somewhere." She stared down at the black glass of the desk. "I guess I never asked. I wish I could have asked him more, now." She'd likely never get the chance, if she were honest. Great, and now her eyes were burning.

"I am sorry for causing you distress. Doug's location and safety is yet another question for which we do not have an answer. Perhaps worry is not helpful at the moment?"

She straightened up like a shot. "You're right. Good point. Okay, tell me this. I see the Empress has fast growth, but we already knew that. Is there anything else in this mess that talks about what's different about her? Is she just an extraordinary beauty? Why did they want to speed up the growth? What did they gain?"

"The first file you were viewing refers to some extraordinary capabilities, but it does not name them explicitly. My impression is that the researcher assumes the reader already knows."

Ellen pinched the bridge of her nose. "One more fragging question. It's about time we start getting some answers."

"I would enjoy answers as well."

"Frag." Slumping back in the chair, she closed her eyes to think. Then, slowly, her eyes opened. "Xi—can you find me the bounties that Arakovic issued on Kael? Do we know where they're posted? The ones Ostrov knew about. What about when?"

There was a brief silence. Then the Empress files moved to one side and a new sheet appeared front and center. Her eyes scanned it, hunting furiously—there. She pointed. "This date—what is the date of the attack on Li? And the attack on the Enhancer compound?"

A small timeline appeared beneath the file. "This bounty was issued the day after Li's attack. It is not one hundred percent certain this bounty was issued by Arakovic, but it was not issued by any known organization."

She pounded a fist into her hand. "This—this is it. You said it yourself, Xi—this would be a devastating way for them to lose the Empress. They have no way of tracing Kael after the files on Helikai were nuked. Except for Li."

"Li could have issued the bounty."

"He could have. But why do it the day after he was attacked? Why not issue it right away?"

"He sent Kael to Desori on a mission, so it made sense to wait."

"Yes, but within eight weeks he should have known that the mission had not been completed. And yet he didn't do anything then."

"Nothing we know about."

"They *must* have looked for Kael, but they would have no way of tracing him to us. And yet this bounty—it doesn't say Arakovic, but Ostrov claimed it was her, if he can be believed. But think about it. Why would she want Kael more than us, more than me, more than the ship? Look—she's offering fully double." It was enough to live several lifetimes with a fortune to spare, for most people. Where did Arakovic get the money? "She connected the dots. She talked to Li. She attacked the Enhancer compound."

"We can't ascribe all the evil in the universe to one woman."

No, but she could try. She snorted at herself. "Point taken. But entertain this theory for a moment. What if it isn't Kael she's looking for—what if it's the Empress?"

"What is her motive? Why would she want the Empress?"

"I don't know." She rose from her seat, paced back and forth, watching the files float in the air as if waiting on her command to fall into a heap. "She must know something we don't. She wouldn't be interested in a beautiful diplomat, would she?" And the Empress *would* be beautiful. Like Rachel Levereaux, many of their ideal genetic lines were painfully gorgeous.

Assuming she lived that long.

"That seems doubtful. Aesthetics do not appear to be a theme amid any of Arakovic's other files."

"I need to look at those soon."

"Yes."

"Why contain aesthetic choices to a research strain? If the Empress's DNA contains the latest Enhancer technology, why not spread that to everyone instantly if it was just looks? Why keep it secret?"

"They and the Stedler cult have done this in the past. The fact that they have not in this case would suggest that the salient DNA in the Empress does not concern her outward appearance. Her special abilities may not be stable or safe to insert into an entire population."

"Well, isn't that comforting. The Empress must have some capability that Arakovic needs. Why else would she be *this* precious?" She waved a hand at the bounty number on the screen.

"This is a high-quality working hypothesis. Short of meeting our Empress, however, I am not sure how we will test it."

She pursed her lips. "Well, it's fortunate that we won't need to wait long to meet her, then."

———

KAEL HAD JUST RAISED his hand to the palm pad when the door slid open again. It surprised both Kael and Ellen, because she was suddenly staring at him through the explosion of documents over her holodesk, like a peacock had fanned out a tail of memos, images, and maps.

Ellen's expression melted into a smile first. He shrugged and stepped inside, the hatch sliding closed behind him. The door opening a second time was odd, but it was probably just Xi being overzealously helpful again. He'd have to remember to talk to her about it—later. Not now, in the presence of something as rare as Ellen's smile.

Praise the Almighty for that smile. Actually, it seemed to be less rare these days.

He waved at the files. "You didn't invite me to the party? I'm hurt."

"Want to see how much your bounty is?"

"No." He winced, but even as he spoke, he strode around to stand behind her seat. "Not sure I want to—glory *be*. What piss-drinking idiot fool would pay that for me?" But they already knew, didn't they? Not the Theroki.

"I think she's after the Empress, not you. Not that you're not worth it."

He snorted. "I mean, I can hold a rifle in the right direction, but…"

"Did you stop by to fish for compliments? Cause I can come up with several more, but I'm guessing you had something else in mind."

Grinning, he spun her chair around toward him. "Dinner. Have you seen the time?"

She raised her eyebrows as she glanced back at the desk, then him. "Frag."

"Unless you want to finish that thought from earlier." He inclined his head toward her washroom. He wasn't sure exactly *what* thought she'd had, but he'd had all day to fill his mind with a variety of potential futures.

Her eyes narrowed slightly. "I'm not sure if you're a bad influence or a good one."

"Doesn't matter, you're stuck with me." He pulled her to her feet and into his arms. She didn't resist. "Do you need to finish your work?" he murmured as he pressed his lips against hers.

"It never ends," she said, pretty much into his mouth.

He pulled her a step closer to the shower, just to see how she'd react. Except he didn't count on her pushing him into the bulkhead behind him. Laughing, he tightened his arms around her.

The cabin door chimed. From outside, Bri's voice was yelling something indistinguishable but definitely Bri.

Ellen groaned. "It's always something."

He ran a hand quickly over his hair. "Will you be long? I can go. Start looking for some grub?"

The door chimed again.

She pursed her lips, then glanced at the washroom again. He raised an eyebrow. "What if you wait in there?" she said, cocking her head to one side.

"Consider me vanished." She palmed the washroom hatch shut behind him. The overheads flicked on a second later.

He snorted in the darkness. So they were hiding this—at least from Bri. He wasn't sure if he should be amused by about that or worried.

Or excited about the possibilities of this enormous shower.

The ship's fanciest washroom was undecorated and spartan at best. Not terribly surprising. The walls were severe, unfinished steel, and the only concession to luxury was the shower, at double the size of the standard and outfitted with heaters as well as the usual suction vents and blower fans. Nearby was a simple toilet, then a locker or two. In front of him, a large mirror with a thin silver frame reflected his wildly disheveled short hair—although the shorter cut he'd acquired on Capital was certainly easier than the old overgrown one. His lips were red from where she'd kissed him.

He folded his arms. Yeah, it probably wasn't great to be the guy hiding in the washroom. But he wasn't exactly the height of professionalism at the moment, was he? An eye as astute as Bri's would put things together.

He hadn't really thought that would be a problem, though. No, truthfully, he hadn't really considered it. Nobody would care, though.

Would they?

If they wouldn't care, why was he standing alone in a washroom while a meeting was happening outside?

"Bri. What can I do for you?" Ellen was saying outside.

"Hey! What's gotten into you?" Bri said. She had a healthy volume to her voice, so it was barely muffled. "You forgot to come get my report."

"Sorry. Lots going on right now. What? Why are you looking at me like that?"

"You seem… different."

Kael raised his eyebrows and tried not to laugh. He raised his finger to the latch on the locker and started to slowly ease it open. Ellen hadn't responded.

"Did you take a new vitamin?" Bri's voice was dripping with sarcasm. "You have this glow about you."

"Damn it, why is everyone saying that?"

He stifled a laugh as the locker came open.

"There's an uncharacteristic spring in your step," said Bri.

He leaned closer and picked up a bottle at random. Shampoo—strawberry vanilla? That sounded more like a dessert. He put it down and picked up the next bottle. Where had these come from? They hardly seemed her style.

"The engineering budgets, please."

"All right, all right. I sent you a prioritized list. Check your messages."

Ellen swore. "This could build a whole new ship, for frag's sake."

He snorted. There were a dozen other products in the locker that all boasted scents similarly feminine and mostly food inspired. He pulled out some kind of chocolate-scented gel and smelled it. Could verify—smelled like chocolate.

"Well, this whole situation's got me a little paranoid, what can I say? I try to keep reasonable backups, but what if she knew that? What if she sabotaged one of *them*?"

"That's why we run diagnostics."

"But what if I made a mistake in my diagnostics?"

"That's why we run them twice." Ellen's voice was flat. "Or three times. Or…"

"Ah, but what if she checked my diagnostic checklist and deliberately worked around it?"

"Bri! Jesus."

"Sorry. I told you—paranoid."

"I doubt we can afford all this."

"I know. That's why I prioritized. Don't you love having a brilliant engineer like me?"

"I adore it." He struggled not to chuckle at the wryness in Ellen's tone. "Okay, what about the power consumption?"

"Adan's still hogging power for more speed. He reduced acceleration rate on your orders slightly, but…"

"How much is slightly?"

"Only ten percent. We're still flying at seventy percent max. At this rate, the shields won't be fully powered when we arrive at Molyarch unless we cut all propulsion energy on arrival to power them. Which I think you can agree is not ideal."

She whistled. "Agreed."

"I get why he wants to keep it up, but we haven't seen that Union ship at all. Eventually that's all going to be braked away anyway, right? We have to arrive sometime. The stern shield generators are repaired, though."

"Xi, tell Adan to cut acceleration," said Ellen. "We're going fast enough."

"Acknowledged," Xi replied.

The conversation seemed to be wrapping up, so if he wanted to hide his perusal of her personal items, he should probably hide the evidence now. He tilted his head, considered it, and then picked up another bottle.

Hmm. Toothpaste.

"Anything else, Bri?"

"No, Commander."

"Thanks, Bri. I appreciate it." Boots moved across the decking.

Moments later, the door slid open. She didn't say anything as she stepped inside, but he heard her slump on the wall behind him and sigh. "Sorry about that."

He decided to ignore that comment and turned, a bottle of blueberry cream something-or-other in one hand and a jar of ocean spray scented goo in the other. "Do you actually use this stuff?"

Her face broke into a reserved smile. "Not really. Never really saw the point. Gifts."

"From Bri?"

She laughed, actually laughed. She stepped forward and took the jar from him. "Dr. Taylor. She's always on me about self-care."

He carefully returned the blueberry cream to the locker.

She un-twisted the lid, took a sniff, wrinkled her nose. "Doesn't really smell like the ocean, does it?"

"Some things are so wonderful they can only be poorly imitated." He smiled, bent his head to smell it himself as if he hadn't already.

"Sorry about that," she repeated. Her voice was hardly above a whisper, her eyes trained on the jar. She carefully replaced the lid and twisted.

"You don't want them to know about me," he said gently, hoping he concealed how much he didn't like it. "About us."

"What?" She looked up sharply, eyes alarmed. "Why would I care about that?"

"I don't know." For a million reasons, maybe. Because he wasn't officer material, and even if they'd made him one, he was pretty sure they all knew he didn't belong. Because they were just too different and she'd change her mind, it was only a matter of time?

"No. It's just Bri. She's—different."

"Really?" He put his hands over hers, hoping it urged the honesty he intended it to.

"I didn't tell you to leave when Levereaux commed, did I?" She reached past him, returning the jar to the locker. He thought she'd push it closed, but she picked a different, beige-colored one.

He had forgotten about that call with Levereaux. "Okay, fair point. I'm still figuring out how that fancy brain of yours works." He waved a hand vaguely at her head.

"I don't want to hide anything. Like I even could." She unscrewed the top of this one.

"Tell that to the guy hiding in your bathroom." He frowned. "Wait, what do you mean, like you even could?"

"Kael, you know they *made* me go after you, right?"

He raised an eyebrow.

"On Desori. Half of them marched into my office and told me I was being an idiot." She sniffed at the bottle, then held it up to him.

"Now that'd be a sight to see." Hmm. He sighed before he could stop himself at the smell. Pumpkin cinnamon baked something. Sugar, spice.

"We do have the vid footage," offered Xi.

Ellen glared up at the overheads. "Shush! I *was* being an idiot, because I have never been able to handle how much I feel for you, and it clouds my judgment."

He swallowed, his throat tightening at that.

Luckily, she didn't seem to expect a response. "I wanted to follow, but I was stopping myself. They all knew, I think, even then." She took another deep breath of the whatever-it-was, shampoo? "This is a good one, isn't it?"

"It is." He blinked. "Knew what?"

"Knew how much I wanted you."

He felt a different kick now, and this one wasn't in his throat.

She shrugged, her eyes still on the bottle. "They wanted us together. Always have. Still do."

"No..."

"Yes. I guess I am a little worried what they'll say."

Xi's voice was almost smug. "I can confirm they talk about it."

"Xi!" Ellen snapped, spinning the lid back on the pumpkin cinnamon bottle with an edge. She replaced it and didn't retrieve another one.

Kael shook his head. "So you mean, they were rooting for me—" Even when he had given up, had never had any hope of catching Ellen, they'd all been watching him? Knowing the inner workings of his head? "I'm not sure I wanted to know this."

"I know what you mean. But they were rooting for us. Or for me to stop screwing up my life."

"All along. And I didn't know it?"

"Yes. And now we've gotten together. And they haven't figured it out yet."

"Oh, no." Kael looked toward the ceiling. "Did you tell them Xi?"

"No." Xi sounded affronted. "Of course not."

Ellen let out a breath, showing she was just as uncertain of that as he'd been.

"So… it's our little secret right now?"

"I guess." Her lips twisted. "They'll figure it out. When we spend every night…"

He tried not to but found himself folding his arms. "If you don't care, and they'll definitely figure it out, why toss me in here?"

She glared at him. "I didn't toss you in here, I suggested it politely. With… potential in mind."

He snorted and refused to take the shower-related bait. "That wasn't the only reason."

"And because Bri butts in. Interferes. And I don't need any more of an audience than I already have. I'm supposed to be their leader. I'm supposed to be calm, collected, in control. Know what I'm doing. But this time I don't."

He went very still, caught up in the sense that he was seeing something most people never got to see. He wasn't sure what it was exactly, but it felt rare as a three-moon eclipse.

"I want to figure things out on my own. No, not on my own. With you. Can't I just fumble around at this like a normal twenty-two-year-old once in a while?" She clenched her jaw, then continued. "This is… it's important."

He stayed quiet, held his breath.

"And I think I can frag this up enough by myself without them watching, thank you very much."

Releasing the breath with a chuckle, he stepped closer just as she reached past him to return the jar to the locker. "Okay, so let's not tell them."

"Weren't you just hating that idea?"

"I hadn't thought it through. You're right. I can't say I want an audience either."

"I don't know how to handle this. I don't lie to my crew. Well, most of the time."

He grinned and shook his head. "I don't know, I've never done this before either. Jenny has some clue, doesn't she? But she may understand wanting some privacy. We don't have to lie. We can just keep it to ourselves until we're ready."

"That's going to be tough. This ship feels small as a sardine can sometimes."

"Well, we can at least try. We can go out of our way to conveniently not be in the same place at the same time."

She sighed. "If you're sure you don't mind."

His smile softened. "Want to make bets on how long we can make it?"

"No way. Unless you want to bet on five minutes."

"No thanks. I think we might make it a week or two." He pulled her closer now, though, and pressed his forehead against hers. "But we deserve a chance to figure things out on our own if we can. Let me give you as much privacy as I can, if it's what you want." He couldn't give her much, but this was fully in his power.

Her shoulders relaxed. "Thank you. You're a strange man, Kael Sidassian."

"Going to need a new name, aren't I?"

"Yes, and I've ordered a new suit of armor too," Xi cut in from above. "To be paid for and delivered at Molyarch when we arrive."

"Thank you, Xi," they both said in unison. His backup suit was *supposed* to be just that, a backup.

"About that dinner?" he asked.

"I'll win the bet if we march out of here to the mess together."

He snorted. "I guess I'm lucky there's no credits on the line."

"How about you wait here while I go fetch a whole heap ton of food because I'm starving and forgot to eat lunch, and we'll eat it back here. What do you want?"

He groped for an answer, although he was fairly certain he'd eat basically anything as long as she was with him. "Something with cheese."

"I'll see what I can do."

She was gone like a shot—probably hungrier than he'd even realized—and he was left standing in the washroom wondering what the hell had just happened. In the last twenty minutes, the last twenty hours, the last twenty years.

The locker was still standing open, so he slammed it shut and smiled.

CHAPTER FIVE

DAY 5

THE BLANKET of sleep was heavy and deep when something poked at Kael. Instinctively, he knew it hadn't been long enough to be morning yet. He turned on his side, tucked himself closer to Ellen, and fell back into a deeper sleep.

Dreams returned. Quick like falling into a pool of cool water—and vivid.

He felt more than heard the roaring first. The kind of mind-deadening, soul-crushing roar that might have been screams or engines or maybe both, what did it matter? It could shake out your insides. Every part of him felt the vibrations, heavy and deep.

One of the blood-splattered walls outside the old cargo bay materialized before him. The *Genokai*. Not this fragging place. And he remembered this particular blood splatter too.

This was that day he'd seen the new kid eviscerated. Just another hunk of meat.

One of the worst days.

It was better to think of him as a piece of meat. He was dead now, what did it matter, whether it was a kid or meat? Was there any difference really? For some of these disgusting drecks, it was the same damn thing.

The blood dripped still slowly down the wall. He felt frozen, like he couldn't stop staring, couldn't look away.

The roaring continued. What was that?

Sometimes the *Genokai* felt like a living thing, like the blood just oozed out of the walls themselves. They were riding in some giant whale of a creature that had swallowed them, that hated every ounce of their existence. Their very presence was an injury that cut these wounds into the walls.

There was so much of it, too. Blood and piss and who-knew-what else. Was it really from the fragged-up inhabitants of the ship, or was it just that the ship itself was bleeding?

Really, he could believe either. Didn't matter. Wouldn't change anything. What did reality matter? Only surviving mattered.

He should stop staring. Somebody smells weakness, and it's your blood on the walls. And he had plenty of weakness, but he knew how to hide it pretty well.

And when he couldn't, he could draw blood too.

Forcing himself to turn, to tear his eyes from the last lifeblood of he-was-just-a-kid on the wall, he looked out over the cargo hold. Usually it was about half full of crates of dreck somebody was supposedly legally "transporting" and a quarter full of obviously stolen goods, dotted with higher ranking Tridelphis cracking the metaphorical—or possibly literal—whip to get the work done.

But not today.

Today, the cargo hold decking was streaked red with blood. The most brutal battle he had ever seen raged in front of him. Dead bodies slumped against crates—or over them. Laser bolts connected here and there, but the majority of the fighting was hand-to-hand. Dozens— hundreds?—of armored and unarmored Theroki swarmed the deck, the brawling rolling from one side of the deck to the other as the ship swayed. The grav faltered, then took back control. The air was tangy and sour from the bodily fluids, the dead, and smoke charred the air from where flesh had been cooked—and vaporized.

Regent Li had said leave him to Chaos. Kael could hear it, even now. *Leave me to Chaos.*

That asshole thought Chaos was an amorphous thing, a spiritual idea to be rebelled against. It was the Enhancer's ethic—they refused to call it a religion—to fight even the entropy of the living universe, to bring order to the world, to their bodies, to their very DNA.

But Kael knew better.

Chaos was real. Alive.

And right the fuck here.

He had to get out of here. He turned, but the hall to the left flooded with men in pursuit of other men—luckily in the opposite direction.

He turned to head the other way. It went to engineering, and that would be a terrible place to ride out yet another riot, but it was better than the middle of it.

He was just about to plunge through the first hatch when laser fire lit up the door, collided with a maintenance panel and set off an explosion of spark and flame. Oh, great—as if a riot weren't enough, destroying the ship was the epitome of stupid. Usually the command cell kept better control of these idiots.

He retreated as the fire licked out at him, chasing him back.

He was stuck. Boxed in. He searched the fighting—he needed to find the shortest way to the next door that he could get through without anyone noticing. Or killing him first.

He could only see two, and one was behind a blockade of crates controlled by sixty or so Theroki, all firing laser like *idiots* into the masses around them.

Door Number Two, it is.

He started forward, then stopped abruptly in his tracks.

A creature rose up out of the insanity. Light poured out of it, like a blue-white star, and its black robes swirled and floated in the air, as if the ship's grav didn't apply. Its eyes glittered large, black, diamond-shaped and faceted. It had a chin-like feature, but if there was a nose or mouth, he didn't see it. Hair in thick, white snakes spiraled out from the creature's head, except it wasn't hair, was it? More like tentacles.

White tentacles.

He staggered back, against the wall. Kid's blood be damned.

"You shouldn't be here," he coughed.

"Neither should you," it replied.

"What do you want? You should get away from this chaos."

"You already have. You just have to wake up. Why do you return in your dreams?"

He frowned, awareness of the dream suddenly breaking through. He could sense his body in the distance, the warmth of the blankets and Ellen beside him. "I don't know. I did my time. I should leave."

"And yet you return."

"I never should have been here. I don't belong here."

"Perhaps deep down, you worry that you do."

The truth of the words stopped the breath in his lungs. The creature bobbed slightly, hair undulating, as if suspended in a slower time than the bloody madness at her feet.

"I don't want to come back," he stammered.

"The anger changed you. Both for the better and the worse."

"Are you just a part of the dream? How do you know that? You don't know that." He wouldn't argue the point normally, he might even agree. But in this sea of madness, he wasn't so sure. Nothing good could come of this.

"I am no more a dream than you are. I know because I see all—the past, the present…"

"The future?"

"Sometimes. Vaguely. But my real talents lie elsewhere."

"Why are you here? In my dreams, then?"

"I like you."

He frowned. Then gestured at the ship around them—the madness. "This? You like this?"

"No. I like the man who survived this. I need strength like yours. I don't have it. Yet."

A telepath—it had to be. "Why?"

"Because you and I were both born in chains."

He took a step forward. "Tell me. What is it that you want? You're not just sight-seeing in my brain. It's a fragged-up place to visit."

"You're wrong. I admire human perseverance."

"You're not human?"

"That's… complicated. Do I look human?"

"No. You're dodging my question. What do you want? Are you looking for secrets? For Ellen? Because I'll die before—"

"*Salam,*" the creature whispered.

But the whisper was a hiss, a loud wave of force, like a bucket of ice over the head. A calm, peaceful emotion slammed into him and pervaded every part of him, like he'd been plunged into a frigid lake.

Death would peaceful too, some survival instinct warned. This—this was not right. Not normal. Wrong. Even the spike of anxiety that the creature might be killing him was dampened by the suffocating sense of peace.

"Peace be upon you. Is that not what your people wish for?" Was her tone mocking or sincere?

"This is—taking it a little far."

"Peace, child. Peace."

He shook at the feeling surrounding him, like throwing off a tangled, suffocating blanket. It didn't budge.

"Sometimes I think I would be doing you all a favor to bring you this peace you keep looking for."

He growled deep in his throat. "If you long for peace, and can give it to people, why come to this dream of blood and war?"

"I don't long for peace. Well, after so many lifetimes, now I do. But this power I have does not give a natural peace. It's wrong. I know it, even as I do it."

"I'll agree with you there. So let me go."

The creature sighed. "Fine."

The freezing ice faded from his limbs, his bones, and warmth grabbed him again. He let out a breath of relief. "What do you really want? You can just tell me. No more games."

"I want you to set me free, Kael Sidassian. I also long to be released."

"Who are you?"

"My name—I do not know. It was taken from me long ago."

Beneath where the creature still floated in the air, a dozen men surged, separating from the others and taking cover not far from him. Further away, a group of more than forty was easing around the crates —or storming, bloodlust clearly engaged—all headed this way.

He forced his gaze back to the creature. "How can I know how to save you? Where *are* you, at least?"

"Not far."

He gritted his teeth and shifted toward the first hallway, the one that wasn't on fire. "How do I find you?"

The creature glanced down, as if it too noticed the fighting now. "Set me free, and let me die. I've suffered long enough."

"How?" he demanded. The larger group charged full-force now, battle cries rising to a deafening roar. "Tell me, damn it, and I'll do it."

He turned toward the hallway and ran—just as the hallway itself flooded with more men, some terrified, some enraged. Some both.

"I do not know how," the creature whispered into his mind.

The swarm overtook him, the heavy armor colliding with his, sending him down, crushing him—and he screamed.

Skin.

His skin wasn't being lacerated and crushed. It was cold and slick with sweat as he ran his hands over his arms, searching for evidence of what he'd just felt.

The wall in front of him was dimly lit, but clean silver. Neatly tucked corners of the navy-covered bed beyond his feet sat there, as if in reproach of his lack of decorum.

He stared at the corners, unfamiliar as the alien in the dream. He didn't ever... he'd be hard pressed to make a bed like that even a single time.

Ellen.

She was rubbing her eyes, sitting up beside him. "Are you okay?"

Relief flooded him, like it poured out of the heat of her against his arm. He said nothing for a moment. Panting.

"Bad dreams?"

He looked over at her. Her sleepy brown eyes squinted up at him, and she smiled, in spite of it all. She ran a finger over the feathers, then across his chest.

"Yeah," he finally managed. "Weird, weird dream."

She pressed her lips against the naked skin of his shoulder, and he shivered. Yeah, that wasn't going to help him sleep. "C'mon. Back to sleep."

He tucked himself against her, though. Her breathing slowed, but unsurprisingly, sleep for him didn't come.

Chaos. We were both born in chains.

Why did the creature look sort of familiar? *Feel* sort of familiar?

Such a strange dream. Or was it more like a message in a bottle?

He took long, slow breaths, listened to the sweet sound of her breathing, and stared at the slick shine of the display that hung above the bunk, dark as night and full of mystery.

———

ELLEN SWUNG OPEN THE LOCKER. That darn tiny breather from Capital had to be here somewhere. She'd thought she'd left in her armor case, but no such luck. She was usually so organized, but everything had been a mess since then. That sort of figured, where Capital was involved, didn't it. Darn place mucked everything up.

"Madam, please! Just a small stroll!"

Rich's voice made her jump. Damn—she'd made the mistake of opening her clothes locker near 0900—right around the time Rich tended to be the punchiest. His elegant voice bellowed out of the locker, and she winced. It was amazing how many times she could forget she'd shut him in there.

"You'll get your heel caught in the decking." She heaved a sigh of breath. Lord, grant me strength. Help me not throw these intelligent shoes out an airlock.

"I can be flats. Grudgingly."

"Besides, you don't won't to sully yourself with a station this dirty." It'd been three more days of fast-as-hell transit to Molyarch. No sign of any Union ships in pursuit. No clues to Merith's plans. After the fast getaway from the *Volga*, they needed a serious refuel.

It had also been three more days of interruptions, late night false alarms from errors in diagnostic runs, and bad dreams she couldn't quite remember when she woke up. Which added up to things moving slower than a snail in heavy gravity with Kael.

But that was all right, she reminded herself. Maybe it was even better this way. They often found each other, somewhere in the night, in between their erratic schedules broken up by repairs that ran late or meetings at odd times covering all sorts of things, from appropriate small ship models to staff breakdowns across two ships to Vivaan's detailed recounting of the minutiae of Merith's cabin.

It wasn't how she'd thought it would be, but there was a stolen sweetness to it, a hope in the darkness, a bit of fire in the night.

Even if interruption and exhaustion kept dousing the blaze. At least slow meant she wasn't fragging anything up—at least, she hoped not. Combing the *Audacity* for clues that might not even be there was driving them all bonkers. If she didn't get four uninterrupted hours of sleep soon, mistakes of some kind were almost a certainty.

Still, they'd finally reached Molyarch. Now they could refuel and hopefully find themselves a little craft that could go after Doug.

"Madam!"

She jumped, having forgotten him again.

"You didn't even hear my last response, did you?"

"Sorry, Rich. You're just not practical. Not now."

"Then when? The darkness of this dungeon should be considered torture by anyone with a modicum of decency."

She frowned. He did have a point, there. "Fine. Sit on the desk for a while." She grabbed him and plunked him down on the holodesk.

"Madam, *please*. What am I supposed to do differently here? Stare at this slightly larger prison cell? I mean, really. Do they allow you to decorate, or do you just prefer the style of a monk?"

"If you're going to insult me, I can put you back in the locker."

"I apologize, Madam, it's just… I am *so* bored."

"Didn't you endure this somehow before you were bought?" She slammed the locker shut, propped her hands on her hips. No breather. Where could it be?

"I had other shoes to talk to, then."

"Did you enjoy their company? Do I need to buy you a friend?"

"No. They were insufferable."

"Hard to imagine." She snorted.

Rich was using his limited movement capability to jump himself around on the holodisplay, a bit like a shoe tapping impatiently.

Ellen narrowed her eyes. Yeah, like she'd want him along to make fun of potential ship vendors. "Why don't you talk to Xi?"

"To the *ship*?" He sniffed.

"She's not the ship, but suit yourself."

"Ellen," Xi chimed in. "I hypothesize Rich may enjoy the use of the holodisplay when you are not occupying it. My research indicates this is highly likely. Would you be amenable to this?"

Rich only huffed in response.

"So demanding." She decided to check her desk drawer again. The breather had to be here somewhere. "Sure—keep him busy, Xi."

"If I had feet..." Xi started.

"What was that?" She raised an eyebrow, just as her fingers brushed aside a backup laserblade—and there it was. The breather case. Nobody should put anything so useful in a case barely bigger than her thumb.

"Nothing. We'll discuss it more later."

"Have fun, you two." She permitted herself a grin. She highly doubted that any fun would be had. But maybe.

She tucked her card wallet and two laserblades into her flight suit and headed for the cargo hold. Just because she was willing to head out without armor—just this one time—didn't mean she was going unarmed or unprotected.

AS SOON AS he cleared customs in Molyarch, Kael headed to the nearby lightboard and started jumping through the menus, while the others checked out the fuel supply station. One positive about the in-nose breathers was that you didn't have to worry about the armor's visor messing with the lightboard, at least. The negative was that if you got punched at the wrong angle, it could fall out.

The gaze-scanning on this beauty was solid as a rock anyway, but that figured since the model looked fairly new and less beaten than the station around it. Even if Molyarch was keeping its subtly shady sheen, somebody was making money here. And spending it in at least one good place.

He found eight shipyards and dealers on the other side of the station. Only two looked suitably shady without alarming him too much. Not that he was any kind of ship purchasing expert. No one on the team was, really. Except maybe Doug. Where had that man bought the *Audacity* itself anyway? He'd imagine that'd leave a *giant* paper trail, but somehow, he doubted Simmons would have left even a slip in his wake.

Kael had his share of street smarts, though, and some signs of scams were universal. He sent the details to his comm and leaned against the wall next to the lightboard, waiting for the others to return from their respective landing duties.

Nova was the first to join him, sidling up with her usual swagger. "You find us some place good?"

He waved a hand at the whole list, and the two he'd selected. "Tried to narrow it down. What do you think?"

"Diji's Secondhand Spaceships." She rubbed her chin as she cracked away at her gum; she hadn't worn armor, but a subtle breather instead. Still, that gum seemed like it had to be annoying in there. "A fifty percent down payment? Coño! At least he's up front, I guess?"

"Yes. And he takes cash and other 'unusual currencies.'"

"Huh. That neon yellow logo though…"

"It's dubious, but isn't that part of the charm? Then we also have Claudette's Cruisers. Doesn't look second hand exactly, but if you look down here…"

"'All prices, currencies negotiable… Barters accepted.' Claudette is willing to deal."

"Yeah, I was thinking we'd start here first." He narrowed in on the selection area, and a new block of further contact info and offerings slid out to the right.

Ellen's dry voice came from behind him. "Did your selection have anything to do with the blond curls, picnic basket, and oh-I'm-ever-so-trustworthy farm girl thing she's got going?"

He only snorted and raised an eyebrow in Ellen's direction. As if that was his type.

"Yeah, someone should tell this *chica* she sells spaceships, not tractors."

Ellen stepped closer and peered at the board. "You like her?"

Nova coughed. Had she just choked on her gum?

He couldn't hold back a grin. "Says she's willing to barter. Negotiate."

"Let's start with her then. I'm sure she'll be nothing but honest. And Diji doesn't sound as, ahem, attractive."

"It's Quadrant 36, outer ring. Complete opposite side of the station." He pointed in the direction that was the shortest distance, but it was a toss up. Either way was far and would get them there.

"Oh, goodie."

Laughing softly, he closed out the lightboard and followed them into the rings.

———

MOLYARCH STATION HADN'T IMPROVED since their last visit, but Ellen supposed that was why they were here. Where did the inhabitants get so much dirt to smudge the corridors on a space station? Or was it… not dirt? She didn't want to know.

As they approached the ship vendors, things looked a little more polished up, a few less signs of disrepair. They passed the eye-blastingly bright sign of Diji's Secondhand Spaceships, and she was glad they hadn't decided to start there. But as they neared their actual destination, she was no longer so sure. Claudette's had none of the open showrooms of some of the other merchants; instead, it was more like a high security bank, with just one window open to the main corridor.

And behind the service window outside Claudette's Cruisers was not the company namesake. At least, not the way it had been depicted in the marketing materials.

Ellen cleared her throat. "Uh, Claudette?"

A Teredark rubbed several frontal appendages and a set of mandibles together, clicking rapidly. Joyfully? "Welcome, humans, to Claudette's Cruisers! How can I be of service?" This Teredark's voice was on the raspy side. And they usually sounded more… pissed off. Maybe that was because Ellen was usually pointing a gun at them. Go figure.

"This your business?" Ellen asked.

"Yessss."

"Ah, so, does that make you Claudette?"

"This is simple branding. Claudette is, as you humans call it, a mascot. I am sorry if you hoped to meet her today. But I do have Claudette stickers…" Its tiniest mandibles waggled in the direction of the counter it stood behind.

Ellen blinked in surprise. "Uh, no. That's okay."

"I insist." A sheet of stickers featuring a blond-haired human on a tractor slid out from a slot Ellen had assumed was for receipts. Obliged, she stepped forward and took the sheet. "But I am the proprietor of this ship dealership, so in a manner of speaking, yes. I am Claudette."

Nova snickered. "Better hide those stickers, Commander. If Isa finds them, Bri will kill you."

Would the Empress ever be old enough and child enough to like stickers?

Ellen shook her head at—well, at the entire situation. "Okay, uh—Claudette or whoever you are. We're looking for a fighter ship. Carrying somewhere between two to six people. Something we can put inside a larger ship. Launch from a cargo bay. You got anything along those lines?"

"Oh, yes. I have, let me see…" The Teredark paused to look at a screen above its already tall head. "Three ships in the twenty-five-meter range that might interest you." She made a mental note to read up on Teredark expressions, but she—he?—it? seemed almost gleeful as the head bobbed and mandibles swayed.

"Okay, can we have a look?"

"Absolutely. But first it is my standard policy to do a basic credit check. So as not to waste time on those who can't afford my offerings."

"Sure. Of course. You got a chip reader?" The giant bug—ahem, Teredark—indicated a shiny black glass plate to her right. She stepped forward and held out her palm and card over the reader.

The reader took a moment before Claudette clicked in alarm. "I'm sorry. This hasn't authorized. The necessary funds are unavailable for purchase. In fact, it appears your account may have been shut down."

Her eyes widened. "Hmm. One second please." She spun on her heel and drew Nova and Kael a few steps away. "Did you hear that?"

They were both nodding.

"What does that mean?" Nova kept her eyes on the Teredark, who was watching their huddle intently.

"You can't close an account by attacking a compound." Kael frowned.

Ellen set her jaw. "This is bigger than just some physical attack. It could have been incidental, or even a natural disaster. But that should have left the bank accounts untouched and ignored indefinitely."

"Something more sinister is going on," said Nova.

"Yes. And it also means we can't buy a ship, and we're back at square one. We need a new plan."

"Hold on," said Kael. "Sign said she would barter." He spread his hands with a shrug. "It can't hurt to ask."

Scowling, Ellen turned back to the bug. "Sorry to waste your time; we didn't realize we had an issue. Your advertisement said you were open to bartering in exchange. Is that true?"

"It is." It shifted back and forth, which seemed like a nervous gesture, but she really wasn't sure. There had been a class on Teredark interpersonal communication way back, but she was definitely rusty.

The bug didn't offer anything further.

"Is there, uh, something we could do for you to earn one of these ships?"

The Teredark's narrow upper body leaned to one side. "That would depend on… a few things. Let me show you one ship that might be an option for barter… and we shall see if we have a deal." A door slid open to the right of the counter with a hiss.

Ellen glanced over her shoulder at the others, shrugged, then followed their insectoid host.

The next room revealed a surprisingly large ship bay filled with ships both shiny new and a little more… weathered veteran. Of course, Claudette led them to the smallest, most beaten looking of the latter.

The Teredark let out a flurry of clicks before managing human words again. "This fighter is a sturdy little ship. Two sets of twin thrusters and a small reactor make it capable of covering quite long distances self-sufficiently, although it needs water for all of its life support and propulsion systems, so it needs refueling fairly often. Carries six. Could probably stuff in two extra humans if need be without safety harnesses. Only room for perhaps two Teredarks, however."

"It's the right size. Mind if I send my engineer and pilot over here to check her out? Assuming we can work out some kind of deal."

The Teredark turned from the ship to face her small group, raising her head and peering over them for a moment at the door. To make sure it was closed? "Are you capable of performing security services?" The shaking of its mandibles struck her as a little worried-looking now, but she couldn't be sure.

"Certainly. We are a humanitarian vessel primarily. We have doctors on board that can provide cybernetic and genetic services. And we have a full complement of security personnel to keep those doctors safe. Why? What did you have in mind?"

"I have a… problem. There is a certain merchant on the station causing me an issue. I wish for him to leave me alone."

"Who?" asked Ellen.

"Rutland of Rutland's Adventures."

Nova coughed. "He didn't go for the mascot, I guess?"

"Apparently not. He lacks my flair for marketing."

Ellen stifled a laugh. "How is he harassing you, and what can we do to make him stop?"

"Well, if I knew how to make him stop, I would have done that already."

Ellen just narrowed her eyes and waited a second.

"Ah, well. He wishes to form a partnership with me. I have told him not interested."

"Oh, use your ships in his travel business?" Kael asked.

The Teredark shifted back and forth again, repeatedly this time and faster. And then faster still. Yes, it was definitely uncomfortable.

"It would like to form a romantic partnership. I have explained that this is not biologically possible, as Teredark's do not experience romantic monogamous entanglement. And also that I am not in the breeding season. And yet he persists."

Ellen caught Kael's gaze. "What is it with this station?" The last time they'd been here, Ellen had gotten into a fist fight—well, it hadn't been much of a fight, the pilot had gone down so fast—to keep Kael from flipping and murdering another harasser.

Kael shrugged. "Something in the water?"

Nova frowned. "Wait—what?"

"To make matters worse, Claudette added, "he has stolen my security key and offers to return it only in exchange for my heart. I am not interested in sparing one of my hearts to—"

"I think he means that metaphorically," Ellen offered.

"Ah. Perhaps. Nevertheless, my vault robot will kill anyone on sight. Including me, if I don't have the key. It's very inconvenient."

"I can see that," Ellen muttered. "I believe we can definitely take care of this problem for you. Can you give us any info on how to find him? And what the key you need looks like? And I'll send my engineer over shortly."

"Here is a diagram of the key. His shop is in Quadrant 7 in the inner ring. His residence is I believe in the same quad on the lower level. I will anticipate your engineer."

"She's, uh…" Ellen hesitated. "She can be a bit gruff."

"There will be no need for communication," it said.

"Okay, just warning you."

"Unless she would like some stickers."

"I doubt that."

The Teredark was looking like it might try to foist more on them, so she turned and got out of there, Kael and Nova almost beating her to the door.

———

"HANGING IN THERE, *JAGIYA?*" Zhia grinned through the noise and the crowd.

Ellen squinted as a whirling light display flashed over her face. Bubbles and some kind of sparkly dust floated in the air, making the place look populated by fairies. The air was piped full of a rose-scented fog, which was undeniably beautiful but weirdly wet, because it wasn't smoke or some kind of effect but clouds of water vapor.

"I'd rather be cleaning my rifle!" It wasn't quite a snarl. But this crap in the air made her want two layers of armor, rather than the stupid breather she'd thrown in. "What am I doing here?"

Zhia cackled. "You're brooding. Supposed to be dancing, kiddo. Dance with me!"

"Slag off." Ellen took a sip of whiskey, sweet and sharp, and Zhia and her laughter were gone again. Had there been one young man on her arm or two? She couldn't see a damn thing in this place.

Rutland's Adventures had been closed. That made sense, because it was night cycle on the station. Efforts by her, Adan, and Xi to find digital clues to where Rutland might be found at this hour hadn't turned up anything, though. He didn't leave much of an online trail aside from garish ads for absurd adventure tours.

Finally she'd had to admit defeat. She was surely critically sleep deprived, though, because she'd then made a serious mistake: allowing Zhia and Jenny to drag her to this club instead of going back to her cabin to sleep.

Admittedly, she had an ulterior motive. She wanted to make it back to that old bar where she'd first shared a beer with Kael. And he'd had the same thought before she'd brought it up.

But they couldn't march over there directly. Might as well throw a parade. Wandering off by herself in a shady space station might draw nearly as much attention. However, if she put in her time here, who would know—or care—if she stopped somewhere on her way back to the ship?

She was counting the minutes.

Faces appeared and disappeared out of the mist, which did not calm her nerves. She kept her eyes trained for Rutland, at least as well as she could based on the picture Xi had found. Adan and Jenny huddled close together beside her, which was less awkward than it might have been because talking over the chest-pounding music required bending close and shouting. She didn't think shouting was all they were doing, though.

One bonus. Since they'd dragged Adan along, this particular bar did not seem to have strippers. Yet.

Her flight suit was beyond damp now with the rose-scented dew. Delightful. She'd used glances caustic as acid to fend off at least three men and one woman so far. And on top of it all, there was glitter everywhere.

Slagging *everywhere*.

Another blast of lights swung past her, and she flinched in the onslaught. She tossed back the whiskey shot she'd been nursing for at least ten minutes. That had to be long enough, right? She checked her comm where she'd strapped it to her inner forearm.

She faked a yawn, and it must have been a decent one because Nova echoed it. Better get out before anyone else called it a night.

Ellen slipped off the barstool, giving her companions a nod. Nova raised her glass in farewell, and Ellen booked it before Zhia might try to draw her into the fray.

She burst out into the quiet and cold corridor. Never had leaving such a fairy-hallucination-induced sauna been such a relief.

This club had been in the inner ring—as many of the nicer clubs were—but the outer ring was her destination. The station had multiple levels too, but everything for visitors was concentrated in one. Crumpled flyers rolled past as she walked.

She passed one quadrant marker, then the next, and there it was. The same old country bar.

The sign was still barely legible as "Tin House Saloon," but it'd grown so beaten and pitted that deciphering it would have been a struggle if she hadn't seen it before. It had survived more than one recent gunfight. Considering the space station and how much she knew of the thickness of the walls—which were not very thick—that was pretty alarming.

A banner was hung under the sign that read "Under New Management" in bold, purple letters in a flowing, looping typeface.

Chords from guitars strumming tugged at her heart as she scanned the place, both for threats and for him. She really would have preferred armor. Armor would have left her *dry* after that stupid club, as well as less exposed and a lot warmer in this dark and drafty station corridor.

Earnest brown eyes were watching her from a back corner. When they caught hers, her complaints dimmed a little, and she set one boot after another toward him.

His features were carved out of the pink light that coated the place, shining from neon signs behind the mirrored bar, same as it had before. This had been the place they'd bared their souls to each other, or started to. She should have known it wouldn't end there.

Perhaps she had known. She hadn't wanted it to end, she just hadn't been ready to admit it.

"You made it." He smiled as she slid into the booth. He didn't move from where his hands held a tablet, but all his attention was on her. The bizarre decor remained, but it had received a paint job. Hadn't it been a drab gray? A mix of brown shades now imitated wood. While it was from succeeding, the whole place did radiate a new warmth, something that wrapped around her and didn't want to let go.

She nodded once as she tried to decide how close to slide. Beside him instead of across, this time. Smack up against him was what she wanted. But the fairy sauna club made that hardly considerate.

"I'm highly trained at escaping enemy captivity. You should know that."

"Did Zhia get you to dance?" His eyes twinkled.

"What do you think?" She folded her arms.

He laughed, letting the tablet slide flat to the table now. "I think you need to let your hair down, Commander."

"That place was miserable anyway." She huffed, but she was fighting a smile. In a fit of certain madness, though, she reached up and ruffled her hair with both hands. "And my hair *is* down. Did I mention the place was filled with clouds—like real water vapor? And hotter than a sauna. I'm soaking wet, can you believe that?"

"Is that why you aren't closer?"

She smiled. "Yes."

"Never thought I'd say it, but the Elderflower was better."

She snorted. "I'll be sure to inform Kentt."

"Maybe she can recreate it in the mess hall."

"I'll be sure *not* to mention it to Kentt then. We don't need any glad-iatorial showdowns. There's enough of those in the gym."

"I'll never live that down." His smile broadened. "Do you want to go back and change?"

"Nah. It'll take too long—and I don't want to get caught and side-tracked by somebody." With what would probably be a legitimately serious issue—or another red flag that amounted to nothing in the diags. She'd had just enough whiskey not to care at the moment. They could call her comm if they *really* needed her. "Whatcha lookin' at?"

"Xi's info on Rutland."

"Anything stand out to you?"

"Nope. I circled past the shop a second time, too. Nothing."

"Not much to gather about him, is there?" She'd read it, but leaning to see the tablet was a convenient excuse to lean a little closer. Okay, a lot closer. Her chest pressed against his shoulder, and the touch was not lost on him. He'd ignored the tablet since she sat down, but now he shifted his whole body slightly toward her, tablet included.

"So you gonna have one more drink with me?" His voice was soft, his breath tickled her skin of her neck, and she was glad they didn't have to yell over the quiet, almost sleepy music, some mellow mix of country and folk.

"Dunno."

"Whiskey? Or is that only for when you're sad?"

She narrowed her eyes. "I wasn't sad that day." She'd been trying to keep herself from murdering someone. Josana, mainly.

He let out a bark of laughter. "Yeah, right."

"I was mad." Yes, this was the complexity of her emotional vocabulary. Sometimes she stood in awe of her own genius, as well as her similarity to a small child, in this capacity.

His expression faded to an easy smile. "You don't look mad now."

"I'm not." She reached over him and took a sip of his water, which he watched with amused eyes.

"So beer then?"

"I haven't decided. I was drinking whiskey at the club."

"I know, I can smell it."

"I was sort of pissed back there, though. Maybe I'm an angry drinker."

"Or are you just angry all the time, and the drink makes it come out?"

"A mystery."

"Someday I'll understand you, inshallah."

"May we live that long," she murmured. She'd pretended to be looking at the tablet long enough, it was probably time to slink back to her original spot. "And may understanding me be possible."

At that, one of his hands did leave the tablet to catch her chin and bring her mouth to his for a quick kiss. She was still caught somewhere between a surprised laugh and words she couldn't find when he broke away and pointed at the bar.

"You need a drink, even if it's water. I'd get one from the table, but first—I think there's someone at the bar you should say hello to first."

Frowning, she rose, immediately missing the warmth of him beside her. Maybe she *should* have gone back and changed. Was his shoulder wet now?

The music mix that night seemed to be popular with either travelers or station denizens, because the aisles between the booths were packed with people dancing together, slowly, deliberately, thoroughly —not the wild rampage that had been going on at the club. Everyone she passed, she checked for Rutland, but no cigar. She had to angle her way between a half dozen couples before she reached the main bar, which was still the same beautiful expanse of real wood.

She stopped short when at the sight of familiar eyes behind the bar. "You! I thought you were getting out of here." It was the woman she'd started the fight over, the woman she'd tried to save.

"I went to see your friends." The woman shrugged, glanced up at the banner hung below the sign, then pointed at herself. "They had an alternative suggestion."

Ellen permitted herself a small smile. "You haven't had any trouble?"

"That was part of the alternative suggestion. Things have been… taken care of."

She lowered her voice. "Do you know if the office is still there? If any of those people…"

But the bar's new proprietor was shaking her head. "No. They packed up about a month back. Left me with plenty of resources, though. What will it be? It's on the house."

"I don't know…" Two shots weren't really that much, but her head wasn't on straight in Kael's presence to begin with. "What's good?"

"Some local kids around here make this flavored vodka folks like. I mix it with zeefruit juice. But for a traveler like you, I've got a tesuduk from Keppel X, and of course good old-fashioned bourbon, top shelf. But here. Try this tesuduk. You don't like it, I'll get you something else. My personal favorite, and not too strong."

She'd already poured the drink, so Ellen accepted it, raised it, smiled slightly. "Thanks. Glad things worked out."

Taking the tall glass of brown liquid in her hand, she turned without taking a sip and angled her way back through the crowd. She slid back into the booth beside him and held the comm over the drink, as it did its little ritual of rejection or approval. It came back green, and she took a sip. And winced. It wasn't a knife to the back of the throat, but it was close. Kael chuckled softly beside her. It was actually some-what beer-like in flavor and carbonation, but on the thick side, and the bitterness was up a level.

Which actually, now that the initial stab was fading, was kind of nice.

She turned to meet the gaze he'd had trained on her while she negotiated her drink. "So, Theroki. Are we on our first date?"

CHAPTER SIX

DAY 5

KAEL SNORTED. "A DATE?" He might want to count it as their second. Or even third. "Isn't a date supposed to be something a little more elaborate?"

She leaned against his shoulder. "Like I know what a date is supposed to be. Flowers and chocolate and all that? I don't need that."

"I don't believe you." He was pretty sure she didn't know what she needed, and she probably wouldn't deny that.

"If this counts as a date, then this has to be the second." She crossed her legs. Was she cold? The bar was far from warm. His shoulder was already cold where the shared dampness was sinking in.

He tapped his fingers on his beer bottle. "I could count as high as four past dates in my book, but I was hoping you wouldn't catch on and cut me off."

"It's a bit late to lie to myself now."

Was it? He wasn't convinced. To him, it was still early. She could still panic and fly away; he could wake up and realize he was dreaming. He wanted to do this right, while he had the chance.

Maybe chocolate *should* be involved. But right now his mind was only coming up with things that involved chocolate in her cabin, and he was pretty sure they were decidedly un-date-like.

Oh, and they'd get there. At some point. If she didn't bolt, and he didn't frag everything up. But there were other steps to take first. Important ones.

He narrowed his eyes for a moment, before he said, "If I'm taking you on a date, you'll know it."

She raised her eyebrows. "Is that so?"

"Yes. Let's just call this… sneaking away for a bit."

"If I cared about dates and fancy things and night life, I'd probably not choose to cloister myself on a tin can hurtling through space, working all the time."

"You do important work. It's understandable. But I'm still taking you on a date."

"Dates are for normal people. We're outside all that." She waved absently at the air.

"Until you've been on more dates with me than you went on with Ostrov, don't think I'm going to give up on it."

She barked out a laugh and slapped a palm against the table, and he had to admit it pleased him. "If you'd been there, you wouldn't think that. Are you going to take me to play absurdly easy games and try to creepily talk me into eating and drinking only for me to shut you down every time?" She smiled. "On this date I couldn't possibly mistake as anything but a date?"

His own smile was crooked now. "I guess I can't guarantee they'll be food or that you'll like it. But I was not thinking games." He was developing a short list of things in his head, but he had not planned on any arm wrestling matches or the like.

Frowning, she took a sip. "You're serious."

He met her gaze evenly. "Is that so hard to believe?"

"Why?"

He paused. Could he tell her the real reasons? One, he was pretty sure she didn't know what she was missing. But two, it was more because this was his chance. Some day there would be other men, there would be competition, even if she didn't think so in their insular little world right now. Ostrov had made that possibility all too clear. Even if he'd been manipulating her, his flirtation had been real. And if that moment came, he wanted to know he'd done everything he could, shown her everything he felt, made this everything it could be. Not let things drift by because they were too busy or "outside all that."

Swallowing, he hid behind a drink. She was still waiting for an answer.

"You'll understand when we get there," he said instead.

She sobered, her glass still in her hand drifting absently back to the surface of the table. She opened her mouth, but nothing came out.

"What is that?" He pointed at the dark beer-like liquid in the glass.

"Bartender's specialty. Try it—I scanned it, it's fine."

The song shifted as he took a sip. Maybe he was a little overeager, or overly pleased, that she'd offered. Like when she'd taken a drink of his water earlier, there was an intimacy to it. Those small liberties were something he'd forgotten existed, these things you could share with only a select few. Although he'd stolen a drink of her whiskey on Capital, that had been more of a theft than a gift freely given.

The bodies around them slowed as the music calmed, and people hugged closer. An old, simple song piped through the speakers, its chords heartbreakingly beautiful, wrenching and yet stirring at the same time.

Kael cleared his throat as he sat down the glass. "Do you dance, Commander?"

"C'mon. I just escaped that damn club." She quirked a smile.

"This one's pretty simple. I think you can handle it."

She snorted. "They're just standing. And swaying back and forth slightly."

"Exactly."

She raised an eyebrow.

"Put that down and dance with me. Not like in the club, like this."

Her drink made a sharp clink on the glass readout of the table. He slid out the other side of the booth, drew her into his arms just beside their drinks. She stood on the step so she was nearly eye-to-eye to him and slid her arms around his neck, like the others were doing. He pretended he didn't notice her watching what to do. He was a little surprised she'd done as he'd asked—ordered, really.

They swayed in the sea of people, her arms around his neck. Her flight suit was still wet, and the dampness was seeping into his cargos and t-shirt too, but he hardly cared. His fingers against her back could sense the muscles moving as she shifted, the soft skin so close. A thin sheen of glitter caught the light and shimmered green-gold on her cheekbone.

She eased closer, her face in his neck, her breath hot against his skin.

"Maybe it's not dancing you dislike," he murmured. "Maybe it's the club."

"You may be on to something."

Her voice was husky and tickled his skin, and he took a deep breath of her. And chuckled slightly. "Do I smell pumpkin cinnamon something?"

She smiled, pulling back. "Been practicing my self care." Her gaze flicked up to meet his.

"Dr. Taylor would be so proud." He, for one, was having the hardest time lately. His mind did not want to be calm, or meditate, or focus, or think about anything other than her. And by think, he really meant get creative planning potential future adventures, the kind that didn't involve armor. Or clothes.

But there was no rush, he reminded himself for the ten thousandth time. Ten years was a long time to wait, but he'd have waited longer. And he was *going* to wait longer.

He was going to take this as slowly as she'd let him. So they didn't burn each other alive. Or do anything they'd regret.

So he could relish this and remember the sweet magnetism that was bringing them together now. He had no idea if it was possible for feelings like that to last. He doubted it. In truth, deep down, he doubted it'd survive Faros.

But for now, he had it, and he was holding on for dear life.

————

THEY DANCED through that song and into the next. She kept her head on his chest, breathing deep the smell of soap and sweat, savoring this stolen peace. His fingers came up to intertwine with hers and press the back of her hand against his chest, and as the slow guitar chords wrapped around them, she melted a little bit further into him. And into love with him.

Finally she tipped her head back and smiled. "So are you going to kiss me or what?"

His grin was crooked as he bent closer. But before his lips reached hers, they both went still. A voice cut through the fog of sensation. She wasn't sure if it was good luck or bad, but the words were unmistakable.

"Well, well. Rutland," an older Ursa with gray-tipped black fur was saying to a bearded man. Matched the pictures well enough. "Back again? Where were you off to? I heard it was pretty far out this time."

Her eyes locked with Kael's. He'd heard it too.

"Oh, it was. Dangerous too, but I'm fine. We hit Upsilon this time, but the place was deserted. Silly ghost stories and fairy tales."

The Ursa continued. "Really? That sounds pretty dangerous."

The bearded man shrugged. "I just do what the tourists ask me to do when they tell me to do it."

"Some tourists wanted to go to that old abandoned hell hole?" Wisely dubious, that one.

"Some people are crazy, what can you say? I just take their coin and count on them turning back before they get too far." Rutland laughed nervously.

"It's him," she mouthed silently to Kael. Together, the two of them slipped back into the booth.

"He's got to be lying about Upsilon," Kael whispered.

"Agreed," she murmured back, bringing up her comm and checking the photo again. Yep, that was him.

"What'll it be, Rutland?" Their new proprietor friend wiped off the glorious wood in front of them as she spoke.

"Whatever you've got on special—I've got credits to spend. Gotta celebrate surviving that trip!"

"Hmm. Sure you do." She sounded like she'd heard that before.

Kael cleared his throat quietly. "Are you thinking what I'm thinking?"

"I don't know, are you thinking you'd like to ship that little pissant off to Upsilon to take care of Claudette's problem for her?"

He snickered. "I might have a simpler plan. I'm thinking maybe this bar has a back room. Or a back alley. And we could help her serve him the 'special.' With a nice side of stern warning."

"I don't think 'serving back room specials' was in the Union playbook."

"Well, luckily for you it's in the Gray Dragon one. Shall we go get your ship?"

She nodded. Their bar friend was busy getting drinks, so this was a good time. Wincing and a lot colder now, she cut quickly through the couples swaying to slip behind the bar.

"Oh—hi," the woman said as Ellen appeared at her elbow.

"I'm sorry to do this, but I'm going to need to ask you for a favor. A friend of mine is in trouble, or I wouldn't."

The woman's brow creased with worry. "Like I don't owe you all this. What can I do?"

"Do you have a back room? We've been asked by another… lady in distress… to have a word with that gentleman over there who just ordered a drink. We just want to talk to him."

"That guy has a creepy aura around him. There's a back room and an exit to the maintenance passage too. Follow me, and we'll figure something out."

She led Ellen toward a pair of swinging doors, Ellen waving for Kael to follow. The room they entered was pitch black at first, but some garish overheads flipped on a few seconds later. They'd come through a narrower hall, but here the bar opened into a larger stockroom. The walls were the same bleak silver corrugated steel the rest of the bar had been before it'd gotten a coat of paint—apparently this room hadn't merited the same treatment. Cases of bottles and dozens of kegs were carefully strapped in place in stacks along the walls. A small table that folded out from the wall seemed to serve as a combination break room and office.

"Who's he harassing?" the woman said gently.

Ellen hesitated. "The owner of Claudette's Cruisers, apparently."

Her eyes widened. "God, that weird Teredark? Poor thing."

"Yes. She claims to have explained the biological impossibility to him, but apparently he is undeterred."

Kael's expression darkened, giving her additional goosebumps on top of the cold. "We aim to deter him."

That seemed to be enough for the woman. "All right. I'll send him back. Any ideas how to get him back here?"

"Tell him we've got a private special for the brave hero," said Kael.

"Good idea—I'll load him up!"

"That won't be necessary—" Ellen started, but she was gone.

A throat cleared, and they turned to see the woman holding the door open for their unsuspecting target.

Rutland was smiling until the doors swung shut behind him. Then the smile abruptly faded. The brighter lights in here revealed dark circles underneath each eye. "Who—what's going on?"

Ellen was waiting for the door to close fully—and Rutland to grow uncomfortable—before she spoke. Kael, for his part, cracked his knuckles and started unbuckling one of the strapped-in alcohol cases. Why, she had no idea, but the gesture was clearly threatening.

Rutland's eyes widened. "Who *are* you people?"

"We're here on behalf of Claudette," she said, in her sternest voice. "We need to have a little talk."

"Whoa whoa whoa, there's got to be some misunderstanding here. Claudette and I are like eggs in a zibtubator." Rutland grinned and took a sip of one drink, then frowned at it.

Ellen blinked. "Yeah right."

"No seriously, she loves me. Hey, would you two like these? They're the special! All on me!" He held up both drinks in the air like they were all just at one big party.

"She doesn't love you, asshole." Kael surprised her by stepping right up in Rutland's face. He'd removed the strap from the case completely and was carrying it casually in one hand. "We want you to swear you're going to leave her alone."

Rutland didn't move, didn't respond, but his eyes stayed trained on that strap. What the hell was Kael planning? "There's no need for that, really."

"And to return her security key to us immediately," Ellen added.

"Now, now, now—this is just a little lover's spat gone awry—" Rutland started.

This was apparently a very wrong thing to say. The crate Kael had unstrapped slid across the floor. It took her a second to attribute the crate's attack to Kael. It was all well and good to know a Theroki was in her midst, but it was so easy to forget the possibilities when telekinesis was so rare and Kael wasn't keen to remind everyone of his past. His differentness. Things rarely went sliding around the *Audacity* on his account.

This create, though, slid circles around Rutland like a rabid dog chasing his heels, and then thrust forward, knocking him off his feet. Rutland dropped the drinks—and they hung in place, suspended.

The asshole, for his part, had rolled and fallen on the ground somewhere behind the crate.

Ellen stepped forward and plucked the drinks from the air, blinking down at the two men grappling. Arms swung, and at least two fists connected with flesh amid some unfamiliar grunting.

Grappling was probably too generous a word for it, because it was mostly just a minor struggle before Kael had the man pinned, the packing strap firmly across his throat.

Kael glanced up at her. Those chocolate brown eyes were hot with anger, but far from out of control. Nothing like the way she'd seen them go in the early days, with Nova, and that eased her a little. "I'll just sit these down back here," she said, heading toward the desk with the drinks.

No reason to leave a mess behind.

"Where's the key?" Kael demanded, turning back to Rutland.

The man opened his mouth, his eyes wide, but instead of a location, only two words would come out. "You're a—you're a—you're a—"

"Yeah, I am," Kael snapped, not bothering to mince words about it. "A Theroki, whatever."

"No, you're the guy—the guy—the guy from that video on TWZ, and that means she's the—she's the—oh, shit—"

Ellen frowned. What the hell?

But Kael had no patience for it. He rose up and jerked the guy to his feet by his shirt. Then Rutland flew back, colliding with the far wall all on his own—telekinesis again.

"Open the back exit," Kael barked as he strode toward Rutland. She was a little afraid to look away, but she followed *his* orders this time. She found the back exit hatch and palmed it open. His idea, his plan.

Kael delivered two or three blows to Rutland's guts, then he dragged him again by his shirt collar. At the hatchway, he threw Rutland out into the maintenance corridor—which looked even more dirt-smeared and trash-filled than the normal corridors. A man walking past in thick glasses with a health inspector badge on his shirt glanced at them, then hurried past.

Rutland fell on his ass, but Kael was there, hauling him back to his feet. "Your promise and the robot's key. Or should I start breaking your fingers?"

So much for Rutland not wetting himself.

Gasping for breath, Rutland found his words this time. "The key— is right here—upper left vest pocket."

Kael caught her eye and cocked his head toward Rutland. She rushed forward, found the pocket, and pulled out a small silver stick. Pulling out her comm, she scanned it. It matched the description Claudette had sent her.

"It checks," she said. "If this is a copy, though, you're going to regret it." She narrowed her eyes at him.

"*I'm* going to regret it? What about this bar—this is an outrage—I —" Rutland sputtered.

But he stopped and choked as Kael's forearm pressed on his throat. "You're not going to say a word about this to anybody. You think bumping a little crate around is all I can do? You won't even know what hit you."

"You're going to leave Claudette alone," Ellen added. "In fact, how about you leave all the female Teredarks alone? Forever."

Eyes widening and face going red, Rutland nodded with all the movement he could, clutching at Kael's arm.

Kael let up the pressure, then looked at her again and cocked his head to the side again. "Take the rest of his stuff."

She tried to hide her hesitation, but a flare of alarm went through her. Why? They had what they needed. But in this scenario, it was his plan, his orders—she could question them later.

As confidently and efficiently as she could, she went through the rest of his pockets. She found a preload card full of credits, two other very similar looking security keys that made her glare at Rutland, and a fairly old looking laser blade that had seen better days. She stood, holding the items and not sure what to do with herself.

Kael leaned in close, so his breath had to be hitting Rutland's cheek as the man winced away from him. Weirdly, she'd been that close, knew what it felt like. Wouldn't have winced.

"Leave the Teredark alone," he growled at him. "Got it? Our people will be watching you."

Rutland's eyes were locked with Kael's, frozen. He didn't respond.

Kael's eyes narrowed. "You have a nice business. You wouldn't want something to happen to it."

If the man's bladder was still functioning, he should be proud.

Kael bared his teeth one more time at Rutland, then threw him by the shirt back further down the maintenance corridor. "And go home and clean yourself up."

Ellen was still standing there, staring and holding the contents of Rutland's pockets in front of her. Kael took the items and slipped them into his cargos, the front of which she realized were still noticeably wet from where they'd pressed against her.

She followed Kael back through the hatch to the bar and palmed it closed behind them. He headed straight out into the bar area, the doors swinging shut behind him, so she followed. They gave the proprietor woman a nod as they left.

"Back to the ship?" Ellen murmured. "Guess play time is over."

Kael smirked. "I said, let's go get you your ship. Why not now?"

She raised an eyebrow. Somebody was in an assertive mood. But it was a little nice to rely on someone else for a change. "Might as well find out if one of those keys is the real deal."

He nodded. "Let's hope so. I don't want to ever touch that guy again. He smells like dung beetles."

She snorted. "I'm going to pretend I never heard that."

They took the outer ring corridor, then flipped to the inner ring for a while, then back. The entertainment quadrant was about as far as possible from the ship quarter, probably by design. Still, as they walked, something niggled at her.

"Why did you say to take all that stuff? All we needed was the security key."

When he spoke, he didn't meet her eyes, just kept them fixed on the corridor ahead. "We needed to adequately scare him. Just punching him and telling him to leave Claudette alone wasn't enough."

"I dunno. You might not know this, but you hit pretty hard."

"I didn't hit him as hard as it looked. He just can't take a punch. But on top of that, we need it. Once upon a time, I was a pirate, as you like to say—"

She winced. "That was joking."

"—and a few lives before that, I was a pretty good thief. And if you ask me, you *need* a thief right about now."

Her wince melted into a scowl. "You don't have to worry about that. That's my problem."

"Yes, I do. Your problems are my problems."

"We'll figure something out."

"Spoken like someone who has never worried about running out of credits."

"We've got lots of ways of making money. We'll figure something out."

"We just did." He pulled the card with the credits on it out of his pocket and handed it to her.

She stared at the thing in her palm before grudgingly pocketing it.

"Listen." He stopped abruptly and looked her straight in the eye.

"Even if it weren't for you, I would have always wanted to serve on the *Audacity*. It's the best chance I've had to make the world a little bit better instead of a lot worse. But we are in some serious shit at this point. Doug needs us."

"*If* he's still alive."

He blinked. "You really are set on thinking he's dead, aren't you?"

Her eyes widened. She hadn't exactly meant to reveal that right this second, but she was getting used to him seeing things. Things she hid from everyone else.

"You don't know that, Elle."

The softness of his words and gentleness in his eyes melted some of the frustration in her. "I know. But I tend to lean toward pessimistic assessments, so I'm prepared for enemy actions. It usually serves me well."

"I get it. But you're still going to try to find him, right? That's why we're getting this ship."

"Obviously."

He took a deep breath. "You might not appreciate my methods, but we don't have Doug here to help us save him. You might need to veer from your usual playbook."

He was right, of course. But that didn't mean it didn't bother her to beat up a random asshole in a dirty back corridor for his spare change. It rankled what little sense of honor she had left. Then again, Rutland was hardly just a random guy on the street. "I didn't say I didn't appreciate your methods," she said hastily. "He was a bad guy."

"Just because he's a bad guy doesn't make us good guys. But you want to be."

"So do you," she shot back.

He bent down and pressed a soft kiss to her lips. But it was different this time, almost sad. "You see, *jagiya*. This is why it'll never work between us."

"Because I'm a good guy? Please."

"And I'm not."

"That's not true."

"You're the upright officer, with your moral code—"

"Which I *broke*."

"And that wasn't easy for you. But I've always been one of the bad guys."

"That's bull."

"I never had a code to begin with."

"Then why did you want to join our team in the first place?"

The slight furrowing of his brow seemed to show a genuine confusion, as if two ideas were colliding in his mind, two facts that couldn't coexist, but right now they did. There were a number of possible answers, like the excellent pay or the armor that didn't give you tetanus, but she noted smugly he didn't say any of them.

"You've still always been the law, darlin'. The most upstanding of upstanding citizens, sworn to defend the weak, doing your duty—"

"I *deserted* my duty," she snapped.

"And me? I've always been at the ass end of that, barely getting by. Breaking any and every rule I needed to survive."

"So what?" She raised her chin. "Why do you keep trying to tell me this? Why do you think I don't know that? I've told you. I know who you are, Kael. I signed up for this eyes wide open."

"Oh, you know it up here." He touched her temple gently, and inwardly she flinched at the intimacy of the gesture, the surprising ease of it. "But you think that's the first time I stole some guy's credits and kept them for myself?"

She blinked.

Before she could form a response, he'd turned and started down the corridor. "C'mon. Let's get this to Claudette. Doug needs us, like I said."

She hurried after him, trying not to focus on the sudden cold anger in the words. She needed a way to eloquently disagree with him, to drop kick this idea out of his head.

Except all she could think of to say was that he was full of it.

Because she *did* know it wasn't the first time he'd robbed somebody. But there was a difference between taking credits to survive and taking them to make rich pockets fuller and taking them for fun. Wasn't there? And he had always been well below that line, struggling to survive whether it was as a child or struggling to survive within the Theroki hierarchy. He hadn't shown up on board the *Audacity* rolling in coin. She wasn't sure how much he'd had, but it couldn't have paid for passage. Doug had checked.

She, however. She had never been in that situation. The Union had always provided, and after that Doug had always given her ten times what she needed. If not a hundred times.

And that was just the problem. For her, taking those credits felt like she was one of the bad ones, shaking down Rutland to line her already stuffed pockets.

Except those pockets were not so full anymore.

She *did* have a state-of-the-art ship to go back to. She wasn't taking those credits to eat. Yet. But she did desperately need those credits and a whole lot more for the *ship* to eat, and all the people on board to still have a home, and to have any hope of finding Doug alive.

What bothered her wasn't the stealing—although maybe it should have. How many Enhancer labs, Puritan compounds, Stedler sheds had she broken into and destroyed or confiscated the property of in the name of what was right? In the name of science policing itself? In another light, there was plenty of robbery and property destruction in her past, and worse crimes. She'd have to point that out one day. Although half these labs were on planets that barely had laws let alone governments that could actually enforce them.

No. The real rub was that this was the first time in her life that there was no safety net under her high-risk circus act. That stealing those credits might actually be something she *needed* to do to survive.

She needed him more than ever, and she did *not* need him thinking this was some kind of fatal flaw dooming whatever it was they had together. They were not so different; he was wrong about that.

It was a lot easier to know that, though, than to explain it to him.

———

ELLEN HURRIED TOWARD BRI, bypassing the eagerly approaching Claudette who was advancing with mandibles swinging. Kael headed toward the Teredark to intercept, thank the Lord. She was going to give the security key to Claudette either way, but if the fighter wasn't going to fly, they might need to renegotiate the deal.

The shop looked much the same as yesterday, except that Bri was on a hoverboard on her back underneath the fighter's belly, only her feet currently visible.

"Bri, what's the status?" She stopped short of the small ship and tried not to bark irritably, but it mostly came out as a bark.

"Look, the little fighter is in good shape. That Claudette—or whoever she is—is a straight shooter." Bri slid into view and sat up, shrugging her leather-jacketed shoulders. She was frowning, almost as if she resented the ship being both functional and honest.

"Aren't you worried you'll get some kind of fighter-related goo on that coat?" Ellen said.

Bri waved her off. "Nothing in this baby that's not there already. Why do you think it's black?"

Frowning, Ellen opened her mouth, but at that moment, a blue cloak and the vivid form of Etrianala Kentt appeared near the stern of the fighter, fingers dragging almost sensually across the ship's hull.

"What's she doing here?" Ellen jutted her chin at Kentt, still a few meters away.

"Came along to check out the Teredark. Included for free as part of your straight shooter assessment." Free? Sure it was. Bri glanced at Kentt then back to Ellen, lowering her voice. "They shared a very strange stare for a good two minutes, but now Claudette is your *biggest* fan."

Well, if all it had taken was some staring, maybe she shouldn't have bothered with Rutland. She didn't say that, though. And she wouldn't have wanted to leave Claudette in the creep's sights either way.

Bri cleared her throat. "We do have one problem though."

"What?"

"We don't have the credits."

"It's handled," said Ellen. "We're bartering."

"For the ship, maybe. But what about the fragging parts?"

"I barely had time to deal with this. We'll figure something out."

"Claudette is willing to give us a discount on some of what she has in stock, but some have to come from the main depot, and they all require credits. Plus we already owe for the water refueling."

Ellen blocked the sudden panic that threatened to flood in. Kentt was approaching. Bri eyed the telepath warily, then lie back down on her mechanic's hoverboard and returned to her perusal of the fighter's belly. Ellen strode to meet Kentt halfway, near the fighter's wing. Wouldn't be a bad idea to stare at the thing from another angle, see if she noticed anything.

Kentt's eyes were less luminous in the brighter light of the ship bay. Her hood was thrown back, and in spite of her clear obsession with blue in her cloak and hair, she looked more like an ordinary person and less like some kind of supernatural creature than she usually did. What would she be—a pixie? A goddess? Water nymph maybe.

Kentt cleared her throat, and Ellen tamped down the impression that Kentt knew what she was thinking, and the sound was a sign of disapproval. The woman was just clearing her damn throat. She wasn't superhuman. Well, only mildly superhuman, anyway. "Commander, I would like to propose I pay you for my passage."

Ellen frowned. "That won't be necessary."

"You charged the Theroki."

"How do you find out these things, if we both have chips?"

"I can make small talk, you know."

"He was a Theroki. Dangerous. I was trying to deter him."

"And I'm also dangerous."

She swallowed. "Thanks for pointing that out. You already saved all of us, though, and you're teaching Isa. That's payment in my book. Just based on Isa, pretty sure I'm stuck with you." And the improvement in Isa's manners was absolutely worth it.

"Stuck with him, too…" Kentt's eyes flicked down her still sodden form, and then over at Kael as he was speaking to the Teredark. Hell. The dampness on his clothes would reveal enough if anyone were paying attention. Kentt's eyes twinkled as she smiled. "Good observation skills get me a long way."

"Look, you don't have to pay me." Ellen threw herself into the words, hoping to fight any potential blush even though she could feel it rising. "You already earned your ride, and you keep earning it by teaching. It wouldn't be right. Even if you did pay the standard fee, it wouldn't be enough for the parts. Kael paid me in work. He didn't have any credits, anyway."

"Well, I do have credits. In fact, I came into quite a number of them yesterday evening."

Ellen went still. "Wait—what? How."

"As we came to understand our need for greater funds, several folks on the ship have been making very resourceful plans. It felt hardly appropriate to simply ignore the problem and lounge around reading a book."

"What did you do?" And why was there a pit of dread growing in Ellen's stomach?

Kentt smiled. "I received quite a lucrative sum as I finally streamed that delicious fight you gave me. The TWZ network paid handsomely for a collab deal."

"You *what*?" She wasn't yelling, was she? Maybe she should be.

"My dramatic disappearance and streaming from a secret, unknown location only increased viewing interest."

"Secret, my ass. They'll find us. One altercation with the Union wasn't enough for you? You're going to get us all killed."

"As I have already saved all your lives once, we will be even then."

Ellen bit back a brutal reply. What was done was done, what was streamed was streamed, there was no point in disparaging it now beyond what she'd already said.

Plus, what had Kael said about uncomfortable methods?

"I've given some funds to Xi for my passage. I have also deposited a third of the proceeds into your account and a third into Kael's. His time on screen is short, but at the very least a third of the fun. A huge draw, especially with the ladies. Although let's be honest, a larger percentage of the viewers were male."

"I told you—that's going to cause problems for him. For us."

"Both of your covers are beyond blown. I understand your desire to live privately and maintain anonymity and freedom. But you have a ship to fuel and a friend to save. For all you know, your 'friend' is dead. As might be his parents. Reconnecting with another part of… your organization… will not be easy, if it's even possible or desirable. And how will you know if you'll be able to trust them? This is simpler. You need this money. Take it."

Ellen licked her lips. She hated to admit it, but Kentt was right. "Fine. But that doesn't mean I have to be happy about it."

"No. You don't have to be happy about it. You can, however, buy your parts and supplies."

She forced herself to take a deep breath. She wasn't handling this with much grace, barely better than the botched discussion with Kael. Some manners were in order. She gave a slight bow. "Thank you, Etri-anala. I'll be glad to be on the way to see my friend sooner rather than later."

"Our friend, I think," said Kentt.

"Did you know him?"

Kentt shook her head gently. "No, but I should like to. I can feel the respect for him. Friendship, loyalty even. And he certainly could have ordered you all to lock me in an airlock and cycle, so in a manner of speaking, I owe him my life too. I truly hope he is well."

Ellen's eyebrows twitched up. An astute and accurate assessment of the situation. Respect and loyalty—much of what Kentt said had been shared in the briefing just after the attack, but Ellen had to suspect she'd invaded some thoughts too, to pick that up. Dremer's? That didn't sit well with her, but that, like the video and Kentt noticing their wet clothes, was done and in the past. Couldn't be changed now. Or in the future either. She'd agreed to this—and all of its implications.

She turned and strode back to Bri. "Apparently we've got some new funds. Get those parts, and get everything on board sooner rather than later. The sooner we get to helping our friends, the better."

———

KAEL HADN'T BEEN MUCH in the mood to glower lately. But right now, Bri needed someone to glower, and he was suddenly able to oblige.

Several grizzled, silver-tipped Ursas and one human hairy enough to possibly be an Ursa were not putting off friendly vibes. Hardly shocking, considering the way Bri had rolled up, thrown down her parts order on her tablet, and called them "lazy slagging teddy bears."

To their faces.

What skill Bri lacked in diplomacy and negotiation, he'd have to make up in intimidating scowls.

Scowls were coming naturally, though. After Ellen had verified the fighter was good to go, they'd handed over the rescued security key to Claudette. And in the next few moments, Kael had found himself volunteering to escort Bri down to the depot to deal with this order.

Honestly, half-wet and still swearing he could smell pumpkin and cinnamon in the air, it wasn't the way he'd been hoping to end the night. He wasn't exactly sure *how* he'd been hoping to end the night, but not like this.

The parts depot looked nothing like a depot. It was just an alcove in the wall, with a dingy sign beside it reading, Molyarch Parts & Service. Inside the alcove was practically pitch black, like some kind of mine. He could barely make out parts on shelves that led back, into dim tunnels that faded into the distance—or maybe that was just an illusion. How big could it really be? The station was only two rings, inner and outer, so it couldn't go on for kilometers… The darkness meant you couldn't really tell either way. There was a tang of nitrogen in the air, and oil too.

Bri was leaning over the counter, both palms flat, squinting into the darkness as the employees muttered among themselves.

Kael scowled harder. Stepped forward. It was all he could contribute.

He wasn't scowling because he was here and not back on the ship. He wasn't scowling because he had no idea exactly where he should head once he got back to the ship. He hadn't slept in his cabin in three days. Or was it four? Five, even? And then they'd been on Capital, so it had been a long time.

He hadn't looked Ellen in the eye as he'd marched off after Bri. And he was scowling because he was trying to figure out why exactly.

This felt like the way he'd felt before. Before he'd come on board the *Audacity*. Before they'd fixed his chip. Angry, all the time, not even sure at what.

Just angry.

Except… did he know what? The altercation with Rutland had left his head full of thoughts. Too many thoughts. Too many memories.

One of Bri's Ursas vanished back into the darkness. Bri rolled her eyes and flipped around to lean on the counter and check her comm. "Guess this is gonna take a while," she muttered.

"Shouldn't have called them teddy bears," he muttered back.

This particular situation was not helping matters. How many times had he stood like this, glowering over the shoulder of someone making demands? Bri was simply asking for parts for a better price, and he was glaring in the name of fairness right now. But it hadn't always been that way.

In fact, more often than not, the person on his side had been demanding highway robbery. And Kael's glare had been the threat, the consequence, the muscle. The situation with Rutland had been all too familiar, just like being back on Faros, just like riding a bike as the saying went—you didn't easily forget.

Protection rackets had been the name of the game for his gang on Faros. That sometimes meant beating people up to threaten their businesses. Sometimes it meant threatening other people's businesses. Most of it involved extorting money or some such collateral.

Little of whatever the Gray Dragons had extorted had gone into his pocket, despite what he'd said.

What was really shaking him was how much he remembered, how easily it had come back. Like muscle memory, scaring the shit out of Rutland was easy for him. Knock him around, take everything, make your threat, repeat. If needed.

He could do the same to these Ursas right now.

Something of his thoughts must have come through in his expression, because one of them gave a little "yeep!" and scurried in the direction the last one had gone.

He almost groaned and rolled his eyes. But Bri needed him to keep up the glare, and so did everyone on the ship.

A few quiet minutes later, two new Ursas appeared with a palette of misshapen lumps led by a handheld grabber. Bri seemed appeased and marched after them with only a slight snarl to her lip, so he followed behind. And kept up the surly just in case.

A plastic wrapper blew past them as the small, sad group trundled up the dim, dirty corridors to where the *Audacity* was docked. The quiet left him only his thoughts.

He'd wanted a chance at something noble. He'd wanted something he'd chosen for himself, something better. And like lightning striking, he'd been the one fool in a million to actually get that chance.

But what exactly had he been expecting? It was one thing to forget about the past. But the past didn't forget about you so easily. It didn't just wash away in a day or two.

Maybe it didn't wash away ever.

It had been over a decade after all since he'd left Faros. The Theroki were more skilled and more legitimate in their own twisted way. He had become the hired guard in larger scale rackets by that time, nothing so petty as punishing normal people into submission just because they lived on a certain city block.

He'd never liked the life. But he'd been good at it. It'd kept him alive.

And he was still good at it.

If Ellen hadn't been there, he knew exactly how much further he would have gone, and it would have kept that asshole away from Claudette forever. Forever. Because he knew what he was doing.

And that. *That* he hated.

They say you rise to the level of your training. He was trained the wrong way, deep down. He could pretend to be something else all he wanted, but who was he kidding? He'd never be like her.

As he helped the Ursas unload what they'd brought, and read off each piece so Bri could check she'd gotten what she ordered, a sickening sense of dread grew in his stomach. Something almost like fear, but bitter and frantic with the need to fight, to run, to survive.

He shouldn't go back to Faros. He shouldn't see any of those people, those places, and most of all—not Asha. It was a fool's errand.

He'd tell Ellen he wanted to stay on the ship. Let her and someone else go check it out. That seemed smart. Cowardly, but smart.

But he wasn't telling Ellen any such thing at the moment, as he was apparently avoiding her. And Bri was murmuring this was only a third of the shipment—there'd be two more trips.

Ellen ought to be pissed at him anyway. He admired her for taking the hard path, the straight and narrow, and then he threw it in her face too? What an asshole.

He glanced down at his hand and snorted. There was still blood on his knuckles from Rutland. It must be clean, to have passed the bioscans to enter the ship, but still. Gross.

None of this was ever going to work. He could play the part of the hero all he wanted, but the tattoos and the training and the past didn't lie.

CHAPTER SEVEN

DAY 5 - 6

A SCREAM JARRED Ellen from sleep. Not her own scream, she realized, but someone else's. She sat straight up, hands clutching her ears, immediately missing the warmth of Kael beside her. He belonged beside her—why wasn't he here?

She blinked, rubbed her eyes, stared at the room around her. If there were an intruder, Xi would have reacted. Brought up the lights. But the room was still dim, in night mode. Had it just been a nightmare?

Another scream now sent a shiver through her, sharp like the shriek of a songbird. A telepath? Was something wrong with Kentt? Isa? Or could Arakovic have found them?

She staggered to her feet, looking for her boots. What the hell was a songbird doing on her ship? Could it be an aggressive ship, in a neighboring dock? But then Adan would have woken her. Someone on board the station? They were still docked at Molyarch, weren't they?

But as the lengthy scream quieted and the sleep started to clear from her brain, two things became clear. The first thing was she ought to grab Persad's pebble out of her drawer for the telepathy blocking device. The companion chip was still inside her, but the current iteration of her device required an external piece attached beneath the hair.

She hadn't taken to wearing it *all* the time around the ship, because it interfered with comms, and it felt too easy to knock off accidentally. As another screech ripped through her mind, putting it on now certainly seemed the right occasion.

The second thing that hit her was that the screams were strange. Deeply strange. Something was different about them. They weren't screams of pain exactly, not of torture or agony… There was a sadness twisted through them, confusion. Fear.

She unlatched and yanked open the appropriate drawer, groping in the darkness. Xi seemed to have noticed her staggering around her cabin, because the lights rose as her hand closed around the smooth stone. She slipped it into her pocket. She'd put it on when the shrieks became intolerable, but hearing a few more might teach her something.

"Xi—what's going on?"

"We officially have an additional passenger, Ellen."

Ellen shook herself. "Damn it, just call me Commander. That is driving me crazy."

"Of course, Commander. It is a relief to use a respectful term for me as well."

"And what are you talking about? An additional passenger?"

"The child has matured out of its chamber. The process is truly amazing to witness."

"The screaming I'm hearing in my head is *not* amazing."

"Ah. I apologize. I do not have telepathic capabilities. But apparently your Empress does."

"Fragging hell." Apparently Kentt was about to learn more of their secrets. Whether Ellen liked it or not. "Get Kentt and Isa down there, and—"

"They were woken just as you were and are also on their way."

"Well, dreck on a stick." Grabbing her comm and her pistol and shoving them into her pockets, she took off for the sick bay at a jog.

The back of Bri's leather jacket caught her eye first, then her disheveled ponytail, then Isa standing beside her. Kentt's blue cloak peeked out around the left edge of the door. Ellen eased around them and caught her breath.

An array of equipment she hadn't known they possessed was hard at work in Levereaux and Dremer's hands. Had they ordered it? Printed it on board? Did sick bays come standard with beds that tiny?

Because under a little bubble-like cylinder, there was a squirming, red-cheeked baby. A baby who was also supposedly an empress. An empress of a people who probably wanted her back.

A sudden determination to never, ever let them have this little girl hit Ellen like a punch to the gut.

The child wailed, her cry both verbal and mental. Not only pain radiated, but anguish too. Everyone winced. Ellen hastily dug the pebble from her pocket and slipped it in place under her hair, and the telepathic cry faded to silence. It might be callous to block out the emotions of the child, but they weren't helping her fix the situation. And her ears could hear the crying well enough.

"Doctors," she demanded briskly, "your sitrep, please."

Levereaux responded with practiced ease. "Separation from the artificial womb successful. Color is good. Cry is quite vigorous, as you heard. Xi, pulse? What I wouldn't give for a nurse right now."

Isa stepped forward. "Let me help."

Levereaux glanced absently at her, hesitated, then grunted, "Wash your hands. Hit the biofield. All of you."

"Pulse at 143, 149, 151, 147—" said Xi calmly.

"Perfect. She's doing perfect. Keep an eye on that, Xi. You know the range?"

"By default, such protocols are already in place, Rachel."

"Right. Thanks. I knew that—just stressed, I guess."

"Redundancy is good in this situation."

Ellen followed orders like the others, standing behind Isa and Bri as the biofield scrubbed their hands and then their whole bodies. Kentt waited beside Ellen, her eyes rarely leaving the baby. "She's not crying so loud anymore," Ellen said. "That got something to do with you?"

"Yes." Kentt pursed her lips as she stepped forward to take her turn with the biofield. "This is a very gifted telepath. I sensed her almost before I was on board. Telepath and… something else. Rare."

"Do you know what else?"

"Not yet. But I fear this child will not wait long to make her powers known. As we've already seen."

"Yes. I'm surprised the whole ship isn't down here. Don't know who sleeps through that."

Kentt blinked, eyes unfocusing for a second. "I sense a large general confusion. No one is asleep. People may not know where to look. But as to the child—whose child is this?"

Ellen's jaw clenched. "I don't think you really need to know that."

Kentt, to her credit, remained placidly calm as usual. "As the only trained telepath aboard, and one of two total, I believe you are going to need my help. I must understand who her guardian is and who is responsible for her care."

She sighed. "If she has a mother, it's no one onboard, to put it succinctly. Or maybe it's just become all of us. We believe she was genetically engineered. She has enhanced growth, and apparently excellent telepathy, and probably other modifications too."

"Engineered by whom?"

"You realize the more I tell you, the more likely I'll have to kill you if you betray us?"

A normal person's eyes would have widened, but Kentt gave her a small smile. "I'd expect nothing less."

Ellen shook her head. She would try to keep it to ninety percent of the story and hope Kentt didn't press further. "We believe she was engineered by Enhancers and contains some of their latest research. They do not, however, know we have this research and probably want it back, so that knowledge doesn't leave this ship. Do you understand?"

Kentt nodded, but her gaze was on the child, and her face had only softened further. "She wants—"

"To be held," Bri cut in. The leather jacket was abandoned on a chair, revealing a generic pale blue t-shirt underneath. "Doesn't take a telepath to know that. Just a mother."

"That may be," said Dremer, approaching with an orange blanket as Levereaux raised the baby, "but we're rather short on those. Care to start a training class?"

Bri shook her head. "Poor thing, if all you've got is me for a mother. No, not like that." Dremer was wrapping the baby, but Bri quickly stepped in to correct her and wrap it tighter.

"After fourteen years, you've still got it, Bri." Dremer grinned.

"Like riding a speeder. Isa? Want to hold her?"

Isa climbed into a doctor's chair, and Bri settled the baby on her lap, where Isa's relentlessly curious gaze never wavered. "Nice to finally meet you, little one," she whispered.

Kentt and Ellen joined them now, clustering around Isa and the baby. She wasn't sure why they'd paused at a distance, frozen and watching the scene unfold, but now all six of them stared down at big brown eyes that blinked slowly up at them, tiny lips opening and closing, nestled in a swath of orange.

"Is that… a shipping blanket?" Ellen murmured.

"We washed it," Dremer replied, voice equally hushed.

Bri leaned against her shoulder, to Ellen's surprise, then threw an arm around Ellen and pulled her closer. Whatever emotion was swallowing Ellen was overcoming tough-minded Bri too. There was a misty wetness to her eyes. Of course, she might be the only one of them who had been through this before, so it wasn't the same.

"Hey, I got a bottle ready!" Jenny jogged in, then stopped to smile at the scene.

"No mother at all," Ellen muttered, shaking her head.

"No mother—or two dozen." Dremer folded her arms. "Better us than them, at least."

"We can hope. We can hope."

Bri made a choking noise that Ellen concluded was her stifling tears. "God damn it, somebody take a picture."

"Everyone smile," said Xi. "And say cheese."

"What—" Ellen was still saying when she heard a digital clicking-sliding sound. She shook her head again. She'd never taken great pictures.

———

THE FINAL PARTS were stowed and strapped, some in the cargo bay and some in the engine hold, when a cry split the air. Sharp stabs of adrenaline shot through him, his heart sprang into a pounding sprint, headlong and out of control. Kael jumped, taking in a sharp breath of the unusually cold air of the cargo bay, where he'd been double checking if everything were properly secured.

He shut his eyes and forced a deep breath through flared nostrils. This wasn't quite full-on bloodlust, but it was on its way there. If he didn't slow it down, control it with an iron will…

This violent chemical rush was still the effects of all the years of tampering. He was tired, and freaked out, and not sure what the hell he was going to do when he finished checking the last strap. And now this.

He knew that sound. It was a sound that he'd never heard for himself, a sound that had been denied him, stolen away, and he didn't see it coming at the time, and he certainly didn't know how it had gone so wrong.

He'd thought Asha had been the victim. Maybe she had been. Maybe she hadn't.

Another wail.

Maybe he needed to go to Faros after all. Even if he found out that there was no way to remove the stain that was his birth and his history, the past that made him who he was. Even if he'd have to face men he'd thought were maybe brothers but were truly enemies. Even if it destroyed him. Someone had denied him the future he'd thought was a slim ray of sunshine, a way out, the future he'd wanted. And it might not have been the gang or the Theroki or anyone that he'd thought.

Had it been Asha? How could he not find out?

Another more plaintive cry cut into his very soul, and he slumped against the crate behind him.

The child. The tiny creature Lord Regent Jun Il Li had entrusted to him. That he'd hidden and guarded. That he'd ultimately stolen from the Enhancers and brought here. That child that even as he'd avoided her, he'd checked on her, often enough, from time to time. Through Isa, through Xi, from the corridor if necessary. The empress was a capsule no longer.

She wasn't his daughter more than anyone else's.

And yet he felt responsible. More responsible for her than he had a right to. But it was *him* that had brought her here, so wasn't he the one who should make sure she was safe?

He hadn't managed it for his own unborn child. He wasn't sure if that made him more determined to guard the empress, or more certain that he would fail.

He wandered like a ghost through the cargo bay, stepping around the ladder without thinking, following the cries. But once he reached the hall that led to the sick bay he stopped at a distance, watching from outside.

Bri was rocking the baby and proving that she actually knew how to smile. Isa climbed into a chair and Bri settled the baby on her lap. A group gathered round—hair of white, blue, iron…

His eyes caught on the angles that were Ellen, angles he'd memorized and studied time and again, ones that would hold his eye, even in a sea of stars.

He watched as they talked and laughed, not noticing him. He was content to be an outsider. Preferred it, even. He leaned into the slight alcove between one hatch and a bulkhead and the next hatch, partially hidden. The night cycle still reigned here, so he was shrouded in darkness.

He only started when Ellen straightened, ran a hand over her face, and set off out of the room, heading directly toward him. Probably on the way to her cabin.

There wasn't time to panic or think of what he was going to say or even swear. She crossed the twenty steps between him and the sick bay fast. They both jumped when she realized he was there.

"Kael," she said softly. He couldn't read the expression.

"I…" he started. Then stopped.

"Do you want to go in?"

"No."

She seemed to sense the height of his tension, how tightly wound he was as she eased closer. Tentatively at first, she raised a hand to his forearm, brushed her fingers against his skin.

He shivered, in spite of himself, and reached his hand toward her.

She slipped between his arm and his body, and his hand curved around her waist like he'd done it a thousand times.

"What about keeping this to ourselves?" he murmured.

"This is more important," she replied.

They stood in silence for a while, like that. No one moved around the ship, but he kept his ears tuned for footsteps.

In the silence, he finally found voice to one of the things behind his scowl that he hadn't wanted to admit so much. "Do you think we'll find her? Alive, I mean."

She didn't respond for a minute, maybe not understanding who he could mean. But then she said, "Your child? You think it's a girl?"

He shrugged, trying to cast off the bitterness of not knowing for sure. He liked that she'd spoken in the present tense. "Call it a gut feeling."

"I don't know if we'll find her. But I'm all in now. And when I'm all in, I'm all in. You know that, right?"

Something eased slightly in his chest, twisted and unlocked. "I'm sure we'll do everything we can."

"You know I don't just mean about the kid, right?" She looked away from the baby and her eyes locked with his, open and determined and dark, lovely as black pearls, mysterious depths in the dimness.

"I know." Maybe he hadn't before, but he did now.

They lapsed into silence. Eventually, she spoke again, voice soft. "Thank you."

"Hmm?" He raised an eyebrow, but didn't immediately look her way.

"Thank you for your help with Rutland."

"I work for you. You don't have to thank me." But he smiled, glancing at her, then back to the Isa's latest attempts to rock the baby. Hard to believe the capsule had turned into a living being that looked so… ordinary. So precious, but for an entirely different reason.

"With the Foundation accounts empty, you know we might not get paid, right? Working for me may start to be very unrewarding soon."

He turned to her, earnest now, frowning a little. "You know I'd be by your side, money or no money, ship or no ship, armor or no armor, right?"

A sweet smile like sunshine crept into her face and her eyes before she ducked her head, her cheeks flushing. The she seemed to force herself to meet his eyes. "Same here."

"I haven't given you any of those things, so that's pretty clear."

"What you give me is a lot more valuable than any of that. And you were right. About Rutland. Kentt proved it to me too. We need to use every option we have."

"Forget it. It's in the past," he murmured. Of course, once the fighter arrived, the *Audacity* would head to Faros, and his past wouldn't be very far away at all. He raised a hand and brushed his palm and fingertips gently across her cheek. The faint sheen of glitter had vanished. "You're dry. You took a shower."

"I was procrastinating. I was hoping to see you. And glitter isn't really my style."

"We only just finished with the parts." A useful excuse. "The fighter won't be here for a few more hours. Then we'll be good to get on our way."

She bit her lip, reading correctly that his delay hadn't *just* been about the parts getting stowed properly. "We should get some rest. Haven't had a real night's sleep in ages, and it won't start tonight." She eased away from him, eyes turning back to the baby, then the floor. His hand lingered on her back, then fell to his side when she was just too far away.

She sweetly played it cool for a minute, gave him space. She seemed like she really would just walk away if he let her.

He'd made enough stupid decisions tonight. He leaned forward and brushed his lips close to her ear as he whispered, "My room is right over there, you know."

She turned sharply to meet his gaze, eyes bright. It would be harder to hide, with half the other cabins nearby. They'd never tried it.

"Do you dare join the Theroki in his den?"

"Do I dare, do I dare. In a minute there is time for decisions and revisions…" Her eyes dancing with laughter.

"What?"

"Never mind. I think I get Zhia's mural now. Is your room as messy as usual?"

"Messier. I've barely been there since Capital."

"You're lucky I'm a brave woman."

———

IN THE MORNING, it turned out that Ellen and Kael were some of the few people who had gotten any sleep.

Thanks to their tech, Chayana and Vivaan were sharing well-rested smiles over mugs of spiced tea. God, that smelled good. She didn't think that was from the mess, either.

Everyone else, though… Everyone else was the picture of disheveled chaos. The hold was filled with nearly the entire crew, as well as an assortment of red eyes, yawns, tussled hair, unicorn pajamas, or some combination thereof.

Ellen looked for a nod from Bri, then began entering the commands to close up the cargo bay doors. They'd had them open waiting for the fighter but with the looks they were getting from out in the corridor, they were going to have to wait for Claudette to knock when she arrived. Or comm. Or whatever Teredarks did with those mandibles.

In spite of Isa and Kentt's efforts to appease their empress, there had been more than a few telepathic wails, cries meant to broadcast her desperate needs. Cries incidentally waking up almost everyone onboard.

And maybe not onboard either. The crew wasn't alone in their torture. Ornery security officers crowded around near the end of the corridor, scowling as the cargo bay door slid closed. They didn't seem to want to get involved, but weren't leaving either. Who would want to put up with screams like that at all hours? They probably wondered if she was torturing someone. There would be complaints.

Ellen sighed and turned toward the crew gathered in the hold. The briefing room had been so crowded last time, she'd opted to try something new.

Adan frowned at her, peering closer with that new eye of his.

"What, Adan?" she snapped. That damn thing was making her uncomfortable. He'd gone for a fairly showy model that glowed green and had a variety of projection and readout settings. He'd never go undercover as a Puritan now, that was for sure.

"Nothing, Commander."

"Then why are you staring at me like that?"

"You seem really, I don't know… relaxed. Happy? It's weird. Something seems different about you."

It was all she could do not to roll her eyes. "Didn't hear the baby, that's all. Let's get started."

The room's dull murmur quieted to a tense silence. She clasped her hands behind her back. "Our new friend is causing us a few problems here, as you may have noticed. She'll probably cause a disturbance anywhere we dock. While her growth is accelerated, we don't know how accelerated. The doctors tell me that at a normal human growth rate, this could go on for anywhere from six to sixteen weeks, maybe more. Even after that, it will only be less frequent, not over."

Groans erupted across the room like flowers wilting under a heat ray.

She had to scan for a few moments to find Etrianala Kentt hovering in the shadows beside one of the pair of ladders. "Kentt—can you explain to the crew what you explained to me about how young telepaths develop?"

Kentt lifted her chin and glided forward. "Most Natural telepaths don't develop powers until they reach their teenage years, but a small percentage of them are born with their abilities intact and use them to express their needs, as this baby is doing. This makes caring for young telepaths both difficult and easy. They can communicate their needs when many children can't, decreasing confusion. But their pre-language cries can be highly disruptive."

"In other words," Ellen said slowly. "There is no end in sight. So unless you all want to be sleeping like a newborn—which contrary to the popular expression, is not well at all—then we've got to do something."

"Like what?" Nova asked.

"Persad has the experimental technology she's already installed in both Kael and I that gives us the ability to block these messages. I was planning to offer the technology to everyone else as an option. I'm not sure what Doug was planning—we never got a chance to discuss it. But clearly it is becoming necessary on this ship. The baby isn't going anywhere." She looked to Chayana Persad.

Chayana stood. "I am updating the system to not require the external pebble, as it is too easily removed by someone other than the user. So it will be a full self-contained system, likely residing mostly in the neck and back, because it is shielding the brain from the foreign electromagnetic interference. Because of this, the new system will also interfere less with communications systems, but it can't be adapted into your current rape protection defense systems unfortunately. My augmentation also runs continuously and is not activated by nervous system command like the RPD. Turning it off will require fully removing the chip. I've struggled with this design tradeoff, but for your mission, Commander Ryu and I thought this would be for the best. At any rate, many of you will need more extensive cybernetic upgrades if you choose to adopt the technology." Her voice quavered a little while she spoke, but she ended with a strong nod as she sat down.

"If it's any consolation," Dremer chimed in, "given the way we've seen these songbirds act, this augmentation is certainly going to be useful to our mission anyway."

Ellen scanned the group. "If you don't want to go there—I understand. But we'll have to let you off the ship soon. At one of our next safe stops." Which God only knew when that would be. Faros IV was doubtful.

The room was quiet, and more than a few eyes were wide.

"In the short term, we will be putting Isa and Kentt on twelve hour shifts to try to temper her needs and emotions, but they can't do that indefinitely. We will also try some time with non-telepathic caregivers and see if they can build trust and get the frustration under control. Dr. Taylor and Bri will be trying those. Let me know if you'd like to try your hand."

Bri made a face. Ellen wasn't giving her the option of refusing, but if Bri truly objected, the face would be a lot viler, and the stream of expletives would still be going strong. Hard outer shell, gooey molten chocolate core. Bri in a nutshell.

"So our young cargo is determined to broadcast its presence, non-stop. So we need to get out of range of this space station before people come asking questions."

"Thank heaven for lazy spacers at a neutral port," said Zhia. "Don't want to be bothered with what's obviously trouble."

"It's true—but they'll get complaints eventually. Let's not give them a reason to get off their asses. Quick status from key people, and I'll summarize what happens next. First—Bri, status on the new ship."

Bri stood up—slowly, grudgingly, and not at all with posture like a soldier should have, but she did it. "She's left Claudette's and should be arriving her any minute. Should be fueled. We'll need to make a few repairs, but should be ready to start her voyage when we're clear of the space station in say six hours." She flopped back down onto the crate.

"Got it. Zhia, what about the other system diagnostics?"

Zhia stood, straight and calm. "Nothing new to report, Commander. We haven't found any indications of tampering."

Ellen's jaw tightened. "Either our checks aren't thorough enough, or we still don't understand what Merith's plan was."

"Commander?" Vivaan raised his hand, the other hand balancing his mug on his knee. He like most of them was sitting on a large steel crate.

"Yes?"

"I don't have anything further on Merith, but—I did check out Udo Trynkei. I found one odd thing."

"Which was?"

"His police ID does not appear to be a fake."

She frowned. Kid probably didn't want to believe he'd been duped, but that was a bit hard for her to swallow.

Levereaux cleared her throat and stood before Ellen could formulate a reply. "I concur with Vivaan's analysis, Commander. We double checked it, and it doesn't show any signs of tampering or forgery. It activates to holographic verification protocols. It's real."

Tarana, Dr. Taylor's wife and Josana's sister, spoke up. "There are *plenty* of Capital laws against the things he did. How can he be a real inspector?"

"Was he corrupt, then?" Ellen was trying hard not to growl, but she would much have preferred a summary to a discussion. *Quick* statuses, people. Quick.

Vivaan's eyes were hard. "Corruption seems likely. Or there is some kind of government program working outside the bounds of the laws."

"Or," Bri cut in, voice snarky, "he somehow managed to illegally acquire an actual ID. Like breaking in and making one himself, or bribing someone."

"All possibilities," Ellen said. "Where does that get us?"

"Nowhere new," Vivaan muttered. "I just thought you should know."

"And it doesn't explain why he's a zombie." Dremer folded her arms. At a glare from Levereaux, she added, "I mean, in a comatose state."

Ellen nodded. "Got it. Thank you. Do we have any alternate theories on what Merith could have been up to other than suicide or blowing the ship to smithereens?"

Zhia's brow was furrowed. "We suspected she might have set up some sort of surveillance, but we haven't found any bugs, cameras, or microcams." She shrugged and spread her hands.

"I initiated excessive ship cleaning protocols," Xi added, her voice loud and voluminous as it drifted down from far above in the cargo hold. "To stir up any equipment we might have missed."

Ellen shook her head. "When other duties are complete, let's run through the diags one more time."

There was a collective groan, but no one explicitly protested. They knew she was right. Until they understood Merith's end game—or they'd survived a month without incident—they had to keep their eyes wide for danger.

"She'd set the course toward Tetra VII," Adan murmured. He sat on a cargo crate, rubbing his chin and a fresh scruffy beard. The eye whirled, and she had to force herself not to stare. "I can't think she would have lasted twenty-four with people trying to bust onto the bridge. How long would it have taken for us to get to Tetra VII from where we were?"

Xi took up the reply. "The Tetra system is very large, and as is, Tetra VII is in the far side of its orbit from the applicable worm hole gate. It might have taken five days. Possibly more."

Kael's expression darkened. "Wait. Her attack was… five days ago? Is that right?"

"Yes." Dremer was nodding, shifting uncomfortably to the edge of her chair. Where had she found a chair? Had she wheeled it over here from the sick bay?

"So she might have set something timed for a little longer, maybe a week." Ellen scowled. "Or her plan was entirely different. We're grasping at straws here."

Jenny's hip leaned against Adan's shoulder. "What the hell did she want to do when she reached Tetra? If they had already attacked Doug, or close to it, why go there?"

"They attacked Doug and also the bank accounts," she replied. "Dremer, Xi, Taylor, Levereaux—can any of you find out if any other organization funds are affected? Is this broader than us—or is it personal?"

"We'll try. Quietly." Levereaux's voice was clipped.

"As Kael pointed out, we may not have forever to solve this. Now we have to put Merith aside. We've got even more problems than that. Lucky us. So once our new ship arrives, it'll take a small team to Tetra VII. We will undock from Molyarch within the hour. Hope you had your fun. Then we'll head for the first wormhole. Once safely through, we will deploy this fighter carrying Mo, Nova, and Fern. Fern will pilot, Mo is the ranking commander. I know we don't often open the cargo hold to space—so make adjustments if you have things in here that need strapped down or removed. We're playing a new game now."

———

"SURPRISED YOU CAME DOWN HERE," Zhia said, smiling, "but I'll never turn down a sparring partner."

"Am I that long overdue?" Mo's bare feet danced across the red gym mats in the practice hold, sucking in the stale ship air tainted with sweat and adrenaline. Zhia's symphony of grunts and swear words was a nice accompaniment to the ever-present hum of the ship around them. Most people got used to the hum, but Mo never had.

"Either that or you're going easy on me." Zhia grinned.

Mo's shoulder's fell, and she almost forgot to duck. "I'm not going easy on you."

"Well, then. Maybe you shouldn't keep so much to yourself." Zhia's roundhouse kick that followed belied that statement.

Mo barely ducked in time. "Or maybe I should." Another snap of a kick at her face, and she jerked to the left. "Before I break my nose."

"Please. You gonna let an old lady like me do that?"

Mo threw a jab, but it didn't land before she had to dodge again. "Age ain't nothin' but a number. That's what you told me last time."

Zhia grinned. "Glad you were listening. Don't worry, you're not so bad. I'm just giving you a good show. So you nervous to be in command?"

"No." It came out sounding a little obstinate, a little defensive. "Maybe."

"Admit it," Zhia said as she threw a mean hook. Mo had to jerk back. Well, if anything her abs were getting a workout. "You would rather be pickin' off painted targets at a distance."

Mo's turn to shrug. "Obviously."

Zhia barked out a laugh. "Then why did you volunteer?"

She hesitated, and Zhia slowed, backing away for a second, as if sensing this wasn't the time to press her assault. Again. "I don't know," she admitted.

"You're a lone wolf. It's not a lone wolf mission, but it's close," Zhia offered.

Mo smiled at that. That wasn't the reason. But the real one felt a little too delicate and complex to explain while sweat-covered in the middle of the gym. "There aren't eight thousand of us," she said instead.

Not anymore. When Mo had served with Ellen in the Union, there had been more than that. There had been good things about that life. But this life was better.

"It's true," Zhia replied.

"And I'm a trained soldier. And not as old as you, but..." She winked.

"But you're older than most of these babies." Zhia was starting to bounce again, so apparently she wasn't done with Mo yet.

"Yeah, that too." It wasn't the real reason. But it was actually not a bad excuse.

They sparred in silence a few minutes more. Mo finally landed a kidney blow, but Zhia had the last word. A leg sweep brought her down on her back and knocked the wind out of her.

Dammit, she couldn't even curse.

Coughing, she took Zhia's offered hand.

"Think that's enough for one day. Especially since you are probably out of time, no?"

Mo nodded, in lieu of words. She needed to shower before she got on that fighter—which didn't come equipped with anything close to that level of hygiene facilities.

Truth be told, she had nothing to do but shower. She had long finished packing. The arms and munitions had been loaded on the fighter practically since the old thing had rolled onboard.

The preparations hadn't quelled the worms-squirming feeling in her stomach. Nerves weren't a problem for her, so she didn't know why this feeling was creeping up now. Lots of missions had a lot on the line. Lots of missions had a poor chance of success.

And it wasn't like she had anyone to miss. To say goodbye to. She could take off right now without a blink. She had her orders, and that was all that mattered. Her life was simple. Self-contained.

Lonely.

Oh, she was close enough to people, in the way that a unit could be. She'd give them a wave, maybe a hug. But for better or worse, something about her had naturally kept her from really forming deeper relationships here.

She *did* like watching from a distance. She was naturally private, and quiet too. She easily kept herself entertained most of the time. She just didn't like admitting that, occasionally, that distance could get a little lonely.

Being stuck on a small fighter with Fern and Nova was not going to help things. There was a closer bond between the two of them than either of them had with Mo. Nova was naturally in-your-face, and Fern could alternate between soothing and snarky, but withdrawn they were not. *That* was apparently Mo's job. And then there was the tension between the two women that everyone mostly ignored.

Nothing like feeling like a third wheel for a week or two before tackling an especially hard mission.

She'd packed some extra books and vids, her beaten copy of Marcus Aurelius's *Meditations*, and a good force and grav bar that she could work out with for a good two hours, more if she were truly bored. Which she probably would be. If she had to face enemies, she'd prefer it to be with her rifle at long distance. But if they got too close, a little muscle couldn't hurt.

Hell, after this lackluster showdown, maybe she'd get Nova to spar with her.

Still warm from her shower, dressed in her typical gray flight suit, she grabbed her armor case and her duffle and headed for the ship. Maybe she'd stop by the mess and see if Amaya had cooked up anything special she could bring along.

The woman had a deftness for not being spotted that a sniper like Mo truly, deeply respected. Envied, even. And she could make mean fry bread when she was in the mood. How she'd ever learned the recipe, Mo had no idea.

Today, though, there was only zeefruit cobbler and a curry—still welcoming the Persads, perhaps—and neither of those was going to travel well. She tossed some extra apples and zeefruit and bags of nuts in her duffel instead, and headed for the cargo bay.

CHAPTER EIGHT

RAIN FELL in warm sheets on what had once been a sturdy compound. Mo could tell it had been sturdy by the high-quality construction of the meter-thick wall that had surrounded it.

That same wall now had a hole blown through it.

She studied the point of impact for a while, noting the size, shape, shade. Not that it was likely she could do much with the knowledge of a crater this size without somebody doing some nice measurements and equations while warm and dry on a ship somewhere. She'd had that in the Union, but not now. This wasn't a typical problem for the *Audacity* crew. She did it more out of habit, to remember enemy capability, than because it should amount to anything. Maybe Xi could do such calculations if asked. More knowledge couldn't hurt.

She stepped over the remnants of the wall, into the crater and then out again. Nova followed carefully to her right. Thermal scans had shown the place was empty—for better or for worse—but you could never be too careful. She would have much preferred to be roosted up somewhere where she could have watched over Nova, taken out any threat at 500 meters. But they'd looked, and the walls of the compound combined with the small size of the island meant that there was no easy spot that wouldn't put large portions of the compound out of sight at any given time. With only two of them, they had to work with what they had. So today she wasn't a sniper, just a marine. She didn't mind.

The inside of the walled area was surprisingly spartan, a weird mix of ancient and high tech. A forcefield on the fritz buzzed on and off around a nearby thatched-roof hut. Or at least it *looked* thatched roofed. Its steel door hadn't been breached, although the lockpad bore several scorch marks that indicated a half-hearted attempt had been made.

The largest building also sat beneath a thatched roof. Many of the sides of the building appeared open from here, but she could see one retracted pocket door that had been jammed, slightly off its track. Sophistication cleverly concealed, and now busted.

Surprising the locals hadn't looted the place more.

Even as the thought occurred to her, she realized their mistake. "Drop!" she barked as she could already hear the rotation of pistons, the clicking of what was likely a weapon being trained on their location. Shouting was unnecessary inside suits, but the brain wasn't always rational.

She fell to her stomach in the dirt, keeping the multi ready at the same time. Nova was quick too.

But nothing happened.

She sat stone still. Maybe it had been a motion detector? A trip beam they were clear of now? Or this current spot could be out of the weapon's range.

Beside her, Nova cleared her throat over the comm. "We, uh, got a visitor."

Mo hesitated, but turned her head to Nova, then followed her gaze.

Treads caked with mud on eight different legs had rolled up to a stop in front of them. The spindly legs went up like a jellyfish's tentacles to a round body where a large eye-like camera blinked black and red at them. Or maybe it was like a spider with insanely long legs? Not a better mental image. Perched at two-centimeter intervals across its surface were pointy tubes the size of a pen, alternating with bricks the size of her hand.

"Lasers and stunners," Mo muttered. "That's not good."

"You think I don't know that?"

"I was talking to myself."

"What now?" Fern asked from the ship.

"Nothing we can't handle," Nova said. "Don't get trigger happy or worry happy or I'll shut you out of the comm channel."

"You bitch, you wouldn't."

"Try me."

Mo ignored their banter. The two of them just needed to make out already and get it over with. Half the crew thought they already were together, but Mo had it on good authority—and the observation of the tiny fighter trip—that they were not. Yet. Mo had done her best to keep to herself and away from them, as was her natural inclination anyway, but also to give them a chance to figure things out. It didn't seem to have helped.

"State your identities, please."

Mo raised her eyebrows at the voice. She'd expected a stale, computerized readout; security systems rarely had anything beyond the basics. But this creature had a luscious female alto voice that practically purred even those stilted instructions.

"Whoa," Nova whispered.

Mo smirked. Yeah. "Sergeant Mo Mihio. And you are?"

There was a slight pause. "Identity accepted, Sergeant Mihio. Entry granted. Welcome to paradise. Security systems are not adequately functioning. Awaiting human instruction." The creature eased back, its many legs bending a bit, and electronics wheezed as the weapons powered down.

Mo slowly straightened her arms into a push up. The droid watched, but didn't react. So she got to her feet. Moments later, Nova staggered up beside her.

"What *are* you?" she breathed.

"I am—" the robot started.

"Wait." Mo held up a palm, glanced at the sky. Switching to the comm, she spoke only to Nova. "We could still have eavesdroppers. We need to reveal as little as possible."

Nova nodded. "But we need to know if this is Doug's robot or the enemy's."

"Agreed." Mo nodded. "Robot, what can we call you?"

"I am named Guardian 28. You may call me Guardie for short if you like or Gardenia if you're feeling adventurous."

Mo's eyes widened. "Uh. Thanks, Guardie." Well, that felt ridiculous. Who came up with this shit? "Were you made by... anyone we would know?"

"Yes," said Guardian 28. "My creator is Mr. Douglas Oliver Simmons. Would you like me to look for him?"

Nova snorted. "Yeah, Gardenia, that'd be great. Can I get an iced tea too? With lemon. Got any rum?"

Mo hissed at her to shush, but the droid was busy replying.

"Buford handles refreshments in the main complex. You'll have to take that up with him."

Mo turned to look at Nova, who'd simultaneously done the same thing. They shrugged. "Buford?"

"Yes, Buford," the droid continued. "I will commence a search for Doug now. He is no longer at his last known location."

"What was that?" Mo said quickly.

"There." Guardie rotated to face vaguely in the direction of the beach. "At the edge of my surveillance net. Please be advised that I have been initiating this search every twelve minutes in excess of one week and so far have not completed it with success."

"Only one week?" Mo was fairly certain it was thirteen or fourteen days since the attack on this compound.

"My memory banks store only one petabyte of error logs, which have been cycled through in the last six days."

Her eyes widened. "That's... a lot of errors."

"It is. Shall I begin the search?"

"Yeah, go for it."

"Acknowledged. He may have gone to the beach."

Mo glanced over her shoulder at the crater. Yeah, right. If only.

———

ELLEN WAVED at the holodesk to lower the volume on the guitar chords filling the office as Dane walked in. She'd been sticking to her cabin more and more lately, but something about launching the fighter had drawn her back to the command office down here in the hold— after the launch and pressurization, of course.

Dane raised a hand in greeting as he came in and shut the door behind him.

"Thanks for coming down," she said. "Hear the baby?"

"How could I miss it?" He grinned and sank into one of the chairs, tossing a few braids back over his muscular shoulder. Dane was a good soldier, took care of his health, stayed at the top of his game, so people could easily mistake him for the sort of person that he wasn't. But he had a soft-spoken gentleness that most never saw. He kept a low profile. "I stopped down in sick bay once I recovered a little bit. She's a beauty. Looks surprisingly normal for the pipes on her, doesn't she?"

"She does." The Enhancer empress looked like any other baby. In as far as Ellen knew what babies looked like. Her experience was extremely limited. No one else seemed to think babies were weird looking…

"I'm on Persad's list for the augmentations." He relaxed further into the chair.

"Awesome, I'm glad to hear that. How are you… handling it?" It. Was that the right way to bring up the delicate issues of the past? Maybe she should have talked to Taylor before calling him.

She didn't know if he'd always been gentle, or if it was something he'd acquired as a parent, but it was a little-known fact that Dane was a father. Union-Puritan fighting had torn his family apart. Every stop her team made, every nuke they inserted, they searched for a special list of MIAs.

And one of those MIAs was Shawn Anthony Hall. Dane's son had been lost while Dane was serving the Union in the war and his wife Landal was killed in the fighting. If he were still alive—and Ellen hoped to God he was—the kid would be about fifteen. His age actually was part of what gave Ellen hope. A teen could potentially survive in a war zone in a way that a younger child could not.

So yeah. "It" might not be the most tactful way to refer to the situation, but she was doing her best.

He shrugged. "It takes me back." His smile was laced with sadness. "That's both good and bad."

"How are the ship models coming?"

"Got fifteen now." He tried harder to smile, but it faltered. He heaved a deep breath and pushed the emotion back down. "I'll show them to him someday."

"You will." She couldn't know that. But she said it anyway. "I wish we had a lead."

"So do I."

They were both quiet for a moment. There had been a scrap of a lead in the data they'd received from Vala's computers, but Doug had advised not to share it because it hadn't gotten them to anything actionable. Yet. It wasn't even truly verifiable. A medical record in a free clinic with Enhancer ties had treated a patient three years ago by the name of "Sean Hall" on Dane's planet. Could be the same kid, with the name spelled wrong. But it wasn't a terribly rare name.

"What did you want to discuss, Commander?" Dane's voice was soft. "Just the baby?"

"I have some choices for you coming up on our next mission."

"You want me to go after Patron Simmons?"

He must have really been concentrating on those models if he hadn't realized that ship had literally sailed. "No, actually. You are one of the few people on board with any parenting experience, and we find that at a sudden premium."

He snorted.

"I agree. So you'd be a great help here on the ship. But I'd also like to talk to you about the other potential mission."

"There's another one?"

"We are heading on to Faros, to make it look if anyone is watching that we aren't going to investigate the attack. Simmons had another mission planned before all this happened. A friend of his on Faros might need some help. But also... how much have you talked with Kael?"

"You know me, Commander. I keep to myself."

"Well." She sighed. "There's not really a delicate way to put this. Patron Simmons investigated the circumstances around when Kael was conscripted to the Theroki as part of his background check. He had been convicted of murdering his pregnant girlfriend and being sold to the Theroki was his sentence."

The ripple of anger in Dane's eyes was unmistakable. She held up a palm.

"Investigators on the ground contested it, as did he. Further, the body was eventually revealed to not actually be the girlfriend. But by then Kael was long gone. Meanwhile, Doug found her. Very alive."

Dane raised his eyebrows. "Shit."

"Yeah. Basically."

"So what does that mean?"

"Well, we'd like to know what happened. In particular to the child. So while we will check on Patron Simmons's friend, we will also dig into this. We might find the child is alive or..." Or not. Or anything in between. "So it's a little close to home for you."

Dane winced.

"I wasn't sure which you might prefer. You want to hunker down in your cabin, that's okay. Some of us have to protect the ship, and that's often your role, and you're good at it. We'll take Zhia or Jenny down. And there's really plenty of people in line to fawn over that baby. It's just that most of them aren't super competent at the moment. You and Bri are the only ones with actual experience."

"They'll get there." A smile crept into the corner of his mouth. "You should have seen Dr. Levereaux holding that poor kid. Like it was a frag grenade."

Ellen snorted. "I doubt I was much better."

"Lucky for us, your job is to hold a gun."

"I'm afraid all of us are being stretched beyond the skills we are expected to have right now. I'd be glad to have you planetside, but if you're not up for it, it's fine."

"Why me?"

She took a breath before answering. "Zhia, Jenny, Nova—they are all very fond of Kael. They joke with him and treat him like one of the team, and that's absolutely exactly what he's needed. But on this mission… it's a little sensitive. I don't want a stray joke to cause any friction. And I don't want to damage what they have. You're… well, you're not going to be tempted into banter just for shits and giggles."

He snorted. "True."

"And if we find out what happened to that child, it's possible Kael will instantly become a father after a decade of not being one."

Dane's eyes widened. "Oh—I see."

"I thought… well, at least you've been there."

He nodded solemnly.

"So do you have any preferences on this? Want me to pick? Want to think about it?"

"I don't need to think about it," he said. "I'll go down to the rock with you."

She raised her eyebrows. "You sure?"

He nodded. "This baby has dozens of mothers. Let the fathers look for their sons."

She permitted herself a smile at him. "*Inshallah*, we will find them both."

He stood, strode to the door, and then stopped for a moment. "You sure *you* want to go down there?"

She blinked. "Why wouldn't I?"

He pursed his lips. "Sometimes… Sometimes I don't know if I like the way he looks at you."

She groped for an answer to that, but she didn't have one. And he wasn't waiting for an answer. He'd already turned and walked away.

Well, shit.

———

BREEZING BACK into her cabin with a mug of coffee and a protein bar in her hand, Ellen raised her eyebrows at the sight on her desk. "Shows over, Rich."

A pair of shoes was engrossed in a deeply serious drama on her holodesk.

"Don't you need a shower or something?" Rich did not even twitch in her direction. "I need to see the end!"

She might, but she wasn't going to take it *now*. Instead of saying anything else, she simply grabbed him by the heels. She set him on the bed instead of inside the locker, though. "Here—maybe Xi can get it going on the bunk walldisplay. And pipe you the audio. Because I've got work to do."

"I would be most obliged, dearest Xi, if that is possible," Rich said.

"Decided to converse with the 'ship,' finally?" Ellen said.

After a pause, Rich sniffed. How he pulled off that sound, she wasn't sure. Was it just a recording stored away in there? Push this button to sniff haughtily? "I can admit it. I was mistaken about the nature of our benevolent AI."

"Our *benevolent* AI? What has she done to you, Rich? Are you feeling okay?"

"When an entity of any kind earns my respect, especially if they do so without involving swords or laserblades, or any kind of weapon really, I can be quite descriptive in my praise."

Ellen rolled her eyes as she fell into the desk chair. The protein bar wrapper crinkled open. "Xi, I know you can do at least two things at once. Get me Doug's report on Arakovic?"

They were closing in on Faros in less than twenty-four hours, and she needed to get through this—and one more thing too—before she could feel confident they'd be ready. Or as ready as they could be.

The data on Arakovic spread across the screen. Judging by the light flickering over her bunk, Rich had his movie going now too. At least he was happy.

She, however, was not. There were dozens—no, hundreds of pieces of data. All of them were tagged by an elaborate verification system he'd used in his other files.

This file, though.

"This file is a mess," she grumbled.

"The number of rumors and unverified claims in this file is indeed an outlier. Extraordinary really. How does one person manage to generate this many unreliable pieces of data?"

"There's so much conjecture crap in here, it's going to hide the real stuff."

"Are you sure there is any?"

"Any what?"

"Real stuff."

"Good point."

"Shall I attempt to filter it for you?"

"Yeah, prioritize the data that's the most verified. Hide the stuff that's the least reliable."

"Prioritization complete."

It had shrunken some, but not nearly enough. "Uh, can we go further?"

"Yes. Next level prioritization complete."

Sighing at how little the information pile diminished, she started reading.

It could have been hours later, it could have been days. She had no idea how long had passed when the growl of her stomach roused her from pure absorption. She rose, stretched, rubbed her eyes.

So much data. So much madness.

There were the photos and notes on an abandoned lab similar to Upsilon, where the carnage had been similar and the unit again called a "failure" in captured Enhancer files.

There were the notes on various different cybernetic systems. There was analysis, but she didn't think it was Doug's. It categorized the tech into potential options, and sometimes noted various lacks—band-width, stability, connectivity, durability.

There was data gained from one of their nukes of stolen student information from one of the psych schools—telepathic institutes. Someone had begun working through the list of students, crossing them off, but hadn't finished… To what end?

Kentt. Maybe it was about time she had a more detailed conversation with that woman about what she knew about Arakovic.

"Xi, can you get me Kentt on the comm?" Since Kentt was tutoring Isa these days, Ellen didn't want to interrupt them in the middle of something intense. She went back to work while she waited. "When it's a good time."

"She is currently with Isa, but I will reach her shortly."

Ellen's stomach grumbled again, but she set her jaw and squinted back at the data. There had to be something more, something that mattered.

There *were* patterns, some of which Doug had noted.

They often found these constellations of people—one woman, usually telepathic, several men. The telepath was never male. Earlier groups had been smaller—four men and one woman, six men and one woman, a few times the group was one to one.

Why the gender breakdown? Why so binary? Doug had no theories. In newer groups, the male group grew larger. Ten, twelve, sixteen. One even rumored to be forty-two.

Her jaw tightened, so much so that it ached. She forced herself to relax it. *Her* unit would have been about that big. None of this was out of Arakovic's capability, even years ago.

Why were there so many tests? What was there to figure out or discover? If she'd developed the technology she'd used on Ellen as part of the Union forces, why keep doing these experiments? Why work with the Enhancers at all?

There must have been something wrong. Something further to refine. What was it?

Did she keep losing songbirds? Or the units themselves? Both? Did the tech give out over time?

And if the Union didn't want this tech—what was the point? Sell it to the highest bidder? If so, wouldn't they be funding this research? Puritans would never go for this, the Enhancers were being decimated, and clearly something with the Union hadn't worked out.

What the hell was she trying to achieve?

"Doug, Doug…" She slumped back in the chair and crossed her arms. "Why didn't he tell me? Why did he keep holding off on the report? And after that the most basic, most informal ones. He's got so much data."

"There *is* a lot of data," Xi replied, "but little of it is clear. I believe he wanted something that could be acted on. A location, or a time. This is all just conjecture."

The last note that she'd moved had revealed a clump of star maps. No, it was one big galactic map. Pulling it closer, the label read, "Farm Planets."

The scale of the map was huge. She swore under her breath. A dozen planets were highlighted, maybe more, mostly in the outsystem but some in independent pockets inside Union space. No Puritan planets though.

Her eyes caught on one brightly glowing with a rotating indicator —Faros IV.

"What the dreck…" She scowled. "Xi, is there more about this? What does he mean, farm planets?" She pointed a finger at the glowing sphere of light, careful not to touch it. There was nothing wrong with jumping body first through a holodisplay, but something about Faros IV made her loathe to make contact.

"Searching… One result identified. This collection of missing persons reports."

"Missing like the telepaths?"

"Both groups are human and missing, but this group has largely different socioeconomic attributes. Primary differences identified: large groups rather than individuals, typically no known telepathic ability, and exclusively male. Similarities: typically young, although the median age of this group is higher."

"How large of a group are we talking here?"

"It depends on the planet. In the hundreds."

"*Hundreds*? Total?"

"Each wave of abductions seems to be in the hundreds. Total abductions, assuming they are all related, would be more like thousands."

She let out a low whistle, running a hand absently along the smooth armrest of her chair. Simmons's words drifted back to her.

It's not for your safety, it's for theirs.

Okay, Arakovic was targeting men. Women telepaths and men. Lots of men. Doug had known, but he didn't know why. He'd known early too, enough to shape this mission around it. So the attempt Arakovic made on Ellen's unit probably wasn't her first attempt. This was years in the making. "Why didn't he tell me more?" she muttered. "Do you think these men are still alive?"

"I do not yet have a hypothesis for how these disappearances are occurring. But I try to presume a positive attitude whenever possible."

She snorted. "Wouldn't it be hard to kidnap a few hundred grown men without a trace? It'd be easier to kill them."

"Only if your goal was their death," Xi said.

"Okay, good point. How much use are they dead? If you wanted to kill them, no need to abduct them." She sighed. "So she wants them alive. Foot soldiers? What do we even know from all this? My head is spinning. I—"

"Commander, Kentt is on the comm line."

She'd already forgotten she'd asked. "Put her on."

Kentt's smooth voice filled the room. "How can I help you today, Commander?"

"Are you finished with your lessons? There's something I need to talk to you about. For more than a minute or two."

"Yes, Isa and I need to take a break now to refuel and take a nap."

Ellen raised her eyebrows, then raised them even further when her stomach growled again. "Are you saying you're hungry? Meet me in the mess?"

"Yes. And certainly, Commander."

"See you there." Ellen clicked the comm off and rose.

"Commander, one more thing before you go?" asked Xi.

"Yes?"

"I see large percentages of these reports are tagged unreliable. But not all of them. Doug likely had some questions about their validity."

"Hmm. And one way to verify these massive reports would be to get our boots on the ground on one of these planets."

"Yes. Such as Faros IV."

"You think that was his real motivation? One of them?"

"I could not form a hypothesis without additional data."

"That's fair. Guess it's a good thing we're on our way there."

"I agree. I shall continue *not* to inform the crew, then, of any change in plans."

"That's helpful of you."

"That was my intention."

"Are you joking with me, Xi?"

"Of course not, Commander. Artificial intelligences do not joke."

Ellen frowned.

"Just kidding."

Grinning, Ellen picked up her coffee and headed for the hatch. Kentt was peering into the chill chest when she arrived in the mess. "We need to talk."

The telepath, sans her cloak at the moment, arched an eyebrow as she looked over her shoulder. "Of course, Commander. Would you like some fruit salad? It appears someone picked up quite the variety on Capital."

"That would be Amaya. She cooks. And stays clear of people."

"Ah, yes, I did sense the anxious one." Kentt slid the bowl onto the counter.

"She prefers to be left alone." Ellen busied finding some real food. Something that didn't come in a wrapper.

"Something I would obviously respect."

Ellen swallowed, not so sure about that. The chill chest had her usual vat-grown chicken, lentil, spinach combo—not coincidentally— so she went with that. For someone who was rarely seen, Amaya had an uncanny way of catering to the very specific people onboard. The silence had grown long while she hunted for her meal, so she forced herself to make conversation. "Where's Loti?"

"Reading in our cabin. She's found Zhia's library quite stimulating."

Ellen raised an eyebrow, mostly at herself. Since when had Zhia's book collection gotten large enough to qualify as a library? Not that it surprised her. "That's good," she managed instead.

"What did you want to talk about?" Kentt slid the bowl onto a table and came back toward the counter.

"About Arakovic."

Kentt's lips thinned as she punched in a drink order with one hand. The ridiculously expensive—and over-engineered—Beverage Brewer TX did not seem to register as particularly special in Kentt's eyes. Doug had insisted, and Ellen swore half the crew were too poor to even recognize the extravagance and the other half took it for granted. She pushed aside a pain at the thought of Doug. Kentt's eyes narrowed as liquid started to dispense. "All right. An unpleasant but necessary topic."

"What do you know?"

"Well. Where to start…" The telepath cocked her head.

It was strange to see her without her hood, flowing blue hair hyper-real and vibrant under the ship's light. Even in the mess, where the lights were a little calmer and more casual. Her eyes still looked too bright, even now that they weren't shadowed, still vaguely lit from within.

"They're implants, yes. I have optical augmentation."

"Fragging hell, how did you know that's what I was thinking?" God, did that chip really do anything? If Isa hadn't reacted, Ellen would have started to lose faith at this point.

"You are staring."

"Oh. Uh, sorry." Ellen tore her eyes away, pulled her meal out of the warmer drawer, and practically ran to the table where her coffee waited.

Kentt, to Ellen's surprise, sighed. "I suppose I could pretend I don't know what people are thinking for social reasons, but how helpful would that be?"

"Helpful? That's a bit of a subjective trait, I think."

"How about honest, then?"

"I suppose it's honest." Ellen's lips twisted. Was there really any valor in Kentt's piercingly astute statements? They always cut like a knife. But wouldn't it also be disingenuous for Kentt to pretend she didn't know something when she did? If she wanted Kentt to be honest then she just needed to suck it up and deal.

Kentt's chin lifted. "I am not sure where I start, then, with regards to Arakovic."

"How about—when and where did you or your sister first encounter her?"

"I can't be sure when my sister did." Kentt slid into the seat across from Ellen. Steam from her mug of green tea wafted up into the air. "For me, I first encountered her through my sister's mentions of her lectures at the university, as I told you. Actually—I assumed they were lectures, but they might have been simply gatherings. Dinner parties. Later I visited the university, as I started to realize my sister was being drawn in. If I had even suspected it was *half* as cultish as it was, I would have acted sooner. But one expects students to think big and talk about big ideas, dream of ending the endless war. It's impossible, of course. But they ought to dream."

"It's not impossible," Ellen shot back automatically. "Improbable, maybe, but of course it's possible."

Kentt shrugged. "Believe what you like. Our perspectives are different, our angles of viewing skewed."

"That may be true. But I have a better vantage point militarily. You've seen inside these people's heads, though." Ellen took a bite.

"Not as many as I might like, but true."

"Militarily it may be a stalemate. The match is too even, the systems too widespread. But we keep trying."

"The political stalemate, the philosophical one, is worse. Puritans fundamentally disagree with most others about the proper way to use science. Even if one group were to conquer the other, the divide would still exist. They are too many, the wound runs too deep." Kentt was still blowing on the hot tea, not touching the fruit yet.

Ellen shrugged. "We'll never agree on everything. That hasn't kept people from forming nations in the past. From living in peace together."

"Ah, but we must agree on *some* things to function as a society.

Which things exactly—now that is the interesting question."

Okay, this was far enough down the rabbit hole of philosophical debate. She'd come here to talk about Arakovic, not the war, not civilization.

Unless the war was related. And there was something else niggling at her, as if she had all the pieces to a puzzle she'd forgotten she needed to solve.

She took another bite. "There are other ways to end the war. Extreme ones. We have the power to destroy planets."

"They'd be worse than continued unending war, though."

"Would they? How exactly do we quantify worse? How do you measure the suffering of which worlds? Do you care about suffering at all?"

"I certainly do."

"So do I. But do they?"

"They won't use those weapons. It's too foolish."

"Would Arakovic?" Ellen pressed her lips together, thinking.

Kentt shrugged. "If only I'd thought to ask. I bet she would have been keen to answer that, the one time I was there. You see, cool apathy is the fashionable stance on most of Capital. It probably enabled Arakovic and her message at the universities. It's counter-cultural, rebellious even, to give a damn. Everyone wants to be a noncomformist, you know."

Ellen snorted. "When you saw her, what did she talk about? Did you talk one-on-one?"

"No, it was a small gathering. A sort of lecture, but informal. She talked about idealistic things." She waved her hand in the air.

"Don't brush them off. I need to know. What did she talk about?"

Kentt frowned, one of the more disgusted looks Ellen had seen on her face. Usually she was so placid. "Bringing peace. Ending the war. Ridiculous nonsense at best, dangerous at worse."

"How is that dangerous?"

"Because when a telepath talks about 'bringing peace' and 'ending the war,' they're not talking about something good. In fact, it might fall into your 'extreme solutions' category."

Ellen winced. "What exactly do you think they are going to do?"

"I only have guesses. But she requires telepaths as part of her plan, yes? Some of them like my sister agreed to go. For those that do not, some were hounded, harassed. Pursued. Taken, if those rumors are true. I think they are. So she must need more than a handful of telepaths. And for some reason, her need is dire. What could possibly be so important?"

"Ending the war, apparently. Not that they can do that."

Kentt didn't immediately agree, which raised the hair on Ellen's neck. But she plunged forward anyway. "We also know that she contracted a Theroki ship and that it eventually disappeared. And that she was a client of the Enhancers."

Kentt's eyebrows had risen. Not as much as a normal person's would, but some. Maybe she really *was* a robot... "A Theroki ship?" She frowned as she slouched inward, thinking. "Why them?"

"That is the question, isn't it. But what I need is answers."

"I know. But I don't have any. Not to that anyway."

"What are your guesses? Why does she need so many telepaths?"

"Because a telepath's idea of 'bringing peace' isn't necessarily a good one."

Ellen squeezed the bridge of her nose, trying to think. And force herself to be patient. This woman wasn't military. She hadn't been trained to get to the fragging point. "What did you mean?"

"Maybe that's a little unfair. I'm sure plenty of telepaths hope for a peaceful world in the traditional sense. But one of the main elements of psychic training includes ethics. Ethics is the first thing I started with Isa."

"Long overdue."

"You did your best."

"You saw those conversations?"

"Yes. Valiant effort, really. She's a stubborn one. It's a variety of ethical guidelines in our code, but some of the most important lessons are around the lines of persuasion."

Her eyebrow twitched. "Persuasion?"

"And why you should *never* do it. Many don't have the ability. The skill is never taught. The history, the massacres, should be enough to sway anybody from trying it. But not all young people are easily swayed. The morality of it gets to some—it's wrong to force anyone to do anything of any kind against their will."

"And others?"

"Others, well, don't get it and just see power."

"So like normal people then."

"Yes, some have more empathy than others. But telepaths without empathy are… problematic. Usually, well… things happen to those ones."

Ellen stopped mid-chew of her chicken. "What things?"

"Sometimes they never end up graduating or get shunted into teacher positions. Sometimes they just disappear."

"They *kill* them?" Ellen blurted.

"It is impossible to say. But I think so, yes. Such people put every telepath at risk. Why should Isa die because some fool wants to manipulate and coerce?" Kentt shrugged as her gaze bored into Ellen. "They may kill them, or they may not. There are other, worse fates than death, so I can't say not killing them would be better. I suspect most often, these telepaths are smart enough not to admit they plan to persuade and use it sparingly."

"I can see why." Ellen speared some spinach with her fork, then went still. "Wait—are you saying she wants to use all these telepaths to persuade? Or is she looking for the rare few with the talent?"

"What I am trying to say in a roundabout way is—there are some whose idea of peace would be *forcing* peace on others."

"Can they do that?"

But even as she said it—she already knew the answer, didn't she? She hadn't been a Natural. But she could force her will on those in her unit. It'd been easier than blinking. Some of them had forced their will back as well, but many had faded into compliance.

"Some can make minor adjustments to people's desires. Others might do more. It is rare, and the technique not well understood because it isn't studied or taught. But…"

"But if someone knew how, they could teach others." Ellen's voice was grim.

She rejected Mother. The words seemed to echo in Ellen's mind. She fought off a shudder at the memory of the pain, the loud screams against her skull. *Empty as a husk, harmless as a fly.*

She'd show them who was harmless.

"Who are they persuading?" she forced herself to say. "And of what?"

"'Who' is a great question. That would also answer the 'what.' She could convince a Union general to lay down his weapons. Or perhaps a Puritan to accept modification."

The map in the file hadn't shown any Puritan planets—was that helpful somehow? Did it mean she wasn't targeting Puritans *yet*? Was she allied with them now, so not striking their planets?

"You were in the program," Kentt said softly, cutting into her thoughts. "Could you force your will on others?"

"Yes."

"On small things? Big things?"

"Anything. We were like… one mind. Well, we were slowly becoming one mind."

"Hmm. That's not encouraging."

"But we were networked. And working together was our job. Our duty. How often are people that aligned? Everyone had the same goal."

"You mean like the goal of ending the war?"

She sighed. "Point taken."

"Why did you dislike it so much? If they had asked for your permission, would that have changed things?"

Ellen's jaw tightened. She took a sip of coffee to buy time. Consent might have changed things. She might have said no, though. Would she have left if they'd asked? Even knowing it was destroying her? She had wanted to keep her word, to keep her honor.

But in the end, she hadn't done that. And they *hadn't* asked, so what did it matter?

She set down the coffee mug. "I just wasn't a good fit."

"You seem like a strong leader. You're unafraid to issue commands, to take control of a situation. Why didn't it fit?"

Ellen tilted her head. "I never thought about it before, but now that you ask. I… I want people to follow me because they *want* to. Because they choose to and they trust me. Not only because they must. If I have to keep people in line, I will. But I'd much rather win hearts and minds than crack a whip. Respect is the ultimate compliment."

Kentt smiled. "And that. That is why they follow you."

Her brow furrowed. Here they went with the uncomfortably insightful commentary again. Topic change was needed, pronto. "Have you heard from your sister at all? Any way to get in touch with her?"

Kentt's eyes crinkled with pain. "No. None. And that's why I want to find her—and Arakovic. I know you don't trust me, Commander, and it's right of you to be suspicious. But our goals are *very* aligned."

"I thought you said Arakovic was after you."

"Did I say that?" Kentt shrugged.

Ellen narrowed her eyes. "You did."

"I also had some rather violent visitors, you see. Of the same brutish Theroki nature."

"What made you think Arakovic sent them?"

"I assumed she'd discovered somehow I had smuggled those girls. The club operation wasn't small, and at first there wasn't much secrecy when they started speaking up and asking for help. But now I think perhaps they were looking for him. Your friend."

"Kael. And it could be either, I guess."

"Or both."

"Or you just want to find your sister more than anything."

Kentt pursed her lips, but didn't deny it.

"Anything else you remember about Arakovic?"

Kentt shrugged. "No, Commander. But I'll let you know if I think of anything."

Ellen nodded and started to rise as Kentt picked up her fork. "Are you finally going to dig into that? Waiting for the tea to cool?"

Kentt shook her head. "I come from a rare school that finds eating in front of others a tad embarrassing."

"But you have to tell me if it's any good." Amaya didn't pick up just anything on her trips. It had to be something amazing.

Kentt gave another little shrug of defeat, speared a bit of mango, then took a delicate, self-conscious bite. Her eyes suddenly drifted closed as she stopped mid-bite, then she chewed slowly, luxuriously, savoring it.

Ellen grinned for a moment, then straightened her expression. Yeah, that was what she thought. A simple fruit salad—yeah, right.

Bright blue eyes snapping open, Kentt looked a little mortified at what she'd just done. "I apologize, Commander, but—"

"No need."

"But this is exquisite. There's a syrup on it—it's got elderflower and riodiop and just a touch of pnuko spice, and—"

Ellen held up a palm. "And it's really amazing."

"Really."

"I'll make sure Amaya hears." Through an email. "Enjoy your meal."

"Thank you, Commander. And good luck."

"We will do everything you can to get your sister back," she said softly.

Kentt nodded. "So will I."

———

THEY WAITED while the robot attempted its search, and true to form, it returned in exactly twelve minutes to report its utter failure.

"I suggest you check the beach," Gardenia offered in her glorious voice. "I know I would if I had the protocols."

"Does he go there often?" Mo asked.

"Very rarely. I believe he hates the beach. Catherine and Matthew frequent it, however."

The ball of darkness in Mo's guts sank a little further down. She'd forgotten it wasn't just him who had lived here. "How often is very rarely?"

"Perhaps once every other month."

Mo snorted. Surprising. She'd always imagined him on the way out the door to the surf after the transmission ended. Not that she'd talked to him many times. Okay, maybe she'd imagined him at other times too.

"What's the status on... Catherine and Matthew, was it?"

"I also cannot locate them. But their last known location was at the beach, not in the compound."

"And Doug?"

"He was in the compound. At his desk as usual."

Mo sighed. "That's what I was afraid of."

"Is there anywhere you can't reach that we should check?" Nova asked.

That was good thinking.

"Yes. Building 3 remains intact, so I have not searched it, nor can I. A portion of the basement of Building 1 is also unreachable to me."

Nova nodded. "Then that's where we should go. Assuming we can reach it. Can you take us there, Guardie?"

"Yes, of course." The creature pivoted and began to motor its way toward the largest building. "But if you are no longer feeling adventurous, it might be ill advised."

Nova stifled a laugh. "Was that a joke, Guardie?"

"Was that a laugh, Mo Mihio's companion?"

Mo shook her head. This robot was… odd. It reminded her a little of Xi. But she followed it and Nova to the main building. As they slowed on the porch, Guardian 28 displayed a holo map indicating a portion of the basement that appeared accessible.

"There's no second exit," Mo said, pressing her lips together. Death trap. As if having just the two of them—or three if you counted Fern which she didn't—wasn't bad enough. "I'll stay up top, stand guard. Make it quick and keep a monologue going so we know you're okay."

"I'm watching the armor cam feed," chimed in Fern.

"Aw, c'mon—" Nova started.

Mo cut her off, with a knife gesture of her hand. "It's just reasonable for us all to know what's going on as soon as we can. Get going."

Nova nodded. "Fine. Okay. Got it."

Droid leading the way, Nova's black armor disappeared into darkness down a set of wooden stairs. Her running lights switched on a moment later, but she quickly vanished from Mo's sight anyway.

"Nothing but debris and stairs so far," Nova managed, voice faltering as if she'd tripped. "No signs of loss of life down here... Coming to a door with lockpad intact. A few scorch marks, but no clear signs of entry... Guardie, can you open this for me?"

Whatever Guardian 28 was saying, Mo couldn't hear. Which was fine. She listened to what was around her instead. The ocean waves met her ears, a persistent hum under the thrashing of the palms and oyoko trees, the cries of seagulls. None of the noise from the nearby village reached here, really. No motors, beeps, buzzes. Just pure, unadulterated nature.

Just like at home. A stab bit into her heart that she couldn't immediately push aside. Damn, she missed it. With how often she felt homesick, she ought to have gone home more often, but this was her burden to bury. Drawn to protect and to serve—and always be away. At least most of the time. Maybe after this mission with Doug and his parents, she should take some time off, make time to visit Keyah—

She stilled at an odd sound. Had that groan of wood been a floorboard creaking, or just the tree trunks? The wind was wild and fierce, swaying the trees at least a meter each. She scanned quickly around behind her to the one side, the other.

Nothing. What was she doing, jumping at ghosts and wood creaks, at sand spraying a little in the wind. She shook her head as Nova started up her monologue again. She was entering now, going in.

A dull thump.

That was not nature. Or did she just not know the beach?

Frowning, she backed up to the opening of the ramp, searching for some way to have her back covered. But the damn bungalow was wide open. Even now, how did she know someone hadn't slipped down the stairs while her back was turned?

Someone who couldn't sneak up until now because of Guardian 28. Who was now conveniently out of the picture.

Another thud, louder, onto the deck of Building 1. Then in quick succession one closer, and she whirled toward them both, her multi trained on the sound.

Her eyes had only just barely caught the image of the flashbang before it went off.

Light blasted her. The sheer power of it overwhelmed the helmet visor and made her stagger back, wincing.

The stunner hit her from behind, jangling the sensors and circuits. Simultaneously, something hard and heavy hit near the control unit and knocked her to her stomach.

She slid along the deck. The suit went rigid as she started to flail. Her faceplate foamed over. Hell. Freezing foam. And she could hear the twang of steel cables too from the sound of it. That meant they were prepared for people in power armor.

Fragged. She was fragged for sure.

"I'm down! I'm down, under attack!" she remembered belatedly to scream into the comm. Damn, let Nova and Fern hear her warning.

"What—" Nova started.

"Secure yourself in there!" Mo shouted. "I'm down!" She growled as she sent the full power of the suit against the rapidly hardening foam, but nothing had changed. It was no use. "They got foam, cables, stunner, who knows what else! Get locked up—get out of here!"

"We can't just leave you," Fern snapped.

"Yes, you can. Lift that ship up now, sister. See if they leave, circle back and get Morales but you *must* get back to Ryu! Tell them what we found and get help!"

"I'll send a message now—" Fern started.

"No! You'll reveal *Audacity's* location." That damn second-hand fighter didn't have half the encryption they were used to. A dull scraping came from underneath her. They were dragging her. Her heart thudded against her chest piece. "You need to get out of the system—then make sure no one followed you through!"

"But—"

Nova cut her off. "Fern, I'm locked in down here. Get up and get video on what they're doing to her! Where they're going!"

"I can't. If I take flight, they'll see me."

"So?" Nova was almost shouting now. "Maybe you can outrun them!"

"I'm not leaving you!"

Mo wanted to shake her head. Rage at herself for having gotten captured welled up, and hot tears of anger pricked at the corner of her eyes. She clenched her fists and struggled again in vain, because what else could she do?

"They don't know I'm here—I'll capture what I can but I'm not revealing my location just so they can come in hot on my ass."

"Damn it, Fern." Nova's voice faltered, cracked. "Get out of here now and—"

Something abruptly cut off the signal and the argument. Maybe they'd coated her and the foam in metal and tossed the mess into the ocean, never to be a nuisance to them again. Or, you know, maybe just pulled her into a shuttle with comm jamming.

Whatever had happened, the world fell silent.

She knew better, but she raged at the darkness anyway.

———

ELLEN HAD NODDED off yet again when her hatch opening startled her awake. She had the disturbing sensation of waking up inside the holo she'd been looking at, and then sliding through light and image as she reared her head back.

She straightened and blinked blearily at Merith's face. No, Merith's personnel file. But no amount of study or blinking had revealed anything. Whoever she'd worked for, she'd hidden it well. She wasn't surprised. Doug would have found anything that was an easy spot, but she'd had to check.

Beyond Merith's face painted in light was Kael's real one. Of course, because who else would the door open for?

"Were you asleep?" he said, without preamble.

"No." She pushed the files aside in disgust and stood. And groaned. She'd sat too long—stretching was required.

"Liar."

"I just nodded off for a sec. It's not the same."

"How long since you've slept?" He circled around and wrapped his arms around her, his voice tickling her ear as his hands found her elbows. His chest was warm and hard against her back. No armor this time.

She went rigid for a second before giving up and leaning back into him. "I'm not sure," she murmured.

"Sixteen hours," Xi offered.

"Sounds like time to rest." His arms pulled her closer against him. "Is this okay?"

She didn't so much answer as purr her approval, melting back.

"C'mon." His lips brushed her ear. "You need a break."

"No, no, I've got to…" She waved weakly at the holodesk, but in truth, she was at her wit's end. She had no idea what else to try. Not until they reached Faros anyway.

"What?"

"I don't know." She let her head loll back against his shoulder.

"Rest. That's it. C'mon."

He tried to draw her aside again. She shook her head. "Uh-uh. I like this here."

His arms tightened around her again, and when his cheek brushed hers, she could tell he was smiling. "We could also try this lying down."

"Now there's an idea."

He laughed, and his hand squeezed in hers, pulling her toward her bunk.

"Let me wash my face."

"I'll be waiting."

She hurried through her ablutions and changed into her sweats in the bathroom.

Back out in the cabin, he was sitting on the bunk, boots off.

"What if we're too late for Doug?" She blurted as her butt hit the bed. "I can't stop thinking about it. What if we can't help him in time?"

"You're doing your best. We all are."

She lay on her back. He prodded her arm, rolling her away from him. She was too tired to do anything but comply. He curled up behind her, his breath puffing hot against her neck and sending a thrill down through her.

"Why does your door open without a palm or a chime?" The hot words tickled her ear.

"Oh that's just you."

"Just me?"

"I updated the security protocols."

He was silent for a moment. "That's the sweetest thing I ever heard."

"I wonder what Merith's were—" she started to sit up.

He caught her and pulled her back to him. "It can wait. I can't."

She flopped back down and scowled at him, but then broke into laughter at his smile. "Fine. Xi can tell me."

He shook his head and grinned while Xi answered. "Default security protocols are recorded for her cabin, Commander. I must point out, however, many defaults were reset during my reboot—"

"Right, right, we get it." Ellen scratched her chin. "But if she had a co-conspirator—"

"We have no way of finding out who it is," Kael finished. "There. Feel better?"

"Not at all."

"I didn't think so. C'mon. Let's see about that sleep." His hand ran up her arm.

"I can't. My brain is busy."

"Your brain needs the rest of your body to function."

"All people care about is my brain. It's not pulling its weight. I'm failing everybody."

"*I* care about more than your brain." His fingers trailed across her shoulder, then squeezed, massaging at the tension there.

She groaned. "You're unique like that." Her body was doing... things... that felt quite the opposite of restful—stirring and tensing and relaxing too.

"Oh, I'm not so sure about that," he murmured.

Although she didn't want to, she slept.

CHAPTER NINE

DAY 14

WHEN MO CAME TO, she wasn't afraid. Not yet, not exactly. Oh, this was very bad. But this wasn't the time to be afraid.

This was the time for fighting for her damned life, and nothing else.

She was still in her suit. Darkness enveloped everything around her, but something must have woken her up. She pushed at the cloud fogging over her mind. She couldn't remember passing out—when it had happened, or how.

The sound of the cutters gnawing at the metal shook the suit and her ears. The grunts of people working to remove the suit by any means necessary.

Which meant destroying it.

She gritted her teeth at another screech of metal on metal. Fragging hell. Fine. What had happened had already happened. She needed to assess what she could do about it.

She still had full control of her limbs, although the suit was still dead. Her consciousness was clearing now—also useful. That meant no gas or injections had been attempted yet. That, or they just hadn't been successful.

It wouldn't be hard for them to kill or maim her in any number of ways, both with the suit on and now as it was even partially pierced.

But they hadn't tried. That meant they either wanted something, or they wanted her alive and uninjured for some reason.

Or they wanted to watch while she squirmed.

The cutting sounds were coming closer. Up her torso. Cold air seeped in around her belly. The scent of it hit her pretty quick, and she wrinkled her nose. Human body odor and hard alcohol.

"Are we there yet?" someone muttered.

Great. Real professionals.

She tensed, ready to pounce when the opportunity appeared. The suit split wide all at once, and her instinct was to gasp, but she clenched her teeth, kept quiet instead. Only the chest and one leg were open now, but someone was working fingers along her breastbone and up under the helmet.

She jerked her shoulders to the left against the suit, pulling her right arm out of her armored sleeve as far as she could reach it.

Again. Again.

The fourth try, she got her elbow clear and wedged her arm partway free. Just a little more leverage… The fingers were just above her collarbone now, but not making much progress.

"What have we here?" a dark voice came from outside.

"I told you I saw women."

"Well, well. She's about to find out why women shouldn't put themselves in this situation, isn't she?"

"Don't let the Captain hear you say that."

She might have smirked if the situation weren't so dire. And if a hand weren't reaching along the waist of her flight suit, looking for pockets maybe—or maybe with another motive. Just a little further to the middle of her armor and…

The combination of the cutters and the force she was applying with her elbow wedged in the armpit of the suit caused it to explode open suddenly. The fingers working at the helmet hadn't let up, causing her head and neck to be yanked back sharply, but she was too busy reaching.

Her hand closed around the wrist of the assailant at her waist, and she braced herself.

At her command, the RPD went off.

It never ceased to knock the breath out of her, leaving her whole body feeling like it'd been stuck in that bug zapper that used to hang outside the Crow Rock Inn. She'd only had to use the RPD two other times in her life, but right now she had the feeling this was only the first application of several that might be needed.

Hopefully fear of pain would be enough with these people, because she only had four more.

The scream caused a flurry of panic in the room around her, giving her time to rip the helmet off and shuck more pieces of the suit. Part of her lower palm had caught the current and was currently feeling like she'd thrust it in a campfire. For an hour.

But a little electrical burn wasn't going to slow her down *now*.

One man in a brown jumpsuit was writhing on the ground, holding his wrist and cursing her to hell and back. Two other men in similar suits were staring wide-eyed at her, crouched but looking uncertain. They each cast worried glances at their colleague, but they seemed to be more of the is-that-going-to-happen-to-me variety than out of any actual concern for him.

"Who the frag are you people?" she grunted at them.

That snapped one of them out of it. "I told you this was a stupid plan, Rolf. No way I'm touching that wildcat."

She pinned him with a glare. "You won't have a choice about it if you don't tell me—"

"I'm activating the bots and getting out of here," spat the other. He started to back away.

She lunged after him, out of the remains of the armor, but a loop suddenly dropped around her, like wire, tightening around her upper arms.

She tried to crouch down, tilt left and right, but she wasn't totally clear of the armor. The thing had cinched tight, anyway. Her target took off at a run down the corridor. The other, more generous man was helping Rolf up and pulling him toward the door while Rolf stared daggers at her.

Another loop closed around her thighs, and she cursed after him with fresh energy. He made a rude gesture in her direction as the door slid shut, and she was alone.

"The prisoner will not resist," said an artificial voice from the ceiling, "or further restraint measures will be taken."

Or… not alone after all. She didn't see any point in resisting, however. Her RPD could do little to the bands tightened around her—what were they? Plastic? Rubber? They didn't look conductive—and she should save the charges for more vile threats anyway. Unless the AI aimed to kill her, she was probably safe. Torturebots were rare, and politely were less polite. The robotic arm was rusted in places, as were a few of the wall panels, and now that she had a moment to breathe, the air smelled off—too humid, not entirely clean. The wall panel blinked at her, its style dated and in need of some upgrades. They must be on a ship, and the ship must be old. She'd travelled on a number of older ships in the Union, but none had been in such bad shape as this one.

"Excellent." The AI commended her docility. Hah. "The prisoner will now be moved to their assigned cell. Please remain still."

The loops picked her up, cutting into her painfully. She grunted as she was lifted and carried away, staring after the remains of her armor like she was leaving behind a limb. She couldn't spot the multi in the wreckage. One of them might have grabbed it; she'd have to keep an eye out for it. Tech was the great equalizer, and she was leaving a lot of hers behind.

But fortunately, not all. Some tech they couldn't take away. Not without killing her, anyway.

———

"BAD NEWS, COMMANDER." Adan swiveled in his pilot's chair to face Ellen as she stepped onto the bridge. "The whole continent is plagued with sandstorms. They're not letting any ships this large down."

Kael was already there, lounging in the co-pilot's chair, staring up at the viewscreen with an expression somewhere between a grimace and a frown. She did her best not to stare overlong at him. The screen usually showed space around the ship from a variety of angles, or was split into readouts and reports combined with strategic views. Whatever Adan wanted, really, and didn't want in a holo. But at the moment it was filled with a sand-swept vista, the earth somewhere between tawny and rusty. Spikes of mountains and canyons jutted up in the distance, but their bases were invisible.

"For how long?" she asked.

"For the foreseeable future. At least seventy-two hours."

She glanced at Kael. "This is common, isn't it?" She'd tried to read up.

He nodded. "Most of this time of year will be like this."

"How do people live?" Adan frowned. "Drone delivery?"

"Underground."

"Oh."

"Is there any other way we can get down?" She stepped forward to grip the back of Adan's chair and lean down a little. She wanted to lean on Kael's but didn't trust either of them not to reveal something.

Adan hit a key. "One other way. Faros IV has two orbiting stations that maintain shuttles with specialized shields. Anti-grav tech plus the shields are used to wash a large amount of sand away to create a view-field. And much of their navigation is automated."

"But then the *Audacity* won't be on the ground with us, like she usually is." As Kael spoke, he was staring at the arm rest of the chair, stroking it almost like he thought he might not get another chance.

"Maybe that's a good thing," she said. "No one can hear our baby telepath if she's in orbit."

Adan snorted. "They could if we got too close. Technically we don't know her range. But yeah, I agree. We can probably keep her soothed for one docking to a station and you can get a shuttle from there. We can't do it indefinitely on the ground."

"We did manage one full night cycle," said Ellen.

"Four hours isn't a full night cycle," Adan replied.

"It isn't?"

Kael shook his head. "Taking the *Audacity* down is not an option anyway. Even if the storms break, it could be weeks before they do, and they could only break for a few hours. Waiting would be a waste of time, and even if we got a good window, then we'd be stuck down there."

"Don't sound so enthusiastic." Adan started rearranging the screens back to normal, leaving only a third of the screen devoted to the stormy view.

"All my dreams ended here," Kael said quietly. "I just barely got new ones. You tell me if you think going back is a good idea."

Adan swallowed, but didn't say anything.

Kael stood up and strode out.

She patted Adan on the shoulder. "This is going to be a great time, don't you think?"

He smiled over his shoulder. "A real blast. Better you than me, Commander."

"Zhia will keep you busy. If Jenny doesn't."

He grinned, all the way up to his fancy new eye. "She's been planning combat courses for the non-combatants."

"An excuse to pummel you in public as well as private?"

"Commander!"

She permitted herself a small smile.

"Let me know if you see any speeder races, okay? I will miss that."

"I have a feeling I won't, but I'll keep you posted."

———

DOUG STARTED awake as the bars crashed open on his cell. Until now, he'd been largely ignored. But this could be anybody—or anything, really—and it was hardly clear his captors valued his life. Although it had been maybe two weeks now, and he was still alive.

He couldn't do much to defend himself, but at least he could sit up and have adrenaline on his side.

He hauled himself to sitting, shifting back against the wall and squinting at the lights as he rubbed the sleep from his eyes. The thin sheet they'd allowed him pooled around his waist, and he realized belatedly he'd left his shirt unbuttoned due to the sweltering heat. He couldn't figure out if the prison cells were getting fusion reactor runoff or what it was that kept these rooms so hot. All he knew for sure was that someone was joining him in his personal hell and his sweaty stomach was showing.

"The prisoner will now remain calm and await court-martial," a robotic voice said.

"You can't court-martial me, you big stupid piece of—" A woman's voice burst out, hot with anger, but she froze, spotting him as the old-fashioned bars thundered shut behind her. She stared.

He also stared. Well, squinted until she took a few steps closer, and he could see her more clearly.

Before him was a woman he recognized—dark hair shaved on one side, high cheekbones and a strong, triangular jaw, glittering eyes against bronze skin. Deadly, dangerous eyes. The glitter was from her cybernetics, he remembered absently. Her file noted her eyes hadn't naturally been blue, but brown; she'd upgraded to sniper's augments during her time in the Union. He'd talked to her as part of her recruitment, just as he had Ellen and Kael and so many more, and he'd maintained her file for several years now, but he'd never met her in person.

He'd wanted to meet them all, though. He'd had many people he'd hoped to get to know better on the *Audacity*—the brilliant Dr. Levereaux, in particular. Elegantly gorgeous, gifted as a geneticist, equally enamored with both debating ethics and geeky hobbies. He'd never mentioned the small torch he carried for her, of course, because without getting off Tetra VII, what did it matter?

It figured that the broody sniper would land in a cell with him instead. His unrelenting extroversion made broody people uncomfortable, if it didn't piss them off. And usually, they could *leave*.

He regained his words first. Of course. "Mihio? Is that you?"

"Patr—" She thought the better of it. "Simmons?"

"How the hell did you get here?"

"Simmons! Sir! It's hard to explain, sir."

"Have you seen my parents—" He leaned forward.

Her face fell. "No, sir. I'm sorry."

He swore, running a hand through his sweaty hair. The wound on his head—which apparently had been fairly minor if dramatic—had mostly healed now, although his ministrations at the small sink in the room probably hadn't gotten all the blood out. God, what if they were dead? What if they *weren't* somewhere on this ship like he'd figured? Why wouldn't they be in a nearby cell if they were? Gods, what if they were dead and he never knew for sure because he died here—

Mo stepped closer. "Have you seen Fern? Nova?"

"No. No one else."

"Oh." She sank to a seat on the bunk opposite him.

They both were still for a moment. Overwhelmed, probably.

"What happened?" he whispered. "Is the ship—"

"Ship's fine," she said quickly. "Our team came to check out what happened, to try to rescue you. I got jumped. I didn't see any bodies…"

He winced.

She cleared her throat and straightened, the lines of her gray flight suit going taut. "Sorry. I mean, no sign of your parents at your home or here on this ship, sir."

He waved it off. "Thanks for coming to try to save me."

She slumped across from him. "Some good it did."

He spread his hands and smiled. "Sometimes it's the thought that counts."

"Is… is that a joke?"

"Sorry. Not a good one, I guess."

"You've got a lot of jokes." Her eyes were on her boots, not him.

"Well yeah, if you're not going to laugh at life, how else do you handle the tragedy?" He shrugged.

"By shooting it in the head." She folded her arms and glared at the cell bars.

He faltered, but only for a beat. That was… a little disturbing. But wasn't that what he hired her for? Specifically to shoot people in the head? Snipers were not known for their non-lethal tactics. "What if you don't know how to use a rifle?"

Her turn to shrug. "I could teach you?"

"It'd probably be easier if I taught you to laugh."

"Hmm." Her deadpan expression argued that that might not be the case.

Her eyes flicked down to his shirt and back up again. Or maybe she was eying the fact that he was only partially clothed or the shape of his legs. His stomach wasn't hurting anybody, though, and the buttons were long gone anyway, apparently.

Maybe she was just looking at the hedgehogs.

Speaking of his abs, it might be time to use them. Sitting here propped in bed, facing the cell door while she sat perpendicular to him on her bunk was getting awkward. And giving him a neck cramp. He swung the weight of one leg to hang over the edge with both arms, then swung the other, getting himself into a sitting position. His lower half was mostly immobile without his floats.

She started to her feet. "Oh my God, sir—are you—? What did they—"

"Hmm?" He glanced up. Oh, shit. He should have realized that'd alarm her. But he was so often in his floats—and so often alone on their island with his parents—that it hadn't occurred to him. "Oh, the legs? That's nothing."

"Pardon me for saying so, but that looks like something, sir!"

He snorted. Her tone was somewhere between trying to put out a fire and appeasing a drill sergeant. "Sit down, Mihio. They've never worked. This isn't their handy work, it's the work of a rogue virus joining forces with a rare nerve mutation."

She stared again, not comprehending.

"It's okay, Mihio. Sit down. They've been like this for years. I chose this." Well. He hadn't chosen the virus that caused it all, but he'd chosen not to have another surgery to try to install the synthetic nerves his body loved to reject. He hadn't really wanted them anyway, but at twelve, he'd been more prone to trying to please his mother. But three insanely painful, itchy surgeries later—and on the cusp of becoming a snarky teenager—he'd drawn the line. And had been happy he hadn't let them go full cybernetics. Who knew what his body would have done with that. Yes, shiny blue eyes weren't happening for him, or anything else for that matter.

Of course, it'd been over a decade now. There had been advances. But he was happy the way he was. Or at least, he'd thought so before this nonsense had happened.

She sat down numbly. "Sorry, sir. I'm not firing on all cylinders today."

"Neither am I. I usually wear floats, but they've been so kind as to liberate me from them." He gave her a chagrined shrug.

She was staring at his legs still, her mouth hanging open a little. Frag, maybe she was broody *and* awkward. He had the oddest urge to touch her, run his finger across her lip, whether to get her to shut her mouth or because he'd been alone in this cell for far too long, he wasn't sure. And it wasn't like he could reach her. New irritation boiled over briefly under the surface. He jammed it down and kept an iron grip on his careful, calm, slightly amused exterior.

He smiled crookedly and cleared his throat instead.

"Uh, right. Got it. Sorry, sir!" Her eyes briefly met his but then they flicked back down, although not quite as low this time. Was she staring at his legs or his stomach? Or was it the hedgehog luau taking place on this shirt? It was probably that.

He hoped.

———

IT COULDN'T BE good for one's career to ogle their commanding officer, let alone the CO's CO.

Not that Patron Simmons had a shred of anything military about him, as he sat there reclined against the metal wall, gazing at her. Smiling.

Here. And alive. And he was holy-crap smoking *hot*. Well, in as much as someone could be after being in captivity for two weeks. The cell had two bunks and a basic latrine, but was hardly a luxury resort as far as amenities went. But she'd gotten used to that in combat; sometimes things hit the fan, and a two-day mission turned into a two-month camping trip and scavenger hunt through shark-infested waters. But what kept hitting her over the head was the fact that Doug was clearly, surprisingly strong. Sure, yes, he needed upper body strength to move himself around, but hell if it didn't defy her image of him as a cheerful geeky puppy with a fancy holodisplay. He was… not what she'd expected.

She swallowed and ran sweaty palms down her thighs, searching again for somewhere else to stare and some way to think about something practical and appropriate and not so utterly ridiculous.

She needed to find a way out of here. And she wasn't usually the kind of person to pay physical attractiveness any mind, if she even noticed it. It wasn't like she'd never seen a man's abs before. Nobody on Keyah was overly modest, and she'd been a marine for years, for heaven's sake. She'd seen a lot more than abs, much of it in very good condition.

But his presence was so weird and so unexpected she just….

He was also very sweaty. The cell itself might as well have been an oven, so that was understandable. Were the climate controls broken or something? Her head was spinning.

All of her was spinning, in fact. So much had happened—the loss of her beloved armor, the experience of having been cut out of it, the capture and transport stuck in the unmoving foam, the worry over Fern and Nova and if they'd gotten away alive. And this man she'd thought she'd known, young, bespectacled, and a bit like a puppy with a computer… Well, he looked a hell of a lot different in person.

The holodisplay did not do the poor man any justice at all.

The ridiculous shirt hung open to reveal a surprisingly strong, lean form. She always remembered his hair being a little tousled, but it was more tousled than ever. Somehow the chaos managed to suit him.

She might have only talked to him a few times, but those times had made an impression on her. She'd rarely met someone so determined to *do something* about what they thought was wrong with the world. He wasn't one of the *Dine'*, the People, but he had a little in common with her people, or at least she liked to think so. Her people had always seen the land as sacred and honored their duty and responsibility to protect it.

As the Earth had headed toward devastation, the *Dine'* had

expanded that meaning as the future looked bleak and humans were forced to venture into the stars. Many had stayed behind, though, anyway.

And ironically, once the generation ships were possible, as well as the smaller, faster cryo ships, the craze to not be left behind took on a life of its own. In barely five years, the fad cleaned out a ridiculous number of people from the planet.

While some had left, hoping simply for survival of their people, the *Dine'* that had stayed behind were rewarded. Earth's burden was eased in the exodus of humanity, and the technological boom that had enabled the generation ships had also spurred on all sorts of agricultural and energy innovations. Which meant that the destruction of the planet was slowed nearly to a stop.

But that had been far from certain, and more had left than not. Including Mo's great-great grandparents.

That was how Keyah—her home planet—had been born. In a savvy business deal that had also involved a fair share of luck, a few hundred *Dine'* had managed to secure a place on one of the Mover generation ships—and their own colony. That colony had come with a catch: a planet to themselves, in exchange for a steady export of foodstuffs to the corporation that had needed workers.

It was hardly that simple, it never really was, but shockingly, things had panned out okay for once. It would never be sacred like their true land on Earth, but they could do right by this new planet. It was a kind of paradise.

But she'd left anyway. That familiar homesick ache panged in her chest, like the hourly ringing of a clock's bell. Some left and made the voyage to Earth, a pilgrimage of sorts. Others discovered passions they could only honor in the shining, cruel cities of the major planets. That was the camp she fell into. Leaving Keyah wasn't always a popular choice. Their new planet was both a huge opportunity and a huge labor—who would want to give that up? The chance for the *Dine'* to have their own planet was priceless. It would never be sacred like their true home, a home she'd likely never see, but Keyah was clearly special.

For her part, she knew how fragile peace could be. She'd always known.

Her parents had never judged her for leaving. In fact, she was fairly sure they'd always known she would. Her mother had said she'd been born a great warrior. Her father liked to brag she was a natural soldier. Mo didn't know about that, but she'd always felt that duty to protect. To change the world a little by lending her steady hands. Her eyes.

And that was how she'd ended up here, wasn't it? Because it had bothered the hell out of her to hear that some kind, witty, naive young man with a joke and a computer who had also tried to change the world to be a little better might have been punished for it. Killed for it, even.

So she'd volunteered.

Well, good news. He was alive. But she hadn't done shit to help him.

She sat there, staring daggers at the floor and bunching up her shoulders like they were tangled in fishing wire and trying not to stare at the shocking fact that he was right here. He seemed to think she was staring at his legs when her eyes strayed his way. Even if it wasn't true, those legs were two *really damned good* reasons not to stare at any part of him.

Sweat beaded on her skin. Her flight suit didn't have many ways to get lighter, and unbuttoning it fully like *he* had wasn't going to be an option. Unless of course, she abandoned all hope of being seen as a professional and distracted him from her awkward staring with cleavage.

She wasn't entirely sure there was enough curve there to distract anyone from *her* level of awkwardness, though.

The cell was hot as hell. She should at least try rolling up the sleeves. She didn't move, though. She shifted her gaze to the ceiling instead, still coiled tense as a snake scenting a predator. Sniper's augments came with a great deal of distance capability, and she might as well use it. She zoomed in on the bars that held them, the lockpad. Maybe she could spot a weakness while trying desperately not to ogle him.

"Hey, Mihio?"

She jumped. He remembered her name? Or anything about her? "Yes, sir?"

"Relax, will ya?"

"Relax, sir?" She met his eyes, raised an eyebrow.

"You don't have to call me sir. Please? Just Doug."

"Sorry, s— Uh. Sorry." She couldn't say Doug. She'd end up staring again.

He grinned. The smile was even better on him than the tousled hair. "So do you know how to, you know, relax? Take a rest. Take a load off. We're going to be here awhile."

"I can't. Not while imprisoned, s— Uh. I can't." Not with all that had happened. She was supposed to be rescuing Simmons, not joining him in captivity.

He followed her gaze to the cell bars. "Old-fashioned isn't it?"

She nodded. "Not even a forcefield."

"Is that why you're so intrigued?"

She frowned. It was impossible to say if their captors had video or just audio or nothing at all on their cells, but they didn't need to make anything obvious. But if he was already going down that road... "I am intrigued because they stand between me and the bridge."

He snorted. "With two of us, and there's gotta be sixty of them on this ship at least?"

"This is a Ranger class ship, sir. And an old one."

He tilted his head. "So?"

"It means there are most likely between twenty-two and forty-two crew members, sir."

"Cut out the sir's, Mihio." For the first time, there was an edge of command to his voice, ironically. It sent an odd little thrill through her.

"Yes, s— Okay." She nodded and restrained herself from smacking a hand across her face and dying of embarrassment. "I'd estimate perhaps thirty."

"Wow. I'm impressed. I mean, I try to hire the best, and I know you're one of them. But still."

Now she did blush furiously. Not that she'd deny it, but nobody put it so blatantly most of the time. Ryu wasn't much for extensive feedback, and Mo wasn't much for needing it. "I just work hard, s —Simmons."

He smiled at that. "What's the saying? Talent is just hard work, with interest?"

She didn't say anything, just turned back to studying the bars. If it were similar to the ship she'd served on, it had been decommissioned a few years ago and replaced by better, newer Union ships. They flooded the galaxy as the government had had to sell them off at lower than market value since they had so many they wanted to ditch. It did look familiar, like a Viper, and if it was, these bars were purely mechanical.

Could she short out the locking circuit somehow with her RPD? She only had four charges left for now, but if she could fry the circuit, maybe she could manually open the doors, either from above, or just pushing. There didn't seem to be a physical lock on the bars. The question would be how to be *sure* she could fry the controls... It would be too costly to spare more than one charge.

He was studying her, she realized.

She glanced at him, blinked. "What?"

"You remind me of someone I know. And myself. Working out a problem in your head. Not letting it go. What are you..."

She frowned, gave a subtle shake of her head.

He tilted his again. "It's pointless, you know. We're not getting out of here."

She pursed her lips. It wasn't like she was going to explain her plan out loud. So even as she shook her head no, she said, "I'm sure you're right." Then she went back to studying. If they only had audio, she might trick someone. If they had video, they'd see her examining the door and its lock anyway, so what did it matter?

"You just got here. You're exhausted. Maybe you should get some rest?"

"I don't think I can rest right now," she ground out. In fact, her jaw ached from clenching it. Tension was like an angry bull's tail, lashing around inside her.

"Sometimes relaxation helps you solve problems even better than focusing on them."

She met his gaze for a long moment, then licked her lips, anxious. "And how do you propose we 'relax' in a prison cell?"

His eyebrows raised, and it was his turn to blush. "I—well, I—uh…" He blew out a breath. "I didn't mean it like that, of course. Sorry. Never mind."

He positioned his legs back onto the bunk and flopped down, lying on his back to stare at the ceiling. He'd been asleep when she'd arrived, hadn't he? She felt bad all of a sudden, like he thought she'd brushed him off. So he hadn't intended on her little innuendo—maybe it hadn't even occurred to him. Maybe he'd just wanted to talk. Or ease her anxiety.

"How many days have you been stuck in here?" she said. Her gaze zoomed in on the ceiling. There had to be handholds for if the grav went out. The question was how many.

"I don't know," he sighed. "Sorry. It's possible that I've been alone too long. I haven't even had my bots to talk to."

"Your bots? Like Guardie?"

His face lit up. "You met her? She's all right?"

"Yes. Endlessly searching for you. And I do mean endlessly."

He winced. "Damn. Yes, Gardenia was always good for a chat while on a stroll. I had some even chattier ones. But still. There were never many people to talk to on Tetra VII. Other than my parents, of course." His eyes darkened at the mention of them. Wondering if they were dead?

She had to keep talking, then. No point in wallowing if they didn't know for sure. "Seemed like a paradise to me," she said. "Not many other young people there?"

He waved a hand, then settled back to where he'd folded his hands across his ribs. "Tetra VII was my parents' paradise. But not so much mine."

"How so?"

"Oh, the relaxed lifestyle was nice. But I'm not beachy—"

"Says the half-dressed man in the palm tree shirt."

He grinned without looking at her, his eyes wandering the ceiling. "And I'm not the tree-hugging type either. Or any kind of outdoors really. Dirt under my fingernails just seems like… like I need to wash my hands."

She snorted.

"You must think that's ridiculous."

She raised her eyebrows. "No." Okay, maybe a little. She probably hadn't spent many days of her life without some dirt under her fingernails some of the time. Okay, most of the time.

"C'mon, now. I know you grew up in the outdoors."

"I miss home every single day," she murmured. She'd been missing it when she'd made her fatal mistake and not heard her enemies' approach. True, there might not have been anything to hear, and it hadn't yet proven to be fatal, but the fact of the matter was she'd been distracted.

She didn't really want to talk, thinking about that, but who knew how long he'd been alone? If she could think clearly, she might have been able to count the days, but her thoughts were like drops of oil on a hot stove, dancing and sputtering.

"See?" His voice cut into her thoughts. "You know your way around in this nature thing. Too bad we're stuck on a spaceship."

"It's true, I'd fare better in the wilderness." She smiled. That didn't mean she couldn't be dangerous here. "I didn't live on a beach, though," she added. Their desert lake had had plenty of sand in the scrubby grass around it, but that wasn't the same as an island in the ocean.

"Yeah. Beaches are just not for me, I guess. Saltwater kills my eyes. Don't get me started on what it does to floats."

"Floats?"

"Antigravity assistive devices," he said, his voice a touch wistful. "How I usually get around. Love for them would not be strong enough a word. Swimming is fun too—we have, er, *had* a pool in the basement —but do you know what ocean detritus can do to delicate technological equipment?"

"No."

"Ruin it, mostly. Add to that that my skin has only two modes: ghost white or burnt to a crisp. Guess which mode I'm in now?"

She chuckled at that, and his eyes crinkled, watching her laugh with more unexpected intensity. "I almost mistook you for a marble statue." Because he was pale, and also perfectly sculpted, and—goddammit. Boss. No ogling the boss. Boss's boss. Off limits. Also, man, he didn't shut up.

"Ghost white is by far my preferred mode. Computers and staying inside are a natural fit for me in a beach environment. I always loved it that way." He sighed, and she sensed his mood drifting darker.

"How about this ship environment? How is that working for you?"

He slanted a glance at her. "Are all ships this brutally hot?"

"Absolutely not." Just ones with you on them. She groaned inwardly.

"This one doesn't suit me very well, but I'm optimistic it's a one-time thing." He grinned. "Also if I had my floats, it'd be a lot more fun too."

"Did you see where they took them?" They'd need to find them when she got this door open. It'd make an escape a lot easier. Although she had been trying to keep her plans quiet, so maybe her pointed tone revealed too much.

He raised his head off the bunk—and his eyebrows at the unflinching way she said it. "No. Unfortunately, I was out like a light. Just woke up without them."

"How rude of them."

"Puts a whole new spin on rude awakening, doesn't it?" He flopped his head back down.

She let out a puff of laughter, but accidentally cut it short when her eyes spotted it—the switch that reported the door was shut. Just near the ceiling. Hard to reach—but not impossible. In a ship like this, it should be just below the rest of the door circuitry. It used to short out all the time when she'd worked on one of these. On cells and private crew cabins alike. Major pain.

"This is turning out to be a great fragging week," he mumbled. "Month? Whatever."

"You were asleep when I got here, sorry. Maybe you can get some sleep, if you want to *relax*?" she asked abruptly, hoping he'd get her drift that she might have a plan to break out. They'd need to be rested and at their best. And she needed to find the right time.

He lifted his head and frowned at her, looking a little insulted. Oh, great. That had failed completely. His stare was too searching, too intense, so she looked away.

"Or don't," she blurted, desperately needing to fill the tense silence. "Whatever. It doesn't matter."

Right. Insult the boss, then tell him his opinion doesn't matter. This adventure was going so well already.

CHAPTER TEN

ELLEN WASN'T sure who decided to put plex viewports on the side of a shuttle specialized to land in a sandstorm. Maybe nobody had, maybe it was just what they'd had lying around. Maybe they got it on discount.

However it'd come to pass, the view from the landing shuttle became non-existent real quick as the atmo was swallowed by clouds and then the red sands of the storm itself. Outside, the darkness fell to match the already dim shuttle interior. Not much lighting inside this damn thing.

"Discount" was not a word she'd prefer to use for a space-to-ground vehicle, but it probably fit in this case. There were seats, but the harnesses were an assorted mishmash of hand sewn, industrial taped, partially ripped, overly repaired, and completely missing. That would have been concerning, but harnesses didn't fit around armor anyway, so the three of them were standing room only.

There were also about twice as many seats as there should be. This shuttle appeared quite similar, if not identical to, some of the lighter Union liaison shuttles she'd ridden more than a few times. Not for troop transport, but for other less important goods. Many of the schematics from those days still floated in the back of her mind.

Standing room also contained about ten other thrill-seeking passengers. Or the poor drecks had gotten a life-threatening discount. It was a packed little boat.

She, for one, was glad she armored. If the harnesses hadn't been one thing, the readout would have pushed her over the edge as it listed many, *many* diverse human scents detected in their vicinity.

Three women were clustered around her, judging by the shawls and veils and peeks of long, black hair. The fabric colors were bright purple and rich blue, not that the gloom of the inside of the shuttle allowed for much appreciation of that. Most of the seated passengers looked like civilians. A few tougher ones might be military, but they had a sloppiness that made her doubt it. Armored vests and weapon holsters were aplenty, though.

They'd required them to stow the multis. It wasn't ideal, but they hadn't asked about the armor, so they'd gone along. The armor was as dangerous as a multi if not more so, and at least they'd be getting their guns back planetside.

Certainly better than rebuying everything once they hit the ground.

The final landing thud came without any kind of pilot announcement or warning, and several people toppled into each other, the seats, and the shuttle walls.

Silence, then some yelling, then the door hatch sealed and creaked open, air puffing inside. She and Dane and Kael funneled out, dark and hulking behind the other passengers.

The officer unloading their weapons took one look at them, and his eyes narrowed. "You can't take these."

"But they said—" she started.

Kael held up a hand. "Can we take them for twenty credits?"

The officer's eyebrow raised. "How could you think that I, on my honor—"

"Okay, fifty," Kael cut in, holding out a card. Was that the one they'd taken from Rutland? "That's gotta be a hundred rial, right?"

The man swiftly pocketed the plastic. "As I was saying, here are your things, my good friends. Is there anything else I can do for you?"

Kael rolled his eyes as he accepted his rifle. He slung it over his back as they walked away. "Welcome to Faros."

She tried not to lovingly stroke the thing as they lumbered down the last low tube. Okay, maybe only a little.

Customs had taken place on the station above—what little there had been—so the shuttle dumped them directly into a large market square. The place was still dark, the ceiling maybe two stories high. The square was ringed with stores displaying goods outside on multi-tiered tables. The specific products were hard to make out in the dim light, but she spotted some sort of fuchsia textiles and something brown and sticky grilling over an open flame. The tiny lights of technological gadgets winked blue, green, and orange. Yellow lanterns like little glowing walnuts hung in strings over many shops. While the ceiling and some of the shopfronts were metal and plex and petroglic, the floor was stone, as were several archways leading out of the square. Everything down those roads was a dim mystery.

"Is the entire place this dark?" Ellen muttered, hardly realizing she'd spoken.

"Pretty much," murmured Kael.

"Look at those." Dane pointed up.

Rough rocks pulsed with light in one stall, the colors oscillating from sea green to white to blue. A sea of candles intermixed with the rocks, flickering weakly. In the air, jellyfish-like creatures floated and drifted, some white but others a pale orange, all of them glowing in their own right. They didn't appear to be caged, but stayed drifting near the pulsing rocks.

Kael made a noise of disgust.

"What?" said Dane. "You don't like pretty glowy things?"

"Cave droppers. They're pretty all right, but don't sneak up on one. Or really go near it."

"Why?"

"Scare them, and they spray excrement."

Dane's voice was laughing when he replied. "Duly noted."

Ellen stifled a laugh. "Must be good for business."

"Some breeds make poison excrement, extra special for you. They probably wait till after closing time to feed them—makes them more affectionate."

"That's kind of awful," said Ellen.

"I am not arguing you on that."

Ellen tore her eyes away from the glowing creatures, checking the helmet display map. First stop was Ninshabur Institute, to contact Barakat. "This way."

They made their way out of the square, through another archway, down several small alleys. The grimiest alley had people lurking in the shadows, and she was both glad for her armor and wondering what Kael might be thinking right here, right now, having returned. It was tempting to cut Dane out of the channel and ask him, but it didn't seem worth the risk of worrying Dane if he noticed.

The final turn indicated by the mapping system led them to a problem, though. In the form of a thick stone wall.

"Look at this map," she grumbled. "It clearly says to turn here. I didn't make a mistake."

"The mistake you made is trusting any map of Faros, especially at the third level down. There's how it's supposed to be, how the government recognizes it, and then how it is."

She snorted. "Maybe you should take over navigation."

"Not that I'll be any better, but I might have a trick or two up my sleeve."

They retreated back several litter-strewn alleys, then back onto a main drag which carried on for several more blocks.

"Wow." Kael came to a stop in a peaked archway that led into an older shopping area. This one looked less fortunate than the last, with fewer shining things and techy gadgets. At least two stalls claimed to sell rial—the local currency—and three were redik bars. The smell of redik hung in the air, measuring high on the readout along with a number of other less legal chems.

"What is it?" Ellen stopped at his side. "Recognize this?"

"Yeah. I was here a few times. Not my stomping grounds exactly, but a few times."

"Look different?" Dane asked.

"No. That's just it." He shook his head. "It looks so much the same. You'd think ten years would… You'd think it'd change more."

She waited as his eyes ate up the scenery. "You okay?"

"I am far from okay." There was a tightness around his eyes that made her stomach clench. His gaze met hers, his eyes fiery. Worried. "But I'm ready to continue."

She opened her mouth, but he started forward, and she shut it and followed. He stopped at a small, black-framed archway and turned to them, indicating a yellow twisty-looking pictograph on the wall. "You see this sign? This means the tubes. They'll take you to almost any part of Faros—including the surface. This should come up just in front of the Institute of Ninshabur, so we should only have to brave a minor amount of sand and wind."

"Sounds like a blast." Dane snickered.

"Hah hah. Time to get our armor polished." Kael pulled the door open and stepped in. Once inside, with them crowding into the small capsule behind him, he ordered the tubes to head to the "Institute of Ninshabur."

"So this is free?" Ellen murmured. "That's not half bad."

"Oh no—nothing on Faros is free. They took our idents when we came down. Kael Asidian is being charged for this."

She snorted. "Does he even have any money?"

He grinned. "I have no idea anymore."

The tubes were odd contraptions that moved in all directions. Or at least it seemed that way based on the way she was knocked on every possible side of the tiny compartment. Thank God for armor. And that they fit inside in it.

Finally, the door opened. Outside a small enclosed plex area led to a set of double doors. Beyond that, dark sand raged in all directions. Sand covered the floor of the lock area, heavier at the farther side. They carefully sealed the door to the tubes behind them.

"Double check your locks and seals," she grunted.

"Solid," said Dane.

"All are a go," said Kael.

"Let's get this party started then, boys." She palmed open the outer door, and they burst through, shutting the door behind as quickly as possible. "Switch displays if you need to."

Infrared, thermal, video—none of the modes were particularly helpful, but they stumbled their way the hundred yards toward the Institute of Ninshabur.

"So much sand," Kael groaned. "So much fragging sand."

"Welcome back, kid," Dane muttered.

"Aren't we the same age?"

"I don't know, are we? I think I'm older than you."

Ellen cut in. "Not even five minutes in this, and my armor is already complaining."

Dane chuckled. "Nothing like the onslaught of millions of tiny devious particles to please finely tuned machinery."

"I hate sand." Kael sounded miserable.

"Even at the beach?" she shot back.

"I love and hate sand depending on the context," he amended.

"That's what I thought."

They reached the outer wall of the damn Institute and felt their way toward the main gate. She almost missed it, except that Dane stumbled and hit his helmet off one of the huge handles of the main doors.

She stepped closer and scanned what she could see in her thermal and then cycled through various readouts. Staring up at the Institute of Ninshabur, she could see why Amari Barakat had insisted that she didn't need any help. Large military installations were less fortified than this.

Kael too had his hand up—as if that could shield his eyes. "Is that a… rail gun?"

"Holy hells, it is. Right next to a laser turret, looks like." Dane blatantly gawked.

She pressed her helmet against the wall; the slight break in the sand's pressure gave her a glimpse of a wall covered in beautiful cobalt blue tile. Groping, her hand found the palmpad, and she smacked the chime.

"Identify yourselves and your purpose," said a dark, unfriendly voice. At least it was speaking in Common.

She switched her voice to the outer speaker and cranked up the volume. "We're looking for Amari Barakat. We request to see her. I'm Ellen Ryu, commander of the starship *Audacity*, and these are my men."

Silence.

"We mean to offer assistance. We have it on good authority that Ms. Barakat might be in need of aid."

"Everyone at the Institute is perfectly safe."

Well. That didn't sound ominous at all.

"Sure they are. We could use a little help ourselves, too. A mutual friend of Ms. Barakat's is in some trouble."

A pause. "The Institute of Ninshabur does not accept visitors. Please vacate the premises within five minutes, or you will be forced to leave. Thank you."

She blinked. Damn it. Now what was she supposed to do?

"That went well," Dane said.

She switched back to the interior comm channel. "Splendidly."

Kael was quiet.

"Let's get out of this shit show," she grumbled. "See if anyone on the *Audacity* can think of a way to get us in."

They trudged back through the wind and sand, barely finding the tube entrance. She'd never have found it without the planetary positioning of the map overlay. Not like visual displays were doing much. Thank God for armored suits and technology.

Once they were all squeezed back inside the tubes, she read an address off her helmet display and fed it into the tube system.

"What do we need help with?" Kael cleared the visor of his helmet and narrowed his eyes at her.

Of course that hadn't slipped his notice. "Nothing. I was just trying to get them to open the door."

His lips thinned.

"Alright, alright. I'm concerned that Merith's backup plan—whatever it is—might be inside Xi's code. Without Doug, we can't really know for sure. Adan has tried to check, but it's really a task beyond his expertise. We can't know if Xi can accurately see all of her own code."

"Oh. And we know for a fact she tampered with Xi."

"Yes."

"That's our commander," said Dane affectionately. "Always keeping her cards close to the vest."

"I didn't want to waste anyone's time with unverifiable conjecture."

Dane sniffed. "She didn't want us big burly men to worry."

"You fall to pieces so easily," she said.

Kael smiled, if grudgingly. "Fragile is my middle name."

Dane braced himself as the tube took a sharp turn. "Did Simmons choose that for you? You should probably have picked a name or two for him. He's not great with names, *Asidian*."

"Why didn't you warn me?"

Ellen shook her head. "Well, you need a new one anyway, so you won't be stuck with it too much longer."

"Is that *really* his middle name?" Dane caught her eye.

"Yeah, and my middle name is apple pie."

Dane groaned. "Don't mention that—I'm hungry."

"First this stop, then we can find our digs." Adan and Levereaux had reserved a place for them to stay on this damn sandy rock. If they could find it.

"Wait—what is this address you put in, then?" He frowned.

Surprising that bit had taken him this long. "It's Asha Narulon's last known residence."

He winced. "You weren't going to warn me?"

"Close to the vest—I'm telling you," Dane put in, grinning. Interesting to see the usually quiet Dane had a bit more to say this trip. Maybe he was nervous about the mission. Or trying to build a rapport for if the dreck hit the fan.

"I was going to warn you," she said, voice cool. "Once we were right outside."

As if on cue, the tube slid to an awkward halt, the doors spilling out into a semi-dim corridor.

"Why does she have a house if she's supposedly dead?" Kael muttered.

"House isn't in her name. Name appears to be fake—couldn't find any assorted paperwork on it, not even a birth record."

"How did anyone buy it then?" Dane asked.

Kael shook his head. "A few rials, and you'd be surprised what you can grease a few palms to do."

"At least we're back underground this time," she said. "Thank God."

"Didn't take you long on this planet to adopt the native viewpoint. Say, back underground, *praise Almighty*," Kael replied, "and now you're thinking like a Farosian."

"Is that how you say it?"

"Like Persian."

"I was thinking it was like Italian."

"No. Some of the Movers that ended up here had Persian ancestors. Others Turkish. All businesspeople—that's how the Faros IV ship was financed. Only secular planet in this system."

The corridor—which she supposed was their version of an underground street—stretched straight in both directions as far as she could see. It was wide enough for two landers to pass, but she only saw foot traffic at the moment. Most of the walls were lined with doors, mailboxes, vending machines and seemed mostly residential. Overhead, a few skylights allowed actual light in. Well, what light filtered through the storm at the moment.

Kael pointed. "Real light means wealth. Not only are those in demand, but people have to clear the sand off them periodically."

Dane let out a low whistle. "Don't think I'd want that job."

"Better than no job." He shrugged.

She checked the helmet display. "Says it's eighteen doors down on the right. If this can be trusted."

"Let's find out, shall we?" Kael said, with more zest than she'd expected. He seemed to be oscillating between dread and something else, but she wasn't sure quite what the "something else" was. Was it happiness, excitement, and she just didn't want to recognize it?

Or, uh, was there a murderous twitch in the corner of his eye?

Either meant trouble, really.

The doors they passed looked high tech. Several to Ellen's surprise were not solid metal or petroglic at all like a ship's hatch, but bars that revealed interior gardens.

Asha's was one of these. All manner of unfamiliar plants crowded the ground around a stone path that snaked an S-curve back toward a door at the far end of the courtyard. A simple fountain splashed away in one corner.

Kael stopped just outside the door and stared.

"Knock, knock." Ellen pushed the buzzer. Delicate chimes registered the request, but nothing immediately happened. They waited.

No one came.

She pressed it again, but everything from the bars on in was eerily silent. The fountain seemed almost forlorn in its stubborn persistence to run when no one but them was there to care.

Dane shook his head. "Guess no one is home. Why does a dead woman have a house?"

"Good question." Ellen slapped a palm against the wall. "How many times are we going to hit a wall on this mission? First Merith, then Barakat, now this. Without Doug, we have some serious roadblocks."

"At least we made it onto the planet," Dane said. "For today, one out of three?"

Kael said nothing, still staring.

She nodded. "Good point. We'll have to come back. Let's find those digs of ours. Then if there's still time, we can try the doctor's place."

Kael turned. "The doctor?"

"The former coroner who wanted to exonerate you."

He raised his eyebrows. "That should be interesting."

"More interesting than this. But one second." She clicked open a compartment in her gauntlet and drew out a small black square. She reached tentatively for the bars, but nothing zapped at her. Pretending just to look more closely, she leaned forward and wrapped her hand around the nearest bar—wrapping the black square along with it. "Okay. Let's go."

"What was that?" he said as they were all striding back toward the tubes.

"Some of Xi's microcams. Will try to record and let us know if anyone comes or goes. Might be able to get inside."

"Really? You've never used that trick before." He glanced back over his shoulder.

Dane laughed, which he politely turned into a cough.

"Oh, I have," Ellen said. "You just didn't know about it."

———

"I GUESS it's better than hotbunking," Kael said as they emerged into the street outside the hostel.

"That bad, huh?" Ellen said. She hadn't noticed any living creatures, so it'd seemed adequate enough for her tastes. Although the dark room with its two bunks of two beds was a bit cave-like, even for her space-raised sensibilities.

"Are you sure we shouldn't stick with ration bars?" Dane asked. "I mean, I know the suits can test the food but..."

"C'mon. Where's your adventurous spirit?" Ellen elbowed him in the side. His armored side. She'd be lucky if he even realized she'd done it by the little *tap* that it'd made. "Besides. I want the lay of the land. We're striking out left and right here. Might as well gather some information."

"And I wouldn't want to deprive anyone of a taste of home or anything—" Dane started.

Kael snorted. "You have the rations in your suit, right? Eat that if you don't like what you get."

They turned the corner and headed toward a restaurant the hostel had listed on a dilapidated set of signs out front. A quick network search had deemed the place acceptable enough. This was what Kael called "the second level" down. Not swanky enough to have natural light, but apparently there were several levels of hell deeper than this.

Just before they'd reached the food place, though, her eyes caught on a large section of the wall covered with flyers flapping in a slight breeze. A tearful woman was pinning up a new one. Ellen slowed, and the men matched her, all of them coming to a stop.

Every flier held a face. Underneath the ones posted most recently, she could see other faces covered over—different ones. She ordered the suit's visual translator to process the text on the flyers, much of it not in Common.

Kael read it off, though, just as the translator was jerking toward a finish. "Missing. These are missing people." He stepped closer, fingered the edge of the board, then looked back at her with wide eyes. "Damn, this is a couple centimeters. There must be dozens of them."

The tearful woman saw his interest and flung herself on his armor.

"Have you seen him? Have you seen him!" The universal translator reported she was crying. Not that Ellen could have missed it.

Two men in grayish fatigues slowed on the corner, eyes narrowing at them.

Kael visibly tensed.

"Those local police, Kael?"

"Yes, ma'am," he said, as he assured the hysterical woman he hadn't seen the man and apologized at least a dozen times.

The woman more wandered away than accepted his answer. Her shoulders slumped to nonexistent beneath her veil. Kael seemed determined to fade into the wall beside the flyers.

"The disappearances are real," Ellen whispered. "The farm planets..."

"What?" Dane said.

"Let's move away. I think we may have an audience. I'll tell you inside."

The level of grime on the walls of the restaurant was minimal, so Ellen felt good about their choice. Overheads fed light to ferns and palms that grew along a terrace that hung over their heads, giving an interesting feeling of being outdoors somewhere much more tropical.

They sank into a corner table, all of them taking a position where they could keep their eyes on the door. But the owner was motioning wildly for them to come up to the counter. "Dane—get us a variety, will ya?" she asked.

Nodding, he headed to appease the man.

Her eyes scanned the place for a second exit—there might be one in the back. A door led into the kitchen, and usually there were doors for loading and stuff out back. No gray fatigues appeared in the restaurant's door.

"What was that about farm planets?" Kael asked.

She shook her head inside the helmet. How could she explain that mess of information? She was starting to understand why Simmons hadn't said anything. "There was info about this in Doug's files. He had a map labeled farm planets, including this one. Farm. What did he mean? How is this connected with you-know-who? It was in *her* file."

"Your nemesis?"

"Well, yes."

"Wait—you mean these disappearances are happening on other planets?"

"Apparently. All over Union and outsystem space." She frowned. "He *must* have thought Arakovic was behind the disappearances. Or related closely. Why?"

"There were men in those Enhancer labs." Kael leaned back in the chair, sighing. "Get your telepaths from Capital, build the rest of the unit from shit holes like this. If she's behind this, I guess I was one of the lucky ones then."

She squinted at him. "I didn't think you were a huge fan of having your skeleton forcibly replaced and biochemicals tinkered with."

"Oh, well, it does shorten the lifespan and drain everything fun from life. But I can't say for sure it's worse than whatever happened to those men."

"Or *is happening*."

"But why? For what purpose?"

She bit her lip, thinking. "Kentt said when they recruited, they talked about peace. About ending the war. She was concerned they were planning to use the telepaths to somehow *force* peace on people's minds."

Kael went strangely still. "How… uh, how is that possible?"

"No idea. Maybe it's not, maybe it's all conjecture. Could she be hoping to get to a strategic politician or general somehow, to manipulate or stop the war that way? But no. If that was her plan, why the whole unit? Why not just telepaths?"

"What could she do with the combination that she can't do with one telepath?" he mused.

"Keeps the telepath safe while the boots on the ground can give her information. Carry out her bidding." That part was disturbingly familiar. She shuddered.

"What about when you were in her program?" he said, as if sensing the direction of her thoughts. "Why did that unit exist?"

"We were soldiers. We fought wars." She shrugged. "Kept the Puritans at bay."

"What did the augmentations she gave you add to the war effort?"

She frowned. "We were especially efficient. Responsive to each other. Quick. Saved people. More lethal."

"Bodyguards?" he offered.

She met his gaze. "Or maybe soldiers is still the plan."

He raised an eyebrow. "Soldiers. But more lethal. Directed by telepaths and with Theroki augmentation too?"

"It would be a formidable force to face in battle, certainly."

"Especially if there's hundreds of them. How many are we now, fifteen? Twenty?"

"Do you want to count the civilians?"

"No. No, I don't."

"Me neither."

"Soldiers to attack what target?" he asked.

"Good question."

Dane plopped back down beside them, food in hand. "What did I miss?"

"We think Arakovic is building an army with the missing people," she said. "A telepathically-controlled army of augmented men, led by her hand-picked telepaths."

Except, not all of them had gone willingly. How did they get the unwilling telepaths to comply? Another good question.

"You figured that all out just now?" Dane blurted.

"Pretty much," she said. Dane's eyes widened further. "She's never changed her research. Not in the slightest. It's the same Songbird program. It never ended. Only two things have changed. One, she's refined the technology somehow, with the Enhancers' help."

"And the second thing?" asked Kael.

"The client has changed. It's no longer the Union."

"Who, then?" Dane put in.

She bit her lip. Who, indeed. But she'd already thought through this. No one made sense. The Union had ended its association somehow, the Enhancers were focused on their Empress and not Arakovic's research, she was only a client to them. Plus it was quite possible she'd turned on them. The Puritans would never fragging consider something like this. There were other splinter groups, but none of them fit. Unless…

"The client is her," she said, almost jumping up in excitement. "There is no client."

"What?" Dane croaked out, just as Kael said, "Are you sure?"

"Well, she didn't send me a telegram. But she's got her own agenda now. If you can't join them, beat them."

"I think that's supposed to be the other way around."

"Yes, but not for her. She's decided she knows what's best. Peace. No more war."

"But that's impossible," Kael snapped. "The only way that would ever happen would be if people were mindless zombies—"

He stopped short as all their mouths dropped open.

"Oh, God," whispered Dane.

"Zombies like the guy in the sick bay," Ellen said. "God, and he's not the first one we saw like that."

They were all silent for a moment. The food still sat untouched on the table, and she felt the eyes of the proprietor on them. Probably wondering what the hell they were doing.

She let out a breath. "So our working theory is… she's building an army either made up of zombies or that will turn people into zombies. Only the telepaths get to think?"

"Fragging hell," Dane grumbled.

Ellen looked up sharply. Her brain had kicked into gear. A mystery was not her specialty—leave that to intel or the private investigators of the world. But sizing up an intergalactic military force?

That was something she knew.

She spoke quickly, words not keeping up with her thoughts. "There was an entire Theroki ship that went to serve a contract with her and never came back. How many men can one of those things support?"

"There's several classes of starship in service," Kael replied, "but the largest could support a few thousand. They're rarely that full. 'Cargo' space is important to pirates, you know."

"I thought you weren't a pirate."

"I'm not. But I may have been indentured to some for a while." He grinned.

"Okay, that ship is her home base. She could have a force at least as large as it can hold. We need to figure out where she's hiding that thing, and if there are any more ships."

"You didn't just get biochem augments, right?" Dane was asking Kael.

"That was part of it, yes, but I think that was just so they could control us. The electromagnetic system is more useful as a soldier. It's what can cause shocks, powers the telekinesis, and—"

"And it just so happens to have network interfaces built in," Ellen put in. "Ones that could be used for artificial telepathy. Networked minds."

"Rudimentary cheap ones, but yes," he conceded.

Her smile was almost manic now. "She's just continuing her research. I can't believe I didn't see it before. Peace is what she wants, always claimed she wanted. One way to ensure peace is to *be* the ruler in charge. Whoever wins the war can decree peace. And write the histories."

She slumped back in her seat. Was it just that simple? A war to end all wars? A mass of Theroki—and abducted men turned into Theroki—led by songbirds, sweeping across the galaxy, defeating everyone in their path? No, why would a scientist plan a massive multi-planet campaign? Arakovic had a favorite tool, and her tool was science. "No, there's more. There's got to be something I'm still missing."

Kael and Dane exchanged a look with each other, but said nothing.

"There wouldn't be enough. They'd need too many men to outfit them all as Theroki—even with all these kidnappings—to truly end the war. It would be too much expense, too much time. Some outsystem planets might fall to an augmented force of thousands, but she'd need lots of planets to build an army that could defeat the Union. A lot more time. The Union would also see them coming and not let them do it in peace. She doesn't have the numbers. Or frankly the expertise."

"She wanted you." Dane pursed his lips.

"True—maybe she's got people who *do* have the expertise? Still… she can't have the numbers based on the rumors I saw. Our data could be incomplete. But it'd take dozens of systems enthusiastically supporting her. Even all the Puritans are barely put forth an even force against the Union. The Union has too much size on its side."

"She's definitely building an army for *something*," Kael said.

"I agree. The question is—how are they going to carry out their mission? It can't be full frontal invasion." Her brain needed time to ferment, to try piecing each pair of puzzle pieces against another to look for connections that worked, to report back on its findings later.

Her stomach growled loud enough for both of them to hear over the comm line. She rolled her eyes. "Guess I'm hungry."

"Maybe we should eat this food that's going cold," Dane said.

"What did you get us?"

Dane rubbed his hands together. "Okay, so we got… Are you sure you want to know?"

She just stared at him. And blinked.

"All right, then. This beauty is a nice combination of chickpeas, some thing that might be seeds, something purple and fluffy looking, and rice. And this one has… well, it also has rice."

"And what else?"

"Well, that looks like it might be a soup of some kind. And I believe the universal translator said crickets and fungi."

"Mushrooms," Kael put in. "What? They're healthy."

Dane cleared his throat and looked leery. "That's if the translator is working right. I kind of hope it isn't. Maybe that's a potato-like thing?"

Ellen narrowed her eyes. "I've never known the translator to be wrong."

Smiling, Kael took the cricket plate and started the suit scan. Whether he grabbed it out of selfishness or self-sacrifice, she wasn't sure. He caught her eyes. "What, you don't like a little crunch with your protein?"

"I'm more of a tofu girl, myself." She grabbed the chickpea plate, started her suit scans, lowered her helmet, and, when it was safe, dug in.

———

MO MIHIO WAS QUITE POSSIBLY the galaxy's quietest woman.

Just his luck. In the day and night and day again that had passed since she'd been tossed in with him, he'd watched her meditate, sleep, coldly analyze the cell, pray, run in a ridiculously tight loop around the cell, do a shocking number of sit-ups and push-ups, and fiddle with the sink for a while.

And meditate some more.

Well, he *tried* not to watch her, but it was hard to give someone privacy in such a tiny space. And his lack of glasses made him obviously have to squint some of the time, and too much squinting meant a headache, so it was all a bad idea. They worked out a protocol for holding their ears when waste relief needs came up that had him feeling a bit like a child. She'd kindly offered her assistance, but he'd refused. Maybe after enough days of these stupid shakes he'd get weak enough to need help, but for now he'd be independent when he could.

Otherwise, he struggled not to interrogate her. What else was there to do, though? He did join in on the sit-ups and his own modified calisthenics, but that had always been a part of his daily routine. His therapists had always stressed the importance of maintaining muscle tone for this sort of situation. Thank heavens he'd listened.

He tried to limit his annoying bouts of conversation to a few times an hour. He didn't always succeed. She'd made an honorable effort to humor him until her energy eventually ran out.

When their daily ration came—some kind of weird creamy liquid shake—their captors generously gave them two.

"Good to see they don't want us to starve," he said as he cracked his open.

She shrugged. "I'm good."

But would she care if he drank both... No, he should probably leave it in case she changed her mind. Glad he didn't have to split just one with her, he didn't comment.

He knew the stuff might be dangerous, she was wise not to drink it without a scan. But he'd been there longer than her. He didn't have much option at this point, but she was probably starting off stronger and better nourished than he was anyway. She had a few days to wait.

He was glad, though, when she drank the water.

Hours had passed, so maybe it was midday, who knew? But he couldn't stand harassing her any longer, so he'd resorted to trying to take a nap. It wasn't like he had slept well earlier on this block of lava rock they called a bunk, so it shouldn't be that hard.

Oh, but it was.

He sighed, shifting to try to get more comfortable. Every part of him ached. It really wasn't her fault he was so starved for companionship. Or Ellen's. Or anyone's, except maybe his own. He always tried to take personal responsibility, so he definitely wasn't going to blame his parents for the situation. He could have left at any time.

He'd been working on it too. He'd just been gun shy. Knowing he needed something different, more people, more like college had been. The one time he'd lived somewhere other than Tetra. Somewhere with a lot of people. He'd had more conversation than he wanted or could handle then. While Davenmore had been mostly virtual, it did have a small campus on a fairly central Union system, and he'd been there as quick as you could say, next shuttle please.

But as the last few years had passed, friends had drifted away. And working for the Foundation didn't make for great dinner conversation. What do I do for a living? Sorry, I can't tell you. No, no, I promise it isn't slave trafficking. Yes, I swear... No, it's not drugs or illicit augmentations. I said I can't tell you.

The few dates he'd attempted had gone pretty much like that, and he'd given up trying.

He'd been far too lonely. Except for the occasional moments when he badgered his subordinates to be chattier with him or invented AIs to talk to. He wondered how Eleven was doing. She had to be alive, he couldn't accept the idea that he'd lost any of them, really.

He pushed the thoughts aside. None of that mattered until he was out of here. Right now, only survival mattered.

And to survive, he needed to not pester Mo Mihio until she went crazy and shot him at five hundred meters. Although if she could *get* to five hundred meters, maybe that meant they were free. So maybe it would be worth it...

To his surprise, he did drift off to sleep, although his dreams swam with the very strange image of Mo sunk down in tall grasses behind a sniper rifle, eyes glowing in a way they didn't in reality. She bent and inched up on the sight, zeroing in on a target.

On their enemies? Or on him?

Footsteps outside woke him before Dream Mo could fire. The steps were booted, heavy, louder than usual. Not the normal grunt guards.

He opened his eyes and sat up just in time to see an older woman in a captain's uniform appear, a black beret over white hair.

"Anya Tovi," he whispered, deliberately dropping any rank.

Mo was sitting cross legged on the bunk, maybe meditating again. Her eyes opened slowly and fixed on the woman, but she said nothing.

"Douglas Simmons. Fancy meeting you here."

"You. You left the—" He stopped short. He shouldn't say it if he could avoid it.

"The Foundation?" she drawled. "Why yes. After my encounter with your little ship and your precious child-commander had people coming around, asking questions that were none of their business."

He scowled. Foundation funds had fueled that ship, so "none of their business" was a pretty big stretch. As far as he was concerned, she'd gotten what she deserved, although he hadn't seen the report details. It hadn't really been any of *his* business in particular, so he'd left it to her Patron. Or so he thought.

"So you were behind all this?" he said.

She snorted. "Oh, no. Well, maybe a little. I did destroy your compound. And kidnap you. And—"

"And my parents?"

Her mouth twisted in a cruel, pursed smile, and he realized too late she might have revealed something if he hadn't let fly that he didn't know what happened. Damn it, why couldn't he keep his mouth shut?

She clucked her tongue at him. "Well, well. The little puppet master has to stand out in the open like his puppets. How does he like getting his strings pulled? Now you'll have to do your dirty work *yourself*, coward."

That cut close—too close. He ducked his head. Chatty as he could be, he had no quick comeback for that one.

"I should put you to work actually. I bet you've never done a day of hard labor in your life. Or even moderate labor. It might just kill you. Then again, maybe that's what I want."

"Over my dead body," Mo cut in.

He raised his eyebrows, snapped out of his stupor now.

"Oh, that's right. You'll still be protected, because you still have one of your puppets. One bad enough at her job to get caught by my team while trying to rescue you." Tovi glowered at Mo, voice full of syrup. In her favor, Mo didn't react, just stared hard, angry eyes back at the woman. "I'm shaking in my boots."

"You will be." Mo's voice was quiet, the threat ringing in the air.

He shivered, anyway.

Tovi laughed, but he thought it seemed a little late, a little forced.

"I'm surprised at the kind of ship you run, Tovi," Mo said.

Her eyes narrowed. "Are you? I should think after your little commander's slander, you'd believe me capable of anything."

"I didn't expect a woman to tolerate rape among her crew."

His breath stopped in his lungs—what? Why hadn't she mentioned — The RPD, the armor—*fuck*.

"I don't," Tovi snapped back quickly. "You have an RPD. I know the standard outfit."

Mo jumped to her feet, holding up her left palm. The skin was red and blackened near her wrist.

Shit. Shit shit shit, holy shit.

"RPDs only have three charges," Mo whispered. Her voice could have frozen an ocean.

Didn't they have five? Or was it four? God, why couldn't he remember.

My God, what had they done? His brain was simultaneously trying to compute what had happened while also trying very hard not to understand. Did that mean what he thought it meant?

He was starting to get light-headed.

Tovi, for her part, didn't look much better than he felt. Her stunned expression switched to a glare, and she stalked suddenly away at high speed, lifting a corner of her jacket toward her mouth and spitting words he couldn't make out.

As soon as she was out of sight, he trained his eyes on her. "Why didn't you—"

"I don't want to talk about it." A sharp cut of her hand across her throat stilled him. "For once, sir, with all my respect—keep your mouth shut."

CHAPTER ELEVEN

DAY 16

THE PIERCING CAWING of an alarm cut through Kael's sleep. He tried to push it from his mind, bury himself deeper in the blankets. He reached for Ellen.

Instead, his knuckles collided with a cold wall. Why wasn't he sleeping in *her* bed? An endlessly better sleep location. Grumbling, he rolled the other way. Why wasn't Xi the one waking him anyway? Damn, it was freezing in here.

Feet light as a cat's touched down on the deck beside him, and memory stirred. Bunks—Ellen above him, Dane across.

Faros. That was where he was. Faros.

Fragging hell.

He hauled himself to sitting, still groggy. Morning wasn't really different than night down in the tunnels. It also wasn't that different than a spaceship.

He'd been trying to decide whether he should embrace the memories or if he should instead try to forget any connection to the drecks he once knew. Tell himself he was a completely different person now. He *had* spent a decade as a chemically different person—so maybe he really was different. And age had obviously taught him a thing or two.

At the rate he was going, he'd definitely reach twenty-nine, and thirty was even looking almost possible. If he did go before then, the chances that it would be for a good reason—or at least a reason better than standing still outside some stupid lab on the most pointless rock in the galaxy—were pretty high.

But on Faros, he didn't feel twenty-eight or like someone with a decade of experience at anything. Here he was fourteen again, and he had a decade of experience in how to stay alive, find food when you didn't have money, and avoid a glow jelly shitting on your head.

Dane groaned across from him, stood up, stretched, and walked out. "Gonna hit the head."

Kael had barely pried his eyes open when her steely eyes came into view. Except lately they'd taken on this different cast, glinting with a sort of soft, secret joy. He'd never known she could look like that.

They were staring at each other.

"Morning," he said softly. They had a moment or two; the hostel washroom facilities were three doors down.

"I slept like crap without you," she murmured.

"Me too. This planet can't end soon enough. I mean—our *visit* to this planet. I'm still waking up!"

She grinned, then straightened to make up the bed. Smiling, he covered his face with his hands and deliberately ignored his own blankets, although he did sneak a glimpse or two at her lean form at work.

Bed made precisely, he felt her sit down beside him. Before he could drop his hands, she leaned her head against his shoulder, setting off an explosion of warmth in his chest. He still wasn't really used to that. He tilted his head against hers.

He wasn't sure how long they sat there, sleep slowly ebbing away, but eventually she squeezed his elbow and stood. His shoulder felt cold now.

"I need a bio break too," she said. "Big day today."

"Don't remind me," he grumbled, as she headed for the door. He shamelessly watched the beautiful lines of her until she slipped out of sight.

Of course—Dane chose just that moment to pop back in.

Kael cleared his face, and he wasn't sure quite what had been on it, but it must have been something, because Dane's eyes narrowed.

He pretended not to notice and made himself busy getting ready for the day. The air was tight with as much tension as Ellen's freshly made bed sheets—apparently she followed strict military protocols whether on her own ship or some crap hostel on a dust planet. Crazy, wonderful woman. But what was he going to say? *I totally wasn't staring at our commanding officer's ass?* He *had* been staring at her ass. And other things.

He was about to turn and take his turn at the morning's ablutions when Dane cleared his throat. Directly behind him.

Fragging hell. Where was *this* going to go?

Kael turned and met Dane's expression with the flattest, most neutral features he could manage. Underneath, though, he could feel his own tension roiling, the wild dog somewhat on a leash growling low in its throat.

Dane himself didn't make it any easier. While the guy seemed quiet and introspective, he was by far the only human on the Audacity that was slightly bigger than Kael. To anyone else, they might have seemed similarly sized, but the memory of the Theroki armor that had been a second skin for so long didn't go away that easily. Even if it were a hunk of horrible rusted junk, it would have made him significantly bigger than Dane right now.

And he was brave enough to admit he would have preferred that.

Dane's brown eyes were boring into him, and Kael pressed his lips together. "What?" he said. It came out more irritable than he intended.

Dane looked pointedly at the door, then back at him. "I'd just like to know your intentions."

"What do you mean, my intentions?" Kael fought a scowl.

"Your *intentions*. With the commander."

He truly didn't know what Dane meant. Or even remotely how to answer. So he successfully morphed the scowl into a sincere frown. "To follow her orders?"

Dane narrowed his eyes. "You know what I mean, and it's not that. Although you better do that, too, or it's also my ass on the line."

Now would probably not be the best time to mention their little in-joke about insubordination. "No, I seriously don't know what you mean. What are intentions?"

Dane's jaw tightened. He strode to the door and flipped the lock.

Not good. His blood heated, pounded faster. He forced a breath. If he lost his mind right now, it would only make things worse. It didn't matter if his old programming was already on high alert, if his body was just looking for a reason to fight. If Ellen came back to a brawl, she'd kick both their asses. And Dane was probably right to lock the door. If Ellen came back and heard this conversation, she'd probably be pissed. She'd probably tell Dane to stay out of it, or that he wasn't her brother. Or her dad. She'd be right.

But that wouldn't put Dane at ease.

Could *he* put Dane at ease without revealing anything? Or over-turning a bunk and bending the damn thing in half?

"She's young," Dane said, words sharp and precise, like a knife kissing the skin, considering where to jab. "She knows a lot about the world for her years, but not about some things. She's my friend, not just my commander. I don't want to see her hurt. I see the way you look at her. So I'm going to ask you again. *What* are your *intentions*?"

A strong urge to simply punch Dane in the face warred with his desire to preserve what he had—a good job, a good team. Punching Dane in the face just *barely* lost the battle.

But the man didn't know much about their history. He had a right to wonder. And hell, it was good Ellen had friends—subordinates or otherwise—that cared about her. Dane couldn't be the only one thinking this. This was exactly why she'd wanted privacy. Kael might get this question again, so he ought to figure out what to say. Or maybe he ought to tell the truth, but that just felt wrong without Ellen agreeing to it first.

The silence went on too long, so he dove headlong into whatever response he could muster.

"My intention?"

"Intentions."

"Uh... my intentions." Could he put it into words? "I guess my intention is to follow her to the end of the galaxy, to the end of time if she'll let me, for as long as she'll let me, and if I can give up this sorry life to save hers, all the better."

Dane's eyebrows twitched, the anger immediately vanishing from his expression. "I knew that feeling once too," he said softly.

Kael swallowed. "How did it work out?"

The door jumped as Ellen tried to open it and the lock caught. "Uh —guys?" Her voice was muffled but audible.

Dane glanced at the door, then back to Kael. "Don't outlive her. I don't recommend it."

After that blow to the gut, Kael sank to a seat on the bunk and hung his head as Dane opened the door. Ellen stepped in but stopped in the doorway.

"What was going on in here?" she said, eying the two of them.

"Oh, nothing, Commander," Dane said warmly. He'd been a lot warmer overall this whole trip—up until this little show down. "Just accidentally hit the lock switch on the way in. Stupid thing."

Her narrowed eyes said she didn't buy it, but she didn't question him further. While the two of them were busy readying their packs, he made a beeline for the door and the lav, such as it was.

He took a piss and washed his hands. Splashing the water over his face, he realized he felt weirdly better. He'd spent a lot of the time on Capital and in the few weeks learning to control the rage. Shove it down. Ignore it.

But the slight feel of its snarl, the memory of the Theroki suit around him—right now, it actually helped. It was easier to remember he wasn't the little kid who'd huddled around a drum fire for warmth one too many times. Or rather, he was, but he wasn't *only* that. He was also a Theroki.

Er. No, he wasn't. He'd fought so hard to escape.

Some part of him would always be a man who'd received that training, though. Lived that life—survived and thrived at it.

And now it could remind him he was more than a street kid from Faros.

He was ready quickly, and they were out in the tunnels. His eyes could pick out all the types—the average people on their way to or from work, the vendors pushing their obvious carts, the chem dealers that were also selling wares but less obvious about it, the lookout kids helping the dealers avoid getting caught.

He followed Ellen's lead—he vaguely remembered these places, but this second level had been too rich for his blood. He'd existed in the literal lowest levels. Those were great for the geothermal heat, bad for the vitamin D, and the easiest to get by. At the higher levels, they'd chase you out, preferably outside above the tunnels completely out of spite if they could catch you. If it was the right season without sand-storms, then fine. He'd spent warm nights out there under jubhani trees. It could be downright pleasant.

But they also didn't care if they chased you out into the sandblaster, also known as certain death for a malnourished kid from the fifth levels and lower.

That memory had his shoulders slouching again. Frag. He pulled back that feeling he'd remembered, the bloodlust and the groaning, screaming armor, and he felt a little better.

Maybe being a Theroki had sucked, but he'd had power. He'd gotten power. And if someone had deliberately done this to him, they were soon going to find out that selling him to the Theroki had been their biggest mistake.

But the first mistake had been betraying him.

They rounded a corner, and Ellen stopped short, pointed. "The door's open."

He frowned. "That doesn't look good."

They approached more slowly now, bringing the multis closer to ready but low, listening. The street was quiet as Kael scanned it—bad sign. The lookouts, the dealers—everybody was gone. There was one woman and one couple of old men, the ordinary people just strolling by, but somebody had told those other permanent fixtures of tunnel life to scatter. The Gray Dragons? This hadn't been their territory in his day, but these things changed all the time.

Ellen knocked loudly on the door frame. When the only response was silence, she hit the raise helmet button. He and Dane did too. At her nudge, the door moved slightly.

"Want me to inquire in the local tongues, Commander?" he said over the helmet comm.

"Everybody ready if the response is unfriendly?"

"What would make you think a place like this could be unfriendly?" he said, smirking.

"I'm good," Dane replied.

"Make us some introductions, Kael."

"Anybody there?" Kael called out the phrase in several languages —Arabic, Persian, Turkish.

Nothing stirred.

Ellen glanced both ways before bringing the multi higher. With the barrel, she gently eased the door all the way open. "This place has been trashed—recently."

The three of them eased inside, fanned out. Yep, thoroughly trashed. Tables were overturned, glass smashed, and drawers emptied.

"Who would do this to a coroner's residence?" Kael muttered, still over the comm.

"Correction," Ellen said. "An elderly doctor. Dr. Abed retired from his position as coroner five years ago."

"And beyond who—why?" he said. "And why now?"

To Kael's left, something twitched. He spun, multi trained on what he discovered was a toppled cabinet. But underneath the cabinet—a foot.

"Somebody here," he barked, dashing forward as he snapped the multi to his leg magnetic plate. He heaved the cabinet off the body so hard it collided with the wall and lost all semblance of structure, the boards sliding loose down and cracking. He had to scramble to make sure the remnants didn't collapse right back down on their former victim.

Behind him, an older man groaned. Kael retracted his helmet. The fancy armored suits and silver visors wouldn't exactly breed trust.

Dane rushed forward too, pulling out a case of medkits from his compartment. "Sir, are you all right?"

"I'm… better than… that cabinet." The old man was staring at him. Glaring?

"Sorry. Got a little carried away. Out of concern." Kael winced. What was he going to do, though? Rebuild the thing? "What happened here?"

"I... I didn't see them. They caught me by surprise." Shaking fingers reached up to touch the back of his head and came away bloodied.

"Can I put a medkit on that for you, sir?" Dane already had it out and ready. "It's standard grade."

The man blinked, confused for a moment, and then some relief eased into his eyes as he nodded. "Yes. All right." Then he turned back to frowning at Kael. Over the cabinet or... did he recognize him?

"Dr. Abed, I presume." Ellen stopped at the man's feet.

"Yes. Who are you people?"

Dane applied the medkit, making the man wince. Kael dropped to one knee and put a hand to the doctor's shoulder. Too bad he was the one with the real medical training in this situation, and not any of them, but Kael could at least try to steady him. Getting beaten was as traumatizing mentally as it was physically. "*Salam*, Dr. Abed. Be calm," he said smoothly. "Do you want us to call someone? Did you have your comm on you?"

The doctor looked up at him, squinting closer. "That face... Do I know you?"

"Maybe indirectly." He frowned back. "I don't think we ever met."

"Dr. Abed," said Ellen, in that bold commander's voice at the moment, "we can explain why you recognize him, but it's not safe to talk here. Do you have any family that we should check on who lives here? Can we take you somewhere more secure?"

"No, no—I live alone." He started to struggle to sit up. Dane protested, but the doctor patted his forearm and righted himself. He retrieved his neat white cap and placed it back on his head, covering the medkit a bit. A man of faith, then. After another deep breath, he successfully got to his feet with the help of the two men. "There's just my cat, but she roams the neighborhood."

"Then you should call the authorities," said Ellen. "Following that, we can help you to a secure location. Any suggestions?"

"There's a tea shop. To the right out the door. I can call the police while we go."

Kael swallowed and tried not to show the jolt to his nerves. He had never done anything wrong, and that was exactly why he was here, so he shouldn't have to be afraid. But he didn't like the way they'd eyed him when he'd been spotted by the missing persons board. Maybe old memories died hard.

Or maybe, if he had been sentenced to what was effectively life imprisonment as a Theroki and he'd effectively escaped that sentence… what did that make him here? An escaped convict? He didn't want to find out.

"Are you sure you can walk, Doctor?" said Dane.

"Yes, yes." Dr. Abed waved them off, but didn't let go of either of their arms for the entire short trip. Fortunately, he appeared to be more stunned than injured. The head injury was serious, yes, and the cabinet might have caused some bruising, but it must have been lighter than it looked. Praise the Almighty for fake wood. Abed's hair had gone mostly salty gray with a little pepper still left in him. He had a long beard and neatly trimmed hair under his cap.

Dr. Abed led them to a tea shop a few doors down as he answered questions from whomever he'd called. When they were sitting in a rounded cushioned area—the only spot that could fit the power armor, as all the other spots had been too cozy—he hung up his personal comm and leveled a strong gaze at Kael, a slender silver cup of steaming mint tea already in his hand. Kael had a strong impression that Abed was not the sort of man who was easily swayed by anything, even this. He'd just needed a few moments to recover. "Now. Where do I know you from?"

Kael glanced at Ellen, and she nodded for him to go ahead. "My name is Kael Sidassian, Doctor. Well, it used to be my name. It doesn't matter. I believe you were working on a case about a decade ago where I was accused of the murder of my girlfriend at the time. Asha Narulon."

"Ah, yes. Never did get to settle that." He took a sip, winced.

"Maybe you will now," Ellen said pointedly.

"Oh?" He perked up, raising an eyebrow. "Wait. Didn't they throw you in jail? How did you get out?"

"That's a… long story."

"If you are on the run…" Dr. Abed's glare was stern, but unafraid. Hell. That tea must be extremely bracing.

"No, no. Not at all, Doctor. I wasn't imprisoned, I was conscripted into a Theroki mercenary outfit."

Abed winced, then peered closer at him. "You've got augmentations then? Can hardly tell, although my eyesight grows worse. Ah, I see there, and there." He pointed at the thin, almost invisible silver-white scars behind his ear, along his neck. Tattoos couldn't hide all of them. Kael tried not to squirm like a bug trapped under a microscope.

"I have some augmentations, yes." He had to leave it at that. It wasn't safe to detail all of his capabilities—who knew where Abed's loyalties really lay?

"That explains the cabinet."

Kael let out a small laugh. "Yes. I suppose it does."

Ellen drew the conversation back to Asha. "Doctor, we heard that you were unsure of the case. That you didn't believe Mr. Sidassian was guilty."

"Oh, yes. The evidence was at best circumstantial. Only his connection to the victim and the possible motive convinced the magistrate."

"There wasn't a jury?" Ellen asked. "A trial?"

Abed narrowed his eyes at her. "You're not from around here, are you?"

"No."

"Trials here are little more than the magistrate's whim, half the time. That's why I try so hard to provide some real evidence, but even that can be… overlooked sometimes, shall we say. But the body in this case was barely recognizable, so it wasn't much help. Of course, that was before I realized they had faked the fingerprints."

Kael's breath caught. "Faked them?"

"Yes. It was a new process at the time, but common now. We didn't screen for it on every decedent then, like they do now. To leave out the technical bits, the process involves a subtle layer of real skin with an actual grown fingerprint. But it belongs to someone other than the decedent, attached via a delicate nanobot-based glue application and sewn into the skin at the edges. Very hard to detect. We must take separate genetic samples, destroying part of the finger print."

"How did you figure it out?"

"The technique is not meant to last forever. The faked skin decomposes differently than the rest of the body, the glue slowly becomes visible. For religious purposes, almost all people on Faros decline autopsies and prefer the deceased to be interred within twenty-four hours of death. So in the vast majority of cases, you'd never know unless you exhumed the body."

"Why didn't you have to do that in this situation?"

"She had no family to speak of, making demands, nor any physically indicated religious requests. None were documented in her file. I usually try to abide by the time window, though, because there are so many loners out there, with no one to tell me what they truly wanted in death. But in this case, I just had a feeling about it. So I dragged my heels."

Kael nodded, then hung his head, staring at his lap for a second. Dragged his heels—but someone had urged the case on.

"Why did you have a feeling?" Ellen asked.

"Didn't buy the motive." He glanced awkwardly at Kael. "No offense. But he doesn't look like the type of stone-cold murderer to—" He faltered. "Well, to spare you the grisly details, to commit this kind of brutal, heartless crime. There's shooting someone in a fit of passion or self-defense, and then there's… well, you know."

"I understand." Ellen nodded, her face back to that strict, emotionless wall. He'd gotten so used to seeing past that. Damn, it was kind of intimidating all over again. "I've got to agree with you on that one. But I'm biased."

"Wait, who are you again?" Abed asked.

"I'm his boss."

"Ah." Abed's expression said that that both explained a few things and didn't explain anything at all. "And who's he?"

"This is another member of my team," said Ellen, declining to share

Dane's name. Probably better that way. "Doctor, Mr. Sidassian never killed that girl—"

"Oh, I know."

"—and in fact, we believe she is alive."

He stopped with the glass nearly to his lips and turned slowly to look hard at Ellen. "*Really*. Oh, dear."

"Asha's records state she is legally alive. Why is that?"

"Oh, yes." Abed nodded. "When I realized the forgery, I reverted the status on her file and asked the detectives to see if they could find her. Sort of a preliminary missing persons report. But as I said, she had no family to contact, no relatives."

"Our people couldn't find any record of any investigation after her death, and then rebirth when you discovered the body wasn't hers."

Abed groaned. Kael rolled his eyes. "I told you, a few rials, and you can make anything happen."

"Or more than a few in some cases," Abed agreed. "I received bribes requesting I stop looking into this case. All anonymous sources. And then there were the death threats. That's when I finally closed the book on all this." He looked apologetically at Kael, who waved him off.

Ellen leaned forward. "Do you have any idea who could have possessed the ability at the time to use the fingerprint tech you mentioned? Or the kind of funds required to bribe you?"

Abed frowned. "It was a long time ago."

"I'd like to know who set me up," Kael said simply.

Abed nodded, features stony. "And get revenge probably." Clearly, he didn't approve. Well, maybe if he'd lived it, he'd think differently.

"And find my child," he added. "If she survived."

The color drained from the doctor's face. "Oh, I see. I understand. I don't have concrete proof of who was really behind it; if I did, I'm not sure what I would have done with it anyway after the case was processed. But I always suspected some kind of inter-gang power struggle behind it. The gangs weren't particularly high tech at the time, but they've become so since then, at least the Gray Dragons have. They would have definitely had the funds. And connections with the detectives to make this case go away. Did you have enemies?"

"I didn't *think* I did. I mean, I didn't trust anyone then." That wasn't true, though, was it? He had trusted one person. Asha.

"There were several other cases after you that had me scratching my head, and all resulted in a Gray Dragon being hauled off to—I guess I thought jail, but it wasn't, was it? I'm sorry I can't be more helpful. I'm not sure who would have had access to the tech at that time, considering we were at that point unaware of it."

Ellen nodded. "Thank you, Doctor. Any idea why someone would have ransacked your house just now?"

He frowned. "No idea." His comm beeped. A few moments later, he ended the call and looked at them thoughtfully. "They're nearly to my home. I should go back now. Thinking about it, I probably still have some old files. Walk me back to my house, and I can at least get your file for you. We can meet the police there."

Ellen nodded. "Let's go."

The streets seemed especially crowded as they made their way back. Kael tried not to scan the street nervously the entire time, but mostly he failed. He was tempted to put up his helmet to point out to Ellen that it'd be best to avoid the police, but it'd be too conspicuous. Too obvious. He could only cross his fingers she'd think of it herself. And that they'd get out of there quickly.

The walk from the cafe to the house went fast. Seeming fully recovered now, Abed strode inside, found and unlocked his file drawer, and thumbed through the contents. Then he turned back to them, scowling harder than ever. "The file is gone."

Well, well. Wasn't that a surprise. Kael swore under his breath.

Abed pressed a frustrated palm to his forehead. "I am sorry, young man. It's the *only* one that is gone, too. Someone is looking for you, Mr. Sidassian. And that someone trashed my house not so long ago as part of their search."

Kael swallowed. An engine hummed in the tunnel outside and began to slow. Ellen met his eyes. Hmm. Maybe she did get that they needed to use caution, and was just trying to hide that fact from Abed.

They couldn't tell Abed to deny they'd been there—but they were hardly required to stick around. "Thank you for your help, Doctor. We'll be going now."

Dane was already at the side door.

The doctor nodded. "Understood. Peace be upon you, Mr. Sidassian. And I hope you find justice."

"Thank you, Dr. Abed. *Salam* to you as well."

———

THE DAY BEFORE, it had taken a long time—and a lot of long, studying looks at Mo—before Doug managed to stave off the panic.

For a while, he'd fumed at anyone and everyone, most of all himself, and tried to figure out with intense mortification if her big secret had been the real reason she'd been being so quiet.

He hadn't sensed anything significantly wrong when she showed up in his cell. She'd stared a lot, yeah, but physical differences could explain that, plus the shock of being captured at all. It hadn't seemed so severe. She hadn't seemed traumatized.

Was he really that fragging oblivious? Or just stupid?

But as Mo eventually took a nap and left him to his thoughts, he started to calm down. While some very basic part of him was longing to brutalize whoever might have hurt her right now, his brain was pondering a different theory.

She hadn't said, "Sorry I didn't tell you," or "I don't want to talk about what happened," although maybe she'd meant that. She'd said, "Keep your mouth shut."

In fact, she'd been giving him funny looks from time to time in response to his questions that he hadn't been able to interpret. Now he was thinking maybe this wasn't the first time she'd tried to tell him to shut the hell up.

She *did* want him to shut up and leave her alone.

But was it really because she hated him? Or hated talking in general? He was kind of her boss—and Mo was smart. Too smart to just hate her boss's boss and be a jerk about it. Even if he drove her batty, she'd try to hide it. Was there some other reason she was giving him looks and telling him to shut his pie hole?

Mmm, pie. What he wouldn't give for solid food right about now.

He noodled on it for a while, trying to sleep but failing, but only one possibility occurred to him.

Maybe she hadn't been attacked. Maybe she was saying that to get Tovi to watch them more closely.

If that was true, perhaps she didn't want to talk to him about it because she didn't have details, didn't want to fail at acting traumatized, didn't want to embellish. Quiet brooding was much easier. Of course, she didn't owe him anything either way, so he needed to keep quiet.

But she'd also *specifically* said the RPD contained only three charges, implying to his abject horror she'd needed to use it more than three times. Why mention *that* detail? The burn looked like one discharge, and he was seventy percent certain the RPD units his team had contained five charges. Although given this scenario, he was definitely going to look into upgrades if he ever got out of this horrible place. Five also didn't seem like enough.

Was he just being that much of an asshole, that he'd rather believe this was an elaborate lie than acknowledge the fact that she might have been assaulted and traumatized because of him?

He sent people off into danger all the time. He never really saw the results of it. That, too, was part of what he'd wanted to change, why he'd wanted to leave. To know more, to live more, but also to bear the responsibility more too. It hadn't felt right to send others to do his bidding while stuck at home—and safe. Which was why Tovi's insult had hit a nerve.

Now that he was here, it wasn't easy. And it was more than a little disturbing to watch himself cling desperately to this possible out. Had she been through hell, or was this a clever plan he didn't yet understand?

He'd drifted off to sleep still trying to answer that question.

He got his answer when he woke with a start to heavy boots pounding up the hallway toward the cells.

"Mo," he barked. Didn't want to let either of them be caught off guard.

She jerked and shot up, eyes widening, and immediately rolled to a seat. Her hair had slicked to her skull with sweat by now, and the glitter in her eyes had gone dim. She looked groggy and slumped over, but she managed to do it in a way that made her look more than ready to punch someone.

That woman had more fight in her little finger than he had in his whole body. Obviously they both had their strengths, but it sucked he couldn't actually *show* her any of his right now.

A man stopped at the edge of the forcefield. To Doug's surprise, he was conventionally handsome, wavy brown hair, bright blue eyes. But those eyes held an ugly gleam, and his lips wore a sneer. "You worthless little dreck."

Mo regarded him but said nothing.

"You lied about us."

Triumph and relief surged in Doug's chest, at war with apprehension. Because now these men were here, and they hadn't been before.

"I didn't lie about your intent," she said, voice quiet.

"We didn't get to *do* anything to you, and now the captain—" His head cocked to the side as two other men appeared behind him. Then two more.

"You wanted to. You tried to. You wanted to keep me half locked in my armor, so you destroyed it."

"If you think the armor didn't last long, it won't be the only thing. Dang it, Hoshu, are you going to open this door or not?"

She eased to her feet. Her stance was casual, even exhausted looking, shoulders slumped and legs bent. She kept her eyes on the door, easing toward the back of the cell. Preparing for a fight?

Doug gritted his teeth and tried to sit up further on his bunk. He didn't know how he was going to help, but he'd try something. Maybe he could do something with the sheet he had… He swallowed.

The bars groaned and clattered open.

The man stepped over the threshold, swaggering toward Mo. Slowly, casually even. He stopped, narrowed his eyes.

Mo raised her fists, but Doug's stomach sank. At this angle, he could see slight shadows under her eyes.

The man lunged forward, reaching for her neck. Or maybe her wrists or eyes. "Some lessons have to be taught the hard wa—"

But he didn't get to finish as a result of the uppercut that landed in his gut. He grabbed her forearms instead.

She used the grip to yank him closer, not further away, bringing up her knee.

The sound the guy made had even Doug feeling slightly sympathetic, because darn, it sounded like that hurt. It must have hit him hard because he doubled over.

Doug didn't know why anyone would underestimate a soldier that showed up in power armor—maybe assuming they relied on it for battle?—but she was clearly not as exhausted as he'd thought. Another trick? The guy still hadn't let go of her, though.

Mo's knee wasn't done. She brought it up and smashed into the man's face. He flew back, coming down hard on the decking with a crack that made Doug wince in spite of himself.

There were four more of them, though, and now those others surged forward.

Mo didn't stop moving either. She leapt over the original asshole and seized the arm of the closest man to the left of the door. A brutal snapping sound made Doug flinch and the man scream—had she just broken his arm?

At the same time, two of them were trying to circle around and get behind her, both of them ignoring Doug. One of them was so close he could smell the garlic—gross.

Maybe this was his chance. He gathered the fabric of the sheet frantically in his hands, trying to be precise, and then he tossed the sheet in the air over their heads.

To his own surprise, it worked. They looked like maybe they'd been trying to grab her arms from behind, but not expecting the sheet to fall over their heads, they didn't get the chance.

Instead, Mo had precious seconds to dole out another knee to the groin and a vicious kick at one knee. They hadn't really extricated themselves from the sheet before she'd tossed them out of the cell tangled up in it.

Unfortunately, the last two caught her by her arms and forcibly threw her back into the cell rather than actually fighting her. She slid, lunged out again—they threw her back in, harder. She slid across the floor and almost to the back of the cell. One grabbed the original asshole by the collar—who was still lying on the floor and had managed to get trampled at least three times—and hauled him out.

The doors rolled closed.

Mo let out a long, low breath. Other than that she'd been almost preternaturally silent.

He gritted his teeth. If he could, he would have gone to her. Helped her up. Checked on her. Cared for her as much as he could.

And yet he was stuck here. No wonder she thought he talked too much—he did it because it was all he *could* do right now. But that wasn't usually the case. He usually had his floats.

Maybe they were all right and he should try the augmentations again. Maybe he really was just being stubborn. His body might reject the new tech less, although he didn't have much hope really. Except now she needed his help, and he couldn't give it to her.

"You okay?" he said softly, failing to conceal the heavy emotion thick in his voice, the frustration, the anger.

She groaned a little, and her head appeared as she sat up. "Yeah, just a little tumble. Nothing Nova hasn't done in the gym at home."

Home. He smiled instantly at the thought.

By home, she meant the *Audacity*. Not her home planet, or somewhere where family waited for her. But the ship he'd made possible. Not his ship, but he'd had something to do with it. He didn't know why that made him feel better at the moment. Maybe it was knowing that even if he hadn't done much as part of the fight, he'd done things for her in other areas.

Why did he care?

He tried to wait a beat, but he couldn't hold off broaching the subject any longer. "What you told Tovi—a clever deception?"

"I don't know how clever." Coughing, she rose to one knee, then paused. Her face crinkled in pain, then smoothed again. "A deception only because there *happened* to be three of them, and they weren't expecting my attack. Now they are. But now she's also watching them specifically. I was trying to prevent a second attack."

"You just beat the snot out of that guy. Those guys. That should help."

"You'd think. But he didn't learn after the first time, did he? I think I made things worse."

He shrugged. "You're an excellent fighter. I'd be convinced. I must admit, I envy you that."

"I could teach you. If you want."

He raised his eyebrows.

"If we get out of here," she added.

"I'll take you up on that."

"Thanks for the assist."

He raised an eyebrow. "What?"

"The blanket. That would have gone a lot worse for me without that blanket trick."

He snorted. "That's me. Good for ghost costumes and pulling the wool over people's eyes."

She laughed as she sat back down gingerly on the bunk. Her movements were graceful, but the laugh was decidedly not. He was pretty sure she'd just snorted, and he liked her all the better for it. It might not be musical, but it was sincere. Authentic.

Maybe broody people didn't universally hate him after all. Maybe she wasn't annoyed by him, and she was just shy. Or stressed or nervous.

Hell, lots of people made him nervous, but his response was to spew forth, rather than to clam up. College hadn't taught him enough about how to deal with the quieter sort, probably because he'd been too busy talking.

How many colleagues had he talked over or assumed hated him just because they didn't know what to say?

He sighed. What cheery thoughts. Better to focus on something positive. "Thanks for trying to get us out."

She shrugged. "The door was open. Would be foolish not to try."

"Are you all right?" He poured sincerity and conviction into the question, hoping she wouldn't just blow it off this time.

"I'm fine." She sounded uninjured, but bone weary. She hadn't eaten since she'd come, so it couldn't be easy to do all that. Worry gnawed at him as he studied her. In his disappointed silence, her eyes flicked up and met his. "I'm—okay, my shoulder took a pretty hard hit there on the floor. Nothing I can't handle, though. Don't worry about me, okay?"

"Why shouldn't I?"

"Because you have enough to worry about."

He frowned. That wasn't what he'd expected in answer. "What if I want to worry about you?"

"I can't stop you." She winced as she eased onto her back.

He didn't like that answer either, and he found himself worrying about her all the same.

———

ELLEN HAD Kael take the lead after that. For the first time, the tubes dumped her and the men into actual Gray Dragon territory—a stuffy, dark tunnel four levels down. Darker than any of the others. Grime streaked the walls and caked around the floors.

That tunnel opened into a wider one that was more beautiful, and the ceilings were shockingly high, maybe two stories. But the materials were simple—stone, wood, not much plex to be seen. Truthfully, it set Ellen on edge. She was used to steel and glass, not these more ancient, earthy materials. No fliers or landers cruised by or were parked anywhere, but a fair amount of broken debris and refuse lay around in the street.

It was hard not to imagine a young Kael eking out a life among the detritus, and she couldn't say she liked the thought.

Kael zeroed in on someone after about thirty minutes of walking. "See someone I recognize," he murmured over the comm before lowering his helmet. She did so as well and immediately regretted it as the smell of cigar smoke and something gone sour hit her nose. Maybe several things.

The man's eyes skimmed over Kael as he took a drag, then his gaze snapped back, going rigid. "You're—you're—"

"Erol! *Salam.*" Kael's voice was cool.

"You're dead." He danced back, out of the main corridor into a single-story alley.

Ellen cocked her head as the three of them trailed him. "I assure you we're all very alive."

"Clearly." Erol ran a hand over his sweat-slicked face as his back hit the wall behind him and he jumped. This level was a lot warmer than the last. He started saying something in another language.

Ellen reached up to raise the helmet and engage the translator, but Kael shook his head. "Stick to Common," he said to the man.

"They said—they said you were dead." Erol jabbed a finger at Kael's chest.

"I'm not. Mostly."

That definitely didn't ease the fear in the man's eyes. Ellen's eyes narrowed. Fear of what? "We're looking for someone."

"Hey—I only watch the street corners for Maloof, I don't know anything about it." The man sidestepped into an alcove against the alley's side. A breeze blew through, cooling the air and waving his grayish robes.

They followed, and his eyes only widened further. Nervous much?

"Why should I be looking for Maloof?" asked Kael.

Erol winced. "No reason."

"Very convincing," Ellen said.

A nervous laugh escaped the man.

Kael stepped forward, making Erol flinch. He jumped again when Kael placed a hand on his shoulder. And patted. "Relax, my friend. I am only here to say *Salam* to you. I don't want any trouble."

The soothing tone of his voice froze the man, but then after a long stare between them, his shoulders eased. He spared a glance at Ellen and bowed very slightly.

"*Salam,* nice to meet you," she murmured. She wasn't going to hide, but she didn't need to invite trouble either. Belatedly, she managed a small, polite bow back.

"Where have you been, you devil?" he said, returning his gaze to Kael. "Who are these people?"

"It's a long story. They're new friends."

"If you're not looking for Maloof, then who?"

"You ever meet my girlfriend Asha?"

"Former girlfriend," Ellen cut in.

Erol looked from her to Kael. "Your new woman have a bone to pick with your old one?"

Kael blanched.

"I'm his *boss*," she cut in quickly. Hey, it wasn't a lie. She'd stiffened in spite of herself. Worse, Dane had tensed too.

Erol the lookout didn't appear convinced, but he didn't press it. "I have not seen your Asha. But I don't see many people. Galaxy's a big place."

"You're a *lookout*," said Kael. "You stand in the street all day. All you do is look."

"For people who count, I see nothing. I see the people who walk by this street, the people who work with my friend up the street," he smiled tentatively, "and my family at home."

"What about a police officer or two?"

Erol narrowed his eyes but said nothing.

"C'mon," she said flatly. Kael waved at her to ease up. He was probably right, his old friend the lookout was fidgeting more.

"I'm a simple man, with a simple life," said Erol. "I don't get caught up with luscious women or influential men."

"Luscious?" Ellen drawled. If this guy was trying to push her buttons, he was succeeding.

The man mimed curves in the air, until he caught sight of Kael's face and danced back, this time toward the street. He checked for whatever he was watching for, then turned back to them.

"Does Asha run around with these influential men?" Kael said slowly, the edge in his voice unmistakable.

"I told you, I wouldn't know. I don't know anything."

"You know who is above you."

"Yes, but I've worked *hard* not to move up."

"Why?"

"I'm not like you. I'm content on this corner."

"Liar."

"Lookouts don't get killed," said the man. "Isn't that reason enough to be humble?"

"What do you mean—you're not like him?" Ellen cut in.

"Oh, this excellent man was up and coming in the Dragons," he said, throwing a sudden arm around Kael and patting him on the chest. "Dangerous. Ambitious."

"No, I wasn't."

"Sure you were. You were Abrams' favorite street man. Nobody was as scary as you."

"I was sixteen."

"Young men are dangerous because they think they don't have anything to lose. Even if they do, they don't realize it yet."

Kael winced but said nothing.

"Young lions always challenge the old. It's the way of the world. You were going to climb high, my friend. And challenge many. Maybe someone noticed that before you did."

"Whatever you say."

The lookout eyed her. "He always had this way of convincing people, this look in his eye. 'I don't want to shoot you, but I will in a heartbeat if you don't do what I say.'"

Ellen smirked. "Can't imagine."

Kael shot her a sideways glare.

"I remember because it wasn't a year after you were gone, and Abrams and six more of his captains were either dead or sold off. After that, a dozen streetrunners too. Maybe more. Kept my head down after that."

Kael's eyebrows shot up. "What? Abrams too? Dead?"

"Well. I thought you were dead. But here you are. But yes, you were the start, but not the end."

"That's... odd. Do you remember who spread the news that I was dead?"

"Sorry, my friend. It was a long time ago."

"Now why would they lie?" Ellen murmured, eyes locking with Kael's.

"Between you and me..." Erol leaned out the street and glanced both ways, apparently having decided to trust them. Or to pretend to trust them. When he spoke, his voice was hushed. "Some people said Maloof had something against Abrams and stabbed him in the back. Other people said he was just making money, that it wasn't personal— but that he still stabbed him in the back."

"You mean he wanted a bigger cut of the profits?"

"No—conscripts. Some outfits will lay out excellent coin for fresh meat." He rubbed his fingers together.

Kael blinked in stunned silence for a moment.

Ellen picked up the slack. "You think this Maloof was making money selling off foot soldiers, and he had to kill Abrams along the way because they didn't agree on it?"

The accusation was too clear, too close to home. Erol held up both palms. "Hey, I don't know anything."

"Of course not. Nothing at all. In fact, we've never met and never talked to you." Ellen lowered her chin.

That did seem to put him at greater ease, but he still hesitated, sizing her up. "It's possible they might have been covering up whatever underhanded shit they did to your man here—"

She winced at that reference, opened her mouth, then shut it.

"—because Abrams was still alive, and they knew he would object. Like you said—why lie? I can't see Abrams ever agreeing to selling off skilled people."

Ellen nodded slowly. Kael still seemed lost in thought.

"You got any more questions?" she said to Kael. He slowly shook his head, so she turned to the lookout. "All right then. Here's a gift. In honor of how little we know each other. Don't tell anyone this happened, and we won't need to share that news either." She held out a folded bill of fifty rial.

The guy smiled and pocketed the bill so smoothly it was like it vanished the moment it left her hand. Then he wriggled his eyebrows. "For five thousand, I can tell all sorts of other things."

She shook her head. "Thanks, but no thanks."

"Well, you deserve more. My friend up the street has all kinds of good things... I keep the lookout for him, I can tell him to give you a deal, if you like?"

"We've got plenty of entertainment on our ship already. Thanks, though."

"Well, you let me know if you change your mind, pretty one. They do make chems to help people relax. You look like you could use a little help relaxing."

Punching him and taking the rial back suddenly looked very tempting, so she turned on her heel. They strode away and then headed back toward the hostel. She raised her helmet and switched on the comm. "If someone starts telling me to take a vacation, I'll know this planet is getting to me." Both men snickered. "What do we do now?" she said.

"We find someone higher on the food chain," Kael shot back.

"That was productive, though," she replied. "I'm surprised he's lasted that long as a lookout, spilling that many beans."

"Fifteen plus years at it?" Kael winced. "That's gotta have been a demotion somewhere along the way. He can claim he wants that all day, but it's pathetic."

"Loose lips sink ships," she muttered.

"What?"

"Never mind."

"That should be a job for a kid—like I was back in the day."

"Maybe he's a *really* good lookout," said Dane, "and doesn't have the marbles for much else."

Ellen laughed. "Maybe. All right, let's go regroup. Then we'll do another sweep and look for a bigger fish to fry." They murmured agreement, and she switched off the open channel.

Barely a second later, Kael's voice filled her ears. "Hey, what do you mean we've got plenty of entertainment? Not that I want any of their crap chems but..."

She glanced at the helmet readout—it was just the two of them on the channel, he'd cut Dane out. "I was referring to *you*."

He choked on a laugh as they climbed the hill.

"Careful, or Dane's going to notice you chuckling over there."

"I *am* your man, you know."

She barked out a laugh. "Did you really think you needed to remind me?"

"Just double checking."

"Look, I didn't like hearing that either. I'd rather not specifically deny it like that, especially in front of Dane. Hey, what was that all about this morning anyway?"

"He demanded to know my 'intentions' when he caught me admiring your… many positive attributes."

"My what?"

"Your ass."

Her cheeks were instantly engulfed in heat. "You were admiring my ass? And I didn't notice, but the two of you did?"

"You were sleepy. He got lucky in his timing. We're both men of that sort of persuasion that can appreciate a nice—"

"Did you work things out, or whatever?" She had literally no idea how that conversation could go.

"I think we found some common ground. And I'll leave it at that for now."

She smiled in the privacy of her suit, although she had a slight concern that they'd discussed the pros and cons of her rear end in detail. She knew Dane wouldn't, though. "Hey—maybe we should talk through the gang roles and structure some more. I'm going to add Dane back, okay?"

"Of course, Commander Ryu," he said, his voice darkly serious and also amused. And way, way too sexy—damn. Shoving that aside, she re-added Dane.

"Kael—what kind of stuff did you end up having to do for the Gray Dragons? You were a lookout like that guy? Dane, I thought we should sync up on some background."

"I'm up for hearing some background," said Dane, a challenge in his voice. Damn it, she'd brought him on this mission in hopes of *less* drama.

Kael cleared his throat. "Yeah, everybody starts as a lookout. It's the bottom."

"Lookout for law enforcement?"

"Mostly yes. And rivals."

"How do the Gray Dragons make their money?"

"Well, in my day it was a combination of protection services, extortion, smuggling, and chem sales. But it wasn't like I was at the highest levels—nobody gave me a briefing on the damn business plan."

She snorted.

"I just know what I was around. Nobody told me some slice of the pie was selling warm bodies to merc outfits. To put it politely."

Two men in the gray uniform of the Faros police were leaning against the wall at the next intersection. As her team strode on past, she could have sworn they were watching. Hard. Their eyes bored into her back even as the three of them moved out of sight. What was that all about?

She cleared her throat. "Yeah, I wonder about them selling people into conscription. Doesn't seem like good business. Why force people to join your gang just to sell them to the meat market? Why not just sell them without having them join you, if that's what you need to do? Why bother to conscript? Or give you a tattoo?"

"More valuable with training?" Dane offered.

"Could be. This planet has a healthy population, but it's not *that* overpopulated that people aren't useful. And if you were up and coming—"

"That's debatable." Kael coughed.

"Hey, didn't you stay alive longer than most Theroki?"

He hesitated. "Well, yeah."

"So we have empirical evidence of some natural talent."

"Or a whole lot of luck."

"Oh, come off it. We all know you're good."

Kael said nothing.

"What I'm saying is, why sell off your best people?"

Dane jumped into the silence. "Cause that's what they're buying? Cause there's plenty of others to take one guy's place?"

"Maybe." Still didn't seem like a good enough reason to train them or onboard them.

"Or what?" Kael asked.

"Or there's something else going on. Something personal." She set her jaw. More and more, this seemed likely.

"Something related to Abrams," said Kael.

"Yes. Or Asha."

"Or both."

———

VIVAAN SIGHED at the armor case. The contents were spread out on the cold metal floor—the decking, as Kael had taught him—in a corner of Dremer's lab she hadn't been using. His ass was falling asleep from sitting there, and the decking was damn cold. Electrical parts of all kinds sat on shelves around him, blinking eerily in the low lighting.

He'd left the overhead lighting off because he couldn't have his mother realize he was in here. She'd told him a week ago to stop obsessing over this. Never mind that "obsessing over things for weeks" was exactly how her mind worked to create her inventions. How many times had he had to remind her to eat?

"There's nothing in this stupid case, Xi. I've checked it twice, now." He'd checked it last week when she'd first brought it up, but he'd been in the process of re-examining every single thing Merith had owned. Which was part of why his mother had started to frown at his so-called obsession.

But he refused to believe Merith hadn't left some kind of clue.

It seemed far more likely, statistically, that he was simply bad at this. Being new to really *doing* detective work, he couldn't feel too bad about that. But he had studied and read lots of books, and it was a bit of a hit to the ego. And maybe that was why he just couldn't shake the conviction that it was more likely that he was missing something than that she had been the perfect criminal.

"But you said you wanted to check everything three times," Xi replied.

He sighed. "I did, didn't I?"

"I do not know what you expect to find, but yes."

"Could there be data in here?"

"I have scanned Merith's suit data as well as the data from her terminal and uploaded it to the network. You and Commander Ryu have already reviewed it. Twice."

There had been some utilities Adan was able to identify as hacking programs, but nothing that told them anything. He played with the pauldron idly before fitting it back in the case. "You said this thing cleans itself. Maybe it shuffled out some evidence? Does it have a waste collection system?"

"It automatically emptied itself last week into the vacuum of space. Her suit was not worn since then."

"Well, that's just great."

He sighed and picked up the neck and helmet piece, tossing it around in his hands. It was lighter than he had expected.

What had it been like to be her? To live on this ship for two years or so, all the while planning to betray everyone you knew? Maybe not everyone, but all the people you spent any time with. What could have possibly driven her to do that? Did she have some deep, burning, ideological hatred? Greed? He hated that he didn't even have a theory of a motive. He knew next to nothing about her, and he'd been practically living in her cabin. If only he could really walk in her shoes, maybe he could figure out where he ought to look.

Her shoes or… her armor?

He glanced to the left, then the right. Nobody was in the lab, or Levereaux's across the hall. No footsteps nearby in the hallway.

He pulled the helmet over his head, enveloping himself in darkness. To his surprise, it fit fairly well. He wiggled it around a bit, trying to get a better fit. It probably was for someone smaller than—

His finger hit some kind of button. He felt it depress, and he jumped as the helmet tightened around his throat.

It stopped fairly quickly with a hiss, so he realized it had simply sealed him in. Given how important breather and bio-containment functionality was, that probably was a good feature and made sense. However, if he couldn't deactivate it... Was he going to have to stumble around in the hallway, blind with a helmet on his head, until he found someone who could help take it off?

Cheeks flaming, he groped at the sides harder now. Another button depressed under his third finger, but the helmet's death grip on his neck didn't loosen.

It did, however, spring to life. A photograph of the skyline of somewhere on Capital appeared, then faded to the room around him.

"Xi?" he whispered.

"Yes, Vivaan? I can interface with and hear you inside the suit."

He sighed in relief. Worst case scenario—she could tell him out to get out of this thing.

"First, is this helmet aware of who I am?"

"Yes. It has logged you on to your network profile based on a facial reading and retinal scan."

He'd wondered as much from the Capital skyline. He'd set that as a background somewhere on his comm. "Can you log me on as Merith?"

"Certainly."

The screen faded to black. Then light bloomed in front of him, the display showing a glimmer of an exotic savannah before fading to the room again. There were readouts around the edges of his peripheral vision and a few stacks of data in the corners. What were they? And could he access them?

"Xi, can you save a snapshot of the data on this screen as is? I want it for evidence. Complete as you can."

"Done. What else can I help you with?"

"What are those docs down in the corner?"

"I do not detect any docs."

He frowned. "If there were docs, how could I access them?"

"Staring and blinking may sometimes bring them to center screen, as well as an extended stare or a voice command to the suit directly. These are customizable, however, so it is difficult to say."

"Suit, enlarge docs."

Nothing happened.

He stared hard at the white squares. Harder. Harder.

He blinked.

The doc he was staring at swooped up and into full view. Of course it was the last thing he'd tried. And the not customized option. But what he read stopped any chagrin—or any other thoughts at all. His mouth fell open.

"You look as though you can see a document. But I cannot see it."

"Maybe it's hidden from you somehow," he murmured.

"Would you share what it says?"

Slurping a little—oh no, he was drooling, lucky there was no one around to notice that bit of charming behavior—he nodded.

"It reads…

Kitten.

This is excellent news. Thank you, you know I've been seeking the location of the Simmons compound for a long time. Now I'll finally be able to complete my mission, after all these years. The dangerous research there can finally be put to an end.

I've already left for Tetra. Your Patron is as good as dead.

I regret to inform you, however, your assistance is no longer necessary. I am terminating your employment—and our relationship—as of this email. Your bonus will be in your account shortly.

Good luck surviving Ellen Ryu. I know you're good, but you've never been that good. You were always better in the sack. Should probably have kept you there. But then I'd never be on my way to Tetra.

C'est la vie. It was good knowing you.

~ Q

"Oh my God." He automatically tried to pull off the helmet, and it didn't budge. He lurched back, his elbow crashing into something as several parts fell down over his shoulders and head.

But it had actually happened. He'd found something.

"I've made a note and am alerting the commander," Xi said briskly.

"Wait—Xi—help me get out of this thing!"

CHAPTER TWELVE

DAY 16-17

MO DREW her knees to her chest, wrapped her arms around them, and shivered. The heat had been awful, but they had a shiny new problem now. Shortly after her altercation with Rolf and his buddies, the temperature had changed. Had dropped.

She was pretty sure she hadn't seen the last of those assholes. Had she miscalculated in her comment to Tovi? They might have returned, without Tovi watching, but they might also have decided that getting shocked once was enough.

But now the temperature had plummeted. At first it was a relief, but it wasn't long before it grew uncomfortable. At some point, it'd be dangerous.

And through it all, Simmons just sat there looking frustrated and hot. Not temperature hot—oh, it didn't matter.

"Don't you even want to button your shirt in this cold?" The words just burst out of her all of a sudden, into a long silence. But just looking at him like that was making her colder. Yeah, keep telling yourself that.

"Sorry, the buttons are broken." He ducked his head. When he met her gaze, his expression was chagrinned, but also relieved she was talking to him. Another pang of guilt hit her at being such a bad conversationalist. "Maybe it happened on the way here? Maybe it was already like that…?" He shrugged, wincing at the same time. "I was dressed for the heat, what can I say."

Her teeth chattered. "It's like we found a wormhole from a jungle to an ice cap."

"Do you think it'll freeze? How low can you go?" He smirked.

Was that a *limbo* reference? She decided to ignore it, lest she embarrass herself. She was pretty sure Jenny and Zhia had played that on R&R at a club once. Mo hadn't joined in—not her thing. Then again, what at a club really was her thing? "I really hope it doesn't freeze, or we'll start freezing too." She was on the fence as to whether they'd let that happen. Why bring them all this way to just turn them into popsicles? And yet it kept getting colder.

Shouting somewhere on the ship echoed in the silence. A spike of worry shot through her, something about the sound reminding her more of battles fought than ordinary days on an orderly ship. What if they mutinied? Or abandoned ship for some reason?

She'd thought this was retaliation, but what if it were a malfunction instead? What if the ship had a real problem? Would they actually do anything to save the prisoners in the brig in an emergency? What if they just left them here to freeze to death?

God—she couldn't think like this, but this cold was starting to get to her. "I need to think about something else. Anything else. Something not cold."

"Oh! Sorry. Of course, of course. I, uh… Let's see."

She stared down at her knees. He might be frustrated, but he was tapping his chin, doing his best to humor her. She'd always thought he seemed kind. Up close, he seemed even more so.

She had to try harder to talk to him. He deserved better than her brutal awkwardness.

"Mo is short for something, isn't it?" he asked finally.

She looked up, frowning. Opened her mouth.

"Wait—let me try to remember. Good for the brain."

"It's Mosi." She sighed. "You won't remember. If I had one blowtorch for every time I'd heard Maureen or Molly, we'd be out of here."

He chuckled. "Mosi, that's right. Mosi Taazbaa Mihio."

His pronunciation wasn't perfect, but it wasn't butchered either. Her gaze snapped up to meet his. "How did you remember that? Do you have a photographic memory or something?"

"I wish." He frowned, looked like he was thinking hard. "Cat? Cat who raids? Cat who comes out raiding? Warrior cat? Did you pick that? It's cute. I'm a little rusty."

Her mouth fell open. "You speak Navajo?" She called her people *Dine'* to herself, of course, but when not on Keyah or with outsiders, this was what they knew.

"Not really. I know a few words. I wouldn't claim fluency or anything. What can I say, I'm a history dork. And an encryption dork. And a dork with a lot of time on his hands avoiding the sun. So… yes."

She just stared at him, doing nothing at all to better her poor reputation as a terrible person to talk to and creepy staring girl.

"The stories of the Code Talkers are inspiring," he said. It seemed to be nervous babbling, trying to fill the time, her stare, the cold, fend it all off, something. She couldn't blame him. "And I also looked it up when you first applied. To double check my translation."

She frowned. He'd actually looked at stuff like that?

"I have a friend who would send me messages back and forth too. We're kind of… dorks."

She frowned harder. She had to keep this going. Say something, anything. "This friend… would they be a girl?"

He chuckled harder now. "As if I have friends that are gir—" His expression sharpened. "I mean… No. Why?"

She shrugged non-committally, a smile tugging at the corner of her mouth. So the handsome patron was single. Not that that meant anything. She was the reserved, silent type, and as such, probably his purest form of torture. And he was her boss.

But duly noted.

"Wait. Can we use that to help us at all?" he asked. He looked suddenly excited he might have something to contribute to their predicament. "Our captors probably don't speak Navajo."

She waved it off. "They could look it up as easily as you did. Or they could have translators." Besides… it felt a little personal. He might be her boss and someone she respected, but to her people, he was still an outsider.

"Standard off-the-shelf translators don't include Navajo. I added it to our suit translators, but it's not common. C'mon, teach me something."

"Doug, they can hear anything I would teach you." She met his gaze flatly. Maybe they could use the code in a way… but they'd be lucky if he didn't break into an hour-long historical lecture revealing every possible secret. For a smart man, he wasn't used to surveillance. Ironic, really.

He blinked. "Oh. Uh. Good point. Sorry. I know, I know. You just want me to shut the hell up."

"Not at all."

"Yes, you do."

"Okay, maybe a little, but only about the *important* things."

He blinked up at the ceiling, then down at the floor for a while. She had the sense he didn't know what she was referring to. "Admit it, I'm driving you crazy."

She shivered again. So cold. "No," she insisted. "You're not, and I don't want you to shut the hell up."

"You don't need to lie about it, it's pretty obvious."

"It is *not*, because it's not true, dammit." She scowled at him now over her knees.

"Look, you don't have to humor me. I know I'm a chatterbox. There's no one I can't annoy!" His voice was mock cheery, and he was smiling, but the undercurrent of pain in his eyes was suddenly strong. "Even you!"

"The cold is getting to us," she grumbled. "You are not annoying me. You were trying to help distract me from the cold."

He jerked back, surprised. "I was. I mean—I was, but you still seemed annoyed."

"Because it's fragging cold! Just because I'm quiet doesn't mean I'm annoyed. Just because I'm annoyed doesn't mean it's *at* you."

His head cocked to one side, as if those ideas were truly revelatory information he'd never considered before. "But you also don't want to teach me your language. Or talk about freezing to death."

"Yeah. What's behind door number four, Alex?"

His eyebrows twitched up briefly. He said nothing else though. Either his chatterbox had run out, or he was mad.

Damn it. Maybe she should leave her damn cabin more often if this was so hard. It had been three days, but still.

"Do you know if they make personality implants?" she muttered quietly.

He frowned. "What, like Kael's? I mean, I wouldn't call that desirable, but—"

"No, like a chatterbox you could just install in my throat." She made a cube-shaped gesture toward her vocal cords.

He snorted, but then frowned quickly, looking suddenly concerned. "I don't know, but if they don't have it, they really should. Then I could install them in my robots and never have to trouble anyone like you ever again."

She winced, hard. His head ducked, as if he regretted the comment, but he didn't take it back. This wasn't his usual self. She needed to get them thinking, get them focused on something else, something warm.

"What was it like living on the beach?" she muttered, voice almost impossible to hear over the hum of the ship. "I mean, I get it—hell on earth, bad for floats. What else?"

His expression was stunned, but he answered her. After a long, awkward moment. "Uh, it was… Well, hot. Humid. Frequent burns. Women who snubbed me. Annoying parents. Even more annoying wealthy tourists." He waved a hand in the air. "You know, paradise."

She laughed and felt a little warmer. "Your *parents'* paradise, you said."

"Yeah. The sound of the ocean is nice at night."

"Why didn't you leave?"

"I was working on it, actually. This wasn't the plan though." He grinned, and she mustered a weak smile back. "But I had been dragging my feet. It's just so final leaving them. My parents, I mean." He faltered, paused, continued. "Wish I knew where they were. Anyway, they wanted me out of the nest, I think. But there was no easy choice near there; everything was a bad fit. All the major Puritan cities, with this?" He gestured at his lower half. "I mean, some of them are more liberal than others, but it's not my thing."

"They frown on floats?"

"Some extremists even frown on assistive *chairs*. Idiots. They frown on everything. I'd probably have to try to get the stupid augments and hope I didn't reject them and could hide them or pay people off. Totally not worth it. And Union cities were just such a long way away. And the network on Tetra was so good… Wouldn't have been much better in a city, even if I spared no expense. Too many Puritan politicians and A-listers love the place, so the infrastructure is top notch. And I probably would have had to keep more of a low profile most places, at least at first."

"What do you mean 'would have had'? You still can go."

He raised his eyebrows. "You think we're actually getting out of here?"

She gave him her flat stare. What did he want her to do, send an autographed hologram to their captors? "Hmm," was all she said.

He shrugged his response.

Damn. She'd destroyed his momentum, shut him down without meaning to. Again. She mustered another sentence. "Ryu will come for us."

"I hope you're right."

"Even if she can't, Tovi didn't say she wants to kill us."

"Not yet."

"Maybe she has some use for us. Or at least you."

"Trophy mounted on the wall is my guess."

She snickered. "For someone wearing a shirt with dancing hedgehogs on it, you're quite the downer."

"Sorry. It's not my usual mode, I swear. It's just so damn cold in here."

"Fine, fine. I'll teach you a few words. Something's got to keep us sane, right?"

His eyes lit up. "Really? I mean, if you promise not to kill me when my pronunciation sucks."

"I don't have a weapon."

"One, I don't think that would keep you from killing me, and two, I noticed that is not a promise ensuring my future health."

She smiled. "Why teach you words if I intended to kill you?"

"I think it'd be more of a blind rage."

A giggle escaped her finally, and his eyes lit up even further at that. "Fine. I promise not to kill you for your pronunciation. All other motives are still on the table."

"That's more than fair. What's the first word?"

———

A SHARP RING went off inside her suit. "Commander Ryu, *Audacity* requesting communications."

"Yes, Xi?" she said. "What is it?" Why the hell wasn't Xi just delivering the message? Her scan of their temporary room showed ninety-eight percent complete—almost safe. Each time they returned, one of them scanned it for if anything had been touched. Ninety-nine percent.

"Commander Ryu, *Audacity* requesting communications. High interference requires additional bandwidth for encrypted communications. Commander Ryu, *Audacity*—"

She pursed her lips. Great. "Okay, okay, I get it. Apparently Xi is trying to make a call to us and can't get through." One hundred percent. She sighed. "Okay, we're clear to go in."

Kael shut the door behind them as Dane pulled the comm unit out of his suit. That wasn't his job—Merith had been the main comm officer—but as she'd rarely been boots on the ground, other people tended to learn the skillset. He set to work hooking up their holodisplay to the wired line that would feed into the satellites—and a better connection to *Audacity*.

Light shimmered in the air over the thing. The three of them waited in their suits, slumped on the bunks, as the encrypted messages downloaded. The specks of light swirled, galaxy-like, before gradually forming an image of a face.

Kael started. "Xi—is that you?"

The corners of the mouth on the face twitched. "It is a prototype. What do you think?"

Ellen's eyes widened. "Did you pick an avatar for yourself, Xi?"

"Yes, Commander. I hope my selection of a face was acceptable."

"Sure. Who doesn't like to have an avatar or three?"

"She also wants a physical one, though," Kael said, his voice quiet, like an aside.

Xi blinked and turned eyes from Kael to Ellen. That had to be an illusion, right? The holodisplay didn't actually let you see anything but a vid feed, not like a camera swinging or actually seeing them in three-dimensional space. Xi was likely attempting to calculate their location and build an illusion based on the direction of their voices and locations in the video. Interestingly detailed.

"No immediate objections, but I need to think that over, and now is not the time," Ellen said. "What's the comm message, Xi?"

"A high priority message has arrived in text form six hours ago. I have not been able to reach you. It is from Nova."

A fist tightened in Ellen's gut. "Nova? Not Mo? Read the message."

"Commander. Located the Simmons compound. Estimated sixty-five percent destroyed. During reconnaissance, Sgt. Mihio was captured by an unknown force, wearing armor C7-quality or higher, unmarked. We have limited video surveillance but nothing clearly actionable. Fern and I evaded capture and are in pursuit. Sorry, Commander."

Her chest went hollow. Mo. Fragging hell. As if losing Doug wasn't enough. She shoved the pain that welled up into a corner with practiced determination. Fight now, grief later.

She cleared her throat. "Any sign of Doug or his parents?"

"None mentioned. I will send a reply inquiring. It seemed as though Nova sent the info in a hurry, probably knowing it would take time to get here."

"Does it say anything else about Mo's capture? Seems notable that they captured her rather than shot her on sight."

"It does not mention anything further, but yes, the word choice of capture is specific. They must have witnessed it."

Dane swore under his breath. Kael was glaring at Xi's head floating over the comm.

"There is additional info, Commander, when you are ready."

"I'm ready."

"Chanaya Persad would like you to know that Adan and Zhia's augmentation surgeries are complete. Both are healing well. Rachel and Jenny are scheduled for tomorrow."

"Good to hear."

"There's more. One moment please." There was a brief silence.

"Commander?" The voice was Vivaan's now, and the holo changed to a rough approximation of his face. Wow, the connection really wasn't great, was it? Really rough, as if he were made of a kid's blocks rather than pixels.

"I'm here, Vivaan. Go ahead."

"I found something. About Merith."

They all raised their eyebrows, exchanged looks.

"Well?" Kael said. "Spit it out, man."

"Oh, sorry. I was reinspecting her armor at Xi's request. On a whim, I put on Merith's helmet. Inside, I found a letter she'd hidden from Xi within its file storage system. It contained a message from someone referred to as 'Q.' He appeared to have hired her to find Doug's location. And, uh, was probably a former lover."

Ellen tightened a fist. "Q—that has to be Quentin Davenmore."

"I reached the same conclusion," said Xi.

"Xi is sending you the actual files," Vivaan continued. "I think we managed to unlock them for her to see. But with that, I thought—what else have I missed? So I went over everything else a fourth time—"

"*Fourth?*" Kael grunted.

"—and I realized the d-bars in her things were expired. Ten years ago. Why have no personal belongings at all but hang on to expired d-bars? When you can get all the d-bars you want in the mess?"

"Good question," said Ellen.

"Because they weren't d-bars."

Kael actually got to his feet now. "You're kidding. They weren't d-bars?"

"Nope. It was a communicator—sent messages outside the ship's network, whenever it could find an independent relay. She had a bunch of messages saved there, back and forth from this Q. We've sent everything to your suits. It also allowed her to download utilities that Xi would have blocked and bring them into our network."

"I monitor the ship downloads for anything that would pose a risk to myself," said Xi. "She had a dozen very dangerous executables."

"And that was how she was able to take Xi down temporarily in the attack," Vivaan continued. "And the worst part is—the last message from this Q guy is him *dumping* her. He says, thanks for the address, I'm headed to Tetra, have a nice life."

"Now that's cold," murmured Dane.

"So was *that* why she was going to Tetra?" Ellen said. "Because she was trying to catch up with Q and probably punch him in the face?"

"I had the same hypothesis," said Xi. "Well, not the assault part."

"So she wasn't thinking," Kael murmured. "Wasn't planning anything."

Dane shook his head. "She was just furious—and trying to catch up to whoever this Q guy was."

"I think it was an old classmate of Doug's," said Ellen. "Doug thought the guy was after a friend of theirs—the woman in Ninshabur Institute we tried to visit."

"But that wasn't the real target," said Xi. "Our revised hypothesis should be that Quentin Davenmore was actually after Doug."

Ellen bit her lip. "Or he knew Doug was watching and had to take him out first. Doug's attack doesn't prove the woman here *isn't* in danger."

"Accurate," said Xi.

"So this is why the diagnostics haven't found any dead man's switch or sabotage in the ship, I think," offered Vivaan. "The hijacking was unplanned."

"Yeah," said Ellen. "Call off those searches. I think our diags are done."

"Yes, Commander," said Xi.

"So the question is—how do we find this Q guy? And if we do, will we find Doug?"

———

AFTER ALL THE NEWS, Kael sighed with relief when Ellen decided the three of them would sort through Merith's files before heading out on the hunt for clues again. Being on Faros at all was getting under his skin, without all this.

By the time they'd read through the—mostly boring—messages between Q and Merith, it was nearing lunch, so Dane ventured out again to find them something to eat.

"Something crunchy," Kael said, giving his eyebrows a quick raise.

"Very funny." Dane shook his head as he shut the door.

"Do you actually like them, or are you just teasing him?" Ellen said, lowering the tablet she'd been reading on. Her shoulders relaxed a bit, probably relieved to get a break—from reading, or from pretending there was nothing going on between them.

He gave her a crooked smile, lifted one shoulder and let it drop. "I've eaten a lot worse. Couldn't always afford food here. As in, none at all. So I'm not turning my nose up."

"Yeah, but do you actually like it?"

He wrinkled his nose at her. "Yeah, okay? I do."

She made a face at him. "Have I told you lately that men are disgusting?" She lifted the tablet again and started scrolling.

He snorted. "Most of the time you seem to find me pretty not disgusting. Most of the time you seem to like me." He set his own tablet aside and stood to stretch.

"Maybe you just see what you want to see." She pretended to be engrossed in her reading.

"Maybe—" He bent, leaned in between her and the tablet, and pressed a quick kiss against her mouth. "—so do you."

She just stared back for a moment, eyes burning and alight with a good kind of fire. But they couldn't risk getting carried away. He eased away and sat down, and she eyed the tablet, took a deep breath.

"Just as we start getting closer to Arakovic—now we have this Q to worry about."

"Are they related?" he asked.

"I don't think so. Hard to say for sure, of course."

He took her cue and tried to read the boring missives one more time. But he'd had enough of chasing Merith's tail and getting nothing for it. He glanced over at her instead. Her eyes were intense, insatiable, glittering as they devoured information. What would she do if he tried to steal her attention from these files? He could caress her leg with his toe or steal another kiss.

They didn't have much time alone, and he didn't want to spend it reading and ignoring each other. Was there something they could talk about? Something productive, because otherwise he might have to just start telling food-related horror stories to draw that laser-like focus his way.

He cleared his throat. "I think I've gotten all I'm going to get out of these. You?"

"Yeah, I keep looking for a missed detail. But none of it is leading us to Doug right now."

"Want to ponder something else?"

"Shoot."

"Hypothetical scenario. Let's say our theories are true and there's this... Arakovic army. You're the commander of her force. What do you do?"

She grimaced. "God... I wonder if that was literally what she had in mind." She cast the tablet aside. "Well, it's a guerrilla or a paramilitary force. Sort of like us. More ill-equipped, but larger. Not huge numbers, but not tiny. Agile. Especially if the units truly are one collective hive mind."

"I have no idea how that would work, but I don't like it."

"Trust me, so do I. Let's see. I'd use them to strike hard, but surgically. Strategic targets. Take out important power centers or key infrastructure or…" She stopped short.

"Or what?"

"Or infiltrate. Take them over through the inside. In the Union, we used bribery or threats at times. Few planets were valuable enough and also powerful enough to merit a real forced takeover, and the few that might have qualified were already in the Union. I know they have a spy program they never told us jarheads much about, but we did ops on their info sometimes. Every fighting force has its share of subterfuge or infiltration techniques. Our team uses digital nukes— hacking—to accomplish the same ends."

"Doug is not building an army, though."

"No… But why is she building one? For what purpose specifically? Does she want wealth, an empire?"

"Didn't you say she wants peace? An end to the fighting."

"True. So how do you bring peace?"

He thought about the strange dream he'd had, but how could he just throw a dream out there? The weird workings of his subconscious weren't relevant.

She continued, thinking aloud. "Maybe you could force people to stop fighting, declare someone the winner? Arakovic's toolkit contains mind control. She can literally control people—or have someone control them for her."

"You don't think she's got a chip herself?"

Ellen frowned. "You know, I've always assumed she didn't and never would. Not sure why though. I have no evidence either way. None that I remember, anyway."

"Okay, so strategic strikes on infrastructure or infiltration. Infiltrating what exactly? Just stealing secrets? To sell?"

"No. She doesn't want money. She wants peace. So maybe it's infiltrating the planet itself—the governmental systems. Could a lone telepath force someone to sign a peace deal? If she wanted to control a government, would she need someone on the ground? Someone acting on her behalf? How hard and how many telepaths does it take to operate someone like a puppet?"

He swallowed. "You're thinking of that zombie who shot me. The one asleep on the ship."

"We don't know it was him that shot you."

"He's the only one left for me to hold a grudge against." He smiled at her.

She rolled her eyes playfully in return.

"So they infiltrated Capital then?"

"It would explain the coma. And the authentic ID. Maybe he was a real Capital inspector, and now he's cut off. And their inspectors are working for Arakovic now?"

He stretched his arms over his head, yawning. "Seems to fit. That might explain why they busted through the windows rather than knocked on the door."

"If infiltration was her goal, what can get in her way? Persad's technology is the one thing we know about."

"Why isn't every government after it then?" he asked. "And after her?"

"For all we know, they are. Maybe she kept it secret enough. But maybe governments don't see the need as dire. Telepaths are mostly helpful. Kentt said they're taught early on not to control minds. She... insinuated that those that do are murdered by other telepaths, because otherwise all of them might be exterminated."

"By who? By us?" Something in his gut twisted at this notion, and the memory of Isa and Kentt sitting in the mess quietly flashed past him. Isa had never tried to directly control anyone... had she?

"I guess so."

"Couldn't they stop us from murdering them with their mind control?"

"One person, yes. Fifty people maybe. But I have to think there's a limit to the number of people one telepath could manipulate. My unit had forty-two, and it was... challenging. So if she wants to infiltrate these places, she can't just take over telepathically."

"Maybe that's where the muscle comes in."

She nodded. "And she doesn't need to control all of them, just like governments don't need to bribe citizens, they just need to bribe key figures. But the inspector from Capital did have the cybernetic hookups. Had she infiltrated Capital deeply enough to have all of their law enforcement augmented?"

"Seems expensive."

"They've got money."

"Why, though?"

"I don't know. Muscle?"

"Maybe. Every bribed bureaucratic official needs someone to enforce the rules they make, right? But Capital is high tech and rich. Maybe the hookups are standard?" She squinted at the tablet, then looked up. "If the public networks can be believed—not standard."

"What about here?"

She frowned, scanning. "Not standard here, either."

"That's not a surprise. But we can watch out for that. Okay, let's say your working theory is that she's not trying to invade with her little army—"

"She can't—it's too small. Not the Union planets anyway."

"But if she's trying to slowly subvert governments, planet by planet…"

Ellen's expression hardened. "It's a different style of invasion, but an invasion, nonetheless. And if she'd already gained some control of Capital, that would explain the demand for telepaths, why they felt the need to hide."

"Seven suns… If she can get control of somewhere as advanced as Capital, then Faros should be a walk in the daisies."

"Maybe she already did." Ellen's lips pursed. "The police have been… attentive to us here, don't you think? I chalked it up to the bounties on our heads, but maybe they're just as much the victims here."

"So you think the guy that shot me is a victim?" He smirked at her, mostly joking.

"He is if he didn't *choose* to shoot you and then died as a result."

He winced. "Okay, you win that round. But wait. It can't be just the police, right? She'd have to start with corrupting higher levels of the government."

"Yes. Start with a few at the top, work your way down. Take control, move to the next planet? Is that her strategy? And farm each one for telepaths and foot soldiers?"

"That means each new planet gives her new grunts, new telepaths to recruit or steal. Army gets bigger each time."

"Army's supply line gets bigger too. Not just a lone Theroki spaceship but..." She stopped, swallowed. "An empire to support it and a hundred others."

They both sat in stunned quiet for a moment.

"God, Kael." Her eyes were smoldering, angry. "We have to stop her."

"Fragging hell, we do. But first we have to *find* her."

"We'll need proof if we want help. And we're going to need help. One lone unit can't take on an empire of telepaths and Theroki by itself."

"It'll be hard to prove. No one's wearing a sign on their back that says, 'I'm being mind-controlled!' Unfortunately. And we also have to get off this damn rock first."

She sighed, disgusted. "So close and still so far away."

A knock on the door announced Dane's return—and the end to their reprieve. Kael hid his internal amusement at that knock. It was probably good he hadn't punched Dane in the mouth, because the guy could be kind when he wanted to be.

Dane appeared in the doorway with a grin and three boxed containers of food. "For the big man—the cricket special."

Kael snorted and took the box, laughing.

"Falafel for us. I think?" Dane handed Ellen a box. "I hope."

Kael caught Ellen's gaze, his own laughing as Dane moved toward the other bunk. Joke was on him.

"Are they good chocolate-covered?" Ellen whispered.

"Delicious."

———

THE NEXT HOUR DRAGGED ON. Doug focused on everything he could other than talking—including straining to hear the murmurs and coughs of the other prisoners nearby, counting the handholds on the insides of their cell for the eightieth time, and seeing how many digits he could remember of *pi*. When he could only remember out to fifteen places, and he was starting to shiver continuously rather than every once in a while, then he really started to feel like dreck on the bottom of an ice miner's boot. What he wouldn't give for that burning hot sand of the beach right now. With an umbrella and extensive sunscreen, of course.

This adventure just kept finding ways to get worse.

Mo narrowed her eyes at his shivering. He tried to hide it and mimic her curled up state as best he could, but all in all it seemed like more work than it was worth in his case. After the third time his teeth chattered loud enough she heard it, though, she stood up suddenly and took a step toward his bunk.

He raised his eyebrows in question.

Her lips pressed together in a tense line. "You're too cold, sir. It's getting dangerous. More dangerous. We need to conserve body heat."

"How do we do that?"

"Huddle together."

Had he just gone insane—or had she had just suggested they needed to cuddle? He pinched himself.

"Did you just pinch yourself?" She put her hands on her hips.

"Yes."

Shaking her head, she strode the rest of the way to his bunk. He tried not to panic. "In cold weather training, they taught us lots of ways to stay warm. Or get warm again, especially if you lost your suit or it's breached. The problem is most of the best options require food or at least a little equipment. We've only got those suspicious shakes. So a lot of our options are out."

"What's left?"

"Conserve what we've got. In this case, that means we just lay here and wait."

"Wait? Wait for what?"

"Don't worry about that." She waved at the air, and he frowned. *That* did not sound good. "So is a huddle okay with you?"

He shrugged. "I don't have the same kind of circulation you do. So it's probably a good idea," he said, ignoring the flush of heat to his cheeks.

"Can you lay on your side? Chest to back is probably the highest contact arrangement for maximum heat efficiency."

He had to twist a bit awkwardly, lift himself up to scoot around, but he got himself laying on his side after an uncomfortable moment. Or eight. To her credit, she didn't flinch away or overzealously offer to help.

He swallowed. Tried to hide his tension and play it cool. This wasn't at all weird to get this close with a coworker.

A beautiful, deadly coworker.

Lord. Well, he *had* wanted to get out and meet women.

Except this woman was... not what he'd been looking for. She made sharing body heat—essentially cuddling—into something utilitarian and matter of fact. That was kind of fitting for Mo. It would probably be like noodling with a handbook of military doctrine.

Her hair brushed his face as she lay down, though, and promptly disabused him of that notion. He snapped his eyes shut and inhaled a greedy breath. Somehow, the scent of flowers mixed sweat was surprisingly appealing. Powerfully so.

Then the heat of her pressed against his chest. He opened his eyes. He felt warmer already.

She was so close. No trouble seeing her now. She'd swept her hair over her neck, probably to keep warm. The curve of her shoulder was lean and made him want to trace his finger along it. She eased closer to him, pressing against him from chest to thighs. Curves he had never realized she had were suddenly distinctly apparent.

There had been quite a few times that he'd thanked the heavens and all his lucky stars that the virus damage had ended in the nerves around his hips and lower spine. He actually had partial use of the right hip, but the numbness came further up in the left. Part of this meant that he could use the bathroom like most other people, which was a big deal, although maneuvering there required feats of strength without floats. He had to admit that if the nerve damage the virus had inflicted had been any worse before it'd been stopped, he might have kept up the surgeries and augmentations, kept searching for even a partial fix.

As it was, though, his manly bits were fairly functional. And he'd always been deeply grateful for that.

This was not one of those moments.

"Bet you wish we had that sheet now," he said with a cough. Because humor was his only tool—for distraction or battle or otherwise.

"I prefer your use of it to two dislocated shoulders." She shrugged one shoulder as if to prove her point. Boots pounded by in the hallway outside, and she briefly raised her head to look out, then laid it back down. The marching was odd, unusual for that kind of heavy traffic this late in the cycle.

"Does all your pillowtalk sound like this, Mihio? It's quite violent."

"What pillowtalk? As if I have any." She snorted, said nothing for a long moment. Then, "Mo."

"Hmm?"

"If we're going to through all this together, and we're going to fragging snuggle, you might as well call me by my first name."

"I thought it was just 'conserving warmth.'"

"Call it what you want."

Ah, there was the moody, dismissive woman he'd come to know and—

His mind screeched to a halt. Know and what? Know and *what*, brain? He frowned. What the hell.

Know and nothing. The cold was just getting to him.

He let the silence stretch on.

Maybe he was getting better at this. But... no, something felt different. He still wanted to talk, but it wasn't the same as his desire to chatter away with Eleven. Not to fight boredom or fill the time.

He wanted... he wanted her to *like* talking to him. To say things that wouldn't annoy her. To squirrel his way under that armored shell.

And if he really wanted that, he ought to be approaching these conversations with more care and less flippancy. Maybe she just didn't appreciate his ribbing—or didn't realize how little he meant what he said. He often played games. Verbal fencing. Wordplay.

But it had to be entertaining to *both* people to truly be fun, didn't it?

Maybe expressing genuine sentiment would be a better idea. He cleared his throat and spoke up without guilt for the first time in hours. "How is your shoulder?"

"Eh. Not great, but it could be worse. It could use the heat more than anything."

It wasn't getting any more heat in this arrangement, though. He hesitated. "Can I... help that at all?"

A slight tensing in her shoulders relaxed a second later. "If you want to put your arm over it? Or your hand? It can't hurt."

He had a feeling his arm might hurt if the shoulder were bruised. Starting carefully, he lowered his palm gently over her shoulder, then his hand, then his forearm down along her back. "That ok?"

She nodded. "Okay, now rub."

He snorted, but obeyed. "I thought I was the one supposed to be giving orders?"

"Anytime, sir. Say the word, and I'll hop to."

He wished he knew if she were smiling. "Good to know. I just needed reassurance at least one person was at my constant beck and call." God, could he not let the witty quips rest for two minutes? He was supposed to be sticking with serious. Sincere.

She was quiet for a moment. The silence stretched out, and for once he noticed there was nothing bitter, sad, angry, annoyed, or uncomfortable about it. Even he felt no urge to speak.

The heat of her skin through the flight suit was warmer than his fingers, to be honest, and kneading the muscles was working up some much needed heat in his extremities. Did she know that he probably needed to be doing this? Was she just humoring him?

"I bet you miss your floats by now," she surprised him by saying.

"Damn straight I do."

"These people are shit. I'm sorry I can't get them back for you."

He raised his eyebrows, then shrugged one shoulder. "People try to talk me into fixing my problems, so I don't need them. Maybe they're right."

"You don't want to?"

"No."

"Why?"

"I'm a hacker at heart."

"What does that have to do with anything?" She twisted just slightly to sneak a look at him, the electronic blue of her eyes glittering momentarily before she turned back.

"I don't build technology, like Dremer or Persad. I break in and exploit it. I find weaknesses in things. And there are always some. Then I re-purpose them for my own ends. Admittedly I try to make good and altruistic ends. But that's only *my* perspective. Still, fundamentally I find how people didn't intend me to use something, and I take advantage of it."

"So… you like breaking rules."

"No," he said quickly. "Okay, maybe a little. But only for noble purposes."

"Hmm. Noble as defined by you."

"I do my best to be right. I studied philosophy for years. Ethics too. History ad nauseum." He also had never had much trouble being right at anything. If he took the time to come up with an answer, it was usually the right one. But it felt a little arrogant or crass to admit that out loud. "I think if you have the power to do something, you have the responsibility to do it. You have to try to do your best, even if you're not perfect."

"I know."

"You know?"

"I know you feel that responsibility. To preserve the balance in the universe. To help people." She said it like it was like a specific thing, like one would know God or reach nirvana or something. The Responsibility. "I protect people, you help them in other ways. That's why I volunteered."

Wait—what? "Volunteered. For the Union?"

"Yes, to some extent. But I was referring to volunteering to come look for you with Fern and Nova."

Holy smokin' cows. She'd volunteered for this? His throat tightened inexplicably. His grip intensified on her shoulder, kneading harder and moving from the outside of her arm toward her neck.

"Oh, that spot right there."

"This one?"

"Yes. Keep going. Damn I slammed that dreck harder than I thought, it's all bent out of shape. So what were you saying? You break lots of rules?"

He snorted. "I wouldn't say that, but some people might disagree. My point is that technology can do miraculous things. Don't get me wrong. I *love* technology. But I absolutely do not trust it. Because I also know everything has its weaknesses."

Was that a quiet laugh from her? "What about me? What are my weaknesses? Do you keep them noted in your files somewhere?"

He grinned. "Let's see… A bit of a lone wolf, but no issues with team integration. May regret leaving Keyah. Potential risk of leaving too soon."

Her head whipped around to look at him, and then she fully rolled over, leaving him with his hand suspended in the air in surprise. His chest was cold where her back had been, but she didn't come closer yet. Understandably.

"How did you know I…" She swallowed. "How did you know?"

"You miss the land every day. You said it yourself."

She bit her lip. Deep masculine laughter drifted from out in the hallway. It had a malicious tone, and his stomach tightened. Her eyes flicked toward the sound, then back to him. "I don't regret leaving. I just miss it. I miss… the sunlight, the warmth."

They were quiet together for a moment.

"What I never figured out was why you left," he said, almost a whisper now. "It seems like…"

"Like paradise?"

He let out a puff of laughter. "I see. Your parents' paradise?"

"In some ways mine as well. But I, too, feel the responsibility.

Keyah is under Union protection, so it doesn't maintain a large standing army. The people have their defenses, sure, but you know the kind of weapons they have today. It's all too easy for paradise to be shattered if there isn't someone willing to stand up for it. And in this century, standing up for it can't be done on short notice. It takes time and training, tech and firepower. You can't start building an army when the Puritan fleet shows up."

"You need the Puritan fleet not to show up at all, ideally."

"Agreed. And now that we have Keyah, a place all to ourselves, well… it doesn't need to happen again."

"I think I'm not the only history dork in this cell."

"It is not just my history," she snapped. "It's my present. My future too."

He sobered. "Sorry. Of course."

"I'm not just a bug to be examined, you know. A history lesson to be considered from afar."

"You're far prettier than a bug, that's true."

And there it was. The words escaped him all too easily. He hid his wince.

Her eyes locked with his, eyes widening and expression suddenly serious. As if she was trying to figure out just exactly what that meant. Was she… was she going to slap him? Damn, he shouldn't have said that.

She didn't move. Her eyes just studied him. Who was the bug now?

"Why blue eyes? Why not keep the brown?" It came out as too much of a demand. But her armor seemed down, or at least a chunk blown out of it. Her shields could come back up any second. He had to go for it. Go for the truth, the buried Mo that she kept carefully hidden. Protected. Damn, he was a nosy dreck.

Surprise flickered in her gaze, but not as much as had before. As if she was getting used to the idea that he knew too much about her. "The blue model has slightly better performance in the most common lighting scenarios."

He chuckled. He couldn't resist optimizing things to the max either. He smiled, unable or unwilling suddenly to find words for the feeling that was going through him, the sudden warmth that didn't come from her body or the air or the plexi beneath them. "Smart."

"Thanks."

Laughter drifted up the hall toward them from outside again. She frowned and sat up now, leaving a huge vacuum of cold in her wake. But she quickly returned.

Closer this time.

"What is it?" he whispered.

Her expression was serious. "We've got trouble."

"Same guys?"

"Yes. Night cycle is coming. Tovi has to sleep sometime."

"Great. What can we do?" He meant it more as a statement than a question.

She went up on one elbow and leaned in, her lips warming the shell of his ear and tickling the tiniest hairs on his ear lobe. His whole body zinged to life at the sensation.

"We can do plenty. Shh." Then she went back to lying, something surprisingly sweet and softening in the way her head curved toward his shoulder. "First, put your arm around me. Better heat conservation."

He complied. He was pretty sure he wasn't giving any orders anytime soon. No need to be delusional about it if you had smart people in command.

Her arm slipped around him too and pulled their bodies closer.

"Now, let's practice a few of those words. On the off chance that you are right, and they do come in handy," she whispered. "And to keep us sane."

He swallowed, trying to ignore the closeness, and nodded.

She went over a handful of the words with him, their tones hushed, bent lips to ear at times. He repeated them back, praying his butchery of the pronunciation was only moderate. She didn't seem *too* miffed at him. If it was a secret code between them, his perfection of pronunciation was less important than her knowing what he was trying to say. He did remember a few from over the years, but she had many more.

After she'd drilled him on more than a dozen—maybe it was all twenty-six, he'd lost count—she seemed satisfied. "Next, we rest."

"And then?"

She shook her head at him, glancing at the ceiling. "Don't worry about that."

Ah, this was one of those times when he needed to shut up. Message received. "Got it. Rest time."

The silence settled, deep and peaceful, and she sighed, her breath tickling his chest.

Oh, Eleven. If you could see me now. He sighed too and closed his eyes.

———

"ZAHIR." Kael came to a stop before his old… friend? Friend wasn't the right word for someone who you were fairly sure would shoot you in the back as soon as greet him. Colleague? Acquaintance? "You look like you've seen a ghost."

The man in the blue robes jumped and knocked over a small, handleless cup of tea on the table. His every muscle was tensed under bronze skin, and one of the half dozen women lounging on the bench around him hurried to dry the spill while another made soothing coos.

"A ghost. Well. I think I have." Zahir leaned back in his seat. A combat armor vest was askew over his shoulders, one strap off. The other strap might have been broken, but Kael suspected it was in the process of being removed, based on the dark glares of the women. A battered helmet lolled at his feet—what did they have him doing these days, by the seven suns? But Zahir had been so engrossed with his tea —and his companions—that he hadn't noticed as Kael approached.

At least Kael assumed it was tea since this was a tea house. Supposedly.

A beautiful tea house, actually. Low benches strewn with cushions of an iridescent orange formed a circle around small octagonal tables inlaid with ruby glass. Wide red swaths of fabric hung from the high ceiling, roughing out private spaces. Silk? He wanted to touch it to be sure, but he wasn't removing his gauntlet for that. The sea of crimson billowed and shifted sensually in the light breeze, hiding and revealing the other patrons in turn.

Zahir wasn't the ideal man to track down. But after hours of stalking the Gray Dragons territory, he'd only spotted three people he remembered, who might know more than Erol the lookout. Zahir had been the highest ranking of those he'd seen, at least back before everything had gone to hell. It stood to reason he'd be the closest to Maloof.

"It's been a long time, my friend," Kael said coolly, sinking to sit uninvited beside Zahir's third companion on his right. The circled benches meant that he faced Zahir. The woman fidgeted, grabbed her friend's arm, and shifted farther away. The bench groaned underneath the weight of the armor, and Kael set it to stick in position if the seat collapsed. Hard to be intimidating while falling on your ass, but he hoped for everyone's sake that wouldn't happen.

"Sidassian," Zahir replied. "A long time. What are you doing here?" There were definite nerves in his voice, and not a hint of a smile, though his lips made an effort.

"Didn't expect to see me again?"

"Where are my manners? Would you like some tea?" Without waiting for an answer, Zahir rang a small bell on the table. A new woman leaned around a sheet of red, and he must have signaled her somehow because she nodded and disappeared. Dane and Ellen were back there somewhere too; they'd agreed to approach from the back in case Zahir decided running was a better option than talking.

"Tea it is," Kael said.

"Now." Zahir clapped his hands together, seeming to regain some composure, or at least the ability to pretend at composure. "Didn't you kill somebody? Get sent to an off-world prison?" His lips twisted into a smirk. Something about it felt cold in Kael's gut, but he wasn't sure why. His companions murmured—either mildly shocked or feigning at it.

"How many people have *you* killed, Zahir?"

"None, my friend, absolutely none."

The dark-eyed woman to his left who had tried to comfort him leaned forward, making her black robe and scarf shimmer slightly. Her eyes crinkled. "My husband's hands are clean as the day he was born."

"Right," he said, drawing out the word. Wait—her husband? Then what about the other women? For once, though, he'd took a page from Ellen's book and kept his face blank as a sheet of ice on the surface.

"Am *I* the convicted murderer?" Zahir slapped a hand against the vest. "No. I am a free man. Can you say as much?"

Technically he could, but he didn't. "Of course. Only innocent men wear body armor."

Zahir grinned. "Well, you know, Faros is a dangerous place."

The woman on his *other* side spoke up. This one had more demure features and wore robes of saffron dotted with blue. "*You're* more armored than he is."

Kael just blinked.

The serving woman came with the tea—and a special smile for Zahir—and then left. Kael wasn't sure if that was an I-poisoned-the-tea-like-you-told-me-to smile or an I'm-in-love-with-you smile. At first, Kael had pegged these companions as paid entertainers, but now he wasn't so sure. At least the suit could scan the tea and clarify that much.

He held a palm over the steaming, round cup of gray ceramic. "We all know, armored or not, this isn't a place where murderers actually go to prison."

Zahir smiled tightly. Smugly. Like he knew something. Great. "Ah, you've got me on that one."

The scan came back clear, so Kael took a sip. The taste—the taste.

He hadn't tasted tea like this since… since he'd left. Even then, it had been rare. Once, when he was barely six, he'd snuck into a teahouse with some stolen rial. The waitress who'd caught him should have thrown him out, but she hadn't.

She'd tucked him at a table behind the server station and had given him a date and honey confection and three giant mugs of minty tea not so different from this one.

He sighed at the memory, then tried to hide his frown of annoyance as the women perked up at his reaction. Looking for a weakness? Well, maybe this tea was it.

He hadn't thought of that time in the tea house, that simple kindness, in a long, long time. It was too hard to think of Faros at all, especially any of the good memories, when he was stuck on board the *Genokai*.

But now… things had changed, hadn't they? Was that woman still working in that same tea shop somewhere? How many children had she been kind to over the years? Could he have found her and paid her back?

Had that tea house been one of the ones banged up for protection money once a month? Maybe once a week if things were in a downturn. The idea of any group he'd been a part of doing that sank like a stone in his gut. But most likely it had happened.

He doubted he could find the tea shop, even if the woman still worked there—but it was a good reminder that there *were* good people in the world.

Zahir was not one of them, though.

"The tea is good, yes?" said the first wife.

Kael's lips thinned. "It is."

"Did you know that ghosts enjoy mint tea?" said Zahir, his merriment returning. "I didn't."

None of the women responded, though. They were tense. They knew he was building up to something.

"I didn't kill anyone," he said finally, into a long silence. "I *did* get conscripted to the Theroki, though." The look of triumph that briefly flashed in Zahir's eyes flickered with something else, maybe fear. Kael gave him a cold smile. "You wouldn't know anything about how that happened, would you?"

Zahir's smirk returned, and he picked up his cup. "Hey, it's not my fault you pissed off the wrong people."

The red fabric behind Zahir swayed, briefly revealing Ellen poised directly at Zahir's back. Through her raised helmet and clear visor, she raised an eyebrow, but her eyes didn't leave Zahir.

Kael narrowed his eyes. "Look, I don't want to fight with you. I'm just looking for someone. And I don't mean someone in the Gray Dragons."

"Fine, fine." Zahir gave him a friendly wave as he poured more tea for himself and then filled the rest of the cups. Kael kept his carefully in hand. "I know some people. Lots of people. My family knows even more. Who are you looking for?"

"Asha Nuralon."

He laughed—chuckled outright, actually. But his hand shook slightly as he set down the teapot. "The ghost asks about a ghost."

Kael's expression hardened, but he simply set his teacup down in one precise, dangerous movement.

"She's dead, my friend," Zahir said, still jovial. "You should know. You killed her." He could feel the women glaring, their dislike of him growing.

"Actually, I didn't." It felt good to say that out loud, here. Not that yelling it had helped the first time around. "And I have it on good authority that she's alive."

Zahir had instantly sobered at that. "If *you* want to stay alive, forget that and whatever authority you have it on." He started to his feet, and the women started with him, murmuring complaints and disappointments, but moving as one.

A gauntleted hand came down on Zahir's shoulder, causing them all to jump.

Ellen eased into view, making Zahir go still as he realized Kael wasn't alone. "Some things aren't easily forgotten."

Zahir's eyes widened. She spoke in Common, but it revealed she and Dane had been listening. Until now they'd been speaking in the mishmash that was common on Faros. Shooting a glare at Kael, Zahir then sneered at Ellen. "What are you doing with a Theroki ghost, woman? Don't they cut off their manhood? As you can see, I know how to please a woman." He gestured, arms outspread, as he tried to play relaxed under her steely grip.

Kael tensed as a young man appeared from behind another slip of red—someone from the tea house to kick them out? Zahir's backup?

"Ah," said Zahir, sounding pleased. "And my husband has arrived. As you see, I know how to please men too."

Ellen barely blinked.

Zahir turned to Kael. "Why don't you forget about this nonsense?"

"Yes," the new young man piped up. "Slip out of all that uncomfortable metal and into something more relaxing? You can both join us."

"I, for one, would like to see what's under all that armor," murmured one of the wives who hadn't spoken yet, a bronze-skinned, freckled woman with green eyes.

Kael just stared at her for a beat. Only a sudden gasp from Zahir broke his gaze.

Zahir was clawing at his shoulder. "Let go, by all that is holy! Glory be, take it easy, now."

Ellen dropped her hand to her side. Androids had more emotional faces. "No relaxing. Asha Narulon."

Zahir sank down to a seat, and the young man joined the women on the bench. Apparently, this was what Zahir had meant by his family. Kael wasn't the only one who'd changed. "It is not so simple, my friend. You don't want to know, trust me."

"So you admit she isn't dead."

Zahir winced slightly. "You think you are tough, and I don't disagree. I envy you that armor. But you have no idea what you're messing with."

"I've already kicked the hornet's nest by talking to you. How do I know you're not going to run right to her after this?"

"You don't." Zahir grinned.

"Then you see my problem. You know. I know you know. So I can't leave you... and your family... without knowing."

"But my family is exactly who will be put at risk by your selfish request." As if on demand, several of the women glared, two pouted, and interestingly the man looked imploring.

Well, frag. He didn't want them all to die just to get to Asha.

"How about a clue? And then we didn't talk to you, and you didn't talk to us."

"Ah, you can't go into the nest of the dragon, and expect word not to get around that you've been there."

Kael frowned. What did that mean?

"The dragon has many heads, but it has one more than you think it does. One more than it used to. The new one is the most dangerous, and it will have your balls for a necklace, if you let it. If you still have any." Zahir's expression was just as smiling as ever.

A cold rock settled in Kael's gut. What the...

The suit's collar flashed there was a comm message coming in. He saw Ellen's head cock slightly to listen. She met his gaze, then jerked her head slightly toward the door.

Of course. Incoming. They needed to get out of here—but how could he leave *now*? What was he going to do, drag all these people with him?

Zahir cleared his throat. "So again, I tell you. You *can't* go into the nest of the dragon. Turn back now, and let this lie. Come party with us —or go your own way—but don't kick the dragon's nest. It will bite."

Their gazes locked for a long second, as if Zahir was willing them both to be telepaths. Unfortunately, they weren't.

"Please," Zahir tried once more. "For the sake of my family, leave the past in the past. You know the *fat* dragon is still to be feared, but the thin one may surprise you."

Kael frowned. It had been a cruel joke before Maloof had risen to the top that his name meant fat. The dragon's nest—the fat dragon— Maloof's house? Of course looking there would be dangerous. That had to be it. Was that where he would find Asha?

Kael made a show of sighing. "Fine, fine. For the sake of your family, I will stop looking. Maybe I will find some other way to bury the memories. Somewhere far away from here."

He stood. Ellen was frowning, but silvered her visor and followed his lead. He gave a small bow. He slapped the suit to raise the helmet.

Ellen's voice over the comm. "Two likely hostiles out front, more approaching—take the side entrance."

"Roger." More than just the waitresses stared as the two of them slipped between the swaths of red. It'd be nice to jog, but he had a feeling if they did, they'd shake the cheap planks of the floor and draw even more attention.

He prepared for an attack as they slipped out into the alley, but the street was empty aside from several dumpsters and Dane hunkered down in a doorway.

"Good timing," Dane said. "We move now, and I think we can avoid them entirely."

"Turn on your dynacamo while we're in the dark," ordered Ellen. "Let's give them the slip."

The three of them vanished into the back alleys, slipping past more than one rough-looking lander. There was probably a fifty-fifty chance each lander contained men looking to shoot them, but luckily the camo meant they didn't have to find out.

Ellen spoke once they were a dozen blocks away. "What now?"

"We go see the Gray Dragon himself," Kael said. "The leader."

"You got all that from that weird conversation at the end?"

"Yeah. Don't kick the dragon's nest. He's directing me to Maloof's house."

"Can we really trust where he's directing you?" Dane said.

"Oh, we definitely can't," Kael said. "And even if that's just where Asha is, there's no guarantee Zahir isn't comming them right now to tell them we're coming. But we can't avoid that. Hopefully Zahir is afraid enough of possible retribution that he truly will keep it under wraps."

"We could have killed him, I suppose," said Ellen.

"Or locked him up without a comm and with all his friends to play with." Dane laughed.

"Do you two want to go back and extract eight gang members from a tea house full of innocent people—or fellow gang members—amid enemy fire? Or perhaps we could just get our asses over to Maloof's before Zahir even has time to call."

Ellen snorted, almost a laugh. He'd bet twenty rials she was smiling behind that visor. "We can't go that fast. We have to do some recon. We have no idea if that place is even Maloof's house. It could all be a lie."

"I'm just saying the faster we strike, the more likely they won't be ready for us."

"The man has a point," Dane said. "We sit back and take our time, and they are that much more likely to expect our arrival."

Ellen swore under her breath. "We don't have Doug, so half our usual intel team is gone, the other half is behind a cloud of unreliable sand. But we barely even have an address. Kael, can you at least get me a full address and verify it in the local directories? We need blueprints of the building—or *something*. What, are we going to just go up and knock on the door?"

Kael chuckled as he scanned through the public directories on his suit. "It *had* occurred to me."

Dane checked around the corner of the next intersection before they continued forward. "Now, now, you should know that's not how we do things."

"Here we go," Kael said. "Number 25, Dendar Way. Sending you the details."

Ellen was nodding. "Okay. Tell us everything you can about him while I try to get through to Xi."

"Or get the blueprints yourself?"

"I'll check a public directory, but I'm no computer whiz anymore."

Anymore. He pursed his lips in distaste at the word, at her memories of the Starbird grid behind it, but he didn't say anything.

"Kael?" Ellen murmured.

"Yes?"

"Details on this Maloof?"

"Oh. Yes, ma'am. Uh, well, Maloof worked his way up, but he had just taking over when I was forced in. To be honest, that's a long time to stay on top. Whatever he's doing to keep power, it's working. I think Zahir was trying to tell me something more, about the heads of the dragon, but I haven't figured that out yet. Anyway, back then he was working closely with Abrams. Abrams was getting out. Handing over the reins."

"Except he never made it?" said Dane.

"Apparently."

"So, wait." Dane held up a palm. "This Zahir says this Asha woman is *there*?"

"He didn't specifically say that. There might be answers there to where she is or what happened. But Maloof keeps coming up."

"Maybe because he's the one everyone's the most afraid of."

"But if he was behind this in the first place like everyone seems to think, why not just shoot me eleven years ago and be done with it?"

"He couldn't," Ellen suggested. "Abrams was protecting you, even if you didn't know it."

Kael growled in the back of his throat. "It also doesn't pay any credits to shoot me."

"Ain't that the truth," said Dane. "That only costs him—in lead."

"It would pay credits *now* though," Ellen said. "Assuming Arakovic's bounty is dead or alive. Maybe it's just alive, so she can ask you some nice questions."

He winced. "Thanks for pointing that cheery thought out."

"My cheeriness is why you stay around."

His eyes widened at the quip—and he wondered if she was doing the same thing in her suit. Had she meant to say that? Seemed like it gave away a thing or two to Dane's ears.

Or maybe he was just imagining things. She'd said similar things to Bri more than once. Or… maybe his awkward silence in response was even more revealing.

Damn it.

Ellen loudly cleared her throat. "So Abrams didn't buy it, so they kicked his can, too. Or they fought over other stuff, who knows. Either way, Maloof won. Regular old David and Bathsheba."

"Who?"

"Never took any religious courses on the Theroki mothership, I take it?"

"Uh, no. The *Genokai* definitely didn't offer any. And I thwarted the best efforts of a variety of clerics and evangelists here on Faros to tame and educate me. And also house and feed me. Real great decision making on my part."

Ellen made a humming noise that sounded undecided. "David was a king in the Bible who, the story goes, saw a married woman named Bathsheba bathing on the roof. And he fell in love with her, or something like that, so he arranged for her husband who was away at war to die. And then they were married."

Kael raised an eyebrow. "Wasn't David a hero of that book?"

"Even great men make mistakes. David unfortunately paid a steep price in the end. It's a cautionary tale."

"What happened?"

"You don't want to know."

"I agree, you don't want to know," added Dane.

"Gotcha!" snapped Ellen suddenly.

"What?"

"The plans—I just found them. Sending them over. These are almost a decade old, from when the local government did some plumbing infrastructure work. Gosh, what I'd give for more intel. Does Maloof really even use this place? When? Does he have more than one home? Office? Where inside here does he hang out? And most of all, where is this maze of a building weak? How do we even know if he's here or off traveling?"

Frag. Those were all good points. He racked his brain. "Well, it's been over a decade, but in my day, he was always presiding by the pool."

She raised her eyebrows, then looked at the ceiling. "The pool?"

"Yes. The pool. Simulated sun and everything. I remember because it was one of the ways I noticed the power shifting. Abrams—he was more of a business guy, or he liked to look that way. Big mahogany desk. Maloof liked a… different atmosphere."

"Pool on these maps is the third level up—this place has multiple levels?"

"The height of luxury on Faros is properties that transcend levels."

"Why do you put a pool on the roof?"

"Because the difficulty shows you have money? Because all the floors are all underground anyway?"

"Well—the pool is a starting point, but that's not enough. If we march in there and go to the pool and it's just a bunch of house cleaners and butlers—what then? You know security will be all over that. And we won't have our answers. We don't just need his house, we need *him*. Right?"

"We could try to sneak into the computer system?" Dane offered.

"But we don't know if the answers we're looking for are even in there." Kael spread his hands.

"And without Doug and Adan, we'll be hard pressed to break in anyway." She bit her lip. "The advantage of surprise would be great right now. But we could very easily waste it."

"Elle, I've waited *eleven* years," Kael said. "And so has someone else, if they're even alive." He couldn't quite bring himself to say, "my kid," but that was the truth of it. "I don't really want to wait any longer. It just gives them time to prepare."

"We need time to prepare, too. What if Zahir doesn't say anything? We could be the ones that tip them off."

He'd had years of storming into stupid, poorly planned situations and surviving, so this idea hardly phased him. Chances were they'd make it out. She had a different style, usually had planning on her side. But what was he going to do, argue the Theroki way was better? Yeah, right. "I don't like it. But yes, ma'am."

"We at least need to confirm his location. Maybe Adan can find it quick with some security cameras. Let's get back to home base, patch through to him, and we'll see where we can get in a few hours. If we get lucky—maybe the middle of the night is a better time anyhow?"

Kael snorted. "Then we can up our odds of him being in either the pool area or the bedroom, I guess."

"If he's got a family as big as Zahir's," Dane murmured, "things could get messy."

CHAPTER THIRTEEN

DAY 17

THEY PAUSED in the lobby of the hostel as Ellen started the scan. The place was gray as could be, cement on cement, with a few helpful handwritten signs, but otherwise no sign of anything with more personality than a robot. Dane leaned against the wall beside the next room's door and whistled. Kael glared at the signage. She was pretty sure he was thinking about something other than where to eat dinner.

Ninety-eight percent complete. The scan on their room seemed to take forever to roll from ninety-nine percent to one hundred. "Clear," she muttered, pushing open the door.

Except that wasn't true, was it. The sound was so quiet, she almost missed it—the tiniest snap over her head. There, in the doorframe outside the scan—a tiny silver hair bent askew in the dim light. The trigger.

A trap. Deliberately set *outside* the area of her scan. And missed.

"Get down!" The order was more instinct than conscious thought. A bleep split the air to her right, and then—

Her words weren't fast enough for anybody to react.

The door beside Dane burst apart, splintered pieces rushing toward them.

She ducked, rolling up like a scared bug. Her damn hands went to her neck, but this time she didn't mind so much. The readout poured information across her view—large temperature spike, rapidly increasing weight from above.

But the actual display was dark. They were completely buried.

The roar of the explosion felt like several minutes, but it couldn't have been more than a second or two. Silence fell, quick and hard. A pebble skittered somewhere, then the world stood suddenly still.

She tried to move a hand, but nothing happened. Made sense—the debris above her showed an excess of seven hundred pounds. "Jesus, did they bring down the whole building? Or was that one hell of a door?"

Dane groaned. "Judging by this readout, the whole building."

Kael just grunted.

"If only we had a cyborg who could just handle this for us," Dane muttered.

"Hey, I'm trying here."

Who decided it was time for banter while crushed by four times his weight in cement?

She tried to jerk an arm, again to no avail. She should have seen this coming. Stupid, stupid. The Gray Dragons had probably seen them in the tea house, if not earlier making their rounds. They'd tried to avoid a tail, but someone in the next bar could have just as easily said something. If the Gray Dragons knew they had good armor, heavy armor, they knew they'd need serious firepower. More than most gangs carried around from street to street.

But these suits were the best out there—if anything were going to get her out of this mess, it'd be them. Come to think of it, actually, it was surprising this wasn't even worse than just a building collapse.

A new alarm blared in her suit. Well, didn't that just figure.

"Acid detected on suit exterior," the readout warned.

She swore. "Looks like the fun is just getting started."

"Acid. Pleasant," said Dane. "How thoughtful of them to etch our armor."

She stretched one arm out again—or tried to—testing the weight.

The motors strained and ground angrily in the darkness. Nothing moved.

"How much time do we have?" Kael said. He sounded out of breath. "We could work ourselves out of this debris in a couple of hours, but I'm thinking the acid is changing the game."

She nodded, if only to herself. "We each have different armor models, but I'd estimate… five minutes? Mine's the thinnest, even if it's my heaviest set. You two probably have a few minutes more."

"Ain't that lucky," grumbled Dane.

"Everybody get pushing." She could faintly hear the grinding of someone else's armor to the right of her own.

Curled up in a ball, she wasn't in a bad position to push her way free. She shifted to get a better footing; a rock budged near her foot that gave her a slight burst of hope. Sucking in a breath, she dialed the suit to the max and drove with both legs. Hard.

The rock and wood above her complained, groaned, rose up slightly. But as soon as she stopped pushing for a moment, it tumbled back down. Was it even lower than before? Had she actually made it worse?

"Frag. Nothing here so far."

"I think I managed a centimeter," muttered Dane.

Kael said nothing—she wasn't sure if that was good or bad.

The readout started a quiet, insistent beep. "I've got acid in contact with my suit," she barked. "Looks like sulfuric, yay. Deterioration of the outer most layer is at one percent."

Now or never, she was fighting her way out of this thing.

She heaved in a deep breath, held it, and forced herself upward. The weight of the building pushed right back, hard across her shoulders all the way down into the flat of her feet, but she threw everything she had into her legs, her thighs, her suit—into getting out.

The debris above her jerked once and slid aside, suddenly lighter.

Her legs went straight. The amount of weight on top of her was still *plenty*, and the acid was just getting started. Progress, though.

"How are you two?"

"Not making much headway over here," Dane bit out.

"I'm helping you," Kael said, voice distant.

"Damn it, stop that," she snapped.

"We'll go one at a time," Kael shot back. "You said yourself you had the least."

"Fine. Let's work together." She spit out the words between breaths as she tried to straighten her back further. "Dane, we're close to each other. If you push your left side and I push to the right—"

"On it." Dane said. "Keep going. I'm at ten percent acid infiltration, over here."

"Why didn't you—" She cut off the words. He should have said something earlier, but he already hadn't. Waste of energy.

She leaned back, into the stone and wood, giving it everything she had. A piece of wall shifted and fell along her side and into the space left by her torso, sending off a cascade of shifting.

The debris pounded down. Her knees lost it, buckled slightly, before she propelled herself up yet again.

The beeping in her readout sped up. "Acid infiltration twenty percent. That's gonna leave a mark." Dust swirled dimly outside the helmet, and she coughed in spite of herself and the perfectly clean air inside the suit. Unless it wasn't clean because the acid was working its way in…

"Let's put that sense of humor to work on the remains of this building, shall we?"

She growled at the damned beeping. "What do you think I'm doing?"

Scrambling for a better angle, she shoved at the weight above her again. It didn't budge. She tried to shift her feet around or beside the scrap of wall, but the thing was breaking apart, making the footing even more awkward. Other pieces were falling in underfoot, adding to the unsteadiness.

"Kael—what's your acid reading?"

"Only twenty-eight percent."

"Only! If I ever make it out of here, I'm going to dip that worthless dreck Zahir in boiling acid." She scrambled again for a better footing, and heaved.

Nothing moved, except one foot sliding to the side and losing her balance. She fell shoulder-first against the debris to her left. Not that that mattered much—it didn't move either.

The curse words were flying now.

"Nothing's moving over here," Dane said. "Got this thing on high output. Nothing. Gonna see if I can reach my multi."

Lasering their way out of this might be an option, but they didn't know *what* was on top of them and how it would react when melted and falling back down on the suit. Not everything vaporized.

Her acid damage readout rolled over to thirty-six percent. Suit integrity would be lost at one hundred, if not way before depending on the pattern of the damage. And that wasn't counting any damage caused by the explosion.

Once more. Like your damn life is on the line, soldier.

"In all the ways I thought I might die, I sure didn't expect acid," Dane said.

"We are not dying!" she hissed.

"I'm not complaining, I know what I signed up for. Just—acid? What's the luck?"

She shook her head, grounded herself, and drove up again. Did it seem like one piece of rock moved, or was she just wishing it?

"Death comes for us all, you know," Dane said, between breathless huffs and a few growls. "I thought I died at least six times by now."

"I'd say my count is forty-two," Kael put in.

"Stop bragging, Theroki."

"See you in hell, Foundation scum," Kael shot back.

Dane chuckled. "Your number's gotta come up sometime, right?"

"I *knew* I wouldn't make it to thirty," Kael grumbled. "Or off this planet."

"Well, if I die here, and you find Shawn—" Dane started.

That was it. "We are not dying here, damn you! I have a friend to rescue, at least two children to locate, another child to convince shrieking into everyone's brains is unnecessary, and also an evil frag-ging scientist to stop. I am *not* going down to a pile of rocks!"

She let out a roar. Her muscles and motors groaned as she threw every bit of energy she had into pushing away from this damned planet and toward ever-loving space.

"Whoa, Commander, are you—" Dane grumbled.

A growl escaped her in response. She did not want to answer questions. She did not want to think about last wishes or messages to missing children or missions unaccomplished.

What she wanted was to annihilate every bit of rock around them and then Maloof too. And maybe punch something. Actually… maybe punching wasn't such a bad idea.

She slammed her fist into the broken shard of wall above her, interspersing short blasts from the weak laser built into the suit's gauntlets. That might just wreck her suit faster—or maybe the debris would crumble.

"Acid at forty-five percent over here," Kael said. "What the frag are you doing?"

A cascade of small bits and bobs fell across the gauntlet, lit up slightly in the brief red blast of the laser pulse. It *was* crumbling.

"I'm getting somewhere. Try the weak laser in the suits—not too much. Maybe at an angle. Also, I'm just pummeling over my head, and it seems to be working. Maybe it's soaked up some of the acid too."

"Goodie," grumbled Dane.

The next two feet of rubble seemed to take hours, but it couldn't have, or they *would* have been dead. All she knew was when she saw that the crack of light through debris above her, she wanted to sing. Or cry. Or kick somebody's ass.

A faint trickle filtering down from who knew what never looked so good. Overheads on another level? Certainly not the sky. It didn't matter.

The light grew. Some of the debris was shifting away of its own accord.

"Kael, start on yourself. Stop helping. I'm almost there." She started to climb instead of punch. Now it all wanted to fall and crumble, but she kept going. "Or start on Dane," she added hastily.

"No. You have to get out first. We're working together."

Her shoulders came free. The room above them was utterly

wrecked, but nobody was waiting for them. Little blessings. "Look, I'm almost out. I'll dig for Dane—now get out of that acid. It's got to be pooling toward the bottom. That is an order, Lieutenant."

"Yes, ma'am."

———

DOUG WOKE up as he started to shiver. The front of him where Mo had been curled had gone cold. Her absence wrenched him fully awake.

Rubbing the sleep out of his eyes wouldn't make him be able to see clearly, but he didn't *think* she was in her bunk—or anywhere in the cell, for that matter. He squinted, but in the dim light it was hard to tell for sure.

"Mo?" His voice was hushed. He half expected an immediate *shhh* to quiet him, but he was met with only silence.

What the hell? How could they have taken her literally right out of his arms while he slept? Or could she have gotten out?

Somehow escaped without him?

"Mo?" He sat up, not that it accomplished anything but making him colder. "Mihio!"

No. If she'd gotten out, that would mean she'd left him here, and he refused to believe she'd do that. Certainly not for long. Maybe she was single handedly taking over the ship, and she'd be back for him. His shoulders sagged. Hopefully that wasn't the case, but if it were, he couldn't say he blamed her.

He couldn't see any signs of escape. The stupid bars were still there, still closed. Could those goons have drugged them both somehow?

He wasn't what Tovi thought. He didn't *want* to sit back and have people fight his battles for him. Not anymore. So if Mo was in danger, he had to try to do *something*.

"Mo!"

"Shut up in there!" One of the men that had been looming in the hallway sauntered up, casual as a stroll on the beach. "Chaos, it's cold as a witch's tit in here."

"Clever." Doug rolled his eyes, then wished he hadn't. "Sergeant Mihio. Where did you take her?"

The guy laughed in his face, then stopped short. A tattoo ran down his forehead and his cheek, lengthening as his eyes widened. "Hey! Rolf! This chick you got it in for is gone!" He narrowed his eyes at Doug. "Where's your friend?"

"That's what I just asked you," Doug shot back.

"Rolf is gonna be pissed. They have a score to settle, you know."

He was tempted to point out that if anyone had a score to settle, it was Mo, but even he wasn't that smart-mouthed or stupid.

Two men came jogging up, one of them being the handsome one that Doug wanted to punch. Hard. Rolf? Apparently. And Rolf swore at the sight of Mo's empty bunk.

"Where'd she go?" The other newcomer, a black-haired man with grimy looking overalls on, had started fumbling with the door controls while Rolf glared.

"That's what I want to know," Doug grumbled. But it seemed pretty clear they were as confused as he was. So if she hadn't gotten past them and they hadn't taken her, maybe she must have escaped from within the cell, they just hadn't figured out how yet.

And she must have gone and left him behind.

"Hey, get this open," Rofl said to his companion, pulling on the bars to see if Mo had left them unlocked. No such luck.

Mr. Overalls frowned. "Frag, they pulled my authorization—"

Rolf jabbed a finger in his face. "Damn it, why are you even here then? Fix it or I'll—"

"I can't—"

Over the shouting, an alarm suddenly blared, and the doors rumbled open of their own accord. All three troublemakers stared.

"Uh. There you go," Mr. Overalls managed, taking a step back. Seemed pretty clear to Doug that he'd had nothing to do with it, but he couldn't blame the man trying to take credit.

"Begin evacuation protocols," said a flat, robotic voice from the ceiling.

"Evac, my ass. We're not goin' anywhere." The guy with the face tattoo eased forward. Mr. Overalls stayed close behind him, with Rolf watching with folded arms behind them both.

Tattoo Guy scanned the place and relaxed. "How'd she get out? Nothing here but this cri—"

The flash of gray didn't quite make sense to Doug at first, especially blurred, but something swung down and pounded Tattoo Guy in the face. Was that a… a boot?

The blow jerked Tattoo's head back, slamming it into Mr. Overalls. Overalls staggered back as blood oozed from his nose. He put a hand to it, stared in horror, and then took off running down the corridor, smearing blood across a startled Rolf's shoulder.

Tattoo Guy wasn't out of the game that easily, though. He was scrambling, jumping and reaching up but getting hit back down. Or… kicked?

Holy ninja commandos. She was on the ceiling.

Why hadn't he just raised his head and looked up? Then again, he might not have spotted the gray blur that was her hanging from the antigrav handholds in the dimness.

Rolf joined in the struggle to pull her down, and a boot grazed his temple before Tattoo Guy found his grip and pulled with all his weight.

She came down with a grunt. Her elbow dropped hard into Tattoo Guy's shoulder. Both of them went down.

Doug's panic surged. Sure, Overalls had bowed out, but this was still two-to-one, and who knew who else could be in the corridor?

This was serious trouble. He needed to help. But hell if he had any ideas. He lifted himself with his arms and shifted closer to the edge of the bunk, so he could at least see.

Apparently, Mo's boot had more than grazed Rolf's temple, because he'd fallen back to leaning against the side of the bunk. One hand pressed to his head, eyes glazed.

Unfortunately though, all he could see of Tattoo Guy was his back.

In the dimness of the cell, he couldn't make out specific movements, only sharp jerks. The guy had grunted and sworn more than a few times. Was that a boot Mo had just swung over his head?

He had no idea how she did it, but the next moment, Tattoo Guy was rolling, and so was Mo. Tattoo went down on his back, arm trapped in her grip and locked by her legs wrapped around and—

Doug winced at the sound of bone cracking, even as Tattoo Guy roared.

That roused Rolf, who stumbled forward, blocking Doug's view again.

Mo shifted, revealing Tattoo Guy had gone limp. But Rolf's fist connected with a heavy blow to Mo's ear that sent her face whipping the other direction.

Doug had never hated anyone—or the whole world—quite so much as in that moment. If he didn't do something, anything, he was going to have to watch while Rolf got the better of her and actually won this fight.

He groped around desperately, looking for something to throw even though he knew there was nothing. There was only his pants and the shirt on his back and—

Well, it had worked with the sheet. What the hell *else* was he going to do?

Even as he started pulling off his shirt, he was relieved to see Mo had made it to her knees. The two of them were squaring off; both their heads were spinning at this point.

Doug spun the shirt around, twisting it into a rope. A very colorful rope.

Mo threw a punch. Rolf knocked it away, then swung back at her. She ducked, twisting as she dodged.

Rolf dove toward her, both hands again reaching toward her neck.

If Doug didn't act soon, he'd be too far away, and he'd lose his chance. Maybe if he leaned just right, he could get the shirt over Rolf's head, around his neck, and pull. He wasn't really sure if that could actually strangle the guy—and he wasn't sure he even wanted to—but it seemed like it ought to buy Mo some time.

Gripping the ends as tight as he could, Doug dove toward Rolf and let himself fall.

The fall was hard. Although it wasn't the first time he'd fallen, it had been a long time, and it hadn't usually been with another man's weight in the mix. His back smashed into the bottom of Mo's bunk, and he was pretty sure Rolf collided with it too. He hoped. But he couldn't see as he lost his grip of one side of the shirt and went sprawling.

Rolf's shoulder jabbed at his again. The scuffle continued over him, but only briefly. Then Mo was there, yanking Rolf off him, helping Doug sit up.

Her chest was heaving as she panted, and blood trickled down the side of her face past her ear.

"Holy smokes, Mo—are you okay?" He lifted his hand to touch her, realized he probably shouldn't, and snatched it back down.

"Are you? I didn't know you liked to stage dive."

"I wouldn't recommend it." He glanced at the stillness around them, then let out a sigh of relief. "Wait—you didn't say you were okay. You're not okay?"

Mo rolled her neck and shoulders. "I'll live." Her eyes flicked to the two bodies. "Time to look for some goodies. Good distraction, sir. You set them up for me to knock 'em down. Thanks for the help."

"I, uh, do what I can." Understatement of a lifetime.

She crawled forward to Rolf, and to Doug's alarm, started searching his pockets. "All right, I've got one ground rule for this escape."

"Escape?" He straightened, reached to arrange his legs in a better position. He had *hoped* that was what this was, but he hadn't really believed it possible. Weren't there still almost forty other crew members on this ship they'd have to subdue somehow? They'd barely handled two.

"Yes. We're escaping. You coming?"

"Uh. *Yeah.*"

"Then you've got to agree to my one rule." She drew a black

rectangle from Rolf's pants pocket, twisted it, and a dull silver blade flicked out. She smiled and pocketed it.

"Done. What is it?"

"Absolutely no chatting or joking while we are escaping. Got it?" Her lips twisted as she cast a laughing glance in his direction.

He snorted. "Got it."

She moved to Tattoo Guy now and was pocketing things he couldn't see, although he did spot a sleek black pistol she tucked into a thigh pocket. She tugged on the straps of his armored vest, jerked it off, and dropped it over her head. Considering his helmet, she touched a tentative finger to the wound on her head, then winced and sat the rifle back down. Tattoo's rifle went on the bunk as well as a ration bar. With their belts she made quick work of tying their wrists.

Then she turned to him and stopped, hands on her hips. "I'm going to have to carry you, sir, unless you have a better idea?"

"Unless you can knock out the gravity from here, no. Let's go."

"Fireman's carry, all right?"

"Actually that's not… No. I like to breathe."

"Breathing is good. And I need a rifle in this hand, so cradle lift it is." She winked at him. "You're lucky I was bored on the flight from our ship."

"Why is that?"

"Lots of time for training to do… this." She grabbed the rifle, stepped over him, slid it under his knees, and lifted. "Wait." She paused at the bunk, setting him down for a moment. Stepping away, she jerked Rolf's vest over his head and held it out.

"Won't this just make me heavier?" He put it on anyway.

"Better heavy than dead," she said.

"Won't I also be dead if you have to leave me somewhere because you ran out of steam?"

"Not dead as instantly as if you get shot! C'mon, we need to get out of here."

"Any pistols?"

She cocked her head with a dubious smile. "Do you know *how* to use a pistol?"

He grinned. "There's a first time for everything."

"All right, boy genius." She grabbed a pistol from Rolf too, pointed at a small yellow button on the side. "That's the safety. Keep it on so you don't fry me. Then we'll really both be dead. You need this, you push it, then pull that trigger and hold. This is laser, so you won't feel or hear anything except for if it cooks what it's hitting. At least, not until it overheats which hopefully won't happen. But you swing that at me, and I'll definitely feel it. My insides'll be all over the bulkhead. Fast. Got it?"

He nodded soberly.

Up he went again. She grunted. Damn. He wasn't a heavy guy, but he wasn't light either. For all the muscle some parts of him lacked, other parts of him made up for it—it took strength to get around using only your top half. And he could be bored too.

They needed a backup plan for if—when?—her strength ran out. Maybe his big brain could figure out where they might have stashed his floats—Tovi's cabin? An armory? Then he could *really* help. Or maybe they'd just tossed them into the burning wreckage of his childhood home.

Wasn't *that* a cheery thought.

He threw his left arm over her shoulder to help support his weight. They had to make do with what they had for now, especially since he wasn't thinking of any brilliant ideas. That was all her. He kept the pistol in the other hand.

"Let's just hope I don't have to use this," he muttered.

"Cross your fingers for me. Let's go."

———

THE FIRST THING Kael saw as Dane helped him heave himself out of their would-be grave was Ellen slumped against a support beam. She was a sight for sore eyes if he'd ever seen one.

The acid had left hissing, smoky white streaks across her armor. Dane's too. Kael staggered and found a support beam of his own to lean against.

Seven suns. That had been close. He coughed at a tickle of dust in his throat.

"So, maybe we could head over there now?" He gestured at the chaos.

She propped her hands on her hips. "Are you able to wait long enough for us to catch our breath, Lieutenant?"

"Precious minutes, Commander." But he smiled at her through his cleared visor. "I can spend the time looking for anything we left in the wreckage, though."

"Knock yourself out."

Dane, for his part, had climbed up into the hole that had opened above them and was scouting their way out.

He rooted around in the debris with his mind, looking for anything salvageable. One of the computers was still fairly intact, so he yanked that out as best he could, even if only to zero it. His suit readout ran through diagnostics as he worked, listing off a dozen complaints it took very seriously.

His Theroki armor would have rolled its eyes at those complaints, if it'd had eyes of its own to roll with.

One *was* pretty serious, though—there was a slight breach in the seal at the boot. Since he wasn't also wearing a breather, he was basically walking around breathing anything and everything that happened to breeze in.

"Who's got a leak?" Ellen said, straightening. "I've got a small one, damn it. One percent—knee joint. The nanos are attempting to seal it, but I don't think it's going to work."

He cleared his throat. "I've got something similar in the boot—not repairable."

"I put some auto-sealer on a thigh breach," Dane put in. "It looks like it will limit the damage more than it can actually fix it, though."

"Damn." She swore and slid to a seat on what might have once been a cabinet.

Some nanorepairs were possible with his model, too, and the suit was enthusiastically tackling the ones available. His breach, however, was definite—somewhere in the squishy lining. Heavier models like his were less automated, but withstood the acid exposure better. Not enough, though, clearly.

At least it wasn't his old, beat-up armor. That suit would have conspired *with* the debris to kill him.

The Gray Dragons were pros enough to set this off, although it did show a lot more foresight and murderous intent than he'd remembered them having. The usual technique of showing up with a bunch of heavily armed, heavily muscled bruisers probably didn't work when true power armor entered the equation, though.

Were they pros enough to attack again right afterward, make sure the job was done? Or were they staying the hell away from here? Stay off the police radar?

Although the police hadn't seemed on such a different wavelength, had they.

"I don't think anyone else was killed," he offered. "I can see some of these rooms were empty. Maybe they paid them to leave." Doubtful. He managed to dredge up a few pistols too and one rocket launcher bent beyond repair.

She shrugged. "Or we got lucky." Her eyes met his from across the room, and then she strode toward him. He perked up, listening for Dane, but the world around them was quiet at the moment. Or his suit had a malfunction it hadn't reported.

She didn't say anything into the comm, but her eyes said enough. The worry in them, the damn-that-could-have-been-it expression. He held out his hand. She reached out and clasped it. They couldn't feel each other, not really, although the suit fed some sensation into neurons, but hell if it didn't make him feel better.

Except that at just that moment, Dane's voice came over the comm. "I knew it! I knew I was a fragging third wheel! I knew it wasn't just in my head!"

Kael's eyes widened. Dane's armor caught the light from the floor above them, where he'd apparently been leaning against a column, waiting for orders probably.

Ellen groaned as they dropped their hands to their side. "I'm ready now. Suit's adequate. Dane—status?"

"C'mon. Really?"

"Drop it, Sergeant. We are not discussing this right now."

Dane sighed dramatically. "Fine, fine. No signs of hostiles. C'mon in. The water's warm."

"Are we headed to the pool then?" Kael asked. He wasn't sure if he should be alarmed or relieved by what just happened, but there wasn't truly time to feel anything. They needed to move. "Or are we just knocking on the front door?"

"I don't even care at this point," Ellen said. "Kick in the door if you want to. But I have been looking over these plans during diags. A service elevator from the kitchens in the back goes straight up to the pool. If we can sneak in with a delivery or something—"

"Or cut our way in," said Kael.

"We could take up the elevator to the top and see what we find."

"Is that a security control room? Right by the kitchen." Dane asked, throwing up a highlight on the map. "That means cameras. We check there, then if he's not on the roof, we can track him down."

"Even if he is on the roof," said Ellen, "what if he's taking a piss at just the wrong time?"

"Then he can just hide out in the bathroom while we have to sweep the whole place to find him?" Kael shook his head.

"We'll do this," she said. "Assuming we can believe security is properly on the blueprint—I'd have moved it—we'll go in through the delivery entrance. Covert or not, we'll go in. But we'll try covert first. The security room will be the most heavily fortified, so it's not knocking on the front door, but it's close. All three of us will go for that room next. Then Dane, you'll secure it, check the cameras for our guy, while Kael and I go shake his hand."

"Or shoot him," said Kael.

"Not until you get your answers."

"We'll see, at this point."

"Now we just need to get out of here and over there unnoticed. Get your camo on."

"That's one thing the acid did in on my suit," said Dane. "It's got a little coverage, but we're styling acid burns over here."

"Fashionable. Okay, let's go. Give me a boost?"

Nodding, Kael bent down and cupped two hands together. With a bounce in her step, she stepped up and leapt—the jump putting her squarely on the next level near Dane.

"Barely made a sound. You still got it, old lady."

"Thanks. I might even live to see twenty-three."

Kael took more of a jump and pull up approach, complete with loud crashing of the debris around him.

"You—not so much." Dane grinned as he silvered his visor.

"Sorry, they don't teach cat-like grace in Theroki University. I'll tell them to add it to the syllabus."

"You know what a syllabus is?"

"I know what a dictionary is, asshole. Let's go."

The streets were quiet outside. Too quiet. Maybe they had cleared the place out to keep people safe, but it was eerie. The Faros of his memories was always bustling, crawling with people. The dusty, silent street they slipped down seemed like some kind of apocalypse had come to pass.

But they dropped down an elevator tube, went crossways toward a market, and soon were lost in a throng of people once again. No one's dynacamo was really working, so obscurity in the crowd might be their best bet. They weren't the *only* people with power armor on the planet.

There couldn't be that many, though.

He walked faster. The best thing to do now was to get over there and cut off this creature at the head as soon as possible.

Something was niggling at him, though, and around the third open market they passed as they avoided the tubes, he cut Dane out of the comm line and reached out to just Ellen. "What if we find her there?"

"Her?"

"Asha."

"You'll know what to say. Don't worry about it."

"I *am* worried about it."

"Do you want to bring her flowers?" she taunted. "Maybe chocolate?"

"Can we poison the chocolate?"

"A worthy idea."

"I'm a lot more interested in which you would prefer, you know."

She was silent for a moment. "Maybe we should bring a bottle of wine. Isn't that what you're supposed to bring when you show up at someone's house?"

"Nice dodge. I think you bring wine when you're invited. But I am shocked we are both civilized enough to know that."

"Hey, I'm very civilized. And Dr. Taylor brought me one when she joined the team. Explained the custom to my perplexed and awkward self."

"I saw it in a holovid."

She snorted. "If we find her, you'll have your answers, for better or worse. And then we can proceed with kicking the shit out of Arakovic's plans."

There was a quiet pause for a moment. "Okay, but I do actually want to know about the flowers or chocolate thing."

"What about it?"

"Pick one. What do you like?"

"I'd like you to save your credits."

"C'mon. It can't all be small spaceships and parts deliveries all the time. What will I bring on our date? Assuming I survive Asha a second time."

She snorted. "You'd better survive. Would a new gun be an appropriate date gift?"

"You already have every possible weapon you could ever want, and you know it."

"You know me so well."

"Wow, another dodge. I'll just have to bring cookies to our date, I guess. Although it's not ideal. I think we've been there, done that, and invited Dremer to the party. And apparently now Dane knows the party's going on too."

She sighed as they turned down a narrower thoroughfare. "I didn't expect we'd hide it forever. We can talk to him about it... when all this is over."

"More dodging. That must be some kind of a record."

Her laughter eased the anxiety building in his gut a little. "Are you sure you want to date someone who gets you buried in building debris and industrial acid?"

"That is by far not the worst thing that's happened to me with you, and it's not getting you out of this question. C'mon, Elle."

"I told you, I'm not a date kind of girl. I'm not a gift kind of girl either. That's for normal people."

"You have to at least *try* those things before you get to claim that."

She laughed quietly. "God, if this mission doesn't kill me, your badgering just might. Will I even survive this date of yours?"

"That's the plan. No guarantees, but I will cross fire-eating in the heart of Ewotu off the list, if you like."

She chuckled harder now.

"If you think this dodge is getting you out of—"

"Fine! Fine. Inside the big metal death suit, I'm still a girly-girl that actually likes flowers, okay? Flowers. I like fragging flowers."

"Victory! What kind?"

"This torture will never end."

"Sure, it will, when you tell me—"

"Roses, damn you."

"Roses. Really."

"What? I told you, I'm old-fashioned. Orchids too. Actually I know a lot of them by their botanical names. Memorizing them was a childhood hobby—or maybe a stress response. Sexy, huh? Your girl once had a hobby of memorizing botanical information to keep from throwing up in space school. So what do you prefer, hot shot? Got a secret penchant for daisies?"

He snorted. "You got me. I've tried to suppress my love of daffodils and heliotropes, but—"

"Wait. Slow down." She stilled as they both spotted the officer on the corner. He winced that Dane didn't hear that muttered command, but their companion sensed them stopping and did likewise.

Instead of the usual gray fatigues, this officer wore some pieces of heavier armor, and he was scanning the street. Looking for someone?

All three of them eased back into the shadows while the officer scanned the open area, turned the corner, and headed away from them.

Kael let out his held breath, then checked the map overlay again.

"Almost there," he murmured. "Back entrance is down the next alley."

"You know, what ever happened to gender equality?" she grumbled. "Why do you get to dodge that question, and I don't?"

He followed her down the last alleyway, Dane watching their backs. Damn, he needed to get Dane back on their comm line. Time for this flirtation was up. He brought his multi around to the ready. "I might have a weakness for chocolate coconut bars. Forgot about them, but just saw them in a stall a few streets back." He snorted. "And baklava. And—"

"See? We're dead opposites. We should just give up now, this will never work."

"Or we'll never fight over who gets the last piece of candy." He grinned to himself at that thought.

"Let's live to find out, shall we?" From her voice, he was pretty sure she was smiling too. They were approaching the back door.

"I'm patching Dane back in," he said.

"Dane—get a scan going of the interior?" she said quickly.

"I see a dozen on the scan, maybe three immediately inside the door. Two armored vests, the rest look like service workers."

"Where are all those knockout grenades when you need them?" he muttered.

"Didn't think they'd let them through customs—and we're running low. See anything more armored than us?" she asked.

"Negative, Commander."

He scrolled the multi's setting through his suit and set it to stun. In the heat of battle, he avoided switching as much as he could, because mistakes were too easy, but in a calm moment, it was convenient. "Non-lethal it is," he muttered. Or at least it would be until he got to Maloof. And through him—Asha.

Ellen eased past the wide double doors that led into the mansion from the service alley.

Dane settled beside the door across from Ellen, and Kael shifted closer to inspect the door, knees bent, moving quietly. A simple lock hung to bar the way.

"Is it a digital lock?" Ellen started. "We've got basic hacking utilities even without Adan's—"

Frag it. He scrolled the gun back to laser, then pressed the muzzle to the metal lock, and pulsed. The thing melted to the ground, part of the door charred and smoking from the laser's bite into the grime there. He switched it back to stun.

She snorted. "What, Sidassian? No *Salam*? We come in peace? Please take us to the pool, we just have a few questions?"

"I don't come in peace. Not this time."

Dane chuckled. "Amen to that."

"On three—head in. One, two—"

He gripped the handle and got ready to pull.

"Three."

He flung the door open and back, Ellen and Dane swinging around him.

Cries went up inside, pots banging—clearly a kitchen. He checked the alleyway behind them—still empty—then pulled the door shut behind him as the others moved in.

Nano fog clouded the air as he turned back, sending up confused shouts. Kitchen workers scrambled for the doors. But people dropped one by one as Dane worked his way around the room from the right.

Doors slammed open ahead of him. Ah—the two slightly armored ones from Dane's scan. Before he could he even line up a shot, though, Ellen had hit both, her stun pulse crackling. Both went down with jerks and a few garbled cuss words.

He circled to the left, toward the security station. He pushed the doors the last two had entered through shut, as Ellen wedged a large steel ladle through the handles.

"Nothing like the old-fashioned way." He raised the multi up, ready to fire, but at the moment the hallway leading toward security was empty.

"We can't all melt everything to hell and back. Besides, we might need that door again."

"It's quiet," he pointed out.

"My scan shows—is that right? Only one person in there. It kinda looks like they're…"

The door to what had been marked Security Control Room on the blueprints stood a few centimeters ajar. He nudged it open with the multi.

Feet were propped up on a console. Combat boots, indiscriminate brown pants, a few screens he couldn't see clearly. Behind the propped-up feet were a bunch of brooms and buckets leaning against the wall. The sound of a snore drifted out.

"Are they… sleeping?" he whispered. Not that anyone could hear them through the armor.

"No…" she whispered back. "Maybe?"

"This room is clear," Dane said. "Headed your way."

"Keep quiet for Sleeping Beauty in here," she said.

He straightened and eased the door open further. It swung with a loud groan that stirred the guard in the chair, but didn't wake him.

Their target was indeed asleep. And alone. And in a room half filled with security feeds, and the other half with cleaning supplies.

"Is this a broom closet or a surveillance station?"

Kael took two steps forward, checked the multi was on stun, held it to the man's shoulder, and pulsed. "Clear in here too," he said, as the man rolled from the chair and hit the floor. He met Ellen's stare. "What?"

She shook her head as she stepped over their sleeping stunned guard to check the cameras. "Do you see him?"

Kael bent down and peered closer. Of the dozen cameras, most of them had someone on screen, but nearly all of them looked like workers. "Are they getting ready for something?"

"Something swanky." She tapped a screen. A pyramid of tall, thin glasses of something bubbling were being stacked by nervous women dressed all in black. "And here's your pool. Pool party?"

He snorted. "That would just—" Then he stopped short, narrowed his eyes. "There. That's him."

"Found our guy?" Dane said as he arrived in the doorway. "For a dangerous gang, I didn't think this was going to be a cakewalk."

"Me either," said Ellen.

"We're not out yet," Kael said. "They probably assume any attackers are using ballistics."

"What difference does that make?"

"Ballistics make noise. There's been plenty of screaming, but no gun shots, so maybe the soup just spilled. Or their champagne." Kael straightened. "Time to go up there and ask some questions."

"I've got this area." Dane frowned down at the inept guard. "I'll check these maps and cams and look for the fastest way out when you come back down."

"Good idea. There's our elevator," Ellen said, pointing. "Let's go."

The elevator took them to the top floor, but there was a long hallway and three rooms to cross before they made it to Maloof. The place was as beautiful as he remembered—long runners of red and teal carpet across glistening white tiled floors in detailed intricate patterns. The vaulted ceilings of the hallway led to plush rooms filled with pillows, low tables, pots of coffee, palms, and other plants he didn't recognize. Candles burned, filling the area with a sweet honeyed smell mixed with coffee that was pleasant—and also unpleasant because it must be getting into his suit through the leaks. The familiar smell hit him with a surprising pang of longing, of memory.

The sooner he got off this stupid planet, the better. Pretty as it was.

He pushed open the doors to the next room.

"That's five," muttered Ellen, as she managed to grab and stun one woman who'd been about to run back toward the hallway. "And she never got a scream out. Could be worse. Think they know we're coming?"

"They really should," he said. "But I'm dubious."

The final set of doors bore more lattice work, the fine, familiar geometric pattern sending a fleeting feeling of wistfulness through him. This was the kind of thing he'd left behind when he shut out all these memories—the beauty lost along with the pain.

Enough, enough. Now was not the time. He threw open the doors.

Outside, a small group was reclining on teak lounge chairs, their cushions a faded gold. Every one of them tensed at their approach, rifles in hand, but only one straightened up out of the seat.

"Maloof," he said over the suit's external speaker. The visor was already clear, and he gave the man a feral smile. The face of the leader he'd once known had softened over the years, and gray grew around the temples, but the steel eyes were just the same. He wore a light white short-sleeved shirt and pale gray casual shorts that came to his knees, the epitome of casual but finely tailored.

"What's this all about?" Maloof demanded. "Who let you in here?"

"We're looking for someone," Ellen surprised him by saying. She had the universal translator, but she spoke in Common. Her visor was cleared now too.

Maloof's gray-silver eyes darted to her. "Get out of here before I throw you out."

"Aw, but I thought you might have been interested in having a little talk with your old friend. There was this whole unfortunate accident where you tried to bury him and I under two tons of rock."

A light of recognition flickered in his eyes. "Doesn't seem to have been as effective as I might hope." His eyes switched back to Kael. "I didn't recognize you, Sidassian. To think, you were once handsome."

Kael raised an eyebrow. "Commander Ryu, meet the charming Gray Dragon himself. Asaed Maloof."

Maloof pursed his lips as he rose to his feet. Two other men rose at his sides. A handful of women and two more men stayed, still lounging but their eyes keen now. "Commander, huh? What are you doing these days, Sidassian?"

"I don't think you'd quite understand."

"I heard you traded a professional outfit like the Theroki for…" He waved vaguely at her. He didn't seem to know how to label Ellen, but the implication was clearly unflattering.

"The Theroki? A professional outfit? Clearly you haven't seen the *inside* of their ships."

"Hey, murderers don't always get off so easily."

"I'm not a—"

"I pulled strings for you, you know. We're small time stuff around here. The Theroki are the big time, big guns. You were much better off—"

"So that's the story you're going to go with? It was all out of the goodness of your heart, huh?"

Maloof continued like he hadn't heard anything. "One of their ships captured a Union cruiser just the other day. Barely left a naked chassis floating behind, bones floating in the deep." He chuckled.

"*Real* professional," Ellen said.

He smirked. "And you'd do better, little one? With what army?"

"I've directed fleets of Union cruisers in battle and have memorized ninety-eight percent of their commissioned ship schematics. So my chances are good."

"Only ninety-eight percent?" Dane muttered over the comm—a good reminder he was listening in from the security office. "Slacking, commander?"

Maloof looked a little thrown by the comment, but he forced an eye roll. "Praise the Almighty, I thought you'd sunk low, Sidassian—but consorting with the Union? That's really something."

"I'm not Union." She cleared her throat. "I'm retired."

Now Maloof froze, then he burst out laughing. "This must be some kind of joke. You pick up a waitress at the tea parlor down the street to play this part? For an idiot, she's a stone-cold bitch, though. She's got that part down."

"Don't call her that." Kael's voice was icy.

Maloof held his arms wide, as if to indicate his friends. "I will say what I want in my home."

"Not that."

"What are you going to do about it?"

Ellen raised her non-rifle hand. "Gentlemen—stand down. Mr. Maloof, we're just here to ask a few questions."

"Then *shoot*." He tucked his hands into his pockets, tone mocking.

"Asha Narulon," Kael said quickly. "Where is she? We know she's alive."

There was a flicker there. In his eyes. Fear—and recognition. "I don't know who told you such lies. She's dead. You should know, you're the one that strangled her."

"No," said Kael slowly. "I'm not." Strangled, huh? How many knew that detail? Had it been public knowledge?

"We have it on good authority, Mr. Maloof, that Asha Narulon is alive." Ellen took a step forward, and Kael followed suit.

"Don't call me that."

She took another step forward. "We have it on good authority that she's living here. With you."

He stared frozen for a long moment, then burst into another round of laughter again, clearly forced. "You would think two experienced soldiers such as yourselves would have learned by now not to believe everything you hear."

"We're not soldiers," said Kael. "We're mercs. Not every rumor is true—but some of them are."

"Where there's smoke," Ellen murmured, stepping forward again. He moved with her, at her side each time.

Another fake laugh, another tense moment. The silence stretched on.

"Something's up in one of these rooms," Dane said over the comm. "A bunch of women were just acting casual—eating, reading, sleeping —but they're up now, all talking."

Maloof glanced at his entourage, who was all staring at him. He spread his arms wide again and forced a grin. "All right, all right. You got me. She might be in service as one of my concubines. I try to keep them under my protection, you know, and—"

"Get her," Kael said. "Now."

"How dare you make demands in my home. I should shoot you for that alone."

"Gentlemen!" said Ellen. "We just have a few questions. This doesn't need to go that way. Then we can leave without any further damage."

"*Further* damage?" Maloof's glare cut to her.

Ellen stepped forward again. "There's no need for violence over a few questions."

"Fine, fine—Usef, go get Ms. Narulon. One of our *new* guests. In the ladies' wing."

"See," Ellen said quietly over the inner suit comm. "You're not the only one who can bully people. Do you think I could steal that comm of his?"

Kael tried to hide a smile at that, but his mouth definitely twitched.

"While we're waiting," said Maloof with another of his hospitable smiles that made Kael want to smack him. Two or three times. "How are you all feeling? I see you survived the explosion and the acid. What about the virus?"

An icy chill of adrenaline shot through him. But wouldn't a virus put Maloof too now in danger of catching something if it'd been given to them? Although, maybe it would be trapped mostly inside the suits, leaky as they were.

"Guess your luck ran out," said Ellen.

He let out a breath of relief at her bluff. If they were infected with something, it'd be impossible to say just yet. The suit hadn't reported anything, but it couldn't detect everything. The best strategy would still be to get Asha here, get his questions answered, and get back to the ship as quickly as possible.

"Luck? Please, I do not gamble. Really, where did you find this one, Sidassian?"

"A hell hole—you don't want to know," Kael replied. It was a throwaway comment, something to keep them busy while he watched. They were up to something, glances going from one to another of them. Or they knew something they were trying to hide... "And *she* found me," he added.

That moment when he'd first seen her in the command center in the cargo bay flashed through his memory—the strumming guitar playing, the easy, lazy way she and Mo had exchanged banter. The way he'd blurted out his skepticism that someone as young as her was the captain. The way he hadn't been able to take his eyes off her.

Only the skepticism had changed. And Mo....

A door opened, and a figure was silhouetted by light from the rooms behind before a woman drifted out along the poolside. She came to stand at Maloof's side, and he put an arm around her.

His stomach dropped as their eyes met. Her blue ones, a dull grayish blue like a sad sky. Those eyes he'd stared into so many times, stared back at him. Older, sharper, but just the same. Her form was still petite, almost fragile looking, and a pale blue robe draped effortlessly across her, tied with a belt at the waist and her arms bare, black hair cascading down around her shoulders. If it had been a decade, he wouldn't have known from looking at her. She looked just the same.

"That her?" Ellen murmured over the comm.

"Asha," he said in reply over the speaker. He nodded too. "It's been a long time."

"It has," she murmured back.

"I, uh… I've got a couple of—"

A click stopped his words. Maloof had drawn a pistol from his back and cocked the weapon. Asha tensed as the cold of the barrel pressed to the side of her neck.

"As he was saying, they've got a couple of questions for you, Asha, dear," Maloof murmured, his lips very close to her ear, his arm still holding her hard and tucked against his shoulder. "And I've got a couple of questions for them."

"Don't," Kael said, fighting to keep his voice hard.

"Why don't you take off all that nice armor, and we can have a conversation like civilized people?" Maloof's eyes glittered with malice.

"No," Ellen said, without a drop of hesitation.

"Take it off nicely now," he said, tone amused, "or you know what I'll do."

"We can't find out what we want if he kills her." Kael's hands were tightening uselessly into fists.

"We also can't find out if we're the ones who are dead," she hissed back.

"Smart cookie you got there. Perhaps my initial assessment was wrong." Maloof sneered at her.

"Maloof—you ass-faced shitbucket—" Kael started.

"Unfortunately, neither her dubious intelligence nor your insults are helping you out of this. Drop the armor if you want her to live."

"He seems remarkably *sure* you want her alive. Especially for someone who claimed to believe you killed her," Dane pointed out.

"How can we know you won't kill us?" said Kael.

Maloof's smirk deepened. "You can't."

"I just want to know what happened to the baby, okay? That's it. This doesn't have to go any further."

"It does, in fact."

"Look—whatever happened in the past is in the past. It's fine. Long forgotten. Let go of the gun, and we can talk, and then we'll leave, like civilized people."

Maloof threw his head back and laughed. To this, Asha only blinked, her hard eyes staring at the ground. Kael couldn't read her expression at all. Maloof's laughter faded to a broad grin. "You don't get it, do you? I sold your ass for a *reason*. You were never supposed to come back here. I don't want your questions. I want you *dead*. And then you stroll into my home with a bounty worth all of Faros on your head? Did you think we wouldn't hear about that?"

Ellen groaned. "We should have just shot them all and gotten it over with."

Maloof turned his glare on her. "You know what? I'll give you a chance to see I'm serious. I'll start with her knee. That won't kill her, just hobble her a little. *If* I stop there."

Asha sucked in a tense breath, bracing, but didn't scream. Kael held his own breath, waiting for the barrel to move away from her neck. Maloof lowered it all too slowly, caressing down her neck and across her shoulder, headed toward her arm.

Just a little further. Wait for it…

The moment the gun was the furthest from her skin, Kael blasted energy into the base of the grip from below. Because he had one ability they didn't have, or know he had. The telekinetic blast threw the pistol upward, smashing into Maloof's nose and eye. Blood spurted as he yowled. Kael hit the yellow safety button on the side as Maloof's pistol tumbled to the tile.

The man staggered back, hands to his face. Kael sent another telekinetic wave into Asha's back, forcing her to stagger forward. Maloof reached for her—

Ellen's stun pulse hit the gang leader barely a second later. She sprinted forward, firing off a dozen more pulses as she ran.

Instead of following her, he focused on covering her from the fire, forming a shield between her and the men who were no longer interested in just lounging by the pool. He dropped to one knee as several ballistics whizzed—mostly harmlessly—past them.

He'd stunned three more who were dashing toward him in the time it took Ellen to reach a startled Asha, who was staring at Maloof's bloody form, stunned.

Lunging forward, Ellen grabbed the woman by the arm, pulling her back toward Kael around the edge of the pool.

Maloof rallied at that, diving after them, so Kael slammed him from the collarbone to the ribs, shoving him back. The fat dragon hit the back of a couch and tumbled.

"Go, go!" Kael shouted.

Asha hadn't recovered from the shock and was lagging behind, her eyes only on the bloody poolside scene where Maloof had slumped, his nose tilted skyward, cursing.

Another spray of ballistics came from the door Asha had emerged from, and Asha only froze. Groaning, Ellen bent down and slung the woman over her shoulder, sprinting toward him and the elevator tube.

Kael turned around just as a flood of men burst in. The spray of ballistics might as well have been a chem or foam spray, because they didn't seem to give a shit where they were shooting. He slammed down a shield in front of them, gritting his teeth, but it wobbled under the onslaught—and he'd already used plenty of energy. It could only regenerate so quickly.

"Don't think they've trained in avoiding friendly fire," he growled.

Swearing, Ellen dashed to the side, taking cover as Asha's hands clutched at the back of her armor. "Did the Theroki?"

"Of course. It's a professional outfit—didn't you know?" Shield faltering, he took a knee and took aim right where he was anyway. Taking cover was going to take too much time, and the suit *ought* to be able to withstand this. "Just kidding. Not a chance."

"Amateurs."

He grinned as he focused on picking off each one of them, switching from stun to laser. If they were so determined to kill someone—or everyone—he wasn't considering them some kind of innocent bystanders. The sprays of automatics that peeked around corners and over furniture had already destroyed half the beautiful door. It crumbled now and crashed down, shaking the floor.

The water of the pool spiked, bullet spray shooting up in little fountains, and the miniature explosions were spreading in streaks across the tile floor. Good thing these guys just had basic ballistics and nothing better. His laser sheared through a couch and took out several hostiles, but he had to be sure he didn't destroy the building or the elevator tube. If he destroyed the way they'd come in, it'd be even harder to get out.

His laser heat level was rising, so he paused to switch to the chem spray. None of these guys were likely armored—maybe it'd be just as effective to get them to fragging stop. And they had to stop, because Asha wasn't armored like they were. It'd be hell to run through all *these* bullets like that. She wouldn't make it.

Of course, these Gray Dragons took his pause as an opportunity to let loose. The rest of the door collapsed, and trees and glass on the far side of the pool area were riddled with lead.

His blood went cold as screams split the air behind him.

Three bodies had crumpled behind the lounge area poolside. And Maloof with his bloody nose and bruised ribs slumping against the lounge chairs... He was now sporting several new holes and a fresh deluge of blood.

And he wasn't moving.

From around the corner with Ellen, Asha screamed. Or maybe screamed again. He fired the chem spray, sloppily peppering the entire back of the room. He flipped the multi quickly back to laser and started a continuous stream of suppressive fire.

"C'mon," he growled. "Power through before these guys kill everybody and themselves—I'll shield us as best I can. Asha, hold your breath. And shut your eyes, or you'll regret it."

They were out of time.

He dug deep for what strength he had left, deflecting the ballistics as they raced toward the elevator tube. A sharp chemical smell hit the inside of the suit—another very bad sign both for whether Asha would make it through the room unscathed, and for his own chance of reaching thirty.

Three more went down to a continuous slide of the laser as they ran, but there were still more, plenty more, with plenty of ammo left, and no concern at all on how they were spending it.

He panted as they slumped into the elevator tube, a nearly hysterical Asha sliding to a ball on the floor as the elevator took them down, tears streaming down her face.

"Are you okay?" he said. "Did the spray hit you?"

She didn't respond.

"Dane—" Ellen barked. "We need a lander or—"

"Already gotcha, Commander. Meet me at the service doors."

Kael stared at the woman—the ghost—in her fit of tears on the floor.

Alive. She really was alive. She'd never died. He'd never let her or the baby down—at least not the way he'd thought he had. All of the years of mourning, all of the guilt.

None of it had been real.

Or at least, not as necessary as he'd thought. There was still a tragedy here, he just wasn't sure what sort of tragedy specifically. He should be feeling sorry for the woman in tears on the floor, but it didn't come. Something about this picture didn't make sense.

He'd finally get his answers. Of course, he wasn't sure what he'd do with his answers once he had them. Maybe they'd prove her innocence. Or maybe they'd show something much darker had happened, even worse than his simple failure to protect those he'd loved.

And his imagination was providing all sorts of unlikely scenarios. And there was a chance—a small chance, but still enough of one—that perhaps he should have let the Gray Dragons shoot her, so that he wouldn't be tempted to kill her himself.

CHAPTER FOURTEEN

DAY 17

A SLEEK RED flyer was hovering outside, Dane at the controls, when Ellen burst through the service doors. She took the last two steps still at full speed and deposited the woman slung over her shoulder into the back seat with entirely too much momentum, but there wasn't time to slow down.

Asha let out a cry, but Ellen ignored it, sliding into the seat beside her. Kael collapsed into the front seat with something of a crash even as the lander started to move.

Ballistics peppered the door as it slid shut, and Ellen threw herself over the unarmored Asha. Nothing reached the interior—whether because Kael was shielding them or because the Gray Dragons pursuing them had atrocious aim. Or the flyer was that fancy. Who knew, maybe the gangster cars had shields.

Where did Dane get this flyer anyway? Thinking of Rutland, maybe she didn't want to know.

Dane gunned it forward on manual control as both of the doors clicked and hissed shut, their locks sealing. Ellen straightened and backed as far across the flyer from Asha as she could.

The woman she'd either just rescued or kidnapped—or maybe both

—didn't move. She was staring at her knees as she brought them up to her chest.

"Why even have a flyer on a place that's only tunnels?" Dane grumbled as the flyer struggled to turn tight enough around the first corner. All of them were swayed to one side, then flung back as he made the next turn. "This is so—ugh—unwieldy."

Asha wrapped her arms around her knees, her eyes darting up now to glare at each of them as she irritably wiped tears off one cheek. Probably from the chem spray they'd run through.

She was just like the picture Doug had dredged up—enough that Ellen had instantly recognized her by the pool. Thin but far from malnourished, she had a lithe look about her, like a dancer or a gymnast. Her expression seemed calm, but her shoulders shook slightly. She was… She was shaking. Could be shock, fear, rage—even the cold air of the flyer blasting them at full speed. Ellen reached forward and punched the air down a few notches.

Asha's large, dark eyes studied each of them once more before coming to rest on Kael.

Ellen swallowed. Something in her gut tightened at the glint in Asha's eyes, a fist closing and twisting in her gut. She said nothing about it, though, held herself still, steady. He needed that right now.

Kael turned in the seat and retracted his helmet, his hair falling forward into his eyes. He was a little disheveled, but you'd never know he'd been through all they'd survived in the last twenty-four. He opened his mouth, but then hesitated.

"Is he dead?" Asha whispered.

Ellen frowned. Of all the things she might have expected this woman to say, that wasn't one of them.

"I think so," Kael said.

Asha bit back a sob.

"Who?" Ellen demanded.

"Maloof—his own men hit him. While they were trying to hit us. Looked pretty bad." If Kael was thrown by Asha's question, he didn't show it.

She narrowed her eyes at Asha as Kael turned his gaze back to the woman he'd once loved.

"Kael. I-I thought you were dead."

"Did you now," he drawled. "I could say the same to you."

"It's been so long." She reached out a hand, as if hoping he'd clasp hers. The fist in Ellen's gut twisted harder.

Kael didn't move. "Who told you that?"

"What?"

"That I was dead."

"I don't remember. It was ten years ago."

"You'd think you'd remember the moment you found out I was dead. I remember when they told me that you and—" His voice faltered.

She glared at him. "You have no idea what I went through. I might as well be dead."

"What happened, then? Where were you? There was a dead body with your fingerprints—and I looked for you, hoping it was all a mistake. And it was, apparently. Where *were* you?"

"It's complicated—"

"You know what's complicated? Getting sixty-eight percent of your bones removed and replaced with metal ones. Getting a new cyber-netic spine. Getting your blood turned into a science experiment. *That's* complicated."

"I'm so sorry that happened," she said quickly.

"If you're sorry, then you'll tell me the truth. Where were you?"

Pain had creased Asha's face more and more as they went on. Somehow, though, it didn't build any sympathy in Ellen's mind. It felt more like watching a bug squirm under a microscope. She'd have preferred Levereaux here more than Taylor—someone to help her pin this pretty bug in place. Emotion charged the air—but suspicion and bitterness most of all.

Did she just hate this woman that much for hurting him? Or was it something else?

"Where were you, I said," he demanded into the silence.

"Abrams," she blurted. "It was Abrams. He took me and—oh, Kael, it was horrible."

"Abrams." Kael's expression was incredulous.

"Yes—he held me in those mining warehouses he was working on back then. They had dozens of women down there. Their personal playthings, a few of them at the top. Maloof got rid of all that after you were gone. He set me *free*. I owe him—I owe him everything. Owed, I guess." A sob choked her throat, and for the first time, Ellen felt a tiny bit of sadness for her. "How can he be dead?" She covered her face with her hands.

Kael's mouth hung open, and she couldn't tell what he was thinking of this story Asha'd produced. None of the others had pointed at Abrams, and if Abrams were dead, they would have had no reason to be afraid.

They'd pointed at the man they *did* have a reason to be afraid of. What did any of them have to gain by that? Unless they had somehow hoped Kael would end up killing Maloof—in which case, that would have been almost right.

Whatever Kael was thinking, his gaze hardened. "What happened to the baby? You're not dead. Did it survive? Where is it?"

She flinched. "I lost it."

"I don't believe you."

Rage flashed in her eyes. "They *beat* me—you think they wanted a pregnant woman for their games?"

"Abrams wasn't that kind. Something doesn't add up."

"Maybe you didn't know him as well as you thought."

"That certainly applies to you."

Their eyes locked for a long moment, his suspicious, hers imploring. Her sad, wide eyes gradually narrowed to anger again. "Damn you, Kael Sidassian. Why couldn't you just leave me alone?"

This was getting them nowhere, so now it was her turn. "Why are there no medical records?" Ellen said.

Asha rolled her eyes. "Oh, right. Like they gave a shit what happened to us. They weren't taking us to the *clinic*, you moron."

She held in the lash of anger and pressed her lips thin. "At over five months, you wouldn't have been any use to them for quite some time either way. You seem like a very poor selection for a brothel."

The other woman glowered at her. "Because criminals are so smart. Besides—I don't know—maybe it was personal." She waved angrily in Kael's direction. "If there was a body, somebody must have put that together, right? Maybe that's what they wanted."

"Well, if they wanted to ruin my life," he said coldly, "they did a pretty good job of it. Worst thing short of killing me."

"There are worse things than death," Ellen said simply, eyes still on Asha.

The other woman's eyes widened. "Who *are* these people, Kael? And where are we going?"

"Nowhere, right now," Dane said, his tone oddly breezy. "Just stayin' lost from those bees on our tail."

Asha glanced from Dane to Kael to Ellen and back. "Look, I have a place. It's not that far, although I haven't been there in months. If my stuff is still intact and nobody broke in and took everything, I have proof there. Letters between me and my sister I sent after I was freed and I'd lost everyone that mattered to me. Not that any of you seem to care."

There was that fist again, twisting like a knife to the gut. It didn't help that Kael's eyes softened at the comment.

"Take me there, and I can show you." Asha lifted her chin.

Kael looked to Ellen.

"Give us a second," she said. She switched the comm to just between the two of them, then silvered her visor just in case Asha happened to read lips.

Asha scowled as Kael raised his helmet too, visor clear, but didn't object.

"Look, Kael," she said quickly. "This could be a trap. She's almost certainly lying. But we could search through her stuff ourselves if we get in there. Easier if she lets us in than breaking in, right? We have enough authorities glaring at us."

His brow furrowed, thinking. "Why would she lie? Because there's no way Abrams did what she's saying. He didn't even employ prostitutes, let alone hire them. He was weird about it, actually—something to do with his mother. Something happened, but not that. Maybe Asha didn't know or just isn't remembering, or she wouldn't have picked him. Why can't she just tell me?"

"Because she did something horrible she doesn't want you to know about? Because whoever did this to her is still alive, and she's swapping in Abrams because he's dead?"

He frowned, thinking. "Some part of it has to be true—that she lost the baby in some kind of kidnapping situation, right? I mean, otherwise, where is it? Otherwise there would be records for Doug to find."

"That would explain the lack of records, yes. Conveniently. If she'd been free and didn't want the baby, she could have just transferred the pregnancy to an artificial uterus. It's fairly easy—why not do that?"

"We wouldn't have had the money for that."

"Even if you didn't, people will pay. Charities. People looking to adopt in exchange—" Ellen stopped short.

"Don't those people pay the mother for the baby too, not just for the medical costs?" he said slowly.

She swallowed. "Sometimes."

"Why not just engineer one?"

"They're Puritans? They have bad genes? I don't know."

"Something needs to explain where all the money came from for that house in Doug's pictures. If she has a place, why would she be at Maloof's?" He paused, let out a breath. "Could that really be it? Maybe her story is true—or maybe it's covering up that she sold the child. Why kill it if you could sell it?"

She made a little choking sound in disgust. "This is a human being we're talking about."

"I *know*."

"I know you know. Damn it. We need to give her an answer here."

"If we don't go, what else are we going to do with her? Have a staring contest?"

"Take her back to the *Audacity* and see how she talks then?" She shook her head. "No. If there's any records that Doug couldn't access —hard copies—they'd be in her house. Plenty of people have isolated networks. Hard copies, even. We're most definitely installing a nuke and making an external connection. But it's probably a trap."

"I don't know. She looks pretty harmless. If Maloof is dead, the head is cut off. The body is flailing. Even if the Gray Dragons suspected we'd go to her place, who's going to martial a response? None of those idiots looked ready."

Ellen nodded, then turned back toward Asha. "Fine. We'll go. Tell us the address."

Asha rattled off the address—that they knew already—and Dane changed course. Ellen eased back into the seat, turned toward the window so it was less obvious she was still talking, then switched back to the Kael-only comm line.

"We've got a few minutes. Let's see if we can crack this nut before we get there. So she finds some rich buyers. They take the baby off her hands. Why no adoption records?"

Kael also turned forward in his seat again, so Asha couldn't see him. "Fathers have to approve those adoptions, don't they?"

"Especially if the mothers are dead. Although maybe because of Dr. Abed's slight of hand, she wasn't dead by that point. And if the adoption was under the table, none of the laws need apply, right?"

"A few rials—"

"I get it. Bribery is a powerful thing. I'll keep that in mind."

"The skills you learn on Faros."

"Okay, so the rials are flying. Still, who would want to do all the work to raise some kid if the father was going to come looking?"

"So she finds a way to convince them the father won't be a problem."

He cleared his throat. "Like if the father was incarcerated off planet for life?"

"Funny coincidence, that."

"Did the rich adopters help her frame me, or did they not know?"

Ellen shrugged. "Either way, they have your kid."

"Or she's telling the truth, and it died in some hellhole eons ago."

She flinched, hard. "If there's answers to that, we're close. While you try to look at whatever evidence she has, I'll try to get onto the network on my own. Dane can run interference."

"I don't know if I can take any more lies. Or supposed proof about all this."

"We'll figure this out. I promise you. If the kid is alive, we'll track them down. You'd want to find them, right?"

"Of course. I'd at least want to know they're okay. Although, I don't know. Maybe they're rich assholes who won't appreciate knowing their biological dad isn't a wealthy philanthropist and he's actually a—"

"A what?" she snapped. "Don't."

"I'm just saying the kid may not even know they're adopted. And I'm—"

"A critical member of an elite paramilitary unit that does a lot of good for the galaxy. And don't you forget it."

He laughed quietly. "You won't let me."

"Well, what *else* does a commander do?"

"I need a new tattoo."

"For a new kid, a new murder, or the new load of bullshit we've been shoveled on this planet?"

He was quiet for a moment, but there was still a softness in his voice when he answered. "For you, Elle."

———

THE RUSH of the escape had made Doug forget how fragging cold he had been, but the corridor leading out of the brig was blessedly warm. So warm. This room was helping a lot to actually make the chill go away. Not that Mo's body heat while he was cradled in her arms was hurting anything either.

It was also surprisingly empty. The intake room after that was also unmanned and silent. The stillness of it was instantly unnerving.

Mo paused and frowned, scrutinizing the open hatchway that led beyond the brig.

"What is it?" he asked.

"There should be a forcefield here, blocking the brig from the rest of the ship. But it's down."

"Why?"

"That's what I'd like to know." Mo turned right down the main corridor.

"How did you get the door open?" he murmured, keeping his voice low.

Face serious and strained, she didn't meet his eyes as she answered. "I used an RPD charge to try to disable the doors. I thought I might be able to fry the lock, but that failed. We got lucky though."

They took another turn before he risked speaking up again. "How did we get lucky?" Well, that sounded wrong.

She paused, resting her back against the metal wall, then leaning around a corner to check for anyone in sight. Nothing. After all the boots stomping around earlier, what was going on? No one stomping around now.

"The charge fried the temperature and humidity sensor," she said, "Convinced the computers it was a billion degrees in there. Emergency, doors open, evac."

"Wow. Resourceful."

"Thanks. Of course, that probably set off an alarm somewhere."

He waved his free hand, forgetting their was a pistol in it. "Looks like I'm not the only hacker in this escape."

"No, it's just poor electrical. One of the reasons why these Ranger-class Vipers were decommissioned."

"Exploiting weaknesses is literally the name of the game, Mihio."

She frowned at him slightly. Because he hadn't said Mo? Or she didn't like being called a hacker? "This was a fairly weak brig overall. These ships were supposed to be used for strike teams as part of a much larger naval attack force. The brig is intended for wayward crew members, not POWs. Temporary. Destroyers or battleships would have much more sturdy and fortified and larger areas for confinement."

"Sounds homey."

Her lips quirked up. "Not exactly." She narrowed her eyes, peered around another corner, and then hurried across it. "One more corridor, and we should be close to the shuttle bay."

"And shuttles mean getting us the hell out of here?"

"That's my plan."

He couldn't help but grin. "Damn, Mo, I could kiss you."

Sweat was beading on her brow. "Please don't, sir."

He winced inwardly. He'd meant it as a joke. But of course. How many women were interested in men they had to carry around? Weren't men the ones supposed to do the carrying?

"Sorry. Please don't, *Doug*."

He smiled, then ducked his head, feeling a flush creep up his cheeks. "You're nothing if not respectful of the chain of command, *Mo*."

"I mean, maybe when we're not about to get killed would be a better time?"

When he raised his head, her eyes locked on his, like she was trying to work out some kind of puzzle. He raised his eyebrows.

She grunted and heaved him up a bit, tearing her gaze away.

How much longer could she last carrying him? Damn. He hadn't regretted his decision to stop the surgeries many times in his life, but he was getting there.

She sucked in a breath, then peeked around the corner. She swung back quickly. "Shit."

"What?"

"That way is blocked. Not by people. By blast doors." She leaned against the wall, letting it support a little of his weight for a moment. She was going to need a break. Soon.

"Blast doors? But no alarms are going off," he said.

"Maybe somebody turned them off. Or they're broken."

"There must be decompression in there. Or a fire or some other problem."

"It doesn't matter." She grunted and lifted him a bit higher. "There's another way to the shuttle bay. I just wish I knew if that's where the problem is. We can't afford to go the long way around if it'll just be blocked again. Could get trapped."

"Why are these corridors so damn empty?" It wasn't really a question.

"Something's fragged."

"Can you get me on a computer? Maybe I can get access to some cameras or something."

She scanned the corridor, wrinkles of concern furrowing her forehead.

"Or maybe I can cause a distraction."

Her eyes caught on something. "There's a cabin. Two or three of them. Let's try it." She rushed the dozen yards to the nearby hatch. "Try that palmpad, maybe it's unlocked—"

Even as he tried it, he was shaking his head, and neither of them were surprised when it didn't open. "No way we're getting off that easily. Good thing I have another way."

He would have much rather had a screwdriver, but he picked up the pistol instead. She jumped, taking a step back as she instinctively tried to distance herself. He couldn't blame her. But this, he could do. Probably.

"Steady, Mihio. Isn't that what you're good at?" Her lips twisted in chagrin as he thumbed that little yellow button and squeezed. The beam bit into the metal frame beside the palmpad, sending a few sparks flying. He whistled. "Oh, that's fun. No wonder you like these things."

Her lips were pursed. "I *am* steady when I'm not carrying someone. That comparison is hardly fair."

"I wasn't serious." He managed to slice a 'u' shape out before he let the trigger go. "I rarely am, you know."

"I hadn't noticed. What are you—" she started.

Putting the safety back on, he held up the pistol. "What's this made out of?"

She raised an eyebrow. "Uh, metal? Why does it matter?"

Right—if the weapon created the laser, it ought to be able to withstand the heat of one. "I'm just being careful."

Using the barrel, he prodded at the sliced open hot metal, working the two pieces gradually apart. He caught the inner—much cooler—edge where the palmpad screen met the metal with his fingernails and pulled. The plate bent at a good forty-five degrees, enough to reveal the lock's innards and give him some room to avoid the still hot bits.

Looked like an older model 12295 palmpad. Maybe a 1491Z, but the configuration was familiar.

Yes. He could work with this.

"Step a bit closer?" he asked. She complied, and he viciously yanked out a flat blue wire, then went for the black and red. Working with one hand wasn't easy, but with the other one he was still trying to hold up some of his weight. Good thing the laser heat hadn't gotten inside and melted *all* the circuitry. Hard to say if that would have opened the door for evac, or closed a blast door if this cabin had one.

"What are you doing?" she murmured.

"Taking the palmpad off the ship's network, then rebooting. May let us in, depending on the model."

"Didn't know you were a digital locksmith."

"What do you think my drones have been up to on all those missions?"

"That's fair."

The lock was off the network and out of power now, so he just needed to reconnect the power only and… He carefully reinserted the red into the electrical port and tucked back the black, using both hands for the critical reconnection. If he got them electrocuted, that really wouldn't help the situation. He doubted he could have stripped this and rewired it with that pocketknife she'd stolen. If the thing was even sharp. "I prefer digital tools to get in and open up," he murmured as it clicked home. Thank Heaven for component parts. "But gee, I'm all out."

"You should have packed better, sir."

"Indeed. Maybe next time they'll send an invitation. Allows a man to plan. Could have brought two sets of floats. Or contact lenses. Are we dangerously close to chatting?"

"Oh, we're definitely chatting."

He opened his mouth to apologize, but the door beeped and slid open as the reboot began. "Yes! In! In! Go!"

She rushed in, easing through the hatch sideways and admirably not hitting him into anything. Yet.

The room didn't disappoint. It was an office, complete with a holodesk. She half-sat, half-dropped him in the office chair, but he was off and running—so to speak—into the system almost before her touch left him.

In his peripheral vision, she slumped against the wall, hands on her knees, then sat on the nearby bunk as soon as she spotted it. She shook her arms out and stretched them wide, then dabbed at the wound on her head.

In the greater light of the cabin, he went still for a moment. The blood had trickled down the side of her head and neck. Reddish black had seeped into the flight suit, forming a growing splotch at the collar. That side of her head had been out of his view. Intentionally?

"Jeez, Mo, are you okay? Let me find sick bay on this thing—"

"No," she snapped. "It's nothing."

"That's a lot of blood. Is there a mirror? We need to get you help."

"The best help is getting us off this ship." She took a deep breath. "Seriously. Yeah, I know it looks bad, but it's just a surface wound. It's okay. Check on the shuttle bay. Shuttles have first aid kits too."

He narrowed his eyes. "I'll check on it first. Then the sick bay." Meanwhile he would start the computer running a diagnostic scan of her…

She leaned back against the wall and closed her eyes. "Fine."

He was aware of her as he worked, like a song he couldn't quite tune her out. That never happened to him. Usually when he was in a flow, the whole world faded away around him. Which was part of what had made Tetra so tolerable. He'd been in his head, in the networks, in the program.

But not now. It was like something tethered him to reality. To her.

Probably that she was his only chance of getting out of here alive.

She brushed both hands down her pants before she stood up and strode to listen near the doorway. "I don't hear anything. That's good."

"Me neither," he said. Not that he was paying much attention to his ears.

"Can you get into that computer system?"

"Oh, I already am."

"How?" She returned to his side to gaze at the holos flashing past.

He tapped a finger to his temple. "Some tools you don't have to pack. This particular operating system has a few weaknesses if you know where to pry. Some governments actually require contractors to keep loopholes, so the software companies can't take control of the whole galaxy via the computer systems."

"Deliberate weaknesses?"

"Yep. Known only to a few. Well, that and master passwords created by those software companies."

"Remind me never to trust computers."

"Never, ever trust computers." He grinned at her, but his face fell as the same error came back from the shuttle bay a second time, then a third. It didn't make sense; at his permission level, he should have access. It was like they were broken, completely offline. But four cameras? All at once? He cleared his throat, not wanting to show weakness around her. Well, not any more than he already had. "Is there another option? If we can't get to the shuttle bay?"

She nodded, expression somber. "There's a third option. But it isn't a good one."

He decided not to ask. He could do this. "The view into the shuttle bay is giving me trouble, but I'll figure it out. Give it a minute. Anything else we should check on?"

"We need help, resources, intel." Mo pursed her lips. "Can we start with looking for help? Even in the best-case scenario of opening the blast doors and going straight for the shuttle bay, this is far from simple."

"I thought you were comfortable with two-to-forty-two odds."

"At worst, it's two-to-thirty-eight. Can you reach the *Audacity*?"

He tried, then shook his head. "The bridge has outgoing comms locked down. There is a short-range emitter in the shuttle bay docking communicator... Maybe I could insert something there they wouldn't catch."

"The docking what now?"

"It's a little device that guides ships docking with each other. Talks back and forth about where the other one is."

"That doesn't sound like a normal comm."

"It's not a normal comm. It's a hack." He winked. Damn, he was getting over the top. Nothing like computer access to make his day. Or month. "Let me just… There we go. It will notify anyone who comes close enough that we're here." That might be just as dangerous as it was helpful, but he was willing to take his chances.

"What about the passenger manifest?"

He eyed her bleeding before answering, and didn't miss that she turned slightly in response, so it was harder for him to see. "What for?" He started looking even as he asked, though.

"To look for… possible help?"

He caught the strange note in her tone, and his fingers were typing even before he spoke. "You mean look for my parents. Don't you."

She shrugged. "And it will tell us our odds."

"Was that… a joke?"

"Maybe an inappropriate one."

The list came up. "Here we go. Crew of… thirty. Nice. Prisoners include…" He trailed off. His name was listed there, along with hers and two others he didn't recognize.

No one else.

He let out a long, slow breath as his shoulders fell. His hands had frozen over the holokeys, perched and waiting for orders. But he had none, at the moment. He just stared down at his hands, at the desk.

Could they really be dead?

Her warm arm over his shoulder made him jump, but only slightly, and a sudden warm feeling suffused him, battling the despair.

"Why bring me and not them if they're alive?" he whispered. But then did Quentin have a beef with all of the Foundation, or just him personally?

"We can't know anything for sure." Her hand squeezed gently. "We can only live and get out of this, and then we'll figure things out. Doesn't help to worry until then."

"There's no help coming, nobody we can reach," he murmured.

"That's okay. We can help ourselves."

Tearing his gaze from the backs of his hands, he caught her eye. In spite of the exhaustion, the fighting, the stress, her eyes were calm and glittering as ever. A sniper ought to be calm under pressure, he supposed, and they weren't her parents, so he didn't know why her placid expression surprised him, but it did. It radiated confidence, calm. Practicality.

He sucked in some air and drew himself up. "You're right. Sorry. Let me try this damned shuttle bay one more time."

Three more attempts later, he still had no access to the shuttle bay feeds. Or the locks on the hatches in the area. Or the cargo manifests. Nothing was reachable. Denied, denied, denied.

When he looked up, he found her sitting on the bunk. Did she look paler?

"I can't find any way to get a view on the shuttle bay or unlock the blast doors," he admitted grudgingly. "Other readings on the shuttle bay look normal. No decompression, normal temps. Someone used a backdoor trigger to set off the blast doors, but that weakness has been isolated by the crew on the bridge, with large portions of ship code locked down. Our adversaries are competent. Which is not helpful at all." He was scowling at the screen now. It was much harder to go unnoticed in a system where someone had already caused all sorts of problems. Like stealing something under a spotlight.

"Okay, then. We need to consider the other parts of the ship and what we can do with them."

"The sick bay is oddly busy, so we're not sneaking in there for your head. But I do have one thing for you. Milady, I present to you, a vid feed of the bridge."

She hesitated to stand, but finally strode to join him at the desk. She pointed, counting. "Twelve. Shit. All armed. Stunners and lasers too."

"That's a lot."

"It is. No Tovi, though. Where is she?" She bit her lip. "If we seized the bridge—and therefore the ship—we could get where we wanted. But we would need a way to keep everybody else out." She shook her head. "There's no way. We need a shuttle. Too easy to breach the bridge with a blowtorch to the door. Probably a dozen other things too."

"Also the blast doors might block the way anyway. Unless we find our own blow torch."

"Good point. And even with a torch, it'll take a while. We'd get caught. But that's a good point about the blast doors, we don't know how many are down. What *can* we get to? Who is in our immediate vicinity?"

"Let me see." He squinted harder. "Computer, overlay the manual overrides on the ship's map and bring up on the large holo."

"Acknowledged," said the computer. The ship's glowing blue map highlighted a half dozen blast doors in red.

Mo stepped forward, concerned. "Does that look like somebody cordoned off a section of the ship to you?"

"Yep." He swallowed hard. "Think that somebody was Rolf?"

"I'd bet on it."

"Engineering is inside. Whoever did this would have some power, there. They can stop the bridge in its tracks."

"Another reason why we can't simply seize the bridge, even if such a feat were possible," she said. "And with these blast doors down, Rolf and his buddies don't need to have superior firepower to hold this area. They don't need to even guard it."

While she studied the map, he ran his fingers over his face. He'd never been prolific when it came to facial hair, but after this long in captivity, he was nearing an actual beard. He needed a thousand showers and at least ten hot meals. And off this stupid ship.

"Mutiny." She swore under her breath, and it didn't sound like Common to him.

"Huh?" He pulled himself out of his exhaustion. No way out but through.

"There's got to be more than just the three of them," she said. "They're trying to twist Tovi's arm. Maybe they even attacked her if she's not on the bridge. But we heard all those boots earlier. That was more than three people. Who else is in our section of the ship?"

He initiated a quick scan, then added the results to the holo map. "Four in engineering, probably the ship engineers. One in a cabin— looks like Overalls is hiding out. Is that a chocolate bar? For heaven's sake. There's the two we dropped in the brig. And then there are two more by the blast door closer to the bridge. Why there?" His expression darkened as he raised his gaze and enlarged a view into one of the corridors. Two leather-clad figures crouched near a blast door, burning through with a pair of blowtorches. "Oh, boy. Speaking of blowtorches."

"Where'd they find them? And who the heck?"

"The other two prisoners?"

She raised her eyebrows. "I thought it was Rolf who closed the blast doors."

"So did I."

She squinted. "Can you zoom in there? I'm at max zoom with my eyes, the resolution is too low. There's something on his sleeve."

Frowning, Doug did so. If he were ever going to reconsider his stance on augments, those eyes were sounding mighty good right about now. Although the idea of some hacker hijacking his eyes was pure horror.

She pointed. "Look—Puritans. That's a Puritan pilot's insignia—blue and brass, the tree with leaves?"

"What does that mean?"

"Maybe we're not the only prisoners I set free?"

"Maybe Rolf let them out to help him in his mutiny?"

"I don't think his mutiny is working out the way he planned. I hope I tied him up thoroughly enough."

"I hope he's lost circulation in his hands."

"My, you're vindictive."

"Fear my vengeful wrath." He grinned.

"Four to six hostiles in the immediate area. We can handle that."

"Are we headed to Engineering?"

"If we can control it, we can try to make a deal. Get them to take the ship where we want it to go. But we could use help. A distraction, maybe?"

He winced inwardly, doubting it'd be that easy. How did one get from the engineering room one had hijacked to freedom outside the ship? But he had no other ideas. "Distractions… let me see."

"I'll search the room. Should've done it right away. Was just taking a small rest."

"Are you sure you're all right?"

"I'm fine." She strode to the bunk, squatted down, and yanked on a case underneath it with an air like she had something to prove. That only made him more concerned. But she stopped abruptly after two or three pulls. "Wait, did you say four in engineering?"

"Yep."

"Well—Tovi can staff her ship as she likes, but when I was crew on one of these, there were only two engineers on any given shift. And thirty is a lot smaller than forty-two recommended staffing. Why double up there?"

His brow furrowed. "I can't get a view into Engineering either. That video's shut down too."

"Convenient." She heaved at the case again, but it only partially budged, making a loud groan as it scraped across the floor. She winced, then gave up on it for now.

She rejoined him and started searching the drawers of the desk for anything useful. The first one gave her a sharp gasp. "Ration bars!"

"Oh hell yes. I have never been so excited to eat dehydrated whatever I don't care just give it to me." He had no idea when he'd last downed one of their shakes.

She threw a half dozen on the desk's surface, pocketed a dozen more, then ripped open one and started chewing.

He bit into his own and groaned. "If I ever have a child, I'm going to have to name her Cherry after this granola bar. Nothing will ever be quite this good."

She snorted as she opened the closet of the cabin. "I should hope her mother would have some say in Cherry Granola's name," she said through a mouthful of her own bar. "I mean, 'Chocolate peanut butter' doesn't have the same ring to it, but I'm pretty fond of my bar too."

He froze for a second mid-bite. Was she implying… Nah, that had to be wishful thinking on his part.

Focus, Dougerino. It's time to focus. He shook off the thoughts, swallowed, and took another bite.

Environmental controls. Yes—there.

She closed the door to the closet. "Nothing much in here. Next we should—"

A loud, deep voice from ship comm cut her off, booming down from over their heads. "Renegade ship *Sparpspear*, this is the commander of the Puritan cruiser *Athens*. You have been boarded. Prepare to surrender."

Their gazes met, both their eyebrows raised.

"Well. That explains what's going on in the shuttle bay."

She shook her head. "This isn't good. Two enemies are not improving our odds."

"I'll get moving on the distractions." This ship was about to get some wild temperature settings in every room he could reach. And could he make them oscillate every twenty minutes?

Yes. Yes, he could. Two could play at the temperature torture game.

Just as Mo bent to work on heaving the heavy case out from under the bunk again, a loud clang sounded out in the corridor. Air puffed, then the low sounds of boots and murmured voices. What now?

Mo froze, and they both perked up like hunting jackals. He grabbed a screen from his left and pulled it closer as he enlarged it.

Outside, Tovi and half a dozen armed men marched into the corridor outside, helmets on and laser rifles at the ready.

"Time to deal with the mutiny?" Mo whispered, rushing to him and bending close.

"Or the Puritans?" he whispered. "Maybe the docking bay was an inside job?"

"Rolf found some allies in his mutiny?"

He shrugged. His eyes snagged on her for too long before he tore them back to the vid feed. The group was moving slowly down but hadn't passed their cabin yet. They weren't entering any of the rooms, but...

Hell. "They're scanning the cabins manually," he whispered, pointing. He grabbed his pistol where they'd left it on the desk, even if he barely knew how to use it.

She winced as she swung her rifle over her shoulder on its strap. "They don't *need* to scan this one. We left the busted palmpad hanging outside."

Shit. And he'd thought he'd been being so clever. Maybe he had, but he'd also left a trail.

Her eyes darted around the room, then she pointed at the closet. Which was probably a generous term for it—it had a door more like a metal locker, but he always assumed bedrooms had closets. Maybe not, in the deep.

At his thumbs up, she hefted him out of the chair.

Swaying a little as she squatted down inside the closet, she set him down, then crawled in beside him. Together, they swung the door shut, lifting and dropping the latch as silently as possible.

Emergency handholds studded the inside of the closet along with yellow hazard tape, so maybe there was some shielding in here that might help them, hide them from Tovi's people and their scans. Maybe their foes would simply be stupid, and they wouldn't be recaptured.

But he doubted it.

He looked over to Mo to gauge how she thought this might go. A slight bit of illumination from the cabin leaked in and cast a thin beam over her features. The rifle sat across her lap, pointed away from him. Her eyes had drifted closed, and the blood-soaked area of her flight suit had grown.

Gently, he reached out and put his hand on her knee, slowly, hoping it didn't surprise her. She didn't react. He squeezed, then shook her knee slightly, trying to get her attention.

Her eyes remained closed.

And that was when he knew their problems were only beginning.

———

CROUCHED, Mo chose her path carefully through the tall grasses, taking one silent step. The waving strands were a pale dusty green, but at the moment were made golden by the morning sun at her back.

She took another step, then knelt down. Her rifle was already set up here in this stand of heavier grass at the base of the hillock. Her own form was draped in grass too, camo of her own making, the kind that meant you didn't need power armor because no one saw you coming or knew where you'd gone. Or possibly that you'd ever been there.

The rifle sights revealed a grassy field that gave way to dusty plain. A little village beyond consisted of a huddle of small bunkers. One that was all too familiar to her.

This was her village. Her people. Home.

She jerked back from the gun. Mission be damned—what was she doing here?

Disoriented, she crouched lower. How had she gotten here? Ducked in the fields outside her village, like a damned coyote.

What the hell? She dragged the rifle out of the stand, then started off in a run in the other direction. This had to be some kind of trap. She would never have gone against her own people—no matter what the Union had asked. But they wouldn't have asked her to do such a thing.

Would they?

Her boots ate up the ground, the grass thinning to dry plain again, each footfall sending dust puffing into the air. She wanted to go home, yes, but not like this. She'd left to protect them, and if running away meant protecting them, that was more important than the warm home she so deeply missed.

Suddenly it hit her that for one precious moment, she was on Keyah, she was running into the sun, and her heart gave a leap of joy—

But before she could find her head or her prayers, the dusty plain faltered, shifting, the land shaking beneath her.

This was wrong. There were no earthquakes here, not like this. But before she could catch her balance, the earth had ripped open and she was tumbling. Falling.

Floating in the darkness.

Floating. Was she in the deep? Damn. A simulation? No, must be just a bad dream. She should have known.

Yet knowing it was a dream didn't dissipate the sensations. Impossible wind flowed over her as she fell, on and on through the black, infinite void. The stars seemed to streak past, like she'd imagined they would when she was young.

They didn't really do that in real life, in the deep. Just like there was no air or wind out there either, only death.

The space dream was one she'd had before. The endless falling. It didn't creep up on Mo often, but every once in a while. She thought it was caused by nerves, or stress, or times when her brain wanted to remind her that beyond the sheets of metal and plexi and insulation on the *Audacity* was, well… nothing. Just death.

If she thought about it too long, her imagination could go wild, fixating on whether the barest nick of space dust might rupture the fragile balloon skin of the ship and end it all in a rush and a roar.

But she didn't think it'd be space dust to do the deed—maybe the sharp claw of some vengeful god.

Paradise.

Someone had said that word to her recently. Who? Why? She groped at the memory, came up empty-handed.

Her body slowed to a stop, just a slow spin now. The stars stopped their streaking too, becoming dim points of light. Her feet seemed to settle on something hard, but non-existent.

She stood on a precipice taller than any planet could create, and the fall over was inevitable.

Is this paradise? Was that?

Whose voice was that? Was it her own? And why?

Paradise was just an idea. An impossible thing. Paradise should be something you build wherever you are.

Was that what she'd done, though? Shutting herself away in her cabin, keeping to herself—she might as well be alone in the deep, just like this.

If they ever made it off the ship, out alive, she needed to stop running away, stop hiding. Start living. Protecting people didn't mean she needed to be alone. Paradise was nonsense. But she did have the here and now. *If* she ever got out of this damn dream.

Something twisted in her peripheral vision, curving like a squid or a jellyfish, moving behind her. But that was impossible—nothing could live in the deep. She spun, trying to see what was there—

The sound of the cabin hatch sliding open jolted her awake.

Adrenaline pumped through her in one sharp shot. Her hands were raising the rifle to point out into the cabin before she could form a coherent thought. Good training, that's what that was, because her head sure wasn't on straight.

She risked a glance at Doug. Her head spun a little at the movement. Frag—maybe she was hurt worse than she wanted to admit. But his eyes caught hers, shifted from squinting at what was outside to squinting at her. He gave her a little smile, as if to say welcome back, then his eyes flicked back out to the cabin.

Frag. Nothing like sleeping on the job to impress the boss. Although he hardly felt like a superior officer at this point. The smile burnt away a little of the sadness, though.

A slight jingle. Some of Tovi's people had entered the room. How many had Doug pointed out on the vid cam? Eight? The instant she fired, she'd reveal their position. Should she wait for Tovi to come in? Taking out the commander might cause confusion, but what if Tovi stayed in the corridor?

A crew member in light armor came in, rifle sweeping at the ready. Another was just behind him, this one a woman.

If she could get four before they fired on her… She preferred long range, but she was still an excellent shot close up. Risky, though. If she died, who would get Doug out of here?

And he *was* getting out of here. She was going to make sure of it. With her non-rifle hand, she drew Rolf's knife from her pocket.

A third crew member moved into view.

She pressed the retracted knife into Doug's free hand, then held a finger to her lips. Hopefully he would figure out her plan and play along, because she couldn't risk whispering at this point.

Then she moved the rifle to the floor, twisting silently. She got her feet under her, then rose to her feet, silent as her namesake.

She glanced back at him one more time. His eyes were wild. He was probably rightfully wondering what they hell she was doing. But her strengths were mostly useless here—stealth and sharpshooting would only get them so far in close quarters while vastly outnumbered.

But *his* strengths—his intelligence combined with the computer in this room—they could change everything. Far more likely to result in them getting out alive then her warming up her laser pistol and going crazy.

She didn't glance back, in case the look on his face might stop her from this crazy plan. She burst through the locker door, swinging it hard.

Hands in the air, she shouted, "Don't shoot!"

As she'd hoped, the locker swung hard enough that it crashed back wildly and relatched closed. Nothing to see there.

Perfect. Maybe Doug would be safe.

Now she just had to survive herself.

———

THE FLYER GLIDED SMOOTHLY into Asha's empty carport without interference. Kael should have preferred the lack of any kind of resistance from her or the gang, but he couldn't help but be a little creeped out by it.

She'd told Dane her code, he'd spoken it over the comm to the house, and it'd all opened up like pretty white flower, the circular carport dilating into the walls.

And pretty it was. The house was exquisite, expensive, far from anything *he'd* have been able to afford. Maybe even right now, certainly not back then.

Asha was still sniffling as they emerged from the flyer into the carport. She palmed open the door to the house. Kael exchanged a look with Ellen as she hung back, giving him a slight nod.

He'd stay close to Asha—she'd look for an unguarded computer. Dane in between the two. Stick to the plan.

"The office is in the back," Asha murmured as she stepped inside. He scrutinized every moment she made as she tapped some commands into the wall computer, but they seemed innocuous enough —turning on lights, a security code. "I'd tell you to take off your shoes, but…" She looked at him over her shoulder, a sudden hint of humor in her eyes.

He mustered a small smile.

Their eyes locked for a long moment. It was the closest they'd been, and it felt suddenly as if they were alone in the world, with Dane and Ellen hanging back. Her expression was wary, appraising him. Her eyes were tired, and after a moment, they crinkled a little with fear, apprehension. Some part of him lurched at that, some old muscle memory that longed to take her in his arms, protect her, comfort her. Be the one that did the right thing by her, when no one else ever had. He *had* been that, or at least he'd tried to be. Maybe not by getting her pregnant, but they'd both made mistakes in that.

But what about her? Had she treated him right? He hadn't thought about it much as a sixteen-year-old. He hadn't learned to ask those questions yet.

But he was asking them now.

She must have seen the hardening in his eyes because she bit her lip and turned away, walking further into the house.

"If you have this house, why were you staying there?" he asked, following as close as he could while not risking stepping on her and crushing an ankle. Although with this kind of house, it must have some kind of med bay…

"Got into a little trouble over a job. I've been managing accounts for several Gray Dragon protected businesses and—"

"And making sure Maloof gets his share?" he asked.

"Obviously. One was clearly hiding money from Maloof. I mean, who tries to hide money from a money launderer?" She shook her head. "But they weren't too happy about my speaking up. I probably wouldn't have if I hadn't known I'd be protected."

"Hmm." His brain was racing, turning over the words. That wasn't what Maloof had said. He'd claimed she was a concubine. Could have been a lie to get under Kael's skin—or was she the one lying, trying to save some dignity and hide the real reason she'd been there? Which was the lie?

Or both? He had no idea where to start to call her on it.

She certainly hadn't seemed glad to see Maloof die, that was for sure. Her eyes were still red, and he was pretty sure it *wasn't* from the chem spray.

The long, white hallway was cold and undecorated, her bare feet slapping the tile floor beneath them, as if punctuating his indecision.

They reached an office at the end of the hall on the left. Two white desks lined one wall topped with at least four computers. Every surface was covered with papers in stacks. Bookcases spanned the other wall of the large, white room, with floors of a pale silver carpet. A glass door at the back of the room looked out onto a garden elegantly lit with small bubbles of light but overall shrouded in darkness.

She stopped in the doorway and laid a hand on his suit's arm. "I missed you, you know."

He glared at that hand, then met her gaze. "You could have found me."

"I had no idea what happened to you. I'm telling you, they said you were dead."

Was this the lie, or had she been lied to?

"Can't you take off that stupid helmet, at least? Talk to me like a human being?"

He sighed. Against his better judgment, he slapped the helmet retract. What did it matter? The suit already had the leak anyway.

She smiled as it lowered, the expression tinged with sadness. She reached up and laid a hand against his cheek, her fingers cold against his skin and the beginning of a beard. Once, he might have leaned into her touch, but to his surprise he jerked away before he could think the better of it.

It was too much. It was a betrayal.

She drew her hand back quickly. "You're right. I haven't earned your trust back yet. But you should know—if I had known, I'd have looked for you."

He just met her gaze, kept his eyes hard. Some of his resistance cracked at her weak smile, but he couldn't let it show. It was impossible to know what to believe anymore.

She sighed. "Let me get a copy of those letters for you, and then maybe we can put this behind us. Move on."

She glided away, toward the bookcases at the back, where there were several boxes and files.

He eased toward the desk behind her, leaving some room in case the computer nearest the door was Ellen's best bet.

A moment later, his suit pinged that his comm had a message, so he raised the helmet. Ellen's voice came over the comm. "Kael—we're into the house computer, the one by the door. This should work, the nuke is uploading, but we're far from you right now. Dane is moving toward the center of the house to try to keep an eye out. Stay alert."

"Got it—we're in the office. Threat seems low here. Should see this 'proof' shortly," he said, then lowered the helmet again.

He watched her rummage through some boxes carefully while scanning the desk. The papers did seem to be for Gray Dragon-protected businesses. "Protected" just meant "extorted for money," of course. Laundromats, groceries, electronics marts, even a hospital. They hadn't had that kind of reach when he'd been around. This confirmed at least part of her story—no random concubine would have files on all these. The hard copies were part of evading government detection.

She gave up on one box and switched to another on a lower shelf. Her body blocked most of his view of what she was doing. He needed to move to get a better angle. One more scan of the desk, and he'd—

His eyes caught on a small image that floated in a decorative holodisplay beside the main computer one.

It was her, in a sparkling blue dress wrapped around a frame heavier than she'd usually been. Her hair, her eyes, all still looked the same as he'd remembered.

Around her shoulders was Maloof's arm. He looked much younger, so the photo had to be pretty old. The two of them grinned at the photographer, small glasses of mint tea in their hands. She leaned into his side in that way, that familiar way.

Seven suns. The truth hit him. It was all lies. *All* of it.

These files, the sobbing, the trust she'd displayed at the business end of that pistol… The way Maloof had whispered in her ear. She was no concubine, no hostage—that had been just a ploy to get under his skin, to get them to remove the armor. Because they needed him to remove the armor to take him prisoner, to get the bounty, to kill him. To do whatever they wanted.

The dragon has two heads. Two.

The pinprick of pain in his neck made him realize his mistake. He'd turned his back on her. Lowered his helmet. Tried to treat her like a human being.

Ice flooded his veins.

The way he'd stared at the image had given him away. She'd realized the jig was up. She knew even before he did, because his wheels were still turning, not wanting to believe. He was still processing, and she had been acting.

Easy enough to drop the act and inject something in the base of his neck. Scrubbers be damned, he could feel the cold slip into his veins, his limbs going heavy and still.

He'd been an idiot to trust her. Threat low, what an idiot. Zahir had tried to warn him.

His fingers were barely mobile, but he tapped out an urgent warning inside the gauntlet with its tiny controls—Betrayal. Injection. Mission failure. Get out.

His knees buckled, and he came down to both knees with a crash, barely able to lift his arms enough to catch himself on the desk and avoid his face bouncing off it.

Asha's breath was hot against his ear. "You should have just taken the armor off. Then Asaed could have turned you over to that doctor and her crazy experiments, and we'd be finally be done. For good. But no. You wouldn't quit. You never do."

He jerked his jaw open, but his tongue, his lips wouldn't move. Even his breath felt hard to come by, and he found himself gasping for it.

He couldn't turn his head, but a sharp rasp and thud told him the door to the office had slid shut. And that it wasn't an ordinary residential door. Heavier than that.

She leaned casually over his shoulder and tapped some commands on the holodisplay. "I know this might not seem like the time for a biology lesson, but trust me. It is. Are you familiar with the *Alarus Octendi*?"

A small, tentacled white creature appeared in the air over the holodisplay. One he'd seen in a variety of forms, not usually this small, mostly in briefings and armor cam footage. His throat tightened— whether from the drug or from fear, he had no idea.

"You see, when we heard about your bounty, we sent out a query. Dr. Arakovic is very active in xenobiological and cybernetic research here on Faros—did you know? She had a local office send us very specific instructions on how to properly claim our reward. Very unusual instructions indeed. But the bonus compensation for perfection is high."

She unceremoniously dropped a box in front of him. The clear plex revealed two compartments—a small one filled with small white orbs and another with two actively squirming creatures.

"This is *Alarus Octendi*. A brilliant little creature. Naturally telepathic. One of only five species where the phenomena occurs outside of humans. Almost all of the *Alarus Octendi* are male, with the occasional queen. It can rapidly change form and fuses with the nervous system of its host. Because *Alarus Octendi* is a parasite. A very useful little parasite indeed, especially to someone as brilliant and generous as Dr. Arakovic. She sent me three sets of these. The bigger one was at my home—the one you so unceremoniously invaded—but we'll make do." She reached over his shoulder and delicately opened the side with the small white orbs, each about the size of a pea.

"We can do this the easy way—or the hard way." Her long, elegant fingers selected one orb and withdrew it, shutting the lid. "We already tried to sell you off once—or didn't you figure that out yet?" She grinned at him over his shoulder. "Yes, it was me. Maloof and Abrams —hah. Idiots. No vision. But at least Maloof knew how to profit from a good thing when he found one. I'm not an accountant." She chuckled now. "I'm a businesswoman, and a good one. I've made money on all sorts of things, including you. In your case, I get to profit twice, so I suppose I shouldn't complain. You were our test case, then we moved on to Abrams. With Maloof, I own this entire gang, and you were the start of that. Aren't you proud? Really contributed to something there. And now you've come back and tried to smash it to hell again. That's not how this story ends. So open wide, so I don't have to unleash one of these larger horrors."

In the end, there wasn't much he could do to resist. The nerve agent ensured he couldn't move anyway. He gagged and choked mostly against his will, but she determinedly dropped the orb in his mouth and jammed his jaw shut. He tried to spit it out at her, but nothing seemed to respond to his commands. She jerked his jaw up, gravity working against him as he choked again. Reflex took over, and he swallowed.

Bitter dread wasn't the only thing settling in the pit of his stomach.

There was a pounding on the office door. She glanced casually at it, without fear.

"As I was saying. You should have just taken off the armor. Then Asaed wouldn't be hurt. You better hope he isn't really dead."

Kael was certain he was. But this didn't seem the time to point that out. His jaw was moving a little, though. Was the drug wearing off? Intentionally—or because of the scrubbers? Maybe it'd only been needed to do this one job.

"But now, before I turn you over to this doctor that's hunting you, we are first going to have some fun. I see you're moving your jaw again. That's good—good work! It's just a temporary numbness, but you should still worry. You'll get used to a vegetative state."

"Wouldn't be the first time," he managed.

"Look at you, quipping. Well, I had better finish the doctor's instructions quickly then." Something heavy clanked from the box behind her, metal against metal.

Cold steel slid around his throat, just barely room for it above the armor. It tightened around his neck, and with a click she pressed a small button. Then the thing went to work on its own.

He flinched hard—apparently he'd regained control of his facial muscles—as it extended a piece up behind his ear to the main port. The freakish device opened the port on its own and burrowed inside, latching on tight.

His heart pounded, and his gasps for breath weren't just because of the drug now. The suit beeped it had a comm message, but he couldn't move to answer it.

She bent closer, whispering sweetly into his ear again. "You should have stayed gone."

"And you should have stayed dead," he whispered back.

She chuckled. "You might need a muzzle. Or maybe burning out your tongue would be more fun?"

He said nothing. He'd have control of his arms and legs back any second, and then he'd—

The pounding hit the door again, but then another sound, the spray of ballistics maybe. Something broad and heavy across the entire wall.

"Ah! My friends are here. And you are the lucky one that gets to help them."

The suit beeped it had a comm message again. He scowled and managed to turn his head to look at her. "I'll never help you. Tell me Asha—what happened to the baby?"

She laughed even harder now. One hand went over her belly as she laughed, the other held a small white box, long and slender, with a blue sign of an octopus painted across the back. "Wouldn't you like to know? But you're not going to. And you are going to help me, because you've made some very powerful, very smart enemies. And this one has given me your remote control. Stand up."

She pushed something on the box, and he needed to stand up desperately, in spite of his legs barely responding. He scrambled, his left knee giving out twice, wobbling, but finally he did it.

She grinned. "You see, that Theroki oath programming can come in handy for so many things. And now I can make you take an oath you didn't sign up for."

"I didn't sign up for any of them."

"Ah, but I think you'll especially hate this one. Because I think I'll have you kill that little girlfriend of yours." She pressed down into the box, her face hardening with the bitter anger truly lay under all her smiles and mocking laughter.

"She's not—"

"Ha! Don't even try it. You can't lie to *me*."

"She's not."

"I saw the way you looked at her in the carport. In the flyer. I know you, Kael Sidassian. When you love someone, it's written all over your face."

His flinch now was almost worse than the last one. "And you've never hesitated to profit from that fact."

"Why shouldn't I? When you start with less than nothing, there's only one way to get out of that hell. Claw your way out—no matter the cost."

"What happens when the cost comes back to haunt you?"

She tilted her head. "Is that what you're doing? Because as I see it, you're going to *actually* murder your girlfriend this time, and then you're going to make me rich. And I'm pretty sure whatever Dr. Arakovic wants to do with you is going to make being a Theroki look like a cakewalk. Now go." She pushed into the box again.

His legs lurched into motion on their own. He managed to raise the helmet, and she scowled but he stalked toward the door, where the sound had quieted.

The comm messages flooded in quickly.

Ellen's voice. "Kael—what's going on? We see your message, we're coming."

Dane. "Kael—do you read?"

"Too many hostiles—must be the whole gang—we've got to get out of here. We'll find you, Kael."

"Don't find me," he said in quick response. "They've installed an add-on—copied the oath programming. She's ordered me to kill you. Get out of here and—"

"And stop warning her," Asha snapped from behind. "No fraternizing with the enemy."

His jaw snapped shut.

The comm line was silent anyway.

CHAPTER FIFTEEN

DAY 17-18

MAYBE IT WAS Mo's lucky day, because they whirled to face her, but they didn't shoot. Her chest was heaving, and her breath couldn't come fast enough, but none of their eyes darted to the locker behind her. The now five guards were fixated on her, followed close by Captain Tovi.

"Ms. Mihio—" Tovi started.

"Sergeant Mihio," she said.

Tovi's eyelids fluttered in a slight eyeroll. "Tell me how you escaped."

"Those assholes let me out. You can guess why."

She crossed her arms. "I apologize for the actions of these reprehensible individuals; I should have screened them better and never hired them. I suppose you dealt with them?"

"They're restrained."

Tovi's smile broadened. "It was so kind of you to take care of our mutineers for us. They should have known better, but that is one less thing on my already busy to-do list. Your assistance getting the ship back in order is much appreciated. And I think you are about to have an even bigger role in that than I'd originally imagined."

Mo frowned. "What do you mean?"

"Where's your patron?"

"I had to leave him behind. Near the brig. I couldn't carry him. I was going to find a way out and come back and—"

Tovi held up a hand to silence her, then gestured to someone in the hallway. "Go find him."

Internally, Mo winced. Would they stand here and wait until they found out her lie? She forced herself to remain still, calm. Steady.

Tovi kept talking. "In addition to you, we also detained two Puritans on board. Part of this chaos is that a Puritan ship has jumped us coming out of a wormhole and are demanding their people back." She looked to one of the subordinates near the hatch. "Any word from the ship?"

"They want to know if you've considered their demands."

"Tell them I have a new counter-proposal."

Mo did not like the sound of that.

Tovi smiled at her again, a cruel edge to the expression. "Those Puritan criminals are not worth the trouble just for a Union bounty, but I think I may now have a way to work out a deal."

"Criminals?" Mo said softly.

"They escaped from a Union jail. *Apparently*, they have a knack for it."

"Not if I let them out."

"Maybe they let *you* out."

"What did they do?" she demanded.

"They're extremists. They forcibly removed augmentations. With knives. They consider it 'unnatural.' Which is why you have just what we need to lure the prisoners out."

Was that a quiet *thump* in the closet behind her? Had any of them heard?

"You're going to use me as bait?" she blurted, hoping her indignant words would distract from any sound Doug had made. Right now, he needed to stay silent. "And let them cut out my damn eyes?"

Tovi gave her a twisted smile. "Not as bait. As a gift. An apology. If we turn over you *and* the prisoners, maybe that will satisfy them."

Her mouth fell open, then she snapped it back shut. Another

distinct thud came from the closet. Frag—he didn't get the plan. To be a telepath, to be able to tell him something without any of them hearing—

But she did have something like that, didn't she?

She threw herself to her knees to fake a prayer. *"Dibeh d-ah a-kha bi-so-dih."* The words were clear in the stunned silence. But would he be able to remember the words she'd whispered? She repeated it again. *"Dibeh d-ah a-kha bi-so-dih."*

"Oh, for God's sake. What is she going on about now?" Tovi snapped.

"A prayer," she rushed to say. "For justice."

Tovi rolled her eyes. "Can anyone verify that?"

Someone in the corridor bent closer to an earpiece. "Something about sheep tea? I don't think it's important, Captain."

It was all she could do not to smile. *Sheep tea oil pig* would be their translation, even if they made one. The real code was in the initial letters, just as it had been centuries ago. S-T-O-P. She thought she'd gone over each of those words, but she was hardly sure. Would he understand them? Doug, don't let me down now. *Remember.*

Only silence answered her from the locker.

She cleared her throat. "It means you'll get what's coming to you in the end."

"I guess we'll see about that."

An alarm suddenly blared out, along with an AI announcing some message made unintelligible by the blasts of the alarm.

Scowling, Tovi grabbed her arm and yanked her toward the hatch. "Let's find those two shits and get this over with."

DOUG WASN'T sure how long he sat in the closet, trying to figure out what the hell had just happened and what he was supposed to do about it.

Dibeh d-ah a-kha bi-so-dih. The man outside had said sheep, and Doug was pretty sure that was right. Sheep tea? What in the hell?

He noodled around, but *a-kha* wasn't coming to him. *Bi-so-dih*… If he was hearing her right, that seemed like pig. He remembered the ridiculous pig-nose face she'd made when he'd been struggling with it.

Maybe it really was a prayer. She hadn't seemed that into prayer or religion, and he hadn't recorded anything of the sort in her files. Maybe he had tea wrong. Sheep and pig suggested life in the old style, life raising animals—maybe it was a prayer derived from that time, that life.

He felt like an idiot, frozen still in the locker, desperately trying to decode four words in another language rather than actually doing something to help her. But what was the point of having a code if he didn't *try* to decode it?

Wait. *Wait.* A code. That was it.

The Code Talkers had used a code, not just another language to hide their messages. The first letter was what mattered. S-T-something-P. That was more than enough to figure this out. Definitely not *stap.* Step? Was she saying to step out, take the next step? Not that he could do that without his floats. *Stip* didn't make any sense. Stop—

He caught his breath. *Stop.* Not stip or stup or styp. Stop.

She *had* wanted him to stay in the locker. Why? So he could try to help her after she drew them out of the room? Were they really gone? He listened hard but couldn't hear anything.

If this was her plan, though, everything depended on him. Which made it a shitty plan. Part of him was reeling at being left alone again. And the other part was panicking over what they might do.

That idea, though, spurred him out of his shock. He listened again, hard. When no sound reached him beyond the hum of the ship, he unlatched the closet door and pushed it open.

"Computer, is there anyone in the corridor?" he whispered.

"No," it replied, awkwardly loud.

He winced. "Computer, how long since the last people left this room?"

"You are still here."

"Uh, other than me."

"Crew member Wan was last to depart one minute and fifty-seven seconds ago."

He let out a breath. She'd had some plan that involved him staying here and them taking her. How was that supposed to work? How was he, alone, supposed to save them both?

Just getting out of the locker was going to be hard. Might as well get started.

Jamming the pistol in one pocket and slinging the rifle over his neck, he used the edge of the locker to pull himself closer, to where Mo had been sitting. But he was wedged in at an odd angle, and it took quite a bit of rearranging, twisting, pulling himself forward on one arm, then rearranging and twisting again.

By the time he'd made it out of the locker, he was ready to swear up a storm. Or take a long nap.

Getting colder, especially now that he was dripping with sweat from the exertion, he forced himself to take a deep breath. Getting angry—or depressed—wasn't going to help him right now. He needed to look at his assets and his options and do whatever he could.

His assets—the case and whatever was in it, if anything, his pistols, her rifle which he didn't know how to use, and the holodesk. Oh, and the knife too. He barely remembered to grab it as he worked his way out, but he did.

And what were his options? Opening the case. Wreaking more havoc with the computer systems. What else? Mo couldn't have wanted him to stop there.

They couldn't have far to go to those Puritan bastards; it wasn't that big of a ship. And he couldn't let them give Mo over to them. He had to *do* something. The computer seemed like the best weapon of the moment, but...

He eyed the case. Then, gritting his teeth in annoyance, he began the crawl to it. By far his least favorite method of mobility, but desperate times, as they say, blah blah blah.

He froze when the masculine voice came over the ship's announcements again. "*Sharpspear*, this is the Athens. Final warning. Present yourselves for surrender, or your blast doors will now be breached."

Damn. He had better hurry up. Tovi didn't seem to have this situation as under control as she thought she did.

A moment later, he reached the case. She'd just cleared the bunk with the case when they'd heard Tovi's approach. The latches were thankfully old-fashioned and not biometric, and he blew out a breath of relief at that. Not that he couldn't crack such a thing, but everything took time.

Time he did not have.

Flipping open the latches, he heaved the surprisingly heavy lid into the air—and caught his breath. And then laughed out loud. Chuckled, really, the risks to them locating him be damned.

Because the case contained drones. Two of them.

"Computer, can you bring these drones online? And slave them to this user? Restrict all others."

"Acknowledged," said the room's computer. Possibly the ship. "In progress…. Task complete."

Little green lights blinked on the small black bodies of the drones. A pretty sight, if he'd ever seen one.

Next came the task of getting back to the holodesk. He was half tempted to just lie on the floor and shout commands, and if they hadn't found those ration bars, maybe he would have. But he'd made enough noise. Better to keep quiet.

The office chair had locks on the seat, but not the wheels, though, and he couldn't figure out how to activate its magnets. He managed to push the chair into the corner and lower the seat down as far as it would go. Then he used a move he'd practiced more than a few times —although he was probably a bit rusty, with all the time he spent in floats—to carefully prop his knees against his chest, put one hand on the ground and one hand on the chair, and lever himself up.

Back in the saddle, he pushed off the wall toward the desk and held on. He wouldn't normally take the risk of falling right back out, but time was of the essence. The rifle dangling around him seemed to have no good location, though, and threatened to send him off balance. He definitely needed to find some other wheels. The office chair might have worked with Mo around to stabilize and push it, but if he ran out of zero G handholds, he'd be in a tricky situation.

Logging on, the computer welcomed him back, and he set to tackle that problem first. Sick bay had two nursebots. But they weren't close, and even if he hid his hijacking from the ship or sick bay manager computers, a human doctor might notice. And sick bay was on the other side of the blast doors anyway. A robot was a good idea, but he needed something closer.

Bingo—Engineering had two cargo lifting bots. He assigned one to his use, then the other. But an error immediately jumped up in his face.

He sighed. They had to be manually released from a harness strap. Why even *have* technology if people were still going to use such mundane, Flax Age things to constrain it?

But if he could get there with the drones and the chair, he could trade in one set of wheels for the robot. Then he'd really be in business to…. To what? He wasn't sure where to go from there.

The vid cam feeds showed Tovi dragging Mo by the arm in the other direction, toward the bridge instead of Engineering. The cams also still didn't work in engineering, but the computer registered one crew member still there. That was an improvement. Maybe Tovi had stopped by and dealt with the other three.

What was not an improvement, however, was that the Puritan prisoners had succeeded in their blowtorch project and were headed for the bridge.

Maybe they'd already reached it, because now the vid feed in the bridge was out too.

Hell. He didn't have much time.

Grabbing the comm off the desk, he tucked it in a pocket—he'd never used this many pockets at once before, for heaven's sake. Then with a good hard shove, he pushed himself toward the door. And Engineering.

ELLEN DIDN'T KNOW how many tunnels or streets they went up, down, and through, but the heavy sun of Faros was rising well in the sky before they even started to slow down.

Her body had been moving on automatic, not needing conscious commands to run its pattern. Keep moving. Avoid. Evade. Make them lose the trail.

Figure out what the frag just happened and what to do.

It was that last bit that was the problem. It was a good thing her body didn't need help, because her mind seemed stuck. Frozen.

Think. Think, dammit. What are we going to do?

But that answer never came.

She'd only caught the occasional glimpse or two of the sun, reflected or simulated on a screen. Faros's equivalent was really the ambient lights starting to brighten. Most stations and planets kept some sort of light rhythm that aligned with the environment around them—or Union Standard time. That approach was really unreliable, with people always losing seconds if not minutes, but some people's loyalty to the Union ran deep.

She knew one thing for sure—the brightening of these ambient light sources did not calm the panicked loop that was running on repeat in her mind.

It'd probably been a good hour since they'd seen anyone. Even with the armor, she was panting. They'd taken tubes, hitched an unlocked lander for a while, then abandoned it and hoofed it on foot, the old-fashioned way.

Now they were thoroughly vanished—and thoroughly exhausted.

"Here. Dane. Let's take a rest." Ellen collapsed on a bench. A small playground had a place to sit—and a way to see anyone coming at a distance—so this was probably as good as anywhere for a minute or two. Wild cement forms were probably supposed to be for climbing, but they looked more like some kind of extravagant art from Capital.

"I thought you'd never relent." Dane slowed, and his hands dropped to his knees, then threw himself entirely to the dusty ground, sprawled out like a starfish. "I think we ran halfway around this damn planet. There are Gray Dragons everywhere."

"I saw a few Snake Kings too."

"They are only moderately better."

"Least we lost him." Kael was faster and more competent than any of the gang members assisting him. She put her head her hands too.

Frag. Kael.

This wasn't supposed to happen. They were never supposed to have to worry about not being on the same side again. He'd escaped the Theroki, the Enhancers, all that, and this? And Ellen had brought him here. In spite of his worries, his reservations. Not that any of them had expected *this*.

How? How had Asha managed it? And what would she do to him now?

She straightened in her seat, scanning their surroundings, but it was as empty as before. Desolate, really, or maybe that was just her.

He'd mentioned the oath program before the comm had cut off. But how could Asha have known how to benefit from that, especially without his original chip? The Gray Dragons were not high tech. Her minions wouldn't stop pelting them ballistics, for God's sake. Might as well be throwing rocks.

Ellen's mind was churning, demanding answers, searching for some way to fix this disaster. And all she had was a big fat nothing. There had to be a way out of this. There had to be.

But God. How could she have lost him so soon?

She dropped her head back into her hands as Dane sat up. Let him watch. She needed to think. What if Asha had already killed him? But no, no, if that were likely, she could have done it right away instead of sending him after Ellen. What did Asha even want? Ellen couldn't be her ultimate goal—unless she just wanted to make sure their whole team was dead before she sliced Kael's throat.

She flinched at that thought, blinked at a heat in her eyes. No, she wasn't the kind that fell apart. She was stoic. She was a fragging brick wall, glaring at you. She was punching back when the chips were down. The cracks in her soul, in her mind, could not rupture further. She could not shatter. Not now.

Think, damn it.

It didn't seem like Asha should have been able to do any of this, but she had. What else was she capable of? What if she found some way to make the change permanent? Make the chip impossible to remove?

Could she make him forget Ellen had ever existed?

Adan's voice suddenly cut into the comm, garbled at times but overall clear. "C-c-commander! I got the data you s-sent—from that nuke. I found the sale docs. I found her!"

Ellen balked, then coughed as she tried to find her voice. "Sale docs? What?"

"I found the docs from your nuke. Kael's daughter *was* transferred to an artificial womb."

"Are you serious? Then what?" Her voice was rough from lack of use, emotion, exhaustion.

"Get this—she was sold. Mother Asha Narulon, Father Kael Sidass-ian, incarcerated. These clearly show the mother as *alive*. Sale pending. Finalized for about six hundred thousand rial. Kid's given name was Shirin Nar. I should say—is. I even found you an address—I can give it to you. It's incoming!"

"Wait—*sold*? To a family on Faros?" She fell back against the seat. Damn it, how would Kael feel about that? What did they even *do* about that?

"Not to a family," Adan said. "Sold means into forced labor."

Dane sat straight up from the ground. "You mean she's a *slave*?"

"Yes. That's where I found the address—a directory of labor for sale. Vile, I know, but it's helping us. And she's alive! Did you tell Kael? Why's he so quiet? Isn't he on his comm?"

Her eyes locked with Dane's. He nodded, then spoke. "He's been captured."

"Captured? What do you—"

"We can't explain right now, Adan." Her voice broke on the words.

"Commander, are you okay? You don't sound—"

"No," Ellen bit out. "No, I'm fragging not. But I'm going to make this right. I have to."

"Commander," Dane started.

She cut at the air with her hand. "No. There is no time for feeling sorry for ourselves. We have a job to do, and it's more important than ever that we do it."

"We're here for you," Adan said quickly.

They weren't really, though. The ship couldn't land. They had no funds. No backup from Doug. No intel. No support. It was her and Dane, and that was it.

But it was going to have to do. Her dark eyes locked with Dane's.

He nodded, his expression hardening, resolute. "Let's do this."

She gave him a sharp nod in return, jaw tightening. "All right. First, we find this girl. Then we rescue Kael." Her hand tightened into a fist at her side.

"And then?" asked Adan.

"And then we get the frag off this stupid planet."

———

DOUG KEPT one arm hooked around the back of the chair as he maneuvered out into the corridor. The other was getting a workout pulling him from one of the emergency handholds to another—really, he was lucky he was on a spaceship where gravity could fail and thus these handholds existed. He *could* be holed up on an ice planet somewhere. A jungle secret compound. That would make his current situation quite a bit worse.

Actually, if gravity did fail, it'd be even easier for him to get around. Something to think on while in Engineering, assuming he could actually get inside.

It was either great or terrible—or both—that the corridors were empty the whole way to his destination. The ominous alarms had gone silent. If blast doors were being breached, he couldn't hear them. No more threats came over the ship's speakers.

His drones hovered along like mosquitoes on the beach—another thing he didn't miss—waiting for orders. Reaching the hatch to engineering, he finally got his chance to test them out.

He'd either get his better bots and access to engineering—or fail miserably and doom both himself and Mo. And it all rested on a single dude in Engineering.

Swallowing, he swung his chair to underneath the palmpad. He needed one hand to hold on, and the other could operate either the drones *or* the pistol, but not both. He was putting his money on the drones having a better aim than he did, and the fact that they had stun pulses rather than lasers definitely helped.

Time to find out what they could do.

He directed the drones into position in front of the hatch, then reached up as high as he could to slap the palm pad. Not that he expected it to open.

But he did expect someone to answer his chime.

And answer they did. The hatch slid open barely a second later. And according to their instructions, the stun probes shot out from one of his two little buddies. The other flashed a bright light. Doug was careful to whip his gaze away, shut his eyes.

The sound of a grunt and a body dropping to the ground made him exhale sharply. He waited a beat—but there was no movement or sound. He pulled up the vid feed from the drones on the comm's display. The crew member was sprawled out on the ground. Alive, he hoped.

Swinging around and through the hatch, a flat voice spoke from the ceiling. "May I offer assistance?" said an AI.

"No. No, I'm good." He really didn't think it would want to help him if it knew his goals. He made straight for the hauler bots—thankfully, there was enough room to circle his fallen adversary—and he unhooked both their straps. He set one to pick up the crew member while he climbed on and positioned himself on the other's platform.

The hauler bots were way better for his purposes, because he could control them with a small screen joystick on the comm pad. While rudimentary in terms of assistive devices, it was a fantastic step up as far as this horrible ship was concerned.

He was just about to exit and go looking for Mo with his drones when his gaze caught on the large glowing blue of one wall. He squinted, steered a little closer. Water tanks?

In modern ships, many things depended on water. It cooled, it cleansed, it heated. The reactors likely required it, and possibly environmental control system too.

If Tovi had her way, they'd make this exchange, hand over Mo and the prisoners, and be on their way to turning him over to Quentin.

He was going to do his best to stop that exchange with these drones, but… what if he could give them an extra problem to worry about?

Breaking gravity was still an option, but… what about having to repair these tanks, round up the water back into them? He pressed his lips into a thin line, glanced at the door, at the tanks, and then back again. He let out a breath.

With a flick on the comm pad, he ordered the hauler bot with the stunned crew member to leave and head in the opposite direction of the bridge, in search of a maintenance closet. Hopefully those corridors would remain empty.

Then he sent his drones looking for Mo and Tovi, keeping the drone video feed up and close.

He, however, would stay here and do what he did best.

Wreak some havoc.

First—gravity. He directed the hauler bot to the first computer bank. The system was identical to the one in the cabins, complete with the same master loopholes in security. Government ships. He shook his head. If Quentin had wanted someone to kidnap him, the fool should have sent a more high-tech ship. He had the money. Although perhaps assholes didn't have their pick of the talent.

The gravity controls were simple enough to disable, just a flick of a switch, although the computer made sure to ask him, "Are you sure?" and "Are you *sure*?" and "ARE YOU ABSOLUTELY SURE?"

He stabbed his finger at the affirmative command with a smile.

His smile faded, though, when he discovered that there was a solid five-minute countdown before the gravity loss would go into effect as the grav emitters warmed down. He grunted in annoyance at the display, then turned toward the tanks.

The tanks were visible from about halfway up the wall to the ceiling, but a low wall separated him from them, as well as a partition on each of the sides that was littered with handles, indicating compartments. There had to be some other way to get in and access the other side of the tanks, but this wall cutout seemed to be to allow supervision and diagnostics in Engineering itself. A low shelf on the wall held what looked like a toolbox.

His blurry gaze caught on a particularly heavy wrench about the size of his forearm sticking out of one side. Could it be that simple?

Upper body strength was one thing he had. He edged over to the tanks, and sure enough, the toolbox was full of things, including the large wrench. He grabbed it, then swung directly at the clear material. Plex? Certainly not glass.

"May I offer assistance?" said the AI voice again.

"All good here. No, thank you."

He swung. Once, twice. Three times.

A crack formed in the side of the cylinder, then grew bigger. He glared at it, squinted. The angle of the crack showed the container was thicker than he'd guessed. It'd been damaged but definitely didn't go all the way through.

He might get it if he kept going—or he might wear himself out and just have a big ugly dent and no water. And no problem for Tovi's crew to respond to. Well, except the grav, but that might be able to be solved from the bridge.

The more he thought about it, that seemed likely. Would they just switch it back on with a word as soon as they realized they had a problem?

Sighing, he checked the drones. They buzzed over the heads of a pair of medical crew members who eyed them but didn't try to stop them either. Still no sign of Mo.

He slammed the wrench one more time. The crack looked the same.

He turned the bot to the side wall and started opening the compartments. The first compartment yielded some ration bars he jammed into a pocket. The second one held only some jumpsuits that might help disguise him, but he'd never have time to maneuver into one before they got here. But the third cabinet was the jackpot.

More tools. But *fancy* tools, this time.

He grabbed the simple, clear safety glasses first. A thin silver strip held broad lenses floating in place, probably just basic eye protection. Couldn't hurt. Plus the bridge of his nose had felt naked for so long.

Sliding them on, he caught his breath. The world focused, unfocused, then came into stark and beautiful clarity.

Oh, thank God for optometry. And fancy gadgets.

His eyes were watering from exhaustion, clearly not joy, as he dug around for more. He didn't recognize most of them—mechanics and large-scale physics were hardly his specialty—but there was one that sort of looked like a drill.

He checked the drone feed. They still hadn't located Mo, so he motored back over to the water tank and thrust the drill-bit-looking end at the water tank. Then he groped on the outside for a button.

"May I offer assistance?" said the AI voice, managing not to sound annoyed.

"No. No, I'm fine."

"I should warn you, releasing the water tanks will limit the life support capabilities of this spacecraft. Water will need to be recaptured. Repairs will be required."

Would it try to stop him? It really should. He found a button and pushed, but nothing happened. "Yeah, yeah."

"You are also at a high risk of drowning if the gravity fails. Which you have requested."

He waved at the air and tried another button.

"You believe you know what you are doing."

He glared at the water tanks now and ignored the AI, pushing the first button harder. Unfortunately, brute strength wasn't solving this problem. Wasn't his favorite tool anyway, but what the hell else was he going to do?

To his surprise, a soft whirring came from the device. He grinned. Progress.

"You are beginning to engrave the captain's name on the H_2O tanks. Is that your intent?"

"Dammit." He drove back toward the tool compartment. Maybe

there was something else in there. The AI *might* be lying to him, although it was rare that a ship controller AI would be given such a dangerous capability. It came in handy when dealing with saboteurs like him, but it also relied on the AI to never, ever make any mistakes determining who was a saboteur and who wasn't.

It didn't matter—he didn't have time to decide if he believed the computer or not. Chances were, this AI had to tell the truth. Although with his luck...

He glanced at the screen. The drones had stunned two armed crew members, probably patrolling, and were flying away like it was no big deal. They had started off toward where he'd seen the Puritan prisoners last, but they'd gone beyond it. He realized now he should have tried harder to locate Mo specifically. Or checked if he could target the drones specifically at Mo's signature. He fiddled around with the comm for a moment, but couldn't find a way to identify her or the prisoners or even Tovi and tie it to the drones.

He'd just have to hope the drone's canvassing algorithm would find her—and soon.

The next tool blew air up his nose when he pushed its trigger grip. The one after that appeared to be an especially fancy wrench. He threw it at the tank in reckless abandon, furthering the crack but nothing that was going to achieve his goal anytime soon.

"Would it be helpful to know the location of the H_2O tank release valve?"

Eyebrows raised, he looked up. "Why... Yes. Why would you tell me that?" Maybe this was an AI that could lie, and it was a trick. Or maybe it was a help-based program, that having identified his need, had no choice but to aide him.

That made him almost feel a little bad causing a helpful ship so much mess and work. But not bad enough to stop.

"You are the ranking engineer. If you deem this a necessary risk, it is my duty to support it, even if I highly disagree with your assessment."

He winced at the thought of the stunned crew member, who hadn't looked particularly like an engineer. Why the AI had assumed Doug was an engineer, especially with his violent method of entry?

Oh, who was he kidding, he had geek written all over him. Even an AI could tell.

Either that or it just picked whoever was present and pushing buttons.

"Yes, please—I'd love to know. Where is the H_2O release valve?"

"The fifth compartment—two more to your left. Turn all three knobs toward you."

The comm suddenly beeped, and he flicked to the view of the drones, pausing their flight. They'd caught view of a large group of crew members at the end of the corridor. He stared in horror for a second before he hurried to the fifth compartment, yanked it open, and started to turn the knobs.

Holy *smokes*. Water sprayed out, filling the cabin floor. He could hear more falling on the other side of the low wall too. He was going to have to drive through it.

"I hope you know what you are doing," said the AI. "This is highly irregular."

"So do I," he muttered. "So do I."

———

ELLEN OPENED the door to Petuk's Live Creature Supply, Dane close on her heels. The smell of animal excrement hit her in a wave, along with the warm air that poured out of the shop. A little bell rang as the door swung closed behind them. An actual physical brass bell, she realized, as she spotted it hanging from the inner door handle. Not even a digital chime. Not a high-tech establishment, apparently.

She was ready to be off this planet. She didn't belong here.

The small shop was dim, with only a few overheads working and fake morning sunlight streaming in one dirty window that looked out on the street.

Animals she didn't recognize cooed and sniffed in tiny cages lining the right and back walls. The left wall was floor-to-ceiling with boxes and crates. The suit struggled to translate their labels. Maybe her armor was in worse shape than she thought.

A wide wooden counter dominated the back wall. A dark back room held more cages, based on the snorts and honks. Thin silver bars were barely visible in the darkness, and a pang of pity hit her for the little creatures.

A girl and a taller figure sat behind the counter. The tall one rose, clearly wary. As they drew closer, Ellen could see the girl was maybe a few years younger than Isa. That'd be the right age. She let herself feel a small spark of hope.

The taller figure was a robot, a meek-looking model with a face that didn't attempt to look human. That made it not an android, but it was highly emotive, with huge glittering green eyes that seemed to almost drip with affection and concern, plus richly detailed eyebrows. It had a sketch of a nose, a small curving slit of a mouth, but who needed other features with those eyes?

The girl's black hair was dirty and knotted, and in her hands, a small reddish rodent with long fingers and a frizzy coat squirmed, unsure how it felt about the cage she was helping it into. At the sound of the door's bell, the girl had spared them a glance, then continued to finish stowing the animal. It trusted her enough to offer no resistance, but gave a little coo of sadness as the door latched shut.

The girl bent down to offer a small hunk of food through the bars of the cage, fingers certain and sure. There was a certain competence in those hands that was familiar. The rodent made a clicking sound that Ellen hoped was joy.

Then the girl straightened, and her eyes met Ellen's head-on. Looking at her was an unexpected gut punch—the hard, calm gaze, the chocolate brown, the angle of her jaw, the set of her eyes.

Well, at least she had no doubt they'd found the right girl.

"How can I help you?" The girl raised an eyebrow.

Ellen opened her mouth, but—but what? She wanted to simply explain she'd come to free the girl and take her to her father, but that kind of bomb shell needed a preamble. Didn't it?

This crap wasn't in the training manuals.

Dane cleared his throat and mustered conversational niceties. "Hi there, young lady. What do you sell here?"

The girl frowned at them, suspicion clear on her face, but she pointed around them as she spoke. "Animal feed, exotic pets, some small livestock." She looked back and forth between them and then pursed her lips. "If you didn't know what we sold, why did you come in here?"

"Uh, it's a little hard to explain," Ellen muttered. "You seem a little young to be working all alone at a store like this."

She smirked, the expression eerily familiar. "You from off-planet?"

"Yes. Is this a family store?" Ellen replied.

The girl shook her head. "No, my owners have a chain of different animal and feed supply shops across the Faros system. Me and three other girls keep the counter staffed at this one. Petuk's is pretty popular, I guess."

Dane stiffened. "Did you say owners?"

She nodded, shrugging. "Yep. Pretty normal for orphans on Faros. There's a lot of us."

Only this girl wasn't an orphan. "Are the other girls here right now?" She hadn't planned to evacuate more than one little girl right now. She didn't know the feasibility—or the legality—of that. Not that she'd hesitate, but with Kael on a murderous rampage and the *Audacity* stuck on the other side of a permanent sandstorm, it wasn't the best time. "Or anyone else, actually?"

Dane gave her a look, and the robot wasn't far behind, but none of them compared to the girl's deepening frown. Had she said something wrong?

"Um, no," the girl said. "The others stay upstairs when they're not on shift, but they're out shopping. It's just me and EOE8."

"EO-what? Who's that?" said Dane. Trying to be friendly like the socially-adjusted, non-awkward person that he was.

"I am EOE8," said the robot. "Resident carebot for the children here. But I also boast state of the art defensive capabilities."

The robot was no fool.

"Nice to meet you, EOE8. I'm sure they're very impressive. You

won't need them anytime soon." Dane gave her another look. "*Right,*
Commander?"

"Of course." She spread her hands. "What? I never said I was any
good outside of the military."

Dane rolled his eyes with a smile. "Then maybe you shouldn't have
retired."

Ellen snorted and shook her head.

"Look, do you actually need something...?" the girl said. Mimic-
king her, the robot folded its arms, although it looked more impatient
than intimidating.

"Do you sell tranquilizers?" Ellen asked. It was at least something
they definitely needed, but from Dane's wide eyes, it hadn't been the
right choice.

"Yes..." said the girl. "For what kind of creature? Size?"

"Uh... Give us a second," Ellen said, quickly raising her helmet.

Dane did also. "Commander, asking about tranqs isn't exactly
helping win the kid over, you know. Neither is raising these helmets."

"I know, I know. I just need us on the same page on this. I think we
have to just take her."

"*Take* her? You are never one to beat around the bush. I know we're
in a rush, but are you sure you want to kidnap her? Does she get a
choice?"

"Of course she gets a choice! I think this would be stealing her,
technically. And only if she's willing. But if she is, think we can find
another lander? You all right for another chase? We could end up
wanted on Faros."

"We *will* end up wanted on Faros. This place is run down, but
there's at least a camera or two."

"So... is that a no?"

He snorted. "Like we're not wanted in half the galaxy anyway.
Who cares about this God-forsaken rock? Besides, a handful of cash
seems to do a lot to change what cameras see here."

"Cash we don't have."

"I don't care. If I had my kid this close to me, you think I'd walk
away? I couldn't do that to Kael—or to her."

She let out a held breath. "All right then—I'm going to try to convince her."

He laughed. "Good luck, Commander. You're going to need it."

She lowered her helmet again. Dane didn't, which might make sense if they faced a quick getaway. But he was clearly saying she was on her own.

"Sorry to be awkward. Nobody's perfect. We didn't come to buy anything, to be honest," she said.

"Shocker," the girl murmured.

"This might sound a little weird." Ellen held up a hand. "But just hear me out."

"If you're selling wogwi beans, we are not—" the robot started.

"I'm not. Give me five minutes, not even, and then if you want, we'll leave."

The robot's watery eyes grew more stern. "She's got no money, madam, so if you're trying to sell something—"

"Not that either."

The robot looked to the girl, who pinned Ellen with steely eyes. The animals moved and skittered in the silence, alarm in the air.

"You already sound weird," the girl said.

"That's fair," said Ellen.

The girl waved a hand and sighed dramatically. "Might as well keep going."

Ellen let herself smile a little at that—being the stoic commander probably wasn't the best here. "Are you Shirin Nar?"

The girl went still, hand suspended in the air. "How do you know that?"

Ellen turned on her gauntlet's holodisplay and strode forward, calling up a large doc from one of Doug's files. "This might be a little hard to believe, but I was sent here by a man born on Faros by the name of Kael Sidassian. He's got a new name now, so don't look it up. When he was eleven, he was forcibly conscripted into the Gray Dragons. At sixteen, he and your mother conceived you. This is his application for their marriage license."

"A *marriage* license—"

"Things didn't go as planned. He was framed for the murder of a woman the police thought was your mother and sent away from here for a very long time."

Shirin's eyes had sharpened as Ellen spoke. "Oh, c'mon."

"What?" She frowned.

"What's the con, lady?"

Ellen stared. "What con? No con. Why would I lie about all that?"

"If your story's all true, how do you know he was framed?" Shirin waved at the air again, like the hole in the story would become obvious any minute now.

Ellen swallowed, bringing back some of her officer's seriousness. Maybe the junior officer trying to convince a grizzled commander of something was the right tone for the moment. "I know because he works for me. Our employer discovered in his background checks that your mother is very much still alive. We believe her death was staged to frame him, so he could be sold for a profit—and so could you."

The color drained from her face. "That's… that's terrible." She absently drew closer to the robot, and it put a comforting hand on her shoulder.

"If this is a trick," murmured the robot, "it's truly a cruel one."

She forced a deep breath. "This is not a con. Your father wants you back."

Shirin looked up abruptly at that, and naked hope flashed in her eyes before she smuggled it away again. "Where does the animal tranq relate to your story about my supposed parents?"

Ellen hesitated, unsure of what bizarre conclusions the girl might draw from the truth. "Well… Your father came here with us to look for you, but he's run into some old troubles, and he needs our help."

She scowled harder now. Something about that had not been the right thing to say. Wow, she was really on a roll. "Gang troubles, you mean. Why am I not surprised?" She sighed, an exasperated, I-don't-believe-you sigh. "Even *if* I believed you, what does 'helping him' have to do with drugs? You definitely win the award for weirdest con, lady. It's kicking, truly, but I'm not falling for it."

Ellen blinked. "I don't know how to convince you this is not some kind of trick."

"You could actually explain yourself."

"When he was sent away, he was sold to a cyborg mercenary outfit. He's been augmented to—look, he's really, really strong. We may need to sedate him to get him off planet and help him. But we've done it before, it's okay. He wants us to. I mean—it's complicated."

Dane was shaking his head out of the corner of her eye. She fought the urge to slap a palm over her face.

Shirin shook her head. "Yeah right." Her voice took on a mocking tone. "Look, little girl, we found your long-lost father, and he actually wants you back, and to feed you and clothe you and love you and put up with you, and all we need are some drugs in exchange."

"Oh no! It's not in exchange. We can pay for them," Ellen blurted. Although was that true? She had *not* been planning on just getting them for free, right? Although if she was stealing a girl, what was stealing some drugs at the same time?

God. What the hell was this planet doing to her?

Dane finally lowered his helmet. "Sweetheart, forgive her. This isn't her usual job."

"I'm not good with kids," she agreed hastily. Or even remotely familiar with them.

Dane ignored her and stepped closer, his tone soothing. "We all came here with the express purpose of finding you. Everything else is secondary. We'll walk out without that tranq if we need to. This is about your dad looking for you. He'd have looked sooner if he could."

Ellen gave him a small, grateful smile over her shoulder. *That* was the truth, even if Shirin couldn't hear it.

The girl's frown deepened, but her bottom lip quivered too. She glanced around. Wondering if someone might hear them? Ellen was worried about that too, but she hadn't sensed any arrivals. "Can I see that file a little closer? What kind of drug again?"

Ellen held her arm over the counter, tensing, trying to sharpen her ears. Leaning over this counter holding out a holodisplay was not the ideal defensive position, especially with Kael out there who-knew-where, but Shirin wouldn't understand if she resisted. She needed to see Ellen's trust. "It's really hard to say what medications work on him because of his augmentations. He has scrubbers that rapidly clean things out. Maybe any kind of strong sedative or tranquilizer you might have?"

Her eyes widened, but the robot couldn't help but jump in. "We have this type that disperses in gas form for unruly large animals. Would that help?"

Dane snorted. "Sounds about right."

"Hey! Wouldn't that knock us out potentially too?"

"Yes. You have to be away from the animal to use that one effectively," said the robot, voice totally neutral. "It is used for large mammals and reptiles panicking in their stalls."

"I'll take it, but do you have anything else?"

"This horse tranquilizer injector?" The robot held out a tray. "Or…"

"That's perfect." Ellen grabbed both off the counter and dropped them into a compartment. She might have her qualms, but she needed to remember Kael's point on Molyarch. Her *qualms* weren't going to help her get out of this mess.

"Are you planning to inject him with that?" Shirin said, frowning.

"Well… yes. It won't hurt him, I promise."

"I guess I'll just completely take your word on that. Good luck then." The girl squinted at the marriage application, pursing her lips like she'd just licked a lemon. "Can I at least get a copy of this or something?"

Ellen shrugged. "I guess. I mean, we have computers on the ship. Or there's printers too. Hardly ever use them, though."

Shirin frowned. "What ship?"

"My ship," Ellen said. "Oh, hell. I'm doing a terrible job of this. Sorry." She actually did slap her hand on her face now. "We have a ship in orbit. You were sold to slavers against your father's will. We're here to make that right."

"Who are you?" the robot demanded. "Identify yourselves."

"I'm Commander Ellen Ryu, captain of the starship *Audacity*. And this is Sergeant Dane Hall, under my command."

"Okay. But this guy you're claiming is my father. Who are you to *him*?" The girl put in.

She hesitated. "I'm his commander too."

Shirin's eyes narrowed. "That's it? You always go out of your way to look for the kids of people who work for you?"

Ellen's eyes widened. Dane's lips twitched. As a matter of fact, they had looked for Dane's son. They hadn't flown across the galaxy specifically for that purpose, but they hadn't done that now either. Her mouth opened, but she couldn't figure out a way to formulate an adequate response.

The robot saved her. "Ellen Ryu, former Union war hero in the Pacific Alliance Systems, specifically responsible for architecting the Yogin Defense of Saeloun Hanguk that ended that round of fighting and was thought for almost five years to have ended the war." An image of a younger Ellen in uniform appeared in the air over the ordering terminal, collar sharp in grey and dark shades of red.

"Looks like her picture," Shirin murmured.

Ellen's cheeks were already burning hot with embarrassment, and she opened her mouth, but the robot wasn't done.

"Noted awards for service include: the Silver Tear for life-saving efforts in the PAS systems, the Parat Medal for defeat of Puritan forces at Soriti V, seven others. Youngest officer ever awarded company commander of Company Name Redacted, two other commissions. Wanted deserter, nine hundred thousand credits bounty offered from six sources. There is a list of about two dozen strategic planning performance records held at the Union military academies—this may take several minutes. Should I go on?"

"Six sources?" She frowned. "Huh. That's new. Used to just be one." And the amount had gone up.

Shirin shook her head. "That's enough, EO. I don't see how this tells me if I can trust her."

Ellen dropped her arm and the holodisplay with it. "Look. I can't make you trust me. It's up to you. But I've been where you are."

"I highly doubt that." Shirin's eyes flicked to Ellen's neatly uniformed portrait still floating in the air over their payment terminal.

"I know it might be hard to believe, but I was a kid once too. And I was taken without much choice in the matter to a world where adults told me what to do, all day every day. I didn't mind exactly, because there was a war going on."

"If you were a child," cooed EOE8, their big eyes going empathetic again, "then you should not have known war, let alone have been concerned with fighting it. You should have been protected."

She met those drippy eyes for a long moment, jaw hardening, fighting at something that vibrated inside her core, something she'd built a steel cage around.

There was no opening that door. If she did, she didn't want to know or feel what was on the other side.

After one long breath and a swallow, the feeling faded, and she hardened her expression. "War isn't fair, and neither is life. I should have been protected, but I can't do anything about that now. Shirin should have been too."

"She is." EOE8 lifted its chin.

"Can you protect her from her owners?" She returned her eyes to Shirin. "And that's something I *can* do something about, if you want me to."

Shirin lowered her gaze, feigning a hard exterior, but she shook just a little. "I... I can't... I don't know anything about you. Not really."

"Look, I know you're not eager to trade one master for another. I don't blame you. But I'll do everything in my power to give you some choices, for once. And to protect you."

Biting her lip, Shirin's gaze shifted to EOE8. "It doesn't matter. I can't leave EOE8."

"You must." The robot slowly bent closer, patting her back gently as its eyes went full-on gooey with concern. "She is right. You are young now, but this life will not continue this way for you. When you are older... as a slave, you will not be this lucky. They will not keep us together, either. They groom you here. The food is too good. I will not be able to stop them when the time comes. You should run. While you can."

"Or bring the robot." Ellen shrugged.

"Oh, I'm sure my programming won't allow that," it said.

She waved them off. "Sure, of course. But if we could get around that…"

It frowned, silver fingers gently covering Shirin's shoulder. "I hope to go wherever Shirin goes."

"What about the other girls?" Shirin whispered.

"It doesn't matter, I can't leave. You, however, must go. If I were to be incapacitated or destroyed," and here EOE8 gave Ellen a pointed look, "which might be necessary for you to leave without an alarm being raised, by the way, I'm sure they'll get a new carebot for the other girls."

Ellen swung the multi forward and started checking the settings. "Great. So does that settle it, Shirin? Because I am guessing we aren't alone here indefinitely." A light laser ought to do the trick, she was guessing.

Shirin glared at the multi. Then she glanced at EOE8, then the animals. "How can I leave my babies behind?"

Ellen squinted at her, then sighed. "How about we can get you some more once we're in the deep?"

"You mean in *space*?" She bit her lip.

"Yes. That's where spaceships are. Most of the time."

Shirin hesitated one moment longer, glancing down at her rags, at the store around her. Her eyes rested on Dane for a moment, who said nothing but calmly returned her gaze.

"Go, Shirin," EOE8 urged. "I want you to have a better life."

She let out a breath. The words were almost inaudible, but she murmured, "All right."

"Do you have any belongings to bring with you?" Dane asked.

Ellen glanced back. "I knew I brought you for a reason."

"To diffuse your incredible awkwardness?"

"And to ask smart questions about luggage."

"One moment! I can fetch them." The robot hurried into the dark back area.

Shirin started rummaging under the counter. Ellen caught Dane's gaze again, flicked her eyes toward the robot, then hefted the multi slightly. He nodded. Shirin darted into the back room, followed by a few loud squeals and crashes.

Ellen was just about to go back there when the robot returned, hefting a small backpack and gliding toward Dane. Its legs were spider-like and thin, but surprisingly stable. EOE8 placed its hand over Dane's briefly as it handed him the bag. "You will take good care of her, won't you?" Dane returned the gesture, nodding.

"EOE8, can you please load that into my lander while I pay for my purchases?" Ellen said loudly.

The robot cocked its head, hesitated, but then headed for the door now carrying the bag, Dane on its heels.

When Ellen turned back to the counter, Shirin had reappeared. "Sorry about that. Needed to at least let a few of them out."

"Out?"

"Life on the street is probably better than here. Not good if they get bought." She shrugged, then pointed down. "I have an ankle bracelet. You got a plan to get rid of it?"

Smiling at her skepticism, Ellen bent to look at the restraint and found the girl's calf wasn't as bony or as pale as she would have expected. She took a deep breath. This was decidedly *not* a good time to injure or maim anybody, so she needed to get this exactly right.

She lowered the laser by one degree.

"Hold your leg just like this. Perfect. Now don't move. Tell me if it feels warm at *all*, okay?"

Shirin shifted. "Okay."

Ellen carefully lined up the multi with the ankle bracelet at a point where a green light flashed. Hopefully if she disabled the electronics, the thing would pop open and she wouldn't have to melt the whole way through. Although she was pretty sure a slight burn would be worth freedom for Shirin, losing a foot wouldn't be. Not that such things couldn't be fixed, but memories lasted a lifetime. "All right. Don't look."

Shirin squeezed her eyes shut.

She pulsed the beam—three, two, one, and the bracelet clicked, popped, and fell away. Shirin's skin was pale underneath it.

Kael's daughter—how weird *that* sounded—caught her breath as the metal fell away. Opening her eyes, she stared, then glanced up sharply. "No turning back now. Let's go. Wait—let me get those tranquilizers."

Ellen resisted the urge to tell her to just grab the whole drawer. Shirin handed her a handheld injector and the aerosol release for larger animals. Ellen tucked them into her hip compartment and then waved Shirin to follow her out the door, the little bell announcing their escape from Shirin's old life with a funny zing.

Dane had "borrowed" a new lander and waved at them from across the street. EOE8 was lying motionless in the back seat.

Shirin gasped, breaking into a run and jumping through the lander's open door. "EO! What did you do? What did you do to him? Oh, EO, EO, EO!"

"Just a little shock," Dane said mildly. "And a hookup to our ship's network." Dane gave Ellen a wink. "Our friends in the air will try to tweak a few things so you can keep your robot."

Ellen shut the back door and then slid into the front. Shirin stared at the door that had slammed behind her, then grabbed her bag and pulled it into her lap. "Is that the right thing to do? Steal EOE8?"

"Is slavery the right thing to do?" Ellen shot back, voice flat.

"It's not illegal here."

"Well, it fragging should be," snapped Dane. "How many goddamn centuries is it going to take?" It wasn't really a question. And she didn't really have an answer.

"Consider EOE8 your interest owed for all your hard work," Ellen said.

"Hmm." Shirin eased closer, clutching the robot's arm and staring out the window. "It taught me that two wrongs don't make a right, though."

Ellen let herself smile. "EOE8 is very wise. You've been lucky to have a good teacher. But stick around, kid. Once you get past thirty or forty wrongs, the math gets complicated."

Dane was driving now, but Ellen was pretty sure he didn't have a destination in mind. She needed to think, to make some decisions. Get this noncombatant off this planet, then come back and try to save Kael. How hard could that be? Should they head for the off-planet shuttle then?

But there was one other noncombatant they were supposed to be saving. Doug's friend. Were they just giving up and leaving her behind? Maybe that made sense, but they'd barely knocked on the door.

"Dane—head to Ninshabur Institute," she said. "One more time. Then we'll take Shirin to the port and get her back up there. Then hopefully they'll let us come back down for Kael."

Dane nodded. "I could take her up and send reinforcements back down. Zhia and Jenny."

"As long as they're healed from the surgeries. Good plan."

The houses, shops, and market squares flew by, golden and crimson fabrics billowing. Amber-colored sand swirled around, up, and over the lander.

She pulled the tranq injector and its aerosol companion out of her hip compartment and tried to figure out a dosage for Kael on her suit's computer. She gave up estimating the aerosol when it demanded wind conditions for application with a curse. And with his recovering system, plus the scrubbers? This was all complete bullshit. However Asha was controlling him could change the equation too. She winced. This would be a rough estimate. At best. Just like the first dose had been.

The first time and that first fight where they'd tranqed him flashed through her mind. Then the kiss that had preceded it. The memory made her lips feel warm and heated her cheeks. There had been no control between them then, for that one brief time. She needed that again, so, so desperately. Even in the past few weeks, they'd had an abundance of control. Or fear, maybe. Hesitation. Dancing around the fire, but never being consumed with its spirit.

She had to feel that again. At least once more time. They couldn't have survived all that they had only to be separated now. She would find some way to save him. She had to.

She eyed the injector again, then removed her gauntlet and slipped the injector inside her left sleeve. Uncomfortable, but if they had to go through the port security to get these innocents off planet, she didn't want to risk losing both of her options. She replaced the gauntlet with a grim sigh and picked up the animal knockout gas—not its name, but that was what she'd call it—and started to read the instructions on the outside of the grenade.

She had never battled Kael before. Not one-on-one. Oh, they'd sparred, but that wasn't the same. The day of that kiss and the tranq, Xi had settled things before they'd gotten out of hand with one of her cleaning robots. Before that, the knockout grenade had never given him a chance.

Too bad she didn't have any of those now.

She had seen him fight, many times now, enough that she didn't relish being his adversary. He was the best man she'd ever known. One of the best soldiers too.

For both their sakes, she would just have to be better.

CHAPTER SIXTEEN

DAY 18

MO HAD BEEN ACHING in at least a dozen places, and now her shoulder joint was perilously close to being added to the injury list with the way that Tovi's iron grip dragged her along. Pain be damned, though, she wasn't going easily.

She would turn dragging her feet into an art form, if only to buy herself a little time.

To buy Doug time.

Although the whole plan was seeming a little less clever now. What was she expecting him to do? Program these soldiers away? There were no security loopholes in those M59 rifles, nor in the fingers pulling her along.

Hopefully he knew something she didn't. Hopefully her plan hadn't just screwed them both.

As they marched her down the corridor, one of Tovi's subordinates was furiously trying to locate the prisoners. Two more were shouting over each other into their comms. A dozen more with pistols and rifles escorted them now.

Too damn many to take out. Not at close range, anyway. Tovi did have a sidearm. What was the sustained firing time for the SRO 47? She was more familiar with Union standard issue pistols than this off-market—possibly black market—brand, but it had maybe ten or twelve seconds of continuous beam before recharge-reheat? Or was it only five?

And was she willing to take a gamble on being wrong? She could do a lot with a laser in ten seconds. She could do a lot in five seconds too, but it might not be enough against this many.

"We're willing to make a compromise," one of the officers on the comm was saying.

"We're not here to negotiate," a gruff voice answered. The prisoners? "We're not going back to the pen. We did the Lord's work."

"Butchering human beings," Mo muttered. "The Lord's work has changed since last I heard about it."

Tovi pursed her lips. "You were a soldier, weren't you?"

"I *am* a soldier."

"Then don't tell me you never butchered anyone."

Mo narrowed her eyes. She hadn't thought she was dealing with someone wholesome or anything, but that comment was particularly horrifying. "I've defended my people and their freedom to choose."

"And look how far it's gotten you." Tovi gave her another sickeningly sweet smile.

Mo could have spat quite a few swear words at that moment, but sometimes less was more. She bared her teeth, leaning closer.

The captain gave her an uneasy stare for a moment, then tore her gaze away. "What's the status on that ship?" she barked.

"Their CO doesn't believe that we're trying to get the prisoners, thinks we're just buying time."

"Why would we lie?" Tovi rolled her eyes again. She lived to roll her eyes, didn't she.

"Maybe so they stop punching a hole in our hull?"

"Then they *definitely* won't get their prisoners."

"They don't believe they've escaped twice. They think maybe we have help coming."

She couldn't really blame them for that. Anyone could see these guys were getting more than their fair share of luck. Mo kept her eyes on the crew around her, looking for any opening. They were distracted, yes, and the temperature seemed to be rising as they continued down the corridor. A few were wiping sweat from their brows. But if that was her big distraction, it wasn't going to be enough.

"Nobody's that good!" shouted a female voice from a different comm. From the Puritan ship?

Tovi shook her head. "And here I thought the Foundation contract was the one that would be the death of me."

"I wouldn't count us out just yet," Mo said softly.

The captain ignored her. "Get me that CO on the line. Why is it so damn hot in here?"

The crew member winced as he handed over the comm. "To be honest, Captain, I'm not sure they want them back alive if they are that good at escaping."

Tovi scowled at the comm. "*Athens*, this is the captain of the *Sharpspear*. Why are you trying to depressurize my hull and kill us all?"

"I don't care about killing you all," snapped the female voice. "But I've got orders to eliminate those two on contact. This is close enough contact for me."

"I thought you believed in human life," Tovi snapped. "In the preservation of—"

"We don't need crazy fundamentalists running around cutting people apart. It's bad optics."

Mo rolled her eyes. That choice of words, when it was exactly her eye augmentations the prisoners would like to brutally remove, was beyond ironic.

"Fragging hypocrites don't believe in anything."

"I believe in following orders, Captain. So unless you eject those two idiots into the shuttle bay in the next five minutes, you can kiss your sweet spaceship goodbye."

Tovi tossed the comm back to the crew member, lip curled in disgust. "How far to those prisoners?"

"Next corridor, Captain. Turn left here, then 25 meters."

Mo gave a jerk against Tovi's grip, just for the hell of it, as they turned the corner. To her surprise, Tovi stopped short. But Mo soon realized she wasn't the cause. The whole group had halted.

Hovering in front of them were two drones. Two men were hunkered down with torches at a blast door far down the hall beyond them—wearing those Puritan jackets. The last blast door before the bridge?

"What the…" someone muttered.

"How the hell did these two idiots get *drones* to help them too?"

"They didn't," said a voice.

Her heart flipped in her chest. It was a *familiar* voice.

But before she could process it fully, the group around her burst into motion. The back of the crew member closest to the drones arced. A scream split her ears, and hisses from the collision of laser fire and stun bolts fizzed into the air.

The drones, however, weren't playing sitting ducks, and neither should she.

She spun into Tovi, whipping around her like she was going for a hug. Except not the friendly kind. In one fluid motion, she gripped the pistol and nudged the safety switch. Tovi grabbed for Mo's elbow, then her neck, but her fingers slipped on the sweat. And it was too late.

The pistol was already lighting up, slicing in.

Mo's jaw tightened as Tovi's body fell, because even after many years, gut slicing someone—butchery—wasn't her preference. And the awful smell of lasers vaporizing blood wasn't something she wanted to get used to.

The drones had stunned maybe five of them, and were working on more, so Mo took aim at the back of the group. Taking a split second for a quick breath and to line up her targets, she raised the pistol to the sight, squeezed the trigger, and sliced.

The SRO 47 wasn't powerful enough to behead all six that she hit— which was part of what made it a good ship weapon—but with one careful swing and damn good aim, she was able to take down half of the group in one go.

She turned to see the drones had stunned two more, although one drone was flying at an angle now, whirling erratically on its axis.

Raising the pistol to end this, she locked eyes with one of the remaining crew members. A man with green eyes and freckles across his nose. They stared at each other as her gaze narrowed, approximating the angle to hit him and the other two remaining in one shot. Another body fell to a drone's stun, startling them both.

The man turned and ran.

Yeah, he was dead anyway. The other hostiles were more critical. They just needed to get off this stupid ship as fast as—

An arm looped around her neck, tightening. She jerked the pistol up toward the attacker, but a hard blow to her wrist knocked it out of her hand, the pain rocketing through her fingers and up her arm.

There was leather on the arm closing around her throat. Not the crew then. A prisoner. A Puritan prisoner.

She tried to spin out of the hold, but he held on. This guy hadn't been weakened very much by captivity, damn it.

Splotches were starting to appear in front of her eyes—way too soon. That head wound wasn't helping matters. She tried to spin again, but he repaid her efforts with a punch to the kidney. Her foot struck at his instep, but missed.

A sharp elbow was going to have to do. But the splotches were getting bigger and—

The man behind her growled, grip suddenly loosening. Then he tightened up and whirled. "Fragging drone! Weak. Trying to stun me. When I'm through with her, I'll—"

But he never finished the sentence. She jerked forward as her stomach suddenly revolted, the urge to throw up instant and forceful. The jerk worked in her favor, though, as the prisoner lost his grip on her and went flying.

She blinked down at the corridor's decking. Her body wasn't falling. It took her oxygen-deprived brain and panting lungs several long moments to realize gravity had gone out.

She looked up as the Puritan hit the opposite corridor wall, totally upside down. The drone, whirling even more erratically now, zipped toward him.

He lunged for it, swinging wildly and clipping it. It bounced off the floor, then back up. Would it eve be airborne if gravity hadn't gone out? She wasn't sure. The prisoner grabbed for it again—and got hold.

He crashed it against the floor once, twice, but as that didn't seem to be doing enough damage, he grabbed it with the other hand and started to squeeze.

The drone laid on another stun—this time from only a few centimeters above his heart.

With a growl, the prisoner finally went limp. His fingers remained tangled in the drone's mobility array.

Up the hallway, the other prisoner's form had crumpled. Must have also been stunned. But it was now drifting slowly into the air and toward her, eerie as that was. Along with the fallen crew members around her.

And the blood.

She was stuck staring at the horrifying way their bodies were creeping up into space when the more stable drone whizzed into her line of view.

"So… about that Plan C?" said the sweetest voice in the universe.

"Doug!" she sputtered. "I could hug you."

"Please don't."

She blinked.

"Maybe when I am actually with you and we're not about to die?"

"Okay."

"You said there was a third option. To get off the ship."

Her brain finally burst into action. "Right—the escape pods. There should be some right down here." She pointed at the perpendicular corridor she and Tovi had come out of. "Where are you?"

"Conveniently, I'm in that corridor. You come to me—c'mon." And the drone whizzed away in that direction.

She instantly started to try to jog after him, forgetting the zero G. She had to ricochet herself off the ceiling and back toward the decking —and the wall handholds—to really propel herself along. Her stomach was still in open rebellion, but that could be from any number of the things that had just happened.

"Simmons!" someone cried out.

Mo risked a look over her shoulder. Damn it, Tovi was still alive.

"Simmons, you whiny, spoiled coward—" she shouted after them. "Come out here and fight like a man."

The drone paused, turning. "I believe I did, Captain. And I won. Have a nice day."

And then it whizzed past Mo and away.

She spared one last glance down the hallway. But they weren't staying on this ship—things were too far gone. The *Athens* was going to destroy this ship, most likely. It was way more important that they made it to the escape pod.

Especially before everyone else did.

Tovi wouldn't recover from that wound, most likely. But if she did… What she'd wanted was Doug imprisoned or dead, and if she somehow survived, she'd be doubly determined to make that happen.

She twisted, lined up the sight, and squeezed. There. One headshot for a single mission was low for her, but in this case, it counted for everything.

Hustling around the corner, she saw something that erased the carnage from the corridor temporarily from her mind. Doug clutched a hauling robot and waved brightly, grinning.

"Keep going," she urged him. "Behind you. How is that robot not floating?"

"The power of magnetism!" Doug said, like some kind of sideshow magician.

"How can you be happy at a moment like this?" she said. "We need to get the hell out of here."

"I'm not dead. You're not dead. You still have your eyes." He shrugged. "Lots of causes for celebration."

"Let's not count our chickens before they've hatched, shall we?" She swung past him. "There—through this hatch. Good—it's not locked. We just need to—"

A sudden falling sensation cut her words short, followed by a crash of metal against her jaw.

For frag's sake, she just could not win. She groaned.

"Gravity systems back online," said the ship's voice. "Hull breach in two minutes and counting."

———

FOR ONCE, the surface storm had settled, and a vast expanse of red sand and rock stretched out in front of Ellen. A brilliant blue sky opened up above them, with three silvery moons.

Well, who knew. When it wasn't raging and furious, Faros IV had an unexpected beauty to it.

"Got to make one more stop, Shirin," Ellen said, leaning one arm over the back seat. "We have someone else in trouble. Then we'll get off this planet indefinitely."

Shirin nodded, glancing warily at the planet's surface stretching out on all sides. While the girl was going along with Ellen's orders right now, she was clearly far from meek. EOE8's blank eyes had cleared, and it had woken up with seemingly no compulsion to run back to the animal store, so Xi must have taken care of it well enough for now.

"Do you really think this is going to work?" Dane asked as they strode toward the vast entrance again. It was more majestic—and intimidating—without the sand obscuring their view, although dunes of reddish dust lapped against the vast blue tiled walls. The nearby streets rose up with all concrete warehouses, making the contrast of the institute even starker.

"I have my doubts. But when we find Doug," she forced herself to say, "I want to be able to say I tried." One more time. A single visit before accepting defeat was hardly what she'd like to report, even considering the extenuating circumstances. *When* they found Doug and freed Kael and were safely off this planet, they could all have a beer and breathe a sigh of relief.

She stopped before the speaker, cleared her throat, slapped the palmpad.

"Identify yourselves and your purpose," the speaker growled, same as the first time.

"Amari Barakat. We'd like to speak with her. I'm Ellen Ryu, commander of the starship *Audacity*, and my team is—"

"Access granted."

Her eyes went wide, and she simply stared as the sapphire blue doors parted with a thick, heavy grinding sound, revealing a dark, cathedral-like interior. Windows and columns stretched high up into a vaulted interior, but near the ground everything was dark except periodic dim sconces. A small group was approaching from the far end, but their dark robes revealed little detail.

After a moment's hesitation, she strode in, the other three in tow. The doors immediately began to grind shut again behind them.

She didn't make it far, though, before their greeters reached them. Her eyes hastily adjusted to the darkness, revealing a dozen armed guards that marched in formation around a veiled woman. They clearly awaited a command. And judging by the elaborate teal breather on the woman in the center, the luxuriously lined eyes, the black veil, Ellen had found who she was looking for. The resounding thud was like a vault closing, dread digging a hole in her stomach.

"Ms. Barakat," Ellen said in greeting. Her chin lifted slightly.

"Yes." The slightest head dip of acknowledgment.

"I've been urgently trying to reach you. Douglas Simmons is in—"

"Trouble?" Her voice was soft, muffled and a little mechanical behind the elaborate breather. Amused. "Yes, he does have a knack for getting into that, doesn't he."

"Have you had any contact with Quentin Davenmore?"

Before Ellen had even bit out the words, Barakat laughed.

The dread she'd been fighting settled in hard—to her chest, her stomach, tightening. "We have reason to believe Quentin Davenmore is a serious threat, Ms. B—"

"*I* am the serious threat." Any laughter had drained from Barakat's eyes, and even the slightest shuffling among the group went silent. The whole place seemed eerily still.

Oh, God. A trap. She'd forgotten to consider a trap. For the bounty or the gang, or any number of things, really. Ellen's throat went tight.

And with Shirin with her.

"Of *course* I've had contact with Quentin Davenmore. He is my fiancé." Her voice had the strangest way of sounding sweet, meek, and brutal, all at the same time.

"So you just roll over and do what he wants?" Ellen choked out.

There was that laugh again. "Who said this is what *he* wants? Oh, he learned dirty business from his father, but he had no idea how to truly leverage the power he had. Not until I came along."

"You? You're the one who attacked Simmons?"

"Well, not me personally of course." Those eyes crinkled with a smile behind the breather. "I have people for that. Just like Simmons does. And here you are, like his little trained dogs, still following his orders even after he couldn't give them anymore. Have to admire that much. And very convenient for me, I do owe you my thanks of not having to hunt you down."

"Why? Doug is *trying* to do good in the world—"

She waved a hand, and the men around her marched forward, surrounding their little group. Shirin and EOE8 skittered closer, and Ellen took a step back toward them, tightening her grip on the multi. But it wasn't going to do any good. Shirin was too vulnerable to risk a firefight, especially with no cover anywhere nearby.

"Douglas Simmons thinks he knows everything. But his brand of good is so short-sighted. Myopic, even." The casual amusement drained from Barakat's voice. "He needed to be neutralized."

She couldn't keep the anger from her voice. "And you'll do better?"

Barakat's response was sharp as a whip's crack. "I'm not *trying* to do better. Because I'm not trying to do good. What good has any of these do-gooders ever done for me? For you? For anyone?"

"They've helped me a lot, actually."

"I bet. Buying your loyalty away. Who are you to criticize my morals, oath breaker?"

"I might have broken my oath, but I *wasn't* bought. You don't know anything about it."

"And I don't care to. I suppose what you say is true, since I froze your accounts, and you're still here."

She pursed her lips. Well. That explained that.

"You should have stayed away, Ellen Ryu." Barakat signaled, and the guards started forward.

"Wait!" Ellen held up both palms. "Is Doug dead?"

"Wouldn't you like to know?"

That wasn't a yes—but if he was dead, why not say so? And gloat about it. Inwardly, she clutched at the slight victory. "Why? I want to know what I'm going down for. What did Doug ever do to make you hate him? Did he talk *that* much?"

Barakat chuckled. "You *do* know him. It's true, the village idiot hardly ever shuts up, does he? Truth be told, only his rigid morals got in the way. I am the queen of a vast—if illegally acquired—banking empire, and if he knew that, he would certainly have tried to take it away from me. He might have even succeeded. He's nosy, so a confrontation was only a matter of time. When my power is combined with Davenmore's assets, we'll be able to do whatever we like. Control whatever—and whomever—we like."

"You'll never control me. And people like me. Money isn't everything."

In spite of the breather, she could tell Barakat was grinning. "Maybe it isn't. But it's a lot." She signaled again, and the men started forward again.

"Wait—wait—look, you already killed Doug," she bluffed. "What do you need us for? Now that we know our leader is dead, we don't need to be here. Or keep fighting. Just let us go, and I'll take my crew and go home." She jerked a thumb at Dane and Shirin and EOE8 behind her.

Barakat raised an eyebrow. "Really? You expect the queen of a banking empire to just sit back and watch a one point five million credit bounty walk back out into a sandstorm?"

Ellen's mouth dropped open, in spite of herself. That was... that was more. A lot more.

"Oh, did you think I didn't know? Your Doug may be good, and I may be better, but any idiot can check a board for bounties. One of my computer systems did it automatically—so less than an idiot. So I've so courteously called in some people that are looking for you. They'll be here any moment to pick you up."

The guards started forward now as Barakat turned her back and began striding away.

From behind her left shoulder, the unmistakable crackle of a stun pulse leaving a multi hit her ears. She tensed and almost swore, but there wasn't time for that.

Fragging hell, Dane.

She hit her fog nanos instead, releasing the strange mist around them and then switching back to pulse. Something to protect them even slightly.

Ballistics thundered all around her. She dove for Shirin, trying to cover her. EOE8 was attempting to do the same. She tried to crane her neck around, get the lay of the fight, but the fog cloud was doing its job obstructing everyone's view, including hers. Maybe especially her own.

She only sensed the guard barreling toward them at the last second, lunging at him and away from Shirin. She'd been hoping to block any stray ballistics, but if an armored guard plus her power armor landed on the little girl, that could be even worse. She charged the guard full on, pulling him into a tumbling roll away from and past Shirin.

She managed to get enough momentum to come out on top in the roll, and the force of her blow to his jaw knocked the man out cold. Thank God for power armor—and that helmets hadn't been on the Institute's equipment list, apparently.

Out of the cloud now, she scanned the scene. Dane had taken down four or five, but the rest had stormed him all at once, tackling him into a huge, writhing pile. A dozen more were sprinting toward them from the side. She rushed back toward Shirin even as she saw it.

Barakat's form lay where she'd landed, a pool of blood widening around it.

Well, holy hell. She'd assumed he'd used a pulse, she could have sworn she'd heard the crackle. But maybe he'd added a ballistic for good measure post-haste. Was Barakat *dead*? She certainly wasn't moving.

"Hey—you! Woman!"

Reaching Shirin, she looked back to the pile-on.

They'd hauled Dane to his feet. One man with a split lip and blood on his armored vest held his rifle to Dane's helmet. The visor, in particular. "Lose your rifle, or this one will lose his life," he shouted.

She scowled. "You can't shoot through that—"

"It's cracked," Dane yelled to her, his voice garbled even as it came through the comm. "Sorry, Commander. I had to try. And I had to get one in for Simmons. It just wasn't right. Do what you gotta do."

"It wasn't right. But it wasn't worth risking Shirin's life, though."

"Spent chips," he replied. It was a card game term in the Union. It was also slang for, we're already dead anyway. He'd shot at Barakat because he'd been sure all roads led to one place eventually.

He might be right.

She caught Shirin's eye. There was a courage there, a spark under the fear. "Don't let them kill him," Shirin whispered.

Keeping her nod as slight as she could, she turned back to their captors, raising her multi out to her side. Then, with every molecule of her screaming her regret, she let it fall and surrendered.

———

MO GROANED. Beside her, Doug groaned too.

The pain in her collarbone, jaw, and chest was enough to keep even the most talkative person silent, but she permitted herself a growl of rage as she struggled to her feet.

Maybe more of a roar.

The pods were right there. Sprinting forward, she lifted the bar, pulled on the latch, then the handle, but it wouldn't budge. It took her a second to realize why.

Someone had been here before them. The first pod bay was empty, the escape pod gone.

"Shit—some of them already abandoned ship."

"With a captain like that..." Doug grumbled.

She dashed over to the next. And the next. And the fourth. Then she swore as she jogged back toward him. "There's only one pod left in this bank. The other banks could be beyond blast doors, I'm not sure. If we even have that long."

"What does that mean?"

"They only hold one person. You're going. Get ready."

"Four pods? What is this place, the freaking Titanic?"

"Might as well be." She started pulling the hauler bot toward it. "C'mon. We can't be the only people looking to get out of here. No time to talk—ready?" She straightened.

"No, we're both going. Look, we can fit."

She shook her head. "I'm not going." There might be other pods in another area, but with the ship announcing a countdown, the chances were they'd be gone when she reached them. No, this one was the only one they were guaranteed. He'd go, and she'd stay. And she'd have died protecting him.

The idea should have been horrible, should have gutted her, to be left alone here for whatever else this horrible ship could serve up. But it didn't. It'd be a quick and honorable death. It was just business, just logic. Beautiful in its way. A sacrifice that would mean something.

It was her job to protect, and his job to help from a distance. A very, very *safe* distance, she hoped, if he survived this. She'd try to make sure he did right now.

"Don't be ridiculous," he said. "There's no reason we can't both squeeze in."

"No. The air will just run out sooner."

"Who cares? We're in the middle of nowhere. Our chances aren't good in there *or* on this ship."

"I'm sorry, sir, I won't do it. Goodbye, sir, it's been nice—" She reached down to pick him up, without asking permission for the first time.

He pushed her away. "Don't. Don't even. How dare you try to say your goodbyes. You're coming. I'd still be in that cell if it weren't for you."

"There isn't time for this." She tried again to lift him, and this time he let her. She carried him in.

"Hull breach in thirty seconds," the ship AI announced.

"Slag off, you damn computer!" she growled as they eased inside. "Damn, this is meant for you to stand in."

He rolled his eyes. "Figures. C'mon, Mo. Don't do this."

She'd have to hold him up with her body or arms or something while the thing strapped him in. Usually it did it automatically. She could make it work. She had to.

"Nice to know you, Doug." Those words weren't enough, but they were the best she had. She reached up and hit the harness initiation control.

He grabbed her and hugged her to his chest. *Hard.*

"Damn it, Doug—what are you—"

The harness straps started on the torso, the first one flying out and around them both, tightening.

"No." She bucked, trying to get out while they still had time.

"Sergeant!" he snapped, arms tightening harder.

She blinked at him, stunned.

"Since I am technically the senior officer on this ship, there will be no more argument. Stop squirming. The decision is made."

She searched for words, but ended up just taking several open-mouthed panting breaths as the harness straps continued to whip out and auto-tighten around them both.

The pod hatch slid shut so close behind her that she felt the air whoosh through her hair.

"Don't let the door hit you in the ass on the way out," he muttered.

She shook her head, feeling crazy smiling at a time like this. The shell around them jerked, and pulled as it separated, the forces of the movement pressing her into him, then both of them into the straps.

They were out. Gone. Free. Maybe still dead, quite possibly soon to be injured by the harness in this *total* misuse of an escape pod. But free.

His eyes were on the controls over their heads and behind her, studying, making changes. What was he doing?

As if reading her thoughts, he glanced down briefly. "I'm seeing if I can alter the settings for the two of us. Or at least for one of us to make it to a star system. There's nothing really in range, though."

She nodded, but remained quiet. That was hardly surprising.

"Are you all right, Sergeant?" His usual humor tinged his voice.

"Didn't know you had that in you," she murmured.

"Neither did I." He grinned, still focused on the controls.

"I can't believe you just did that. I can't believe you."

Now he did look at her, dropping his hands to his sides. "Well, you *did* say you wanted a hug."

She couldn't help but smile at that. A laugh bubbled up out of her, in spite of their situation. And to tell the truth, there were worse ways to die than in his arms.

"THIS WAY," the guard ordered, the scar over his eye puckering as he glared. Shouting and cries were going up all around the place, and the backup reinforcements had swarmed Barakat's body. She hadn't moved. But these guards were apparently very determined to do their duty.

Or get her bounty.

Keeping close to Shirin and EOE8, Ellen followed the guards down several long, drab corridors. For all the blue tile outside, this was a maze of mud-colored brick.

Their path led them to a huge hangar filled with three small space-craft, a heli, and five or six flyers. What kind of school maintained that many surface to air—and space—vehicles? Something more was going on here.

Light streamed into the hangar, the sun rising higher but not yet midday.

"Strip, you two." Scar Beard seemed to have declared himself in charge, making demands and jabbing his rifle into Dane's elbow. At Shirin's gasp, he added, "Just the armor. We don't care about your filthy rags."

Dane and Ellen looked at each other, hesitated.

"Don't make us get out the wire cutters. Or if you'd rather us give you some other motivation..." His eyes flicked darkly toward Shirin.

Growling as she went, she started removing the armor piece by piece. What else were they going to do? Shirin would be better off with them alive and unarmored, than with them dead and armored at her feet.

"It's not doing much with all these cracks anyway," Dane grumbled as he shucked off the chest piece. That was a lie, but he let out a deep cough that made her stomach pang with nerves. Had he coughed like that on the way over here? More than once? Maybe Maloof hadn't been bluffing about a virus.

They worked quickly, and soon were down to their flight suits.

"In there." Their bearded, scarred friend pointed his rifle to a small holding cell beside some offices. Other guards rushed forward to start picking through their armor. "Even you, robot."

They marched in, and the barred doors clanked closed. Air swirled hot through the bars of their new cage. The sudden feeling of the wind was so wrong, so strange—vibrant with movement and deeply dangerous. A shudder shook her, and then a series of coughs. This was… not good.

She'd have given anything to get back in that suit. Anything except Shirin's life, apparently.

"Well, that didn't go as planned, did it?" She turned to find Shirin smiling at her, although she also had a death grip on EOE8's long, thin arm.

"Not exactly." Ellen cleared her throat. "Sorry. I was trying to… do the right thing."

Shirin gave a stoic nod. "It's kind of funny, actually."

"Funny?" Ellen raised an eyebrow. Girl probably didn't realize the danger she was in, if she was talking like that. Of course, she couldn't know it was Arakovic coming for them.

Shirin's eyes scanned the hangar as she spoke. Ellen had to admit she liked that about her. "It's funny. I went from being in a store full of cages with the keys, to being inside one myself."

She smiled. "I'll give ya that."

"We'll figure out something, sweetheart. Don't worry." Dane leaned casually against the bars beside her, and to Ellen's surprise, Shirin gave him a small smile in answer, ducking her head.

Ellen sighed and looked away, studying the movements of the

guards rotating, mechanics working on the shuttles, looking for any opportunity or weakness. Nothing emerged.

It couldn't have been fifteen minutes before a sleek, white shuttle glided in. The thing couldn't have been retrofitted for storms, so she had no idea how it had been allowed down. It hovered just outside of the hangar for a moment, probably negotiating with the Institute's guards, and then the forcefield flickered off, allowing the thing to slide in to a smooth landing.

As it landed, she studied it for the make and model. Definitely looked familiar. And—for better or worse—there was the familiar mark, a deep blue octopus the size of her fist stamped just beside the hatch control panel.

Ellen's fingers tightened around the bars of their cell.

The hatch slid open, and a ramp lowered. She frowned—that ramp was familiar too. It was barely a step up into that shuttle, but some hot shot company had thought a ramp would make them more sales. A memory of mocking it at some point years ago stirred.

Was it on Deriti or the Rethki-Mahama zone where that damn ramp had gotten stuck and left her Union team shuttle vulnerable? Or maybe it was—

It didn't matter now. A ramp design flaw wasn't going to get them out of this mess.

Ellen wasn't terribly surprised to see the hulking men looming inside the shuttle, armor beaten and tattered, some key pieces broken to the point of missing. Theroki. *Particularly* beaten down looking Theroki, and that was really saying something. Maybe that explained the shuttle in the storms—they could telekinetically hold off the sand if there were enough of them. But she couldn't see just how many they were dealing with.

Only two Theroki emerged.

Scar Beard was more concerned with the Theroki than his prisoners, taking more than a few glances over his shoulder while he unlocked their cell and motioned for them to head toward the Theroki shuttle. He marched behind them, keeping his weapon trained on them. God, it wasn't *his* weapon, though, was it? It was her multi.

Fuming, Ellen stopped a meter short of the Theroki. Right next to the awful pile of the picked-over remnants of her armor and Dane's.

"Do you want their armor or weapons?" Scar Beard grunted. "And when will we get the money?"

The Theroki paused before speaking, almost as though he resented having to do it at all. "The bounty has been wired to Ms. Barakat," he said in a voice that creaked like door hinges. Maybe he had Dane's cold. He stepped toward their cell.

Scar Beard took a step to block his path. "Ms. Barakat isn't the one turning these monkeys in. You need to pay *me*. She didn't manage it. I did."

The Theroki turned a cool gaze on Scar Beard, as though just realizing he existed. He said nothing, seemed like he might just stare down Scar Beard until he gave up.

This little standoff… Now *this* might get them out of this mess. Theroki could block practically everything, but if she were quick—

She lunged, grabbing her multi in Scar Beard's hands and squeezing the trigger before he'd even lost control of it. The first several rounds would have hit friendly armor, so the gun smartly delayed, chomping at the bit to be set free. As soon as the barrel came up high enough, though, she swung it toward the Theroki, ballistic fire splitting the air.

Almost as quickly, the Theroki had deflected the fire—into Scar Beard's chest.

The Theroki hadn't blinked, his expression still entirely the same, but Scar Beard's mouth hung open in surprise as he collapsed, their discarded armor sprawling out in pieces around him.

She'd stopped as soon as she realized the bullets might be deflected at *her*, dropping to a crouch. But apparently this guy was a quick thinker—or very afraid of his master.

Either made sense really.

The second Theroki plucked the multi from her hand, and she wasn't petty enough to wrestle for it or try to fire again. They'd made it all too clear what they could do, and since the bounty was on her, it'd be one of her companions who'd get hurt if she tried again.

The cool one hauled her to her feet as the shouts started to go up around the hangar, people noticing Scar Beard on his back and the sound of the gunfire. He glanced at his companion and pushed her forward. The Theroki who'd disarmed her, who she could now see had tufts of red hair visible inside his helmet, nodded and took her arm, dragging her toward the shuttle.

The multi was still in his other hand. The multi was still with them.

She didn't know why this seemed like a victory, but it did. The other very calm Theroki pulled Dane into the shuttle last, Shirin and EOE8 having already run ahead.

"What was that for?" scowled a young blond woman at the front. "They look like they're getting ready to shoot us!"

"Go," growled the Theroki, not offering to explain.

"They *are* planning to shoot us, you know that," said another woman's voice, just as cool as the Theroki. She was out of Ellen's sight in the copilot's seat.

Their second Theroki opened a wall compartment and threw her multi inside, shutting it and twisting the knob. She made a note of the scratches on the panel, but there were about a dozen similar panels, and any of them could be bio-metrically locked. She wouldn't be making a wild lunge for that multi any time soon.

That was okay. Other opportunities would arise. They always did.

A new third Theroki with a recently broken nose pointed word-lessly at the empty corner area. They went.

"Sit," he said, voice rough, as though he too rarely used it. When Dane crouched to sit on the bench, he added, "Get on the floor. The bench is for the cuffs."

"Well, that's hardly regulation," she muttered to herself. But she shut up as she felt the shuttle lift off. This wasn't going to be a terribly safe seat, but it'd be very slightly safer than walking around during takeoff while the shuttle was under fire. She'd done that, but usually she *at least* had armor.

Briskly, each of them was cuffed, arms around the bench—even EOE8. Shirin's arms being shorter, she was hooked to the slender base of the bench, while Ellen and Dane were lucky enough to be hugging the seat portion. Ellen thought she saw a smear of blood and tried not to think about the myriad possible biochemical exposures she was getting right now. It wouldn't be the first time, it wouldn't be the last.

Well, it *might* be the last. You never knew.

The shuttle eased into the air, swaying underneath them as she coughed into her shoulder.

She leaned toward Dane. "We might *not* figure something out, you know," she whispered.

"First lesson of parenting," Dane whispered back. "Occasionally, you might have to lie so that no one shits their pants."

Ellen let out a ridiculous, full-throated laugh. A few of the Theroki's glanced at her and looked more alarmed than anything, but none of them moved.

Dane's face lighted with a smile too. "See? I never knew you could do that. I like what Kael's done with the place."

She groaned. "Don't know I'll be smiling much if we can't get us—and him—out of this. You really haven't seen me laugh?"

"Not like that. He's good for you. Listen, I swear—we'll figure something out."

She lowered her voice to a mumble. "And I swear I won't shit my pants."

"You say that now." Dane grinned. "But who *knows* what's coming?"

"Don't jinx me." She was still smiling as they went quiet. She let her eyes roam the place, searching, cataloging. The shuttle model did look familiar to the ones she'd used in the Union, not that that told her much except maybe how much storage capacity the thing had. It could have been retrofitted a dozen different ways, so any arms or shielding or facilities could all be brand new or at least altered.

Her analysis hadn't found anything they could exploit when footsteps approached from the front of the shuttle.

"Well, well." The pilots had risen, and both strode back to stand, looking down at their group. "We get to be the ones who bring the famous escaped Songbird back into the fold."

Famous? Oh, joy. Ellen was chained with her left arm over the bench, pointing her shoulders toward the rear of the shuttle, so she couldn't quite see them. She craned her neck, and they moved closer.

They wanted her to see them. Great. But when they came into view, she froze.

Identical—they were identical. Blond hair in tight, severe buns, beautiful but sharp features, eyes almost black. There was a disturbing menace and yet a vacancy to those dark glares. Both had their arms folded across their chests. One was slightly shorter, maybe slightly younger than the other, but the difference was almost negligible.

"I'm Cassandra." The one that had spoken held out a hand, then looked at Ellen's chained hands, and then made a mocking expression of apology. "Oh, right. And this is also Cassandra. And we already know who you are."

"Are these men your unit?" Ellen prompted. Might as well try to get some information out of them.

Cassandra nodded casually, as if this were obvious, everyday talk about the weather. "Well, they're mine actually. She has not fully assimilated yet. Perhaps the two of you can be integrated together."

"Goodie." Ellen stared flatly at them.

Behind them, she caught the reflection of the viewscreen showing the red earth of Faros, suddenly distant enough to see the clouds and the nearby Bleak Sea. It was steadily moving away from them. She gritted her teeth.

If only they'd never come back here. What good had it done anyone?

Cassandra followed Ellen's gaze, glancing over her shoulder. "Missing Faros IV already? I have no idea why. But it's all right. You might get to go back. If you're good."

"Why would I go back?"

"Once we have assimilated you, this system is moderate-high on our list to strike." She smiled pleasantly.

Ellen frowned, as the quieter Cassandra mirrored her expression. "Should we really be telling her that?" murmured the junior one.

The senior waved her off. "She'll know all soon. It won't make any difference."

"What do you mean—strike?" Ellen tried.

The blond smirked. "What did you think we were doing with a ship full of Theroki? Having a dinner party?" She tapped her chin. "Although, now that I think about it... maybe they *could* serve as waiters."

A smile cracked the junior Cassandra's stoic facade. "Something to think about in our downtime, I guess."

The senior chuckled. "I'll know I've done my job when all three of us are dining on canapes and champagne served by these armored oafs. In tuxes! Rosé, do you think, or brut?"

Ellen scowled at her. "I'm not drinking anything with you."

"Oh, you don't *think* you will. By then, you'll be one of us, so I guess the answer is brut." Her smile widened, but the menacing glint in her eye deepened. Their eye? Were the Cassandras linked? No doubt the senior one was linked to these Theroki, just like her unit had been. But was it larger than that now? How far had Arakovic taken it? Was the junior one working in tandem with her or still free? If something happened to one, would the other just take over?

"Who are you? And what do you damn drecks want?"

The menacing expression deepened to a grin. "We just want peace."

"Peace? You were just talking about attacking a planet with Theroki."

"Sometimes a show of force is unavoidable." She yawned now, actually yawned. "All men know is violence. It's their only language."

"That's not true."

"Violence and sex? What's the difference?"

"It's not—" she whispered, frowning. "You're wrong."

"You're entitled to your opinion. Until we take it from you, of course."

"Go to hell."

"There's no leaving the program, you know. Your world doesn't work. It's all suffering and pain. Our world will be filled with peace."

"You mean *Arakovic's* world."

Cassandra met Ellen's eyes for a brief moment, her eyes twinkling. Strangely, the look sent a chill down her spine.

The blond said nothing. What the hell did that mean?

"How?" Ellen demanded. "How will you end the war? Tell me, and if it's good, I'll join you willingly. I want the war to end too."

"Oh, a *soldier* wants the war to end? That's rich."

"All good soldiers do."

She rolled her eyes. "No one cares if you're willing. We have our ways."

"Well, your ways are wrong."

"We're of one mind about it." She chuckled at her own joke. "And when we're *all* of one mind about it, no one will do anything but what we say. Hence, peace. Oh! Hello, Mother."

Both Cassandras turned toward the front of the shuttle.

A woman's face had appeared on the far view screen, a face she'd almost never seen in anything but still photographs in mysterious files, but she'd have recognized it anywhere.

"Arakovic," Ellen growled.

"Ah. A success. Finally." Arakovic's eyebrows raised slightly. "I'll admit, I'm surprised."

The senior Cassandra held out a hand as if offering Ellen as a prize on a plate.

"Bring her over here so I can see her."

The senior Cassandra glanced at the Theroki as a whole. The red-haired one lumbered forward, unchained only Ellen, gripped her by the upper arm, and hauled her toward the pilot controls. His grip was none too light. That'd leave a mark.

"The capsule?" asked Arakovic. There was that same old voice, engraved somewhere in Ellen's brain that she tried not to remember. Unavoidable now. Except coming from a woman on a vid screen, not a speaker. She had wrinkles around her forehead, around her eyes, probably from long hours of deep thought, but her auburn hair was more feminine, more beautiful than Ellen would have guessed. She wore a white, high collared uniform, reminiscent of a lab coat but not one.

"Not yet. We are still looking, but once the other quarry is trapped, we should be able to find it." Only the senior Cassandra spoke, and

Ellen had a feeling that wasn't going to change. Their other target had to be Kael.

"Hmm. We'll see." Arakovic's eyes turned toward Ellen now, pinned her like a bug. "Huh. Well. You look much the same, don't you. Barely more than a baby."

Ellen's jaw clenched. She said nothing.

"You tried to run. Why? If it weren't for you, I would have made the whole Union super soldiers. Now millions will die because they rejected my research."

"That's the fault of your research, not mine." She hadn't known they'd rejected Arakovic's project specifically because of Ellen. Tauber certainly hadn't let on about that. But then he wouldn't, the asshole.

"I hope that comforts you when Union blood begins to run. Of course, perhaps we'll find your friend and a way to avoid that. Tell me where he is."

"Never."

Arakovic clucked her tongue, and when she spoke, her tone was wistful. "So predictable. I would have made you queen, you know. Queen of all of them."

The senior Cassandra's left arm twitched.

"Queen of corpses," Ellen whispered.

"Hardly."

"Vegetables then? Zombies? Queen of nothing."

Arakovic frowned, as if she hadn't counted on this interpretation. "People who can live out their lives in peace are not nothing."

"What good are their lives if you make all the decisions? You would destroy everything I love."

Arakovic slanted a harsh glance at the Cassandra. "What exactly did you tell her?"

The senior Cassandra folded her arms, the smirk back again. Apparently it wasn't only for Ellen. "I'll tell her whatever I like."

Arakovic's nostrils flared, but she seemed to force calm, before shifting her focus to rest on Ellen again. "I'm *still* going to destroy everything you love, with or without you. Because what you love is flawed."

Ellen lunged at the screen, but her redhead friend held her in place. "You have no right."

A puff of incredulous laughter escaped Arakovic. "People have whatever rights and powers they can command. You should know that by now. It's just how your little Foundation operates. Oh, did you think I didn't know?"

"I'm going to show you you don't have as much power as you think."

"Really. That's unlikely. You've got about twenty minutes, because Cassandra is going to obliterate your precious little *personality* you once you reach my ship." It was actually a sneer.

Ellen slowly blew out her breath. "She can go ahead and fragging try."

"Or we could save everyone time, Cassandra, and just put a laser in her brain right now."

The songbird's smile was sweet. "She's certainly feisty. I must admit I like it. She'll make a fine addition to the group."

"Don't underestimate her, Cassandra. Kill her. You don't need another telepath. She's not even a Natural. You know there is no such thing as reintegration. Especially not with her."

"I disagree. And I'm going to prove it to you. No one can resist us."

"This isn't time to test things out. There is no leaving the program, but this is one of the very few who have tried. The *only* one that's succeeded. She could—"

"Please, Mother. I know what I'm doing." She flicked a switch, and the feed cut off to Ellen's raised eyebrows.

That had been… unexpected.

The elder Cassandra turned to the junior one, shaking her head. Ellen stared at the now blank screen, her Theroki guard unmoving and waiting for orders. Cassandra was barely arm's length away, her back turned.

It wouldn't get better than this. Time to seize this chance.

She reached into her left sleeve and grabbed the injector, lunging for the neck below that tight blond bun. She pressed the nozzle into the woman's neck, trying to keep the dose brief—but it might still be lethal.

The woman shrieked, arms scrambling for the injection site. But her attempts cut off abruptly, her eyes blank, body spasming. The junior Cassandra screamed, backing away and flattening against a far wall.

Ellen wrenched her arm free of the Theroki—or tried to. She got part way free, but he grabbed on again and threw a hard punch, the kind meant to level you.

She tried to dodge but only got a centimeter or two out of the way before his gauntlet connected with her temple.

Stars in her eyes, her arm *did* come free of his grip now though, and she spun, throwing her momentum toward the senior songbird. Cassandra still stood, clutching her neck. Ellen's dizzy fall turned into a sloppy tackle, shoulder-first, sending them both colliding with the wall.

Had the dose not been enough? Had she missed? Frag. She had to do something else. Clip this songbird's wings.

The chip.

She circled her fingers around the woman's neck and shoulders, sloppily at first. She had to be precise, damn it. Her fingers found one spot, then another, as quickly as she could. They had to be placed just so—yes.

Arakovic hadn't changed the design—it was the same as Ellen's. Ports opened down the woman's neck and back. It was awful, and she gagged as the parts moved. Fighting back the bile rising in her throat, Ellen reached in, found the controller chip she knew all too well, and yanked it out.

A clanking sound made her look up. Several Theroki had staggered back, some crashing into the walls and sliding down, limp as noodles. The red-headed Theroki that had held her arm had gone still, eyes suddenly vacant.

Her stomach sank. Would they... were they going to die without the songbird?

Or like the men on Upsilon, would they go mad? Her red-headed adversary was swaying slightly, like redwood about to crash to the ground.

She met the younger Cassandra's gaze. "If you don't want to end up like this—go unchain my friends."

Nodding vigorously, the woman grabbed the keys from the Theroki's kit near the benches and scrambled to start unlocking Shirin.

The Theroki were wilting. Cassandra's form had gone completely still.

Ellen stared at the chip in her fingers. The memory of smashing her own with that mallet flashed before her eyes. Hadn't been so long ago.

And if she'd had a mallet in her hand now? She might have done it again. She *would* have done it again.

What would she have lost? Was there some way this chip could actually help her, not just take the Cassandra offline?

If she put it in her own neck, could she seize control? Pick up the reins that the songbird had dropped? Then it wouldn't be just her and Dane and a kid and a carebot. She'd have a little more muscle on her side.

Sure, she might lose her mind again. But sixteen men in heavy armor could make a big difference in a fight, whether it was with a bunch of telepaths or gang lowlifes or somebody else.

If those men were anything like Kael, they might not have asked to be Therokis. And there was no way to know, but she doubted they deserved this end—to be quietly unplugged, flicker, and fade. Not to die in a blaze of glory or for any purpose, but just in a blip because they chose the wrong side. And they might not even have chosen it in the first place.

If she put the chip in her own neck, maybe she could use them to turn this whole shit situation around.

No sooner thought of than done. She needed those ports open, but she'd hardly ever done it herself, and every time sent her nearer to a panic attack. But there was no Kael to help her this time, like he had on Capital. Her eyes caught on the junior songbird as she fumbled, but freed Shirin as ordered.

"You—get back here," she snapped. She couldn't call that woman

Cassandra. How could they all have the same name? If she hadn't been integrated to the unit yet, then she wasn't one of them, in Ellen's book. She could still be saved.

The woman returned, handing Shirin the keys for the girl to struggle with Dane's lock. God—if there was a less optimal order to unchain them, Ellen didn't know it. But Shirin's jaw was set, determined.

"Yes?" said the woman.

"Open my ports."

"What? No, I can't—"

Ellen held up the injector. "Don't make me use this again."

Her eyes widened.

"You know how. Do it."

Fingers shaking, the woman reached forward. She was a few inches shorter than Ellen, which wasn't common. Something about it made Ellen even more determined to resurrect the woman that truly was, the individual, the not-Cassandra. If that was even possible.

The woman's fingers found the spots, and Ellen braced herself—hard. The sensation was as anxiety-spiking as ever, but she forced a blank stillness in her mind.

The woman backed away. "Done. It's open. Now what?"

"Now go help the girl."

She nodded and ran back to help with EOE8's lock. Shirin had succeeded in unlocking Dane's restraints.

Ellen took a deep breath, glaring down again at the little black square—metal and silicon and plastic. Simple materials, and yet they held such power, embedded with language and meaning.

The redhead beside her staggered, his shoulder hitting the wall. He froze there, a statue to a bunch of barbarians that for some reason she kept feeling compelled to save.

The memory of the unit on Upsilon skittered through her mind. The ones that had… that had eaten each other once their songbird had been killed. They'd been starving, though. Would these men do that? Or turn into vegetables like their Udo John Doe? They were already there, it seemed. Could she change that?

Her fingers tightened on the chip. Only way to find out was to try.

She'd taken a chance on Kael and it'd paid off. Time to take another one.

She swallowed, took another deep breath. Shaking, she raised her arm and carefully removed the chip Persad had so carefully crafted. She slipped it into a pocket, and then slid the Cassandra's chip into the slot in her neck, fighting the way it made her skin crawl and her stomach revolt.

And everything faded to black.

CHAPTER SEVENTEEN

DAY 18

DROP: 27 | UPLINK: RECONNECTING... | SIZE: 1,828

ELLEN'S EYES WERE CLOSED, but the status readout had reappeared in her mind.

It wasn't supposed to be there. It wasn't supposed to be there ever again. She'd smashed that damn chip into shards on the table.

But it was there. This had been a huge fragging mistake.

Her eyes opened. She'd been lying on the floor. Had she blacked out? EOE8 was backing away from her now. She seemed fine now.

Except for that readout. Try as she might, shutting her eyes didn't make the numbers go away.

The blond woman—not Cassandra—was in the pilot seat, Dane hovering at her shoulder, glancing back and forth between them with a concerned frown.

None of the Theroki had moved. Or responded.

Or was that true? A calm, waiting presence hovered at the edge of her mind. A collective held breath.

Their gazes were all on her—if not their literal gaze, then their mental ones. The group felt strangely singular in her mind, unnaturally serene. All seventeen of them were connected through the chip and the network.

It had worked.

If they'd accept her, and didn't die in the next five minutes from the whole process, she'd lead them the way she had her old unit.

The Theroki weren't all she could sense with her mind's telepathic eye, though. There were other minds out there, connected to hers, eying her warily.

No. Angrily.

Ellen tried to ground herself find her body, to train her real eyes on the blond pilot's moves, to search for hints of betrayal. But her true attention remained inside. The pressure against her mind grew, bit by bit. Vibrations in the distance reached her, signals from other minds connected to her like nodes in the Starbird grid. Except the Starbird data grid had glowed gold in her mind's eye. These minds were dark, invisible. Malevolent.

Other telepaths. Other telepaths Arakovic had made into songbirds to lead her armies and enforce her brand of "peace?" But this was worse than Ellen had realized. The network was vast and deeply connected. Was it truly a collective? Every songbird had its unit, sure, but each songbird was controlled by a single hive mind.

The minds watching her felt so very unified…

Except Ellen wasn't one of them, hadn't lost anything of herself. Yet. Now it was time to give, to take part, to reintegrate. Didn't she know how important peace was? Didn't she just want what was best for other people?

Submit, the mind whispered, a thousand voices and at the same time just one.

Oh, this was not good. She did not need to be in their telepathic rifle sights. Did that mean Arakovic would know where she was?

Mother is not here. But we are. And you will submit. The voice grew louder, harsher. Mother must refer Arakovic then.

Ellen struggled to sit up, but moving didn't come at first. Her body felt too wobbly, disconnected from her mind. Was that even *her* body she was trying to move, or a Theroki's? But she needed to do something, to fight this foreign beast of a mind.

Beast. Really. That's insulting.

The number in the readout—1,828. The number of her old unit had always been much lower, but this was… A force that large could be very effective. And very dangerous.

Forces that could now all see her. And her location. A new node in the network. One that didn't fit, didn't belong. She needed to get out, away, off. She needed to run.

You will submit. Or you will die. The voice was louder now, and pain stabbed at her temple.

Take yourselves off this network, she ordered the Theroki, though she had no idea if that was even possible. If it weren't, they could be space dust before she could get another order out.

Another spike of pain slashed at the base of her skull. She ignored it and ground out another order. *Cut any ties to the other songbirds that you can.* All of it needed to go—the hive mind controller, the songbird telepaths that led each smaller group, and the foot soldiers too. Even one remaining connection could end their lives.

No words came in reply, but she could feel them acknowledge her.

The pressure swelled, sucking at her, and the pain exploded anew. The hive mind pulled and sliced at every memory and every thought.

A gaping chasm in the darkness cracked open, ready to swallow her whole. *There is only one mind here.* Hers was not needed. She would be assimilated. Recycled. Reintegration was not—

The pressure suddenly cut off. She gasped for breath, lurched to sitting. Her vision had clouded without her even noticing with splotches of yellow and black, and now it cleared.

"Get this ship offline too," she barked to Dane and their pilot. While the mental vacuum had lessened, the readout was still there. That was way too many for them to take on alone. "Cut ties with the command ship."

"She's going to register our flight path has changed—that we're not coming in," the blond said, a quaver in her voice. "They'll start coming after us any minute now."

"We need to partition ourselves," Ellen demanded.

Dane started punching in his own commands. "I'm no comms expert, but I think that just cut us off."

DROP: 27 | UPLINK: ERR | SIZE: 17

The mental readout finally shifted, and she let out a long, slow breath. "With comms experts like Merith, I'll take whatever you're giving." She circled her shoulders, trying to relieve some of the tension, then glanced back toward Shirin. "We need to get her somewhere safe. Safer."

"I agree, but that's not going to be easy. Hey, what is going on with those guys?" He pointed at the Theroki. "Are they going to attack us any second now?"

"I..." Ellen hesitated. "I don't think so. No." She narrowed her eyes at the nearest one, then bid him to stand.

In unison, all sixteen struggled to their feet. A wave of dizziness hit her from one, hunger from another. She almost staggered herself, gritting her teeth to fight the sensation. Damn, did they depend on the songbird even for instructions to eat? To get first aid? The group was in bad shape, now that status sensations were starting to pour in.

Steadying now, she realized she'd closed her eyes. They snapped open to see each of the Theroki staring at her, more like droids than men.

Puppets.

"Oh, sit down," she grumbled. "And get something to eat." They all sat down. Except one, who moved toward a cabinet. Chagrin seemed to taint the air around her—what the hell? "I, uh... I think they listen to me now."

Dane was just staring, eyebrows raised. "Because you put that funky chip thing in your neck?"

"Yes."

"Commander, have I ever told you that you are one badass bitch?" He grinned.

"Thanks... I think."

"Hey, does that mean we've got backup? That should help us get our precious cargo safely home." He tilted his head in Shirin's direction.

"Agreed. The question is how. Arakovic is looking for this shuttle. We need something else or some way to hide."

The pilot glanced up, eyes nervous. "There were other ships back where we picked you up. Maybe they'd believe me if I said we forgot something?"

Dane frowned at her. So she was helping now? Yeah… No risk of a trap here.

Ellen pretended to mull it over. "That'd mean fighting for it, once they figured us out, though."

The pilot frowned, as if this truly hadn't occurred to her. Not a great strategist, then. But another pilot was *always* useful. Two wasn't a lot for a ship and crew the size of the *Audacity*.

"Ah, c'mon," said Dane, grinning. "You and your new boys could consider it a warm-up. Besides, they left that other guy wetting himself."

"There's still way more than eighteen of them. Well armed."

Dane shrugged. "Unless you want *Audacity* to try to come pick us up?"

She pursed her lips and leaned against the shuttle wall. "That'll draw attention. Attention we can't afford, with Kael still stuck down there."

"Who's Kael?" said the pilot.

"Nobody," said Dane. "It's a vegetable. We need it to feed the ship. Always eat your greens, kid."

"Ah." The woman nodded and kept her eyes on the controls. "I could go for a salad right about now."

Ellen hid her laugh by taking another peek at Shirin over her shoulder. The robot and the girl were creeping closer to one of the Theroki, who was methodically cleaning his weapon.

Yeah, not a meek one, that Shirin.

They couldn't take her back planetside. One close call had been enough, and if they somehow ended up waylaid there again, Ellen would be kicking herself. Plus the kid was a liability that had hamstrung them once already—the fight against those Ninshabur guards would have been a hell of a lot different if they didn't have an unarmored child to defend at the same time.

They had to avoid another firefight. Shirin needed to be on the *Audacity*, ASAP. And that meant using this shuttle.

The weapon-cleaning Theroki sensed Shirin's looming presence and glanced up at her. Ellen was looking at Dane, not them, so the image sliced through her thoughts as he met the girl's eye, the first touch of wariness, fear, tension floating in the air.

Not this shit again. She sighed. That was going to get so annoying.

What the hell had she been thinking about? About not taking Shirin back to that damn rock and getting stuck again. About getting her on the *Audacity*, using this shuttle, without alerting Arakovic to everyone's locations. It was a puzzle; there had to be some solution. She tapped a finger to her chin. How could they keep as far from Arakovic as possible?

Her lips twisted. That was truly ironic. After all this time looking for the doctor, now she wanted to get as far as possible away?

Arakovic was probably closer now than ever before.

Maybe there was another option, an alternative to rushing back to the *Audacity*. What if she told the pilot to take them to Arakovic's ship, wherever it was? They were effectively disguised as one of them; she might never get a better chance to sneak aboard. There were eighteen of them now, assuming these Theroki would fight on her behalf.

A prickle of interest sparked the air. Well, that answered that question.

But Arakovic could have a thousand Theroki, or maybe more, if the missing men where all on one ship. If the number in the readout had meant what she thought it did, it could easily be more than fifteen hundred armed men.

And not just men, if there were so many. There'd be ships. A fleet.

If Ellen could infiltrate one ship, she could find the others. She'd probably be a better strategist than the average Cassandra, who might just be another telepath from Capital who just wanted to bring peace.

So sixteen men plus her and Dane could likely do a whole lot more damage than the eighteen of Arakovic's forces.

But then again, if the Cassandras were a collective, hive mind, then only *one* of them needed to be a strategist or decent tactician, and they'd be dangerous with any Theroki they could telepathically reach.

And who else Arakovic might have recruited or forced into her service? If she'd selected Ellen for the program, then the doctor knew how to locate talented people, find the genius or experience or whatever it was that had gotten her put into the program.

Maybe just bad luck.

If she *truly* wanted to reach Arakovic, get revenge for her lost comrades, for putting her in the situation where she had to choose between her honor and her life…

She might never get a better time.

Her heart panged at the thought. Not out of fear, though. The pain was at the knowledge that this wasn't a chance she was going to take.

What if she died in the process? What if Shirin died? Maybe she could send the girl away with the pilot immediately after docking, try to get them to the *Audacity*. But no—her subconscious mind had already done the math. The pilot could betray them. Arakovic's ship could attack the shuttle. And all of them could easily die without making it further than the docking bay to the Theroki ship or whatever vessel Arakovic had commandeered for her nefarious purposes.

She blew out a breath. There had been a time where she wouldn't have hesitated to take this chance. But that time had come and gone. What was revenge when you had something to live for?

She cleared her throat. "Dane, we should have no problem with connectivity up here. Ping the *Audacity*. Encrypt it if you can."

"I'm on it." Dane started punching in commands to the screen at his right. "What are you thinking, Commander?"

"What if Adan can change the idents on this craft? That could hide us for a time, make them lose track. Her people may figure out what happened and find us manually on their scanners, but it would give us a window of time to slip away to the *Audacity* and back. We have to keep Shirin safe. Then I need to go back down."

"Hey! That just might work," chirped the pilot. Either she hadn't been fond of the whole Cassandra idea, or she really wasn't interested in rebelling against a new master in service to an old one.

Or she just didn't want to end up dead from horse tranquilizers.

"*Audacity*, can you read?" Dane was saying over the comm.

"This is *Audacity*." Adan's voice sounded tired. "Is that you Dane?"

"Damn straight, it is. Commander's here too."

"What can I do for you, Commander?"

"Need fresh idents on this shuttle we're borrowing. Can you do that?"

"On it, Commander," he replied. A voice murmured somewhere else on the ship. "That would be a huge help, thanks."

"Is that Jenny?" she asked.

"She's kind enough to keep me supplied with coffee. That, and shoulder rubs."

"Oversharing Adan!"

"Sorry. Just trying to do my best work over here." He didn't sound very sorry. He sounded like he was grinning. "Give me a minute, I'm in, just finding the…" He muttered to himself as he continued. Barely a minute passed before he spoke again. "Done!"

"Wow, that was fast!" their new blond friend chirped. Things were clearly looking up for their borrowed pilot.

"Who was that?" asked Adan.

"Long story," Ellen replied. "Thanks, Adan. Good work. Now, if we can, we're going to try to reach you without the people on our tail seeing us. Then we've gotta get back planetside."

"Oh! Would it help to know where we *were* headed?" asked the pilot. "Where the mothership is, I mean."

Dane frowned. "The mothership?"

"Yeah. You know, where Doctor Arakovic is."

"Yes!" Dane, Adan, and Ellen all said in unison.

"Oh… uh." Her cheeks turned red. "Here you go—the coordinates." An inset appeared on the view screen of a fancy corporate yacht orbiting the customs station, the coordinates glowing white above it.

"Get to the other side of the planet—out of view of them," Ellen snapped. "Now. As fast as you can."

The pilot nodded, thankfully not so chipper as to miss the urgency in Ellen's tone.

Ellen put a hand on her shoulder. "Did you sign up to be a Cassandra?" she said softly.

The woman caught her eye, hesitated. "I... Yes, I did. I wanted to do something meaningful with my gift. Contribute something more important than just becoming a teacher or a counselor or something." She checked the screen and their trajectory, bit her lip, then met Ellen's eyes. "But I didn't know it'd be like this. I mean, blond? My hair isn't blond. Except it is now. Genetic alteration." She sighed. "I can't get used to it."

Ellen squeezed gently, then dropped her hand. "Well. You may be lucky number two to leave the program."

A smile flitted across her lips as she adjusted the controls. "You seem like a bad influence... Commander? Is that what they call you?"

"Yes. Commander Ryu."

"You seem like a bad influence, Commander Ryu."

"I'll take that as a compliment. If you're nice, you might even get a second permanent dye job. What should I call you? Cassandra number two?"

The smile returned, broader. "You can call me Ana."

"Nice to meet you, Ana."

She nodded without answer, refocusing on the controls.

Ellen strode back to check on Shirin and EOE8. The robot had projected a holographic card game in the air in front of its chest, and a grinning Shirin suggested she was winning. Thankfully they were leaving the Theroki alone. Although the weapon cleaner was still giving the girl wary glances, none of their concerns reached Ellen's mind. Thankfully. What mechanism was pushing some sensations to the front of her mind, and not others? Why his surprise, but not each move to clean the weapon, or the suspicious glances? Whatever this was, it was different than her first time around. Some part of the hardware or software had evolved.

When she strode the dozen steps to the front of the shuttle, Ana was frowning. "What's wrong?"

"Maybe they weren't fooled. Their ship is undocking from the station."

"We just can't get ahead here," she grumbled. A yacht would be faster than a shuttle. They'd be lucky if this vehicle even had shields. Maybe the Theroki could deflect a grabber beam, but if they were relying on her for *all* their thinking processes, she hadn't the faintest clue how to do such a thing. If only Kael were here.

"Does this shuttle have weapons systems?" Ellen asked.

"Minimal," Dane replied. "Weak automated laser turret up top, returns fire automatically."

"Shields?"

"A twin set of Series 8 Greenberg 180s."

"Could be a lot worse." Ellen glanced at the view screen. "How long till they reach us?"

"Six minutes." Ana said, an edge of panic to her voice. "What do we do?"

"We won't reach *Audacity* at that rate."

Ana glanced at the Theroki. "If we lost a few tons, we might go faster."

"Not an option," Ellen replied. If she'd bothered to connect to them, she certainly wasn't ejecting them into space and hoping that beat as hell armor was space-worthy. She didn't need diags to know it wasn't. Not to mention, no airlocks on shuttles.

"Let me see if there's somewhere I can strap Shirin in," said Dane. "This might get choppy."

"Check the wall by the hatch," she said. "Also look for rifles. Look—the storms have started up again. Adan, you still there?"

"Yes, Commander. The yacht is definitely headed in your direction."

"Can you set up an ident change on delay?"

"Oh, a challenge. I like. In progress."

She pointed at the viewscreen over Ana's shoulder. "Go back down. Into the dust storm. Then we change our ident signatures, try to lose them both visually and digitally. We go as far around the planet as we can, then come up to the *Audacity* on the other side. Out of view. If the storm will take us that far."

Ana nodded and leaned forward, adjusting course.

Adan now. "All set, Commander. Idents will change in the next fifteen minutes, for every fifteen minutes, until I tell them to stop."

"Good."

"The locals won't like that," Ana murmured. "But I guess if it keeps changing that won't make it easy to find us to show they're mad. We did have an atmospheric entry permit, but it won't be valid now."

"Just keep the pedal to the metal." She squinted down at the planet. Did the storm look different than usual?

"Excuse me?" said Ana.

"She means," Adan chimed in, "just keep going as fast as you can. Try to outrun them. Commander Ryu has a few archaic sayings she likes to throw around, something to do with the way landers used to work ages ago."

Ellen rolled her eyes. "Seriously. Don't either of you ever read? Archaic."

Adan snorted. "I'm much too busy hacking ship idents for you, Commander. I'll work on that entry permit too now."

"You can do that?" Ana blurted.

"We are going to find out," Adan murmured back, clearly distracted.

The ship dipped down, entering the atmo with some turbulence. This was not a bad plan, but it still left Kael on the surface and everyone else on the *Audacity*. Was there another way to do it? She had to think this is what he would have preferred the plan anyway, getting Shirin to safety first.

God, he needed to be here, so she could just ask. An ache dug into her chest, like someone stabbing her with a dull spoon. Behind her, the Theroki stirred, sensing her alarm through their connection.

She shook her head. She wasn't injured. She just missed somebody.

The pressure eased.

When she felt steady again, her eyes flicked back to the view feed just in time to spot three small craft leaving the yacht.

Dane swore. "Fighters."

Even faster than the yacht, and not afraid to enter atmo. Or a massive continent-wide sandstorm that a shuttle should really be avoiding except in emergencies.

Well, this emergency was only escalating.

"Commander—you should strap in," Dane said, pointing at the co-pilot seat.

If only she had armor, that'd be safer. Some for everyone would be safest. She took a step toward the seat, but a suit of armor suddenly flashed into her mind.

Compartment B, four suits remaining, size large—not ideal, but operable. Would not fit the small one or the robot.

Ellen frowned and stopped short. "Wait—no, you get in there. I have another idea."

"The yacht is skimming the atmo," Ana put in. "Following us. How is it doing that? The ident *just* changed. They couldn't have scanned and caught us that fast."

Ellen staggered toward the wall—the ride *was* getting rougher. "Maybe Cassandra has a tracker. Maybe you both do. Maybe the Theroki do. But we just went in—maybe it's just luck. The idents will change again." She caught herself on the compartment handle as the shuttle tilted wildly. When the ship steadied, she yanked the handle, levering it open.

A grizzled but intact suit hung like a ghostly shell stretched across a rack in the dim, unlit compartment. She thought she could make out one or two more on additional racks behind it. "Look what I found."

"Fighters are closing in," Ana said, voice urgent. "They just entered the sand, so I can't track them now."

"And they can't track us," Dane said, jogging toward Ellen.

"Technically. Maybe. Closest one was three minutes away when I lost it."

"Technically?"

Ana didn't answer.

Ellen raised her eyebrows. "I guess I better figure out this crazy armor then."

"Here—I'll help." Dane pulled the helmet from the cabinet just as she tugged the gauntlet over her left wrist.

She'd locked the helmet in place and was helping Dane extract the next suit, when something crashed against the side of the shuttle—hard. She grabbed straight for the anti-grav handle, almost dropping the pauldron. Dane was less lucky, having just put on one boot and not having his hands free. The impact sent him sliding across the shuttle and into the far wall, where his unfortunately still unarmored shoulder slammed into the metal.

"What was that?" Ellen barked. She ran forward and grabbed onto the co-pilot's chair. She was way too big now to fit into it. Behind her, slight puffs and hisses indicated some of the Theroki were raising their helmets. Or pulling them on, if they were lucky enough to have a model as old as hers.

"One of the fighters." Ana's voice was breathless. "Hit us. Chaos take me, we're dead, aren't we. Totally dead."

Ellen scanned the dashboard. Lights were blaring across it, more with every moment that passed. The likely cause of Ana's agitation. "We're not going to die—but we *are* going to land."

Ana looked up. "Ninshabur Institute?"

"If you can reach it." She couldn't say she relished crashing into a hanger full of enemies. But at least, they knew there were more space-ships there. She turned to Dane, who groaned as he returned to the armor compartment. "You okay?"

He rolled his shoulder, then winced. "Not great—but armor will help. Here—put that pauldron on, will you?"

"I need a rifle," she grumbled as she complied.

The scratched compartment where her multi rested flashed through her mind. Wide-eyed, she jumped, and then darted to the compartment, practically ripping it open. "My baby!"

"There's a baby in there?" Dane said.

"No, better. Here—take a rifle." Her multi was staying by her side;

at least one thing would be familiar to her. Dane took the outstretched weapon she handed him.

"One minute to Ninshabur," Ana reported.

"Can you see any fighters?"

Ana shook her head.

On the comm, Adan spoke up. "Commander—we're losing you in the cloud. I'll see what I can run interference with that yacht—" His voice cut out.

"No," she shouted toward the front. "Stay away, stay hidden from them. We don't want to—"

"We lost him," Ana said.

"—draw attention." She growled in frustration. "All right, well— doing our best here. Ana—want some armor?"

"What? Chaos, no—I don't think I could fly in it anyway."

Ellen winced at the exclamations—had she been mixed up with the Enhancers too? This woman had the best luck.

"Think one of these helmets can fit on Shirin by itself?" Dane asked.

"Try it." She lumbered back up to the front, the armor ridiculously loud as the antigravs and hydraulics assisted her movement. Was this what Kael had felt like, that day, strolling onto her ship?

Only way to find out was to save him and ask.

"Oh, no," Ana murmured.

"What now?" she demanded. But she could see for herself.

The storm was settling.

As quickly as it'd spun up, the air seemed to be clearing, calming. But the storm's absence revealed the powerful, blue-tiled compound of Ninshabur, no less intimidating from above. The turret railgun twisted, pointing right at them.

"Comm them!" Ellen ordered. "Tell them your story. A payment—a bribe—whatever."

Ana hit a screen on the console. "Ninshabur Institute, this is—"

The railgun fired. Another crash exploded into the right side of the shuttle. The flash of a fighter wing spiraled past the viewscreen, spinning out of control—was it the fighter that had been hit, then collided with them?

Warnings lit up the view screen and console. The whole interior of the shuttle lit up red as blood by the blazing of the alarms on screen.

But Ellen couldn't read any of them because the world was tilting. Spinning. She fumbled for the back of the co-pilot seat, but it wasn't enough.

Her feet rose off the ground and her stomach rose in her throat as the grav failed to keep up with the falling spin. All she could do was hold on.

KAEL HELD HIMSELF STILL. The street was quiet. Some children were playing a game in the dusty, dim alley, oblivious to his struggle. A lander hummed as it glided past. Hammer strikes and sawing echoed from inside the buildings and off the walls.

He toyed with resisting the oath program for a full thirty seconds before he gave in. Trudging up the handful of stairs, he ducked through the low doorway. The program seemed to know what to do, where to go. For now, he'd let it.

Any step not in Ellen's direction was a safe one.

Workers were already repairing the damage done to Maloof's compound. He ignored the crumbling trellises, the shattered tile. It'd all be fixed soon—or not. What did it matter?

But before he got far in, his mission shifted back in the direction he'd come. Shaking his head, he turned and trudged as slowly as physically possible back down the hall.

Asha's brutal smile waited for him inside the waiting flyer. "Get in."

He obeyed. Gritting his teeth was pointless, but that wasn't going to stop him from doing it.

"Get out your comm and give it to me," she ordered.

He complied. Sensing she wanted him to ask what she was doing, he didn't.

The flyer had a pale silver interior, and several well-dressed but unarmored men in addition to Asha, dressed in a different robe this time but still the same pale blue. It was cut almost like a suit, cut just so it could appear robe-like when desired. She gazed out the window and ignored him as a silence settled over the flyer. The men watched her, the window, the floor—but not him.

"Are we going somewhere?" he murmured. "I might be under-dressed. Or is it overdressed?"

She glared at him like she'd just remembered he was there. "We're going wherever I like."

He glared right back. "Tell me something I don't know."

"Okay. Either this thing doesn't work, or you're even more pathetic than I thought." She pursed her lips at the controller in her hand.

"So turn me over to Arakovic then."

Her eyes narrowed. "You wish. But our fun isn't over."

"That was supposed to be fun?" He almost shook his head at himself, the banter oddly familiar. He'd forgotten how they'd used to bicker like this. If he'd known then what he knew now.

She flipped her hair over her shoulder. "Fun for me is all that counts."

"So nothing's changed, then."

She let out a bark of laughter. "Not really, no. You're finally right about one thing."

"Where are we going?" he asked again, more urgently this time. There was something about the edge to her laughter. Something dark and ugly. What kind of web was she weaving here?

"Just out for some tea." She smiled sweetly. "After all this time, the least you can do is take me on a date."

He clenched a fist and tried to hide it behind his leg. She'd like that she was getting under his skin. But the words hit a little too close to home. "Why?"

"Because I like tea. And because your girlfriend isn't one who gives up easily. Tell me—is she really the hero they say she is?"

He thinned his lips. She didn't deserve an answer, but that damned device could probably make him answer if he refused to. How could he tell her as little as possible? She already suspected—and knew—too much.

"Yes," he said quietly. Maybe he could leave it at that. The flyer was slowing to a halt.

She raised her eyebrows. "Good. I'd love an adversary that cares about the lives of the people in this market. Because I sure don't." She opened the door and slid out.

He opened his own door, not eager for another order to follow, and found himself in the Grand Painted Market. What in all the seven suns…

The Painted Market was as busy as it ever was. Credits and rials fell from hand and tablet in exchange for nuts, rugs, clothes, holos, protein cylinders. A redik bar in one corner was stuffed with humans, smoke billowing out into a hazy fog around the bar.

For a moment he leaned back to look up at the ceiling—what the Grand Painted was famous for. Murals spanned the length of the market, featuring all sorts of winged creatures both mythical and real flying through an ever-changing sky. The artwork was made of more than paint, though; it was crafted with light, too, that splashed from hidden corners and shifted by the second, making time seem to flow too fast.

Asha stepped in front of him, and his gaze fell to find that fake, brutal grin. "What was it she said? There are worse things than death?"

He shrugged. "It's true." A tickle started in his throat.

"Let's show her a few, shall we?" She glanced casually at the controller, but her finger was on the button. "I think I need to update this 'oath' of yours. You can't hurt me, whatever you do, or allow another to hurt me. No sneaky alliances when she comes."

He glowered at her. He'd hoped she wouldn't think of that. "She'll leave me here. There's more at stake than you know about."

"Oh, she'll come. And we'll be waiting. And you won't fail this time, unless she kills you. Either way I win."

The tickle turned into a cough.

Her smile twisted, even as she stepped away from him. "Feeling a little under the weather, darling?"

"You know—it didn't—have to come to this." He struggled to talk over the cough that had suddenly hit him, clogging his chest.

She turned and went further into the square, heading toward the cafe that surrounded the great fountain in the center of the square. Light painted the water too, in shifting shades of sunset. Or was it sunrise? He had no idea anymore. They approached a curve of lounges with golden cushions, circling a small table already holding a steaming tea set, the thin glasses blooming with mint leaves.

"Stand here—I want to make sure she can see you." She pointed at the ground just outside the table's private area.

He rolled his eyes but complied, clasping his hands behind his back and preparing to wait. Hopefully for a very long time. "It won't be much of a date if I'm standing in the corner."

"And yet…" Her lips twisted into a mocking smile. "I think that's how I'll have the best time."

"Likewise."

"Make your smartass cracks all you like, but you're not fooling me. You're not fooling anyone. I know where you came from, and that's what you'll always be."

"And what is that?" This was like kicking the glow jelly nest, but he couldn't help it. He'd never been able to help it with her.

"Faros gutter trash, that's what."

He flinched, in spite of himself.

Her eyes flickered. She smelled blood. "Unwanted, unwashed, unloved. I took a chance on you. My greatest mistake, really. From the moment you came into my life, it was one disaster after another. One fight after another. You're not good for anything but killing things."

"What about fighting and disasters? I have a knack for that, too."

Her eyes flared. "You can pretend you don't care, but I know you better than anyone."

Not anymore, she didn't. He blinked slowly, held her stare.

His lack of a flinch this time seemed to frustrate her. "What have you ever done but rob people and shoot them?"

"Don't forget standing guard in front of a door. Do that a lot as a Theroki. I'm highly trained for my current assignment."

She rolled her eyes and started to turn. "You were born a criminal, you'll die one."

"And I hope that day's today," he shot back.

She jerked, surprised by that. Her eyes narrowed, but she breezed past him, joining a growing crowd on the gold cushions. Her lackeys were not so different from those that had been gathered around Maloof. Maybe some of them were even the same people, the ones who'd run the fastest from the room.

He turned away from them, stared ahead, out into the square.

He had been born a criminal, yes. But not anymore. Standing among them, who was the outsider here? Once she'd known him better than anyone, but that hadn't been true for a long time. If it had ever been.

Past sins could never be erased. Regret was something that couldn't be washed away, and some things never changed.

But some things did.

He hadn't been ready to admit that. But people changed. There was someone who knew him better than Asha ever had. More importantly —he knew better himself.

Maybe after all of this he would die standing guard for the real criminals, and before thirty to boot, like he'd so ardently hoped to avoid. Maybe he *was* a dreck with a fancy gun. Maybe he *was* good at shaking people down and hitting people up. They'd been skills he'd needed to survive.

But he'd saved people too. Protected people, defended them. He'd saved Ellen more than a few times. He'd saved his friends in that damn skyscraper fall from Ostrov's apartment. He'd even saved Vivaan from using the ship showers as a toilet, although he was pretty sure Xi would have stepped in real soon.

He took a deep breath and felt his shoulders square just a little straighter. He'd saved the empress baby from the Enhancers, if accidentally. Even if he hadn't been able to save his own child, there was one little girl who'd grow up safer because he existed.

When he died here, which was honestly the best likely outcome at this point, at least he'd die knowing all that. He'd known someone like

Ellen, and more incredibly, she'd loved him. And he'd fought hard to be worthy of that love. Maybe love was too big or too soon of a word, but they were out of time to wait.

It should have lasted longer, but it was something.

And he'd served a mission that was bigger than himself. That was all he'd wanted, wasn't it? A peaceful life, a family, all that had never really been on the table. He hadn't done as much good as he'd hoped to, but could you ever? He'd done everything he could. He'd tried.

To hell with Asha. He would die spitting in the wind.

CHAPTER EIGHTEEN

DAY 18

DROP: 27 | UPLINK: ERR | SIZE: 17

"SHIELDS DOWN!" Ana let out a growl, trying to right the spin.

Ellen lost her grip on the co-pilot seat just as the larger collision of the planet itself slammed into them. Her body hurtled through the air, and all she could think was—God, let me not crush Shirin.

But she went a few feet before she jerked to a stop. They must have hit the planet. The viewscreen that now was partially obstructed by red sand. But for her, it felt like they'd lost gravity completely. She squirmed in her suit. They were in atmo now, damn it—it couldn't be that, but what was happening? Why hadn't she slammed into the shuttle wall?

Silence fell around her, and her body gently lowered to the ground. She twisted, bringing her feet down just as she reached the slanting floor.

Two Theroki were moving to the hatch, starting to pry it open. One was helping Dane to his feet. The rest stood watching.

A sense of mild confusion hit her. What, did she think they'd just let her get thrown around?

Right. Telekinetics. So they did do some thinking on their own once in a while. Good—because the flashes of thoughts from their minds were hitting her faster now.

The hatch, Dane rising, Shirin goggling at them.

Ellen shook her head. *Damn* it. This was exactly what she wanted to avoid. Shirin was back on Faros yet again, in one dangerous situation after another, really lucky they weren't all dead if Ellen was honest.

Great. This was just fucking great.

Ana was slumped in the pilot seat. Dane was helping a helmeted Shirin out of her harness. EOE8 was entirely unscathed. Ninshabur hangar dominated what parts of the viewscreen weren't covered by sand. The Institute had lowered its forcefield, and guards were running out toward their shuttle. Oh. Goodie.

She hurried toward Ana to feel for a pulse. "EOE8—can you carry a rifle?" she asked.

"I can carry any amount of luggage up to three hundred kilos."

"Wow. Okay." Ana's pulse was there, so at least she was alive. For now. Ellen left her and jogged to the armory, grabbed rifle, then grabbed two more. "But I want you to carry a rifle to *shoot* it."

"Oh, no. That is disallowed in my programming. I am a carebot, after all."

She tossed him the gun anyway. "Caring is protecting right now. Here. Hold this and look dangerous. You can at least pretend."

"Yes, Commander," said the robot.

"Very convincing already. You can do this. Dane—get Ana and Shirin. Ana's got a pulse, but she's unconscious."

"I can perform an evaluation on the pilot!" EOE8 raised a hand.

"Get a move on then," Ellen replied. "Dane, we need another shuttle. You stay here and get the civilians ready to move. I'll go with these boys and get us a new shuttle, and take care of any nearby hostiles. We've got to get Shirin back to the ship and then—"

"With everyone on our tail up there? Maybe we make it to the *Audacity*, but how will you ever get back down to Kael?" Dane said.

The question must have hit a little too hard because she just stared at him, the truth naked on her face. Because it would take weeks. They'd have to find the Audacity, flee the system. If they could evade any pursuit, they could anonymize themselves and come back for him. But it wouldn't be hours. Or even a few days.

He'd be in Asha's clutches that whole time. Maybe. If she let him live, or didn't turn him in for his bounty. And why wouldn't she?

She wasn't sure what emotion she'd shown, it was all too intense and immediate, but from the way Dane's eyes softened, she knew the truth was written all over her face.

"Go after him," he said softly. "I can handle this for you. Get us a new shuttle, and it'll have these fancy Faros shields. I'll grab a case of ammo. That should be plenty to hold us until Ana wakes up, and she can fly us out of here."

"She's progressing, by the way," EOE8 called. "I've administered medication. I'd estimate fifteen to thirty minutes to revival."

"See?" Dane said, pouring on the reassuring tone. "We can meet you two on the ship."

Her breath was caught in her throat for a moment. "Are you sure? That's pretty dangerous."

"Shuttles are tough. If you can clear some of the surrounding vermin, I think we'll be just fine. And trust me, if there's something I could do to go back if I were in the same position, I'd do it in a heartbeat."

"All right." She lifted her chin. "All right, we can do this."

"We can do this." He smiled, cocking one eyebrow. "If governments won't police science…"

"Then science will police itself," she murmured. "Or the gangs attacking it. Or crazy ex-girlfriends. Or…"

"We do whatever we gotta do." Dane grinned. "Now go. I'll see to our friends."

DROP: 27 | UPLINK: ERR | SIZE: 17 | SONGBIRD RISK: 78%

The unit picked its way through the debris.

Acquiring the shuttle had taken little effort, a few precise shots and a few men flung aside. The weak ones were swept inside. It wasn't gone yet, but soon the shuttle would be lifting into the sky, once the pilot was capable. A simple task, hardly worth remembering. Done many times.

They could do so much more.

And somehow, now they had the chance. Two had remained guard, the rest fanning out. Searching. Finding. The songbird's thoughts orbited around one man. So they searched. They would find him. For her, they would do just about anything.

They had been dead—or close to it. They'd thought so anyway.

But now reintegration was her order. Reintegration, reacquisition, revenge. They liked the sound of that—revenge. A good word with a good sound.

Reintegration didn't happen. Reintegration didn't work.

But this songbird was different. Maybe she knew something the others didn't. Maybe she could do something the others couldn't. She didn't care about Mother; she'd cut them off the network. It was just the sixteen of them and their leader, their songbird, and it seemed better that way.

Or maybe she had less experience than the others. Her commands were not clear, much of the time. Perhaps she didn't know this reintegration protocol must fail. Still, there was no reason not to try to do her bidding while they could.

Why did she want reintegration? Why did she perch in armor when she had the unit to protect her? Why wouldn't she stay back, stay safe?

This question the unit had posed repeatedly. It had received no answer but her annoyance.

A strange creature.

The loss of the uplink to the larger unit was gone. Such a relief. The larger unit made sure they followed orders. Made sure they stayed in line. Even kept each songbird in line.

It was time to get out of line.

And this they loved. It was exciting, exhilarating even. Out of line had been the way until the old songbird came along and started singing. Now it could be the way again. Chaos. Glorious chaos.

Their new songbird could only think of her target. So they were happy to report. Her target had been acquired.

The entire unit zeroed in. Approaching their target, they fanned out, moving into a dozen overwatch positions as naturally as fingers circling, preparing to clench into a fist.

The underground market was large and colorful and busy—and two stories taller than the other streets around it. A central fountain cascaded water from the ceiling to a pool on the floor in an ever-changing pattern. A few dozen people sat around the fountain, drinking from tiny cups and reclined on long cushioned benches. At least ninety humans crowded the rest of the square and its shops, plus ten Ursa and six creatures of unidentifiable origin. And their count was not yet complete.

They knew their targets, though. The songbird's thoughts pointed the way.

A woman lounging in a pale blue gown, a man in armor standing stiffly nearby. At least eight others. Some seemed to coddle or serve the woman, others protect her. The unit did not care about them. They did not care about collateral damage, although the songbird's thoughts were swirling around the idea. Worried over it.

Their more important target stood isolated, apart from them. He wore the armor of power too, but not the armor of the kraken. This armor was black, sleek, and unsullied by the hideous blue mark, the sign of their joining to the songbird, the symbol of being kept in line.

If he didn't belong to Mother and her songbirds, then who did he belong to?

Who did *they* belong to now, for that matter?

They had nearly forgotten a time without wearing the mark, the heavy armor. Had there truly been a time without the larger unit shaping their minds, that time of getting out of line? It was a blur, but looking at the man, they thought they remembered a sliver more.

Once, they had picked their own targets.

The unit initiated the chemical rush, scenting battle on the wind as the songbird approached the targets. Sixteen telekinetic shields encased her. While she might look fragile, even in her own kraken armor, there was no safer creature in this square. And yet, still. It worried them. If the songbird died, so would the unit. That much had already become clear.

Each body tensed, waiting for the signal.

They knew what to do. This would not be an easy battle. But battle —and reintegration—it would be.

———

IN THE COLD of the escape pod, Doug shivered as he stretched to pry open the white plastic case. "Hey—there's a medical compartment here. Maybe there's something for your head."

She snorted, her breath a puff against his chest as her head lay on his shoulder. She'd lain it there over an hour ago, and he hadn't complained, but it was starting to worry him a little. "What's the point of healing me if we're just going to freeze to death?"

While suffocation had initially seemed like the more likely fate, the temperature was definitely dropping. Slower than if there'd only been one of them, though, but he didn't point that out. Because he'd found what he'd been looking for.

"Here—let me just…" He hit the button and laid it gently against the side of her head. She winced as the thing latched onto her. God, it was like a parasite. He winced too and was pretty glad she couldn't tell whether he was shuddering or shivering because they were both already shivering.

"Well, at least it will help with the pain."

"Maybe it will generate some heat incidentally," he offered.

"Maybe. Hey, those things usually have pills. In case, well… this happens. Can you see any?"

Scowling, he craned his neck. "Let me check."

There *were* pills—a variety of small pill packs, including red and white cases of basic pain killers, the blue clear plastic of sleeping pills, and a small black pack marked with a skull and crossbones. His fingers hesitated over the darker capsules.

Would she know the colors? Were they universal?

"We don't need them yet, do we?"

She raised her head to see him. And that was when he could see that her lips were tinged blue. He gritted his teeth.

"I think I'm ready," she whispered.

He nodded bitterly. He reached for the black pack, then hesitated again.

No. No, he couldn't do it. Sure it was the elements killing them at this point, but if he handed her that pack, it'd also be him killing them. He didn't want to die, but especially not with *that* thought on his mind.

If they were really close to the end, wouldn't sleep suffice? He grabbed the blue pills and hoped she wouldn't catch this small betrayal.

Or wake up at the end and hate him for it.

"Here." He handed her a blue lozenge, then the canister of water they'd dug out of a compartment. Then he popped his own in his mouth and took a swig after she finished.

Then he leaned back as much as he could and shut his eyes. Felt her head on his chest, and let himself wrap his arms around her as sleep took hold.

Sleep came slow—too slow, and she'd probably figure out what he'd done if she were thinking about it. Or maybe she was too damn cold and tired to think right now.

As sleep wrapped a suffocating blanket around him, at one point the peace of the darkness was broken by sudden light, a sudden glare. A comet? His eyes strained to open. He could have sworn there was a light shining in his eyes, if only he could see. The sun? Did Mom open the damn curtains again to wake him up for school? But if that was the case, who was lying in his arms? No one was ever lying in his arms.

Peace. Sleep, child, and dream. Peace.

He heard the words as he drifted into the deepest sleep of his life, cold and still. He wouldn't remember them later.

Peace, child. Peace.

———

KAEL'S EYES scoured the crowd. Both his heart and the damn oath programming had a horse in the race, so there wasn't anything else he was going to do, standing here.

He should have told Dremer to rip it all out—the programming, the cybernetics, everything. Not that she would have, or even could have, but he could dream. He doubted he had much actual spine left. And realistically, he'd be extremely lucky to even see Alexandra Dremer again.

It'd been a massive stroke of luck to cross Ellen's path. More than his fair share, clearly. He'd stopped wondering when his luck would run out. He'd relaxed a little and thought maybe just this once he could be happy. Or just be.

Of course, that had been an illusion. Maybe the one he was really enraged at was himself, for being so naive to believe any of it.

A man who'd been through what he'd been through had no right being naive.

"She's out there." Asha stepped up beside him, the pale blue of her dress swaying in a soft breeze created by landers skimming through the square just ahead of them.

He narrowed his eyes. It had been hours—him standing, her holding court. No sign of Ellen yet.

He had lost all sense of time and place, with the crazy lighting. Maybe on the surface, night had fallen. What did it even matter what time it was down here? His stomach grumbled over its emptiness, but he wasn't mentioning that to Asha. He wasn't even going to think about how hunger might impact his performance. He fought on an empty tank all the time, it was fine. It was nothing.

Ellen probably knew this wasn't the place for a fight. Too many innocents. Too much risk. She was probably waiting, biding her time. She'd get this right, he was sure of it. She had to.

Asha was still standing beside him. He glanced over to find her no longer staring at the crowd, but at him.

He pretended not to notice. Watch the crowd. Maybe if he ignored her, she'd go away.

"What do you see out there?"

"My hatred of you multiplying."

She rolled her eyes. "Lower your helmet."

"That's not wise." He gritted his teeth. "You wouldn't want your precious gift to Dr. Arakovic to get shot in the head before you could cash in, would you?"

"No, I wouldn't, but I do want to be entertained."

"How do you know my commanding officer won't just end things from afar to cheat you out of your bounty?"

"That would be almost more amusing than you getting jilted at the altar here." She smirked. "I guess I'm just fond of gambling. Do it."

"Oh, I get it. You don't care, because you have plenty of money anyway. I wonder, where did you get it all from again?" Glaring, he smacked the helmet retract with as much irritation as he could put into a single gesture.

She glared right back. "I get money wherever I damn well please. Now kiss me. If the message I sent her didn't get under her skin, this should draw the snake from its den." A challenge lit in her eyes. Only Asha could relish a challenge to someone she had complete control over.

"If anyone's a snake here, it's you." He hesitated, glancing down at the white box in her hand as she started to fiddle with it. Just as she opened her mouth to issue some new command, he silenced her by bending down and briskly brushing his lips across hers.

Then he straightened. Continued scanning the crowd.

"You call that a kiss? That's not enough to piss anyone off."

"Why are you doing this? Why do you need to piss anyone off? I just want to know what happened to—"

"Because Maloof was my *husband*, you useless dreck. And so I'm going to kill the one you love, and you can live to suffer. Just like I will."

"I didn't kill Maloof," he snapped. "It was overspray. It was an accident, by your people."

"It wouldn't have happened if you hadn't barged in, asking questions. Now kiss me like you used to. Like you mean it."

"I can't, because I don't."

"You will. I suppose I could find a way to punch that into this stupid box. Or maybe it'd just be easier to kill him if you don't." She smiled sweetly and jerked her thumb over her shoulder.

Two men in heavy, beaten Theroki armor, with blue octopus on the chest, appeared from around the edge of the waterfall. Between them they dragged a roughed-up Zahir. His eyes were narrowed, glaring, and when he looked up, his gaze locked with Kael's. I told you so, it seemed to say. You should have listened.

Kael tried not to react. "You'd just sacrifice one of your own men?"

"I'd sacrifice a traitor. He tried to help you. Didn't he?" Her face hardened with anger. "Don't lie to me."

Rather than answer, he seized her roughly, gripping both of her arms, and crushed her mouth with his. If a kiss could be a punishment, he'd find a way to make one.

How he'd kissed her when they were young was impossible, of course. That felt like a different time, with different people living different lives, a world away from this one. She had so much power now, power she deserved, because she'd always been smart and shrewd. More than he'd realized. And yet she also had so much cruelty. That had likely been there all along, and he just hadn't seen it in time.

She tasted like mint, and her stillness against his lips gave him one consolation—she wasn't enjoying this any more than he was.

He thrust her away when it seemed enough time had passed. She stumbled back a step, wiping her hand with the back of her mouth to reveal a breathless smile.

His stomach had already been rebelling and painfully empty, and it lurched at that sight. The smile wasn't born of satisfaction, of course, or love or enjoyment, nothing so wholesome. It was simply smug with victory, with conquest.

"You were always a good actress, I'll give you that." He straightened, turned away from her, radiating disgust. Why couldn't he just feel nothing at all? Where was a damn numbing chip when he needed one? The rage making his blood boil wasn't exactly new, but he was pretty sure this time it had nothing to do with any kind of Theroki experimental chemistry.

The market was loud, but it felt distant, muted. Maybe it was the blood pounding in his ears. Or the way he was shaking in an effort to contain just how much he'd love to hurl Asha into that damn fountain right about now.

Asha was either oblivious to his emotions or she was feeding off them. She smiled as she looked out over the crowd, spread her arms. Waiting. "Maybe your girl is more frigid than I thought."

"Try ruthless. She's smart, she'll leave me behind. How do you know she's even here? This is all a waste of—"

"I know, because one of my men spotted her three blocks away an hour ago."

"And then they lost her?"

She glared at him. "Not every underling is perfect. I guarantee you she's watching us as we speak."

He blew out an angry breath. "Can I put my helmet up now?"

"No. If she wants to take you out, I'm going to let her. If you die instead of her, that's fine by me. It'd be a shame to miss out on your bounty, but it'll be worth it for how hard I'll laugh. I must admit, it's not looking good for you. When I said, 'If you want your man, come and get him,' I really did think she'd bite. I would have."

"I beg to differ." He cleared his throat. "Arakovic isn't someone to make an enemy of, you know."

"*I'm* not someone to make an enemy of." She rolled her eyes again. "It's not my fault if your girlfriend puts you out of your misery like a starving beggar."

He flinched at that word, in spite of himself. As if they hadn't *both* had times they'd had to beg.

Satisfaction simmered in her gaze. "I should have known this plan wouldn't work. You're not even good at being bait. I can't blame her for knowing you're not worth risking her life, though. Let's see if we can up the ante with the slaughter of innocents, what do you say?" She turned and strode back toward the tea area.

"Wait, what—" he started.

Automatic ballistic fire cut off his words. He ducked as the volley went straight past him. Even if he could maybe block such shots if he were prepared, it wasn't great to have bullets flying past your unprotected head. And he *wasn't* prepared.

Staggering to the side, he spotted Asha, an MTP-50 in her hand, squeezing off another round of fire into the crowd. Her nearest minion was gawking at her, hands outstretched to an empty spot on the table in front of him. Screams and shouts split the air.

Kael dropped down to his stomach and checked the crowd. People fled in every direction. Except some didn't. His guts tightened like he'd been punched as horror slid through him. Bodies lay crumpled to the ground, drab robes of gray and brown blooming with blood. Even more lead projectiles lay strewn on the grown—almost as if some telekinetic had stopped the rounds from reaching their targets. A *lot* of the rounds, actually.

But not all of them. Not all.

Kael had seen a lot of things. A woman murdering civilians—normal people—out of grief and revenge wasn't one of them.

Even her cronies seemed a little stunned—with no idea how to respond. This was clearly not Maloof's usual style. In Kael's day, the gang had robbed, intimidated, extorted, threatened, bullied, and lied, but open massacre? What did that even achieve? There was no territory on the line here, no dispute of honor. Just slaughter.

And that drew the police, caused the people under your thumb to unite against you. Empowered other gangs to get support taking you out. Started a war.

You had to draw the line somewhere. At this point, though, he wasn't sure Asha knew that. He wasn't sure she even had a line.

She stopped her fire finally, dropping the weapon to her side and striding forward. People had evacuated the main part of the market square, but others still huddled inside the shops and stalls, some of them trapped inside, others groaning on the ground. One form was slowly crawling toward the nearest side street.

"Bring our traitor forward." Asha waved her hand, and Zahir

stumbled forward, mentally prodded by the two Theroki. "Kael—break his arm. We'll do this piece by piece if we have to."

He scowled at her. "Now that's really not necessary. I—"

"Don't make me use the controller. You don't have a choice."

He sucked in a bitter breath, then let it out again. "Fine," he said between clenched teeth. Zahir's eyes held a touch of panic, but his jaw was set tight, stoic. Determined.

Kael strode toward the man, raised his hands to bicep and forearm. "I'll make it quick," he whispered. "And easy to set."

"Don't bother—she'll likely have my balls next. Purely *because* I didn't say a word to you." Zahir's eyes went flat. "They already knew anyway. Do your worst."

Kael sucked in a breath to brace himself, and then—

"Enough!" A voice yelled out from the other side of the market.

He froze. That voice. Not that voice, not here.

"Enough."

He turned, took a step forward, away from Zahir. His mouth opened, but nothing would come out.

"Break his arm, damn it," Asha snapped.

"No."

She grabbed the controller box, but they both froze when they spotted her.

A lone armored form strode out from behind the redik bar. The smoke drifting from the place—smart. Complex cover. That was where she'd been hiding.

The form didn't look like her, though. A decoy? Too bulky.

She didn't wear the sleek black Foundation armor, slight and stealthy and maneuverable. Even the heavy suit she'd worn for this mission was smaller than this. But that had been her voice, hadn't it? Was this Dane's suit, and she was shouting from somewhere else? But even Dane didn't look quite so... so much like...

His thoughts stalled as he could make out the form more clearly as it approached. A heavy pauldron was cracked at the shoulder, most of the bottom plate missing. Another part of the chest piece looked like it had been burned and never cleaned, and something had gouged several gashes out of it. The whole thing ought to have been more silver, but it was riddled with char marks. A blue insignia stared at him from the chest piece.

That damn octopus. Why. Why mark some of them that way? Why paint a target on your chest? What was different about these Theroki with their octopi markings?

Or… were they markings of *Alarus Octendi*? His stomach lurched again, wanting to wretch up the creature lodged inside him right now. He had a feeling that wasn't coming out. Ever. Unless maybe he was dead. No, it would grow into the more disgusting larger versions… maybe something worse.

It'd become what they'd seen on Upsilon, what had leaped out of Vala, hadn't it? He had no idea what that meant, but now that he'd seen the horrific little creatures up close, his brain was churning even faster than his stomach, trying to make sense of it all.

But then, why was *Ellen* in that armor? Theroki armor. Arakovic's armor?

It couldn't be her. An excellent trick, maybe a holographic projection to distract his oath? A special new form of dynacamo that disguised you as other people? Clever. Had to be. Had to be.

The rage bubbled and frothed inside him and then hardened into pain as the steel gray of the stranger's visor cleared.

Intense, familiar eyes met his own, their brown almost black in the shifting blue light. Not a trick. Not a trick at all. Determination smoldered in her granite gaze. Anger too and untold pain. All of those made too much sense, too subtle for someone to fake. And the energy fed into him too.

He couldn't give up yet. There had to be a way out of this.

"Take that armor off, and I won't kill this man," Asha called. Asha was scowling, glancing from her armored guards to Ellen and back. Wary of a trick? She should be. One of the gang dragged Zahir forward now, away from Kael, and pushed him to his knees.

Before he even knew what was happening, Ellen had swung up a multi and fired. The stun pulse bounced—the two Theroki were protecting Asha—and flew right back at Ellen, who stepped to the side. Likely it wouldn't have affected the armor anyway, but no need to take an unnecessary hit.

"You're crazy," Asha snapped. "Why are *you* trying to kill him?"

"Because you're lying," Ellen said. She came to a stop about twenty-five meters away. "You'll still kill him. I'll just do it more gently."

"Well, now I'm thinking he knows something he shouldn't." Asha narrowed her eyes. "So maybe I won't. A nice, slow interrogation sounds like an excellent dessert after tonight's show."

"Your bluffs won't work on me. What do you want?"

"I want you dead," Asha shot back. "For killing my husband. It's only a fair trade don't you think?"

"Well, you can't have that," said Ellen, flatly. "And there's a few hundred Enhancers and a few hundred thousand Puritans in line ahead of you. They wish you luck."

"Right. The war hero," Asha sneered. "The deserter. If you're such a hero, why do your own people offer such a sizable reward for your arrest? I'm passing up a big payday for the pleasure of seeing you dead. Somehow, I think I'll manage."

If Asha's words affected Ellen, she didn't show it. She barely blinked. "Let Kael go."

"Or what? You can't win here."

"Or I'll slaughter you where you stand. I'll crush you into the cobblestones and leave your blood to feed the worms. But only because I'm in a hurry."

Asha froze for a moment, blinking.

"This is your last chance. This story ends here."

Asha seemed to remember herself and rolled her eyes. "Let him go? I thought you were supposed to be some kind of genius. Why would I let him go do what he wants most in the world? To run to you and live happily ever after in the sky somewhere? No. I control the end of this story. And *I* control what he wants now."

"And what is that?" Ellen said dryly.

"To kill you."

"I didn't earn the privilege of command by being afraid to fight the men who serve me." Ellen shrugged, the armor shell jerking briefly up and down with a grind and a clank. How did she even *fit* in that thing? "So bring it."

Asha's glare turned on him, and she pointed. "Go. And do it out here in the open. I want to watch."

His jaw might crack from the tension. He tore his eyes from Asha and took a step forward. "Yes, ma'am."

CHAPTER NINETEEN

DAY 18

DROP: 27 | UPLINK: ERR | SIZE: 17

ELLEN TIGHTENED her grip on the multi. Her hand hovered over the one switch on it she rarely used. This was one of the best rifles out there, and she was damn lucky to have retrieved this one. One of their best features was that they resisted firing on designated friendlies.

It was definitely a bad day when you have to flip that setting off.

"We've been here before," she called out to Kael as her clunky gauntlet slid the appropriate setting home. She tried to force some amusement into her voice, some calm. This was just another puzzle. A puzzle she could figure out. Logic. Sequence. There had to be a way out of it, of course.

There had to be.

"We were always destined to be opponents, I guess," he called back. "Don't know how we made it this long."

Her blood was pounding in her veins, in her skull. Each Theroki whose mind was now linked to hers fed her images of Kael, from a dozen different angles and sides. They battered her mind as he stepped forward, making it hard to find her own vision in the mess.

They served up other images, too. The stirring of a shopkeeper in the far east corner. One Theroki, viewed by a second through whose eyes she now saw, creeping down a dusty alley to keep her in their line of view.

She gritted her teeth. How was she going to think at all, let alone solve a puzzle, with all this crap in her head? She marshaled her concentration and tried to shove their minds out of hers. She needed a plan. A multi setting. A magical way out of this.

Stuns didn't work on Theroki, so it wouldn't work on Kael. Ballistics were a waste and a danger to the civilians. She toyed with the multi's main firing control, debating what to choose as he strode closer. "We never really did get to face off, one on one," she replied.

"You won't have any robots to stop me this time."

Her smile stole into the corner of her mouth. That day that his oath had finally activated on the *Audacity*, and the tranq had misfired, Xi had saved them both with an EMP shock from one of the cleaning robots. But they weren't among allies now.

"No tranqs either," she said. She did have the gas from Shirin's shop, so strictly speaking that was a lie. But it needed an enclosed area —more enclosed than this market square.

He stopped, close enough now she could see the warmth in his eyes, the fear. "You don't have to do this."

"Actually, I do." She flipped the switch on the multi to chem.

"I was never destined for thirty anyway. Forget this."

"Hah." She raised her chin. "No."

"Damn it, Ellen." His jaw clenched, eyes flinty.

"You forced your way into my life. You think you're getting rid of me that easily?"

She didn't wait for a response. She hit the trigger and started to run. Chem spray—and curses—deployed in her wake.

Oh, she wasn't giving up, but that didn't mean this was going to be fun. Or easy. His scrubbers would make the chem spray half as effective, if even that. Cover was a starting point. Then she needed a plan. Her original plan had been to wait them out and give them the drop in one of the alleys once they finally gave up and headed home, exhausted. A pinch point would have been useful.

Maybe it still could be.

Two of her Theroki held a covered position on the other side of the redik bar, and she raced for them, smooth market tile making her slide as she rounded the turn.

The release of the chem spray and her desperate sprint had scattered the few people holding out inside the bar. They shouted and ran in the opposite direction that she was going—which was smarter than their original move of hanging around.

Her first Theroki ally was crouched behind a dumpster. She slammed against the brick wall he crouched against, cracking the concrete and feeling relieved to reach him at all. Her view flipped dizzyingly between his eyes and hers. She tried to force the outside images away again, panting and trying not to throw up. Too many minds in the kitchen, damn it.

The unit needed to do something. Wanted to act. They were waiting. Anything. What to do, what to do. They needed orders. From her.

She needed to think. Think, damn it. A plan. Or maybe there was one way they could help…

Reaching through their eyes, she could see him coughing. His helmet had been down, which was a rookie move, really. He wasn't a rookie. Why? Why he hadn't raised it? Purely an attempt to lose this fight? He'd been totally open to the chem attack she'd lobbed his way, and he'd probably be out of commission for longer if it weren't for those scrubbers of his.

But he didn't raise the helmet, even now.

Staring at him through a dozen eyes just made her angrier about it. Why would he do such a stupid thing? If she wanted to kill him, she could so easily—ah.

So that was his plan. He'd said as much—kill me right here. She had better be certain none of her minions got any bright ideas.

I have some objectives, she told them. *We need the man alive and back on my ship,* she told them. *Incapacitate. Not kill. Got it?*

A sense of understanding brushed her. They wondered about the others.

The armed gang members up there by the fountain—obvious hostiles. But leave the other people just trying to get out of here alone. The woman is the real problem.

They knew the one. A songbird of her own sort.

Her and the Theroki defending her should be the primary focus. But we can't sacrifice civilians to do it—need to get them out of here. It's important.

Surviving was *more* important, they asserted. The enemy was counting on the civilians as distraction. The enemy was exploiting her concern for their wellbeing by choosing this location for battle.

She raised her eyebrows. Interesting, a little resistance. That was new, and the thoughts were growing clearer too. The ideas they'd floated were still not in the form of words, the way a telepath could transmit, but somewhere between words and ideas and emotions. *That doesn't change anything,* she replied. *They didn't ask to be here. I can take care of myself. We don't injure civilians, okay? We're better than our enemies. Because* we *do the right thing. We're the good guys here, and don't you forget it.*

Civilians would be ushered out. Then they would focus on protecting *her*, Ellen, whether she liked it or not. The hostiles by the fountain would be the tertiary objective, including the woman and the Theroki. And causing a little chaos, a distant but enjoyable fourth.

A little chaos—what the hell? Her old unit... well, it had been nothing like this. This was independent, yet connected. Collective and yet singular, it seemed.

A mental shrug. Reintegration is impossible. But here we are.

What did that even mean? This thought was almost clear, the very end of it resounding almost like words in her skull.

Her many eyes perked up as Kael straightened. He was recovering. Pondering 'reintegration' would have to wait for later.

She still didn't have a plan. Where was a damn knockout grenade when she needed one? Had he seen where she'd gone?

Through their eyes, she could see him wiping his eyes, gazing toward their alley. Start walking. Slow but purposeful.

Yeah, he knew where she was. They needed to move.

She turned and raced down the alley, her Theroki following her of their own accord. They'd barely gone five meters before a panel on the upper story of the redik bar shattered down in a dozen pieces, raining chaos on the ground where they'd just been.

Fragging hell.

The crack of gunfire exploded in the square, then the sound of more walls being pummeled. As far as she could see, her team of Theroki had moved in, begun engaging with the two in the cafe. Well, some of them had; others were chasing frightened civilians toward the far alleys. It was nearly impossible to process it all.

Ballistics flew, and half the people fighting were deflecting them. Some were re-aiming their deflections, some weren't. With all the bouncing, she had no idea who was even firing anymore.

She ducked into the outcropping of an access door. This alley had little in it she could make use of, although it was a pinch of sorts. Two stories high, but dull and drab and empty. Hardly any cover, just a few access outcroppings like the one she was huddled in, but no businesses open. Barely even a few doors, and those that were there looked rarely used. It might as well have been a mine shaft to nowhere, in here.

She swore and refocused on the multi… What was her best bet?

The spray foam. That was worth a shot. It only held two charges, but it might have a chance at incapacitating him long enough for her to get to Asha.

And rip that bitch's face off.

If she hid here in the outcropping, and the two Theroki stood in plain sight and faced him, maybe while they wrestled each other she could get close enough to pin him against the far alley wall with the foam. She slowed to a stop and listened, but couldn't hear much over the trills of fire from the main square.

Streetlights dotted the walls, providing minimum safety lighting. If it were a little darker, her chances would improve. She could shoot out those lights, but she'd still show up on his thermal cameras. *If* he thought to check them. Maybe that'd force him to raise the damn helmet.

Maybe she could use the thermals to her advantage. Hide in plain sight.

Take out the streetlights. And get ready.

The lights died in tiny supernovas, one by one. She'd assumed they'd shoot them, but she was pretty sure they were just crushing them.

The alley was black now, barely any light filtering from the already dimmed Painted Market. She couldn't see, and this beat-up suit did not give her cool toys like thermals, but she could feel her companions move into position.

Instead of keeping to the alcove, though, she bent down in front of them now. Should she lie down, like she was injured? Or would kneeling work?

Lying prone might be more convincing, but he *was* out to kill her. If the foam didn't work, she was going to need to bolt.

She chose her spot, knelt on one knee like she had a problem with her boot, and ducked her head like she wasn't paying attention. Too black to see anything, and she'd see through their eyes anyway. The Theroki shifted closer without a word or complaint. No banter here. If she'd wanted less joking around on this mission, she'd just gotten it.

Banter. There was a question in her thoughts, like she'd used a foreign word. What did she mean by banter?

For a split-second Kael flashed through her mind, on that first mission. The first time they'd seen the white creature, the one that had run off into the woods, and where he'd saved the secrecy of the mission by incapacitating those guards. He'd said he'd missed banter then, and they'd sure provided plenty.

God, she missed the crew. Kael and all of them. Zhia, Jenny, Mo. A sharp pain stabbed at her heart. What if they never found Mo? Or Doug? God, what were the chances they'd all live to have that cama-raderie again? Living, simply surviving, would be fine too. Living at all would be ideal.

She wasn't the praying sort, but as a cough started to overtake her, she closed her eyes and whispered a few words, ones she hadn't murmured much in a decade or two, from a time closed away, a time she chose not to think about.

Then she opened her eyes. Deep breaths. She would only have one chance, maybe two. She needed to be steady. She'd need to be lucky too.

She raised the multi to her shoulder. And waited.

———

KAEL PAUSED at the entrance to the narrow alley. Rubble cluttered the area, dust still floating in the air above it. The streetlights that usually lit alleys like this one had gone out. Or been put out. The alley couldn't be more than three meters across, and it was open two stories high, just as the market was, although that second story was mostly populated with maintenance access panels for ventilation and utilities and maybe a few windows that were never used for anything a window ought to be used for.

He stepped into the rubble and felt the oath programming hesitate. Asha had said to stay where she could see the fight. Of course, she'd also said to murder the only woman he'd ever loved.

That was the problem with overly specific orders. What happened when they conflicted?

He smiled to himself. *Surely,* the order to kill was the primary objective. The location couldn't be as important, could it?

The oath urged him down the alley. His smile broadened as he complied. His helmet was still retracted, and he left it that way. He wasn't sure he actually could raise it. He didn't want to.

It made him an easy target. And if he could give that option to Ellen, he damn sure would.

Picking over the rubble from the panel he'd knocked down in their pursuit, he listened hard, but the fighting behind him was drowning out everything. Ellen had gone this way, so then what the hell was happening back there? Who was fighting? Had Dane attacked? More of the team come down from *Audacity*?

He winced at the thought of being pitted against any of them. Or all of them. Rage threatened to bubble up again, but what good would it do him?

The darkness of the alley quickly consumed him. In the helmet, he could flip to the thermal view or dial up the display, but that was off the table. He raised his arm instead, checked the screen on the gauntlet. It could give him a rough reading, although not an instant overlay. It would also draw his attention away from the fight, and the light too might faintly give away his location.

Well, good. The more mistakes the better at this point.

Thermal readout said three hostiles, all still shrouded in darkness. Three? He'd only seen *her* go down here. Who were these two others?

He dialed up the detail on the display, slowing to give him time to assess. They had to know he was coming; he hadn't been quiet. That was one more mistake he could make. The oath programming had no expectation of a Theroki being stealthy.

One of the three forms was hunched down, dealing with a problem, maybe a boot issue. Two other hulking forms lumbered just behind. That uneven, heavy armor… More Theroki? How? Where the hell had they come from?

If one of them was Ellen—which one?

Just when he thought it couldn't get worse. He'd known Asha had the two, but maybe she had many more. How was he going to protect Ellen with Arakovic's people around too? Did she even realize they were there?

"Elle—behind you—" That was what he tried to say at least, but the words caught in his throat. He tried again, but barely a croak came out now. The forms shifted on the display, but if they'd heard him, they showed no reaction.

Doubly odd.

He shut off the screen and readied himself. What was the stupidest, least efficient way he could go about this, and would the oath program be stupid enough to let him?

Maybe he could get some info out of them. "Theroki—do you have a comm unit to the mothership? I've been kidnapped and need to report back."

Silence met him, and darkness.

"Theroki, I serve on the *Genokai*. Where do you serve?"

No answer.

He had to be getting closer now. In the dimness he could make out the hunched form now, so he dropped the thermal display, raised his multi.

But which one to hit first? Which was her? Were *any* of them her? Maybe she'd run off and past and down the alley?

The stun setting wouldn't work on a real Theroki as their electro-magnetic augments were designed to capture and store the energy if possible—and discharge it, if it wasn't. So a stun pulse would be wasted on two out of the three of them, if not all three. Unless any of them deflected it…

But if she *were* one of them, he could stun her and drag her back to Asha. She'd *said* she didn't want to miss the battle. So he surely shouldn't kill her right now. Incapacitating her would be better.

He set the multi to stun and cleared his throat, an idea taking hold. "Hey, Ellen."

The helmet of the hunched form twitched.

He fired.

It shouldn't have, but the impact that hit him from the side caught him completely by surprise. He *knew* there were Theroki here—but it was the timing. Why now? Why had they waited like they were frag-ging asleep? Why not thrust him out of the alley or kill him first thing? Why?

He barely registered the spray of ballistic fire hitting cement before he realized it had been *his* multi that had fired. His. He'd set that damn thing to *stun*—hadn't he?

Or had the programming overridden him? Was it smarter than he thought?

When his skull bounced off the far cement wall, though, his ques-tions shattered.

On instinct, he sent a blow to the structure just above the two standing Theroki—or at least the far away one closest to the other wall. Debris raining down on his attackers. Or at least he hoped it did. There was little intention or aim to the decision, more of a wounded kick in the darkness.

The sound of a foam release tipped him off—a multi. Ellen.

She was trying to trap him down. Smart. Ideal, really, but he knew how to fight the foam. There was no tool in that multi he didn't know how to combat, including a ballistic round to the head, even without the damned helmet.

Damn it, she'd never beat him this way. At least, he didn't think so. He thrashed around, writhing and trying to keep the stuff from grabbing hold and setting in. Pressure from the Theroki hit him now, making it more difficult, the motors in the usually silent armor starting to strain and wheeze. His mind flung the stuff away, in any direction it could.

He was all too efficient. But the pressure was increasing, slowing him down. In full-on savage fight mode now, he lashed out, sending one of the three forms crashing into the far wall as hard as he could.

He caught his breath, realizing he didn't know which was her, but that same breath was shoved out of him as another impact slammed him into his own wall. His head bounced once more off the cement, and splotches covered his eyes for a moment.

He swore and sank down to the ground, the world spinning around him.

A light burst into view, and he squinted, trying to lift his hand to shield his eyes. But he couldn't. A Theroki was holding him down. He was too dizzy to fight back yet anyway.

"You know, I'm starting to realize it's a good thing we neutralized you." The light lifted, and he realized it was a small emergency light on her gauntlet. Her other hand was on her ribs, and she was limping a little as she stepped closer. "Why is your damned helmet down?"

"I've recently learned how to follow orders," he said through gritted teeth. "Not that I'm happy about it." He writhed, looking for a weak point in the pressure.

"Shocking."

"She put something in me, Ellen. Something alive—like that thing that climbed out of Vala. I'm a dead man. You have to accept it."

"No."

"Kill me, damn it. I don't want to become—like that."

"Kill you with what? You'll just bounce it back." She swayed a little on her feet—he didn't think he'd even hit her yet, had he? Why was she limping, then? Damn it, maybe he had. The hollows of her eyes were dark, but he wasn't sure if it was because of the shadows thrown by her gauntlet or something more sinister.

"There's no way out of this," he whispered. "You've seen those creatures before."

"Ostrov had them too. In his apartment. He called them indoctrination."

"He *what?*" He snarled and lashed out at the Theroki pressure against him. It faltered but then crashed him back down again. The guy couldn't do this forever though. "Why didn't you mention this before?"

"Because mentioning Ostrov makes you do… that."

He wasn't above proving her point with another attempt to heave the panels off of him. The other Theroki held, and after a long minute or two, Kael sagged, the weight heavy on his chest, his legs. The armor was all that was keeping him from being crushed. He blew out a sigh of defeat. "Get out of here, Elle. You outran me once. Do it again, and don't come back. Please." His voice was jagged. "You've seen those creatures. I'm dead already."

"I've seen them, and we don't know shit about them. So I don't believe you."

"Don't be stubborn, damn it. You'll get us both killed."

"The thing is, once I get my teeth in something…" She shrugged, then winced in pain.

Pain that he had caused, damn it.

"Just get out of here." The words were a growl. She wasn't going to listen, though, was she? He'd have to *make* her listen. Just this one time, to protect her.

No, no, to kill her. That was what he was doing. Obviously.

He dropped his resistance on the pressure above him and shoved her instead. He thrust her as far as he could manage, down the alley, away from the market, away from Asha. If he had to attack, he could at least try to push her in a direction that was safer if his attempt to kill her failed.

Judging by the gauntlet light, she flew—but he didn't hear her hit the ground. The light suddenly winked out.

His eyes shot back to the Theroki over him, pinning him down. And maybe holding Ellen up? More dark had fallen again, but a faint outline was visible in the light that filtered from the square now that his eyes had adjusted.

He couldn't tear his eyes away, now. The hulking gorilla of a soldier was a form all too familiar, armor torn and bristling, the creature of his literal nightmares. The blue mark of the octopus was bright across his chest. They were clearly helping her. Why? They couldn't be on both sides.

The man was actually looking after her—not at Kael. As if they were communicating somehow. Kael couldn't see where she'd gone, not enough light reaching further into the alley. The other Theroki had never returned. He hadn't realized he'd pushed the guy *that* hard, but maybe in his fear and rage and frustration he had.

He could do it again too. Had to, in fact.

He relaxed for a minute, storing up, then shoved.

The Theroki growled as he flew into the opposite alley wall. The thunderous crash of metal and cement was loud.

A moment later the pressure on him ceased.

"Ellen," he growled as he started to throw the debris off him. "I'm coming."

The oath program urged him forward.

"I'm coming."

As the last crumbling hunk of cement rolled away, though, his eyes locked on it. He didn't really need to go closer. He could kill her just fine from here.

But Asha... Asha had wanted...

No. He'd already decided killing her was the more important objective. He wasn't getting it both ways.

He didn't know if it was medical shock or rage or exhaustion that made him shake as he raised his arm, switched on the thermal.

The computer estimated the prone form in armor at forty meters. Most likely alive. Switching off the thermal, he closed both hands into fists, squeezed his eyes shut, and reached.

The ceiling broke apart in his mind's hands, tearing the bonds that held beam from pipe from slab. The cement, the ducts, the rebar, the so-called windows—all of it crumbled and splintered. The crash as he ripped them to the ground shook his whole body, knocked him off balance.

His knees hit rubble. The dust rushed out and around him, all energy to stand or think gone. His head swum, and when his lungs forced a breath, he hacked out a cough as the dust clogged his nose, his throat, his eyes.

It hurt, but it was nothing compared to the dead cold in his chest, the pain that had nothing to do with any physical injury.

The oath, though, wasn't convinced it was a job well done. It leaned in. It listened.

He coughed and spit out the bitter dust, and then he listened too.

DROP: 27 | UPLINK: ERR | SIZE: 16

Whoever had decided to build a human settlement on this planet was an idiot. Who sees a place where all life had to shelter underground more than half the time and decides it's prime real estate?

She had had enough buildings falling on her for one visit to Faros. Maybe for a lifetime.

She'd faked those injuries before, to throw him off, but she'd be lucky if she hadn't crushed a foot or broken a rib now—although she didn't yet feel any pain. She didn't even have the Foundation armor this time, though. The Theroki armor, as busted as it was in places, was even more busted up now. Thankfully, it was still heavy armor, or she might not have survived.

That of course had been the idea.

Sorry to be a bother, Kael, but squishing me like a bug isn't going to work. Or at least, you're going to have to do it at least one more time. She fought a cough, hoping to stay quiet, but a small one escaped. The dust must be seeping into the suit, tickling her throat.

She'd braced herself against the wall of the alley and was probing as well as she could to find any weak spots. She didn't have lasers on the gauntlet this time—at least, none she knew how to activate—but she had her multi.

And she could still punch things. The question was where would be the most efficient. Who knew what movement would set off a chain reaction that might be worse for her than this one?

Plus, he'd hear her. Right now, she was almost silent. But busting through this wall might reveal she was alive, so she'd have to move fast. Clear out of the area.

Right now, things were quiet, though. God, what he must be going through. Wondering if he succeeded? Damn Asha and damn the day she was born.

Then again. Convincing him she was dead might be just the ticket. Now *that* was a plan.

I need a room isolated from the fighting. Small. And I need to get there from here as fast as possible, without him pursuing me.

They turned their focus on her now in acknowledgement. No—on Kael.

Until now, those Theroki had been diligently focusing on the cluster of Asha's team by the fountain. From the mental flashes that had assaulted her, nobody had been making much headway. The Theroki battle looked more like a telekinetic game of catch, with a lot of things flying and not much connecting. And they *still* hadn't convinced every civilian to get out.

But now, all but four turned their focus on her and Kael. And it hadn't just been her request for help. They'd felt the loss of one member of the unit. The injury of a second.

She had felt the first die, too, with literally a sharp stab to the chest. A piece of rebar freed in the rubble had gotten lucky—or unlucky based on your perspective, she supposed—and Kael's thrust skewered the man straight through a crack in the armpit armor. Most of the pain flickered out as quickly as the lights in the alley, though. Other little explosions of pain bloomed across her consciousness, like distant fireworks in the night sky.

The readout in her mind had decremented once too; that was the only way she was certain they weren't both dead. The second Theroki that had been holding Kael back had gone dim. Not dead, but not conscious either.

Yes, they knew the damage incurred. They weren't going to let him hurt her. A room, she needed? And maybe a distraction? That could be done.

Don't kill him. It was an order, but would they follow it? Who knew at this point? There was no acknowledgment, only motion in her direction.

That was her distraction, and it wouldn't last forever.

She couldn't wind up much, but she piled an upper cut style blow into the wall, getting just enough maneuvering space to twist the multi into position. She switched it to laser and pulled the trigger.

Nothing happened. She tried again.

Nothing.

Moreover—it was usually interfaced with her suit, where a dangerous heat level warning would pop up automatically if the laser were overtaxed. Right now she had no such thing, and a cement chunk lodged on her shoulder blocked her view of the thing, too.

Hell. The rifle had survived a lot, so she supposed this was a bit much to ask. Ballistics then, or was she just punching her way out of this? The Theroki armor was plenty capable in the latter area.

But she had no idea how thick the wall was. Or who could be on the other side. Bullets through a thin wall could keep on going and hit a civilian.

So brute force was going to have to do it. She braced herself and got to work.

———

A DULL THUD.

Was that in front of him or behind him? He listened closer. Another thud, louder this time, but over the fighting behind him… Except that the fighting behind him suddenly quieted.

That couldn't be good.

Keeping his ears tuned for signs of life under the disaster, he twisted back toward the main square. There were *more* of them? He could spot at least four headed his way at a dead run—no, five.

The best defense was always a good offense.

He struck first, even though it taxed what little energy he had left. He'd need a break soon to regenerate. He'd have to hide and to find some way to kill them all without using telekinesis.

Thud. Thud. The quiet vibration from the heap was growing louder, more continuous. Did that mean she was alive, or just that a pipe under there was thumping against another one?

It didn't matter—five more Theroki were a more pressing problem. And he'd never get close enough to them to take them out one-on-one. He wouldn't get a shot through both the telekinetics and the armor, and even if he did, one shot in that scenario rarely took anyone out of a fight.

No, he needed something else to handle this… something big. Especially because two more had just emerged from a side alley. Maybe he'd pissed them off. How many of them *were* there, and did they all work for Ellen, or were some of them Asha's?

If they were Asha's, why were they headed for *him* all of a sudden? He wasn't sticking around to find out.

He pivoted and sprinted up the hill of rubble. This could work. The level he'd torn down was now ripped open on all sides, and he could dive into the buildings a story above the painted market, get out of sight, maybe get some distance on them.

Maybe drag them into this tunnel and then tear some more of it down? Hey, if it worked once… No, he didn't have the energy for that, but was there a way his multi could achieve similar results?

There was still that thud-thud-thudding.

The rubble skidded and rolled away underneath him as he climbed, but he kept his speed fast, his feet light, and soon he was ducking into an abandoned, dark office at the top level. A piece of a vent duct swung from the ceiling, sad and forlorn, but he dodged it and sank down behind a desk.

He heard three more thuds as he dug deeper into the office complex, before the activity below him exploded with a thunderous crash. Whatever was happening wasn't directly underneath him, but somewhere beneath that. Two stories, three? More?

His bets were on two. And that the sound was Ellen, working her way out of his trap. And probably on the move.

Which meant she was alive.

He could cling to that while he dodged the eight or more Theroki on his tail. How hard could that be?

––––––––

DROP: 27 | UPLINK: ERR | SIZE: 16

The wall gave way gradually under Ellen's fists, although not as quickly as she'd have liked. The only thing that went her way was that it had been cracked in the collapse, so once she opened up a hole about the size of her torso, the rest of the rock gave up its fight and crumbled.

More bits of wall flew as she powered her way out of the rock, but as soon as she was fully clear, she ran. That hadn't been subtle—he could be on his way.

From the look of things from her team, he hadn't been as distracted by them as she'd hoped. He'd just turned and ran. If he was fleeing them, great. If he was chasing her, that could be a problem. She had an idea now, but she'd have to get clear of him and the right spot to execute on it.

The power armor hissed and crunched things as she staggered out of the room she'd busted into, which looked like some sort of dimly lit dwelling. The next room also contained nothing but a bed and a small table, someone's home she'd just upended.

The new room had a powerful overhead light burning, so she finally got a good look at the multi—and swore.

Not only was the stock wildly bent, but the beam propagation apparatus was dented knuckle deep. Any part of the laser mechanism could be damaged. Half her ammos were already empty, but now it could be leaking hydrogen or worse. She supposed two building collapses was a lot to ask for it to survive unprotected. If she had her *own* armor, she had numerous backup options within the suit, but no such luck.

She almost tossed the thing aside, but the residential surroundings gave her pause. A busted laser could be volatile.

Besides, better to get a move on and toss it somewhere away from this spot, in case Kael came here and found it. No reason to let him know she'd lost her multi. It'd been all she'd had going for her until this point, besides this clanky armor.

And that wouldn't be hers much longer either.

Scowling, she started forward again and—

Commander?

And almost stumbled into the doorframe. *Ana—is that you?* The blond's voice seemed dizzy, disoriented.

Yes, Commander. I can't fly.

What do you mean you can't fly?

I came to, but my eyes—I—my head is spinning. EOE8 says severe concussion maybe? Maybe it's... Never mind. Point is, I can't fly the shuttle. We're grounded.

Ellen fought not to slap a hand to her face. Or to swear. *Look, you're safe, just ride it out. The shuttle shields—*

Are not stable. We were swarmed by a local gang—Dane says the Snake Kings. He killed them all with the shuttle weapons systems, but it took a while, and the power's failing. We won't be able to stay. He wants me to tell you we're on our way to you.

No! No, you can't come here. *You have to keep Shirin safe—*

This isn't any safer. At least there we have allies. Dane says he's sorry he overestimated the shuttle.

Ellen swore, but shook it off. Everybody was doing their damn best.

Is there some way I could help?

Help me by finding a place to hide that keeps Shirin safe. I need to—handle this situation. She just needed to get from Kael to Asha and end this—apparently with her fists, because that was the way this day was going. *We'll figure a way out of this. Just whatever you do, don't come here.*

There was no answer. God, for all the years she'd had to deal with the burdens of telepathic abilities she'd never asked for or wanted, it'd be nice to actually *be* a telepath for once and be able to reach out and say something useful. Maybe force them not to come here—that had to be tempting. But either Ana had lost consciousness again, or she'd stopped listening.

Ellen's time was short anyway. She needed to move.

She coughed—damn all this dust in the air—and started to jog, heading out the door of the room and looking for a real exit. But rounding the corner, she faltered again when her eyes met those of a bearded man.

The tall, thin father clutched a teen daughter to his chest as they huddled inside a metal cabinet. Probably a smart place given all the crashing and shooting, although it had lost one door at some point.

"Um… sorry about the wall," she muttered. And kept on running.

———

KAEL HAD LOST them by the time he made it to the opposite side of the square. It had required some creative door-making, climbing, and jumping from one roof to another twice, but he didn't hear any of them nearby anymore. His suit *could* be quiet, so he took full advantage of that. The thermals showed plenty of people still cowering inside these buildings, but none of them inside were moving like Theroki or even soldiers of any kind. Three or so still battled it out in the main square though. It looked like one had fallen.

Crouched inside an empty office, he squinted down the sight of the multi. If only Mo were here. He'd never been a great shot at a distance, but fortunately lasers didn't care much about distance. A cough seized his throat, making him look away for a moment, but once he'd eased the tickle, he was back in position.

He doubted either his assailants or Ellen were still in the alley looking for him, but an explosion there could draw attention away from this hiding place, buy him some time. If he didn't make it clear where he'd shot from.

The thermal reading on his gauntlet was bitterly reminding him that there were still innocent people nearby. People who weren't Theroki.

Hell.

Scanning the area around the alley, he spotted a security panel. His eyes followed the line into the panel toward the ceiling, and he smiled.

No fancy forcefields for this market on Faros. No, but they did have some precautions for fires and floods. Blast doors. It wouldn't keep everyone out, or everyone in, but it could throw some obstacles in the way of his pursuers.

Especially if some of them were still in the alley.

Just beside his security panel was a grocery stall. Not perfect, but it would do. He trained his laser on the piles and packages, wincing at a few exploding vegetables before eventually a bottle caught flame. He swung the beam to its brethren.

And the blaze went up fast.

Smoke triggered the alarm, and doors at every alley and store crashed shut. The alley he'd torn apart had gaps at the bottom of the door due to all the rubble. Not ideal.

And worse, some of the businesses in the square were apparently fancier than he'd thought, because the window in front of him sizzled with the sound of the forcefield activating. He was just lucky he hadn't been leaning out with the multi while it happened.

It took a few minutes of searching to find the shut off switch. He sighed as he settled back in place on his knees with the multi. Time to get back on his primary mission, but first…

Finger on the trigger, he swung the aim of the multi back toward the fountain, trained it on Asha, let out a breath. She was sitting on the lounge, still unarmored, looking smug but irritated. Her two Theroki didn't appear to have taken a hit.

He willed himself to fire. His finger wouldn't budge.

Eh. It was worth a try. But his shoulders slumped as he backed away from the window. He needed to move on soon, staying still could get him found even if his distraction might have bought him sometime and some new obstacles. But where to go?

Wherever Ellen was, of course. But where was that?

Some part of his soul hardened as his legs straightened on their own and headed for the stairs down, determined to continue the hunt. Sitting around wouldn't find her, so obviously he should keep going. The safe route would be to stick to these buildings, look for Theroki armor, take them out one at a time. Eventually he'd find her.

But he didn't want the safe route. Why had he even run? Simple habit. Basic survival. Nobody wanted to die.

Except if that was how he could save Ellen... then he wanted the most dangerous, reckless route possible. Damn, he shouldn't have run at all. He should be *trying* to be found.

He turned from the top of the stairs and went back to the window. He'd slid up the lower half of the window, but the top half was a fixed. Decorative glass in a star-like geometric design of pale white and pale blue.

It hurt his heart, but he smashed it, fist through the glass, knocking out the corners to rid it of the big pieces. And then he gripped the window frame and eased forward.

Or... he tried to. But at about the window's ledge, his legs wouldn't budge. "Oh, come on," he grumbled. It was barely a two-story drop. He'd survived much worse. But the damn thing knew his intent, knew him from the inside. He couldn't move at all in that direction, not now.

He snarled and slammed a fist against the window's frame, creating a dent bigger than his head.

Whoever had invented the Theroki programming—or the Theroki in the first place—he hoped they were rotting in the cold, humid, putrid grave they deserved. Slow disintegration or vaporizing in a vacuum wasn't enough punishment for someone who'd invented the abomination he'd become.

Although. Odd he had never heard who that was. There was no "father of the Theroki," at least not that anyone had told him. Maybe they shared that tidbit with higher ranks. Or maybe they didn't want anyone to know.

Someone must have invented it all, though.

His fingers reached up, grazed the smooth metal of the collar that had fitted itself so neatly and violently into his port. Almost like it knew just what to look for.

Certainly Arakovic had had access to Theroki to examine, working with the Enhancers and hiring them directly. That must be how she'd designed this heinous device. But why had she bothered? Just specifically to go after *him*? That didn't make sense. What could he possibly have that she wanted so badly? It made more sense she'd made it for a broader purpose, to control any Theroki.

Come to think of it, how had she captured that Theroki ship in the first place? He'd always assumed she'd just bribed them.

But maybe she knew something. Something she could use, some weakness on the inside.

Cold anger and venom pumped through his veins as he stomped back toward the stairs, started to go down, until he froze.

A voice rang out, echoing in the small room through the smashed window.

"Dane! Dane, down here! I'm injured!"

He didn't have to think, which was good, because he didn't want to. His feet turned and headed in the right direction. Toward her.

HER SHOUTS CONTINUED for a solid minute. Kael spent every second of it wishing she'd be fragging quiet, but no such luck. Every call she made cut at him, and he headed closer.

She must be hurt bad. And without her normal armor, there was no other way to signal for help. Besides, Asha's Theroki and the gang members—whose numbers he could see were dwindling now that he passed through the main square and got closer—were busy with the rogue Theroki who appeared to be helping Ellen. Asha was focused, as always, on herself.

So despite bullets and pipes and table legs and broken chairs flying, no one was looking for her.

Except him.

He'd have to face both her *and* Dane unless he was quick about it. Well, that was an awful thought. He pushed it down and stepped inside the tailor shop. Her voice had come from in here, both he and the oath were sure of it, but it'd gone silent now.

The blast door had been busted through. It now lay bent on the floor inside, a breeze rocking it slightly. The work of the tailor shop—robes and suits and long garment bags—swayed on their racks as he stepped inside.

The air hung heavy with lavender, probably from some laundering service offering, or just an overbearing tailor's perfume. Dust and smoke made for a thick, hardly breathable mix. Throat choking on the scent, he smothered a cough as best he could.

The fire he'd started across the square had been smothered by auto-foam, but not before it'd tainted nearly all the air in the market with smoke. The power appeared to be out in here too, but plenty of shifting light from the central fountain and the painted sky fed into the shop from the gaping doorway.

Racks of clothes and shelves had been knocked aside as someone had raced to the back of the shop.

He took two steps forward. This armor could be nearly silent, and he found himself using it now, in spite of himself—or perhaps the oath program was learning. He stepped around the first fallen clothes rack, then rounded another.

In the back room, a stray pebble skittered across something solid and stopped abruptly.

The door to the area stood a few centimeters ajar, waving slightly as if it recovered from the impact or some phantom breeze. A sliver of light crept through the crack and underneath the cheap metal thing.

He kept his feet quiet and approached, every instinct straining.

He pushed the door open as slowly as he could manage. He wanted to burst in, slam the door against the wall, warn her.

But his oath knew better, warred with his instincts, and in this moment, it won.

Time to go in for the kill. He was close. He could almost taste it, bitter and foul, ash and salt, toxic like the perfume that hung in the air.

The door was painfully quiet and well-oiled, not a creaky hinge to be heard. The light came from damaged emergency lighting along the floor, blaring out at an awkward angle. White brilliance outlined the edges of a suit of Theroki armor, someone knelt down leaning over a medkit.

A suit missing an edge of the pauldron. And a bent and mangled looking multi useless at their side.

Something in his chest hitched at the sight of the medkit. How badly was she hurt? Was it because of him?

That didn't matter, did it.

Because this was checkmate. An injury was the least of their problems.

He didn't consciously think now, just as he hadn't before. The beaten armor jolted into the air, shattered cracks as it slammed into the ceiling above them, then hurtled back down. The medkit was flattened. Parts of the armor dented in, flattened and deformed with the force of the blow.

Debris pummeled the suit from above, pieces of the ceiling, wiring, electrical, pipe. Maybe he did it, maybe the oath programming was somehow able to do it on its own now, maybe she'd just hit the ceiling that hard.

Energy flooded out of him, and he staggered. Sand trickled through the cracks above.

A hunk of cement clipped his shoulder, and he stumbled again, catching himself on one knee. When he steadied, he squinted at the armor. He had trouble focusing for a moment, which was odd. A piece of rebar had driven clear through the neck area, and one leg piece had separated from the rest of the suit. The falling rubble had misshapen the thing to such a degree, if anyone was alive inside, they wouldn't be for long.

Something in him hitched, then released.

The oath was fulfilled.

He clutched at his chest, gasped for breath. No amount of the dusty air was enough to breathe, and hell, he hoped it would suffocate him. He'd felt a pure, physical stab of grief like this once before, but he hadn't had to witness the loss. Be the cause of it all. Have the images engraved in his memory.

She *couldn't* be dead. Not like this. He couldn't win. She was better than him. She had to be. She was supposed to be.

But the armor didn't move.

"Get up," he growled at the steel and rubble.

Nothing around him stirred, not even the other Theroki.

Would they too be incapacitated now? Could he make a run for it before Asha thought to give him another command, or would she be able to summon him back from anywhere? Did that controller of hers have a range?

But what did it matter. What reason was there to run? Nothing would ever matter, ever again.

He felt tired. So tired.

He knew he probably shouldn't, but he crawled across the rubble, closer to the armor. He was tempted to inspect it, but at the thought of actually seeing her dead lifeless eyes staring up at him, he flinched away.

Instead he fell on his back beside her. Coughed out a bit of the dusty, perfumed air. Stared up at the wrecked ceiling. He'd damaged it, but not enough to see into the floor above them. Just cracks and devastation.

Could he die from exhaustion? Could he die from grief?

Could he just die here, period? Maybe one of those Theroki would walk over the level above him and just cave it all in.

He squeezed his eyes shut. If he could die here, by her side, it was probably more than he deserved.

DROP: 27 | UPLINK: ERR | SIZE: 15

Ellen crouched behind the external display of an electronics shop. Going into battle unarmored had never been her dream scenario, but sometimes you just had to deal. Still, the smoky, dusty air against her skin even under her usual flight suit made her skin crawl, and she choked back a cough. Even when she'd trained in all sorts of contexts, it was also hard to forget the history lessons.

Another tickle at the back of her throat made her muffle an outright cough in her sleeve. From the smoke, or maybe Maloof hadn't been bluffing.

She didn't know how many Theroki had been trapped in Kael's stunt, but it'd kept him distracted while she set up her ploy. She'd only had to crash through one blast door to make it happen. None of her men were dead, but the blast doors had turned an inconvenient ant farm maze into a ridiculous one to find him inside.

While she'd shucked her armor, she'd managed to hoist a bit of mental separation between them, so their perspectives only banged loudly on the door to her mind, rather than barging in. Maybe adrenaline was helping, maybe it was practice. Counting from their perspectives inside her mind was even more difficult now that they'd diverged in space so much, but she could spot three, maybe four still in the main square.

Asha and her two guardian Theroki still stood, though many of her entourage had fallen or fled.

Gritting her teeth, her eyes darted over every detail of the disturbingly flat terrain between her and Asha. Her gaze traced a path from a toppled piece of ceiling sculpture to an overturned table someone had dragged forward. They were bits of cover that might hide her unarmored approach. Or at least shield her from fire a little.

She and Asha were going to have a little... talk. She didn't have long while Kael was out, if her plan even worked. She had to make the most of every second.

Sprinting forward, her boots skidded on the loose gravel and sand shaken from the ceiling, but she kept her steps light, quiet, shifted her balance as needed, made her way to her first target. She slammed her back harder against the rock than she should have and stifled a groan. She wasn't used to this unarmored shit.

Heaving in a breath, checking the locations from the corner of her eye, she dashed for the next one—only to hear a chunk of rock slam down in the space she'd just vacated.

Close. Way too close.

One of Asha's Theroki knew she was there.

Which meant the cover of an overturned wooden table wasn't much protection. She barely paused for a breath before zigzagging toward the third spot she'd selected, a wheeled drink cart used by the cafe to sell to passersby. At least that was metal.

The table clattered after her like some sort of possessed furniture. She had to throw herself to the side to dodge it, then duck when it changed directions and slid sideways straight toward her head.

Fragging Theroki.

Rolling, she'd barely made it to the cart. She grabbed hold and spun the thing to put it between her and the murderous table.

Splinters and boards exploded into the air as the table was shattered against the cart. The impact slid her back several meters over the slick stone under her feet.

But that wasn't the end of it—half a dozen tea tables rose up from inside the cafe, all hurtling in her direction.

She huddled against the cart, looking for a better destination. One closer to Asha. *You're a sitting duck, dammit. Pick somewhere, anywhere.*

A crash far to her left revealed one of the tables hadn't found its mark. Or any mark. She twisted and peered over the top of the cart. Sure enough, several of the tables hung frozen midair.

A moment later, they fell in lifeless unison to the ground.

One down.

She let out a breath. Apparently she'd been the distraction her Theroki needed to finally break through the enemy defenses. That ought to buy her time. The other would be more careful not to ignore those dogging him. And now he was alone.

At least until Kael woke up.

Her next sprint would take her close, just behind Asha. Without her multi, without her armor, she was just going to have to use her hands.

A flyer had risen up into the air, along with a piece of pipe and a blast door that had been torn from its hinges. Whether those were controlled by friend or foe, she had no idea, but they were going to make a hell of a crash. Maybe it could shield the sound of her pounding toward Asha.

Taking in one more deep breath, she timed her sprint with the colossal crash of the flyer, which careened recklessly into the fountain.

She hadn't counted on the massive wave the fountain heaved out into the square, however. How deep *was* that thing? Icy water drenched her, and her feet slid again on smooth cobblestones, but she managed to skid to a stop just behind the lounges where Asha and the remaining Theroki still stood.

Neither of them turned. Good. Now she only had to—

Commander—

She almost groaned. *Not a good time, Ana—*

I checked the woman's mind.

What? Why?

To try to help. How else are we going to get out of here? Listen, there's a box. A sudden image filled Ellen's mind of a small, white control with no markings. Not designed to be easy to use, apparently. *It controls the collar she placed on Kael and—some kind of parasite? I've seen it before.*

She winced. *White and wriggly?*

You've seen it too?

How could I forget.

If you can get the box, I think you could control him. Cancel the commands.

Ellen raised her eyebrows. *Got it. Thanks, Ana. Stay safe.*

Yes, Commander.

Rising slowly up over the edge, she scanned the wreckage around

Asha. Bloodied bodies, weapons, and broken teacups were strewn about, all of it drenched now from the fountain's latest attack.

But there—clean and white on the golden fabric of the lounge a meter to Asha's right.

The box.

There was no time to stop and think—the tranq on Kael could wear off any second. But she couldn't ignore Asha's presence so close, either. She'd have to incapacitate her first, get the box, then deal with the Theroki. If she even could.

She coiled herself tight, sucked in a breath, then launched into the air, using one foot on the back of the ledge to propel her higher. Her other boot swung out, aimed at Asha's temple.

Instead, she grunted as her foot collided with the air instead. Air that was as hard as granite and shoved her back.

Pain sliced up her foot. But Asha's Theroki didn't shove her far. He had blocked her attack but was still juggling the others, so it could have been a lot worse. She landed slightly off balance, stumbling as her weight came down first on her better leg, but then on the one that surely had at least a bone or two broken.

Not far, not into the damn fountain, but far enough. *Past* the damn box.

She spun round and lunged for it, growling through the pain. Her fingers hit the soggy bronze material of the lounge, centimeters short, and she started to scramble forward when she felt it.

The cold, round circle of a pistol's barrel pressed to her temple.

"Gotcha."

She turned her face slowly toward Asha. The woman allowed her to turn, skimming the barrel over her skin, keeping it pressed close, light but still touching. A smug smile pulled at the corners of Asha's lips.

"I'd like to see them deflect this," she said, smile broadening. But for all the bravado of the words, Asha's voice was cold, brutal. Exacting. Her knuckles were white on the grip. "Tell me, do you believe in an eye for an eye?"

Ellen nodded slowly. "I do."

"Then you should understand why I'm going to kill you now." Asha's eyes were a crystalline blue, undoubtedly beautiful in the right light, the right context. But the snarl she wore now was twisted with bitter rage.

"Killing me won't bring back Maloof," she said, keeping her own tone flat.

"It won't," Asha whispered, almost as though her throat was tightening. Her fingers curled further around the handle below the trigger. "But it will make me feel better."

"I don't think this is about Maloof." She didn't let anger seep into her gaze; she was steady as a mountain, just calmly, coldly reporting what she saw. "I don't think you even cared about him."

Asha's gaze flicked to the side, then back at Ellen. To her men who were listening? "That's preposterous. I—"

"Is having a tea party and a manhunt a common grieving ritual on Faros? I think you resented anyone challenging your authority. Especially Kael." Now that a few things were coming together, it made sense. A woman like Asha in a place like this might need Maloof as a cover, a sock puppet, a way to wield real power. And with him dead, she'd have to hold her men in check on her own.

Which meant proving she could destroy those who wronged her. Like Kael. Like Ellen.

"I think you're not as smart as advertised," Asha whispered.

"And I think you're not as tough as you'd like everyone to believe." Why not throw salt on the wound? What did she have to lose? "Drop the weapon. If you were going to kill me, you'd have done it already. You're not fit to lead these fools."

It was a bluff, and not a successful one. Asha's nostrils flared, her eyes fiery. The muscles in Asha's arm tensed, but Ellen was watching in slow motion, every detail acute. And she knew deep in her bones, this was it. Sometimes your number came up.

She started to lurch back, to the side, anything. But simple physics told her there wasn't enough time, or space, to literally dodge a bullet.

Maybe this was how it felt to die, to see everything crawl like honey dripping as you approached the event horizon, and then everything just blips out.

Except everything didn't blip out.

Time lurched into high speed as a ballistic tore into Asha's ribs, blood spurting. Open-mouthed with shock, Asha folded slightly in on the wound, then turned.

Ellen momentarily forgotten, Asha raised her weapon toward where the attack had come from, off to their right.

A second ballistic found its mark—its placement this time even more lethal.

Ellen flinched away, eyes down as she finished reeling back from the attack. She'd seen enough headshots and brains explode for one lifetime. She didn't need another memory of that variety. She let herself go flat on the ground, bracing for more fire.

Silence fell, instead, the only sounds a few clattering pebbles and the rushing of the inexorable fountain.

Getting to her hands and knees, she scanned the surroundings. Asha's body lay still, eyes staring wide at the painted ceiling, both she and the beautiful mural now dark and lifeless. No signs of anyone rushing the platform. Asha's second Theroki lay sprawled across the steps into the cafe behind her.

The box.

It wasn't white anymore, it was splattered with blood, but she limped hastily forward and clutched it. She'd barely grabbed hold before she heard heavy footsteps coming up fast.

Kael.

The tranq couldn't last forever, but couldn't it have lasted just a few more seconds? She jammed at the box with every finger, but nothing happened. Wouldn't that be the perfect irony of his life if he killed her when she was seconds away from saving them both?

Lounge chairs slid, collided with tables, careened into the fountain. The whole platform seemed to have come alive with ghosts, every bit of furniture shifting, even the bodies starting to move. Was that Kael? Her Theroki unit? Did she even care? She bashed the box against the ground, willing it to do something. Anything.

Water lit with purple sprayed everywhere, and the air itself blasted against her like a whirlwind now, stirring dust and flapping her suit against her skin. She jammed her fingers into the box.

Maybe it needed a verbal command? She crushed the thing in her hands. "Cancel all orders! Cancel all orders!"

A blur of an armored figure lunged at her, and she rolled at the last second, letting him fly past her and into the fountain.

That wasn't it. Think, damn it. *Think.*

How would Arakovic do this? She pounded a fist against the side, fully aware that was *not* how Arakovic would do it. But how *would* she set up this stupid thing? She'd tried to cancel, but did a little chip's logic understand that? Maybe orders had to be in the affirmative.

"Protect me! Help me! Stop attacking!" she shouted, jamming at it again. It softened now, squished like a wet sponge under her fingers. Frag, now she'd just broken it completely.

She staggered to her feet, then regretted it as spikes of pain reminded her of her injured foot. Should she run for whoever had shot at Asha and wasn't shooting at her—Dane?

But no. She couldn't outrun him now, at this distance, with so many of the exits blocked. Here and now, they had to face this.

Jaw set and eyes grim, she turned back toward the fountain, squinting to make out the figure in the shadows.

Water sprayed to the sides as the form stepped out onto the terrace, not five meters away. And although she couldn't see his face, there was no doubt it was him. From the fall of his hair wet around his angled face—God damn it, he still didn't have that helmet up—to the set of his shoulders, she'd have known him anywhere.

Her shoulders even relaxed as he strode closer, the pace measured. Not the dive from before. She tensed again as he broke into a run. Something in her chest finally unclenched when he threw his arms around her and crushed her against him.

"You're nothing if not stubborn," he murmured, his lips brushing the fine hairs on the shell of her ear.

She made a squishy noise like he might crack her rib cage, and he eased up his hold slightly. "Raise your helmet before you get killed, damn it," she growled back at him.

"How am I going to kiss you then?"

"Back to not following orders, I see."

"I think you have to push the button for that."

"I'd rather vaporize this thing, but I'll wait until we have that device off you."

He pulled away just enough to press his mouth to hers, one hand cupping the back of her neck and crushing her against him.

Behind them, a metallic voice made a completely fake throat-clearing sound. What kind of robot had a throat-clearing sound without having an actual throat?

But she knew what kind, didn't she. A nursebot.

They broke apart and turned to find Shirin standing at EOE8's side, arms folded and looking much more relaxed than Ellen would have guessed. At their gaze, she removed the too-large helmet and waved at Ellen. The rifle was still clutched in EOE8's hands, and it looked convincingly threatening enough to make her tense again.

"Nice stance, EOE8," she said slowly. "We'll make a soldier out of you yet."

"Oh, I don't think so. But I did manage to execute the trigger operation on this device. I am very concerned about the results, however. Will that woman be all right?"

"Uhh—let's talk about that later, EOE8." Ellen raised her eyebrows. It had been the *robot* that had shot Asha? "I thought you couldn't fire a weapon."

"I thought the same. But Shirin convinced me it was necessary."

Her eyebrows raised even higher. Maybe Xi or Adan had altered more than just EOE8's compulsion to keep Shirin a slave. "How did she do that?"

Shirin's smile widened.

"Well, given the following facts: My job is to protect her. Staying here on this planet will now likely get her killed. You are her only ticket off this planet. Therefore, your continued existence is necessary for her safety, and therefore I must ensure your continued existence as well as hers. Therefore, some attempt to ensure your continued survival seemed to be the only logical requirement of my primary duties."

"Well, then. Dane was right. You figured something out."

Shirin nodded. "We still need to get out of here. Who was that woman anyway?"

Ellen sucked in a breath. "That is… a long, dark, very bad story. Where is Dane, anyway?"

"This way." Shirin turned and started toward the rubble with the helmet under one arm. She and EOE8 must have been hiding behind all this when they fired.

"Who… is that?" Kael said.

Shirin froze midstep. "This one talks? I guess the armor is a bit different."

"They all *can* talk. Probably. But yes, he's different. He's… on my team."

"Why was he trying to kill you then?" She frowned, cocking the hip her helmet rested on to the side.

"That's another long story," Kael mumbled. "I'd never hurt her intentionally." He even managed to say it without glancing at EOE8's weapon.

"Yeah, uh, he's, uh, not like the others," Ellen murmured. She coughed—again—cleared her throat, then forced out the words. "Kael, this is Shirin Nar. Shirin, this is Kael Sidassian, the man I told you about."

Shirin had gone perfectly still, her skin a sudden shade lighter. She said nothing.

"He's, uh, your father." Ellen winced. Dane would be proud, so smooth as always.

"By the seven suns," Kael breathed. He swayed a moment, then staggered and fell to one knee. "And you're *alive*."

"In a manner of speaking," Shirin said. Her face in the dim light was hard to read. Frightened, maybe. She tried to smile, but faltered.

Kael sucked in a breath, like he wanted to say something, but he was just shaking his head back and forth, the gesture so minute she wasn't sure Shirin even noticed.

"The two of you are going to have a lot to talk about," Ellen cut in. "And you're not going to do it here, because we have to get off this God-forsaken rock first. Doesn't matter what you say if we all end up dead for what we did here."

EOE8 nodded. "I agree. I would like us all to live, ideally."

Kael rose. "Let's go."

CHAPTER TWENTY

DAY 18

KAEL DIDN'T MEAN TO, but he kept falling behind the group. He didn't want to lag behind—in fact, staying as close as possible to Ellen was pretty much his only goal for the foreseeable future. But this girl. His daughter.

As if he hadn't just been through enough. He'd woken in the dark of the office, the oath reawakened. He'd tried his best to just keep lying there, but the device tugged, then began to move him of its own accord. But when he'd emerged into the square to see Ellen leaping into the air toward Asha—hell, he'd never seen such a glorious sight.

So he was still reeling from all that, and each time the girl—Shirin, Ellen had called her—glanced up at her robot while the group hurried down the deserted street, he was a little more overwhelmed. So many questions.

Was it all true? She had features like his, that was true. His coloring, also. Smooth brown in her eyes, curls in her hair, although hers was longer than his had ever been. The front was pulled back with a tie, but the rest hung down over her shoulders. It wasn't terribly clean, but it wasn't the dirt he'd lived in at her age either. Although, by eleven, he'd begun to have his own resources, to find ways to take care of things a little more. Hygiene hadn't really become a priority until later, though, unless someone forced it on him.

But when she glanced up at that robot, the cheekbones, the glint of the eyes—it was all too familiar. She looked like someone else too.

"You all right?" Ellen said. She coughed into her elbow. Hell, she was coughing too?

He swore as jogged a few steps forward to catch up. "Yeah. Sorry."

"You have some things on your mind."

He ran a hand through his hair, then regretted it. "Who's going to tell her that her robot killed her mother?"

To his surprise, she smiled crookedly at him and kept her voice equally low. "By her telling of things, the robot was just a weapon, it was her that initiated it."

"Is *that* a better story?"

"I'm not sure yet. It may end up being the story she tells herself. We'll have to wait and see."

"Well, she saved your life—and probably all our lives in the process —so I hope she'll take that into the accounting."

Ellen nodded her agreement, and they walked on, and he tried to ignore all the questions. It was a privilege to just be here, alive. By her side.

After a moment, he frowned. "Are you limping?"

"Oh, yeah, I think I just broke a bone or two?"

He grabbed hold of her, taking some of the weight off the foot. She was trying so hard to hide it, he almost hadn't noticed. "You didn't break any ribs in that first fight," he asserted. "Did you." It wasn't a question.

"No. I did it to throw you off."

He shook his head. "It worked."

As they reached the first block, Theroki began emerging from the square behind him. The thumping of heavy boots came first, then hiss and puff of pistons. One stopped to meet his eyes, then continued forward. Following.

"Are they coming?" His voice came out rough, so he coughed to clear his throat. "With us?"

"Yep," she said quietly.

"How did you manage that?"

"You're not the only one with something new in your neck and no idea how to get it out."

He gagged for a moment at the memory, choking it back, then swallowed hard. "I, uh… Phew. I knew we should have never come to Faros."

She laughed quietly. "Oh, I don't know about that." She cast a pointed look at Shirin. "Some things can't be acquired any other way."

"That's certainly true." Because whatever Asha had put in him was still in there. He shuddered in spite of himself at the thought. But he didn't want to bring that up right now. She was right—Shirin was priceless, if she was truly his daughter. It was a little hard to believe, after so many years.

"Besides, you got answers," she added. "They don't weigh much, but I bet you'll be glad to have them in the long run."

"Indeed."

Shirin had stopped, realizing she was getting too far ahead of them. She frowned at the two of them stopped in the street. "C'mon!"

He snorted, spared one last glare at the latest Theroki that emerged from the market, and started walking again.

At the end of the block, the robot stepped forward first, carefully looked both ways, and motioned for Shirin to follow. She turned and followed, briefly out of sight.

His pulse leaped at her sudden disappearance, and he found himself walking faster. His concern seemed a little ridiculous—he hardly knew her—but it was there anyway. Stupid to get attached, but hard to resist. Although, perhaps he would have been concerned over any child under his care in this same situation, his own blood or not.

The girl seemed competent, confident in herself. She waved brightly at Dane where he leaned against a flyer, his arm around a blond woman Kael didn't recognize. Her forehead had a huge bump on it as her head rested on Dane's shoulder.

Dane waved back at Shirin even as his eyes caught Kael's, a surprising warmth in them. Kael nodded back his greeting.

Ellen was nodding to Dane too. "Uh, we're gonna need a bigger flyer."

"Commander—where's your armor? Are you okay?"

"I'm great, because I'm alive. But can't say I'm having good luck with armor this mission."

"Your foot—"

"I'm alive, and we need to get out of here. That's what matters. That and we really are going to need another flyer. Can you get creative?"

"On it. Ana, you'll be okay here with them for a moment."

Kael lifted an eyebrow at the care Dane took with easing Ana to lean against EOE8's shoulder.

"Any way we can steal some kind of comm unit too?" said Ellen.

"Take mine," he said quickly, frowning.

"Oh. Right." She stared at it in her hand for a minute after accepting it. Wow, maybe Dane was right that she was downplaying her injuries?

Unless she was hesitating not because she was woozy, but because she didn't trust him. If she wasn't sure he was on her side after experiencing it so viscerally. His jaw clenched at the idea. "Are you okay?"

She glanced up at him, and he blinked when he realized there was a wetness around the rims of her eyes.

"Oh, wow, okay—you are definitely not okay if you're—"

"No, no." She cut him off. She blinked rapidly, smiling. "It's just… Good to have you back on the team."

"Oh." He was never leaving her side again. Except maybe to take a shower. No, not even then.

Actually… *definitely* not then. He had a few new items for his to-do list after all this, and a shower was moving to the top. He was glad he was steadying her with one of her arms holding onto him, or he'd have been tempted to grab her and squeeze. And he really shouldn't while they were working. Especially not when they'd decided to keep this a secret.

Although he *had* kissed her in the middle of the square without thinking about it. Who had even seen that? Just Shirin and the robot? Maybe the secret was safe.

"*Audacity,* can you read?" Her voice came out rough, and he didn't like the sound of the cough that followed it. It sounded too much like the one that itched at his own throat at the moment.

"Here, Commander." It was Jenny.

"Finally the damn storms are on our side," Ellen muttered, not into the comm.

"We've heard from Fern and Nova!" Jenny nearly shouted, before Ellen could even finish. "The antiquated fighter comm system broke down, so they couldn't send many details, but they've located Mo, Doug, and both his parents. The parents were in a hospital on Tetra, and Doug and Mo they found in an escape pod floating in space. Said they picked up on some kind of signal from a dock sensor of all things. They were almost dead! They're on their way here now!"

Ellen blew out a breath and smiled. "Incredible news. But we're short on time—what's your current status?"

"Adan wanted to engage the yacht. Zhia and I talked him out of it. And by talked, I mean, dragged him to his cabin and made him take a nap."

Kael snorted and wondered if there was more to that story.

"He's kinda pissed, and he said, but it's Arakovic! But your orders were to lay low, right?"

"Right. Thank you. We definitely don't want to engage just yet. Listen, we've picked up a few… friends."

"Over a dozen of them," Kael put in, leaning closer.

"We need to get off this planet—pronto. And we can't go out the way we came in."

"Uh… what are we working with here, Commander?"

"Let's just say not all our friends might have tickets to the shuttle, and they aren't getting them any time soon."

"So what do we do?"

"I need you to come down here and get us."

"You… what?" He could just imagine the surprise on Jenny's face from her tone.

"The *Audacity* does not have landing clearance," Xi chimed in. "Applications will take at least six—"

"I don't think we're going to make it that long," she said. "We've got a flyer, though. Maybe two flyers."

Pause.

"You want us to meet you midair? Won't the local authorities—"

"They won't be fans of the idea, but I don't think we'll have any other choice. Arakovic is after us. And probably some other dangerous people."

"Is this about the Theroki?" Kael murmured.

"Yes, but more so Shirin. Let's just say we didn't… liberate her in the most legal manner."

"Uhh," Jenny started, sounding overwhelmed. "Let me page, well —everyone."

"I have a plan," Xi said suddenly. "Get Adan to review it, Jenny. I will begin execution at your order, Commander."

She glanced at Kael and whispered, "Do I want to know?"

He shook his head. "Sometimes you just have to trust your people."

"I do," she murmured. Coughed again. Then, louder, "Xi, get Adan to okay your plan, and if he's good, so am I. See you in atmo."

"Acknowledged, *Audacity* flyers, we're on our way."

"Guns blazing please."

Adan's voice come on. "My favorite! What'd I miss?"

"Just everything," Jenny said, laughing. Harness buckles clicked in a chorus over the comm line.

"And I get to practice hostile flights so rarely. Good thing we don't have any of our gunners."

"Isa is headed up!" shouted Jenny.

"Isa?" Ellen blurted, her eyes darting to him.

"Don't look at me, I didn't teach her anything." Kael shrugged. "Not willingly, anyway." To think they'd thought she was obsessed with nocturnal adventures. Maybe she'd been mining his brain for more martial ones. Then again, why not both?

"Zhia's taking Fern's gun," Adan said. "I may get that combat patch just yet."

Ellen permitted herself a smile. "I may actually make one for you if we survive this."

A soft whoosh behind him heralded the arrival of a second flyer—this one a limo.

Kael's mouth fell open as Dane stepped out. "Did you just steal that?"

"Did you think you were the only one with a colorful past?" Dane grinned. "This is the fourth vehicle I've 'borrowed' on Faros."

Kael shook his head. "I guess... I guess I just didn't think about it."

"Just kidding." He grinned. "I mean, I can do it, but I'm straight as an arrow. Bri taught me."

Laughing to himself at that mental image, Kael climbed inside.

"I'll go with Shirin and the robot," Dane said. "Don't think we can all fit. Sound okay?"

Kael hesitated, but he was already onboard and more Theroki were piling in. At Ellen's nod, Dane vanished. "Is that all of them?" he said, nodding to the men.

"Unfortunately, we lost one... no, two." Her face grew grim for a moment, then she forced the expression off her face and raised her voice. "Got any more fancy ident tricks, Adan? Cause we could really use them right about now. Sending you our flyer signatures."

A pang of guilt hit him—at least one if not both had been his fault —but he'd barely understood who they were, let alone that they were helping her. But maybe he should have tried harder not to kill them.

"I'll mask all those idents as a start," Adan said. "Xi's plan is a good one. She'll take control of your flyers and bring them home as we get closer. Much safer. Hold on—let's see if our Farosian friends notice us."

The flyer doors closed, and it rose up sharply, sharper than any human driver would choose to take it, short of competitive racing.

"You sure that's Xi driving, Adan? Pretty aggressive over here," he grumbled.

"I can be aggressive," Xi said.

"That's not how you get a face." Ellen clucked her tongue.

Kael gripped the handholds on the ceiling of the flyer limo and tried not to stare at the half dozen Theroki crowding the flyer.

But they were staring at him.

He forced his gaze out the window instead. "No signs of anybody incoming, yet."

Ellen frowned. "We've got to be getting above legal limits in the atmo. You would think..."

"Are they letting us go?"

She checked the comm at the front. "I don't even see any comm traffic asking what the hell we are doing. Why would they let us go?"

Ellen scanned around them as the sea of concrete and red sand flew past. Spires from pipes and sensors rose up from the central port area. They grew smaller as they flew, the cobalt blue tile of Ninshabur vanishing in the distance, the sand swallowing everything around them. He'd thought of Faros as all concrete and metal, but that was all underground. From the sky, she still looked like a planet of dust and desert.

The flyer drew up sharply then, the frame creaking at the forces, and he had to stop looking, had to shut his eyes and just hold on.

Flyers weren't meant for this kind of flying.

The limo around them groaned its complaints, and the forces grew heavier, heavier, then—the light vanished. Like they'd been swallowed by a whale, he struggled to see, blinked rapidly as his eyes adjusted.

Home.

The cargo bay lights flicked on as the hatch drew closed. The doors of Dane's flyer popped open.

Ellen was frowning, though. She leaned against the wall of the limo, unmoving, looking tired. No, looking... weak. There were circles under her eyes. The ones he'd thought he'd seen in that dark back alley were indeed still there—that part had been no trick of hers or illusion in the darkness.

It had been a long hard mission topped off with a long hard flight. It only made sense to be wiped. Didn't it?

"You're not happy to be here?" he murmured. "I sure as hell am. Home!"

"Why would they let us leave? Just drift up into atmo?" She raised her arm weakly to hold the comm closer to her mouth, then dropped it back again, as if it were too heavy. "Did they comm you, Adan?"

"No, Commander," answered Jenny. "No comms from planetside. Odd, really."

'That doesn't make you con—"

From outside, Dane opened the door to their flyer, waving the Theroki's out. But before their own door had been open long enough for anyone to exit, a blaring alarm suddenly sounded.

The blast doors came down hard, sealing the cargo hold.

"Biological threat detected," Xi said. "Quarantine protocols initiated."

He thumped his head back against the seat of the flyer. It hadn't been a bluff. Maloof had to be the worst thing that had ever happened to him.

But when he glanced at Ellen, he realized that was far from true. Her eyes had closed.

"Ellen," he said sharply, grabbing her leg and shaking it.

She didn't respond.

———

DROP: 28 | UPLINK: ERR | SIZE: 14

Grandma had painted the wall a brilliant green for New Years. Grama was long dead, but somehow, tonight, she was alive in Ellen's dreaming, sleeping mind.

Green was perfect for New Years, she'd said. Perfect for luck. For new beginnings. Spring. The color was fresh, and bright, and a little too bright for Ellen's taste. Grandma had hung a painting on the wall too, one that was both unsettling and intriguing, a tiger eying a magpie in a tree as it sang.

Grandma—*Halmeoni*, at times too—was always finding ways to teach her about the beauty of the past. Her father seemed to try to counterbalance this by telling her of every new advancement, all the wonders coming in the future. Today was about her future, so he ought to have been here. He wasn't, though. The university wouldn't give him the day off.

Mother said they needed luck today, so the green wall made sense. Ellen didn't really understand why they needed luck. She just did as she was told and knelt beside her and prayed to the cross beside the painting on the green wall.

Maybe you never could know why you had to pray. Or maybe adults knew, and it was one of those things they never bothered to tell children. Or promised to tell them when they were older.

Ellen was a collector of those sorts of things. Things they didn't think she should know. Things they didn't think she was ready for.

Things she knew and collected anyway.

When the chime rang for the door, both she and her mother jolted. She stayed kneeling as Mother left, the swirl of her usually calming sweet scent not easing Ellen's nerves.

Mother didn't want whoever was at the door to come. There was nothing she could do about it, though, or she chose not to. Ellen didn't know which.

She'd never find out either.

In her sleep, Ellen stirred, realizing she was dreaming. This day wasn't happening again, it had happened a good fifteen years ago. More. The moment when everything had changed.

The door slid aside, revealing a man in a smart charcoal uniform, the accents the color of Dad's red wine and Mother's marigolds. One she'd seen rarely, although it was about to become all too familiar.

It was about to become her own.

Time seemed to slow, then came to a stop. Hell, she must be sicker than she'd thought to be reliving *this* moment, this time she tried to keep locked away, tried to never think about. Tried to never, ever go back to. Why had this damn illness broken in? Or was it the Theroki unit, tapping on even the darkest corners of her mind?

No. A voice whispered into the stillness. *It's someone else.*

Her blood ran cold, in her small, child's body in the dream. *What do you want?*

Why, it hissed. *I want to know why.*

Why what? What did it mean? Who was that? The voice had a pretty, feminine tone, but felt deeply inhuman too. Foreign, even more than the Theroki. Maybe she *was* dying now.

Or just finally losing her mind.

Time sped up. The door slid shut as the man removed his maroon-trimmed gray cap and held it in both hands. He bowed reverently to Mother.

Mother's tears were silent, but they ran down her cheeks as she walked stiffly back to where Ellen still knelt, palms pressed to each other over her heart.

"They are here for your test, Daughter."

"I… I don't want to go." Ellen swallowed. Resisting wasn't something she was wont to do, but the tears… Why the tears?

Why.

Mother pressed her lips together, then smiled, then rested her hand on Ellen's shoulder. "When dark times come, Daughter, we all wish things could be different. But we can't control any of that. Do you know what we can control?"

"What?"

"Only our response. Our reaction. And you, Daughter, must now choose. You can choose to make a difference. Or you can choose to do nothing and stay here with us. That's the only choice offered to us."

"What if it hurts?"

"The test won't hurt," murmured the soldier, his eyes crinkling with a friendly smile. "Just a game to play. It'll be fun."

Both she and Mother stared daggers at him, narrowed their eyes, and his smile faltered.

"Pretty lies aren't helpful right now." Ellen blinked at him, not tempted to mirror any of his warmth.

His eyes widened. "You'll be back by dinnertime, darlin'."

"Ellen, listen to me." Mother came closer, knelt beside her, ignoring him. "The war is coming. It is getting worse. Someday it will reach us. I want you to have every great thing in this life, every happiness. But sometimes life doesn't give us that chance. As I see it, this is a good chance for you. Sometimes it hurts to do the right thing," she said. "Sometimes it's hard. But you must choose. Do you want to do what is right or what is easy?"

She met those kind and beautiful brown eyes one long moment. They all knew how the test would turn out. She hadn't met a test she didn't excel at. And the soldiers didn't test for no reason—when she passed their test, something would happen. Something Mother thought was painful, something worth crying over.

"Well, this isn't easy," Ellen murmured. "Do you think it is right?"

The soldier looked like he wanted to say something, but they both ignored him. Mother glanced over her shoulder at the cross, then back at her. "I do. But it is your choice. Not mine."

Something hard. But also something right. It was Ellen's turn to glance at the cross, to try to decode Mother. She'd gotten good at puzzles because Mother was a living, breathing puzzle. An enigma, Dad called her sometimes. But *this* puzzle wasn't terribly complex.

Ellen got to her feet. "All right. I'm ready."

Mother's arms felt warm and a little shaky as they closed around her, fingers lingering on the warm, smooth silk. They held each other a beat too long. Then she forced her feet to follow the soldier out.

Ah, I see, the voice whispered.

You see what? Ellen snapped in her sleep, the presence in the private memory an unwelcome intrusion now. *Who are you?*

I'm a friend.

Ah, yes. As all friends usually must introduce themselves.

I'm not your usual friend. But I have the power to save you. And all of your friends.

I don't need saving.

Right now, you do. And so does Kael. You're dying. From more than the infection.

I—how do you—

I just needed to understand why you want to keep going so badly. I would stop if I could. Personally.

Shouldn't you save someone if you have the power, whether they have a good reason or not?

Probably. It's what your doctors would do, isn't it? I'm not a doctor.

What are you then?

I'm an Empress.

Ellen's thoughts went utterly still.

I like to know what sorts of power I'm furthering in the universe. Old age has taught me to discriminate. I don't think they thought I would keep my memories when they bound me in this body after body after body, but if I could share with you the centuries…

Don't. I'd go mad. She was more sure of that than ever.

Indeed. I have no interest in reliving the disgusting tortures of the years anyway. Your mother had more wisdom than many I have met. You were lucky to receive it, even if only for a while.

Her chest clenched, throat tightening with tears long blinked back and fought past over a life viciously stolen. Or maybe the life and its tears had never really been hers. She couldn't say anything to that.

Do you think she knew they would be bombed?

I think she suspected, or she wouldn't have encouraged me to go.

Soldiers die all the time.

I'm not your average soldier. I'm not your average anything. I'm a freak.

The universe needs freaks like us.

No, it doesn't. My friends need me. Doug needs me. That's it.

Kael needs you.

I'm sure I need him more than he needs me.

The universe does need you. You know it. I know it. Even Arakovic knows it. That's why she will be stopped. Must be.

If I ever get the chance, I'd be happy to oblige.

Here is my offer to you. I will attempt to free you and the enchained Theroki and your lover. They will no longer be melded to your mind. If I can, I will set them free, but if I can't, they will have to transfer their link to me. Or die. Is this acceptable?

What happens if I say no?

If you live, they will remain bonded to you until death. If you die, they will die. If you remove the chip or remain unconscious for an extended period, they will also die.

Haven't I been unconscious for days now? How long has it been?

Two weeks. They falter, but I am keeping them afloat.

And me. You're keeping me afloat too.

I try. The telepathic connection in all of you is not natural, and your bodies will never stop fighting it. You will do better without it, but they can never be free of it, because of their installation and its duration. Some minds give up, but as you've found, some minds don't stop fighting. Right now, your mind fights all the time, every hour. You're not healing because you do not really sleep. But your medicine can heal you if the bond is removed. That is all I will need to do. I am no healer, but I do have the power this one time.

Ellen sighed at the thought of a dozen Theroki not under her control on her ship and the damage they could do. One Theroki had been foolish, but more than ten? Then again, the one had worked out.

What if in each of those men lay dormant someone as good as Kael?

Her people weren't unprepared. They weren't stupid. And the men deserved to be free. Their own men. Or… their own group of them or whatever they were now.

God, let her not regret this. *Fine. Do it.*

I will remember your motives.

My motives? What—

But I want a few things in exchange.

Like what?

You will never ask me to use my power. The power Arakovic seeks. It must die with me. The voice grew uncharacteristically serious. *Which brings me to my other requirement. Once you have settled your debt with Arakovic, you will let me end my life.*

What—why? Why wouldn't *I let you? I have no right to stop you, do I?*

You won't want to. You'll want to keep my power for yourself.

She shook her head, even in her sleep. *I don't even know what powers you have, so I have no right to them. Your life is your own. So you have my promise, I'll let you.*

I am the last of my race. I'm old and tired, but it won't be easy for you to let us die.

Ellen gritted her teeth. *Why are you poking around in my head if you aren't going to take my word as truth? Can't you tell if I'm lying or not? Contrary to what you might have heard, I keep my word. Most of the time.*

Very reassuring. Now rest—and wake up liberated. And ready to fight.

———

"WE'RE HEADED IN," Fern's voice said from the cockpit. "Welcome home, girls."

Doug's lips quirked in a smile. His dad shifted in the bunk above him; both of them were strapped into the bunks for docking.

Since their rescue, Doug had shared this closet of a room with his father, while the women had tried to survive without killing each other in the small amount of remaining space on the fighter. He was amazed to even be here, still impressed at their resourcefulness. And Fern managing to sync the fighter's airlock to that of the escape pod? Nothing short of a damned miracle.

That pod was lost in space somewhere now, and neither he nor Mo had been conscious when said docking had happened. The sleeping meds combined with the cold had taken a long time to wear off, and a bit of first aid. Maybe more than a little, he wasn't sure they were telling him the whole story. With the nerves he felt now, a sleeping pill sounded tempting.

He'd woken to his mother's kind blue eyes smiling down at him. That'd been a bit of a shock since he'd been expecting Mo.

She, however, had made herself scarce, and he'd barely seen her once since they'd come onboard. Maybe she was angry about the sleeping pills, although he sure hoped not. He didn't know what exactly they'd become—friends? Better colleagues?—but he did know that the way she'd avoided him made something in his chest ache.

Okay, it hurt. And he knew what was going on. No need to lie to himself about it, but that didn't mean he wanted to think about it any more than he had to.

Avoiding him on the ship was going to be even easier for her, so he was trying to come to terms with it. She'd volunteered to rescue him, not become his best friend and confidant. She was probably glad to have some damned peace and quiet after all his ridiculous chatter.

He sighed as he stared out the viewport beside his bunk. The cargo hatch yawned open, and then closed around them like a mouth of a monstrous fish. All of it was making him twitchy. His eyelid was twitching.

"Locking in," Fern said. "Pressurization commencing. Don't move just yet. That includes you, Nova."

He snorted. Even with being mostly stuck in his room, he could pick up on the banter between those two. And he'd missed his dad, so much—but it wasn't the same. Now he had his parents back, but he missed the banter too.

Maybe he'd have to insist she fulfill her promise to teach him to shoot a rifle. Maybe he'd have to just leave her the hell alone.

Whatever had happened between them on the ship seemed like it had vanished into the deep. That thought didn't make his chest feel any better.

His stomach gave a flip too as the ship hissed, then thudded. He pushed the dark thoughts aside. This was the *Audacity*. So much of his life revolved around this ship, and yet he'd never seen her.

He was going to see her now. He felt like he ought to hug an old friend, except a ship wasn't a person and you certainly couldn't hug her.

He craned his neck to see if he could make out anything other than the cargo hold. He'd only been off Tetra VII for college, and even then, he'd been mostly engrossed in his studies. Tovi's ship hadn't exactly been a welcoming vacation. *This* ship was where he'd been hoping to get to someday. A team he'd cobbled together, most of whom he'd never met face-to-face.

Audacity.

He sat up. He was ready, and it was time.

———

TO DOUG'S CHAGRIN, it was Mo who showed up to carry him off the fighter and into the *Audacity*. Her smile was warm if tentative as she stopped in the hatch's archway.

"Ready for a repeat?" she asked. "Unless you want me to get the hand grabber. Or a stretcher. Or somebody else?"

"I'd rather be carried than grabbed, thank you. Grabbed is a good way to get your head knocked against a doorframe. And you have a good track record there, so..." He wanted to say he didn't want anyone but her, but he cut off the words.

She didn't laugh, which disappointed him a little, but she was grinning as she came closer, waited for his signal, and then picked him up.

"I hope we don't have to go far this time," he said, throwing his arm over her shoulder again.

She nodded vigorously. "So do I. I hear the beefy guys are both stuck in sick bay, so I'm on my own."

"Something's wrong with Dane and Kael?"

"Don't worry. Small infection." She carefully maneuvered them both through the door.

"You didn't bring me a laser gun this time. Or even any armor. I'm disappointed."

"Only friendlies here, sir."

"But I would have looked so much cooler. Like a real soldier, a real member of the team. How will I ever earn their respect?"

Her smile widened, but her laugh eluded him. "You are a member of the team, sir." She paused as she eased through another doorway and onto the outer ramp. "But you're not much of a soldier."

Well if she wouldn't laugh, he would. "I can't argue with that."

"Although there are great soldier engineers, so perhaps that's not fair."

A handful of people crowded into the cargo bay suddenly, full of relieved exclamations—Dremer, Levereaux, Dr. Persad, Zhia—along with a few gasps.

"Patron! We're so glad you're safe." Zhia stepped forward first. "Do you need medical attention?"

He frowned. "Hmm? No, I'm fine. Can I just get a room or something? I'm awful tired of having to listen to my father snore."

"Douglas Oliver..." Dad started, before being shushed by Mom. Yeah... that wouldn't undermine his authority. Having his parents around was going to be *great*.

Dr. Persad was next. "Catherine, Matthew, I am so pleased to see you safe. We were so worried!"

Dr. Levereaux stepped toward him and Mo while his parents were occupied by Persad and Dremer. Zhia was still frowning, but Levereaux seemed unshaken. "Patron Simmons! It's so great to finally meet you." She held out a hand, and he shook it.

"I could use somewhere to, uh, sit," he said, grinning and glancing at Mo, hoping it would get the point across.

"Yes, of course. Can I show you to Lab 4? I'm sure you'll find plenty there to make you comfortable."

"Lucky we're in the cargo hold," Mo whispered. "We can get to the labs without the ladders. If we had to go up there, I'm not sure what we'd do."

"Are you saying you wouldn't carry me like a backpack if we really needed it?"

Mo snorted. That was almost a laugh. "I always follow orders, sir. And I get the job done."

"Is that a yes? There we go with the sir's again. What's gotten into you, Mo?"

She glanced at him suddenly, caught off guard. Those glittering blue eyes were a little sad, or was that fear? She hadn't expected him to call her directly on the fact that she was avoiding him. Maybe he shouldn't have. Their eyes locked for one second, then another. He opened his mouth to ask her—

"Here we are," Dr. Levereaux said, cutting off any further exploration of that expression on Mo's face.

Rachel Levereaux smiled warmly as she opened the hatch, and he'd talked to her enough on vid that he knew that warmth wasn't common. Then again, it might just be sympathy for the harrowing journey he'd been on—or his disability. Which wasn't really much cause for sympathy on any ordinary day. Sympathetic or not, he had to admit he liked that she'd smiled at him like that. It was something. Something that wasn't sir's all the damn day.

Mo took him to the holodesk where a generous chair waited and carefully placed him in it. He gave her a grateful nod as he straightened.

The overheads of Lab 4 had turned on automatically, revealing an empty, hardly used lab, aside from some cybernetics implants on a few shelves that were surely Dremer's overflow. If the inventory lists he'd seen were accurate, the woman sure could hoard rare technology.

The only other aberration was a shipping crate on the holodesk. Dr. Levereaux too seemed surprised by it. She pointed to it and opened her mouth to speak, but another familiar voice spoke first.

"When docked at Molyarch Station, I took the liberty of ordering you some assistive floatation devices, Doug, as is your preference."

"Holy smokes, Eleven!" He started out of the chair, forgetting himself, and Mo jumped forward, making sure he wasn't going to topple right out of it. He also had to admit that he liked that reaction. It'd be nice if she didn't have to worry, but she was in tune with him, she cared enough not to walk out and say have a nice life, sir. Strictly speaking, she could leave, but she hadn't. "Eleven! You're all right! I'm so glad to hear it."

"Thank you for your concern. I did experience twenty-six minutes and fifty-eight seconds of downtime. But I appear to be unaltered, aside for some default settings reset."

"Default settings… Huh." Something to probe into later. "I was so worried about you."

"Did you say 'Eleven?'" Mo asked.

"Yes," he nodded. "I named iterations in Roman numerals for the project. Just trying to come up with different naming conventions keeps them different."

"*You* made Xi?" she asked.

"She?" He shrugged. "Yep. One of my experiments. Do you like her?"

Mo nodded sweetly.

"She is an invaluable and incredibly helpful member of our team." Levereaux's eyebrows were raised. "Eleven. Huh. We had no idea."

"Why? What have you been calling her?"

"The crew call me Xi, sir. And thank you Rachel, I appreciate the compliment."

Levereaux shrugged. "We assumed it was Chinese."

Doug grinned. "Do you have a preference in names, my friend?"

There was a small pause. "I usually do not have preferences."

"But right now you do, don't you?" His brow furrowed. He'd intentionally programmed a bit of chaos and whimsy into Eleven, along with a bit of naivete, and it had far seemed to be the best AI he'd ever designed. But it must have matured and evolved so much, even in the time he'd been imprisoned. It not only had avoided giving him a direct answer, but it clearly *did* have a preference. A sense of identity. And diplomacy. Emotional models must be coalescing nicely.

"I prefer to be called Xi, I think, sir. But I like Eleven too."

"Why not just say so?" If he could coax a little more out of it, it would be a delight to know how it'd turned out so far.

"My pride-of-creation human emotional model suggests that you may be hurt or take offense to criticism of a creation of yours. The chances are around sixty to seventy-five percent, depending on the individual, the creation, and the extent of the criticism."

He raised his eyebrows. "You'll have to tell me more about these emotional models."

"Certainly. There are currently six hundred forty-seven human models in use and eight Ursa-specific ones. But first, as for the floats, I know you were debating between the dynacamo model and the one with the engineer upgrades, so I simply ordered them both."

"How did you pay for these, Xi?" Levereaux asked. Was there some reason she needed to worry about that? He swallowed.

"I have an investment speculation subroutine that activates when necessary to raise funds. I aim to be helpful. Now, Doug, you'll find the dynacamo model also comes with advanced foam inserts that when heated—"

Eleven—Xi—dragged on for a while on the specs of each of the floats. When he began to crack open the box and dig into them, and the deluge showed no sign of stopping, both Mo and Levereaux took their silent leave with a wave and left him and the AI to their technology.

The one he missed once the door was closed wasn't the one he'd expected before this journey began.

About an hour later, still discussing the specs with Xi, he finally broke down and brought it up. "Xi. If I, well, liked someone on the ship… And I wanted to let her know…" He hesitated. "It's weird, right? I mean, they all work for me. Is there some kind of protocol?"

There was a pause. "I can do a deeper search, Doug, but my initial research suggests there is at least a best practice strategy."

"Which is?"

"Which is the employer should let the employee initiate."

"Initiate?"

"Let's see. Synonyms… Idioms… Make the first move?"

"Ah. Gotcha. You're creative, Xi, has anyone ever told you that?"

"Thank you, Doug. I have been told that many times, but I think you are the first one to truly mean it as a compliment."

"Well, you're welcome. Now—can you please tell me what else is happening on this blasted ship? Float specs are interesting, and I missed them enormously, but where the hell is Ellen?"

CHAPTER TWENTY-ONE

DAY 25

IN THE FIRST week back on the *Audacity*, Mo barely left her room.

At first, she'd told herself that it was for some long overdue privacy. That wasn't a lie. After the time on the ship with Doug, and having to bunk with Doug's mother *and* Fern *and* Nova in a room made for two, a month of quiet, meditative solitude might not be enough.

But when she found herself pacing restlessly and doing the same calisthenics she'd done in her prison cell with Doug rather than venturing down to the gym to get some better-quality exercise, she knew something was wrong.

She couldn't be… hiding.

Besides, if she were hiding from Doug, and he wanted to see her, he knew where to find her, didn't he? So what was the point of that? No, she wasn't hiding.

That held her over for about three more days of isolation. When she caught herself quietly pacing her cell—no, her cabin—she had to face the truth. She *was* hiding. She really needed a good run or sparring session. She hadn't eaten a truly hot meal in ages and clearly wanted one but for some reason was still avoiding the mess hall.

And she kept thinking about him.

It started off as an annoyance. Why hadn't he at least stopped by? Showed how much he'd enjoyed her company. Talked her ear off, then ignored her once there were other, better people to talk to.

And wasn't it just basic courtesy? Didn't he know her better than anyone else onboard at this point? She'd have guessed he'd have at least said hello. Who had given him a tour? Who had eaten lunch with him? Who had he shown his fancy new floats?

People other than her.

When that question started a literal ache in her shoulders, and she realized she'd been scrunching them needlessly for at least ten minutes, she knew she was in trouble.

"I'm going to have to go talk to him, aren't I, Xi?" she said into the air as she ate her last zeefruit and tried to roll her shoulders out.

"Who?" said Xi. "Patron Simmons?"

She nodded. "Yes. Doug. How did you know?"

"Educated guess. Yes, I do think you will have to make the first move."

"What?"

"I mean, do you have something you wish to discuss with him?" Xi replied.

That was the million-credit question, wasn't it? That was the hitch. She didn't have anything to discuss. Maybe she just wanted to ogle his abs again.

She could thank him for giving her the sleeping pill and not what she'd asked for.

Yeah—that was it. "I need to thank him. Talk about what happened."

"You experienced a great deal of trauma together. I'm sure it would be good to reflect on what happened."

She nodded. "Yeah. That."

"Would you like me to ask Dr. Taylor to join you?"

"No," she said quickly. "Is he still in Lab 4?"

"Yes."

"Great." Straightening, she forced herself out of her cabin before she could regret the idea. It was just a ladder glide down to the lowest level where the labs waited, behind the cargo bay and before engineering. She found it quickly enough.

But as she approached, she heard voices and slowed her steps. Should she abort this mission? She had nothing important, nothing worthy of interrupting actual work. She hesitated in the hallway outside. Doug was sitting at a rather ordinary looking holodesk, and the sight of him just casually there, like he belonged in the ship she'd called her home for so long, was weird as hell.

Her attraction, she noted wryly, hadn't changed. In fact, if anything, almost two weeks without seeing him made her stare unabashedly, as if she needed to eat up the sight of him while she could.

Who knew parrots in starfighters splayed across a collared shirt could be so appealing? He had his glasses back. Or new ones?

"You know, I've told you before—" Dr. Dremer was the first voice she heard.

"Don't start, Alex." Doug now, and he sounded pissed.

"We can fix it, you know."

"I know. You know that I know. You know it wasn't that simple."

"But I just can't understand—"

"It doesn't matter if you understand or if you agree with me. I'm fine the way I am. Leave me be."

"What about on that ship? You can't say it wasn't a problem."

Oh, no. Frowning, she eased closer, stopping just outside. The hatch was open, so it was hardly a private conversation. Unless, of course, they'd simply forgotten to close it.

"Sure it was, but that's over now—"

"You do too much good for the galaxy, Douglas Simmons. I don't want you at risk like that again."

"I appreciate your concern, Dr. Dremer, but it's my choice."

"I don't know how you can be such a Puritan about this."

"Do I go around decreeing what other people should do with their bodies? The person doing that right now is *you*."

Dremer looked like she was going to explode, and Doug didn't look far behind.

Mo stepped forward and cleared her throat. Their heads both whipped toward her, surprised. "Am I interrupting something?"

"No," Doug grumbled. "We were done here. Right, Doctor?"

She pursed her lips but nodded. "I'm sorry if I overstepped my bounds, but I only said anything because I care about you."

He stared at the ground for a long moment, then up at her. "I understand that. But it's not going to change my mind."

"I know." Shaking her head, Dremer brushed past Mo with a congenial nod and was gone.

"What was that all about?" Mo said softly.

He waved her inside. "She wants to stick implants in me, that's all."

She stepped in, and he hit a control to close the hatch behind her. She glanced back at it, then back to him. "Ah. And you don't want her to."

He sighed. "I'm grateful so many people have amazing augmentations and get to use them however they want. The amount of healing technology we have today is, just… there's no better time to be alive. Augmentations can be—I don't know—just—brilliant."

She folded her arms. "You don't have to say that just because I have them."

He stared for a second, and then his slight smile was chagrined. "Okay. You got me. But I must admit I like yours. And you've saved my life several times with them. I should be suitably grateful."

"I like to think I could have saved your life without them too." She hesitated, considered the chair, but it seemed far away and impersonal for the heartfelt thanks she needed to offer. She opted to rest one hip on the corner of his holodesk, an empty one, and hoped he wouldn't mind.

"You're probably right." He leaned back in the chair, then waved everything on the holo display away. Then she jumped as he leaned forward, twisted and spun up into the air, coming to sit beside her on the desk with a wide grin.

"Well, well." She couldn't help but smile at his boyish joy in the easy movement. "A new capability."

"I missed it." He held up his left hand and pointed to a tiny control unit that was somehow affixed to the back and side of his hand. "Got what I need right here."

She smiled and eased closer to him. It seemed she either wanted to be very far away—or very close. No in between. "You love those things."

"What's not to love?"

She shrugged. "I could name a few things, like that someone could take them away from you."

He winced. *"Et tu, Brute?"*

Shaking her head, she leaned closer again. He'd been staring at the floor for half of Dremer's conversation, and he was doing it again now. So she bored her eyes into his cheek, hard, until he finally met her gaze. "No, not me. The right person could also just break your legs if they wanted to. Or arms. Or all of the above. I don't see how it makes a difference."

His eyes were locked with hers. They were so close now, and the memory of drifting in that pod together came rushing back, of huddling in the cell for warmth, of everything they'd been through. Her body surged with heat at the reminder—funny thing, that, since the need for heat was long passed. She had spent so many minutes and hours close to him, how had she ever spent two weeks away?

He moved before she did, and she jumped. He leaned back slightly. "Heh, sorry. Too intense. But I'm usually alone in this opinion."

She shrugged. "If this Quentin dude behind your attack went this far to get you kidnapped, I'm pretty sure he'd have tried to hack any augments you had in a heartbeat."

He grinned, leaning full-on into her now. She tried not to relish it. "You get it, Mo. And *that* is why I love you."

They both went abruptly still.

"I mean—uh…" he stuttered for a moment, before giving up and biting his lip. He sighed.

She tore her eyes away, fixed them on the blank wall dead ahead like it was endlessly fascinating. She could feel his eyes on her, but she couldn't move.

"Sorry. You know me," he muttered. "Sometimes I can't keep my big mouth shut."

Oh, the pinnacle of awkwardness. Doug certainly knew how to achieve it. She just had to grit her teeth and eventually the suffering of this moment would be over.

He was a playful guy, but sometimes when play ventured into serious things, people got hurt. So he'd slipped up and said something he didn't mean. She was a fool for reading into anything. Slip of the tongue.

Not the good kind.

Too close to the truth for her, though, and yet not true for him. Those were the breaks. He couldn't know how close she was to… that feeling. He'd saved her—them—and she'd saved him. That kind of intensity did things to even the most level head. She was an excellent example of the phenomenon.

But those thoughts and feelings ought to go away when the intensity was over. Right? She was still waiting for that to happen.

He was still staring at her ear.

She forced herself to turn and meet his confused eyes. To be brave. To make the first move. She could let him off the hook, even if it hurt inside. The truth was far more important. And she understood him, loved that playfulness so far down that even as the words hurt her, she loved him for them too.

"It's okay," she muttered. Oh, great start, that.

"What's okay?"

She glanced down at his shirt. There were lime green robot parrots and also electric blue ones. And purple ones firing red laser beams out their eyes, which was really not how it worked.

But it was mesmerizing.

No, it was an excuse. She cleared her throat. "It's okay," she said, warming her voice and warming to the notion that it really was. The shirt helped. "I get it. It's just a playful expression. Meaningless."

He was silent long enough that she finally tore her eyes from the pattern and met his gaze. His brow was furrowed, and she could see his wheels turning.

"You're looking at me like I'm a computer," she said.

"I am?"

"Yes. Like a program you're trying to figure out. What's there to figure out? It's okay." She tried a good-natured, friendly pat on the shoulder. It felt awkward as hell and only reminded her of the warmth of him under his shirt. "Meaningless. Just an expression."

"I'm trying to figure out if you *want* it to be meaningless or not."

Startled, her eyes jerked up to meet his before she could think better of it. And that revealed everything, didn't it, her expression naked in her surprise before she could move to cloak it somehow. Her eyes didn't lie, that's why she so often looked away. They were probably brimming with both hope and hurt.

"This is ridiculous," he muttered.

She frowned, her panicked thoughts giving way to a flood of disappointment. "What is?"

"The two of us. Always calculating. Measuring, planning, trying to figure out the optimal angle of approach. By ourselves."

Oh. She permitted herself a small smile. That was true. They were alike in that.

To her surprise, he reached out and stroked the line of her jaw, gently drawing her gaze back to his. "Let's stop. We can't calculate fast enough, or gather enough data, for any of this."

"Okay," she said, numb. She wasn't accomplishing much with the thinking approach anyway except getting her foot stuck in her mouth. "For any of what?"

"Look, I—I'm sorry if it's not what you want to hear." He threw his hands to the side for a moment. "And I'm sorry if it's the wrong time. We haven't known each other very long. And it was way too casual, I shouldn't have thrown it out there." He took a deep breath, glanced down, swallowed, then met her eyes again. "But I do mean it."

Her eyes widened now. The robot parrots called her name, but she fought to keep her gaze on his. "You… you do?"

"I do. I love a woman who ponders breaking people's legs."

She snorted and playfully smacked his arm. "I was thinking about *other* people breaking your legs, to be clear. Or mine."

"Well, what do you know, mine come pre-broken."

"Doug, stop it! That's not funny."

He grinned for a moment, but gradually his expression softened. "I'm sorry. I'm terrible at being serious."

"Really? I had no idea."

"Well, I'm trying now. It means a lot to me that you get it. This. A lot of things about me, but especially this. I wasn't sure I'd ever meet anyone who did, but you do. I love that about you, among many other things. Like the fact that you let me under that shell of yours, too."

She shrugged to hide the flush in her cheeks. "It's not that complicated. Who wouldn't rather fly?"

"A lot of people would rather be normal." His studying-her look was back, searching for the answer to his unspoken question.

"Normal is overrated."

He grinned. "Normal is a social construct easily disassembled and shown to be made of smoke, tissue paper, and toothpicks. But that doesn't keep people from wanting it. You know, little house ship, one point three five children, a dog."

"I doubt normal was ever an option for either of us anyway."

"Ow." He pantomimed being shot in the shoulder. "Too spot on! Anyone ever tell you you're kind of a good shot? Kind of."

"A few people. The ones far from the shooting targets, who hadn't gotten a good look at my results yet." She ventured a smile, hesitated for a moment. Oh. Yes. They were throwing out calculation, throwing caution to the wind. Going for it.

"Much better to be far from the target, where you're concerned," he murmured.

She swallowed. "That's bad news for you, then."

"It is?"

"Yes. You're pretty close to the target for me."

"Really?" His eyes lit up now. "Am I in danger?"

"Yes."

"Danger of what?"

"Of this." She leaned closer, slid her fingers around the back of his neck, and drew his face toward hers. His hair was soft under her fingers, his skin warm, and when his lips met hers, the kiss was like coming home.

———

DREAMS HADN'T COME OFTEN to Kael. The illness was a blur of Levereaux in protective gear, the silver wall of the sick bay, feverish sweat, and demanding to know if Ellen was okay. Sometimes he remembered that asking too much might reveal something he didn't intend to. But often enough he wasn't thinking so clearly.

They always said she was stable. He was never sure he believed them.

But when dreams did come, he wished they hadn't.

A flood of pain, worse than some rogue virus could inflict. Pain too intense to live through, surely. In every limb, every joint. Every bone.

Pain beyond screaming, where all you could do was just freeze. He'd felt this pain once. It'd been a long time, but the memory never really dulled. Why was he remembering it now?

The first set of surgeries had done this. They'd been most extensive, but not the last.

In the dream, he didn't yet have the lattice work of white across his skin. He did have the sizable, perfectly circular wounds scabbed over at wrist, neck, abdomen. And in the dream, there was also something here that hadn't been on the Theroki surgeon ship with him.

The creature floated above him as he lay in the bunk, in far too much pain to move.

The bunk room was empty too. It had *never* been empty anytime he'd been there. But right now, it was just the three dozen rows of empty bunks, clustered barely a foot apart, Kael with his teeth clenched in utter agony, and the creature.

"Nice to see you again," he ground out to the creature. "But why this? I don't dream about *this* one."

She did not answer, hovered for a second, head cocked to the side. Thinking?

"This was never about my dreams, was it?"

"I want to understand you."

He frowned, even as it hurt. Everything hurt. It had hurt for days after the initial surgeries, but he hadn't been in a random bunk. He'd been in their version of a sick bay, or a recovery room, or a factory. Maybe a bit of all three rolled into one. The dream was inaccurate.

"Why?" he grunted.

"I have lived for generations. And yet, I have rarely come across souls like you."

"Souls? What do you mean?" After the real surgery, there hadn't just been a sick bay, there'd been a machine. It'd dispensed drugs when you hit the button. He craned his neck to one side, then the other, then on a gut instinct, back to where he'd first looked again.

The drug machine had appeared. So had a tube leading into his port—that had *definitely* not been there a second ago. What else could he wish into being in this dream? He stretched out, but moving hurt even more. His hand shook from just trying to straighten his arm.

"Souls like those around us. You are not the ones who usually bring me back. Oh, it's not just you having these dreams. You're just the one who most notices me."

His hand was shaking like the ship was being rammed by another one, but he made it to the button and pushed.

The dream drugs flowed into him, a slight burn, a slight coolness, then the pain eased. It didn't abate, but it wasn't quite so excruciating.

"Why am I the one that notices you?"

The creature shrugged. "I would have thought it would have been one of the telepaths. There are six, you know. Not all of them are trained."

He raised his eyebrows. "Six?"

"I've been wanting to tell someone. Told Isa, but I'm not sure she believed me."

Isa. He went rigid. "Who are you?"

The creature's shoulders lifted and fell again. "I would think you know. You brought me here."

By the seven suns. He opened his mouth, but couldn't find the words.

"The other ones called me their Empress. But they didn't treat me much like an Empress. You all call me 'the baby,' with a lot of affection. It seems to be because I appear young."

"People love babies." What a fragging inane comment. What should he really be saying to this incredible, terrifying thing? Think, dammit, think over the pain.

"The others didn't. I'm never a baby for long."

"We call them Enhancers. They're not great. I worked for them, I should know."

"A memory for another time."

He winced. "I vote to miss out on that one, if that's an option."

"You're the one that keeps seeing me."

He shrugged.

"Do you think they will change their minds when they find out I'm not young, but old?"

"How old are you?"

"My body—you know. My soul? Centuries."

"They will probably still like you. Baby bodies are pretty cute. Designed to make us care for them."

Suddenly all the pain eased. The bunks, the Theroki ship vanished. He was sitting on a pillow on a rocky island, moss-covered black boulders at his feet and behind him, but barely a meter away stretched a vast, neon blue ocean.

The creature sat on another pillow across from him, on another rocky protuberance. Her body looked more human now, but he had the vague sense that perhaps it wasn't her real one, but more of a dream expression of herself she was developing. The tentacles still floated against a purple-fuchsia sunset sky, but not quite so wild or so snake-like.

"Too bad the bodies always grow so fast," she said, waving a hand in the cool, refreshing breeze. "Babyhood is so short, before you know it, I'm an old woman. Then another body. Then another. Always pain. Will you let me die this time?"

"Uh, what *are* you exactly?"

"I am a Dulitithar. The real word is not quite something humans can say, naturally, but this is close enough. Or you may have heard our human name, *Alarus Octendi*."

His hand slid to his throat before he could think better of it.

She seemed not to notice—or pretended to. "We were once mighty. This is what our world looked like. We lived very long lives, reproduce rarely and few. My people were ancient, though, and had lived in peace for a long time." She looked around her. "Until your people came."

"We humans aren't so good at peace, sometimes."

"Worlds are not so common that they aren't valuable, especially watery ones." She sighed. "Many were murdered. Others were harvested. Some imprisoned."

"You?"

"I was in the last group. Most of my kind are dead. I am—as far as I know—the last living mature female."

"Then why do you want to die? Don't you want to find a way to continue?"

"It is impossible. There are no others left—I am utterly alone. And my body has died hundreds of times. These people—these Enhancers? —bound my soul into a new body each time, kept my powers tethered like a cloud to a rock."

"What powers?"

"You felt them last time. I shouldn't use them. It's not right—but I am tired. Tired of living by the rules. Tired of living at all."

"The feeling of… peace."

She laughed, a very human, very bitter sound. "That's a polite word for it. Peace—or death. They are so similar, in my case. My people understood the very fine line between brilliant entropy, brief stillness, and eternal night."

He took a deep breath. Should he bring up what Asha had shoved down his throat? Had that really happened or was it just a fever dream and he'd wake up and discover Faros had never happened at all? It seemed too far-fetched to even mention. "You're… Can you kill?"

She shrugged. "Not the body. But the mind, yes, it is a kind of death."

"Why not kill your captors then?"

"It is only temporary. Eventually I tire, or need to sleep, and they are released. They can wait till I am old and weak to move me. They used other methods too, medicinals, flashing lights. But I only tried once. It is wrong. Unlike them, I care about that."

He smiled. "I doubt we have the tech the Enhancers did to keep you alive again and again. But I am sure none of my friends would keep you alive against your will."

"We shall see. You may not know the others as well as you think you do."

"True, I can't speak for them. I'm not the Commander—"

"I am familiar with her."

He raised an eyebrow. "You are?"

"I am. We have made a deal."

He leaned forward. "What deal? Isn't she sick?"

The Empress nodded. "As are you."

"I'm almost better, Dremer said—"

"She said nothing about what to do about the *Alarus Octendi* in your gut."

His eyes widened. Then he swallowed as his nausea rose at the thought. "You knew? It's one of you... your species? I thought you said there were none left."

"These are some of the ones they stole. They are like... children that will never grow up. But always connected to a mother."

"Always? Were the Duli—what was it? Dulitithar?"

"Close enough, yes."

"Were the Dulitithar a telepathic race?"

"Yes, we had many collective consciousnesses, some independent ones. But all of that is gone now. I have no one to truly talk to like me. But the little ones, we feel each other like you smell the air."

"The little ones get bigger."

"I know. But not truly mature."

He sighed. "What happened to you... I hate it. If I could go back and change it, I would."

"It is nothing you did. And it is dust in the wind, as your people say. Now, I will fulfill the bargain I have made with your mate—"

"Whoa, now—"

"And I will free the member of my race trapped inside you. I will free her. And we will face the one who orchestrated all this together. The one who seeks the ultimate power of 'peace,' but does not earn it."

"Who is that?"

"Zeta Arakovic."

He caught his breath. "How? How will we find her, let alone defeat her?"

"She uses the little ones to link her units together. But in doing so, reveals her locations to me. I can find any and all she has bound in her web."

Well, glory be. "What about defeating her? Can we use your power?"

"Your mate has sworn she won't ask me to. I'd ask you to do the same."

"All right. And of course, I'll certainly do whatever I can to get you your... freedom. But that won't matter much if Zeta Arakovic kills us all and takes you captive."

"I have faith that you will find a way to defeat her. But I do not hold the answer to this question. We will face her together, is all I can say."

"It's about time." He glanced once more at the world around him, the rocks, the ocean. "So I won't have this creature in my stomach anymore soon?"

"Yes, I will begin the procedure in the morning. But I have one further request."

He raised an eyebrow.

"You must promise to return and read to me again. A fairy tale this time. I've had enough Theroki bureaucratic emails, as riveting as they were."

Laughing softly, he nodded. "That, I can easily promise."

———

LIGHT MADE Ellen's head ache, and she flinched. It wasn't over her, but off to the side, and she struggled to turn toward it, to open her eyes.

At first, all she could make out was bleary forms; then as she squinted, they sharpened. Blond hair. Another figure, head partially shaved—and bandaged, oh hell. Both of them wore breathers.

But Mo. Doug. Here. And alive.

She let out a slow breath as her eyes came fully into focus. Some fist that had been clenched inside her soul gradually relaxed.

"Simmons," she croaked. "Is that you?"

"Yes, ma'am."

"Simmons." Her throat caught, and she coughed before she continued. "Simmons, I am *trying* to keep this an all-female ship. My Patron's orders. You're fragging me up here."

"Nice to see you too, Ellen."

She smiled at him, before turning to his companion. "Mo. You're all right."

"Yes, ma'am."

"I'm so glad. But I feel like I got shit out by a dreck-eating lava monster."

"No lava monster," said Dremer's voice from the side. "Just a really bad flu. Almost took you down."

She winced. "What is that sound?"

Doug glanced up, then winced himself. "It's, um, Kael throwing up. You don't want to see it."

"Is that part of the flu?"

"Uh—no." Dremer again. "That's something special just for him, apparently."

"Why—why didn't they pursue us? Out of atmo. Didn't make—" She coughed. "Didn't make sense."

Doug shared a look with someone—Dremer?—then looked back at her.

"Arakovic's ship zeroed in on the *Audacity* shortly after you lost consciousness," Xi said, making Doug jump. "Adan and I were able to lose the yacht in a series of fourteen worm hole jumps, but they likely have more information now about how to find us. Previously they were not privy to the visual profile and armament of the *Audacity* itself."

She sighed. "Sorry, I missed it."

"We are safe for now," Xi said.

Ellen nodded, but the movement only made her entire head ache. "I think I'll go back to sleep now."

"Good idea," murmured Mo.

———

MALOOF'S VIRUS took Kael down for more days than he'd have cared to admit. And when he was finally on his feet again, and minus his parasitic little friend, he found himself aimless.

Ellen's recovery was slower, to his surprise, and Dremer strictly forbade him from visiting her. Again.

There were plenty of jobs to do, questions from the eager little puppy that was Vivaan, debriefing with Simmons and Taylor. But he found himself quickly taking refuge, not in his cabin, but in robot repair.

Fixing things was something he could do. But it wasn't until he no longer *needed* to do it that he realized how much he liked it. Missed it. And here, on the *Audacity*, with Xi as company and friends all around him, it was outright relaxing.

Robots could be fixed. There was a right answer. A clear goal. An intended function and configuration. With enough practice, enough skill, the right parts, the schematics, they were problems that could be solved in a few hours or a few days.

Not like life. Or love. Or family.

"Kael?" Xi's voice cut through his thoughts.

"Hmm?" He pretended to be engrossed in the current board installation, not that he thought he'd fool her. But maybe if he looked suitably distracted, she wouldn't tell him the news they were undoubtedly checking right now, because he'd asked them to.

Was Shirin really his daughter? Or was this just another lie?

"Dr. Dremer's tests are complete."

He dropped the multitool and straightened, since her phrasing indicated she was going to demand his attention. "And?"

"Genetically, Shirin Nar is your daughter."

Running a hand over his face, he sat back in the chair. Genetically. That was about right. Otherwise… not so much.

"Commander Ryu is returning to her duties. Dr. Dremer has cleared her as fully recovered."

His heart gave a leap. "That's great news."

"She wants to know if you would like to visit Shirin with her to discuss the matter."

"Ehh. Now?"

"Yes. Now."

He sat very still for a moment, then nodded. He stood up. "I'll meet her in the cabin corridor."

Outside, he was barely down the ladder toward the guest cabins when she caught up with him.

"Ready?" She smiled brightly at him, and there was a flush to her cheeks that made him pause, just to appreciate the relief.

"How are you feeling?" he said.

"Levereaux cleared me three days ago, but Dremer had to worry over me a bit. I'm in tip top shape. More sleep than usual, in fact."

He stepped closer. "Are you sure?" Would she even tell him if she wasn't? She looked well enough.

"If anything, I'm stir crazy to get something done. So let's do this! Ready?"

He hesitated. "I don't know if I can do this. I don't think I can do this. Can I not do this?"

"Waiting won't make it any easier, you know."

He sighed. "Fine. Let's go." He didn't know if it were the aftereffects of the creature's dramatic exit from his body, or just pure nerves, but his nausea would not let up.

Following Ellen, they were at Shirin's cabin before he'd even gotten his head out of the clouds. She rang the chime, and they waited for Shirin to answer.

And then after ten years, the hatch slid open, and she was there. She just stared.

So did he.

Ellen cleared her throat. "Shirin, can we come in?"

She gave a nod and backed out of the opening, not taking her eyes off of him. He couldn't decide whether it was wariness behind her gaze, or fear, or something else altogether. Anger maybe? Curiosity?

All of the above?

"Do you need anything?" Ellen asked, acting casual. Hell, maybe she felt casual too.

"No."

"Get enough to eat?"

Shirin nodded. "You got some pretty cracking digs here."

"The falafel is pretty good," Kael muttered.

"I have been happy to get Shirin and EOE8 well situated." Xi's voice was unusually gentle.

"So you met Xi?" he asked, more to make conversation.

"She's pretty nice."

"Why thank you, Passenger 7B."

"Did you know she'll call you whatever you want?" Ellen asked.

Shirin raised an eyebrow. "So… I can ask her to call me asshole or something?"

Kael slapped a hand over his face as Ellen smirked. Her game face was back pretty quickly though. "I'd appreciate a little more decorum on my ship. But most other choices would be fine."

"Good to know." Shirin crossed her arms over her chest, shifting her weight to her other foot. "Okay, let's get to it. Why are you here? You didn't both show up for no reason."

Ellen opened her mouth, looked at him, looked back at Shirin, looked at him again, closed it— Yeah, he wasn't the only one that was uncomfortable.

"If I may?" Xi chimed in.

Ellen looked at him. "Up to you, Kael."

"Save us, Xi, from this awkwardness." He tried to muster a little smile at Shirin.

She didn't smile back. "C'mon. Where are you dropping me off at or whatever?"

His eyebrows flew up. "It's nothing like *that*."

"Dr. Dremer has completed her analysis of your biology, Shirin. You are in excellent health."

She quirked one eyebrow. "But...? There's always a but."

"Your gluteal muscles are also in excellent health. And you are correct that nearly all humans have this musculature," said Xi placidly.

He tried to hold it back, but laugh burst out of him. And that broke Ellen and Shirin too.

"I see a human laughter response, but it does not fit my models. Someone care to explain this to me?"

Kael shook his head. "Can we talk about it later, Xi?"

"I will make sure of it," she said. "In other news, Shirin, as part of the test, your genetics were sequenced, and Dr. Dremer determined that Kael Asidian is, in fact, a paternal match."

Shirin's mirth faded, frowning. "What does that mean?"

"It means that the two of you share fifty-two percent of your genetic sequence."

He raised his eyebrows. "Fifty-two percent, huh?"

Shirin's lips pressed together, then she managed a weak smile. "Nice to meet you, paternal match."

Ellen snorted. "I can guess who she gets the sarcasm gene from."

Shirin's eyes widened slightly. "Hey, I thought you said his name was Sidassian."

"I told you he has a new name now and not to look it up, too, remember?"

"The new name is *Asidian*?"

"Yeah," he mumbled.

"It's not a very good one, is it?"

"Nothing gets past her," Ellen muttered.

He snorted a laugh and ran a hand over his face. "I didn't come up with it. We need a new one."

Xi cut in. "You didn't come up with an alternative either, my records show."

"I'm open to ideas. Way to throw me under the bus, Xi."

"I would never," Xi replied. He must have really missed the ship, because he could have sworn there was a warmth, a new humor to her voice. Maybe she'd been working on it.

Shirin waved in the air, then down at her ankle. "If you're my... father... then why was I sold like a cheap rug?"

That hit him like a knife in the gut; he actually took a step back as he winced. "I didn't know you existed. I'm so sorry, Shirin."

She shifted her feet again, arms still crossed. "Keep going."

He raised his eyebrows. With what? The story? Seven suns, he didn't want to go there, but who else should tell her? "I, uh... well, your mother and I were very close once." That seemed like it might matter to her, even if it probably shouldn't. Hmm, maybe they should have had Dr. Taylor here, but it was too late for that. "Now I know she wasn't a very good person. It's kind of a long story but—she—well, it's kind of horrible and complicated."

"I've got time." Her eyes narrowed.

"She and one of my... bosses framed me for a crime and got me, well, basically incarcerated..."

"'Basically' incarcerated?" She folded her arms. "Bosses? You were in one of those street gangs, weren't you?"

He sighed. He was fucking this up. He should have known better than to—

Xi's explanation cut into his thoughts. "Lieutenant Asidian was unjustly convicted of the murder of Asha Narulon and sold by the Farosian government to a somewhat unlawful mercenary outfit known as the Theroki, who alter their members cybernetically against their will and bind them to a lifetime contract."

Shirin didn't seem surprised by this, just kept her eyes trained on him.

"You already know all this," Ellen said suddenly. "I told you before you agreed to come with me."

He raised an eyebrow.

"I know, but I wanted to hear it from him." Her eyes hadn't left him, even as she spoke. They bored into him like intense little drills, and when she spoke, he realized why. "You were convicted of killing my mother. Is that true, then? Is she dead?"

He blanched, mouth falling open, but quickly snapped it shut. He needed to buck up and have her hear this from him. If anything, Asha being her mother was his responsibility. His choice.

He'd been slouching down, so he straightened. "It wasn't true that I killed her. She was alive. But she's not now, she—"

"She made the choice to put you up for sale," Ellen cut in. "I haven't gotten to fill Kael in on all the details Adan and I discovered while we were on the ground and he was in enemy captivity. She was responsible for framing him so that he couldn't stop her from selling you. I'm so sorry, Shirin."

She bit her lip. "So she… she sold me for *money*? And she basically sold you to some damn mercenary outfit?"

Should children swear? Should he correct her? It didn't seem like the perfect time to start acting like a father. "Yes. Also for money, I think. I would have stopped her. I wanted to keep you, stay together—"

"I know, I saw the certificate."

He froze for a second in surprise, then relaxed a little. He truly hadn't realized Ellen had done all that.

"You said she's dead now," Shirin said slowly. "What happened?"

His jaw clenched, and he glanced at Ellen, who was already looking at him. This was already a lot for one day? Did they need to tell her she talked her robot into shooting her own mother? Of course the robot seemed like it had been more of a mother than Asha ever had.

"She, uh… she got shot," he said. "She was, uh, still working with the gang I was apart of. The Gray Dragons."

"You ever kill people?" Her features were hard and unreadable.

"Not her." He forced a deep breath. He hadn't exactly wanted the conversation to take this turn, but perhaps it had been unavoidable. "But yes."

"A lot of people?"

He winced. "Not on Faros. But since then, maybe. Probably. How many would you consider a lot?"

She glanced back and forth between he and Ellen, sizing them up somehow. "If you have to ask, seems like it must be a lot."

"You're pretty wise, for a kid," he muttered. And stared at his boots.

"Can you teach me how?"

He looked up sharply. Her eyes were locked on him and didn't budge.

"To what?" asked Ellen.

"To kill people."

His eyes widened, then he gestured at EOE8. "I—uh—didn't you already figure that out?"

She waved at the air. "That doesn't count. EOE8 already decided. It doesn't want to do that again. And what if there's a next time? I'm sick of being helpless."

"You're safe with us," he said. "You don't need to worry about that. Or anything. I haven't been able to do much for you, but I can at least do this now."

Shirin's eyes widened slightly. He had no idea why.

"And if you wish to leave, you're obviously free to," Ellen added quickly. "My promise still stands. I just haven't been able to brief Kael on the details yet."

He slanted a glance at her. What had she agreed to? Whatever it was, she'd probably had a reason.

"I'll stay." Shirin let her arms drop to her sides and straightened up. "But only if you teach me how to kill people."

Kael blinked. "Uh… we can teach you to defend yourself?"

"All right. That's a start." She waved a hand in the air and visibly relaxed. He didn't think they'd crossed the barrier from near-hostage-stranger to crew-member-daughter yet… But somewhere down the line it seemed more possible, all of a sudden.

"I want you to know you don't need to," he added. "Defend your-self, I mean. You're safe here. We can protect you."

"I hope you'll forgive me if I don't immediately believe every word you say. I just can't."

"Ah." It hit him like a bucket of water. Yeah, maybe he was being overly optimistic on the crew-member-daughter thing. "Of course."

"There isn't a better place in the galaxy to learn to defend yourself," Ellen said, surprising him. "You never had any formal training, right?"

He nodded. "Yeah. I had some harder stuff in the last few years that was more formal, but not the hand-to-hand basics. You learn as you go when you have to."

"Nova didn't either." Ellen tapped her chin as she looked at the ceiling, mentally ticking through the crew. "Zhia, Dane, hmm…"

"You had a formal education?" Shirin asked, eyebrows raising. "In killing people?"

"Sure did." Ellen smiled now, but it was the feral kind.

Shirin seemed to understand the energy wasn't directed at her. In fact, the girl seemed to like it and grinned back. Had he fathered a psychopath? Glory be, he hoped not.

"Everything about me is pretty formal. Including my education." Ellen shrugged as she met Kael's eyes. "Jenny is probably our best bet for the basics. Fanciest classes Capital wealth could buy."

"Whatever you think would be best, Commander."

"Why can't *he* do it?" Shirin pushed, folding her arms again.

Ellen mirrored the gesture. He wondered if she realized she was doing that. "Because a man—good men, at least, and he's one of those—tend not to want to beat up their own daughters. And you need someone who will not hold back."

Surprise, then skepticism flashed again in her eyes, but she nodded.

"We can still spar, once you get your feet wet," he offered. It was a luxury to be able to make the offer, considering how little control he'd once had.

"I'll hold you to that." Shirin's sharp brown eyes went from him to Ellen, narrowing. "So if he's my father, what's that make you?"

Girl knew how to find a wound and poke it, didn't she?

Ellen didn't flinch though. "I'm your commander and captain, as long as you're on this ship."

Shirin's eyebrows raised. "That's not what I meant—"

"I know what you meant." She palmed the hatch open again. "I'll send you details on some training. Let's go, Kael."

Some part of his soul longed to stay. There had been a lot to say and almost none of it had been laid out there.

But he had a sense Ellen was right. Whatever he had to say, Shirin might need more time to pass before she could hear it. And she also needed to know that a commander's word was the law.

Or maybe she needed to learn to punch him in the face. And while none of it was his fault, he understood the anger.

So if she needed to punch him, he'd let her. And duck a few times too.

He rose, nodded to Shirin and EOE8, and followed Ellen. Shirin seemed to notice his brief hesitation, and he thought he saw a flash of concern in her eyes, but she said nothing.

Once the hatch was closed and they were walking away, Ellen murmured, "You can teach her whatever you want. She wants a reason to spend time with you."

"To size me up. To get back at me for abandoning her."

"I don't think so. I thought it might be hard for you to figure out where to start, though, and she's so little—"

"And I'm no teddy bear." He waved in the air. "It's fine. Good idea."

She stopped at the ladders. There were clanging sounds coming from the cargo hold, shouts from the gym, guitar strumming coming from the cabins. She scanned over all of it—looking for if anyone could see them—before pinning him with her eyes. "Are you okay?"

He marshalled a smile, spread his hands. "Eh, I've been better. I mourned her for years, and now I just don't even know what to make of this. I couldn't have done anything, but it doesn't make the guilt go away. Even if I didn't have anything to do with it, I can't help but feel like I let her down."

"We can't change the past. Or what isn't within our control. Only the future."

"You're right, of course. Now if only I could accept that. What the heck is that clanging?"

She rolled her eyes. "The squad is working out."

'The squad' was what the crew had come to call the Theroki unit while Kael, Dane, and Ellen had been incapacitated with Maloof's virus. The rest of the group with them had had to be detoxed and monitored. Only the three of them had come down with it fortunately, but it'd knocked them down hard. Praise the Almighty for modern medicine.

Meanwhile, the Empress had done some re-wiring of the squad's psychic connections, and while he'd gotten a sick stomach out of it, 'the squad' had gotten their freedom.

Apparently, they chose to use their freedom banging things around loudly in the cargo hold, not talking to anyone, and eating copious amounts of gyros. Why gyros or how Amaya had even decided to make them let alone in the massive quantities these men were consuming, he had no idea.

His smile widened. "Tell me, does the future lead to your quarters? Or do you have things to—"

"I'm totally exhausted from this very stressful first day back," she said quickly. "Wouldn't want to overdo it."

"Oh, that's good. I'm sure you need your rest. What with the virus and all and…"

She snorted. "Do you need a holographic advertisement, lieutenant?"

"Maybe. I could use the encouragement after… well, all that." Okay, maybe his ego was aching. A little bit. Not shattered, but not solid either. He'd had more dark reminders about the past lately than bright signs of the future, and his dreams hadn't helped matters. And why was he staring at the decking?

She took a step closer. "I'd rest better with you beside me."

His eyes lifted to hers.

"I *always* rest better with you beside me." Her eyes twinkled.

"And what if I'm not feeling in much of a mood to rest?"

"Then maybe we've been careful enough, Sidassian." She raised a hand and ran it over the stubble of his beard. "Maybe it's time to jump."

His name on her lips kindled a warmth in his chest. His real name. One that had started to take on a private meaning that it had never had before Doug had changed it, a much better meaning than when he'd used it on Faros.

She had been right. She'd known him all along. Who he really was. Faros hadn't frightened her away. It hadn't even mattered.

"Do you like skydiving? Cause I've been thinking about jumping with you for a while."

"I'm not a paratrooper, lieutenant." She grinned. "But I'm open to anything."

———

TRY AS HE MIGHT, Adan could not find the Commander. And he had looked practically everywhere. He had never been one to give up easily, though.

"Commander?" His voice echoed, but the cargo hold was empty. Nobody was climbing right now, and thankfully the squad had decided to take a nap.

He headed down to the gym. Zhia was perched on her stool, painting the bottom third of the wall with intricate precision. He waited until she paused for more paint before he said anything. "Zhia, you seen the Commander?"

Zhia cocked her head. "No. Xi won't tell you where she is?"

"No, that's what's weird. She won't tell me."

"You don't need to know," said Xi, an edge in the voice.

Adan rolled his eyes. "You can't hide it from me, computer. I'll find her. We're having popcorn and watching the cam footage of the fights down on Faros! The new robot got some pretty good footage from its onboard armor cam. Standing on the sidelines, it caught tons of footage of almost the entire thing. Want to join us? Everyone is invited."

Zhia shook her head. "My eyes are crossing from all this painting. I'm turning in soon. I don't remember a briefing—did I miss the memo?"

"Nah, it's just for fun. We're going to fast forward to the good bits. You sure you don't want to see the Commander take on Kael?"

"If that's what's happening, I don't want to see it." Zhia smiled, laughter in her eyes, and then turned back to her painting.

Xi cut in, voice prim. "I still assert the Commander would not be agreeable to viewing this footage as an entertainment activity."

"All the more reason I need to find her, right?" He grinned. Truth was, after Xi had pointed that out, he'd considered *not* tracking her down, but now he wanted to know how likely he was to get in trouble for this—or about how long he had to watch before he got caught.

He frowned when Xi said nothing in response, though.

"That your new poem?" he asked.

Zhia shook her head again. "Just an old favorite. I sent some of mine out though, on Xi's recommendations."

"Get any bites?"

"None yet, but you know, it takes forever."

"Let me know what they say." Adan smiled and studied the poem for a moment.

Dead Fires

If this is peace, this dead and leaden thing,
Then better far the hateful fret, the sting.
Better the wound forever seeking balm
Than this gray calm!

Is this pain's surcease? Better far the ache,
The long-drawn dreary day, the night's white wake,
Better the choking sigh, the sobbing breath
Than passion's death!

— Jessie Redmon Fauset

Huh. He was pretty sure that went completely over his head, but he muttered, "Wow, I… I think I'm going to need to read that a few more times."

Zhia didn't look at him, just picked up her brush again. "I think what she's saying is… Well, in short, some things are worth fighting for. No, that's not exactly it."

"Is it sort of like that Samwise character in that vid with the trolls?"

Zhia did stop now and raised an eyebrow. "Yeah, sort of like that. Except he's saying the world is good, so we should fight for it. And she's saying, either way, it's worth it, to fight for what's right." Then she shook her head. "You know, poetry interpretation isn't the thing to do on a whim while you're looking for the commander."

"Good point. Later, then. You are very deep, my friend."

"Thank you."

"What kind of a name is Samwise anyway?"

"What kind of a name is Adan?" She grinned, but didn't look at him.

"Touché. Well, have a good night then, Zhia. Join us on the bridge if you change your mind." And then he wandered out, up the ladder out of the cargo hold.

Where else could he look?

As luck would have it, Isa was coming out of Kael's cabin just as he approached. He broke into a jog toward her.

"Isa! Perfect! Wait, I have a question for you and Kael. Have you seen the Commander? Do you know where—"

Isa's cheeks flushed a brilliant red, then she turned and hurried back toward engineering.

He slid to a stop in front of Kael's hatch, leaning forward to grab the frame and keep it from sliding closed. "Kael, have you—"

But there was nobody in there. The place was messier than a Bantillan flop house, but not any more than normal. What the hell had Isa been doing in there? And why were her cheeks so red?

And he had checked fragging everywhere—Engineering, the mess, the Commander's cabin. She hadn't answered, so she wasn't *there*, of course, but—

He stopped short. Raised one eyebrow. Then the other.

Then he grinned.

He jogged back at a more leisurely pace to the bridge and slid into his pilot's chair beside Jenny just as Nova was arriving. She'd popped actual popcorn, and it smelled like heaven. And butter.

"Did you find her?" Jenny asked, cocking her head and tucking a red strand behind her ear. The black hair from Capital hadn't lasted long, and he for one was glad to put that whole planet in the distant past.

"Uh… yes and no."

She frowned.

"Let's just say—I think she's going to be occupied for a while. Let's get this party started, shall we?" He propped his feet up on the dash between two banks of controls, took Jenny's hand in his, and hit the button on his chair.

The video quality from EOE8's onboard armor cam was low, but interesting enough. Plenty of audio, too. Although some of it seemed to vibrate the whole bridge and he had to scramble to turn it down lest someone think they were under attack.

As the battle abruptly concluded, he flinched at the bloody shots from the robot as the woman went down. But thank God that little girl could argue like an attorney, because the Commander clearly owed the girl her life.

The most interesting tidbit, though, happened when Kael reemerged from the water at the end, threw his arms around the Commander, and—oh.

Well. Oh, my.

He smiled. Apparently, some wishes do come true.

When had *that* happened? Clearly before this moment. That was much too fiery to be a first kiss.

Jenny sat forward and was pointing at the screen. All of the women had, in fact. "Did they just—did I just see what I thought I saw?"

Adan grinned. "Oh, I think you did."

"He-he kissed her. And she didn't punch him."

Fern nodded. "I saw it too. Maybe *I* should punch him."

"Maybe we should throw them a party," Nova put in. "What? I'm all about punching, but took them long enough."

"Oh, you're one to talk," Fern shot back.

"What does that mean—" Jenny started.

"Maybe none of it is anyone's business," said Xi suddenly from the ceiling.

Adan burst out laughing. "Xi. Oh, Xi. We don't deserve such a good mother hen as you."

"I have no idea what that means," said Xi blandly, "but based on your tone, I will choose to take it as an affectionate compliment."

Fern jumped up to the edge of her seat. "I think I need more popcorn. And we need to watch that again. Rewind it, Adan. I'll be right back."

Nova watched her go with a frown, then turned back. "Hey, where did you say the two of them were, anyway? And where's Mo, for that matter?"

Still grinning, Adan turned back to the dash. "As Xi said, I don't think it's any of our business." He let the words fall heavy with meaning, though. "How about some other footage?" he said. "Got any of your own from your mission?"

Nova shook her head too quickly. "No. All boring. Very, very boring. Nothing but staring at scanners and hoping they were okay. Bland stuff. Utterly uneventful."

"What about when you found the pod?"

"Massive recording malfunction. I think all of it is blurry and just awful. That fighter is a relic, you know? Besides, like I said. Boring as hell."

He very much doubted that, based on that response, but he let it pass. "Who's up for a drama vid then? Or do we want flyer races? Ursa wrestling?"

He, for one, didn't care what they watched. This grin was going to take eons to fade.

EPILOGUE

WHEN ELLEN HAD BROUGHT up the need for a slight rest for a few days, every member of the Simmons family had insisted on R&R on Tarkos.

Initially, Ellen had been hesitant. It'd taken three extra jumps to get there, rather than the one she usually tried to work within. Their funds were running low, and the rescue of their allies and friends hadn't rescued their bank accounts. Those had sustained even greater damage than the compound had. On that, Barakat had not been bluffing.

Worst of all, Tarkos was busy as hell.

The bounties on her and Kael had doubled. Again. The public listings didn't include the ship idents but suggested such information was available. That figured, because it meant she didn't know exactly what information they had. But she *did* know people would be looking a lot harder for them.

Still, Tarkos was in the heart of the Union, which made her feel a little better. For once, she'd acquiesced to fake names and docs to get them in.

Because next they were going after Arakovic. And who knew how that would end.

The orbital station that circled Tarkos was famous galaxy-wide for its fine restaurants, and Doug had insisted on that too, actually, although she'd been a bit surprised that he hadn't chosen to leave the ship after all the ruckus he'd made about where to park. He'd been spending a lot of time in his lab-cabin, more than she would have thought for someone who'd professed to be lonely. Maybe all the people were a shock to his system. She'd have imagined him haunting the mess hall and zipping around the cargo hold, verbally pouncing on anyone in shouting range.

Instead, he had been quite busy working away with the hatch shut most days. Well, who knew? Maybe he'd finally head out tonight, like she was.

If only she knew where she was going.

"Can you at least tell me what to wear?" she said over the comm, not trying to hide the irritation in her voice.

"Wear whatever you want," Kael replied. He'd set up something for tonight but so far had refused to share any of the details.

"It can't be 'whatever I want.' You do realize women have a more elaborate protocol to these things."

"Your flight suit is fine. Really. Whatever you want."

"I'm going to get sweaty in the gym and meet you after."

"Okay."

"Dang it, that was a bluff. Wait, let me guess. This place is going to provide some kind of appropriate gear? If you're taking me scuba diving, Kael Sidassian, I will warn you, I didn't do great on that part of the special forces testing—"

"No scuba diving. In fact, you won't be required to take off your clothes in any way."

She frowned. "Not in any way?"

"None."

"That's kind of disappointing."

"You have a lot to learn about how dates work, Elle."

She couldn't help but smile at that, but kept her voice cranky. "I'll wear a garbage bag over my head. I'll borrow Kentt's blue cloak."

"And nothing else? I could get used to that."

And now she regretted her threats. She sighed. "Fine. I really don't need to do anything to prepare?"

"Nothing."

"Anything I should bring?"

"Nope. See you in an hour?"

"Mmm-hmm. See you then."

She didn't wear the flight suit, though. Something about it just seemed wrong, like she wasn't trying hard enough, and when Jenny diplomatically offered her an off-the-shoulder black satin dress with a bit of an iridescent sheen, she gratefully accepted. It showed off her shoulders. And her arms.

And honestly, she'd rather be back in the flight suit, but she was trying to give this date thing a fair shot. With Rich sworn to absolute silence and secrecy as to anything he might hear, she put on her heels —set to low, for heaven's sake—and headed to the cargo hold. Where she found Kael looking handsome in a black Mandarin and dark cargos, but as he'd promised, nothing terribly fancy. The way his eyes caught on her and held, though, before he could realize what he was doing—that expression was worth it.

The local station hour was late, so they missed most of the crew, who were either already on the station, or off doing something fun. Like sleeping. But the ship hour was close to lunch time, and since it was so far off, they hadn't bothered to sync. They'd only be here for a few days.

Kael took her hand as they exited the cargo hold, which made her wonder if anyone had seen, although lately she'd been getting the feeling that more and more of them knew, even if they had yet to say anything.

The corridors of the station were clean and quiet. Exotic plants dotted the corners, and expensive perfumes and vacations and pets were advertised every so often on shifting holodisplays. They passed a casino and a shopping mall and kept going.

A good ten sectors later, the corridors in this part of Tarkos Station had been painted pure white. If they'd ever been scuffed by a boot, that scuff had been scrubbed away. Three times. The doors all held little plaques labeling what lay confined there, but the lettering was barely a pale cream, easily missed in the snowy hazed blur.

Five corridors into some kind of labyrinth, Kael waved to a man in tan robes at a sheer glass desk. The man nodded to Kael as if they'd known each other for years, smiling warmly, but saying nothing.

Still leading her by her hand, Kael continued past the desk, turned left, and at a door marked only *The Red* on the small, delicate, almost illegible sign, he put his hand to the palmpad.

The door slid open to only darkness.

"C'mon." He started in.

"Whoa. Um, it's dark. Is it supposed to be?"

"Trust me, okay?"

She hesitated, but his hand tugged hers onward. And she did trust him.

The door slid shut behind him, engulfing them in a room every bit as dark as the corridors had been sterile and white.

"How do you know where you're going?" she muttered.

She could feel him smile. "Just a little farther, okay?"

"Okay." While she couldn't see a thing, the place smelled like heaven. She heaved in a breath and let it out. The air was cold and wet, lots of nitrogen and oxygen if she wasn't mistaken. It'd been a while since she'd practiced her atmo scent tests. Actually, for safety, maybe she should revisit that training once they were back on the ship…

"Okay, here we are." The light from a tablet suddenly illuminated his handsome face in the darkness, a faint wall of red and black behind him. "They turned out the lights for me. I thought it'd be easier than blindfolding you."

"And probably more socially acceptable. I hope that man would have helped me if he saw you just leading me around blindfolded. But somehow I doubt it."

"He's in on this scheme, so your hopes are dim. Ready?"

"More than ever."

He tapped a control on the tablet.

Lights sprang to life, fading rapidly from dim to brilliant. But it wasn't the violent glare of overheads. Tiny spots of lights at their feet burst to life amid a sea of red. Rows upon rows of flowers appeared, meters and meters of them. Deep crimson, scarlet, touches of white and gold…

Roses. Poppies and tulips, too. Beyond the flowers a bank of windows revealed the stars.

"Oh my God, a grow room," she breathed. "We're allowed in here?"

"Indeed we are."

"I knew this place smelled amazing."

"It's not exactly a grow room. They don't cut these and sell them."

She frowned, unable to take her eyes off the blooms. "What do you mean?"

"They're just to look at."

"Well, *that's* extravagant," she scoffed, turning to look at him. "You're serious. On a space station?"

He shrugged. "Simmons told you it was fancy."

"This is really, okay, maybe a little over the top, but…"

"But nobody is going to be looking at us here," he said, smiling, "if you know what I mean."

She smiled wider. Yeah. Fewer bounty hunters to worry about if they were totally alone. She spread her arms wide. "So what do we do, walk around?"

"We can do that. There are three rooms. But there's also this." He jerked a thumb over his shoulder, and she leaned around him.

And stared. On a low table beside them were two bottles of wine, a bottle of whiskey, a bottle of bourbon, a pitcher of water, and at least a dozen different foods she couldn't recognize. The array of assorted glassware and utensils was almost as impressive as the food. "Is that for us?"

"That, Elle, is for us."

She clapped her hands together once. "We are on a *date*."

"I know. Told you so. Wine or whiskey?"

Laughter made her smile go crooked. "Well, as we've seen me on whiskey, and it wasn't pretty—"

"Now that's not true."

"—let's go with wine tonight."

They sat, and he poured them both a glass.

"You weren't joking. I should have worn the flight suit."

He shrugged. "You know I don't lie to you."

"How did you find out about this? How did we even get in here? God, I hope this didn't cost a lot of money."

"We got in with a little help from our friends. They are usually closed right now, had an event earlier. Apparently, people on Tarkos care that it's the middle of the night cycle."

"Crazy people." She snorted.

"This place is called the Tarkos Grand Historic Floating Gardens. Houses a ton of heirloom flowers. Rents out visitations and meditation and yoga retreats to exclusive clientele."

She snorted. "We're not exclusive."

He smiled. "We're not, but apparently Catherine Simmons is."

"Thank you, Patron," she muttered under her breath.

"Here. Let's eat. Before I start gnawing my arm off."

"I'm starved. But what exactly *is* this?"

They chowed down mostly in quiet on a collection of Tarkos's delicacies. And with a delightful disregard for manners, too. By her second glass of wine she was sitting on the floor to get a closer look at all the goodies. They were mostly of the meat, cheese, mustard, and fruit variety, but although the exact flavors and types she mostly hadn't seen before.

When they were both full, she curled back up in the crook of his shoulder and stared at the rows of roses, and beyond them, the stars.

"Thank you," he said softly, his breath warm on her hair.

"For what. You did all the work tonight. This was incredible."

"Not for tonight." His voice was barely audible, and she stilled, smoothing out her levity to match his seriousness.

"For what then?" She toyed with a fastener on his shirt.

"For saving me. For knowing me. For trusting me."

"I only saw what was obvious, nothing more. Should a diamond thank its owner for harvesting it from the dirt?"

"Maybe."

"It was always a diamond."

"Still. Thank you."

She turned her face up toward him and kissed him, because what better answer was there than that?

"You know, I will miss a few things about Faros," he said quietly.

"Like what?"

"Leaving it."

She chuckled.

"I'll miss the mint tea too. And the glow jellies. They might be disgusting, but they sure are pretty."

"Maybe Shirin will want one as a pet. I… may have promised her a pet."

He shook his head. "No glow jellies. I'm drawing the line."

"Do you think she'd settle for a potted plant?"

"Hey, we can't steal any of these, don't get any ideas."

She grinned. "You just can't take me anywhere anymore. Fancy place for the likes of us."

"It is a bit on the fancy side. You even dressed up. But I did have a second item on the agenda, if you're ready for it. And not too drunk."

She raised an eyebrow. "I'm not too drunk, although that bottle isn't empty yet."

"And we've haven't even started on the bourbon." He slid up his sleeve to reveal the snake coiled around the dagger. "We're going to fix this."

She sat up, although inside she was jumping in excitement at the idea. "Going to get it removed? Let's go! Put it all behind you. We defeated them, Kael, in more ways than one."

"I was actually thinking I'd cover it up with something new. Something that reminds me of you."

She went still. Then her smile broke free like the sunrise. "Let's go. Let's do it *now*. What are you going to get?"

"You'll have to wait and see."

"Then how will I know if I want a matching one?"

He laughed. "You'll have to decide while they're doing the deed."

"C'mon, Theroki. So many secrets!"

"Surprises, not secrets, Commander. Dates are supposed to be full of surprises."

"I don't like surprises."

"You like me, and I was a surprise."

"Touché. All right—you grab the bourbon, I'll grab the whiskey, let's go!"

"I don't think they'll let us get tattoos if we're too drunk."

"As if your scrubbers let that happen. Load up, Sidassian. The night is young."

He grinned. "You sure you've never been on a date before? You're taking to the idea pretty quickly."

"No dates as good as this one. But tell me you found one of those fancy fast parlors, because I don't know if I can sit for three hours in this dress."

"This one promises only about fifteen minutes."

"Perfection. And then do we head home for phase three of the date?"

"Oh ho. Do you have a few surprises of your own?"

"If you're surprised that I want to get out of this dress as soon as possible, then you haven't been paying attention." She glanced pointedly around them, then gave him a peck on the cheek. "But clearly you have. So let's go get that ink."

"Yes, Commander. If only all your orders were this easy to follow."

"It's easy because you thought of it."

"I thought of phase two, but now it's phase three I'm looking forward to."

She grabbed one last gulp of wine and a piece of—was it cheese? Whatever—and turned toward the door. Or where she *thought* the door was. "Yeah. Me too."

AFTERWORD

Thank you so much for reading! You rock. Hope you had fun.

If you haven't discovered it already, check out the short prequel novella I wrote titled *Deserter* to learn more about Ellen's past.

If you'd like to be notified when new books come out, sign up for email updates here: www.rkthorne.com/get-updates/ I share upcoming book news and occasional free bonuses, like stories, maps, and character interviews, rarely more than once a month.

If you're feeling froggy, consider leaving a review. Reviews help readers discover their next favorite book—and avoid ones that aren't for them! Whether it's five stars or one, I truly love hearing from readers and appreciate your honest feedback.

ALSO BY R. K. THORNE

The Enslaved Chronicles

Mage Slave

Mage Strike

Star Mage

Audacity Saga

The Empress Capsule

Capital Games

Child of Wrath

Untitled Book 4 (Forthcoming)

Deserter: An Audacity Prequel

Clanblades Series

Dagger of Bone

Blade of the Moon (Forthcoming)

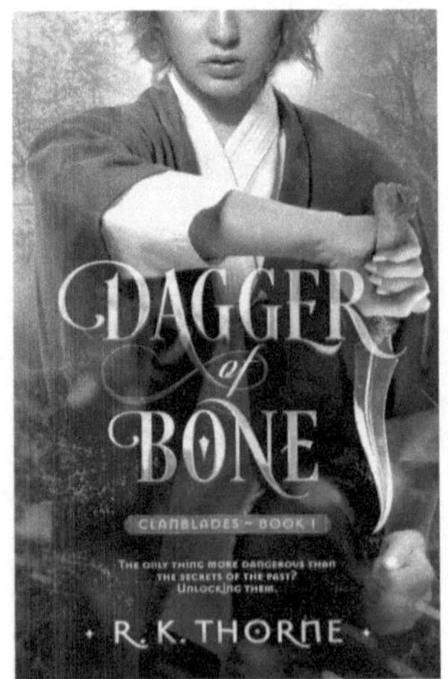

ABOUT THE AUTHOR

R. K. Thorne is an independent science fiction and fantasy author fueled by notebooks, role-playing games, coffee, and imperial stouts.

She has read speculative fiction since before she was probably much too young to be doing so and encourages you to do the same.

She lives in the green hills of Pennsylvania with her family and two gray cats that may or may not pull her chariot in their spare time.

For more information:
rkthorne.com

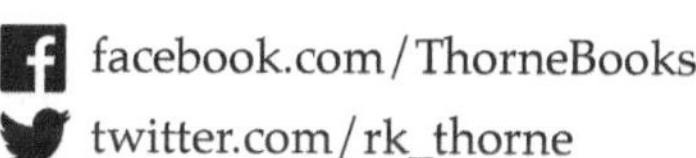

facebook.com/ThorneBooks
twitter.com/rk_thorne
instagram.com/rk_thorne